T0112047

THE LOST NOVELS OF BRAM STOKER

Edited by

STEPHEN JONES

A HERMAN GRAF BOOK

Skyhorse Publishing

Copyright 2012 © by Skyhorse Publishing

Preface and Introductions copyright © Stephen Jones 2012

All Rights Reserved. No part of this book may be reproduced in any manner without the express written consent of the publisher, except in the case of brief excerpts in critical reviews or articles. All inquiries should be addressed to Skyhorse Publishing, 307 West 36th Street, 11th Floor, New York, NY 10018.

Skyhorse Publishing books may be purchased in bulk at special discounts for sales promotion, corporate gifts, fund-raising, or educational purposes. Special editions can also be created to specifications. For details, contact the Special Sales Department, Skyhorse Publishing, 307 West 36th Street, 11th Floor, New York, NY 10018 or info@skyhorsepublishing.com.

Skyhorse® and Skyhorse Publishing® are registered trademarks of Skyhorse Publishing, Inc.®, a Delaware corporation.

www.skyhorsepublishing.com

10 9 8 7 6 5 4 3

Library of Congress Cataloging-in-Publication Data is available on file.

ISBN: 978-1-62087-178-2

Printed in the United States of America

Table of Contents

Bram Stoker
1906

PREFACE

THE MAN WHO CREATED DRACULA

Stephen Jones

IT IS, PERHAPS, somewhat ironic that Bram Stoker wrote one of the most successful and influential supernatural novels of the late nineteenth century. It became so popular that even today—100 years after the death of its author—the name of the book's titular character is more recognized around the world than that of his Irish creator.

That character which Stoker originated is, of course, the infamous vampire, Count Dracula: *His face was a strong, a very strong, aquiline, with high bridge of the thin nose and peculiarly arched nostrils, with lofty domed forehead, and hair growing scantily round the temples but profusely elsewhere. His eyebrows were very massive, almost meeting over the nose, and with bushy hair that seemed to curl in its own profusion. The mouth, so far as I could see it under the heavy moustache, was fixed and rather cruel-looking, with peculiarly sharp white teeth. These protruded over the lips, whose remarkable ruddiness showed astonishing vitality in a man of his years. For the rest, his ears were pale, and at the tops extremely pointed. The chin was broad and strong, and the cheeks firm though thin. The general effect was one of extraordinary pallor.*

However, the man who created Dracula could not have had a more prosaic start to life.

The third of seven children, Abraham "Bram" Stoker was born on November 8th, 1847, at 15 Marino Crescent, Clontarf, situated on the north side of Dublin. His parents were civil servant Abraham Stoker (1799-1876) and social reformer and writer Charlotte Mathilda Blake Thornley (1818-1901). Raised as a Protestant, he was baptized at the Church of Ireland Parish of Clontarf.

A somewhat sickly child, Stoker was bedridden until the age of seven and his mother is said to have read him the type of scary stories that may have influenced his later literary career. After starting private school, the young boy soon made a full recovery and, as he later observed: "I was naturally thoughtful, and the leisure of long illness gave opportunity for many thoughts which were fruitful according to their kind in later years."

From 1864 to 1870 he attended Trinity College, Dublin, where the former invalid excelled at athletics (he was named University Athlete) and graduated with honors in mathematics.

As a member of the University Philosophical Society, he presented a paper on "Sensationalism in Fiction and Society" and, as president, he proposed his friend Oscar Wilde for membership.

While still a student, Stoker developed an interest in the theater that resulted in him becoming a part-time drama critic for the *Dublin Evening Mail*, which just so happened to be co-owned by the Irish Gothic writer Joseph Sheridan Le Fanu.

His reviews soon began to attract notice, and in December 1876 he wrote a favorable critique of Henry Irving's *Hamlet*, which was being staged at Dublin's Theatre Royal.

So impressed by this review was Irving—probably the greatest actor–manager of his generation—that he invited the young critic to dinner at the hotel where he was staying, and the two men quickly became friends. "Soul had looked into soul!" Stoker later wrote. "From that hour began a friendship as profound, as close, as lasting as can be between two men."

By this time Stoker was working as a civil servant in Dublin. His literary ambitions were already beginning to become apparent, not only through his unpaid theater reviews, but also with the appearance of short stories in various periodicals and the publication of a ponderous nonfiction work, *The Duties of Clerks of Petty Sessions in Ireland* (1879).

In December 1878 Stoker married aspiring actress Florence Balcombe, his neighbor and a celebrated beauty whose former suitors included Oscar Wilde. The couple moved to London five days after the wedding, where Stoker became the business manager for the Royal Lyceum Theatre in London's West End, which Henry Irving owned. He also took on the role of Irving's personal assistant, employing actors, arranging tours, and answering correspondence—a position that helped Stoker gain entry into London's high society.

As the novelist Hall Caine (the "Hommy-Beg" to whom *Dracula* is dedicated) later observed in a newspaper article about his friend's relationship with Irving: "I say without hesitation that I have never seen, never do I expect to see, such absorption of one man's life in the life of another . . . with Irving's life, poor Bram's had really ended."

Irving's frequent costar at the Lyceum, the actress Ellen Terry, paid her own tribute to Stoker, describing him as "one of the most kind and tender-hearted of men. He filled a difficult position with great tact, and was not so universally abused as most business mangers."

In a short interview with Jane Stoddard ("Lorna") that appeared in *British Weekly*, July 1st, 1897, Stoker maintained that London was the best possible place to reside for someone with literary ambitions: "A writer will find a chance here if he is good for anything, and recognition is only a matter of time," he remarked.

With the financial security and social introductions that Stoker's close relationship with Henry Irving brought the family, on December 31st 1879, Florence gave birth to the couple's only child, Irving Noel Thornley Stoker.

As part of Irving's theatrical company, Stoker traveled widely, visiting the United States on a number of occasions and meeting President Theodore "Teddy" Roosevelt, Mark Twain, and his literary idol, Walt Whitman. In later years he also visited his disgraced and destitute friend Oscar Wilde in France.

During this busy period, Stoker was not only running the Lyceum for Irving, but he was also on the literary staff of the *London Daily Telegraph*. He had published his first novel, *The Primrose Path*, as a magazine serial in 1875, and this was followed by *The Snake's Pass* (1890), *The Watter's Mou'* (1895), *The Shoulder of Shasta* (1895), and his most famous work of all, *Dracula* (1897).

Originally titled *The Un-Dead*, the name of Bram Stoker's seminal work was changed to *Dracula*—after its blood-drinking protagonist—shortly before it was published in an edition of 3,000 copies by Archibald Constable & Co. Ltd. on May 26th, 1897 (the year of Queen Victoria's Diamond Jubilee). A variant "colonial" edition, for distribution in India and the British Colonies, was printed from the same plates and issued around the same time by Hutchinson & Co.

Two days prior to the official publication, and perhaps with some kind of celebrity endorsement in mind, Stoker sent former Prime Minister William Gladstone an advance copy of the novel along with an explanatory note: "It is a story of a vampire—the old Medieval vampire but recrudescent today. It has, I think, pretty well all the vampire legend as to limitations and those may in some way interest you who have made so bold a guess at 'immortualiadidity.' The book is necessarily full of horrors and terrors, but I trust that these are calculated to cleanse the mind by pity and terror. At any rate, there is nothing base in the book and though superstition is fought in it with the weapons of superstition, I hope it is not irreverent."

In the interview in the *British Weekly*, Stoker revealed that he had spent around three years working on the book and that he had always been interested in the vampire legend.

"It is undoubtedly," said Stoker, "a very fascinating theme, since it touches both on mystery and fact. In the Middle Ages the terror of the vampire depopulated whole villages."

Asked if there was any historical basis for the legend, he replied: "It rested, I imagine, on some such case as this. A person may have fallen into a death-like trance and been buried before the time. Afterwards the body may have been dug up and found alive, and from this a horror seized upon the people, and in their ignorance they imagined that a vampire was about. The more hysterical, through excess of fear, might themselves fall into trances in the same way, and so the story grew that one vampire might enslave many others and make them like himself. Even in the single villages it was believed that there might be many such creatures. When once the panic seized the population, their only thought was to escape."

Stoker went on to list those countries where, in his opinion, the vampire legend was most prevalent: "In certain parts of Styria it has survived longest and with most intensity," he explained, "but the legend is common to many countries, to China, Iceland, Germany, Saxony, Turkey, the Chersonese, Russia, Poland, Italy, France, and England, besides all the Tartar communities."

Reputedly inspired by fellow Irishman J. Sheridan Le Fanu's 1872 novella *Carmilla* and a nightmare Stoker had in which he saw a woman trying to kiss a man on the throat, *Dracula* is an epistolary novel made up of fictional letters, diary entries, telegrams, ship's logs, and newspaper clippings. Before he commenced writing the book, the author spent several years researching European folklore, liberally referencing Emily de Laszowska Gerard's article "Transylvanian Superstitions" (1885) and her travel guide *The Land Beyond the Forest* (1888), but he never actually traveled to Eastern Europe.

He did, however, spend his summer holidays in the North Yorkshire seaside town of Whitby (where the Count first steps foot on English soil), and other locations that may have served as inspiration including the crypts of St. Michan's Church in Dublin and Slains Castle on the coast of Cruden Bay, northeast Scotland.

As Stoker explained, "No one book that I know of will give you all the facts. I learned a good deal from E. Gerard's *Essays on Roumanian Superstitions*, which first appeared in the nineteenth century and were afterwards published in a couple of volumes. I also learned something from Mr. Baring-Gould's [*The Book of*] *Were-Wolves*. Mr. Gould has promised a book on vampires, but I do not know whether he has made any progress with it."

A chance supper-club meeting in 1890 with Arminius Vambery, a professor of Oriental languages from the University of Budapest, may have also resulted in Stoker first learning about the exploits of a fifteenth-century Romanian *voivode* named Vlad Dracula of Wallachia (in that country's language, *dracul* means either "dragon" or "devil"). This warrior-prince was also known as "Vlad Tepes" or "Vlad the Impaler," the latter after his propensity for impaling his enemies alive on sharply pointed wooden stakes.

Vambery *may* have been the model for occult expert Abraham Van Helsing, although researchers have put forward several other candidates. However, most sources agree that the author based the Count himself on his charismatic employer, Henry Irving (1838-1905), whose biography Stoker wrote and which was published in two volumes as *Personal Reminiscences of Henry Irving* in 1906.

In a letter to the author, Sherlock Holmes's creator Sir Arthur Conan Doyle enthused: "I write to tell you how very much I have enjoyed reading *Dracula* . . . I think it is the best story of diablerie which I have read for many years," while the literary critic for the *Daily Mail* newspaper compared it to *The Mysteries of Udolpho*, *Frankenstein*, and *The Fall of the House of Usher*, declaring that "*Dracula* is even more apalling in its gloomy fascination than any one of these."

Stoker's mother, Charlotte, even wrote to her son to congratulate him on the book: "My dear, it is splendid, a thousand miles beyond anything you have ever written before, and I feel certain will place you very high in the writers of the day."

Although it was not the first literary work on the subject, *Dracula* is widely regarded as the first novel to popularize the legend of the blood-drinking "vampire" amongst the general public. Despite not being an instant bestseller, the book was reasonably well received by the critics and public alike and has never been out of print since it was first published. However, it only achieved its iconic status as a classic work of supernatural fiction following the movie versions of the twentieth century.

The first US edition appeared in 1899 from Doubleday & McClure Co. of New York, and it has been suggested that the novel has been in the public domain in America since its original publication because Stoker did not follow the correct copyright procedure.

What is perhaps less well known is that when *Dracula* was reissued in April 1901 as a sixpenny yellow-covered paperback by Constable, the book was published in an abridged, easier-to-read edition for which the author cut around 25,000 words of the original text and made some minor revisions. A subsequent edition from William Rider & Son Ltd. in 1912 corrected many of the typographical errors that had been carried over from the first edition.

For the first foreign translation of the novel, an abridged 1901 Icelandic edition entitled *Makt Myrkranna* (*Powers of Darkness*), Stoker wrote a unique tongue-in-cheek preface in which he claimed that the book was actually based on fact:

"I am quite convinced that there is no doubt whatever that the events here described really took place, however unbelievable and incomprehensible they might appear at first sight . . . I state again that this mysterious tragedy which is here described is completely true in all its external respects, though naturally I have reached a different conclusion on certain points than those involved in the story."

When asked if there were any moral lessons to be learned from the novel, the author diplomatically remarked: "I suppose that every book of the kind must contain some lesson, but I prefer that readers should find it out for themselves."

For many decades it was believed that Stoker's original 541-page typescript for *Dracula* had been lost, before a hand-corrected copy (which, amongst other things, revealed that his character's original name had been "Count Wampyr") was discovered in a barn in northwestern Pennsylvania in the early 1980s. Sold at auction by Christie's, it is now owned by Paul Allen, the cofounder of Microsoft.

The author's original research notes for the novel are kept in a specially made box in the Rosenbach Museum & Library in the center of Philadelphia.

Although he would never again write a book as polished or popular as *Dracula*, Bram Stoker refused to give up his literary ambitions. For the rest of his life he continued to turn out a string of novels in various genres to mixed success. *Dracula* was followed by *Miss Betty* (1898), *The Mystery of the Sea* (1902), *The Jewel of Seven Stars* (1903), *The Man* (aka *The Gates of Life*, 1905), *Lady Athlyne* (1908), *The Lady of the Shroud* (1909), and *The Lair of the White Worm* (1911).

Under the Sunset (1881) comprised eight disturbing fairy stories for children, illustrated by W. Fitzgerald and W.V. Cockburn, while *Snowbound: The Record of a Theatrical Touring Party* (1908) contained fifteen interconnected stories set on a snowbound train.

Stoker had always hoped that Henry Irving would play Count Dracula on the stage, but that never happened before the actor's death in 1905. However, at 10:15 a.m. on May 18th, 1897—a few weeks before the publication of the novel—the author himself supervised a single four-hour read-through of his own hastily assembled theatrical version at the Royal Lyceum Theatre in London.

Entitled *Dracula* or *The Un-Dead*, the one-off production comprising a prologue and five acts was publicly staged purely for the purpose of copyright protection and to register the play with the Lord Chamberlain's office.

In the manner of the day, the first actor to ever portray the Count was listed simply in the cast as "Mr. Jones." This was most probably T. Arthur Jones, who was appearing in a production of *Madame Sans-Genet* at the theater at the time. Ellen Terry's daughter, Edith Craig, took the part of Mina Harker.

Following a devastating fire in 1898 that destroyed most of the sets and costumes, the Lyceum Theatre fell into bankruptcy and was forced to close in July 1902. From then on Stoker had to depend on royalties from *Dracula* and his other literary works to support his family.

The author was apparently not a big fan of literary agents and, although they reportedly did not make him a wealthy man, as a qualified barrister he negotiated himself a royalty of almost twenty percent on *Dracula*, which is more than most authors receive today. "Some men nowadays are making ten thousand a year by their novels," he said, "and it seems hardly fair that they should pay ten or five percent of this great sum to a middleman. By a dozen letters or so in the course of the year they could settle all their literary business on their own account."

Having suffered the first of two strokes shortly after Irving's death seven years earlier, Stoker died in bed in London on April 20th, 1912— the same week as the sinking of the *Titanic*. The death certificate listed "exhaustion" and "locomotor ataxy" (a term which, in those days, was sometimes used by doctors as a euphemism for the final stages of tertiary syphilis) amongst the causes of death.

The semi-impoverished author was sixty-four years old. He was cremated two days later and his ashes were placed in a marble urn in Golders Green Crematorium.

Stoker's passing was barely noticed by the press. A brief obituary in *The Times* for April 22nd, 1912, dismissed him as "a master of a particularly florid and creepy kind of fiction, represented by *Dracula* and other novels."

However, just like its immortal vampire, his most popular novel refused to die.

In an attempt to raise much-needed funds, on July 7th, 1913, Florence Stoker sold off her husband's library, some original manuscripts, and his working notes for *Dracula* at Sotheby's in London. The auction realized £400, 12s for what the widow later referred to as "rubbish," with the "original notes and data" for *Dracula* going to a New York book dealer for £2, 2s.

Meanwhile, a posthumous collection of supernatural tales, *Dracula's Guest and Other Weird Stories*, was published by George Routledge & Sons Ltd. in December that same year.

The book took its title from an early chapter reputedly deleted by the publisher from the original manuscript. It is more likely an early draft that Stoker rewrote for the final novel. The book also contained such memorable short stories as "The Judge's House," "The Squaw," and "The Burial of the Rats."

More than a quarter of a century after that marathon read-through at the Lyceum, the author's widow finally granted the rights to a stage adaptation of *Dracula* to Hamilton Deane, and the play had its premiere at the Grand Theatre in Derby in 1924. Edmund Blake became the first actor to portray the Count on stage, while Deane himself took on the role of Van Helsing.

For the play's successful repertory tour and subsequent London engagement in 1927, twenty-two-year-old Raymond Huntley donned the vampire's cape, but he still had to supply his own evening clothes.

Having seen the play during a business trip to London, American publisher and producer Horace Liveright bought dramatic rights and hired playwright John L. Balderston to adapt it for the New York stage. The revised production, starring Hungarian actor Bela Lugosi and Edward Van Sloan, debuted at the Fulton Theatre on October 5th, 1927, and ran for thirty-three weeks on Broadway and a further record-breaking two years on tour.

Unfortunately, although the stage production generated more than $2 million, Liveright failed to pay Florence Stoker all the royalties she was owed before his premature death from pneumonia in 1933.

Although two unsubstantiated "lost" films, *Die Zwölfte stunde* (*The Twelfth Hour*, 1920) and *Drakula halála* (*Dracula's Death*, 1921), are claimed by some sources to be based on Bram Stoker's novel, the first movie adaptation of *Dracula* is still generally considered to be F. W. (Friedrich Wilhelm) Murnau's *Nosferatu, eine symphonie des grauens* (*Nosferatu, a Symphony of Horror*). Made in Germany in 1922, it starred the appropriately named Max Schreck (whose name literally means "fright" in German) as "Count Orlock."

As Stoker's literary executrix, Florence used attorneys for the British Incorporated Society of Authors to sue the filmmakers, claiming that they had neither sought permission nor paid royalties, and she eventually won her case in July 1925. Although the suit called for the destruction of the negative and all prints of the film, by that time the unauthorized movie had been widely distributed and copies survived.

Florence Stoker died in 1937 at the age of seventy-eight, and her ashes were scattered in the Gardens of Rest at Golders Green Crematorium. Upon his death in September 1961, the ashes of Noel Thornley Stoker were added to his father's urn.

The first Hollywood version of *Dracula* was released by Universal on St. Valentine's Day, 1931. Billed as "the strangest love story of all," Tod Browning's movie was based on the stage play by Deane and Balderston and reunited from that production Bela Lugosi as the Count and Edward Van Sloan as his dignified nemesis, Van Helsing. A Spanish-language version was filmed simultaneously on the same sets with Carlos Villarías as a bestial Conde Drácula.

In 1958, British actor Christopher Lee took over the role in Hammer Films's *Dracula* (aka *Horror of Dracula*), the first version of Stoker's novel to be filmed in color. Peter Cushing was cast as an athletic Dr. Van Helsing, and the actors re-created their roles in several sequels and remakes over the following couple of decades.

Other actors to portray the Count on screen have included Lon Chaney Jr., John Carradine, Jack Palance, Paul Naschy, Louis Jourdan, Frank Langella, Klaus Kinski, Leslie Nielsen, Gary Oldman, Patrick Bergin, Rutger Hauer, and Marc Warren, amongst numerous others.

Over the decades since Bram Stoker's novel was first published, the image of Count Dracula has become as iconic as that of Marilyn Monroe, James Dean, and Mickey Mouse, and, according to records, the number of movies made about the character is second only to those featuring Sir Arthur Conan Doyle's Sherlock Holmes.

However, although *Dracula* will always remain Bram Stoker's most famous work, it was by no means the only supernatural novel that the author wrote . . .

STEPHEN JONES is one of Britain's most acclaimed anthologists of horror and dark fantasy. He has more than 120 books to his credit, including collections by M.R. James, Rudyard Kipling, Robert E. Howard, Clark Ashton Smith and H.P. Lovecraft, and has won numerous awards for his work, including three World Fantasy Awards and four Bram Stoker Awards. You can visit his web site at www.stephenjoneseditor.com

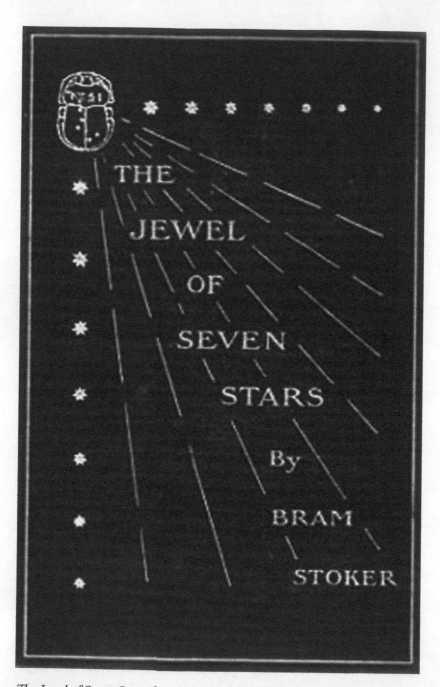

The Jewel of Seven Stars, first edition cover, Heinemann, London, 1903

INTRODUCTION

THE JEWEL OF SEVEN STARS
(1903)

IF *DRACULA* WAS Bram Stoker's "vampire book," then *The Jewel of Seven Stars*—the author's second-best-known work—can be regarded as his "mummy novel."

Published only a year after his previous book, *The Mystery of the Sea*, *The Jewel of Seven Stars* appeared from William Heinemann of London in June 1903. It was a time when much of Edwardian society was keenly interested in occult matters and the new discoveries in Egyptian archaeology, and the author's eighth novel is the story of an obsessive archaeologist's attempts to revive an ancient Egyptian queen of evil.

Although Stoker's working notes for *The Jewel of Seven Stars* have never been discovered, it has been suggested that he most likely based his immortal Queen Tera on either Queen Hatshepsut, who ruled ancient Egypt from 1473 to 1458 BC, or Sobekneferu, the daughter of Pharaoh Amenemhat III, who became ruler of Egypt in the closing years of the Twelfth Dynasty.

Trinity College, where Stoker had been a student, was a noted center for the study of Orientalism, and there is no doubt that due to his connection with Sir Henry Irving, the author would have mixed socially with some of the leading Egyptologists and archaeologists of his day, including controversial custodian and author E. A. Wallis Budge (who is referenced by name in the book).

The Jewel of Seven Stars is not, as some have claimed, the first mummy story—it was preceded by Richard Marsh's *The Beetle* (1897) and Guy Boothby's *Pharos the Egyptian* (1899), along with such short

stories as Théophile Gautier's "The Mummy's Foot" ("Le Pied de mo-
mie," 1840) and Arthur Conan Doyle's "Lot No.249" (1892) and "The
Ring of Toth" (1894). However, like *Dracula* before it, the book did
much to popularize its exotic subject matter to a wider public.

Occult scholar and author John William Brodie-Innes, a leading
member of the Hermetic Order of the Golden Dawn's Amen-Ra Temple
in Edinburgh, Scotland, wrote to Stoker in 1903 as soon as he finished
reading the novel: "It is not only a good book, it is a great book," he
declared, going on to add, "It seems to me in some ways you have got
clearer light on some problems which some of us have been fumbling
after in the dark long enough . . ."

The novel appeared in America in 1904 with much hyperbole from
Harper & Brothers Publishers: *An absorbing story of Egyptian Mystery
suggesting Edgar Allan Poe in its methods of induction, intricacies of plot
and thrilling suspense. The reader is carried away from the prosaic present
to the enthralling yesterday of ancient Egypt. Mystic arts and superstitions
are made by a most unique and convincing plot to seem alluringly possible.*

Upon its original publication, *The Jewel of Seven Stars* received some
criticism due to its decidedly downbeat conclusion. As a result, shortly
before Stoker's death in 1912, the publisher of a popular cheap edition
insisted on a happier ending, complete with a new wedding coda.

It is not known whether the author (who's health was steadily de-
teriorating at the time due to Bright's disease) or the publisher made
these anodyne changes, but, along with the new material, the whole of
Chapter XVI: "Powers – Old and New" was deleted for a revised UK
edition issued by William Rider & Son Ltd. This excluded section was
subsequently reprinted as a stand-alone story entitled "The Bridal of
Death."

As would happen again with his final novel, *The Lair of the White
Worm*, many readers of this rewritten text were disappointed and regarded it as out of keeping with the rest of the book. However, the abridged

version of the novel is the one that most people are familiar with, and the original ending was only restored to the British edition in 1996.

The Jewel of Seven Stars has been filmed four times, but never under its original title. It was first adapted as a TV movie for the British series *Mystery and Imagination* under the somewhat prosaic title *The Curse of the Mummy*. Originally broadcast in February 1970, Isobel Black portrayed the possessed Margaret Trelawny and Donald Churchill was the scheming Corbeck.

Exploitatively retitled *Blood from the Mummy's Tomb* by Hammer Films just a year later, Andrew Kier starred as obsessed archaeologist Julian Fuchs after Peter Cushing left the production when his wife died, and Valerie Leon portrayed both Fuchs's daughter and the reanimated Queen Tera.

Nine years later it was remade again, this time as *The Awakening* (1980), on a significantly bigger budget. Hollywood star Charlton Heston was cast as archaeologist Matthew Corbeck, who believed that his daughter Margaret (Stephanie Zimbalist) had been possessed by the evil Queen Kara.

Oddly, instead of reissuing Bram Stoker's original novel, the producers had the movie novelized by British horror author R. Chetwynd-Hayes.

At least *Bram Stoker's Legend of the Mummy* (1997) acknowledged its source material up front. Louis Gossett Jr. portrayed John Corbeck, and Rachel Naples was the 3,000-year-old Queen Tera, looking to re-create her spirit in another body.

Despite not being quite so influential as *Dracula*, *The Jewel of Seven Stars* still casts its mystic shadow over contemporary horror fiction and, like the grisly artifacts taken from Queen Tera's ancient tomb, is ripe for rediscovery.

S.J.

THE JEWEL OF SEVEN STARS
(1903)

Table of Contents

CHAPTER I

A SUMMONS IN THE NIGHT

IT ALL SEEMED so real that I could hardly imagine that it had ever occurred before; and yet each episode came, not as a fresh step in the logic of things, but as something expected. It is in such a wise that memory plays its pranks for good or ill; for pleasure or pain; for wea l or woe. It is thus that life is bittersweet, and that which has been done becomes eternal.

Again, the light skiff, ceasing to shoot through the lazy water as when the oars flashed and dripped, glided out of the fierce July sunlight into the cool shade of the great drooping willow branches—I standing up in the swaying boat, she sitting still and with deft fingers guarding herself from stray twigs or the freedom of the resilience of moving boughs. Again, the water looked golden-brown under the canopy of translucent green; and the grassy bank was of emerald hue. Again, we sat in the cool shade, with the myriad noises of nature both without and within our bower merging into that drowsy hum in whose sufficing environment the great world with its disturbing trouble, and its more disturbing joys, can be effectually forgotten. Again, in that blissful solitude the young girl lost the convention of her prim, narrow upbringing, and told me in a natural, dreamy way of the loneliness of her new life. With an undertone of sadness she made me feel how in that spacious home each one of the household was isolated by the personal magnificence of her father and herself; that there confidence had no altar, and sympathy no shrine; and that there even her father's face was as distant as the old country life seemed now. Once more, the wisdom of my manhood and the experience of my years laid themselves at the girl's feet. It was seemingly their own doing; for the individual "I" had no say in the matter, but only just obeyed imperative orders. And once again the flying seconds multiplied themselves endlessly. For it is in the arcana of dreams that existences merge and renew themselves, change and yet keep the same—like the soul of a musician in a fugue. And so memory swooned, again and again, in sleep.

It seems that there is never to be any perfect rest. Even in Eden the snake rears its head among the laden boughs of the Tree of Knowledge. The silence of the dreamless night is broken by the roar of the avalanche; the hissing of sudden floods; the clanging of the engine bell marking its sweep through a sleeping American town; the clanking of distant paddles over the sea. . . . Whatever it is, it is breaking the charm of my Eden. The canopy of greenery above us, starred with diamond-points of light, seems to quiver in the ceaseless beat of paddles; and the restless bell seems as though it would never cease. . . .

All at once the gates of Sleep were thrown wide open, and my waking ears took in the cause of the disturbing sounds. Waking existence is prosaic enough—there was somebody knocking and ringing at someone's street door.

I was pretty well accustomed in my Jermyn Street chambers to passing sounds; usually I did not concern myself, sleeping or waking, with the doings, however noisy, of my neighbours. But this noise was too continuous, too insistent, too imperative to be ignored. There was some active intelligence behind that ceaseless sound; and some stress or need behind the intelligence. I was not altogether selfish, and at the thought of someone's need I was, without premeditation, out of bed. Instinctively I looked at my watch. It was just three o'clock; there was a faint edging of grey round the green blind which darkened my room. It was evident that the knocking and ringing were at the door of our own house; and it was evident, too, that there was no one awake to answer the call. I slipped on my dressing-gown and slippers, and went down to the hall door. When I opened it there stood a dapper groom, with one hand pressed unflinchingly on the electric bell whilst with the other he raised a ceaseless clangour with the knocker. The instant he saw me the noise ceased; one hand went up instinctively to the brim of his hat, and the other produced a letter from his pocket. A neat brougham was opposite the door, the horses were breathing heavily as though they had come fast. A policeman, with his night lantern still alight at his belt, stood by, attracted to the spot by the noise.

"Beg pardon, sir, I'm sorry for disturbing you, but my orders was imperative; I was not to lose a moment, but to knock and ring till someone came. May I ask you, sir, if Mr. Malcolm Ross lives here?"

"I am Mr. Malcolm Ross."

"Then this letter is for you, sir, and the bro'am is for you too, sir!"

I took, with a strange curiosity, the letter which he handed to me. As a barrister I had had, of course, odd experiences now and then, including sudden demands upon my time; but never anything like this. I stepped back into the hall, closing the door to, but leaving it ajar; then I switched on the electric light. The letter was directed in a strange hand, a woman's. It began at once without "dear sir" or any such address:

"You said you would like to help me if I needed it; and I believe you meant what you said. The time has come sooner than I expected. I am in dreadful trouble, and do not know where to turn, or to whom to apply. An attempt has, I fear, been made to murder my Father; though, thank God, he still lives. But he is quite unconscious. The doctors and police have been sent for; but there is no one here whom I can depend on. Come at once if you are able to; and forgive me if you can. I suppose I shall realise later what I have done in asking such a favour; but at present I cannot think. Come! Come at once! MARGARET TRELAWNY."

Pain and exultation struggled in my mind as I read; but the mastering thought was that she was in trouble and had called on me—me! My dreaming of her, then, was not altogether without a cause. I called out to the groom:

"Wait! I shall be with you in a minute!" Then I flew upstairs.

A very few minutes sufficed to wash and dress; and we were soon driving through the streets as fast as the horses could go. It was market morning, and when we got out on Picadilly there was an endless stream of carts coming from the west; but for the rest the roadway was clear, and we went quickly. I had told the groom to come into the brougham with me so that he could tell me what had happened as we went along. He sat awkwardly, with his hat on his knees as he spoke.

"Miss Trelawny, sir, sent a man to tell us to get out a carriage at once; and when we was ready she come herself and gave me the letter and told Morgan—the coachman, sir—to fly. She said as I was to lose not a second, but to keep knocking till someone come."

"Yes, I know, I know—you told me! What I want to know is, why she sent for me. What happened in the house?"

"I don't quite know myself, sir; except that master was found in his room senseless, with the sheets all bloody, and a wound on his head. He couldn't be waked nohow. Twas Miss Trelawny herself as found him."

"How did she come to find him at such an hour? It was late in the night, I suppose?"

"I don't know, sir; I didn't hear nothing at all of the details."

As he could tell me no more, I stopped the carriage for a moment to let him get out on the box; then I turned the matter over in my mind as I sat alone. There were many things which I could have asked the servant; and for a few moments after he had gone I was angry with myself for not having used my opportunity. On second thought, however, I was glad the temptation was gone. I felt that it would be more delicate to learn what I wanted to know of Miss Trelawny's surroundings from herself, rather than from her servants.

We bowled swiftly along Knightsbridge, the small noise of our well-appointed vehicle sounding hollowly in the morning air. We turned up the Kensington Palace Road and presently stopped opposite a great house on the left-hand side, nearer, so far as I could judge, the Notting Hill than the Kensington end of the avenue. It was a truly fine house, not only with regard to size but to architecture. Even in the dim grey light of the morning, which tends to diminish the size of things, it looked big.

Miss Trelawny met me in the hall. She was not in any way shy. She seemed to rule all around her with a sort of high-bred dominance, all the more remarkable as she was greatly agitated and as pale as snow. In the great hall were several servants, the men standing together near the hall door, and the women clinging together in the further corners and doorways. A police superintendent had been talking to Miss Trelawny; two men in uniform and one plain-clothes man stood near him. As she took my hand impulsively there was a look of relief in her eyes, and she gave a gentle sigh of relief. Her salutation was simple.

"I knew you would come!"

The clasp of the hand can mean a great deal, even when it is not intended to mean anything especially. Miss Trelawny's hand somehow became lost in my own. It was not that it was a small hand; it was fine and flexible, with long delicate fingers—a rare and beautiful hand; it was the unconscious self-surrender. And though at the moment I could not dwell on the cause of the thrill which swept me, it came back to me later.

She turned and said to the police superintendent:

"This is Mr. Malcolm Ross." The police officer saluted as he answered:

"I know Mr. Malcolm Ross, miss. Perhaps he will remember I had the honour of working with him in the Brixton Coining case." I had not at first glance noticed who it was, my whole attention having been taken with Miss Trelawny.

"Of course, Superintendent Dolan, I remember very well!" I said as we shook hands. I could not but note that the acquaintanceship seemed a relief to Miss Trelawny. There was a certain vague uneasiness in her manner which took my attention; instinctively I felt that it would be less embarrassing for her to speak with me alone. So I said to the Superintendent:

"Perhaps it will be better if Miss Trelawny will see me alone for a few minutes. You, of course, have already heard all she knows; and I shall understand better how things are if I may ask some questions. I will then talk the matter over with you if I may."

"I shall be glad to be of what service I can, sir," he answered heartily.

Following Miss Trelawny, I moved over to a dainty room which opened from the hall and looked out on the garden at the back of the house. When we had entered and I had closed the door she said:

"I will thank you later for your goodness in coming to me in my trouble; but at present you can best help me when you know the facts."

"Go on," I said. "Tell me all you know and spare no detail, however trivial it may at the present time seem to be." She went on at once:

"I was awakened by some sound; I do not know what. I only know that it came through my sleep; for all at once I found myself awake, with my heart beating wildly, listening anxiously for some sound from my Father's room. My room is next Father's, and I can often hear him moving about before I fall asleep. He works late at night, sometimes very late indeed; so that when I wake early, as I do occasionally, or in the grey of the dawn, I hear him still moving. I tried once to remonstrate with him about staying up so late, as it cannot be good for him; but I never ventured to repeat the experiment. You know how stern and cold he can be—at least you may remember what I told you about him; and when he is polite in this mood he is dreadful. When he is angry I can bear it much better; but when he is slow and deliberate, and the side of his mouth lifts up to show the sharp teeth, I think I feel—well, I don't know how! Last night I got up softly and stole to the door, for I really feared to disturb him. There was not any noise of moving, and no kind of cry at all; but there was a queer kind of dragging sound, and a slow, heavy breathing. Oh! it was dreadful, waiting there in the dark and the silence, and fearing—fearing I did not know what!

"At last I took my courage a deux mains, and turning the handle as softly as I could, I opened the door a tiny bit. It was quite dark within; I could just see the outline of the windows. But in the darkness the sound of breathing, becoming more distinct, was appalling. As I listened, this continued; but there was no other sound. I pushed the door open all at once. I was afraid to open it slowly; I felt as if there might be some dreadful thing behind it ready to pounce out on me! Then I switched on the electric light, and stepped into the room. I looked first at the bed. The sheets were all crumpled up, so that I knew Father had been in bed; but there was a great dark red patch in the centre of the bed, and spreading to the edge of it, that made my heart stand still. As I was gazing at it the sound of the breathing came across the room, and my eyes followed to it. There was Father on his right side with the other arm under him, just as if his dead body had been thrown there all in a heap. The track of blood went across the room up to the bed, and there was a pool all around him which looked terribly red and glittering as I bent over to examine him. The place where he lay was right in front of the big safe. He was in his pyjamas. The left sleeve was torn, showing his bare arm, and stretched out toward the safe. It looked—oh! so terrible, patched all with blood, and with the flesh torn or cut all around a gold chain bangle on his wrist. I did not know he wore such a thing, and it seemed to give me a new shock of surprise."

She paused a moment; and as I wished to relieve her by a moment's divergence of thought, I said:

"Oh, that need not surprise you. You will see the most unlikely men wearing bangles. I have seen a judge condemn a man to death, and the wrist of the hand he held up had a gold bangle." She did not seem to heed much the words or the idea; the pause, however, relieved her somewhat, and she went on in a steadier voice:

"I did not lose a moment in summoning aid, for I feared he might bleed to death. I rang the bell, and then went out and called for help as loudly as I could. In what must have been a very short time—though it seemed an incredibly long one to me—some of the servants came running up; and then others, till the room seemed full of staring eyes, and dishevelled hair, and night clothes of all sorts.

"We lifted Father on a sofa; and the housekeeper, Mrs. Grant, who seemed to have her wits about her more than any of us, began to look where the flow of blood came from. In a few seconds it became apparent that it came from the arm which was bare. There was a deep wound-
-not clean-cut as with a knife, but like a jagged rent or tear—close to the wrist, which seemed to have cut into the vein. Mrs. Grant tied a handkerchief round the cut, and screwed it up tight with a silver paper-cutter; and the flow of blood seemed to be checked at once. By this time I had come to my senses—or such of them as remained; and I sent off one man for the doctor and another for the police. When they had gone, I felt that, except for the servants, I was all alone in the house, and that I knew nothing—of my Father or anything else; and a great longing came to me to have someone with me who could help me. Then I thought of you and your kind offer in the boat under the willow-tree; and, without waiting to think, I told the men to get a carriage ready at once, and I scribbled a note and sent it on to you."

She paused. I did not like to say just then anything of how I felt. I looked at her; I think she understood, for her eyes were raised to mine for a moment and then fell, leaving her cheeks as red as peony roses. With a manifest effort she went on with her story:

"The Doctor was with us in an incredibly short time. The groom had met him letting himself into his house with his latchkey, and he came here running. He made a proper tourniquet for poor Father's arm, and then went home to get some appliances. I dare say he will be back almost immediately. Then a policeman came, and sent a message to the station; and very soon the Superintendent was here. Then you came."

There was a long pause, and I ventured to take her hand for an instant. Without a word more we opened the door, and joined the Superintendent in the hall. He hurried up to us, saying as he came:

"I have been examining everything myself, and have sent off a message to Scotland Yard. You see, Mr. Ross, there seemed so much that was odd about the case that I thought we had better have the best man of the Criminal Investigation Department that we could get. So I sent a note asking to have Sergeant Daw sent at once. You remember him, sir, in that American poisoning case at Hoxton."

"Oh yes," I said, "I remember him well; in that and other cases, for I have benefited several times by his skill and acumen. He has a mind that works as truly as any that I know. When I have been for the defence, and believed my man was innocent, I was glad to have him against us!"

"That is high praise, sir!" said the Superintendent gratified: "I am glad you approve of my choice; that I did well in sending for him."

I answered heartily:

"Could not be better. I do not doubt that between you we shall get at the facts—and what lies behind them!"

We ascended to Mr. Trelawny's room, where we found everything exactly as his daughter had described.

There came a ring at the house bell, and a minute later a man was shown into the room. A young man with aquiline features, keen grey eyes, and a forehead that stood out square and broad as that of a thinker. In his hand he had a black bag which he at once opened. Miss Trelawny introduced us: "Doctor Winchester, Mr. Ross, Superintendent Dolan." We bowed mutually, and he, without a moment's delay, began his work. We all waited, and eagerly watched him as he proceeded to dress the wound. As he went on he turned now and again to call the Superintendent's attention to some point about the wound, the latter proceeding to enter the fact at once in his notebook.

"See! several parallel cuts or scratches beginning on the left side of the wrist and in some places endangering the radial artery.

"These small wounds here, deep and jagged, seem as if made with a blunt instrument. This in particular would seem as if made with some kind of sharp wedge; the flesh round it seems torn as if with lateral pressure."

Turning to Miss Trelawny he said presently:

"Do you think we might remove this bangle? It is not absolutely necessary, as it will fall lower on the wrist where it can hang loosely; but it might add to the patient's comfort later on." The poor girl flushed deeply as she answered in a low voice:

"I do not know. I—I have only recently come to live with my Father; and I know so little of his life or his ideas that I fear I can hardly judge in such a matter. The Doctor, after a keen glance at her, said in a very kindly way:

"Forgive me! I did not know. But in any case you need not be distressed. It is not required at present to move it. Were it so I should do so at once on my own responsibility. If it be necessary later on, we can easily remove it with a file. Your Father doubtless has some object in keeping it as it is. See! there is a tiny key attached to it. . . . ." As he was speaking he stopped and bent lower, taking from my hand the candle which I held and lowering it till its light fell on the bangle. Then motioning me to hold the candle in the same position, he took from his pocket a magnifying-glass which he adjusted. When he had made a careful examination he stood up and handed the magnifying-glass to Dolan, saying as he did so:

"You had better examine it yourself. That is no ordinary bangle. The gold is wrought over triple steel links; see where it is worn away. It is manifestly not meant to be removed lightly; and it would need more than an ordinary file to do it."

The Superintendent bent his great body; but not getting close enough that way knelt down by the sofa as the Doctor had done. He examined the bangle minutely, turning it slowly round so that no particle of it escaped observation. Then he stood up and handed the magnifying-glass to me. "When you have examined it yourself," he said, "let the lady look at it if she will," and he commenced to write at length in his notebook.

I made a simple alteration in his suggestion. I held out the glass toward Miss Trelawny, saying:

"Had you not better examine it first?" She drew back, slightly raising her hand in disclaimer, as she said impulsively:

"Oh no! Father would doubtless have shown it to me had he wished me to see it. I would not like to without his consent." Then she added, doubtless fearing lest her delicacy of view should give offence to the rest of us:

"Of course it is right that you should see it. You have to examine and consider everything; and indeed—indeed I am grateful to you. . ."

She turned away; I could see that she was crying quietly. It was evident to me that even in the midst of her trouble and anxiety there was a chagrin that she knew so little of her father; and that her ignorance had to be shown at such a time and amongst so many strangers. That they were all men did not make the shame more easy to bear, though there was a certain relief in it. Trying to interpret her feelings I could not but think that she must have been glad that no woman's eyes—of understanding greater than man's—were upon her in that hour.

When I stood up from my examination, which verified to me that of the Doctor, the latter resumed his place beside the couch and went on with his ministrations. Superintendent Dolan said to me in a whisper:

"I think we are fortunate in our doctor!" I nodded, and was about to add something in praise of his acumen, when there came a low tapping at the door.

CHAPTER II

STRANGE INSTRUCTIONS

SUPERINTENDENT DOLAN WENT quietly to the door; by a sort of natural understanding he had taken possession of affairs in the room. The rest of us waited. He opened the door a little way; and then with a gesture of manifest relief threw it wide, and a young man stepped in. A young man clean-shaven, tall and slight; with an eagle face and bright, quick eyes that seemed to take in everything around him at a glance. As he came in, the Superintendent held out his hand; the two men shook hands warmly.

"I came at once, sir, the moment I got your message. I am glad I still have your confidence."

"That you'll always have," said the Superintendent heartily. "I have not forgotten our old Bow Street days, and I never shall!" Then, without a word of preliminary, he began to tell everything he knew up to the moment of the newcomer's entry. Sergeant Daw asked a few questions—a very few—when it was necessary for his understanding of circumstances or the relative positions of persons; but as a rule Dolan, who knew his work thoroughly, forestalled every query, and explained all necessary matters as he went on. Sergeant Daw threw occasionally swift glances round him; now at one of us; now at the room or some part of it; now at the wounded man lying senseless on the sofa.

When the Superintendent had finished, the Sergeant turned to me and said:

"Perhaps you remember me, sir. I was with you in that Hoxton case."

"I remember you very well," I said as I held out my hand. The Superintendent spoke again:

"You understand, Sergeant Daw, that you are put in full charge of this case."

"Under you I hope, sir," he interrupted. The other shook his head and smiled as he said:

"It seems to me that this is a case that will take all a man's time and his brains. I have other work to do; but I shall be more than interested, and if I can help in any possible way I shall be glad to do so!"

"All right, sir," said the other, accepting his responsibility with a sort of modified salute; straightway he began his investigation.

First he came over to the Doctor and, having learned his name and address, asked him to write a full report which he could use, and which he could refer to headquarters if necessary. Doctor Winchester bowed gravely as he promised. Then the Sergeant approached me and said sotto voce:

"I like the look of your doctor. I think we can work together!" Turning to Miss Trelawny he asked:

"Please let me know what you can of your Father; his ways of life, his history—in fact of anything of whatsoever kind which interests him, or in which he may be concerned." I was about to interrupt to tell him what she had already said of her ignorance in all matters of her father and his ways, but her warning hand was raised to me pointedly and she spoke herself.

"Alas! I know little or nothing. Superintendent Dolan and Mr. Ross know already all I can say."

"Well, ma'am, we must be content to do what we can," said the officer genially. "I'll begin by making a minute examination. You say that you were outside the door when you heard the noise?"

"I was in my room when I heard the queer sound—indeed it must have been the early part of whatever it was which woke me. I came out of my room at once. Father's door was shut, and I could see the whole landing and the upper slopes of the staircase. No one could have left by the door unknown to me, if that is what you mean!"

"That is just what I do mean, miss. If every one who knows anything will tell me as well as that, we shall soon get to the bottom of this."

He then went over to the bed, looked at it carefully, and asked: "Has the bed been touched?"

"Not to my knowledge," said Miss Trelawny, "but I shall ask Mrs. Grant—the housekeeper," she added as she rang the bell. Mrs. Grant answered it in person. "Come in," said Miss Trelawny. "These gentlemen want to know, Mrs. Grant, if the bed has been touched."

"Not by me, ma'am."

"Then," said Miss Trelawny, turning to Sergeant Daw, "it cannot have been touched by any one. Either Mrs. Grant or I myself was here all the time, and I do not think any of the servants who came when I gave the alarm were near the bed at all. You see, Father lay here just under the great safe, and every one crowded round him. We sent them all away in a very short time." Daw, with a motion of his hand, asked us all to stay at the other side of the room whilst with a magnifying-glass he examined the bed, taking care as he moved each fold of the bed-clothes to replace it in exact position. Then he examined with his magnifying-glass the floor beside it, taking especial pains where the blood had trickled over the side of the bed, which was of heavy red wood handsomely carved. Inch by inch, down on his knees, carefully avoiding any touch with the stains on the floor, he followed the blood-marks over to the spot, close under the great safe, where the body had lain. All around and about this spot he went for a radius of some yards; but seemingly did not meet with anything to arrest special attention. Then he examined the front of the safe; round the lock, and along the bottom and top of the double doors, more especially at the places of their touching in front.

Next he went to the windows, which were fastened down with the hasps.

"Were the shutters closed?" he asked Miss Trelawny in a casual way as though he expected the negative answer, which came.

All this time Doctor Winchester was attending to his patient; now dressing the wounds in the wrist or making minute examination all over the head and throat, and over the heart. More than once he put his nose to the mouth of the senseless man and sniffed. Each time he did so he finished up by unconsciously looking round the room, as though in search of something.

Then we heard the deep strong voice of the Detective:

"So far as I can see, the object was to bring that key to the lock of the safe. There seems to be some secret in the mechanism that I am unable to guess at, though I served a year in Chubb's before I joined the police. It is a combination lock of seven letters; but there seems to be a way of locking even the combination. It is one of Chatwood's; I shall call at their place and find out something about it." Then turning to the Doctor, as though his own work were for the present done, he said:

"Have you anything you can tell me at once, Doctor, which will not interfere with your full report? If there is any doubt I can wait, but the sooner I know something definite the better." Doctor Winchester answered at once:

"For my own part I see no reason in waiting. I shall make a full report of course. But in the meantime I shall tell you all I know—which is after all not very much, and all I think—which is less definite. There is no wound on the head which could account for the state of stupor in which the patient continues. I must, therefore, take it that either he has been drugged or is under some hypnotic influence. So far as I can judge, he has not been drugged—at least by means of any drug of whose qualities I am aware. Of course, there is ordinarily in this room so much of a mummy smell that it is difficult to be certain about anything having a delicate aroma. I dare say that you have noticed the peculiar Egyptians scents, bitumen, nard, aromatic gums and spices, and so forth. It is quite possible that somewhere in this room, amongst the curios and hidden by stronger scents, is some substance or liquid which may have the effect we see. It is possible that the patient has taken some drug, and that he may in some sleeping phase have injured himself. I do not think this is likely; and circumstances, other than those which I have myself been investigating, may prove that this surmise is not correct. But in the meantime it is possible; and must, till it be disproved, be kept within our purview." Here Sergeant Daw interrupted:

"That may be, but if so, we should be able to find the instrument with which the wrist was injured. There would be marks of blood somewhere."

"Exactly so!" said the Doctor, fixing his glasses as though preparing for an argument. "But if it be that the patient has used some strange drug, it may be one that does not take effect at once. As we are as yet ignorant of its potentialities—if, indeed, the whole surmise is correct at all—we must be prepared at all points."

Here Miss Trelawny joined in the conversation:

"That would be quite right, so far as the action of the drug was concerned; but according to the second part of your surmise the wound may have been self-inflicted, and this after the drug had taken effect."

"True!" said the Detective and the Doctor simultaneously. She went on:

"As however, Doctor, your guess does not exhaust the possibilities, we must bear in mind that some other variant of the same root-idea may be correct. I take it, therefore, that our first search, to be made on this assumption, must be for the weapon with which the injury was done to my Father's wrist."

"Perhaps he put the weapon in the safe before he became quite unconscious," said I, giving voice foolishly to a half-formed thought.

"That could not be," said the Doctor quickly. "At least I think it could hardly be," he added cautiously, with a brief bow to me. "You see, the left hand is covered with blood; but there is no blood mark whatever on the safe."

"Quite right!" I said, and there was a long pause.

The first to break the silence was the Doctor.

"We shall want a nurse here as soon as possible; and I know the very one to suit. I shall go at once to get her if I can. I must ask that till I return some of you will remain constantly with the patient. It may be necessary to remove him to another room later on; but in the meantime he is best left here. Miss Trelawny, may I take it that either you or Mrs. Grant will remain here—not merely in the room, but close to the patient and watchful of him—till I return?"

She bowed in reply, and took a seat beside the sofa. The Doctor gave her some directions as to what she should do in case her father should become conscious before his return.

The next to move was Superintendent Dolan, who came close to Sergeant Daw as he said:

"I had better return now to the station—unless, of course, you should wish me to remain for a while."

He answered, "Is Johnny Wright still in your division?"

"Yes! Would you like him to be with you?" The other nodded reply. "Then I will send him on to you as soon as can be arranged. He shall then stay with you as long as you wish. I will tell him that he is to take his instructions entirely from you."

The Sergeant accompanied him to the door, saying as he went:

"Thank you, sir; you are always thoughtful for men who are working with you. It is a pleasure to me to be with you again. I shall go back to Scotland Yard and report to my chief. Then I shall call at Chatwood's; and I shall return here as soon as possible. I suppose I may take it, miss, that I may put up here for a day or two, if required. It may be some help, or possibly some comfort to you, if I am about, until we unravel this mystery."

"I shall be very grateful to you." He looked keenly at her for a few seconds before he spoke again.

"Before I go have I permission to look about your Father's table and desk? There might be something which would give us a clue—or a lead at all events." Her answer was so unequivocal as almost to surprise him.

"You have the fullest possible permission to do anything which may help us in this dreadful trouble—to discover what it is that is wrong with my Father, or which may shield him in the future!"

He began at once a systematic search of the dressing-table, and after that of the writing-table in the room. In one of the drawers he found a letter sealed; this he brought at once across the room and handed to Miss Trelawny.

"A letter—directed to me—and in my Father's hand!" she said as she eagerly opened it. I watched her face as she began to read; but seeing at once that Sergeant Daw kept his keen eyes on her face, unflinchingly watching every flitting expression, I kept my eyes henceforth fixed on his. When Miss Trelawny had read her letter through, I had in my mind a conviction, which, however, I kept locked in my own heart. Amongst the suspicions in the mind of the Detective was one, rather perhaps potential than definite, of Miss Trelawny herself.

For several minutes Miss Trelawny held the letter in her hand with her eyes downcast, thinking. Then she read it carefully again; this time the varying expressions were intensified, and I thought I could easily follow them. When she had finished the second reading, she paused again. Then, though with some reluctance, she handed the letter to the Detective. He read it eagerly but with unchanging face; read it a second time, and then handed it back with a bow. She paused a little again, and then handed it to me. As she did so she raised her eyes to mine for a single moment appealingly; a swift blush spread over her pale cheeks and forehead.

With mingled feelings I took it, but, all said, I was glad. She did not show any perturbation in giving the letter to the Detective—she might not have shown any to anyone else. But to me . . . I feared to follow the thought further; but read on, conscious that the eyes of both Miss Trelawny and the Detective were fixed on me.

"MY DEAR DAUGHTER, I want you to take this letter as an instruction—absolute and imperative, and admitting of no deviation whatever—in case anything untoward or unexpected by you or by others should happen to me. If I should be suddenly and mysteriously stricken down—either by sickness, accident or attack—you must follow these directions implicitly. If I am not already in my bedroom when you are made cognisant of my state, I am to be brought there as quickly as possible. Even should I be dead, my body is to be brought there. Thenceforth, until I am either conscious and able to give instructions on my own account, or buried, I am never to be left alone—not for a single instant. From nightfall to sunrise at least two persons must remain in the room. It will be well that a trained nurse be in the room from time to time, and will note any symptoms, either permanent or changing, which may strike her. My solicitors, Marvin & Jewkes, of 27B Lincoln's Inn, have full instructions in case of my death; and Mr. Marvin has himself undertaken to see personally my wishes carried out. I should advise you, my dear Daughter, seeing that you have no relative to apply to, to get some friend whom you can trust to either remain within the house where instant communication can be made, or to come nightly to aid in the watching, or to be within call. Such friend may be either male or female; but, whichever it may be, there should be added one other watcher or attendant at hand of the opposite sex. Understand, that it is of the very essence of my wish that there should be, awake and exercising themselves to my purposes, both masculine and feminine intelligences. Once more, my dear Margaret, let me impress on you the need for observation and just reasoning to conclusions, howsoever strange. If I am taken ill or injured, this will be no ordinary occasion; and I wish to warn you, so that your guarding may be complete.

"Nothing in my room—I speak of the curios—must be removed or displaced in any way, or for any cause whatever. I have a special reason and a special purpose in the placing of each; so that any moving of them would thwart my plans.

"Should you want money or counsel in anything, Mr. Marvin will carry out your wishes; to the which he has my full instructions."

"ABEL TRELAWNY."

I read the letter a second time before speaking, for I feared to betray myself. The choice of a friend might be a momentous occasion for me. I had already ground for hope, that she had asked me to help her in the first throe of her trouble; but love makes its own doubtings, and I feared. My thoughts seemed to whirl with lightning rapidity, and in a few seconds a whole process of reasoning became formulated. I must not volunteer to be the friend that the father advised his daughter to have to aid her in her vigil; and yet that one glance had a lesson which I must not ignore. Also, did not she, when she wanted help, send to me—to me a stranger, except for one meeting at a dance and one brief afternoon of companionship on the river? Would it not humiliate her to make her ask me twice? Humiliate her! No! that pain I could at all events save her; it is not humiliation to refuse. So, as I handed her back the letter, I said:

"I know you will forgive me, Miss Trelawny, if I presume too much; but if you will permit me to aid in the watching I shall be proud. Though the occasion is a sad one, I shall be so far happy to be allowed the privilege."

Despite her manifest and painful effort at self-control, the red tide swept her face and neck. Even her eyes seemed suffused, and in stern contrast with her pale cheeks when the tide had rolled back. She answered in a low voice:

"I shall be very grateful for your help!" Then in an afterthought she added:

"But you must not let me be selfish in my need! I know you have many duties to engage you; and though I shall value your help highly—most highly—it would not be fair to monopolise your time."

"As to that," I answered at once, "my time is yours. I can for today easily arrange my work so that I can come here in the afternoon and stay till morning. After that, if the occasion still demands it, I can so arrange my work that I shall have more time still at my disposal."

She was much moved. I could see the tears gather in her eyes, and she turned away her head. The Detective spoke:

"I am glad you will be here, Mr. Ross. I shall be in the house myself, as Miss Trelawny will allow me, if my people in Scotland Yard will permit. That letter seems to put a different complexion on everything; though the mystery remains greater than ever. If you can wait here an hour or two I shall go to headquarters, and then to the safe-makers. After that I shall return; and you can go away easier in your mind, for I shall be here."

When he had gone, we two, Miss Trelawny and I, remained in silence. At last she raised her eyes and looked at me for a moment; after that I would not have exchanged places with a king. For a while she busied herself round the extemporised bedside of her father. Then, asking me to be sure not to take my eyes off him till she returned, she hurried out.

In a few minutes she came back with Mrs. Grant and two maids and a couple of men, who bore the entire frame and furniture of a light iron bed. This they proceeded to put together and to make. When the work was completed, and the servants had withdrawn, she said to me:

"It will be well to be all ready when the Doctor returns. He will surely want to have Father put to bed; and a proper bed will be better for him than the sofa." She then got a chair close beside her father, and sat down watching him.

I went about the room, taking accurate note of all I saw. And truly there were enough things in the room to evoke the curiosity of any man—even though the attendant circumstances were less strange. The whole place, excepting those articles of furniture necessary to a well-furnished bedroom, was filled with magnificent curios, chiefly Egyptian. As the room was of immense size there was opportunity for the placing of a large number of them, even if, as with these, they were of huge proportions.

Whilst I was still investigating the room there came the sound of wheels on the gravel outside the house. There was a ring at the hall door, and a few minutes later, after a preliminary tap at the door and an answering "Come in!" Doctor Winchester entered, followed by a young woman in the dark dress of a nurse.

"I have been fortunate!" he said as he came in. "I found her at once and free. Miss Trelawny, this is Nurse Kennedy!"

CHAPTER III

THE WATCHERS

I WAS STRUCK by the way the two young women looked at each other. I suppose I have been so much in the habit of weighing up in my own mind the personality of witnesses and of forming judgment by their unconscious action and mode of bearing themselves, that the habit extends to my life outside as well as within the court-house. At this moment of my life anything that interested Miss Trelawny interested me; and as she had been struck by the newcomer I instinctively weighed her up also. By comparison of the two I seemed somehow to gain a new knowledge of Miss Trelawny. Certainly, the two women made a good contrast. Miss Trelawny was of fine figure; dark, straight-featured. She had marvellous eyes; great, wide-open, and as black and soft as velvet, with a mysterious depth. To look in them was like gazing at a black mirror such as Doctor Dee used in his wizard rites. I heard an old gentleman at the picnic, a great oriental traveller, describe the effect of her eyes "as looking at night at the great distant lamps of a mosque through the open door." The eyebrows were typical. Finely arched and rich in long curling hair, they seemed like the proper architectural environment of the deep, splendid eyes. Her hair was black also, but was as fine as silk. Generally black hair is a type of animal strength and seems as if some strong expression of the forces of a strong nature; but in this case there could be no such thought. There were refinement and high breeding; and though there was no suggestion of weakness, any sense of power there was, was rather spiritual than animal. The whole harmony of her being seemed complete. Carriage, figure, hair, eyes; the mobile, full mouth, whose scarlet lips and white teeth seemed to light up the lower part of the face—as the eyes did the upper; the wide sweep of the jaw from chin to ear; the long, fine fingers; the hand which seemed to move from the wrist as though it had a sentience of its own. All these perfections went to make up a personality that dominated either by its grace, its sweetness, its beauty, or its charm.

Nurse Kennedy, on the other hand, was rather under than over a woman's average height. She was firm and thickset, with full limbs and broad, strong, capable hands. Her colour was in the general effect that of an autumn leaf. The yellow-brown hair was thick and long, and the golden-brown eyes sparkled from the freckled, sunburnt skin. Her rosy cheeks gave a general idea of rich brown. The red lips and white teeth did not alter the colour scheme, but only emphasized it. She had a snub nose—there was no possible doubt about it; but like such noses in general it showed a nature generous, untiring, and full of good-nature. Her broad white forehead, which even the freckles had spared, was full of forceful thought and reason.

Doctor Winchester had on their journey from the hospital, coached her in the necessary particulars, and without a word she took charge of the patient and set to work. Having examined the new-made bed and shaken the pillows, she spoke to the Doctor, who gave instructions; presently we all four, stepping together, lifted the unconscious man from the sofa.

Early in the afternoon, when Sergeant Daw had returned, I called at my rooms in Jermyn Street, and sent out such clothes, books and papers as I should be likely to want within a few days. Then I went on to keep my legal engagements.

The Court sat late that day as an important case was ending; it was striking six as I drove in at the gate of the Kensington Palace Road. I found myself installed in a large room close to the sick chamber.

That night we were not yet regularly organised for watching, so that the early part of the evening showed an unevenly balanced guard. Nurse Kennedy, who had been on duty all day, was lying down, as she had arranged to come on again by twelve o'clock. Doctor Winchester, who was dining in the house, remained in the room until dinner was announced; and went back at once when it was over. During dinner Mrs. Grant remained in the room, and with her Sergeant Daw, who wished to complete a minute examination which he had undertaken of everything in the room and near it. At nine o'clock Miss Trelawny and I went in to relieve the Doctor. She had lain down for a few hours in the afternoon so as to be refreshed for her work at night. She told me that she had determined that for this night at least she would sit up and watch. I did not try to dissuade her, for I knew that her mind was made up. Then and there I made up my mind that I would watch with her—unless, of course, I should see that she really did not wish it. I said nothing of my intentions for the present. We came in on tiptoe, so silently that the Doctor, who was bending over the bed, did not hear us, and seemed a little startled when suddenly looking up he saw our eyes upon him. I felt that the mystery of the whole thing was getting on his nerves, as it had already got on the nerves of some others of us. He was, I fancied, a little annoyed with himself for having been so startled, and at once began to talk in a hurried manner as though to get over our idea of his embarrassment:

"I am really and absolutely at my wits' end to find any fit cause for this stupor. I have made again as accurate an examination as I know how, and I am satisfied that there is no injury to the brain, that is, no external injury. Indeed, all his vital organs seem unimpaired. I have given him, as you know, food several times and it has manifestly done him good. His breathing is strong and regular, and his pulse is slower and stronger than it was this morning. I cannot find evidence of any known drug, and his unconsciousness does not resemble any of the many cases of hypnotic sleep which I saw in the Charcot Hospital in Paris. And as to these wounds"——he laid his finger gently on the bandaged wrist which lay outside the coverlet as he spoke, "I do not know what to make of them. They might have been made by a carding-machine; but that supposition is untenable. It is within the bounds of possibility that they might have been made by a wild animal if it had taken care to sharpen its claws. That too is, I take it, impossible. By the way, have you any strange pets here in the house; anything of an exceptional kind, such as a tiger-cat or anything out of the common?" Miss Trelawny smiled a sad smile which made my heart ache, as she made answer:

"Oh no! Father does not like animals about the house, unless they are dead and mummied." This was said with a touch of bitterness— or jealousy, I could hardly tell which. "Even my poor kitten was only allowed in the house on sufferance; and though he is the dearest and best-conducted cat in the world, he is now on a sort of parole, and is not allowed into this room."

As she was speaking a faint rattling of the door handle was heard. Instantly Miss Trelawny's face brightened. She sprang up and went over to the door, saying as she went:

"There he is! That is my Silvio. He stands on his hind legs and ratt-les the door handle when he wants to come into a room." She opened the door, speaking to the cat as though he were a baby: "Did him want his movver? Come then; but he must stay with her!" She lifted the cat, and came back with him in her arms. He was certainly a magnificent animal. A chinchilla grey Persian with long silky hair; a really lordly animal with a haughty bearing despite his gentleness; and with great paws which spread out as he placed them on the ground. Whilst she was fondling him, he suddenly gave a wriggle like an eel and slipped out of her arms. He ran across the room and stood opposite a low table on which stood the mummy of an animal, and began to mew and snarl. Miss Trelawny was after him in an instant and lifted him in her arms, kicking and struggling and wriggling to get away; but not biting or scratching, for evidently he loved his beautiful mistress. He ceased to make a noise the moment he was in her arms; in a whisper she admonished him:

"O you naughty Silvio! You have broken your parole that mother gave for you. Now, say goodnight to the gentlemen, and come away to mother's room!" As she was speaking she held out the cat's paw to me to shake. As I did so I could not but admire its size and beauty. "Why," said I, "his paw seems like a little boxing-glove full of claws." She smiled:

"So it ought to. Don't you notice that my Silvio has seven toes, see!" she opened the paw; and surely enough there were seven separate claws, each of them sheathed in a delicate, fine, shell-like case. As I gently stroked the foot the claws emerged and one of them accidentally—there was no anger now and the cat was purring—stuck into my hand. Instinctively I said as I drew back:

"Why, his claws are like razors!"

Doctor Winchester had come close to us and was bending over looking at the cat's claws; as I spoke he said in a quick, sharp way:

"Eh!" I could hear the quick intake of his breath. Whilst I was stroking the now quiescent cat, the Doctor went to the table and tore off a piece of blotting-paper from the writing-pad and came back. He laid the paper on his palm and, with a simple "pardon me!" to Miss Trelawny, placed the cat's paw on it and pressed it down with his other hand. The haughty cat seemed to resent somewhat the familiarity, and tried to draw its foot away. This was plainly what the Doctor wanted, for in the act the cat opened the sheaths of its claws and made several reefs in the soft paper. Then Miss Trelawny took her pet away. She returned in a couple of minutes; as she came in she said:

"It is most odd about that mummy! When Silvio came into the room first—indeed I took him in as a kitten to show to Father—he went on just the same way. He jumped up on the table, and tried to scratch and bite the mummy. That was what made Father so angry, and brought the decree of banishment on poor Silvio. Only his parole, given through me, kept him in the house."

Whilst she had been gone, Doctor Winchester had taken the bandage from her father's wrist. The wound was now quite clear, as the separate cuts showed out in fierce red lines. The Doctor folded the blotting-paper across the line of punctures made by the cat's claws, and held it down close to the wound. As he did so, he looked up triumphantly and beckoned us over to him.

The cuts in the paper corresponded with the wounds in the wrist! No explanation was needed, as he said:

"It would have been better if master Silvio had not broken his parole!"

We were all silent for a little while. Suddenly Miss Trelawny said:

"But Silvio was not in here last night!"

"Are you sure? Could you prove that if necessary?" She hesitated before replying:

"I am certain of it; but I fear it would be difficult to prove. Silvio sleeps in a basket in my room. I certainly put him to bed last night; I remember distinctly laying his little blanket over him, and tucking him in. This morning I took him out of the basket myself. I certainly never noticed him in here; though, of course, that would not mean much, for I was too concerned about poor father, and too much occupied with him, to notice even Silvio."

The Doctor shook his head as he said with a certain sadness:

"Well, at any rate it is no use trying to prove anything now. Any cat in the world would have cleaned blood-marks—did any exist—from his paws in a hundredth part of the time that has elapsed."

Again we were all silent; and again the silence was broken by Miss Trelawny:

"But now that I think of it, it could not have been poor Silvio that injured Father. My door was shut when I first heard the sound; and Father's was shut when I listened at it. When I went in, the injury had been done; so that it must have been before Silvio could possibly have got in." This reasoning commended itself, especially to me as a barrister, for it was proof to satisfy a jury. It gave me a distinct pleasure to have Silvio acquitted of the crime—possibly because he was Miss Trelawny's cat and was loved by her. Happy cat! Silvio's mistress was manifestly pleased as I said:

"Verdict, 'not guilty!'" Doctor Winchester after a pause observed:

"My apologies to master Silvio on this occasion; but I am still puzzled to know why he is so keen against that mummy. Is he the same toward the other mummies in the house? There are, I suppose, a lot of them. I saw three in the hall as I came in."

"There are lots of them," she answered. "I sometimes don't know whether I am in a private house or the British Museum. But Silvio never concerns himself about any of them except that particular one. I suppose it must be because it is of an animal, not a man or a woman."

"Perhaps it is of a cat!" said the Doctor as he started up and went across the room to look at the mummy more closely. "Yes," he went on, "it is the mummy of a cat; and a very fine one, too. If it hadn't been a special favourite of some very special person it would never have received so much honour. See! A painted case and obsidian eyes-just like a human mummy. It is an extraordinary thing, that knowledge of kind to kind. Here is a dead cat—that is all; it is perhaps four or five thousand years old—and another cat of another breed, in what is practically another world, is ready to fly at it, just as it would if it were not dead. I should like to experiment a bit about that cat if you don't mind, Miss Trelawny." She hesitated before replying:

"Of course, do anything you may think necessary or wise; but I hope it will not be anything to hurt or worry my poor Silvio." The Doctor smiled as he answered:

"Oh, Silvio would be all right: it is the other one that my sympathies would be reserved for."

"How do you mean?"

"Master Silvio will do the attacking; the other one will do the suffering."

"Suffering?" There was a note of pain in her voice. The Doctor smiled more broadly:

"Oh, please make your mind easy as to that. The other won't suffer as we understand it; except perhaps in his structure and outfit."

"What on earth do you mean?"

"Simply this, my dear young lady, that the antagonist will be a mummy cat like this one. There are, I take it, plenty of them to be had in Museum Street. I shall get one and place it here instead of that one— you won't think that a temporary exchange will violate your Father's instructions, I hope. We shall then find out, to begin with, whether Silvio objects to all mummy cats, or only to this one in particular."

"I don't know," she said doubtfully. "Father's instructions seem very uncompromising." Then after a pause she went on: "But of course under the circumstances anything that is to be ultimately for his good must be done. I suppose there can't be anything very particular about the mummy of a cat."

Doctor Winchester said nothing. He sat rigid, with so grave a look on his face that his extra gravity passed on to me; and in its enlightening perturbation I began to realise more than I had yet done the strangeness of the case in which I was now so deeply concerned. When once this

thought had begun there was no end to it. Indeed it grew, and blossomed, and reproduced itself in a thousand different ways. The room
and all in it gave grounds for strange thoughts. There were so many
ancient relics that unconsciously one was taken back to strange lands
and strange times. There were so many mummies or mummy objects,
round which there seemed to cling for ever the penetrating odours of
bitumen, and spices and gums—"Nard and Circassia's balmy smells"—
that one was unable to forget the past. Of course, there was but little
light in the room, and that carefully shaded; so that there was no glare
anywhere. None of that direct light which can manifest itself as a power
or an entity, and so make for companionship. The room was a large
one, and lofty in proportion to its size. In its vastness was place for a
multitude of things not often found in a bedchamber. In far corners of
the room were shadows of uncanny shape. More than once as I thought,
the multitudinous presence of the dead and the past took such hold
on me that I caught myself looking round fearfully as though some
strange personality or influence was present. Even the manifest presence
of Doctor Winchester and Miss Trelawny could not altogether comfort
or satisfy me at such moments. It was with a distinct sense of relief that
I saw a new personality in the room in the shape of Nurse Kennedy.
There was no doubt that that business-like, self-reliant, capable young
woman added an element of security to such wild imaginings as my
own. She had a quality of common sense that seemed to pervade everything around her, as though it were some kind of emanation. Up to
that moment I had been building fancies around the sick man; so that
finally all about him, including myself, had become involved in them,
or enmeshed, or saturated, or. . .But now that she had come, he relapsed
into his proper perspective as a patient; the room was a sick-room, and
the shadows lost their fearsome quality. The only thing which it could
not altogether abrogate was the strange Egyptian smell. You may put a
mummy in a glass case and hermetically seal it so that no corroding air

can get within; but all the same it will exhale its odour. One might think that four or five thousand years would exhaust the olfactory qualities of anything; but experience teaches us that these smells remain, and that their secrets are unknown to us. Today they are as much mysteries as they were when the embalmers put the body in the bath of natron. . . .

All at once I sat up. I had become lost in an absorbing reverie. The Egyptian smell had seemed to get on my nerves—on my memory—on my very will.

At that moment I had a thought which was like an inspiration. If I was influenced in such a manner by the smell, might it not be that the sick man, who lived half his life or more in the atmosphere, had gradually and by slow but sure process taken into his system something which had permeated him to such degree that it had a new power derived from quantity—or strength—or. . .

I was becoming lost again in a reverie. This would not do. I must take such precaution that I could remain awake, or free from such entrancing thought. I had had but half a night's sleep last night; and this night I must remain awake. Without stating my intention, for I feared that I might add to the trouble and uneasiness of Miss Trelawny, I went downstairs and out of the house. I soon found a chemist's shop, and came away with a respirator. When I got back, it was ten o'clock; the Doctor was going for the night. The Nurse came with him to the door of the sick-room, taking her last instructions. Miss Trelawny sat still beside the bed. Sergeant Daw, who had entered as the Doctor went out, was some little distance off.

When Nurse Kennedy joined us, we arranged that she should sit up till two o'clock, when Miss Trelawny would relieve her. Thus, in accordance with Mr. Trelawny's instructions, there would always be a man and a woman in the room; and each one of us would overlap, so that at no time would a new set of watchers come on duty without some one to tell of what—if anything—had occurred. I lay down on a sofa in my own room, having arranged that one of the servants should call me a little before twelve. In a few moments I was asleep.

When I was waked, it took me several seconds to get back my thoughts so as to recognise my own identity and surroundings. The short sleep had, however, done me good, and I could look on things around me in a more practical light than I had been able to do earlier in the evening. I bathed my face, and thus refreshed went into the sick-room. I moved very softly. The Nurse was sitting by the bed, quiet and alert; the Detective sat in an arm-chair across the room in deep shadow. He did not move when I crossed, until I got close to him, when he said in a dull whisper:

"It is all right; I have not been asleep!" An unnecessary thing to say, I thought—it always is, unless it be untrue in spirit. When I told him that his watch was over; that he might go to bed till I should call him at six o'clock, he seemed relieved and went with alacrity. At the door he turned and, coming back to me, said in a whisper:

"I sleep lightly and I shall have my pistols with me. I won't feel so heavy-headed when I get out of this mummy smell."

He too, then, had shared my experience of drowsiness!

I asked the Nurse if she wanted anything. I noticed that she had a vinaigrette in her lap. Doubtless she, too, had felt some of the influence which had so affected me. She said that she had all she required, but that if she should want anything she would at once let me know. I wished to keep her from noticing my respirator, so I went to the chair in the shadow where her back was toward me. Here I quietly put it on, and made myself comfortable.

For what seemed a long time, I sat and thought and thought. It was a wild medley of thoughts, as might have been expected from the experiences of the previous day and night. Again I found myself thinking of the Egyptian smell; and I remember that I felt a delicious satisfaction that I did not experience it as I had done. The respirator was doing its work.

It must have been that the passing of this disturbing thought made for repose of mind, which is the corollary of bodily rest, for, though I really cannot remember being asleep or waking from it, I saw a vision—I dreamed a dream, I scarcely know which.

I was still in the room, seated in the chair. I had on my respirator and knew that I breathed freely. The Nurse sat in her chair with her back toward me. She sat quite still. The sick man lay as still as the dead. It was rather like the picture of a scene than the reality; all were still and silent; and the stillness and silence were continuous. Outside, in the distance I could hear the sounds of a city, the occasional roll of wheels, the shout of a reveller, the far-away echo of whistles and the rumbling of trains. The light was very, very low; the reflection of it under the green-shaded lamp was a dim relief to the darkness, rather than light. The green silk fringe of the lamp had merely the colour of an emerald seen in the moonlight. The room, for all its darkness, was full of shadows. It seemed in my whirling thoughts as though all the real things had become shadows—shadows which moved, for they passed the dim outline of the high windows. Shadows which had sentience. I even thought there was sound, a faint sound as of the mew of a cat— the rustle of drapery and a metallic clink as of metal faintly touching metal. I sat as one entranced. At last I felt, as in nightmare, that this was sleep, and that in the passing of its portals all my will had gone.

All at once my senses were full awake. A shriek rang in my ears. The room was filled suddenly with a blaze of light. There was the sound of pistol shots—one, two; and a haze of white smoke in the room. When my waking eyes regained their power, I could have shrieked with horror myself at what I saw before me.

CHAPTER IV

THE SECOND ATTEMPT

THE SIGHT WHICH met my eyes had the horror of a dream within a dream, with the certainty of reality added. The room was as I had seen it last; except that the shadowy look had gone in the glare of the many lights, and every article in it stood stark and solidly real.

By the empty bed sat Nurse Kennedy, as my eyes had last seen her, sitting bolt upright in the arm-chair beside the bed. She had placed a pillow behind her, so that her back might be erect; but her neck was fixed as that of one in a cataleptic trance. She was, to all intents and purposes, turned into stone. There was no special expression on her face—no fear, no horror; nothing such as might be expected of one in such a condition. Her open eyes showed neither wonder nor interest. She was simply a negative existence, warm, breathing, placid; but absolutely unconscious of the world around her. The bedclothes were disarranged, as though the patient had been drawn from under them without throwing them back. The corner of the upper sheet hung upon the floor; close by it lay one of the bandages with which the Doctor had dressed the wounded wrist. Another and another lay further along the floor, as though forming a clue to where the sick man now lay. This was almost exactly where he had been found on the previous night, under the great safe. Again, the left arm lay toward the safe. But there had been a new outrage, an attempt had been made to sever the arm close to the bangle which held the tiny key. A heavy "kukri" knife—one of the leaf-shaped knives which the Gurkhas and others of the hill tribes of

India use with such effect—had been taken from its place on the wall, and with it the attempt had been made. It was manifest that just at the moment of striking, the blow had been arrested, for only the point of the knife and not the edge of the blade had struck the flesh. As it was, the outer side of the arm had been cut to the bone and the blood was pouring out. In addition, the former wound in front of the arm had been cut or torn about terribly, one of the cuts seemed to jet out blood as if with each pulsation of the heart. By the side of her father knelt Miss Trelawny, her white nightdress stained with the blood in which she knelt. In the middle of the room Sergeant Daw, in his shirt and trousers and stocking feet, was putting fresh cartridges into his revolver in a dazed mechanical kind of way. His eyes were red and heavy, and he seemed only half awake, and less than half conscious of what was going on around him. Several servants, bearing lights of various kinds, were clustered round the doorway.

As I rose from my chair and came forward, Miss Trelawny raised her eyes toward me. When she saw me she shrieked and started to her feet, pointing towards me. Never shall I forget the strange picture she made, with her white drapery all smeared with blood which, as she rose from the pool, ran in streaks toward her bare feet. I believe that I had only been asleep; that whatever influence had worked on Mr. Trelawny and Nurse Kennedy—and in less degree on Sergeant Daw—had not touched me. The respirator had been of some service, though it had not kept off the tragedy whose dire evidences were before me. I can understand now—I could understand even then—the fright, added to that which had gone before, which my appearance must have evoked. I had still on the respirator, which covered mouth and nose; my hair had been tossed in my sleep. Coming suddenly forward, thus enwrapped and dishevelled, in that horrified crowd, I must have had, in the strange mixture of lights, an extraordinary and terrifying appearance. It was well that I recognised all this in time to avert another catastrophe; for the half-dazed, mechanically-acting Detective put in the cartridges and had raised his revolver to shoot at me when I succeeded in wrenching off the respirator and shouting to him to hold his hand. In this also he acted mechanically; the red, half-awake eyes had not in them even then the intention of conscious action. The danger, however, was averted. The relief of the situation, strangely enough, came in a simple fashion. Mrs. Grant, seeing that her young mistress had on only her nightdress, had gone to fetch a dressing-gown, which she now threw over her. This simple act brought us all back to the region of fact. With a long breath, one and all seemed to devote themselves to the most pressing matter before us, that of staunching the flow of blood from the arm of the wounded man. Even as the thought of action came, I rejoiced; for the bleeding was very proof that Mr. Trelawny still lived.

Last night's lesson was not thrown away. More than one of those present knew now what to do in such an emergency, and within a few seconds willing hands were at work on a tourniquet. A man was at once despatched for the doctor, and several of the servants disappeared to make themselves respectable. We lifted Mr. Trelawny on to the sofa where he had lain yesterday; and, having done what we could for him, turned our attention to the Nurse. In all the turmoil she had not stirred; she sat there as before, erect and rigid, breathing softly and naturally and with a placid smile. As it was manifestly of no use to attempt anything with her till the doctor had come, we began to think of the general situation.

Mrs. Grant had by this time taken her mistress away and changed her clothes; for she was back presently in a dressing-gown and slippers, and with the traces of blood removed from her hands. She was now much calmer, though she trembled sadly; and her face was ghastly white. When she had looked at her father's wrist, I holding the tourniquet, she turned her eyes round the room, resting them now and again on each one of us present in turn, but seeming to find no comfort.

It was so apparent to me that she did not know where to begin or whom to trust that, to reassure her, I said:

"I am all right now; I was only asleep." Her voice had a gulp in it as she said in a low voice:

"Asleep! You! and my Father in danger! I thought you were on the watch!" I felt the sting of justice in the reproach; but I really wanted to help her, so I answered:

"Only asleep. It is bad enough, I know; but there is something more than an "only" round us here. Had it not been that I took a definite precaution I might have been like the Nurse there." She turned her eyes swiftly on the weird figure, sitting grimly upright like a painted statue; and then her face softened. With the action of habitual courtesy she said:

"Forgive me! I did not mean to be rude. But I am in such distress and fear that I hardly know what I am saying. Oh, it is dreadful! I fear for fresh trouble and horror and mystery every moment." This cut me to the very heart, and out of the heart's fulness I spoke:

"Don't give me a thought! I don't deserve it. I was on guard, and yet I slept. All that I can say is that I didn't mean to, and I tried to avoid it; but it was over me before I knew it. Anyhow, it is done now; and can't be undone. Probably some day we may understand it all; but now let us try to get at some idea of what has happened. Tell me what you remember!" The effort to recollect seemed to stimulate her; she became calmer as she spoke:

"I was asleep, and woke suddenly with the same horrible feeling on me that Father was in great and immediate danger. I jumped up and ran, just as I was, into his room. It was nearly pitch dark, but as I opened the door there was light enough to see Father's nightdress as he lay on the floor under the safe, just as on that first awful night. Then I think I must have gone mad for a moment." She stopped and shuddered. My eyes lit on Sergeant Daw, still fiddling in an aimless way with the revolver. Mindful of my work with the tourniquet, I said calmly:

"Now tell us, Sergeant Daw, what did you fire at?" The policeman seemed to pull himself together with the habit of obedience. Looking around at the servants remaining in the room, he said with that air of importance which, I take it, is the regulation attitude of an official of the law before strangers:

"Don't you think, sir, that we can allow the servants to go away? We can then better go into the matter." I nodded approval; the servants took the hint and withdrew, though unwillingly, the last one closing the door behind him. Then the Detective went on:

"I think I had better tell you my impressions, sir, rather than recount my actions. That is, so far as I remember them." There was a mortified deference now in his manner, which probably arose from his consciousness of the awkward position in which he found himself. "I went to sleep half-dressed—as I am now, with a revolver under my pillow. It was the last thing I remember thinking of. I do not know how long I slept. I had turned off the electric light, and it was quite dark. I thought I heard a scream; but I can't be sure, for I felt thick-headed as a man does when he is called too soon after an extra long stretch of work. Not that such was the case this time. Anyhow my thoughts flew to the pistol. I took it out, and ran on to the landing. Then I heard a sort of scream, or rather a call for help, and ran into this room. The room was dark, for the lamp beside the Nurse was out, and the only light was that from the landing, coming through the open door. Miss Trelawny was kneeling on the floor beside her father, and was screaming. I thought I saw something move between me and the window; so, without thinking, and being half dazed and only half awake, I shot at it. It moved a little more to the right between the windows, and I shot again. Then you came up out of the big chair with all that muffling on your face. It seemed to me, being as I say half dazed and half awake—I know, sir, you will take this into account—as if it had been you, being in the same direction as the thing I had fired at. And so I was about to fire again when you pulled off the wrap." Here I asked him—I was cross-examining now and felt at home:

"You say you thought I was the thing you fired at. What thing?" The man scratched his head, but made no reply.

"Come, sir," I said, "what thing; what was it like?" The answer came in a low voice:

"I don't know, sir. I thought there was something; but what it was, or what it was like, I haven't the faintest notion. I suppose it was because I had been thinking of the pistol before I went to sleep, and because when I came in here I was half dazed and only half awake—which I hope you will in future, sir, always remember." He clung to that formula of excuse as though it were his sheet-anchor. I did not want to antagonise the man; on the contrary I wanted to have him with us. Besides, I had on me at that time myself the shadow of my own default; so I said as kindly as I knew how:

"Quite right! Sergeant. Your impulse was correct; though of course in the half-somnolent condition in which you were, and perhaps partly affected by the same influence—whatever it may be—which made me sleep and which has put the Nurse in that cataleptic trance, it could not be expected that you would paused to weigh matters. But now, whilst the matter is fresh, let me see exactly where you stood and where I sat. We shall be able to trace the course of your bullets." The prospect of action and the exercise of his habitual skill seemed to brace him at once; he seemed a different man as he set about his work. I asked Mrs. Grant to hold the tourniquet, and went and stood where he had stood and looked where, in the darkness, he had pointed. I could not but notice the mechanical exactness of his mind, as when he showed me where he had stood, or drew, as a matter of course, the revolver from his pistol pocket, and pointed with it. The chair from which I had risen still stood in its place. Then I asked him to point with his hand only, as I wished to move in the track of his shot.

Just behind my chair, and a little back of it, stood a high buhl cabinet. The glass door was shattered. I asked:

"Was this the direction of your first shot or your second?" The answer came promptly.

"The second; the first was over there!"

He turned a little to the left, more toward the wall where the great safe stood, and pointed. I followed the direction of his hand and came to the low table whereon rested, amongst other curios, the mummy of the cat which had raised Silvio's ire. I got a candle and easily found the mark of the bullet. It had broken a little glass vase and a tazza of black basalt, exquisitely engraved with hieroglyphics, the graven lines being filled with some faint green cement and the whole thing being polished to an equal surface. The bullet, flattened against the wall, lay on the table.

I then went to the broken cabinet. It was evidently a receptacle for valuable curios; for in it were some great scarabs of gold, agate, green jasper, amethyst, lapis lazuli, opal, granite, and blue-green china. None of these things happily were touched. The bullet had gone through the back of the cabinet; but no other damage, save the shattering of the glass, had been done. I could not but notice the strange arrangement of the curios on the shelf of the cabinet. All the scarabs, rings, amulets, &c. were arranged in an uneven oval round an exquisitely-carved golden miniature figure of a hawk-headed God crowned with a disk and plumes. I did not wait to look further at present, for my attention was demanded by more pressing things; but I determined to make a more minute examination when I should have time. It was evident that some of the strange Egyptian smell clung to these old curios; through the broken glass came an added whiff of spice and gum and bitumen, almost stronger than those I had already noticed as coming from others in the room.

All this had really taken but a few minutes. I was surprised when my eye met, through the chinks between the dark window blinds and the window cases, the brighter light of the coming dawn. When I went back to the sofa and took the tourniquet from Mrs. Grant, she went over and pulled up the blinds.

It would be hard to imagine anything more ghastly than the appearance of the room with the faint grey light of early morning coming in upon it. As the windows faced north, any light that came was a fixed grey light without any of the rosy possibility of dawn which comes in the eastern quarter of heaven. The electric lights seemed dull and yet glaring; and every shadow was of a hard intensity. There was nothing of morning freshness; nothing of the softness of night. All was hard and cold and inexpressibly dreary. The face of the senseless man on the sofa seemed of a ghastly yellow; and the Nurse's face had taken a suggestion of green from the shade of the lamp near her. Only Miss Trelawny's face looked white; and it was of a pallor which made my heart ache. It looked as if nothing on God's earth could ever again bring back to it the colour of life and happiness.

It was a relief to us all when Doctor Winchester came in, breathless with running. He only asked one question:

"Can anyone tell me anything of how this wound was gotten?" On seeing the headshake which went round us under his glance, he said no more, but applied himself to his surgical work. For an instant he looked up at the Nurse sitting so still; but then bent himself to his task, a grave frown contracting his brows. It was not till the arteries were tied and the wounds completely dressed that he spoke again, except, of course, when he had asked for anything to be handed to him or to be done for him. When Mr. Trelawny's wounds had been thoroughly cared for, he said to Miss Trelawny:

"What about Nurse Kennedy?" She answered at once:

"I really do not know. I found her when I came into the room at half-past two o'clock, sitting exactly as she does now. We have not moved her, or changed her position. She has not wakened since. Even Sergeant Daw's pistol-shots did not disturb her."

"Pistol-shots? Have you then discovered any cause for this new outrage?" The rest were silent, so I answered:

"We have discovered nothing. I was in the room watching with the Nurse. Earlier in the evening I fancied that the mummy smells were making me drowsy, so I went out and got a respirator. I had it on when I came on duty; but it did not keep me from going to sleep. I awoke to see the room full of people; that is, Miss Trelawny and Sergeant Daw, being only half awake and still stupefied by the same scent or influence which had affected us, fancied that he saw something moving through the shadowy darkness of the room, and fired twice. When I rose out of my chair, with my face swathed in the respirator, he took me for the cause of the trouble. Naturally enough, he was about to fire again, when I was fortunately in time to manifest my identity. Mr. Trelawny was lying beside the safe, just as he was found last night; and was bleeding profusely from the new wound in his wrist. We lifted him on the sofa, and made a tourniquet. That is, literally and absolutely, all that any of us know as yet. We have not touched the knife, which you see lies close by the pool of blood. Look!" I said, going over and lifting it. "The point is red with the blood which has dried."

Doctor Winchester stood quite still a few minutes before speaking:

"Then the doings of this night are quite as mysterious as those of last night?"

"Quite!" I answered. He said nothing in reply, but turning to Miss Trelawny said:

"We had better take Nurse Kennedy into another room. I suppose there is nothing to prevent it?"

"Nothing! Please, Mrs. Grant, see that Nurse Kennedy's room is ready; and ask two of the men to come and carry her in." Mrs. Grant went out immediately; and in a few minutes came back saying:

"The room is quite ready; and the men are here." By her direction two footmen came into the room and, lifting up the rigid body of Nurse Kennedy under the supervision of the Doctor, carried her out of the room. Miss Trelawny remained with me in the sick chamber, and Mrs. Grant went with the Doctor into the Nurse's room.

When we were alone Miss Trelawny came over to me, and taking both my hands in hers, said:

"I hope you won't remember what I said. I did not mean it, and I was distraught." I did not make reply; but I held her hands and kissed them. There are different ways of kissing a lady's hands. This way was intended as homage and respect; and it was accepted as such in the high-bred, dignified way which marked Miss Trelawny's bearing and every movement. I went over to the sofa and looked down at the senseless man. The dawn had come much nearer in the last few minutes, and there was something of the clearness of day in the light. As I looked at the stern, cold, set face, now as white as a marble monument in the pale grey light, I could not but feel that there was some deep mystery beyond all that had happened within the last twenty-six hours. Those beetling brows screened some massive purpose; that high, broad forehead held some finished train of reasoning, which the broad chin and massive jaw would help to carry into effect. As I looked and wondered, there began to steal over me again that phase of wandering thought which had last night heralded the approach of sleep. I resisted it, and held myself sternly to the present. This was easier to do when Miss Trelawny came close to me, and, leaning her forehead against my shoulder, began to cry silently. Then all the manhood in me woke, and to present purpose. It was of little use trying to speak; words were inadequate to thought. But we understood each other; she did not draw away when I put arm protectingly over her shoulder as I used to do with my little sister long ago when in her childish trouble she would come to her big brother to be comforted. That very act or attitude of protection made me more resolute in my purpose, and seemed to clear my brain of idle, dreamy wandering in thought. With an instinct of greater protection, however, I took away my arm as I heard the Doctor's footstep outside the door.

When Doctor Winchester came in he looked intently at the patient before speaking. His brows were set, and his mouth was a thin, hard line. Presently he said:

"There is much in common between the sleep of your Father and Nurse Kennedy. Whatever influence has brought it about has probably worked the same way in both cases. In Kennedy's case the coma is less marked. I cannot but feel, however, that with her we may be able to do more and more quickly than with this patient, as our hands are not tied. I have placed her in a draught; and already she shows some signs, though very faint ones, of ordinary unconsciousness. The rigidity of her limbs is less, and her skin seems more sensitive—or perhaps I should say less insensitive—to pain."

"How is it, then," I asked, "that Mr. Trelawny is still in this state of insensibility; and yet, so far as we know, his body has not had such rigidity at all?"

"That I cannot answer. The problem is one which we may solve in a few hours; or it may need a few days. But it will be a useful lesson in diagnosis to us all; and perhaps to many and many others after us, who knows!" he added, with the genuine fire of an enthusiast.

As the morning wore on, he flitted perpetually between the two rooms, watching anxiously over both patients. He made Mrs. Grant remain with the Nurse, but either Miss Trelawny or I, generally both of us, remained with the wounded man. We each managed, however, to get bathed and dressed; the Doctor and Mrs. Grant remained with Mr. Trelawny whilst we had breakfast.

Sergeant Daw went off to report at Scotland Yard the progress of the night; and then to the local station to arrange for the coming of his comrade, Wright, as fixed with Superintendent Dolan. When he returned I could not but think that he had been hauled over the coals for shooting in a sick-room; or perhaps for shooting at all without certain and proper cause. His remark to me enlightened me in the matter:

"A good character is worth something, sir, in spite of what some of them say. See! I've still got leave to carry my revolver."

That day was a long and anxious one. Toward nightfall Nurse Kennedy so far improved that the rigidity of her limbs entirely disappeared. She still breathed quietly and regularly; but the fixed expression of her face, though it was a calm enough expression, gave place to fallen eyelids and the negative look of sleep. Doctor Winchester had, towards evening, brought two more nurses, one of whom was to remain with Nurse Kennedy and the other to share in the watching with Miss Trelawny, who had insisted on remaining up herself. She had, in order to prepare for the duty, slept for several hours in the afternoon. We had all taken counsel together, and had arranged thus for the watching in Mr. Trelawny's room. Mrs. Grant was to remain beside the patient till twelve, when Miss Trelawny would relieve her. The new nurse was to sit in Miss Trelawny's room, and to visit the sick chamber each quarter of an hour. The Doctor would remain till twelve; when I was to relieve him. One or other of the detectives was to remain within hail of the room all night; and to pay periodical visits to see that all was well. Thus, the watchers would be watched; and the possibility of such events as last night, when the watchers were both overcome, would be avoided.

When the sun set, a strange and grave anxiety fell on all of us; and in our separate ways we prepared for the vigil. Doctor Winchester had evidently been thinking of my respirator, for he told me he would go out and get one. Indeed, he took to the idea so kindly that I persuaded Miss Trelawny also to have one which she could put on when her time for watching came.

And so the night drew on.

CHAPTER V

MORE STRANGE INSTRUCTIONS

WHEN I CAME from my room at half-past eleven o'clock I found all well in the sick-room. The new nurse, prim, neat, and watchful, sat in the chair by the bedside where Nurse Kennedy had sat last night. A little way off, between the bed and the safe, sat Dr. Winchester alert and wakeful, but looking strange and almost comic with the respirator over mouth and nose. As I stood in the doorway looking at them I heard a slight sound; turning round I saw the new detective, who nodded, held up the finger of silence and withdrew quietly. Hitherto no one of the watchers was overcome by sleep.

I took a chair outside the door. As yet there was no need for me to risk coming again under the subtle influence of last night. Naturally my thoughts went revolving round the main incidents of the last day and night, and I found myself arriving at strange conclusions, doubts, conjectures; but I did not lose myself, as on last night, in trains of thought. The sense of the present was ever with me, and I really felt as should a sentry on guard. Thinking is not a slow process; and when it is earnest the time can pass quickly. It seemed a very short time indeed till the door, usually left ajar, was pulled open and Dr. Winchester emerged, taking off his respirator as he came. His act, when he had it off, was demostrative of his keenness. He turned up the outside of the wrap and smelled it carefully.

"I am going now," he said. "I shall come early in the morning; unless, of course, I am sent for before. But all seems well tonight."

The next to appear was Sergeant Daw, who went quietly into the room and took the seat vacated by the Doctor. I still remained outside; but every few minutes looked into the room. This was rather a form than a matter of utility, for the room was so dark that coming even from the dimly-lighted corridor it was hard to distinguish anything.

A little before twelve o'clock Miss Trelawny came from her room. Before coming to her father's she went into that occupied by Nurse Kennedy. After a couple of minutes she came out, looking, I thought, a trifle more cheerful. She had her respirator in her hand, but before putting it on, asked me if anything special had occurred since she had gone to lie down. I answered in a whisper—there was no loud talking in the house tonight—that all was safe, was well. She then put on her respirator, and I mine; and we entered the room. The Detective and the Nurse rose up, and we took their places. Sergeant Daw was the last to go out; he closed the door behind him as we had arranged.

For a while I sat quiet, my heart beating. The place was grimly dark. The only light was a faint one from the top of the lamp which threw a white circle on the high ceiling, except the emerald sheen of the shade as the light took its under edges. Even the light only seemed to emphasize the blackness of the shadows. These presently began to seem, as on last night, to have a sentience of their own. I did not myself feel in the least sleepy; and each time I went softly over to look at the patient, which I did about every ten minutes, I could see that Miss Trelawny was keenly alert. Every quarter of an hour one or other of the policemen looked in through the partly opened door. Each time both Miss Trelawny and I said through our mufflers, "all right," and the door was closed again.

As the time wore on, the silence and the darkness seemed to increase. The circle of light on the ceiling was still there, but it seemed less brilliant than at first. The green edging of the lamp-shade became like Maori greenstone rather than emerald. The sounds of the night without the house, and the starlight spreading pale lines along the edges of the window-cases, made the pall of black within more solemn and more mysterious.

We heard the clock in the corridor chiming the quarters with its silver bell till two o'clock; and then a strange feeling came over me. I could see from Miss Trelawny's movement as she looked round, that she also had some new sensation. The new detective had just looked in; we two were alone with the unconscious patient for another quarter of an hour.

My heart began to beat wildly. There was a sense of fear over me. Not for myself; my fear was impersonal. It seemed as though some new person had entered the room, and that a strong intelligence was awake close to me. Something brushed against my leg. I put my hand down hastily and touched the furry coat of Silvio. With a very faint far-away sound of a snarl he turned and scratched at me. I felt blood on my hand. I rose gently and came over to the bedside. Miss Trelawny, too, had stood up and was looking behind her, as though there was something close to her. Her eyes were wild, and her breast rose and fell as though she were fighting for air. When I touched her she did not seem to feel me; she worked her hands in front of her, as though she was fending off something.

There was not an instant to lose. I seized her in my arms and rushed over to the door, threw it open, and strode into the passage, calling loudly:

"Help! Help!"

In an instant the two Detectives, Mrs. Grant, and the Nurse appeared on the scene. Close on their heels came several of the servants, both men and women. Immediately Mrs. Grant came near enough, I placed Miss Trelawny in her arms, and rushed back into the room, turning up the electric light as soon as I could lay my hand on it. Sergeant Daw and the Nurse followed me.

We were just in time. Close under the great safe, where on the two succesive nights he had been found, lay Mr. Trelawny with his left arm, bare save for the bandages, stretched out. Close by his side was a leaf-shaped Egyptian knife which had lain amongst the curios on the shelf of the broken cabinet. Its point was stuck in the parquet floor, whence had been removed the blood-stained rug.

But there was no sign of disturbance anywhere; nor any sign of any one or anything unusual. The Policemen and I searched the room accurately, whilst the Nurse and two of the servants lifted the wounded man back to bed; but no sign or clue could we get. Very soon Miss Trelawny returned to the room. She was pale but collected. When she came close to me she said in a low voice:

"I felt myself fainting. I did not know why; but I was afraid!"

The only other shock I had was when Miss Trelawny cried out to me, as I placed my hand on the bed to lean over and look carefully at her father:

"You are wounded. Look! look! your hand is bloody. There is blood on the sheets!" I had, in the excitement, quite forgotten Silvio's scratch. As I looked at it, the recollection came back to me; but before I could say a word Miss Trelawny had caught hold of my hand and lifted it up. When she saw the parallel lines of the cuts she cried out again:

"It is the same wound as Father's!" Then she laid my hand down gently but quickly, and said to me and to Sergeant Daw:

"Come to my room! Silvio is there in his basket." We followed her, and found Silvio sitting in his basket awake. He was licking his paws. The Detective said:

"He is there sure enough; but why licking his paws?"

Margaret—Miss Trelawny—gave a moan as she bent over and took one of the forepaws in her hand; but the cat seemed to resent it and snarled. At that Mrs. Grant came into the room. When she saw that we were looking at the cat she said:

"The Nurse tells me that Silvio was asleep on Nurse Kennedy's bed ever since you went to your Father's room until a while ago. He came there just after you had gone to master's room. Nurse says that Nurse Kennedy is moaning and muttering in her sleep as though she had a nightmare. I think we should send for Dr. Winchester."

"Do so at once, please!" said Miss Trelawny; and we went back to the room.

For a while Miss Trelawny stood looking at her father, with her brows wrinkled. Then, turning to me, as though her mind were made up, she said:

"Don't you think we should have a consultation on Father? Of course I have every confidence in Doctor Winchester; he seems an immensely clever young man. But he is a young man; and there must be men who have devoted themselves to this branch of science. Such a man would have more knowledge and more experience; and his knowledge and experience might help to throw light on poor Father's case. As it is, Doctor Winchester seems to be quite in the dark. Oh! I don't know what to do. It is all so terrible!" Here she broke down a little and cried; and I tried to comfort her.

Doctor Winchester arrived quickly. His first thought was for his patient; but when he found him without further harm, he visited Nurse Kennedy. When he saw her, a hopeful look came into his eyes. Taking a towel, he dipped a corner of it in cold water and flicked on the face. The skin coloured, and she stirred slightly. He said to the new nurse—Sister Doris he called her:

"She is all right. She will wake in a few hours at latest. She may be dizzy and distraught at first, or perhaps hysterical. If so, you know how to treat her."

"Yes, sir!" answered Sister Doris demurely; and we went back to Mr. Trelawny's room. As soon as we had entered, Mrs. Grant and the Nurse went out so that only Doctor Winchester, Miss Trelawny, and myself remained in the room. When the door had been closed Doctor Winchester asked me as to what had occurred. I told him fully, giving exactly every detail so far as I could remember. Throughout my narrative, which did not take long, however, he kept asking me questions as to who had been present and the order in which each one had come into the room. He asked other things, but nothing of any importance; these were all that took my attention, or remained in my memory. When our conversation was finished, he said in a very decided way indeed, to Miss Trelawny:

"I think, Miss Trelawny, that we had better have a consultation on this case." She answered at once, seemingly a little to his surprise:

"I am glad you have mentioned it. I quite agree. Who would you suggest?"

"Have you any choice yourself?" he asked. "Any one to whom your Father is known? Has he ever consulted any one?"

"Not to my knowledge. But I hope you will choose whoever you think would be best. My dear Father should have all the help that can be had; and I shall be deeply obliged by your choosing. Who is the best man in London—anywhere else—in such a case?"

"There are several good men; but they are scattered all over the world. Somehow, the brain specialist is born, not made; though a lot of hard work goes to the completing of him and fitting him for his work. He comes from no country. The most daring investigator up to the present is Chiuni, the Japanese; but he is rather a surgical experimentalist than a practitioner. Then there is Zammerfest of Uppsala, and Fenelon of the University of Paris, and Morfessi of Naples. These, of course, are in addition to our own men, Morrison of Aberdeen and Richardson of Birmingham. But before them all I would put Frere of King's College. Of all that I have named he best unites theory and practice. He has no hobbies—that have been discovered at all events; and his experience is immense. It is the regret of all of us who admire him that the nerve so firm and the hand so dexterous must yield to time. For my own part I would rather have Frere than any one living."

"Then," said Miss Trelawny decisively, "let us have Doctor Frere—by the way, is he 'Doctor' or 'Mister'?—as early as we can get him in the morning!"

A weight seemed removed from him, and he spoke with greater ease and geniality than he had yet shown:

"He is Sir James Frere. I shall go to him myself as early as it is possibly to see him, and shall ask him to come here at once." Then turning to me he said:

"You had better let me dress your hand."

"It is nothing," I said.

"Nevertheless it should be seen to. A scratch from any animal might turn out dangerous; there is nothing like being safe." I submitted; forthwith he began to dress my hand. He examined with a magnifying-glass the several parallel wounds, and compared them with the slip of blotting-paper, marked with Silvio's claws, which he took from his pocket-book. He put back the paper, simply remarking:

"It's a pity that Silvio slips in—and out—just when he shouldn't."

The morning wore slowly on. By ten o'clock Nurse Kennedy had so far recovered that she was able to sit up and talk intelligibly. But she was still hazy in her thoughts; and could not remember anything that had happened on the previous night, after her taking her place by the sick-bed. As yet she seemed neither to know nor care what had happened.

It was nearly eleven o'clock when Doctor Winchester returned with Sir James Frere. Somehow I felt my heart sink when from the landing I saw them in the hall below; I knew that Miss Trelawny was to have the pain of telling yet another stranger of her ignorance of her father's life.

Sir James Frere was a man who commanded attention followed by respect. He knew so thoroughly what he wanted himself, that he placed at once on one side all wishes and ideas of less definite persons. The mere flash of his piercing eyes, or the set of his resolute mouth, or the lowering of his great eyebrows, seemed to compel immediate and willing obedience to his wishes. Somehow, when we had all been introduced and he was well amongst us, all sense of mystery seemed to melt away. It was with a hopeful spirit that I saw him pass into the sick-room with Doctor Winchester.

They remained in the room a long time; once they sent for the Nurse, the new one, Sister Doris, but she did not remain long. Again they both went into Nurse Kennedy's room. He sent out the nurse attendant on her. Doctor Winchester told me afterward that Nurse Kennedy, though she was ignorant of later matters, gave full and satisfactory answers to all Doctor Frere's questions relating to her patient up to the time she became unconscious. Then they went to the study, where they remained so long, and their voices raised in heated discussion seemed in such determined opposition, that I began to feel uneasy. As for Miss Trelawny, she was almost in a state of collapse from nervousness before they joined us. Poor girl! she had had a sadly anxious time of it, and her nervous strength had almost broken down.

They came out at last, Sir James first, his grave face looking as unenlightening as that of the sphinx. Doctor Winchester followed him closely; his face was pale, but with that kind of pallor which looked like a reaction. It gave me the idea that it had been red not long before. Sir James asked that Miss Trelawny would come into the study. He suggested that I should come also. When we had enterd, Sir James turned to me and said:

"I understand from Doctor Winchester that you are a friend of Miss Trelawny, and that you have already considerable knowledge of this case. Perhaps it will be well that you should be with us. I know you already as a keen lawyer, Mr. Ross, though I never had the pleasure of meeting you. As Doctor Winchester tells me that there are some strange matters outside this case which seem to puzzle him—and others—and in which he thinks you may yet be specially interested, it might be as well that you should know every phase of the case. For myself I do not take much account of mysteries—except those of science; and as there seems to be some idea of an attempt at assassination or robbery, all I can say is that if assassins were at work they ought to take some elementary lessons in anatomy before their next job, for they seem thoroughly ignorant. If robbery were their purpose, they seem to have worked with marvellous inefficiency. That, however, is not my business." Here he took a big pinch of snuff, and turning to Miss Trelawny, went on: "Now as to the patient. Leaving out the cause of his illness, all we can say at present is that he appears to be suffering from a marked attack of catalepsy. At present nothing can be done, except to sustain his strength. The treatment of my friend Doctor Winchester is mainly such as I approve of; and I am confident that should any slight change arise he will be able to deal with it satisfactorily. It is an interesting case—most interesting; and should any new or abnormal development arise I shall be happy to come at any time. There is just one thing to which I wish to call your attention; and I put it to you, Miss Trelawny, directly, since it is your responsibility. Doctor Winchester informs me that you are not yourself free in the matter, but are bound by an instruction given by your Father in case just such a condition of things should arise. I would strongly advise that the patient be removed to another room; or, as an alternative, that those mummies and all such things should be removed from his chamber. Why, it's enough to put any man into an abnormal condition, to have such an assemblage of horrors round him, and to breathe the atmosphere which they exhale. You have evidence already of how such mephitic odour may act. That nurse—Kennedy, I think you said, Doctor—isn't yet out of her state of catalepsy; and you, Mr. Ross, have, I am told, experienced something of the same effects. I know this"—here his eyebrows came down more than ever, and his mouth hardened—"if I were in charge here I should insist on the patient having a different atmosphere; or I would throw up the case. Doctor Winchester already knows that I can only be again consulted on this condition being fulfilled. But I trust that you will see your way, as a good daughter to my mind should, to looking to your Father's health and sanity rather than to any whim of his—whether supported or not by a foregoing fear, or by any number of "penny dreadful" mysteries. The day has hardly come yet, I am glad to say, when the British Museum and St. Thomas's Hospital have exchanged their normal functions. Good-day, Miss Trelawny. I earnestly hope that I may soon see your Father restored. Remember, that should you fulfil the elementary condition which I have laid down, I am at your service day or night. Good-morning, Mr. Ross. I hope you will be able to report to me soon, Doctor Winchester."

When he had gone we stood silent, till the rumble of his carriage wheels died away. The first to speak was Doctor Winchester:

"I think it well to say that to my mind, speaking purely as a physician, he is quite right. I feel as if I could have assaulted him when he made it a condition of not giving up the case; but all the same he is right as to treatment. He does not understand that there is something odd about this special case; and he will not realise the knot that we are all tied up in by Mr. Trelawny's instructions. Of course—" He was interrupted by Miss Trelawny:

"Doctor Winchester, do you, too, wish to give up the case; or are you willing to continue it under the conditions you know?"

"Give it up! Less now than ever. Miss Trelawny, I shall never give it up, so long as life is left to him or any of us!" She said nothing, but held out her hand, which he took warmly.

"Now," said she, "if Sir James Frere is a type of the cult of Specialists, I want no more of them. To start with, he does not seem to know any more than you do about my Father's condition; and if he were a hundredth part as much interested in it as you are, he would not stand on such punctilio. Of course, I am only too anxious about my poor Father; and if I can see a way to meet either of Sir James Frere's conditions, I shall do so. I shall ask Mr. Marvin to come here today, and advise me as to the limit of Father's wishes. If he thinks I am free to act in any way on my own responsibility, I shall not hesitate to do so." Then Doctor Winchester took his leave.

Miss Trelawny sat down and wrote a letter to Mr. Marvin, telling him of the state of affairs, and asking him to come and see her and to bring with him any papers which might throw any light on the subject. She sent the letter off with a carriage to bring back the solicitor; we waited with what patience we could for his coming.

It is not a very long journey for oneself from Kensington Palace Gardens to Lincoln's Inn Fields; but it seemed endlessly long when waiting for someone else to take it. All things, however, are amenable to Time; it was less than an hour all told when Mr. Marvin was with us.

He recognised Miss Trelawny's impatience, and when he had learned sufficient of her father's illness, he said to her:

"Whenever you are ready I can go with you into particulars regarding your Father's wishes."

"Whenever you like," she said, with an evident ignorance of his meaning. "Why not now?" He looked at me, as to a fellow man of business, and stammered out:

"We are not alone."

"I have brought Mr. Ross here on purpose," she answered. "He knows so much at present, that I want him to know more." The solicitor was a little disconcerted, a thing which those knowing him only in courts would hardly have believed. He answered, however, with some hesitation:

"But, my dear young lady—Your Father's wishes!—Confidence between father and child—"

Here she interrupted him; there was a tinge of red in her pale cheeks as she did so:

"Do you really think that applies to the present circumstances, Mr. Marvin? My Father never told me anything of his affairs; and I can now, in this sad extremity, only learn his wishes through a gentleman who is a stranger to me and of whom I never even heard till I got my Father's letter, written to be shown to me only in extremity. Mr. Ross is a new friend; but he has all my confidence, and I should like him to be present. Unless, of course," she added, "such a thing is forbidden by my Father. Oh! forgive me, Mr. Marvin, if I seem rude; but I have been in such dreadful trouble and anxiety lately, that I have hardly command of myself." She covered her eyes with her hand for a few seconds; we two men looked at each other and waited, trying to appear unmoved. She went on more firmly; she had recovered herself:

"Please! please do not think I am ungrateful to you for your kindness in coming here and so quickly. I really am grateful; and I have every confidence in your judgment. If you wish, or think it best, we can be alone." I stood up; but Mr. Marvin made a dissentient gesture. He was evidently pleased with her attitude; there was geniality in his voice and manner as he spoke:

"Not at all! Not at all! There is no restriction on your Father's part; and on my own I am quite willing. Indeed, all told, it may be better. From what you have said of Mr. Trelawny's illness, and the other— incidental—matters, it will be well in case of any grave eventuality, that it was understood from the first, that circumstances were ruled by your Father's own imperative instructions. For, please understand me, his instructions are imperative—most imperative. They are so unyielding that he has given me a Power of Attorney, under which I have undertaken to act, authorising me to see his written wishes carried out.

Please believe me once for all, that he intended fully everything mentioned in that letter to you! Whilst he is alive he is to remain in his own room; and none of his property is to be removed from it under any circumstances whatever. He has even given an inventory of the articles which are not to be displaced."

Miss Trelawny was silent. She looked somewhat distressed; so, thinking that I understood the immediate cause, I asked:

"May we see the list?" Miss Trelawny's face at once brightened; but it fell again as the lawyer answered promptly—he was evidently prepared for the question:

"Not unless I am compelled to take action on the Power of Attorney. I have brought that instrument with me. You will recognise, Mr. Ross"—he said this with a sort of business conviction which I had noticed in his professional work, as he handed me the deed—"how strongly it is worded, and how the grantor made his wishes apparent in such a way as to leave no loophole. It is his own wording, except for certain legal formalities; and I assure you I have seldom seen a more iron-clad document. Even I myself have no power to make the slightest relaxation of the instructions, without committing a distinct breach of faith. And that, I need not tell you, is impossible." He evidently added the last words in order to prevent an appeal to his personal consideration. He did not like the seeming harshness of his words, however, for he added:

"I do hope, Miss Trelawny, that you understand that I am willing—frankly and unequivocally willing—to do anything I can, within the limits of my power, to relieve your distress. But your Father had, in all his doings, some purpose of his own which he did not disclose to me. So far as I can see, there is not a word of his instructions that he had not thought over fully. Whatever idea he had in his mind was the idea of a lifetime; he had studied it in every possible phase, and was prepared to guard it at every point.

"Now I fear I have distressed you, and I am truly sorry for it; for I see you have much—too much—to bear already. But I have no alternative. If you want to consult me at any time about anything, I promise you I will come without a moment's delay, at any hour of the day or night. There is my private address," he scribbled in his pocket-book as he spoke, "and under it the address of my club, where I am generally to be found in the evening." He tore out the paper and handed it to her. She thanked him. He shook hands with her and with me and withdrew.

As soon as the hall door was shut on him, Mrs. Grant tapped at the door and came in. There was such a look of distress in her face that Miss Trelawny stood up, deadly white, and asked her:

"What is it, Mrs. Grant? What is it? Any new trouble?"

"I grieve to say, miss, that the servants, all but two, have given notice and want to leave the house today. They have talked the matter over among themselves; the butler has spoken for the rest. He says as how they are willing to forego their wages, and even to pay their legal obligations instead of notice; but that go today they must."

"What reason do they give?"

"None, miss. They say as how they're sorry, but that they've nothing to say. I asked Jane, the upper housemaid, miss, who is not with the rest but stops on; and she tells me confidential that they've got some notion in their silly heads that the house is haunted!"

We ought to have laughed, but we didn't. I could not look in Miss Trelawny's face and laugh. The pain and horror there showed no sudden paroxysm of fear; there was a fixed idea of which this was a confirmation. For myself, it seemed as if my brain had found a voice. But the voice was not complete; there was some other thought, darker and deeper, which lay behind it, whose voice had not sounded as yet.

CHAPTER VI

SUSPICIONS

THE FIRST TO get full self-command was Miss Trelawny. There was a haughty dignity in her bearing as she said:

"Very well, Mrs. Grant; let them go! Pay them up to today, and a month's wages. They have hitherto been very good servants; and the occasion of their leaving is not an ordinary one. We must not expect much faithfulness from any one who is beset with fears. Those who remain are to have in future double wages; and please send these to me presently when I send word." Mrs. Grant bristled with smothered indignation; all the housekeeper in her was outraged by such generous treatment of servants who had combined to give notice:

"They don't deserve it, miss; them to go on so, after the way they have been treated here. Never in my life have I seen servants so well treated or anyone so good to them and gracious to them as you have been. They might be in the household of a King for treatment. And now, just as there is trouble, to go and act like this. It's abominable, that's what it is!"

Miss Trelawny was very gentle with her, and smothered her ruffled dignity; so that presently she went away with, in her manner, a lesser measure of hostility to the undeserving. In quite a different frame of mind she returned presently to ask if her mistress would like her to engage a full staff of other servants, or at any rate try to do so. "For you know, ma'am," she went on, "when once a scare has been established in the servants' hall, it's wellnigh impossible to get rid of it. Servants may come; but they go away just as quick. There's no holding them. They simply won't stay; or even if they work out their month's notice, they lead you that life that you wish every hour of the day that you hadn't kept them. The women are bad enough, the huzzies; but the men are worse!" There was neither anxiety nor indignation in Miss Trelawny's voice or manner as she said:

"I think, Mrs. Grant, we had better try to do with those we have. Whilst my dear Father is ill we shall not be having any company, so that there will be only three now in the house to attend to. If those servants who are willing to stay are not enough, I should only get sufficient to help them to do the work. It will not, I should think, be difficult to get a few maids; perhaps some that you know already. And please bear in mind, that those whom you get, and who are suitable and will stay, are henceforth to have the same wages as those who are remaining. Of course, Mrs. Grant, you well enough understand that though I do not group you in any way with the servants, the rule of double salary applies to you too." As she spoke she extended her long, fine-shaped hand, which the other took and then, raising it to her lips, kissed it impressively with the freedom of an elder woman to a younger. I could not but admire the generosity of her treatment of her servants. In my mind I endorsed Mrs. Grant's sotto voce remark as she left the room:

"No wonder the house is like a King's house, when the mistress is a Princess!"

"A Princess!" That was it. The idea seemed to satisfy my mind, and to bring back in a wave of light the first moment when she swept across my vision at the ball in Belgrave Square. A queenly figure! tall and slim, bending, swaying, undulating as the lily or the lotos. Clad in a flowing gown of some filmy black material shot with gold. For ornament in her hair she wore an old Egyptian jewel, a tiny crystal disk, set between rising plumes carved in lapis lazuli. On her wrist was a broad bangle or bracelet of antique work, in the shape of a pair of spreading wings wrought in gold, with the feathers made of coloured gems. For all her gracious bearing toward me, when our hostess introduced me, I was then afraid of her. It was only when later, at the picnic on the river, I had come to realise her sweet and gentle, that my awe changed to something else.

For a while she sat, making some notes or memoranda. Then putting them away, she sent for the faithful servants. I thought that she had better have this interview alone, and so left her. When I came back there were traces of tears in her eyes.

The next phase in which I had a part was even more disturbing, and infinitely more painful. Late in the afternoon Sergeant Daw came into the study where I was sitting. After closing the door carefully and looking all round the room to make certain that we were alone, he came close to me.

"What is it?" I asked him. "I see you wish to speak to me privately."

"Quite so, sir! May I speak in absolute confidence?"

"Of course you may. In anything that is for the good of Miss Trelawny—and of course Mr. Trelawny—you may be perfectly frank. I take it that we both want to serve them to the best of our powers." He hesitated before replying:

"Of course you know that I have my duty to do; and I think you know me well enough to know that I will do it. I am a policeman—a detective; and it is my duty to find out the facts of any case I am put on, without fear or favour to anyone. I would rather speak to you alone, in confidence if I may, without reference to any duty of anyone to anyone, except mine to Scotland Yard."

"Of course! of course!" I answered mechanically, my heart sinking, I did not know why. "Be quite frank with me. I assure you of my confidence."

"Thank you, sir. I take it that what I say is not to pass beyond you— not to anyone. Not to Miss Trelawny herself, or even to Mr. Trelawny when he becomes well again."

"Certainly, if you make it a condition!" I said a little more stiffly. The man recognised the change in my voice or manner, and said apologetically:

"Excuse me, sir, but I am going outside my duty in speaking to you at all on the subject. I know you, however, of old; and I feel that I can trust you. Not your word, sir, that is all right; but your discretion!"

I bowed. "Go on!" I said. He began at once:

"I have gone over this case, sir, till my brain begins to reel; but I can't find any ordinary solution of it. At the time of each attempt no one has seemingly come into the house; and certainly no one has got out. What does it strike you is the inference?"

"That the somebody—or the something—was in the house already," I answered, smiling in spite of myself.

"That's just what I think," he said, with a manifest sigh of relief. "Very well! Who can be that someone?"

"'Someone, or something,' was what I said," I answered.

"Let us make it 'someone,' Mr. Ross! That cat, though he might have scratched or bit, never pulled the old gentleman out of bed, and tried to get the bangle with the key off his arm. Such things are all very well in books where your amateur detectives, who know everything before it's done, can fit them into theories; but in Scotland Yard, where the men aren't all idiots either, we generally find that when crime is done, or attempted, it's people, not things, that are at the bottom of it."

"Then make it 'people' by all means, Sergeant."

"We were speaking of 'someone,' sir."

"Quite right. Someone, be it!"

"Did it ever strike you, sir, that on each of the three separate occasions where outrage was effected, or attempted, there was one person who was the first to be present and to give the alarm?"

"Let me see! Miss Trelawny, I believe, gave the alarm on the first occasion. I was present myself, if fast asleep, on the second; and so was Nurse Kennedy. When I woke there were several people in the room; you were one of them. I understand that on that occasion also Miss Trelawny was before you. At the last attempt I was Miss Trelawny fainted. I carried her out and went back. In returning, I was first; and I think you were close behind me."

Sergeant Daw thought for a moment before replying:

"She was present, or first, in the room on all the occasions; there was only damage done in the first and second!"

The inference was one which I, as a lawyer, could not mistake. I thought the best thing to do was to meet it half-way. I have always found that the best way to encounter an inference is to cause it to be turned into a statement.

"You mean," I said, "that as on the only occasions when actual harm was done, Miss Trelawny's being the first to discover it is a proof that she did it; or was in some way connected with the attempt, as well as the discovery?"

"I didn't venture to put it as clear as that; but that is where the doubt which I had leads." Sergeant Daw was a man of courage; he evidently did not shrink from any conclusion of his reasoning on facts.

We were both silent for a while. Fears began crowding in on my own mind. Not doubts of Miss Trelawny, or of any act of hers; but fears lest such acts should be misunderstood. There was evidently a mystery somewhere; and if no solution to it could be found, the doubt would be cast on someone. In such cases the guesses of the majority are bound to follow the line of least resistance; and if it could be proved that any personal gain to anyone could follow Mr. Trelawny's death, should such ensue, it might prove a difficult task for anyone to prove innocence in the face of suspicious facts. I found myself instinctively taking that deferential course which, until the plan of battle of the prosecution is unfolded, is so safe an attitude for the defence. It would never do for me, at this stage, to combat any theories which a detective might form. I could best help Miss Trelawny by listening and understanding. When the time should come for the dissipation and obliteration of the theories, I should be quite willing to use all my militant ardour, and all the weapons at my command.

"You will of course do your duty, I know," I said, "and without fear. What course do you intend to take?"

"I don't know as yet, sir. You see, up to now it isn't with me even a suspicion. If any one else told me that that sweet young lady had a hand in such a matter, I would think him a fool; but I am bound to follow my own conclusions. I know well that just as unlikely persons have been proved guilty, when a whole court—all except the prosecution who knew the facts, and the judge who had taught his mind to wait—would have sworn to innocence. I wouldn't, for all the world, wrong such a young lady; more especial when she has such a cruel weight to bear. And you will be sure that I won't say a word that'll prompt anyone else to make such a charge. That's why I speak to you in confidence, man to man. You are skilled in proofs; that is your profession. Mine only gets so far as suspicions, and what we call our own proofs—which are nothing but ex parte evidence after all. You know Miss Trelawny better than I do; and though I watch round the sick-room, and go where I like about the house and in and out of it, I haven't the same opportunities as you have of knowing the lady and what her life is, or her means are; or of anything else which might give me a clue to her actions. If I were to try to find out from her, it would at once arouse her suspicions. Then, if she were guilty, all possibility of ultimate proof would go; for she would easily find a way to baffle discovery. But if she be innocent, as I hope she is, it would be doing a cruel wrong to accuse her. I have thought the matter over according to my lights before I spoke to you; and if I have taken a liberty, sir, I am truly sorry."

"No liberty in the world, Daw," I said warmly, for the man's courage and honesty and consideration compelled respect. "I am glad you have spoken to me so frankly. We both want to find out the truth; and there is so much about this case that is strange—so strange as to go beyond all experiences—that to aim at truth is our only chance of making anything clear in the long-run—no matter what our views are, or what object we wish to achieve ultimately!" The Sergeant looked pleased as he went on:

"I thought, therefore, that if you had it once in your mind that somebody else held to such a possibility, you would by degrees get proof; or at any rate such ideas as would convince yourself, either for or against it. Then we would come to some conclusion; or at any rate we should so exhaust all other possibilities that the most likely one would remain as the nearest thing to proof, or strong suspicion, that we could get. After that we should have to—"

Just at this moment the door opened and Miss Trelawny entered the room. The moment she saw us she drew back quickly, saying:

"Oh, I beg pardon! I did not know you were here, and engaged." By the time I had stood up, she was about to go back.

"Do come in," I said; "Sergeant Daw and I were only talking matters over."

Whilst she was hesitating, Mrs. Grant appeared, saying as she entered the room: "Doctor Winchester is come, miss, and is asking for you."

I obeyed Miss Trelawny's look; together we left the room.

When the Doctor had made his examination, he told us that there was seemingly no change. He added that nevertheless he would like to stay in the house that night is he might. Miss Trelawny looked glad, and sent word to Mrs. Grant to get a room ready for him. Later in the day, when he and I happened to be alone together, he said suddenly:

"I have arranged to stay here tonight because I want to have a talk with you. And as I wish it to be quite private, I thought the least suspicious way would be to have a cigar together late in the evening when

Miss Trelawny is watching her father." We still kept to our arrangement that either the sick man's daughter or I should be on watch all night. We were to share the duty at the early hours of the morning. I was anxious about this, for I knew from our conversation that the Detective would watch in secret himself, and would be particularly alert about that time.

The day passed uneventfully. Miss Trelawny slept in the afternoon; and after dinner went to relieve the Nurse. Mrs. Grant remained with her, Sergeant Daw being on duty in the corridor. Doctor Winchester and I took our coffee in the library. When we had lit our cigars he said quietly:

"Now that we are alone I want to have a confidential talk. We are 'tiled,' of course; for the present at all events?"

"Quite so!" I said, my heart sinking as I thought of my conversation with Sergeant Daw in the morning, and of the disturbing and harrowing fears which it had left in my mind. He went on:

"This case is enough to try the sanity of all of us concerned in it. The more I think of it, the madder I seem to get; and the two lines, each continually strengthened, seem to pull harder in opposite directions."

"What two lines?" He looked at me keenly for a moment before replying. Doctor Winchester's look at such moments was apt to be disconcerting. It would have been so to me had I had a personal part, other than my interest in Miss Trelawny, in the matter. As it was, however, I stood it unruffled. I was now an attorney in the case; an amicus curiae in one sense, in another retained for the defence. The mere thought that in this clever man's mind were two lines, equally strong and opposite, was in itself so consoling as to neutralise my anxiety as to a new attack. As he began to speak, the Doctor's face wore an inscrutable smile; this, however, gave place to a stern gravity as he proceeded:

"Two lines: Fact and—Fancy! In the first there is this whole thing; attacks, attempts at robbery and murder; stupefyings; organised catalepsy which points to either criminal hypnotism and thought suggestion, or some simple form of poisoning unclassified yet in our toxicology. In the other there is some influence at work which is not classified in any book that I know—outside the pages of romance. I never felt in my life so strongly the truth of Hamlet's words:

'There are more things in Heaven and earth . . . Than are dreamt of in your philosophy.'

"Let us take the 'Fact' side first. Here we have a man in his home; amidst his own household; plenty of servants of different classes in the house, which forbids the possibility of an organised attempt made from the servants' hall. He is wealthy, learned, clever. From his physiognomy there is no doubting that he is a man of iron will and determined purpose. His daughter—his only child, I take it, a young girl bright and clever—is sleeping in the very next room to his. There is seemingly no possible reason for expecting any attack or disturbance of any kind; and no reasonable opportunity for any outsider to effect it. And yet we have an attack made; a brutal and remorseless attack, made in the middle of the night. Discovery is made quickly; made with that rapidity which in criminal cases generally is found to be not accidental, but of premeditated intent. The attacker, or attackers, are manifestly disturbed before the completion of their work, whatever their ultimate intent may have been. And yet there is no possible sign of their escape; no clue, no disturbance of anything; no open door or window; no sound. Nothing whatever to show who had done the deed, or even that a deed has been done; except the victim, and his surroundings incidental to the deed!

"The next night a similar attempt is made, though the house is full of wakeful people; and though there are on watch in the room and around it a detective officer, a trained nurse, an earnest friend, and the man's own daughter. The nurse is thrown into a catalepsy, and the watching friend—though protected by a respirator—into a deep sleep. Even the detective is so far overcome with some phase of stupor that he fires off his pistol in the sick-room, and can't even tell what he thought he was firing at. That respirator of yours is the only thing that seems to have a bearing on the 'fact' side of the affair. That you did not lose your head as the others did—the effect in such case being in proportion to the amount of time each remained in the room—points to the probability that the stupefying medium was not hypnotic, whatever else it may have been. But again, there is a fact which is contradictory. Miss Trelawny, who was in the room more than any of you—for she was in and out all the time and did her share of permanent watching also—did not seem to be affected at all. This would show that the influence, whatever it is, does not affect generally—unless, of course, it was that she was in some way inured to it. If it should turn out that it be some strange exhalation from some of those Egyptian curios, that might account for it; only, we are then face to face with the fact that Mr. Trelawny, who was most of all in the room—who, in fact, lived more than half his life in it—was affected worst of all. What kind of influence could it be which would account for all these different and contradictory effects? No! the more I think of this form of the dilemma, the more I am bewildered! Why, even if it were that the attack, the physical attack, on Mr. Trelawny had been made by some one residing in the house and not within the sphere of suspicion, the oddness of the stupefyings would still remain a mystery. It is not easy to put anyone into a catalepsy. Indeed, so far as is known yet in science, there is no way to achieve such an object at will. The crux of the whole matter is Miss Trelawny, who seems to be subject to none of the influences, or possibly of the variants of the same influence at work. Through all she goes unscathed, except for that one slight semi-faint. It is most strange!"

I listened with a sinking heart; for, though his manner was not illuminative of distrust, his argument was disturbing. Although it was not so direct as the suspicion of the Detective, it seemed to single out

Miss Trelawny as different from all others concerned; and in a mystery to be alone is to be suspected, ultimately if not immediately. I thought it better not to say anything. In such a case silence is indeed golden; and if I said nothing now I might have less to defend, or explain, or take back later. I was, therefore, secretly glad that his form of putting his argument did not require any answer from me—for the present, at all events. Doctor Winchester did not seem to expect any answer—a fact which, when I recognised it, gave my pleasure, I hardly knew why. He paused for a while, sitting with his chin in his hand, his eyes staring at vacancy, whilst his brows were fixed. His cigar was held limp between his fingers; he had apparently forgotten it. In an even voice, as though commencing exactly where he had left off, he resumed his argument:

"The other horn of the dilemma is a different affair altogether; and if we once enter on it we must leave everything in the shape of science and experience behind us. I confess that it has its fascinations for me; though at every new thought I find myself romancing in a way that makes me pull up suddenly and look facts resolutely in the face. I sometimes wonder whether the influence or emanation from the sick-room at times affects me as it did the others—the Detective, for instance. Of course it may be that if it is anything chemical, any drug, for example, in vaporeal form, its effects may be cumulative. But then, what could there be that could produce such an effect? The room is, I know, full of mummy smell; and no wonder, with so many relics from the tomb, let alone the actual mummy of that animal which Silvio attacked. By the way, I am going to test him tomorrow; I have been on the trace of a mummy cat, and am to get possession of it in the morning. When I bring it here we shall find out if it be a fact that racial instinct can survive a few thousand years in the grave. However, to get back to the subject in hand. These very mummy smells arise from the presence of substances, and combinations of substances, which the Egyptian priests, who were the learned men and scientists of their time, found by the experience of centuries to be strong enough to arrest the natural forces of decay. There must be powerful agencies at work to effect such a purpose; and it is possible that we may have here some rare substance or combination whose qualities and powers are not understood in this later and more prosaic age. I wonder if Mr. Trelawny has any knowledge, or even suspicion, of such a kind? I only know this for certain, that a worse atmosphere for a sick chamber could not possibly be imagined; and I admire the courage of Sir James Frere in refusing to have anything to do with a case under such conditions. These instructions of Mr. Trelawny to his daughter, and from what you have told me, the care with which he has protected his wishes through his solicitor, show that he suspected something, at any rate. Indeed, it would almost seem as if he expected something to happen. . . .I wonder if it would be possible to learn anything about that! Surely his papers would show or suggest something. . . . It is a difficult matter to tackle; but it might have to be done. His present condition cannot go on for ever; and if anything should happen there would have to be an inquest. In such case full examination would have to be made into everything. . . .As it stands, the police evidence would show a murderous attack more than once repeated. As no clue is apparent, it would be necessary to seek one in a motive."

He was silent. The last words seemed to come in a lower and lower tone as he went on. It had the effect of hopelessness. It came to me as a conviction that now was my time to find out if he had any definite suspicion; and as if in obedience to some command, I asked:

"Do you suspect anyone?" He seemed in a way startled rather than surprised as he turned his eyes on me:

"Suspect anyone? Any thing, you mean. I certainly suspect that there is some influence; but at present my suspicion is held within such limit. Later on, if there be any sufficiently definite conclusion to my reasoning, or my thinking—for there are not proper data for reasoning—I may suspect; at present however—"

He stopped suddenly and looked at the door. There was a faint sound as the handle turned. My own heart seemed to stand still. There was over me some grim, vague apprehension. The interruption in the morning, when I was talking with the Detective, came back upon me with a rush.

The door opened, and Miss Trelawny entered the room.

When she saw us, she started back; and a deep flush swept her face. For a few seconds she paused; at such a time a few succeeding seconds seem to lengthen in geometrical progression. The strain upon me, and, as I could easily see, on the Doctor also, relaxed as she spoke:

"Oh, forgive me, I did not know that you were engaged. I was looking for you, Doctor Winchester, to ask you if I might go to bed tonight with safety, as you will be here. I feel so tired and worn-out that I fear I may break down; and tonight I would certainly not be of any use." Doctor Winchester answered heartily:

"Do! Do go to bed by all means, and get a good night's sleep. God knows! you want it. I am more than glad you have made the suggestion, for I feared when I saw you tonight that I might have you on my hands a patient next."

She gave a sigh of relief, and the tired look seemed to melt from her face. Never shall I forget the deep, earnest look in her great, beautiful black eyes as she said to me:

"You will guard Father tonight, won't you, with Doctor Winchester? I am so anxious about him that every second brings new fears. But I am really worn-out; and if I don't get a good sleep, I think I shall go mad. I will change my room for tonight. I'm afraid that if I stay so close to Father's room I shall multiply every sound into a new terror. But, of course, you will have me waked if there be any cause. I shall be in the bedroom of the little suite next the boudoir off the hall. I had those rooms when first I came to live with Father, and I had no care then. . . .It will be easier to rest there; and perhaps for a few hours I may forget. I shall be all right in the morning. Good-night!"

When I had closed the door behind her and come back to the little table at which we had been sitting, Doctor Winchester said:

"That poor girl is overwrought to a terrible degree. I am delighted that she is to get a rest. It will be life to her; and in the morning she will be all right. Her nervous system is on the verge of a breakdown. Did you notice how fearfully disturbed she was, and how red she got when she came in and found us talking? An ordinary thing like that, in her own house with her own guests, wouldn't under normal circumstances disturb her!"

I was about to tell him, as an explanation in her defence, how her entrance was a repetition of her finding the Detective and myself alone together earlier in the day, when I remembered that that conversation was so private that even an allusion to it might be awkward in evoking curiosity. So I remained silent.

We stood up to go to the sick-room; but as we took our way through the dimly-lighted corridor I could not help thinking, again and again, and again—ay, and for many a day after—how strange it was that she had interrupted me on two such occasions when touching on such a theme.

There was certainly some strange web of accidents, in whose meshes we were all involved.

CHAPTER VII

THE TRAVELLER'S LOSS

THAT NIGHT EVERYTHING went well. Knowing that Miss Trelawny herself was not on guard, Doctor Winchester and I doubled our vigilance. The Nurses and Mrs. Grant kept watch, and the Detectives made their visit each quarter of an hour. All night the patient remained in his trance. He looked healthy, and his chest rose and fell with the easy breathing of a child. But he never stirred; only for his breathing he might have been of marble. Doctor Winchester and I wore our respirators, and irksome they were on that intolerably hot night. Between midnight and three o'clock I felt anxious, and had once more that creepy feeling to which these last few nights had accustomed me; but the grey of the dawn, stealing round the edges of the blinds, came with inexpressible relief, followed by restfulness, went through the household. During the hot night my ears, strained to every sound, had been almost painfully troubled; as though my brain or sensoria were in anxious touch with them. Every breath of the Nurse or the rustle of her dress; every soft pat of slippered feet, as the Policeman went his rounds; every moment of watching life, seemed to be a new impetus to guardianship. Something of the same feeling must have been abroad in the house; now and again I could hear upstairs the sound of restless feet, and more than once downstairs the opening of a window. With the coming of the dawn, however, all this ceased, and the whole household seemed to rest. Doctor Winchester went home when Sister Doris came to relieve Mrs. Grant. He was, I think, a little disappointed or chagrined that nothing of an exceptional nature had happened during his long night vigil.

At eight o'clock Miss Trelawny joined us, and I was amazed as well as delighted to see how much good her night's sleep had done her. She was fairly radiant; just as I had seen her at our first meeting and at the picnic. There was even a suggestion of colour in her cheeks, which, however, looked startlingly white in contrast with her black brows and scarlet lips. With her restored strength, there seemed to have come a tenderness even exceeding that which she had at first shown to her sick father. I could not but be moved by the loving touches as she fixed his pillows and brushed the hair from his forehead.

I was wearied out myself with my long spell of watching; and now that she was on guard I started off to be, blinking my tired eyes in the full light and feeling the weariness of a sleepless night on me all at once.

I had a good sleep, and after lunch I was about to start out to walk to Jermyn Street, when I noticed an importunate man at the hall door. The servant in charge was the one called Morris, formerly the "odd man," but since the exodus of the servants promoted to be butler pro tem. The stranger was speaking rather loudly, so that there was no difficulty in understanding his grievance. The servant man was respectful in both words and demeanour; but he stood squarely in front of the great double door, so that the other could not enter. The first words which I heard from the visitor sufficiently explained the situation:

"That's all very well, but I tell you I must see Mr. Trelawny! What is the use of your saying I can't, when I tell you I must. You put me off, and off, and off! I came here at nine; you said then that he was not up, and that as he was not well he could not be disturbed. I came at twelve; and you told me again he was not up. I asked then to see any of his household; you told me that Miss Trelawny was not up. Now I come again at three, and you tell me he is still in bed, and is not awake yet. Where is Miss Trelawny? 'She is occupied and must not be disturbed!' Well, she must be disturbed! Or some one must. I am here about Mr. Trelawny's special business; and I have come from a place where servants always begin by saying No. 'No' isn't good enough for me this time! I've had three years of it, waiting outside doors and tents when it took longer to get in than it did into the tombs; and then you would think, too, the men inside were as dead as the mummies. I've had about enough of it, I tell you. And when I come home, and find the door of the man I've been working for barred, in just the same way and with the same old answers, it stirs me up the wrong way. Did Mr. Trelawny leave orders that he would not see me when I should come?"

He paused and excitedly mopped his forehead. The servant answered very respectfully:

"I am very sorry, sir, if in doing my duty I have given any offence. But I have my orders, and must obey them. If you would like to leave any message, I will give it to Miss Trelawny; and if you will leave your address, she can communicate with you if she wishes." The answer came in such a way that it was easy to see that the speaker was a kind-hearted man, and a just one.

"My good fellow, I have no fault to find with you personally; and I am sorry if I have hurt your feelings. I must be just, even if I am angry. But it is enough to anger any man to find himself in the position I am. Time is pressing. There is not an hour—not a minute—to lose! And yet here I am, kicking my heels for six hours; knowing all the time that your master will be a hundred times angrier than I am, when he hears how the time has been fooled away. He would rather be waked out of a thousand sleeps than not see me just at present—and before it is too late. My God! it's simply dreadful, after all I've gone through, to have my work spoiled at the last and be foiled in the very doorway by a stupid flunkey! Is there no one with sense in the house; or with authority, even if he hasn't got sense? I could mighty soon convince him that your master must be awakened; even if he sleeps like the Seven Sleepers—"

There was no mistaking the man's sincerity, or the urgency and importance of his business; from his point of view at any rate. I stepped forward.

"Morris," I said, "you had better tell Miss Trelawny that this gentleman wants to see her particularly. If she is busy, ask Mrs. Grant to tell her."

"Very good, sir!" he answered in a tone of relief, and hurried away.

I took the stranger into the little boudoir across the hall. As we went he asked me:

"Are you the secretary?"

"No! I am a friend of Miss Trelawny's. My name is Ross."

"Thank you very much, Mr. Ross, for your kindness!" he said. "My name is Corbeck. I would give you my card, but they don't use cards where I've come from. And if I had had any, I suppose they, too, would have gone last night—"

He stopped suddenly, as though conscious that he had said too much. We both remained silent; as we waited I took stock of him. A short, sturdy man, brown as a coffee-berry; possibly inclined to be fat, but now lean exceedingly. The deep wrinkles in his face and neck were not merely from time and exposure; there were those unmistakable signs where flesh or fat has fallen away, and the skin has become loose. The neck was simply an intricate surface of seams and wrinkles, and sun-scarred with the burning of the Desert. The Far East, the Tropic Seasons, and the Desert—each can have its colour mark. But all three are quite different; and an eye which has once known, can thenceforth easily distinguish them. The dusky pallor of one; the fierce red-brown of the other; and of the third, the dark, ingrained burning, as though it had become a permanent colour. Mr. Corbeck had a big head, massive and full; with shaggy, dark red-brown hair, but bald on the temples. His forehead was a fine one, high and broad; with, to use the terms of physiognomy, the frontal sinus boldly marked. The squareness of it showed "ratiocination";

and the fulness under the eyes "language". He had the short, broad nose that marks energy; the square chin-marked despite a thick, unkempt beard-and massive jaw that showed great resolution.

"No bad man for the Desert!" I thought as I looked.

Miss Trelawny came very quickly. When Mr. Corbeck saw her, he seemed somewhat surprised. But his annoyance and excitement had not disappeared; quite enough remained to cover up any such secondary and purely exoteric feeling as surprise. But as she spoke he never took his eyes off her; and I made a mental note that I would find some early opportunity of investigating the cause of his surprise. She began with an apology which quite smoothed down his ruffled feelings:

"Of course, had my Father been well you would not have been kept waiting. Indeed, had not I been on duty in the sick-room when you called the first time, I should have seen you at once. Now will you kindly tell me what is the matter which so presses?" He looked at me and hesitated. She spoke at once:

"You may say before Mr. Ross anything which you can tell me. He has my fullest confidence, and is helping me in my trouble. I do not think you quite understand how serious my Father's condition is. For three days he has not waked, or given any sign of consciousness; and I am in terrible trouble about him. Unhappily I am in great ignorance of my Father and his life. I only came to live with him a year ago; and I know nothing whatever of his affairs. I do not even know who you are, or in what way your business is associated with him." She said this with a little deprecating smile, all conventional and altogether graceful; as though to express in the most genuine way her absurd ignorance.

He looked steadily at her for perhaps a quarter of a minute; then he spoke, beginning at once as though his mind were made up and his confidence established:

"My name is Eugene Corbeck. I am a Master of Arts and Doctor of Laws and Master of Surgery of Cambridge; Doctor of Letters of

Oxford; Doctor of Science and Doctor of Languages of London University; Doctor of Philosophy of Berlin; Doctor of Oriental Languages of Paris. I have some other degrees, honorary and otherwise, but I need not trouble you with them. Those I have name will show you that I am sufficiently feathered with diplomas to fly into even a sick-room. Early in life—fortunately for my interests and pleasures, but unfortunately for my pocket—I fell in with Egyptology. I must have been bitten by some powerful scarab, for I took it bad. I went out tomb-hunting; and managed to get a living of a sort, and to learn some things that you can't get out of books. I was in pretty low water when I met your Father, who was doing some explorations on his own account; and since then I haven't found that I have many unsatisfied wants. He is a real patron of the arts; no mad Egyptologist can ever hope for a better chief!"

He spoke with feeling; and I was glad to see that Miss Trelawny coloured up with pleasure at the praise of her father. I could not help noticing, however, that Mr. Corbeck was, in a measure, speaking as if against time. I took it that he wished, while speaking, to study his ground; to see how far he would be justified in taking into confidence the two strangers before him. As he went on, I could see that his confidence kept increasing. When I thought of it afterward, and remembered what he had said, I realised that the measure of the information which he gave us marked his growing trust.

"I have been several times out on expeditions in Egypt for your Father; and I have always found it a delight to work for him. Many of his treasures—and he has some rare ones, I tell you—he has procured through me, either by my exploration or by purchase—or—or—otherwise. Your Father, Miss Trelawny, has a rare knowledge. He sometimes makes up his mind that he wants to find a particular thing, of whose existence—if it still exists—he has become aware; and he will follow it all over the world till he gets it. I've been on just such a chase now."

He stopped suddenly, as suddenly as though his mouth had been shut by the jerk of a string. We waited; when he went on he spoke with a caution that was new to him, as though he wished to forestall our asking any questions:

"I am not at liberty to mention anything of my mission; where it was to, what it was for, or anything at all about it. Such matters are in confidence between Mr. Trelawny and myself; I am pledged to absolute secrecy."

He paused, and an embarrassed look crept over his face. Suddenly he said:

"You are sure, Miss Trelawny, your Father is not well enough to see me today?"

A look of wonderment was on her face in turn. But it cleared at once;—she stood up, saying in a tone in which dignity and gracious-ness were blended:

"Come and see for yourself!" She moved toward her father's room; he followed, and I brought up the rear.

Mr. Corbeck entered the sick-room as though he knew it. There is an unconscious attitude or bearing to persons in new surroundings which there is no mistaking. Even in his anxiety to see his powerful friend, he glanced for a moment round the room, as at a familiar place. Then all his attention became fixed on the bed. I watched him narrowly, for somehow I felt that on this man depended much of our enlightenment regarding the strange matter in which we were involved.

It was not that I doubted him. The man was of transparent honesty; it was this very quality which we had to dread. He was of that coura-geous, fixed trueness to his undertaking, that if he should deem it his duty to guard a secret he would do it to the last. The case before us was, at least, an unusual one; and it would, consequently, require more liberal recognition of bounds of the duty of secrecy than would hold under ordinary conditions. To us, ignorance was helplessness. If we could learn anything of the past we might at least form some idea of the conditions antecedent to the attack; and might, so, achieve some means of helping the patient to recovery. There were curios which might be removed. . . .My thoughts were beginning to whirl once again; I pulled myself up sharply and watched. There was a look of infinite pity on the sun-stained, rugged face as he gazed at his friend, lying so helpless. The sternness of Mr. Trelawny's face had not relaxed in sleep; but somehow it made the helplessness more marked. It would not have troubled one to see a weak or an ordinary face under such conditions; but this purposeful, masterful man, lying before us wrapped in impenetrable sleep, had all the pathos of a great ruin. The sight was not a new one to us; but I could see that Miss Trelawny, like myself, was moved afresh by it in the presence of the stranger. Mr. Corbeck's face grew stern. All the pity died away; and in its stead came a grim, hard look which boded ill for whoever had been the cause of this mighty downfall. This look in turn gave place to one of decision; the volcanic energy of the man was working to some definite purpose. He glanced around at us; and as his eyes lighted on Nurse Kennedy his eyebrows went up a trifle. She noted the look, and glanced interrogatively at Miss Trelawny, who flashed back a reply with a glance. She went quietly from the room, closing the door behind her. Mr. Corbeck looked first at me, with a strong man's natural impulse to learn from a man rather than a woman; then at Miss Trelawny, with a remembrance of the duty of courtesy, and said:

"Tell me all about it. How it began and when!" Miss Trelawny looked at me appeallingly; and forthwith I told him all that I knew. He seemed to make no motion during the whole time; but insensibly the bronze face became steel. When, at the end, I told him of Mr. Marvin's visit and of the Power of Attorney, his look began to brighten. And when, seeing his interest in the matter, I went more into detail as to its terms, he spoke:

"Good! Now I know where my duty lies!"

With a sinking heart I heard him. Such a phrase, coming at such a time, seemed to close the door to my hopes of enlightenment.

"What do you mean?" I asked, feeling that my question was a feeble one.

His answer emphasized my fears:

"Trelawny knows what he is doing. He had some definite purpose in all that he did; and we must not thwart him. He evidently expected something to happen, and guarded himself at all points."

"Not at all points!" I said impulsively. "There must have been a weak spot somewhere, or he wouldn't be lying here like that!" Somehow his impassiveness surprised me. I had expected that he would find a valid argument in my phrase; but it did not move him, at least not in the way I thought. Something like a smile flickered over his swarthy face as he answered me:

"This is not the end! Trelawny did not guard himself to no purpose. Doubtless, he expected this too; or at any rate the possibility of it."

"Do you know what he expected, or from what source?" The questioner was Miss Trelawny.

The answer came at once: "No! I know nothing of either. I can guess . . . ." He stopped suddenly.

"Guess what?" The suppressed excitement in the girl's voice was akin to anguish. The steely look came over the swarthy face again; but there was tenderness and courtesy in both voice and manner as he replied:

"Believe me, I would do anything I honestly could to relieve you anxiety. But in this I have a higher duty."

"What duty?"

"Silence!" As he spoke the word, the strong mouth closed like a steel trap.

We all remained silent for a few minutes. In the intensity of our thinking, the silence became a positive thing; the small sounds of life within and without the house seemed intrusive. The first to break it was Miss Trelawny. I had seen an idea—a hope—flash in her eyes; but she steadied herself before speaking:

"What was the urgent subject on which you wanted to see me, knowing that my Father was—not available?" The pause showed her mastery of her thoughts.

The instantaneous change in Mr. Corbeck was almost ludicrous. His start of surprise, coming close upon his iron-clad impassiveness, was like a pantomimic change. But all idea of comedy was swept away by the tragic earnestness with which he remembered his original purpose.

"My God!" he said, as he raised his hand from the chair back on which it rested, and beat it down with a violence which would in itself have arrested attention. His brows corrugated as he went on: "I quite forgot! What a loss! Now of all times! Just at the moment of success! He lying there helpless, and my tongue tied! Not able to raise hand or foot in my ignorance of his wishes!"

"What is it? Oh, do tell us! I am so anxious about my dear Father! Is it any new trouble? I hope not! oh, I hope not! I have had such anxiety and trouble already! It alarms me afresh to hear you speak so! Won't you tell me something to allay this terrible anxiety and uncertainty?"

He drew his sturdy form up to his full height as he said:

"Alas! I cannot, may not, tell you anything. It is his secret." He pointed to the bed. "And yet—and yet I came here for his advice, his counsel, his assistance. And he lies there helpless. . . . And time is flying by us! It may soon be too late!"

"What is it? what is it?" broke in Miss Trelawny in a sort of passion of anxiety, her face drawn with pain. "Oh, speak! Say something! This anxiety, and horror, and mystery are killing me!" Mr. Corbeck calmed himself by a great effort.

"I may not tell you details; but I have had a great loss. My mission, in which I have spent three years, was successful. I discovered all that I sought—and more; and brought them home with me safely. Treasures, priceless in themselves, but doubly precious to him by whose wishes and instructions I sought them. I arrived in London only last night, and when I woke this morning my precious charge was stolen. Stolen in some mysterious way. Not a soul in London knew that I was arriving. No one but myself knew what was in the shabby portmanteau that I carried. My room had but one door, and that I locked and bolted. The room was high in the house, five stories up, so that no entrance could have been obtained by the window. Indeed, I had closed the window myself and shut the hasp, for I wished to be secure in every way. This morning the hasp was untouched. . . .And yet my portmanteau was empty. The lamps were gone! . . .There! it is out. I went to Egypt to search for a set of antique lamps which Mr. Trelawny wished to trace. With incredible labour, and through many dangers, I followed them. I brought them safe home. . . .And now!" He turned away much moved. Even his iron nature was breaking down under the sense of loss.

Miss Trelawny stepped over and laid her hand on his arm. I looked at her in amazement. All the passion and pain which had so moved her seemed to have taken the form of resolution. Her form was erect, her eyes blazed; energy was manifest in every nerve and fibre of her being. Even her voice was full of nervous power as she spoke. It was apparent that she was a marvellously strong woman, and that her strength could answer when called upon.

"We must act at once! My Father's wishes must be carried out if it is possible to us. Mr. Ross, you are a lawyer. We have actually in the house a man whom you consider one of the best detectives in London. Surely we can do something. We can begin at once!" Mr. Corbeck took new life from her enthusiasm.

"Good! You are your Father's daughter!" was all he said. But his admiration for her energy was manifested by the impulsive way in which he took her hand. I moved over to the door. I was going to bring

Sergeant Daw; and from her look of approval, I knew that Margaret—Miss Trelawny—understood. I was at the door when Mr. Corbeck called me back.

"One moment," he said, "before we bring a stranger on the scene. It must be borne in mind that he is not to know what you know now, that the lamps were the objects of a prolonged and difficult and dangerous search. All I can tell him, all that he must know from any source, is that some of my property has been stolen. I must describe some of the lamps, especially one, for it is of gold; and my fear is lest the thief, ignorant of its historic worth, may, in order to cover up his crime, have it melted. I would willingly pay ten, twenty, a hundred, a thousand times its intrinsic value rather than have it destroyed. I shall tell him only what is necessary. So, please, let me answer any questions he may ask; unless, of course, I ask you or refer to either of you for the answer." We both nodded acquiescence. Then a thought struck me and I said:

"By the way, if it be necessary to keep this matter quiet it will be better to have it if possible a private job for the Detective. If once a thing gets to Scotland Yard it is out of our power to keep it quiet, and further secrecy may be impossible. I shall sound Sergeant Daw before he comes up. If I say nothing, it will mean that he accepts the task and will deal with it privately." Mr. Corbeck answered at once:

"Secrecy is everything. The one thing I dread is that the lamps, or some of them, may be destroyed at once." To my intense astonishment Miss Trelawny spoke out at once, but quietly, in a decided voice:

"They will not be destroyed; nor any of them!" Mr. Corbeck actually smiled in amazement.

"How on earth do you know?" he asked. Her answer was still more incomprehensible:

"I don't know how I know it; but know it I do. I feel it all through me; as though it were a conviction which has been with me all my life!"

CHAPTER VIII

THE FINDING OF THE LAMPS

SERGEANT DAW AT first made some demur; but finally agreed to advise privately on a matter which might be suggested to him. He added that I was to remember that he only undertook to advise; for if action were required he might have to refer the matter to headquarters. With this understanding I left him in the study, and brought Miss Trelawny and Mr. Corbeck to him. Nurse Kennedy resumed her place at the bedside before we left the room.

I could not but admire the cautious, cool-headed precision with which the traveller stated his case. He did not seem to conceal anything, and yet he gave the least possible description of the objects missing. He did not enlarge on the mystery of the case; he seemed to look on it as an ordinary hotel theft. Knowing, as I did, that his one object was to recover the articles before their identity could be obliterated, I could see the rare intellectual skill with which he gave the necessary matter and held back all else, though without seeming to do so. "Truly," thought I, "this man has learned the lesson of the Eastern bazaars; and with Western intellect has improved upon his masters!" He quite conveyed his idea to the Detective, who, after thinking the matter over for a few moments, said:

"Pot or scale? that is the question."

"What does that mean?" asked the other, keenly alert.

"An old thieves phrase from Birmingham. I thought that in these days of slang everyone knew that. In old times at Brum, which had a lot of small metal industries, the gold- and silver-smiths used to buy metal from almost anyone who came along. And as metal in small quantities could generally be had cheap when they didn't ask where it came from, it got to be a custom to ask only one thing—whether the customer wanted the goods melted, in which case the buyer made the price, and the melting—pot was always on the fire. If it was to be preserved in its present state at the buyer's option, it went into the scale and fetched standard price for old metal.

"There is a good deal of such work done still, and in other places than Brum. When we're looking for stolen watches we often come across the works, and it's not possible to identify wheels and springs out of a heap; but it's not often that we come across cases that are wanted. Now, in the present instance much will depend on whether the thief is a good man—that's what they call a man who knows his work. A first-class crook will know whether a thing is of more value than merely the metal in it; and in such case he would put it with someone who could place it later on—in America or France, perhaps. By the way, do you think anyone but yourself could identify your lamps?"

"No one but myself!"

"Are there others like them?"

"Not that I know of," answered Mr. Corbeck; "though there may be others that resemble them in many particulars." The Detective paused before asking again: "Would any other skilled person—at the British Museum, for instance, or a dealer, or a collector like Mr. Trelawny, know the value—the artistic value—of the lamps?"

"Certainly! Anyone with a head on his houlders would see at a glance that the things were valuable."

The Detective's face brightened. "Then there is a chance. If your door was locked and the window shut, the goods were not stolen by the chance of a chambermaid or a boots coming along. Whoever did the job went after it special; and he ain't going to part with his swag without his price. This must be a case of notice to the pawnbrokers. There's one good thing about it, anyhow, that the hue and cry needn't be given. We needn't tell Scotland Yard unless you like; we can work the thing privately. If you wish to keep the thing dark, as you told me at the first, that is our chance." Mr. Corbeck, after a pause, said quietly:

"I suppose you couldn't hazard a suggestion as to how the robbery was effected?" The Policeman smiled the smile of knowledge and experience.

"In a very simple way, I have no doubt, sir. That is how all these mysterious crimes turn out in the long-run. The criminal knows his work and all the tricks of it; and he is always on the watch for chances. Moreover, he knows by experience what these chances are likely to be, and how they usually come. The other person is only careful; he doesn't know all the tricks and pits that may be made for him, and by some little oversight or other he falls into the trap. When we know all about this case, you will wonder that you did not see the method of it all along!" This seemed to annoy Mr. Corbeck a little; there was decided heat in his manner as he answered:

"Look here, my good friend, there is not anything simple about this case—except that the things were taken. The window was closed; the fireplace was bricked up. There is only one door to the room, and that I locked and bolted. There is no transom; I have heard all about hotel robberies through the transom. I never left my room in the night. I looked at the things before going to bed; and I went to look at them again when I woke up. If you can rig up any kind of simple robbery out of these facts you are a clever man. That's all I say; clever enough to go right away and get my things back." Miss Trelawny laid her hand upon his arm in a soothing way, and said quietly:

"Do not distress yourself unnecessarily. I am sure they will turn up." Sergeant Daw turned to her so quickly that I could not help remembering vividly his suspicions of her, already formed, as he said:

"May I ask, miss, on what you base that opinion?"

I dreaded to hear her answer, given to ears already awake to suspicion; but it came to me as a new pain or shock all the same:

"I cannot tell you how I know. But I am sure of it!" The Detective looked at her for some seconds in silence, and then threw a quick glance at me.

Presently he had a little more conversation with Mr. Corbeck as to his own movements, the details of the hotel and the room, and the means of identifying the goods. Then he went away to commence his inquiries, Mr. Corbeck impressing on him the necessity for secrecy lest the thief should get wind of his danger and destroy the lamps. Mr. Corbeck promised, when going away to attend to various matters of his own business, to return early in the evening, and to stay in the house.

All that day Miss Trelawny was in better spirits and looked in better strength than she had yet been, despite the new shock and annoyance of the theft which must ultimately bring so much disappointment to her father.

We spent most of the day looking over the curio treasures of Mr. Trelawny. From what I had heard from Mr. Corbeck I began to have some idea of the vastness of his enterprise in the world of Egyptian research; and with this light everything around me began to have a new interest. As I went on, the interest grew; any lingering doubts which I might have had changed to wonder and admiration. The house seemed to be a veritable storehouse of marvels of antique art. In addition to the curios, big and little, in Mr. Trelawny's own room—from the great sarcophagi down to the scarabs of all kinds in the cabinets—the great hall, the staircase landings, the study, and even the boudoir were full of antique pieces which would have made a collector's mouth water.

Miss Trelawny from the first came with me, and looked with growing interest at everything. After having examined some cabinets of exquisite amulets she said to me in quite a naive way:

"You will hardly believe that I have of late seldom even looked at any of these things. It is only since Father has been ill that I seem to have even any curiosity about them. But now, they grow and grow on me to quite an absorbing degree. I wonder if it is that the collector's blood which I have in my veins is beginning to manifest itself. If so, the strange thing is that I have not felt the call of it before. Of course I know most of the big things, and have examined them more or less; but really, in a sort of way I have always taken them for granted, as though they had always been there. I have noticed the same thing now and again with family pictures, and the way they are taken for granted by the family. If you will let me examine them with you it will be delightful!"

It was a joy to me to hear her talk in such a way; and her last suggestion quite thrilled me. Together we went round the various rooms and passages, examining and admiring the magnificent curios. There was such a bewildering amount and variety of objects that we could only glance at most of them; but as we went along we arranged that we should take them seriatim, day by day, and examine them more closely. In the hall was a sort of big frame of floriated steel work which Margaret said her father used for lifting the heavy stone lids of the sarcophagi. It was not heavy and could be moved about easily enough. By aid of this we raised the covers in turn and looked at the endless series of hieroglyphic pictures cut in most of them. In spite of her profession of ignorance Margaret knew a good deal about them; her year of life with her father had had unconsciously its daily and hourly lesson. She was a remarkably clever and acute-minded girl, and with a prodigious memory; so that her store of knowledge, gathered unthinkingly bit by bit, had grown to proportions that many a scholar might have envied.

And yet it was all so naive and unconscious; so girlish and simple. She was so fresh in her views and ideas, and had so little thought of self, that in her companionship I forgot for the time all the troubles and mysteries which enmeshed the house; and I felt like a boy again. . . .

The most interesting of the sarcophagi were undoubtedly the three in Mr. Trelawny's room. Of these, two were of dark stone, one of porphyry and the other of a sort of ironstone. These were wrought with some hieroglyphs. But the third was strikingly different. It was of some yellow-brown substance of the dominating colour effect of Mexican onyx, which it resembled in many ways, excepting that the natural pattern of its convolutions was less marked. Here and there were patches almost transparent—certainly translucent. The whole chest, cover and all, was wrought with hundreds, perhaps thousands, of minute hieroglyphics, seemingly in an endless series. Back, front, sides, edges, bottom, all had their quota of the dainty pictures, the deep blue of their colouring showing up fresh and sharply edge in the yellow stone. It was very long, nearly nine feet; and perhaps a yard wide. The sides undulated, so that there was no hard line. Even the corners took such excellent curves that they pleased the eye. "Truly," I said, "this must have been made for a giant!"

"Or for a giantess!" said Margaret.

This sarcophagus stood near to one of the windows. It was in one respect different from all the other sarcophagi in the place. All the others in the house, of whatever material—granite, porphyry, ironstone, basalt, slate, or wood—were quite simple in form within. Some of them were plain of interior surface; others were engraved, in whole or part, with hieroglyphics. But each and all of them had no protuberances or uneven surface anywhere. They might have been used for baths; indeed, they resembled in many ways Roman baths of stone or marble which I had seen. Inside this, however, was a raised space, outlined like a human figure. I asked Margaret if she could explain it in any way. For answer she said:

"Father never wished to speak about this. It attracted my attention from the first; but when I asked him about it he said: 'I shall tell you all about it some day, little girl—if I live! But not yet! The story is not yet told, as I hope to tell it to you! Some day, perhaps soon, I shall know all; and then we shall go over it together. And a mighty interesting story you will find it—from first to last!' Once afterward I said, rather lightly I am afraid: 'Is that story of the sarcophagus told yet, Father?' He shook his head, and looked at me gravely as he said: 'Not yet, little girl; but it will be—if I live—if I live!' His repeating that phrase about his living rather frightened me; I never ventured to ask him again."

Somehow this thrilled me. I could not exactly say how or why; but it seemed like a gleam of light at last. There are, I think, moments when the mind accepts something as true; though it can account for neither the course of the thought, nor, if there be more than one thought, the connection between them. Hitherto we had been in such outer darkness regarding Mr. Trelawny, and the strange visitation which had fallen on him, that anything which afforded a clue, even of the faintest and most shadowy kind, had at the outset the enlightening satisfaction of a certainty. Here were two lights of our puzzle. The first that Mr. Trelawny associated with this particular curio a doubt of his own living. The second that he had some purpose or expectation with regard to it, which he would not disclose, even to his daughter, till complete. Again it was to be borne in mind that this sarcophagus differed internally from all the others. What meant that odd raised place? I said nothing to Miss Trelawny, for I feared lest I should either frighten her or buoy her up with future hopes; but I made up my mind that I would take an early opportunity for further investigation.

Close beside the sarcophagus was a low table of green stone with red veins in it, like bloodstone. The feet were fashioned like the paws of a jackal, and round each leg was twined a full-throated snake wrought exquisitely in pure gold. On it rested a strange and very beautiful coffer or casket of stone of a peculiar shape. It was something like a small coffin, except that the longer sides, instead of being cut off square like the upper or level part were continued to a point. Thus it was an irregular septahedron, there being two planes on each of the two sides, one end and a top and bottom. The stone, of one piece of which it was wrought, was such as I had never seen before. At the base it was of a full green, the colour of emerald without, of course, its gleam. It was not by any means dull, however, either in colour or substance, and was of infinite hardness and fineness of texture. The surface was almost that of a jewel. The colour grew lighter as it rose, with gradation so fine as to be imperceptible, changing to a fine yellow almost of the colour of "mandarin" china. It was quite unlike anything I had ever seen, and did not resemble any stone or gem that I knew. I took it to be some unique mother-stone, or matrix of some gem. It was wrought all over, except in a few spots, with fine hieroglyphics, exquisitely done and coloured with the same blue-green cement or pigment that appeared on the sarcophagus. In length it was about two feet and a half; in breadth about half this, and was nearly a foot high. The vacant spaces were irregularly distributed about the top running to the pointed end. These places seemed less opaque than the rest of the stone. I tried to lift up the lid so that I might see if they were translucent; but it was securely fixed. It fitted so exactly that the whole coffer seemed like a single piece of stone mysteriously hollowed from within. On the sides and edges were some odd-looking protuberances wrought just as finely as any other portion of the coffer which had been sculptured by manifest design in the cutting of the stone. They had queer-shaped holes or hollows, different in each; and, like the rest, were covered with the hieroglyphic figures, cut finely and filled in with the same blue-green cement.

On the other side of the great sarcophagus stood another small table of alabaster, exquisitely chased with symbolic figures of gods and the signs of the zodiac. On this table stood a case of about a foot square composed of slabs of rock crystal set in a skeleton of bands of red gold, beautifully engraved with hieroglyphics, and coloured with a blue green, very much the tint of the figures on the sarcophagus and the coffer. The whole work was quite modern.

But if the case was modern what it held was not. Within, on a cushion of cloth of gold as fine as silk, and with the peculiar softness of old gold, rested a mummy hand, so perfect that it startled one to see it. A woman's hand, fine and long, with slim tapering fingers and nearly as perfect as when it was given to the embalmer thousands of years before. In the embalming it had lost nothing of its beautiful shape; even the wrist seemed to maintain its pliability as the gentle curve lay on the cushion. The skin was of a rich creamy or old ivory colour; a dusky fair skin which suggested heat, but heat in shadow. The great peculiarity of it, as a hand, was that it had in all seven fingers, there being two middle and two index fingers. The upper end of the wrist was jagged, as though it had been broken off, and was stained with a red-brown stain. On the cushion near the hand was a small scarab, exquisitely wrought of emerald.

"That is another of Father's mysteries. When I asked him about it he said that it was perhaps the most valuable thing he had, except one. When I asked him what that one was, he refused to tell me, and forbade me to ask him anything concerning it. 'I will tell you,' he said, 'all about it, too, in good time—if I live!'"

"If I live!" the phrase again. These three things grouped together, the Sarcophagus, the Coffer, and the Hand, seemed to make a trilogy of mystery indeed!

At this time Miss Trelawny was sent for on some domestic matter. I looked at the other curios in the room; but they did not seem to have anything like the same charm for me, now that she was away. Later on in the day I was sent for to the boudoir where she was consulting with Mrs. Grant as to the lodgment of Mr. Corbeck. They were in doubt as to whether he should have a room close to Mr. Trelawny's or quite away from it, and had thought it well to ask my advice on the subject. I came to the conclusion that he had better not be too near; for the first at all events, he could easily be moved closer if necessary. When Mrs. Grant had gone, I asked Miss Trelawny how it came that the furniture of this room, the boudoir in which we were, was so different from the other rooms of the house.

"Father's forethought!" she answered. "When I first came, he thought, and rightly enough, that I might get frightened with so many records of death and the tomb everywhere. So he had this room and the little suite off it—that door opens into the sitting-room—where I slept last night, furnished with pretty things. You see, they are all beautiful. That cabinet belonged to the great Napoleon."

"There is nothing Egyptian in these rooms at all then?" I asked, rather to show interest in what she had said than anything else, for the furnishing of the room was apparent. "What a lovely cabinet! May I look at it?"

"Of course! with the greatest pleasure!" she answered, with a smile. "Its finishing, within and without, Father says, is absolutely complete." I stepped over and looked at it closely. It was made of tulip wood, inlaid in patterns; and was mounted in ormolu. I pulled open one of the drawers, a deep one where I could see the work to great advantage. As I pulled it, something rattled inside as though rolling; there was a tinkle as of metal on metal.

"Hullo!" I said. "There is something in here. Perhaps I had better not open it."

"There is nothing that I know of," she answered. "Some of the housemaids may have used it to put something by for the time and forgotten it. Open it by all means!"

I pulled open the drawer; as I did so, both Miss Trelawny and I started back in amazement.

There before our eyes lay a number of ancient Egyptian lamps, of various sizes and of strangely varied shapes.

We leaned over them and looked closely. My own heart was beating like a trip-hammer; and I could see by the heaving of Margaret's bosom that she was strangely excited.

Whilst we looked, afraid to touch and almost afraid to think, there was a ring at the front door; immediately afterwards Mr. Corbeck, followed by Sergeant Daw, came into the hall. The door of the boudoir was open, and when they saw us Mr. Corbeck came running in, followed more slowly by the Detective. There was a sort of chastened joy in his face and manner as he said impulsively:

"Rejoice with me, my dear Miss Trelawny, my luggage has come and all my things are intact!" Then his face fell as he added, "Except the lamps. The lamps that were worth all the rest a thousand times. . . ." He stopped, struck by the strange pallor of her face. Then his eyes, following her look and mine, lit on the cluster of lamps in the drawer. He gave a sort of cry of surprise and joy as he bent over and touched them: "My lamps! My lamps! Then they are safe—safe—safe! . . . But how, in the name of God—of all the Gods—did they come here?"

We all stood silent. The Detective made a deep sound of in-taking breath. I looked at him, and as he caught my glance he turned his eyes on Miss Trelawny whose back was toward him.

There was in them the same look of suspicion which had been there when he had spoken to me of her being the first to find her father on the occasions of the attacks.

CHAPTER IX

THE NEED OF KNOWLEDGE

MR. CORBECK SEEMED to go almost off his head at the recovery of the lamps. He took them up one by one and looked them all over tenderly, as though they were things that he loved. In his delight and excitement he breathed so hard that it seemed almost like a cat purring. Sergeant Daw said quietly, his voice breaking the silence like a discord in a melody:

"Are you quite sure those lamps are the ones you had, and that were stolen?"

His answer was in an indignant tone: "Sure! Of course I'm sure. There isn't another set of lamps like these in the world!"

"So far as you know!" The Detective's words were smooth enough, but his manner was so exasperating that I was sure he had some motive in it; so I waited in silence. He went on:

"Of course there may be some in the British Museum; or Mr. Trelawny may have had these already. There's nothing new under the sun, you know, Mr. Corbeck; not even in Egypt. These may be the originals, and yours may have been the copies. Are there any points by which you can identify these as yours?"

Mr. Corbeck was really angry by this time. He forgot his reserve; and in his indignation poured forth a torrent of almost incoherent, but enlightening, broken sentences:

"Identify! Copies of them! British Museum! Rot! Perhaps they keep a set in Scotland Yard for teaching idiot policemen Egyptology! Do

I know them? When I have carried them about my body, in the desert, for three months; and lay awake night after night to watch them! When I have looked them over with a magnifying-glass, hour after hour, till my eyes ached; till every tiny blotch, and chip, and dinge became as familiar to me as his chart to a captain; as familiar as they doubtless have been all the time to every thick-headed area-prowler within the bounds of mortality. See here, young man, look at these!" He ranged the lamps in a row on the top of the cabinet. "Did you ever see a set of lamps of these shapes—of any one of these shapes? Look at these dominant figures on them! Did you ever see so complete a set—even in Scotland Yard; even in Bow Street? Look! one on each, the seven forms of Hathor. Look at that figure of the Ka of a Princess of the Two Egypts, standing between Ra and Osiris in the Boat of the Dead, with the Eye of Sleep, supported on legs, bending before her; and Harmochis rising in the north. Will you find that in the British Museum—or Bow Street? Or perhaps your studies in the Gizeh Museum, or the Fitzwilliam, or Paris, or Leyden, or Berlin, have shown you that the episode is common in hieroglyphics; and that this is only a copy. Perhaps you can tell me what that figure of Ptah-Seker-Ausar holding the Tet wrapped in the Sceptre of Papyrus means? Did you ever see it before; even in the British Museum, or Gizeh, or Scotland Yard?"

He broke off suddenly; and then went on in quite a different way:

"Look here! it seems to me that the thick-headed idiot is myself! I beg your pardon, old fellow, for my rudeness. I quite lost my temper at the suggestion that I do not know these lamps. You don't mind, do you?" The Detective answered heartily:

"Lord, sir, not I. I like to see folks angry when I am dealing with them, whether they are on my side or the other. It is when people are angry that you learn the truth from them. I keep cool; that is my trade! Do you know, you have told me more about those lamps in the past two minutes than when you filled me up with details of how to identify them."

Mr. Corbeck grunted; he was not pleased at having given himself away. All at once he turned to me and said in his natural way:

"Now tell me how you got them back?" I was so surprised that I said without thinking:

"We didn't get them back!" The traveller laughed openly.

"What on earth do you mean?" he asked. "You didn't get them back! Why, there they are before your eyes! We found you looking at them when we came in." By this time I had recovered my surprise and had my wits about me.

"Why, that's just it," I said. "We had only come across them, by accident, that very moment!"

Mr. Corbeck drew back and looked hard at Miss Trelawny and myself; turning his eyes from one to the other as he asked:

"Do you mean to tell me that no one brought them here; that you found them in that drawer? That, so to speak, no one at all brought them back?"

"I suppose someone must have brought them here; they couldn't have come of their own accord. But who it was, or when, or how, neither of us knows. We shall have to make inquiry, and see if any of the servants know anything of it."

We all stood silent for several seconds. It seemed a long time. The first to speak was the Detective, who said in an unconscious way:

"Well, I'm damned! I beg your pardon, miss!" Then his mouth shut like a steel trap.

We called up the servants, one by one, and asked them if they knew anything of some articles placed in a drawer in the boudoir; but none of them could throw any light on the circumstance. We did not tell them what the articles were; or let them see them.

Mr. Corbeck packed the lamps in cotton wool, and placed them in a tin box. This, I may mention incidentally, was then brought up to the detectives' room, where one of the men stood guard over them with a revolver the whole night. Next day we got a small safe into the house, and placed them in it. There were two different keys. One of them I kept myself; the other I placed in my drawer in the Safe Deposit vault. We were all determined that the lamps should not be lost again.

About an hour after we had found the lamps, Doctor Winchester arrived. He had a large parcel with him, which, when unwrapped, proved to be the mummy of a cat. With Miss Trelawny's permission he placed this in the boudoir; and Silvio was brought close to it. To the surprise of us all, however, except perhaps Doctor Winchester, he did not manifest the least annoyance; he took no notice of it whatever. He stood on the table close beside it, purring loudly. Then, following out his plan, the Doctor brought him into Mr. Trelawny's room, we all following. Doctor Winchester was excited; Miss Trelawny anxious. I was more than interested myself, for I began to have a glimmering of the Doctor's idea. The Detective was calmly and coldly superior; but Mr. Corbeck, who was an enthusiast, was full of eager curiosity.

The moment Doctor Winchester got into the room, Silvio began to mew and wriggle; and jumping out of his arms, ran over to the cat mummy and began to scratch angrily at it. Miss Trelawny had some difficulty in taking him away; but so soon as he was out of the room he became quiet. When she came back there was a clamour of comments:

"I thought so!" from the Doctor.

"What can it mean?" from Miss Trelawny.

"That's a very strange thing!" from Mr. Corbeck.

"Odd! but it doesn't prove anything!" from the Detective.

"I suspend my judgment!" from myself, thinking it advisable to say something.

Then by common consent we dropped the theme—for the present.

In my room that evening I was making some notes of what had happened, when there came a low tap on the door. In obedience to my summons Sergeant Daw came in, carefully closing the door behind him.

"Well, Sergeant," said I, "sit down. What is it?"

"I wanted to speak to you, sir, about those lamps." I nodded and waited: he went on: "You know that that room where they were found opens directly into the room where Miss Trelawny slept last night?"

"Yes."

"During the night a window somewhere in that part of the house was opened, and shut again. I heard it, and took a look round; but I could see no sign of anything."

"Yes, I know that!" I said; "I heard a window moved myself."

"Does nothing strike you as strange about it, sir?"

"Strange!" I said; "Strange! why it's all the most bewildering, maddening thing I have ever encountered. It is all so strange that one seems to wonder, and simply waits for what will happen next. But what do you mean by strange?"

The Detective paused, as if choosing his words to begin; and then said deliberately:

"You see, I am not one who believes in magic and such things. I am for facts all the time; and I always find in the long-run that there is a reason and a cause for everything. This new gentleman says these things were stolen out of his room in the hotel. The lamps, I take it from some things he has said, really belong to Mr. Trelawny. His daughter, the lady of the house, having left the room she usually occupies, sleeps that night on the ground floor. A window is heard to open and shut during the night. When we, who have been during the day trying to find a clue to the robbery, come to the house, we find the stolen goods in a room close to where she slept, and opening out of it!"

He stopped. I felt that same sense of pain and apprehension, which I had experienced when he had spoken to me before, creeping, or rather rushing, over me again. I had to face the matter out, however. My relations with her, and the feeling toward her which I now knew full well meant a very deep love and devotion, demanded so much. I said as calmly as I could, for I knew the keen eyes of the skilful investigator were on me:

"And the inference?"

He answered with the cool audacity of conviction:

"The inference to me is that there was no robbery at all. The goods were taken by someone to this house, where they were received through a window on the ground floor. They were placed in the cabinet, ready to be discovered when the proper time should come!"

Somehow I felt relieved; the assumption was too monstrous. I did not want, however, my relief to be apparent, so I answered as gravely as I could:

"And who do you suppose brought them to the house?"

"I keep my mind open as to that. Possibly Mr. Corbeck himself; the matter might be too risky to trust to a third party."

"Then the natural extension of your inference is that Mr. Corbeck is a liar and a fraud; and that he is in conspiracy with Miss Trelawny to deceive someone or other about those lamps."

"Those are harsh words, Mr. Ross. They're so plain-spoken that they bring a man up standing, and make new doubts for him. But I have to go where my reason points. It may be that there is another party than Miss Trelawny in it. Indeed, if it hadn't been for the other matter that set me thinking and bred doubts of its own about her, I wouldn't dream of mixing her up in this. But I'm safe on Corbeck. Whoever else is in it, he is! The things couldn't have been taken without his connivance—if what he says is true. If it isn't—well! he is a liar anyhow. I would think it a bad job to have him stay in the house with so many valuables, only that it will give me and my mate a chance of watching him. We'll keep a pretty good look-out, too, I tell you. He's up in my room now, guarding those lamps; but Johnny Wright is there too. I go on before he comes off; so there won't be much chance of another house-breaking. Of course, Mr. Ross, all this, too, is between you and me."

"Quite so! You may depend on my silence!" I said; and he went away to keep a close eye on the Egyptologist.

It seemed as though all my painful experiences were to go in pairs, and that the sequence of the previous day was to be repeated; for before long I had another private visit from Doctor Winchester who had now paid his nightly visit to his patient and was on his way home. He took the seat which I proffered and began at once:

"This is a strange affair altogether. Miss Trelawny has just been telling me about the stolen lamps, and of the finding of them in the Napoleon cabinet. It would seem to be another complication of the mystery; and yet, do you know, it is a relief to me. I have exhausted all human and natural possibilities of the case, and am beginning to fall back on superhuman and supernatural possibilities. Here are such strange things that, if I am not going mad, I think we must have a solution before long. I wonder if I might ask some questions and some help from Mr. Corbeck, without making further complications and embarrassing us. He seems to know an amazing amount regarding Egypt and all relating to it. Perhaps he wouldn't mind translating a little bit of hieroglyphic. It is child's play to him. What do you think?"

When I had thought the matter over a few seconds I spoke. We wanted all the help we could get. For myself, I had perfect confidence in both men; and any comparing notes, or mutual assistance, might bring good results. Such could hardly bring evil.

"By all means I should ask him. He seems an extraordinarily learned man in Egyptology; and he seems to me a good fellow as well as an enthusiast. By the way, it will be necessary to be a little guarded as to whom you speak regarding any information which he may give you."

"Of course!" he answered. "Indeed I should not dream of saying anything to anybody, excepting yourself. We have to remember that when Mr. Trelawny recovers he may not like to think that we have been chattering unduly over his affairs."

"Look here!" I said, "why not stay for a while: and I shall ask him to come and have a pipe with us. We can then talk over things."

He acquiesced: so I went to the room where Mr. Corbeck was, and brought him back with me. I thought the detectives were pleased at his going. On the way to my room he said:

"I don't half like leaving those things there, with only those men to guard them. They're a deal sight too precious to be left to the police!"

From which it would appear that suspicion was not confined to Sergeant Daw.

Mr. Corbeck and Doctor Winchester, after a quick glance at each other, became at once on most friendly terms. The traveller professed his willingness to be of any assistance which he could, provided, he added, that it was anything about which he was free to speak. This was not very promising; but Doctor Winchester began at once:

"I want you, if you will, to translate some hieroglyphic for me."

"Certainly, with the greatest pleasure, so far as I can. For I may tell you that hieroglyphic writing is not quite mastered yet; though we are getting at it! We are getting at it! What is the inscription?"

"There are two," he answered. "One of them I shall bring here."

He went out, and returned in a minute with the mummy cat which he had that evening introduced to Silvio. The scholar took it; and, after a short examination, said:

"There is nothing especial in this. It is an appeal to Bast, the Lady of Bubastis, to give her good bread and milk in the Elysian Fields. There may be more inside; and if you will care to unroll it, I will do my best. I do not think, however, that there is anything special. From the method of wrapping I should say it is from the Delta; and of a late period, when such mummy work was common and cheap. What is the other inscription you wish me to see?"

"The inscription on the mummy cat in Mr. Trelawny's room."

Mr. Corbeck's face fell. "No!" he said, "I cannot do that! I am, for the present at all events, practically bound to secrecy regarding any of the things in Mr. Trelawny's room."

Doctor Winchester's comment and my own were made at the same moment. I said only the one word "Checkmate!" from which I think he may have gathered that I guessed more of his idea and purpose than perhaps I had intentionally conveyed to him. He murmured:

"Practically bound to secrecy?"

Mr. Corbeck at once took up the challenge conveyed:

"Do not misunderstand me! I am not bound by any definite pledge of secrecy; but I am bound in honour to respect Mr. Trelawny's confidence, given to me, I may tell you, in a very large measure. Regarding many of the objects in his room he has a definite purpose in view; and it would not be either right or becoming for me, his trusted friend and confidant, to forestall that purpose. Mr. Trelawny, you may know— or rather you do not know or you would not have so construed my remark—is a scholar, a very great scholar. He has worked for years toward a certain end. For this he has spared no labour, no expense, no personal danger or self-denial. He is on the line of a result which will place him amongst the foremost discoverers or investigators of his age. And now, just at the time when any hour might bring him success, he is stricken down!"

He stopped, seemingly overcome with emotion. After a time he recovered himself and went on:

"Again, do not misunderstand me as to another point. I have said that Mr. Trelawny has made much confidence with me; but I do not mean to lead you to believe that I know all his plans, or his aims or objects. I know the period which he has been studying; and the definite historical individual whose life he has been investigating, and whose records he has been following up one by one with infinite patience.

But beyond this I know nothing. That he has some aim or object in the completion of this knowledge I am convinced. What it is I may guess; but I must say nothing. Please to remember, gentlemen, that I have voluntarily accepted the position of recipient of a partial confidence. I have respected that; and I must ask any of my friends to do the same."

He spoke with great dignity; and he grew, moment by moment, in the respect and esteem of both Doctor Winchester and myself. We understood that he had not done speaking; so we waited in silence till he continued:

"I have spoken this much, although I know well that even such a hint as either of you might gather from my words might jeopardise the success of his work. But I am convinced that you both wish to help him—and his daughter," he said this looking me fairly between the eyes, "to the best of your power, honestly and unselfishly. He is so stricken down, and the manner of it is so mysterious that I cannot but think that it is in some way a result of his own work. That he calculated on some set-back is manifest to us all. God knows! I am willing to do what I can, and to use any knowledge I have in his behalf. I arrived in England full of exultation at the thought that I had fulfilled the mission with which he had trusted me. I had got what he said were the last objects of his search; and I felt assured that he would now be able to begin the experiment of which he had often hinted to me. It is too dreadful that at just such a time such a calamity should have fallen on him. Doctor Winchester, you are a physician; and, if your face does not belie you, you are a clever and a bold one. Is there no way which you can devise to wake this man from his unnatural stupor?"

There was a pause; then the answer came slowly and deliberately:

"There is no ordinary remedy that I know of. There might possibly be some extraordinary one. But there would be no use in trying to find it, except on one condition."

"And that?"

"Knowledge! I am completely ignorant of Egyptian matters, language, writing, history, secrets, medicines, poisons, occult powers—all
that go to make up the mystery of that mysterious land. This disease,
or condition, or whatever it may be called, from which Mr. Trelawny is
suffering, is in some way connected with Egypt. I have had a suspicion
of this from the first; and later it grew into a certainty, though without
proof. What you have said tonight confirms my conjecture, and makes
me believe that a proof is to be had. I do not think that you quite know
all that has gone on in this house since the night of the attack—of the
finding of Mr. Trelawny's body. Now I propose that we confide in you.
If Mr. Ross agrees, I shall ask him to tell you. He is more skilled than
I am in putting facts before other people. He can speak by his brief; and
in this case he has the best of all briefs, the experience of his own eyes
and ears, and the evidence that he has himself taken on the spot from
participators in, or spectators of, what has happened. When you know
all, you will, I hope, be in a position to judge as to whether you can
best help Mr. Trelawny, and further his secret wishes, by your silence
or your speech."

I nodded approval. Mr. Corbeck jumped up, and in his impulsive
way held out a hand to each.

"Done!" he said. "I acknowledge the honour of your confidence;
and on my part I pledge myself that if I find my duty to Mr. Trelawny's
wishes will, in his own interest, allow my lips to open on his affairs,
I shall speak so freely as I may."

Accordingly I began, and told him, as exactly as I could, everything that had happened from the moment of my waking at the knocking
on the door in Jermyn Street. The only reservations I made were as to
my own feeling toward Miss Trelawny and the matters of small import to the main subject which followed it; and my conversations with
Sergeant Daw, which were in themselves private, and which would have
demanded discretionary silence in any case. As I spoke, Mr. Corbeck

followed with breathless interest. Sometimes he would stand up and pace about the room in uncontrollable excitement; and then recover himself suddenly, and sit down again. Sometimes he would be about to speak, but would, with an effort, restrain himself. I think the narration helped me to make up my own mind; for even as I talked, things seemed to appear in a clearer light. Things big and little, in relation of their importance to the case, fell into proper perspective. The story up to date became coherent, except as to its cause, which seemed a greater mystery than ever. This is the merit of entire, or collected, narrative. Isolated facts, doubts, suspicions, conjectures, give way to a homogeneity which is convincing.

That Mr. Corbeck was convinced was evident. He did not go through any process of explanation or limitation, but spoke right out at once to the point, and fearlessly like a man:

"That settles me! There is in activity some Force that needs special care. If we all go on working in the dark we shall get in one another's way, and by hampering each other, undo the good that any or each of us, working in different directions, might do. It seems to me that the first thing we have to accomplish is to get Mr. Trelawny waked out of that unnatural sleep. That he can be waked is apparent from the way the Nurse has recovered; though what additional harm may have been done to him in the time he has been lying in that room I suppose no one can tell. We must chance that, however. He has lain there, and whatever the effect might be, it is there now; and we have, and shall have, to deal with it as a fact. A day more or less won't hurt in the long-run. It is late now; and we shall probably have tomorrow a task before us that will require our energies afresh. You, Doctor, will want to get to your sleep; for I suppose you have other work as well as this to do tomorrow. As for you, Mr. Ross, I understand that you are to have a spell of watching in the sick-room tonight. I shall get you a book which will help to pass the time for you. I shall go and look for it in the library. I know where it was when I was here last; and I don't suppose Mr. Trelawny has used it since. He knew long ago all that was in it which was or might be of interest to him. But it will be necessary, or at least helpful, to understand other things which I shall tell you later. You will be able to tell Doctor Winchester all that would aid him. For I take it that our work will branch out pretty soon. We shall each have our own end to hold up; and it will take each of us all our time and understanding to get through his own tasks. It will not be necessary for you to read the whole book. All that will interest you—with regard to our matter I mean of course, for the whole book is interesting as a record of travel in a country then quite unknown—is the preface, and two or three chapters which I shall mark for you."

He shook hands warmly with Doctor Winchester who had stood up to go.

Whilst he was away I sat lonely, thinking. As I thought, the world around me seemed to be illimitably great. The only little spot in which I was interested seemed like a tiny speck in the midst of a wilderness. Without and around it were darkness and unknown danger, pressing in from every side. And the central figure in our little oasis was one of sweetness and beauty. A figure one could love; could work for; could die for . . . !

Mr. Corbeck came back in a very short time with the book; he had found it at once in the spot where he had seen it three years before. Having placed in it several slips of paper, marking the places where I was to read, he put it into my hands, saying:

"That is what started Mr. Trelawny; what started me when I read it; and which will, I have no doubt, be to you an interesting beginning to a special study—whatever the end may be. If, indeed, any of us here may ever see the end."

At the door he paused and said:

"I want to take back one thing. That Detective is a good fellow. What you have told me of him puts him in a new light. The best proof of it is that I can go quietly to sleep tonight, and leave the lamps in his care!"

When he had gone I took the book with me, put on my respirator, and went to my spell of duty in the sick-room!

CHAPTER X

THE VALLEY OF THE SORCERER

I PLACED THE book on the little table on which the shaded lamp rested and moved the screen to one side. Thus I could have the light on my book; and by looking up, see the bed, and the Nurse, and the door. I cannot say that the conditions were enjoyable, or calculated to allow of that absorption in the subject which is advisable for effective study. However, I composed myself to the work as well as I could. The book was one which, on the very face of it, required special attention. It was a folio in Dutch, printed in Amsterdam in 1650. Some one had made a literal translation, writing generally the English word under the Dutch, so that the grammatical differences between the two tongues made even the reading of the translation a difficult matter. One had to dodge backward and forward among the words. This was in addition to the difficulty of deciphering a strange handwriting of two hundred years ago. I found, however, that after a short time I got into the habit of following in conventional English the Dutch construction; and, as I became more familiar with the writing, my task became easier.

At first the circumstances of the room, and the fear lest Miss Trelawny should return unexpectedly and find me reading the book, disturbed me somewhat. For we had arranged amongst us, before Doctor Winchester had gone home, that she was not to be brought into the range of the coming investigation. We considered that there might be some shock to a woman's mind in matters of apparent mystery; and further, that she, being Mr. Trelawny's daughter, might be placed in a difficult position with him afterward if she took part in, or even had a personal knowledge of, the disregarding of his expressed wishes. But when I remembered that she did not come on nursing duty till two o'clock, the fear of interruption passed away. I had still nearly three hours before me. Nurse Kennedy sat in her chair by the bedside, patient and alert. A clock ticked on the landing; other clocks in the house ticked; the life of the city without manifested itself in the distant hum, now and again swelling into a roar as a breeze floating westward took the concourse of sounds with it. But still the dominant idea was of silence. The light on my book, and the soothing fringe of green silk round the shade intensified, whenever I looked up, the gloom of the sick-room. With every line I read, this seemed to grow deeper and deeper; so that when my eyes came back to the page the light seemed to dazzle me. I stuck to my work, however, and presently began to get sufficiently into the subject to become interested in it.

The book was by one Nicholas van Huyn of Hoorn. In the preface he told how, attracted by the work of John Greaves of Merton College, Pyramidographia, he himself visited Egypt, where he became so interested in its wonders that he devoted some years of his life to visiting strange places, and exploring the ruins of many temples and tombs. He had come across many variants of the story of the building of the Pyramids as told by the Arabian historian, Ibn Abd Alhokin, some of which he set down. These I did not stop to read, but went on to the marked pages.

As soon as I began to read these, however, there grew on me some sense of a disturbing influence. Once or twice I looked to see if the Nurse had moved, for there was a feeling as though some one were near me. Nurse Kennedy sat in her place, as steady and alert as ever; and I came back to my book again.

The narrative went on to tell how, after passing for several days through the mountains to the east of Aswan, the explorer came to a certain place. Here I give his own words, simply putting the translation into modern English:

"Toward evening we came to the entrance of a narrow, deep valley, running east and west. I wished to proceed through this; for the sun, now nearly down on the horizon, showed a wide opening beyond the narrowing of the cliffs. But the fellaheen absolutely refused to enter the valley at such a time, alleging that they might be caught by the night before they could emerge from the other end. At first they would give no reason for their fear. They had hitherto gone anywhere I wished, and at any time, without demur. On being pressed, however, they said that the place was the Valley of the Sorcerer, where none might come in the night. On being asked to tell of the Sorcerer, they refused, saying that there was no name, and that they knew nothing. On the next morning, however, when the sun was up and shining down the valley, their fears had somewhat passed away. Then they told me that a great Sorcerer in ancient days—'millions of millions of years' was the term they used— a King or a Queen, they could not say which, was buried there. They could not give the name, persisting to the last that there was no name; and that anyone who should name it would waste away in life so that at death nothing of him would remain to be raised again in the Other World. In passing through the valley they kept together in a cluster, hurrying on in front of me. None dared to remain behind. They gave, as their reason for so proceeding, that the arms of the Sorcerer were long, and that it was dangerous to be the last. The which was of little comfort to me who of this necessity took that honourable post. In the narrowest part of the valley, on the south side, was a great cliff of rock, rising sheer, of smooth and even surface. Hereon were graven certain cabalistic signs, and many figures of men and animals, fishes, reptiles and birds; suns and stars; and many quaint symbols. Some of these latter were disjointed limbs and features, such as arms and legs, fingers, eyes, noses, ears, and lips. Mysterious symbols which will puzzle the Recording Angel to interpret at the Judgment Day. The cliff faced exactly north. There was something about it so strange, and so different from the other carved rocks which I had visited, that I called a halt and spent the day in examining the rock front as well as I could with my telescope. The Egyptians of my company were terribly afraid, and used every kind of persuasion to induce me to pass on. I stayed till late in the afternoon, by which time I had failed to make out aright the entry of any tomb, for I suspected that such was the purpose of the sculpture of the rock. By this time the men were rebellious; and I had to leave the valley if I did not wish my whole retinue to desert. But I secretly made up my mind to discover the tomb, and explore it. To this end I went further into the mountains, where I met with an Arab Sheik who was willing to take service with me. The Arabs were not bound by the same superstitious fears as the Egyptians; Sheik Abu Some and his following were willing to take a part in the explorations.

"When I returned to the valley with these Bedouins, I made effort to climb the face of the rock, but failed, it being of one impenetrable smoothness. The stone, generally flat and smooth by nature, had been chiselled to completeness. That there had been projecting steps was manifest, for there remained, untouched by the wondrous climate of that strange land, the marks of saw and chisel and mallet where the steps had been cut or broken away.

"Being thus baffled of winning the tomb from below, and being unprovided with ladders to scale, I found a way by much circuitous journeying to the top of the cliff. Thence I caused myself to be lowered by ropes, till I had investigated that portion of the rock face wherein I expected to find the opening. I found that there was an entrance, closed however by a great stone slab. This was cut in the rock more than a hundred feet up, being two-thirds the height of the cliff. The hieroglyphic and cabalistic symbols cut in the rock were so managed as to disguise it. The cutting was deep, and was continued through the rock and the portals of the doorway, and through the great slab which formed the door itself. This was fixed in place with such incredible exactness that no stone chisel or cutting implement which I had with me could find a lodgment in the interstices. I used much force, however; and by many heavy strokes won a way into the tomb, for such I found it to be. The stone door having fallen into the entrance I passed over it into the tomb, noting as I went a long iron chain which hung coiled on a bracket close to the doorway.

"The tomb I found to be complete, after the manner of the finest Egyptian tombs, with chamber and shaft leading down to the corridor, ending in the Mummy Pit. It had the table of pictures, which seems some kind of record—whose meaning is now for ever lost—graven in a wondrous colour on a wondrous stone.

"All the walls of the chamber and the passage were carved with strange writings in the uncanny form mentioned. The huge stone coffin or sarcophagus in the deep pit was marvellously graven throughout with signs. The Arab chief and two others who ventured into the tomb with me, and who were evidently used to such grim explorations, managed to take the cover from the sarcophagus without breaking it. At which they wondered; for such good fortune, they said, did not usually attend such efforts. Indeed they seemed not over careful; and did handle the various furniture of the tomb with such little concern that, only for its great strength and thickness, even the coffin itself might have been injured. Which gave me much concern, for it was very beautifully wrought of rare stone, such as I had no knowledge of. Much I grieved that it were not possible to carry it away. But time and desert journeyings forbade such; I could only take with me such small matters as could be carried on the person.

"Within the sarcophagus was a body, manifestly of a woman, swathed with many wrappings of linen, as is usual with all mummies. From certain embroiderings thereon, I gathered that she was of high rank. Across the breast was one hand, unwrapped. In the mummies which I had seen, the arms and hands are within the wrappings, and certain adornments of wood, shaped and painted to resemble arms and hands, lie outside the enwrapped body.

"But this hand was strange to see, for it was the real hand of her who lay enwrapped there; the arm projecting from the cerements being of flesh, seemingly made as like marble in the process of embalming. Arm and hand were of dusky white, being of the hue of ivory that hath lain long in air. The skin and the nails were complete and whole, as though the body had been placed for burial over night. I touched the hand and moved it, the arm being something flexible as a live arm; though stiff with long disuse, as are the arms of those faqueers which I have seen in the Indees. There was, too, an added wonder that on this ancient hand were no less than seven fingers, the same all being fine and long, and of great beauty. Sooth to say, it made me shudder and my flesh creep to touch that hand that had lain there undisturbed for so many thousands of years, and yet was like unto living flesh. Underneath the hand, as though guarded by it, lay a huge jewel of ruby; a great stone of wondrous bigness, for the ruby is in the main a small jewel. This one was of wondrous colour, being as of fine blood whereon the light shineth. But its wonder lay not in its size or colour, though these were, as I have said, of priceless rarity; but in that the light of it shone from seven stars, each of seven points, as clearly as though the stars were in reality there imprisoned. When that the hand was lifted, the sight of that wondrous stone lying there struck me with a shock almost to momentary paralysis. I stood gazing on it, as did those with me, as though it were that faded head of the Gorgon Medusa with the snakes in her hair, whose sight struck into stone those who beheld. So strong was the feeling that I wanted to hurry away from the place. So, too, those with me; therefore, taking this rare jewel, together with certain amulets of strangeness and richness being wrought of jewel-stones, I made haste to depart. I would have remained longer, and made further research in the wrappings of the mummy, but that I feared so to do. For it came to me all at once that I was in a desert place, with strange men who were with me because they were not over-scrupulous. That we were in a lone cavern of the dead, an hundred feet above the ground, where none could find me were ill done to me, nor would any ever seek. But in secret I determined that I would come again, though with more secure following. Moreover, was I tempted to seek further, as in examining the wrappings I saw many things of strange import in that wondrous tomb; including a casket of eccentric shape made of some strange stone, which methought might have contained other jewels, inasmuch as it had secure lodgment in the great sarcophagus itself. There was in the tomb also another coffer which, though of rare proportion and adornment, was more simply shaped. It was of ironstone of great thickness; but the cover was lightly cemented down with what seemed gum and Paris plaster, as though to insure that no air could penetrate. The Arabs with me so insisted in its opening, thinking that from its thickness much treasure was stored therein, that I consented thereto. But their hope was a false one, as it proved. Within, closely packed, stood four jars finely wrought and carved with various adornments. Of these one was the head of a man, another of a dog, another of a jackal, and another of a hawk. I had before known that such burial urns as these were used to contain the entrails and other organs of the mummied dead; but on opening these, for the fastening of wax, though complete, was thin, and yielded easily, we found that they held but oil. The Bedouins, spilling most of the oil in the process, groped with their hands in the jars lest treasure should have been there concealed. But their searching was of no avail; no treasure was there. I was warned of my danger by seeing in the eyes of the Arabs certain covetous glances. Whereon, in order to hasten their departure, I wrought upon those fears of superstition which even in these callous men were apparent. The chief of the Bedouins ascended from the Pit to give the signal to those above to raise us; and I, not caring to remain with the men whom I mistrusted, followed him immediately. The others did not come at once; from which I feared that they were rifling the tomb afresh on their own account. I refrained to speak of it, however, lest worse should befall. At last they came. One of them, who ascended first, in landing at the top of the cliff lost his foothold and fell below. He was instantly killed. The other followed, but in safety. The chief came next, and I came last. Before coming away I pulled into its place again, as well as I could, the slab of stone that covered the entrance to the tomb. I wished, if possible, to preserve it for my own examination should I come again.

"When we all stood on the hill above the cliff, the burning sun that was bright and full of glory was good to see after the darkness and strange mystery of the tomb. Even was I glad that the poor Arab who fell down the cliff and lay dead below, lay in the sunlight and not in that gloomy cavern. I would fain have gone with my companions to seek him and give him sepulture of some kind; but the Sheik made light of it, and sent two of his men to see to it whilst we went on our way.

"That night as we camped, one of the men only returned, saying that a lion of the desert had killed his companion after that they had buried the dead man in a deep sand without the valley, and had covered the spot where he lay with many great rocks, so that jackals or other preying beasts might not dig him up again as is their wont.

"Later, in the light of the fire round which the men sat or lay, I saw him exhibit to his fellows something white which they seemed to regard with special awe and reverence. So I drew near silently, and saw that it was none other than the white hand of the mummy which had lain protecting the Jewel in the great sarcophagus. I heard the Bedouin tell how he had found it on the body of him who had fallen from the cliff. There was no mistaking it, for there were the seven fingers which I had noted before. This man must have wrenched it off the dead body whilst his chief and I were otherwise engaged; and from the awe of the others I doubted not that he had hoped to use it as an Amulet, or charm. Whereas if powers it had, they were not for him who had taken it from the dead; since his death followed hard upon his theft. Already his Amulet had had an awesome baptism; for the wrist of the dead hand was stained with red as though it had been dipped in recent blood.

"That night I was in certain fear lest there should be some violence done to me; for if the poor dead hand was so valued as a charm, what must be the worth in such wise of the rare Jewel which it had guarded. Though only the chief knew of it, my doubt was perhaps even greater; for he could so order matters as to have me at his mercy when he would. I guarded myself, therefore, with wakefulness so well as I could, determined that at my earliest opportunity I should leave this party, and complete my journeying home, first to the Nile bank, and then down its course to Alexandria; with other guides who knew not what strange matters I had with me.

"At last there came over me a disposition of sleep, so potent that I felt it would be resistless. Fearing attack, or that being searched in my sleep the Bedouin might find the Star Jewel which he had seen me place with others in my dress, I took it out unobserved and held it in my hand. It seemed to give back the light of the flickering fire and the light of the stars—for there was no moon—with equal fidelity; and I could note that on its reverse it was graven deeply with certain signs such as I had seen in the tomb. As I sank into the unconsciousness of sleep, the graven Star Jewel was hidden in the hollow of my clenched hand.

"I waked out of sleep with the light of the morning sun on my face. I sat up and looked around me. The fire was out, and the camp was desolate; save for one figure which lay prone close to me. It was that of the Arab chief, who lay on his back, dead. His face was almost black; and his eyes were open, and staring horribly up at the sky, as though he saw there some dreadful vision. He had evidently been strangled; for on looking, I found on his throat the red marks where fingers had pressed. There seemed so many of these marks that I counted them. There were seven; and all parallel, except the thumb mark, as though made with one hand. This thrilled me as I thought of the mummy hand with the seven fingers.

"Even there, in the open desert, it seemed as if there could be enchantments!

"In my surprise, as I bent over him, I opened my right hand, which up to now I had held shut with the feeling, instinctive even in sleep, of keeping safe that which it held. As I did so, the Star Jewel held there fell out and struck the dead man on the mouth. Mirabile dictu there came forth at once from the dead mouth a great gush of blood, in which the red jewel was for the moment lost. I turned the dead man over to look for it, and found that he lay with his right hand bent under him as though he had fallen on it; and in it he held a great knife, keen of point and edge, such as Arabs carry at the belt. It may have been that he was about to murder me when vengeance came on him, whether from man or God, or the Gods of Old, I know not. Suffice it, that when I found my Ruby Jewel, which shone up as a living star from the mess of blood wherein it lay, I paused not, but fled from the place. I journeyed on alone through the hot desert, till, by God's grace, I came upon an Arab tribe camping by a well, who gave me salt. With them I rested till they had set me on my way.

"I know not what became of the mummy hand, or of those who had it. What strife, or suspicion, or disaster, or greed went with it I know not; but some such cause there must have been, since those who had it fled with it. It doubtless is used as a charm of potence by some desert tribe.

"At the earliest opportunity I made examination of the Star Ruby, as I wished to try to understand what was graven on it. The symbols—whose meaning, however, I could not understand—were as follows . . ."

Twice, whilst I had been reading this engrossing narrative, I had thought that I had seen across the page streaks of shade, which the weirdness of the subject had made to seem like the shadow of a hand. On the first of these occasions I found that the illusion came from the fringe of green silk around the lamp; but on the second I had looked up, and my eyes had lit on the mummy hand across the room on which the starlight was falling under the edge of the blind. It was of little wonder that I had connected it with such a narrative; for if my eyes told me truly, here, in this room with me, was the very hand of which the traveller Van Huyn had written. I looked over at the bed; and it comforted me to think that the Nurse still sat there, calm and wakeful. At such a time, with such surrounds, during such a narrative, it was well to have assurance of the presence of some living person.

I sat looking at the book on the table before me; and so many strange thoughts crowded on me that my mind began to whirl. It was almost as if the light on the white fingers in front of me was beginning to have some hypnotic effect. All at once, all thoughts seemed to stop; and for an instant the world and time stood still.

There lay a real hand across the book! What was there to so overcome me, as was the case? I knew the hand that I saw on the book—and loved it. Margaret Trelawny's hand was a joy to me to see—to touch; and yet at that moment, coming after other marvellous things, it had a strangely moving effect on me. It was but momentary, however, and had passed even before her voice had reached me.

"What disturbs you? What are you staring at the book for? I thought for an instant that you must have been overcome again!" I jumped up.

"I was reading," I said, "an old book from the library." As I spoke I closed it and put it under my arm. "I shall now put it back, as I understand that your Father wishes all things, especially books, kept in their proper places." My words were intentionally misleading; for I did not wish her to know what I was reading, and thought it best not to wake her curiosity by leaving the book about. I went away, but not to the library; I left the book in my room where I could get it when I had had my sleep in the day. When I returned Nurse Kennedy was ready to go to bed; so Miss Trelawny watched with me in the room. I did not want any book whilst she was present. We sat close together and talked in a whisper whilst the moments flew by. It was with surprise that I noted the edge of the curtains changing from grey to yellow light. What we talked of had nothing to do with the sick man, except in so far that all which concerned his daughter must ultimately concern him. But it had nothing to say to Egypt, or mummies, or the dead, or caves, or Bedouin chiefs. I could well take note in the growing light that Margaret's hand had not seven fingers, but five; for it lay in mine.

When Doctor Winchester arrived in the morning and had made his visit to his patient, he came to see me as I sat in the dining-room having a little meal—breakfast or supper, I hardly knew which it was—before I went to lie down. Mr. Corbeck came in at the same time; and we resumed out conversation where we had left it the night before. I told Mr. Corbeck that I had read the chapter about the finding of the tomb, and that I thought Doctor Winchester should read it, too. The latter said that, if he might, he would take it with him; he had that morning to make a railway journey to Ipswich, and would read it on the train. He said he would bring it back with him when he came again in the evening. I went up to my room to bring it down; but I could not find it anywhere. I had a distinct recollection of having left it on the little table beside my bed, when I had come up after Miss Trelawny's going on duty into the sick-room. It was very strange; for the book was not of a kind that any of the servants would be likely to take. I had to come back and explain to the others that I could not find it.

When Doctor Winchester had gone, Mr. Corbeck, who seemed to know the Dutchman's work by heart, talked the whole matter over with me. I told him that I was interrupted by a change of nurses, just as I had come to the description of the ring. He smiled as he said:

"So far as that is concerned, you need not be disappointed. Not in Van Huyn's time, nor for nearly two centuries later, could the meaning of that engraving have been understood. It was only when the work was taken up and followed by Young and Champollion, by Birch and Lepsius and Rosellini and Salvolini, by Mariette Bey and by Wallis Budge and Flinders Petrie and the other scholars of their times that great results ensued, and that the true meaning of hieroglyphic was known.

"Later, I shall explain to you, if Mr. Trelawny does not explain it himself, or if he does not forbid me to, what it means in that particular place. I think it will be better for you to know what followed Van Huyn's narrative; for with the description of the stone, and the account of his bringing it to Holland at the termination of his travels, the episode ends. Ends so far as his book is concerned. The chief thing about the book is that it sets others thinking—and acting. Amongst them were Mr. Trelawny and myself. Mr. Trelawny is a good linguist of the Orient, but he does not know Northern tongues. As for me I have a faculty for learning languages; and when I was pursuing my studies in Leyden I learned Dutch so that I might more easily make references in the library there. Thus it was, that at the very time when Mr. Trelawny, who, in making his great collection of works on Egypt, had, through a booksellers' catalogue, acquired this volume with the manuscript translation, was studying it, I was reading another copy, in original Dutch, in Leyden. We were both struck by the description of the lonely tomb in the rock; cut so high up as to be inaccessible to ordinary seekers: with all means of reaching it carefully obliterated; and yet with such an elaborate ornamentation of the smoothed surface of the cliff as Van Huyn has described. It also struck us both as an odd thing—for in the years between Van Huyn's time and our own the general knowledge of Egyptian curios and records has increased marvellously—that in the case of such a tomb, made in such a place, and which must have cost an immense sum of money, there was no seeming record or effigy to point out who lay within. Moreover, the very name of the place, 'the Valley of the Sorcerer', had, in a prosaid age, attractions of its own. When we met, which we did through his seeking the assistance of other Egyptologists in his work, we talked over this as we did over many other things; and we determined to make search for the mysterious valley. Whilst we were waiting to start on the travel, for many things were required which Mr. Trelawny undertook to see to himself, I went to Holland to try if I could by any traces verify Van Huyn's narrative. I went straight to Hoorn, and set patiently to work to find the house of the traveller and his descendants, if any. I need not trouble you with details of my seeking—and finding. Hoorn is a place that has not changed much since Van Huyn's time, except that it has lost the place which it held amongst commercial cities. Its externals are such as they had been then; in such a sleepy old place a century or two does not count for much. I found the house, and discovered that none of the descendants were alive. I searched records; but only to one end—death and extinction. Then I set me to work to find what had become of his treasures; for that such a traveller must have had great treasures was apparent. I traced a good many to museums in Leyden, Utrecht, and Amsterdam; and some few to the private houses of rich collectors. At last, in the shop of an old watchmaker and jeweller at Hoorn, I found what he considered his chiefest treasure; a great ruby, carven like a scarab, with seven stars, and engraven with hieroglyphics. The old man did not know hieroglyphic character, and in his old-world, sleepy life, the philological discoveries of recent years had not reached him. He did not know anything of Van Huyn, except that such a person had been, and that his name was, during two centuries, venerated in the town as a great traveller. He valued the jewel as only a rare stone, spoiled in part by the cutting; and though he was at first loth to part with such an unique gem, he became amenable ultimately to commercial reason. I had a full purse, since I bought for Mr. Trelawny, who is, as I suppose you know, immensely wealthy. I was shortly on my way back to London, with the Star Ruby safe in my pocket-book; and in my heart a joy and exultation which knew no bounds.

"For here we were with proof of Van Huyn's wonderful story. The jewel was put in security in Mr. Trelawny's great safe; and we started out on our journey of exploration in full hope.

"Mr. Trelawny was, at the last, loth to leave his young wife whom he dearly loved; but she, who loved him equally, knew his longing to prosecute the search. So keeping to herself, as all good women do, all her anxieties—which in her case were special—she bade him follow out his bent."

CHAPTER XI

A QUEEN'S TOMB

"MR. TRELAWNY'S HOPE was at least as great as my own. He is not so volatile a man as I am, prone to ups and downs of hope and despair; but he has a fixed purpose which crystallises hope into belief. At times I had feared that there might have been two such stones, or that the adventures of Van Huyn were traveller's fictions, based on some ordinary acquisition of the curio in Alexandria or Cairo, or London or Amsterdam. But Mr. Trelawny never faltered in his belief. We had many things to distract our minds from belief or disbelief. This was soon after Arabi Pasha, and Egypt was so safe place for travellers, especially if they were English. But Mr. Trelawny is a fearless man; and I almost come to think at times that I am not a coward myself. We got together a band of Arabs whom one or other of us had known in former trips to the desert, and whom we could trust; that is, we did not distrust them as much as others. We were numerous enough to protect ourselves from chance marauding bands, and we took with us large impedimenta. We had secured the consent and passive co-operation of the officials still friendly to Britain; in the acquiring of which consent I need hardly say that Mr. Trelawny's riches were of chief importance. We found our way in dhahabiyehs to Aswan; whence, having got some Arabs from the Sheik and having given our usual backsheesh, we set out on our journey through the desert.

"Well, after much wandering and trying every winding in the interminable jumble of hills, we came at last at nightfall on just such a valley as Van Huyn had described. A valley with high, steep cliffs; narrowing in the centre, and widening out to the eastern and western ends. At daylight we were opposite the cliff and could easily note the opening high up in the rock, and the hieroglyphic figures which were evidently intended originally to conceal it.

"But the signs which had baffled Van Huyn and those of his time—and later, were no secrets to us. The host of scholars who have given their brains and their lives to this work, had wrested open the mysterious prison-house of Egyptian language. On the hewn face of the rocky cliff we, who had learned the secrets, could read what the Theban priesthood had had there inscribed nearly fifty centuries before.

"For that the external inscription was the work of the priesthood—and a hostile priesthood at that—there could be no living doubt. The inscription on the rock, written in hieroglyphic, ran thus:

'Hither the Gods come not at any summons. The "Nameless One" has insulted them and is for ever alone. Go not nigh, lest their vengeance wither you away!'

'The warning must have been a terribly potent one at the time it was written and for thousands of years afterwards; even when the language in which it was given had become a dead mystery to the people of the land. The tradition of such a terror lasts longer than its cause. Even in the symbols used there was an added significance of alliteration. 'For ever' is given in the hieroglyphics as 'millions of years'. This symbol was repeated nine times, in three groups of three; and after each group a symbol of the Upper World, the Under World, and the Sky. So that for this Lonely One there could be, through the vengeance of all the Gods, resurrection in neither the World of Sunlight, in the World of the Dead, or for the soul in the region of the Gods.

"Neither Mr. Trelawny nor I dared to tell any of our people what the writing meant. For though they did not believe in the religion whence the curse came, or in the Gods whose vengeance was threatened, yet

they were so superstitious that they would probably, had they known of
it, have thrown up the whole task and run away.

"Their ignorance, however, and our discretion preserved us. We
made an encampment close at hand, but behind a jutting rock a little
further along the valley, so that they might not have the inscription
always before them. For even that traditional name of the place: 'The
Valley of the Sorcerer', had a fear for them; and for us through them.
With the timber which we had brought, we made a ladder up the face
of the rock. We hung a pulley on a beam fixed to project from the
top of the cliff. We found the great slab of rock, which formed the
door, placed clumsily in its place and secured by a few stones. Its own
weight kept it in safe position. In order to enter, we had to push it in;
and we passed over it. We found the great coil of chain which Van
Huyn had described fastened into the rock. There were, however, abun-
dant evidences amid the wreckage of the great stone door, which had
revolved on iron hinges at top and bottom, that ample provision had
been originally made for closing and fastening it from within.

"Mr. Trelawny and I went alone into the tomb. We had brought
plenty of lights with us; and we fixed them as we went along. We wished
to get a complete survey at first, and then make examination of all in
detail. As we went on, we were filled with ever-increasing wonder and
delight. The tomb was one of the most magnificent and beautiful which
either of us had ever seen. From the elaborate nature of the sculpture
and painting, and the perfection of the workmanship, it was evident
that the tomb was prepared during the lifetime of her for whose resting-
place it was intended. The drawing of the hieroglyphic pictures was
fine, and the colouring superb; and in that high cavern, far away from
even the damp of the Nile-flood, all was as fresh as when the artists had
laid down their palettes. There was one thing which we could not avoid
seeing. That although the cutting on the outside rock was the work of
the priesthood, the smoothing of the cliff face was probably a part of

the tomb-builder's original design. The symbolism of the painting and cutting within all gave the same idea. The outer cavern, partly natural and partly hewn, was regarded architecturally as only an ante-chamber. At the end of it, so that it would face the east, was a pillared portico, hewn out of the solid rock. The pillars were massive and were seven-sided, a thing which we had not come across in any other tomb. Sculptured on the architrave was the Boat of the Moon, containing Hathor, cow-headed and bearing the disk and plumes, and the dog-headed Hapi, the God of the North. It was steered by Harpocrates towards the north, represented by the Pole Star surrounded by Draco and Ursa Major. In the latter the stars that form what we call the 'Plough' were cut larger than any of the other stars; and were filled with gold so that, in the light of torches, they seemed to flame with a special significance. Passing within the portico, we found two of the architectural features of a rock tomb, the Chamber, or Chapel, and the Pit, all complete as Van Huyn had noticed, though in his day the names given to these parts by the Egyptians of old were unknown.

"The Stele, or record, which had its place low down on the western wall, was so remarkable that we examined it minutely, even before going on our way to find the mummy which was the object of our search. This Stele was a great slab of lapis lazuli, cut all over with hieroglyphic figures of small size and of much beauty. The cutting was filled in with some cement of exceeding fineness, and of the colour of pure vermilion. The inscription began:

'Tera, Queen of the Egypts, daughter of Antef, Monarch of the North and the South.' 'Daughter of the Sun,' 'Queen of the Diadems.'

"It then set out, in full record, the history of her life and reign.

'The signs of sovereignty were given with a truly feminine profusion of adornment. The united Crowns of Upper and Lower Egypt were, in especial, cut with exquisite precision. It was new to us both to find the Hejet and the Desher—the White and the Red crowns of Upper and Lower Egypt—on the Stele of a queen; for it was a rule, without exception in the records, that in ancient Egypt either crown was worn only by a king; though they are to be found on goddesses. Later on we found an explanation, of which I shall say more presently.

"Such an inscription was in itself a matter so startling as to arrest attention from anyone anywhere at any time; but you can have no conception of the effect which it had upon us. Though our eyes were not the first which had seen it, they were the first which could see it with understanding since first the slab of rock was fixed in the cliff opening nearly five thousand years before. To us was given to read this message from the dead. This message of one who had warred against the Gods of Old, and claimed to have controlled them at a time when the hierarchy professed to be the only means of exciting their fears or gaining their good will.

"The walls of the upper chamber of the Pit and the sarcophagus Chamber were profusely inscribed; all the inscriptions, except that on the Stele, being coloured with bluish-green pigment. The effect when seen sideways as the eye caught the green facets, was that of an old, discoloured Indian turquoise.

"We descended the Pit by the aid of the tackle we had brought with us. Trelawny went first. It was a deep pit, more than seventy feet; but it had never been filled up. The passage at the bottom sloped up to the sarcophagus Chamber, and was longer than is usually found. It had not been walled up.

"Within, we found a great sarcophagus of yellow stone. But that I need not describe; you have seen it in Mr. Trelawny's chamber. The cover of it lay on the ground; it had not been cemented, and was just as Van Huyn had described it. Needless to say, we were excited as we looked within. There must, however, be one sense of disappointment. I could not help feeling how different must have been the sight which met the Dutch traveller's eyes when he looked within and found that white hand lying lifelike above the shrouding mummy cloths. It is true that a part of the arm was there, white and ivory like.

"But there was a thrill to us which came not to Van Huyn!

"The end of the wrist was covered with dried blood! It was as though the body had bled after death! The jagged ends of the broken wrist were rough with the clotted blood; through this the white bone, sticking out, looked like the matrix of opal. The blood had streamed down and stained the brown wrappings as with rust. Here, then, was full confirmation of the narrative. With such evidence of the narrator's truth before us, we could not doubt the other matters which he had told, such as the blood on the mummy hand, or marks of the seven fingers on the throat of the strangled Sheik.

"I shall not trouble you with details of all we saw, or how we learned all we knew. Part of it was from knowledge common to scholars; part we read on the Stele in the tomb, and in the sculptures and hieroglyphic paintings on the walls.

"Queen Tera was of the Eleventh, or Theban Dynasty of Egyptian Kings which held sway between the twenty-ninth and twenty-fifth centuries before Christ. She succeeded as the only child of her father, Antef. She must have been a girl of extraordinary character as well as ability, for she was but a young girl when her father died. Her youth and sex encouraged the ambitious priesthood, which had then achieved immense power. By their wealth and numbers and learning they dominated all Egypt, more especially the Upper portion. They were then secretly ready to make an effort for the achievement of their bold and long-considered design, that of transferring the governing power from a Kingship to a Hierarchy. But King Antef had suspected some such movement, and had taken the precaution of securing to his daughter the allegiance of the army. He had also had her taught statecraft, and had even made her learned in the lore of the very priests themselves. He had used those of one cult against the other; each being hopeful of some present gain on its own part by the influence of the King, or of some ultimate gain from its own influence over his daughter. Thus, the Princess had been brought up amongst scribes, and was herself no mean artist. Many of these things were told on the walls in pictures or in hieroglyphic writing of great beauty; and we came to the conclusion that not a few of them had been done by the Princess herself. It was not without cause that she was inscribed on the Stele as 'Protector of the Arts'.

"But the King had gone to further lengths, and had had his daughter taught magic, by which she had power over Sleep and Will. This was real magic—'black' magic; not the magic of the temples, which, I may explain, was of the harmless or 'white' order, and was intended to impress rather than to effect. She had been an apt pupil; and had gone further than her teachers. Her power and her resources had given her great opportunities, of which she had availed herself to the full. She had won secrets from nature in strange ways; and had even gone to the length of going down into the tomb herself, having been swathed and coffined and left as dead for a whole month. The priests had tried to make out that the real Princess Tera had died in the experiment, and that another girl had been substituted; but she had conclusively proved their error. All this was told in pictures of great merit. It was probably in her time that the impulse was given in the restoring the artistic greatness of the Fourth Dynasty which had found its perfection in the days of Chufu.

"In the Chamber of the sarcophagus were pictures and writings to show that she had achieved victory over Sleep. Indeed, there was everywhere a symbolism, wonderful even in a land and an age of symbolism. Prominence was given to the fact that she, though a Queen, claimed all the privileges of kingship and masculinity. In one place she was pictured in man's dress, and wearing the White and Red Crowns. In the following picture she was in female dress, but still wearing the Crowns of Upper and Lower Egypt, while the discarded male raiment lay at her feet. In every picture where hope, or aim, of resurrection was expressed there was the added symbol of the North; and in many places—always in representations of important events, past, present, or future—was a grouping of the stars of the Plough. She evidently regarded this constellation as in some way peculiarly associated with herself.

"Perhaps the most remarkable statement in the records, both on the Stele and in the mural writings, was that Queen Tera had power to compel the Gods. This, by the way, was not an isolated belief in Egyptian history; but was different in its cause. She had engraved on a ruby, carved like a scarab, and having seven stars of seven points, Master Words to compel all the Gods, both of the Upper and the Under Worlds.

"In the statement it was plainly set forth that the hatred of the priests was, she knew, stored up for her, and that they would after her death try to suppress her name. This was a terrible revenge, I may tell you, in Egyptian mythology; for without a name no one can after death be introduced to the Gods, or have prayers said for him. Therefore, she had intended her resurrection to be after a long time and in a more northern land, under the constellation whose seven stars had ruled her birth. To this end, her hand was to be in the air—'unwrapped'—and in it the Jewel of Seven Stars, so that wherever there was air she might move even as her Ka could move! This, after thinking it over, Mr. Trelawny and I agreed meant that her body could become astral at command, and so move, particle by particle, and become whole again when and where required. Then there was a piece of writing in which allusion was made to a chest or casket in which were contained all the Gods, and Will, and Sleep, the two latter being personified by symbols. The box was mentioned as with seven sides. It was not much of a surprise to us when, underneath the feet of the mummy, we found the seven-sided casket, which you have also seen in Mr. Trelawny's room. On the underneath part of the wrapping—linen of the left foot was painted, in the same vermilion colour as that used in the Stele, the hieroglyphic symbol for much water, and underneath the right foot the symbol of the earth. We made out the symbolism to be that her body, immortal and transferable at will, ruled both the land and water, air and fire— the latter being exemplified by the light of the Jewel Stone, and further by the flint and iron which lay outside the mummy wrappings.

"As we lifted the casket from the sarcophagus, we noticed on its sides the strange protuberances which you have already seen; but we were unable at the time to account for them. There were a few amulets in the sarcophagus, but none of any special worth or significance. We took it that if there were such, they were within the wrappings; or more probably in the strange casket underneath the mummy's feet. This, however, we could not open. There were signs of there being a cover; certainly the upper portion and the lower were each in one piece. The fine line, a little way from the top, appeared to be where the cover was fixed; but it was made with such exquisite fineness and finish that the joining could hardly be seen. Certainly the top could not be moved. We took it, that it was in some way fastened from within. I tell you all this in order that you may understand things with which you may be in contact later. You must suspend your judgment entirely. Such strange things have happened regarding this mummy and all around it, that there is a necessity for new belief somewhere. It is absolutely impossible to reconcile certain things which have happened with the ordinary currents of life or knowledge.

"We stayed around the Valley of the Sorcerer, till we had copied roughly all the drawings and writings on the walls, ceiling and floor. We took with us the Stele of lapis lazuli, whose graven record was coloured with vermilion pigment. We took the sarcophagus and the mummy; the stone chest with the alabaster jars; the tables of bloodstone and alabaster and onyx and carnelian; and the ivory pillow whose arch rested on 'buckles', round each of which was twisted an uraeus wrought in gold. We took all the articles which lay in the Chapel, and the Mummy Pit; the wooden boats with crews and the ushaptiu figures, and the symbolic amulets.

"When coming away we took down the ladders, and at a distance buried them in the sand under a cliff, which we noted so that if necessary we might find them again. Then with our heavy baggage, we set out on our laborious journey back to the Nile. It was no easy task, I tell you, to bring the case with that great sarcophagus over the desert. We had a rough cart and sufficient men to draw it; but the progress seemed terribly slow, for we were anxious to get our treasures into a place of safety. The night was an anxious time with us, for we feared attack from some marauding band. But more still we feared some of those with us. They were, after all, but predatory, unscrupulous men; and we had with us a considerable bulk of precious things. They, or at least the dangerous ones amongst them, did not know why it was so precious; they took it for granted that it was material treasure of some kind that we carried. We had taken the mummy from the sarcophagus, and packed it for safety of travel in a separate case. During the first night two attempts were made to steal things from the cart; and two men were found dead in the morning.

"On the second night there came on a violent storm, one of those terrible simooms of the desert which makes one feel his helplessness. We were overwhelmed with drifting sand. Some of our Bedouins had fled before the storm, hoping to find shelter; the rest of us, wrapped in our bournous, endured with what patience we could. In the morning, when the storm had passed, we recovered from under the piles of sand what we could of our impedimenta. We found the case in which the mummy had been packed all broken, but the mummy itself could nowhere be found. We searched everywhere around, and dug up the sand which had piled around us; but in vain. We did not know what to do, for Trelawny had his heart set on taking home that mummy. We waited a whole day in hopes that the Bedouins, who had fled, would return; we had a blind hope that they might have in some way removed the mummy from the cart, and would restore it. That night, just before dawn, Mr. Trelawny woke me up and whispered in my ear:

"'We must go back to the tomb in the Valley of the Sorcerer. Show no hesitation in the morning when I give the orders! If you ask any questions as to where we are going it will create suspicion, and will defeat our purpose.'

"'All right!' I answered. 'But why shall we go there?' His answer seemed to thrill through me as though it had struck some chord ready tuned within:

"'We shall find the mummy there! I am sure of it!' Then anticipating doubt or argument he added:

"'Wait, and you shall see!' and he sank back into his blanket again.

"The Arabs were surprised when we retraced our steps; and some of them were not satisfied. There was a good deal of friction, and there were several desertions; so that it was with a diminished following that we took our way eastward again. At first the Sheik did not manifest any curiosity as to our definite destination; but when it became apparent that we were again making for the Valley of the Sorcerer, he too showed concern. This grew as we drew near; till finally at the entrance of the valley he halted and refused to go further. He said he would await our return if we chose to go on alone. That he would wait three days; but if by that time we had not returned he would leave. No offer of money would tempt him to depart from this resolution. The only concession he would make was that he would find the ladders and bring them near the cliff. This he did; and then, with the rest of the troop, he went back to wait at the entrance of the valley.

"Mr. Trelawny and I took ropes and torches, and again ascended to the tomb. It was evident that someone had been there in our absence, for the stone slab which protected the entrance to the tomb was lying flat inside, and a rope was dangling from the cliff summit. Within, there was another rope hanging into the shaft of the Mummy Pit. We looked at each other; but neither said a word. We fixed our own rope, and as arranged Trelawny descended first, I following at once. It was not till we stood together at the foot of the shaft that the thought flashed across me that we might be in some sort of a trap; that someone might descend the rope from the cliff, and by cutting the rope by which we had lowered ourselves into the Pit, bury us there alive. The thought was horrifying; but it was too late to do anything. I remained silent. We both had torches, so that there was ample light as we passed through the passage and entered the Chamber where the sarcophagus had stood. The first thing noticeable was the emptiness of the place. Despite all its magnificent adornment, the tomb was made a desolation by the absence of the great sarcophagus, to hold which it was hewn in the rock; of the chest with the alabaster jars; of the tables which had held the implements and food for the use of the dead, and the ushaptiu figures.

"It was made more infinitely desolate still by the shrouded figure of the mummy of Queen Tera which lay on the floor where the great sarcophagus had stood! Beside it lay, in the strange contorted attitudes of violent death, three of the Arabs who had deserted from our party. Their faces were black, and their hands and necks were smeared with blood which had burst from mouth and nose and eyes.

"On the throat of each were the marks, now blackening, of a hand of seven fingers.

"Trelawny and I drew close, and clutched each other in awe and fear as we looked.

"For, most wonderful of all, across the breast of the mummied Queen lay a hand of seven fingers, ivory white, the wrist only showing a scar like a jagged red line, from which seemed to depend drops of blood."

CHAPTER XII

THE MAGIC COFFER

"WHEN WE RECOVERED our amazement, which seemed to last unduly long, we did not lose any time carrying the mummy through the passage, and hoisting it up the Pit shaft. I went first, to receive it at the top. As I looked down, I saw Mr. Trelawny lift the severed hand and put it in his breast, manifestly to save it from being injured or lost. We left the dead Arabs where they lay. With our ropes we lowered our precious burden to the ground; and then took it to the entrance of the valley where our escort was to wait. To our astonishment we found them on the move. When we remonstrated with the Sheik, he answered that he had fulfilled his contract to the letter; he had waited the three days as arranged. I thought that he was lying to cover up his base intention of deserting us; and I found when we compared notes that Trelawny had the same suspicion. It was not till we arrived at Cairo that we found he was correct. It was the 3rd of November 1884 when we entered the Mummy Pit for the second time; we had reason to remember the date.

"We had lost three whole days of our reckoning—out of our lives—whilst we had stood wondering in that chamber of the dead. Was it strange, then, that we had a superstitious feeling with regard to the dead Queen Tera and all belonging to her? Is it any wonder that it rests with us now, with a bewildering sense of some power outside ourselves or our comprehension? Will it be any wonder if it go down to the grave with us at the appointed time? If, indeed, there be any graves for us who have robbed the dead!" He was silent for quite a minute before he went on:

"We got to Cairo all right, and from there to Alexandria, where we were to take ship by the Messagerie service to Marseilles, and go thence by express to London. But

'The best-laid schemes o' mice and men Gang aft agley.'

At Alexandria, Trelawny found waiting a cable stating that Mrs. Trelawny had died in giving birth to a daughter.

"Her stricken husband hurried off at once by the Orient Express; and I had to bring the treasure alone to the desolate house. I got to London all safe; there seemed to be some special good fortune to our journey. When I got to this house, the funeral had long been over. The child had been put out to nurse, and Mr. Trelawny had so far recovered from the shock of his loss that he had set himself to take up again the broken threads of his life and his work. That he had had a shock, and a bad one, was apparent. The sudden grey in his black hair was proof enough in itself; but in addition, the strong cast of his features had become set and stern. Since he received that cable in the shipping office at Alexandria I have never seen a happy smile on his face.

"Work is the best thing in such a case; and to his work he devoted himself heart and soul. The strange tragedy of his loss and gain—for the child was born after the mother's death—took place during the time that we stood in that trance in the Mummy Pit of Queen Tera. It seemed to have become in some way associated with his Egyptian studies, and more especially with the mysteries connected with the Queen. He told me very little about his daughter; but that two forces struggled in his mind regarding her was apparent. I could see that he loved, almost idolised her. Yet he could never forget that her birth had cost her mother's life. Also, there was something whose existence seemed to wring his father's heart, though he would never tell me what it was. Again, he once said in a moment of relaxation of his purpose of silence:

"'She is unlike her mother; but in both feature and colour she has a marvellous resemblance to the pictures of Queen Tera.'

"He said that he had sent her away to people who would care for her as he could not; and that till she became a woman she should have all the simple pleasures that a young girl might have, and that were best for her. I would often have talked with him about her; but he would never say much. Once he said to me: 'There are reasons why I should not speak more than is necessary. Some day you will know— and understand!' I respected his reticence; and beyond asking after her on my return after a journey, I have never spoken of her again. I had never seen her till I did so in your presence.

"Well, when the treasures which we had—ah!—taken from the tomb had been brought here, Mr. Trelawny arranged their disposition himself. The mummy, all except the severed hand, he placed in the great ironstone sarcophagus in the hall. This was wrought for the Theban High Priest Uni, and is, as you may have remarked, all inscribed with wonderful invocations to the old Gods of Egypt. The rest of the things from the tomb he disposed about his own room, as you have seen. Amongst them he placed, for special reasons of his own, the mummy hand. I think he regards this as the most sacred of his possessions, with perhaps one exception. That is the carven ruby which he calls the 'Jewel of Seven Stars', which he keeps in that great safe which is locked and guarded by various devices, as you know.

"I dare say you find this tedious; but I have had to explain it, so that you should understand all up to the present. It was a long time after my return with the mummy of Queen Tera when Mr. Trelawny re-opened the subject with me. He had been several times to Egypt, sometimes with me and sometimes alone; and I had been several trips, on my own account or for him. But in all that time, nearly sixteen years, he never mentioned the subject, unless when some pressing occasion suggested, if it did not necessitate, a reference.

"One morning early he sent for me in a hurry; I was then studying in the British Museum, and had rooms in Hart Street. When I came, he was all on fire with excitement. I had not seen him in such a glow since before the news of his wife's death. He took me at once into his room. The window blinds were down and the shutters closed; not a ray of daylight came in. The ordinary lights in the room were not lit, but there were a lot of powerful electric lamps, fifty candle-power at least, arranged on one side of the room. The little bloodstone table on which the heptagonal coffer stands was drawn to the centre of the room. The coffer looked exquisite in the glare of light which shone on it. It actually seemed to glow as if lit in some way from within.

"'What do you think of it?' he asked.

"'It is like a jewel,' I answered. 'You may well call it the "sorcerer's Magic Coffer," if it often looks like that. It almost seems to be alive.'

"'Do you know why it seems so?'

"'From the glare of the light, I suppose?'

"'Light of course,' he answered, 'but it is rather the disposition of light.' As he spoke he turned up the ordinary lights of the room and switched off the special ones. The effect on the stone box was surprising; in a second it lost all its glowing effect. It was still a very beautiful stone, as always; but it was stone and no more.

"'Do you notice anything about the arrangement of the lamps?' he asked.

"'No!'

"'They were in the shape of the stars in the Plough, as the stars are in the ruby!' The statement came to me with a certain sense of conviction. I do not know why, except that there had been so many mysterious associations with the mummy and all belonging to it that any new one seemed enlightening. I listened as Trelawny went on to explain:

"'For sixteen years I have never ceased to think of that adventure, or to try to find a clue to the mysteries which came before us; but never until last night did I seem to find a solution. I think I must have dreamed of it, for I woke all on fire about it. I jumped out of bed with a determination of doing something, before I quite knew what it was that I wished to do. Then, all at once, the purpose was clear before me. There were allusions in the writing on the walls of the tomb to the seven stars of the Great Bear that go to make up the Plough; and the North was again and again emphasized. The same symbols were repeated with regard to the "Magic Box", as we called it. We had already noticed those peculiar translucent spaces in the stone of the box. You remember the hieroglyphic writing had told that the jewel came from the heart of an aerolite, and that the coffer was cut from it also. It might be, I thought, that the light of the seven stars, shining in the right direction, might have some effect on the box, or something within it. I raised the blind and looked out. The Plough was high in the heavens, and both its stars and the Pole Star were straight opposite the window. I pulled the table with the coffer out into the light, and shifted it until the translucent patches were in the direction of the stars. Instantly the box began to glow, as you saw it under the lamps, though but slightly. I waited and waited; but the sky clouded over, and the light died away. So I got wires and lamps—you know how often I use them in experiments—and tried the effect of electric light. It took me some time to get the lamps properly placed, so that they would correspond to the parts of the stone, but the moment I got them right the whole thing began to glow as you have seen it.

"'I could get no further, however. There was evidently something wanting. All at once it came to me that if light could have some effect there should be in the tomb some means of producing light, for there could not be starlight in the Mummy Pit in the cavern. Then the whole thing seemed to become clear. On the bloodstone table, which has a hollow carved in its top, into which the bottom of the coffer fits, I laid the Magic Coffer; and I at once saw that the odd protuberances so carefully wrought in the substance of the stone corresponded in a way to the stars in the constellation. These, then, were to hold lights.'

"'Eureka!' I cried. 'All we want now is the lamps.'" I tried placing the electric lights on, or close to, the protuberances. But the glow never came to the stone. So the conviction grew on me that there were special lamps made for the purpose. If we could find them, a step on the road to solving the mystery should be gained.

"'But what about the lamps?' I asked. 'Where are they? When are we to discover them? How are we to know them if we do find them? What—'

"He stopped me at once:

"'One thing at a time!' he said quietly. 'Your first question contains all the rest. Where are these lamps? I shall tell you: In the tomb!'

"'In the tomb!' I repeated in surprise. 'Why you and I searched the place ourselves from end to end; and there was not a sign of a lamp. Not a sign of anything remaining when we came away the first time; or on the second, except the bodies of the Arabs.'

"Whilst I was speaking, he had uncoiled some large sheets of paper which he had brought in his hand from his own room. These he spread out on the great table, keeping their edges down with books and weights. I knew them at a glance; they were the careful copies which he had made of our first transcripts from the writing in the tomb. When he had all ready, he turned to me and said slowly:

"'Do you remember wondering, when we examined the tomb, at the lack of one thing which is usually found in such a tomb?'

"'Yes! There was no serdab.'

"'The Serdab, I may perhaps explain,' said Mr. Corbeck to me, 'is a sort of niche built or hewn in the wall of a tomb. Those which have as yet been examined bear no inscriptions, and contain only effigies of the dead for whom the tomb was made.' Then he went on with his narrative:

"Trelawny, when he saw that I had caught his meaning, went on speaking with something of his old enthusiasm:

"'I have come to the conclusion that there must be a serdab—a secret one. We were dull not to have thought of it before. We might have known that the maker of such a tomb—a woman, who had shown in other ways such a sense of beauty and completeness, and who had finished every detail with a feminine richness of elaboration—would not have neglected such an architectural feature. Even if it had not its own special significance in ritual, she would have had it as an adornment. Others had had it, and she liked her own work to be complete. Depend upon it, there was—there is—a serdab; and that in it, when it is discovered, we shall find the lamps. Of course, had we known then what we now know or at all events surmise, that there were lamps, we might have suspected some hidden spot, some cachet. I am going to ask you to go out to Egypt again; to seek the tomb; to find the serdab; and to bring back the lamps!'

"'And if I find there is no serdab; or if discovering it I find no lamps in it, what then?' He smiled grimly with that saturnine smile of his, so rarely seen for years past, as he spoke slowly:

"'Then you will have to hustle till you find them!'

"'Good!' I said. He pointed to one of the sheets.

"'Here are the transcripts from the Chapel at the south and the east. I have been looking over the writings again; and I find that in seven places round this corner are the symbols of the constellation which we call the Plough, which Queen Tera held to rule her birth and her destiny. I have examined them carefully, and I notice that they are all representations of the grouping of the stars, as the constellation appears in different parts of the heavens. They are all astronomically correct; and as in the real sky the Pointers indicate the Pole Star, so these all point to one spot in the wall where usually the serdab is to be found!'

"'Bravo!' I shouted, for such a piece of reasoning demanded applause. He seemed pleased as he went on:

"'When you are in the tomb, examine this spot. There is probably some spring or mechanical contrivance for opening the receptacle. What it may be, there is no use guessing. You will know what best to do, when you are on the spot.'

"I started the next week for Egypt; and never rested till I stood again in the tomb. I had found some of our old following; and was fairly well provided with help. The country was now in a condition very different to that in which it had been sixteen years before; there was no need for troops or armed men.

"I climbed the rock face alone. There was no difficulty, for in that fine climate the woodwork of the ladder was still dependable. It was easy to see that in the years that had elapsed there had been other visitors to the tomb; and my heart sank within me when I thought that some of them might by chance have come across the secret place. It would be a bitter discovery indeed to find that they had forestalled me; and that my journey had been in vain.

"The bitterness was realised when I lit my torches, and passed between the seven-sided columns to the Chapel of the tomb.

"There, in the very spot where I had expected to find it, was the opening of a serdab. And the serdab was empty.

"But the Chapel was not empty; for the dried-up body of a man in Arab dress lay close under the opening, as though he had been stricken down. I examined all round the walls to see if Trelawny's surmise was correct; and I found that in all the positions of the stars as given, the Pointers of the Plough indicated a spot to the left hand, or south side, of the opening of the serdab, where was a single star in gold.

"I pressed this, and it gave way. The stone which had marked the front of the serdab, and which lay back against the wall within, moved slightly. On further examining the other side of the opening, I found a similar spot, indicated by other representations of the constellation; but this was itself a figure of the seven stars, and each was wrought in burnished gold. I pressed each star in turn; but without result. Then it struck me that if the opening spring was on the left, this on the right might have been intended for the simultaneous pressure of all the stars by one hand of seven fingers. By using both my hands, I managed to effect this.

"With a loud click, a metal figure seemed to dart from close to the opening of the serdab; the stone slowly swung back to its place, and shut with a click. The glimpse which I had of the descending figure appalled me for the moment. It was like that grim guardian which, according to the Arabian historian Ibn Abd Alhokin, the builder of the Pyramids, King Saurid Ibn Salhouk placed in the Western Pyramid to defend its treasure: 'A marble figure, upright, with lance in hand; with on his head a serpent wreathed. When any approached, the serpent would bite him on one side, and twining about his throat and killing him, would return again to his place.'

"I knew well that such a figure was not wrought to pleasantry; and that to brave it was no child's play. The dead Arab at my feet was proof of what could be done! So I examined again along the wall; and found here and there chippings as if someone had been tapping with a heavy hammer. This then had been what happened: The grave-robber, more expert at his work than we had been, and suspecting the presence of a hidden serdab, had made essay to find it. He had struck the spring by chance; had released the avenging 'Treasurer', as the Arabian writer designated him. The issue spoke for itself. I got a piece of wood, and, standing at a safe distance, pressed with the end of it upon the star.

"Instantly the stone flew back. The hidden figure within darted forward and thrust out its lance. Then it rose up and disappeared. I thought I might now safely press on the seven stars; and did so. Again the stone rolled back; and the 'Treasurer' flashed by to his hidden lair.

"I repeated both experiments several times; with always the same result. I should have liked to examine the mechanism of that figure of such malignant mobility; but it was not possible without such tools as could not easily be had. It might be necessary to cut into a whole section of the rock. Some day I hope to go back, properly equipped, and attempt it.

"Perhaps you do not know that the entrance to a serdab is almost always very narrow; sometimes a hand can hardly be inserted. Two things I learned from this serdab. The first was that the lamps, if lamps at all there had been, could not have been of large size; and secondly, that they would be in some way associated with Hathor, whose symbol, the hawk in a square with the right top corner forming a smaller square, was cut in relief on the wall within, and coloured the bright vermilion which we had found on the Stele. Hathor is the goddess who in Egyptian mythology answers to Venus of the Greeks, in as far as she is the presiding deity of beauty and pleasure. In the Egyptian mythology, however, each God has many forms; and in some aspects Hathor has to do with the idea of resurrection. There are seven forms or variants of the Goddess; why should not these correspond in some way to the seven lamps! That there had been such lamps, I was convinced. The first grave-robber had met his death; the second had found the contents of the serdab. The first attempt had been made years since; the state of the body proved this. I had no clue to the second attempt. It might have been long ago; or it might have been recently. If, however, others had been to the tomb, it was probable that the lamps had been taken long ago. Well! all the more difficult would be my search; for undertaken it must be!

"That was nearly three years ago; and for all that time I have been like the man in the Arabian Nights, seeking old lamps, not for new, but for cash. I dared not say what I was looking for, or attempt to give any description; for such would have defeated my purpose. But I had in my own mind at the start a vague idea of what I must find. In process of time this grew more and more clear; till at last I almost overshot my mark by searching for something which might have been wrong.

"The disappointments I suffered, and the wild-goose chases I made, would fill a volume; but I persevered. At last, not two months ago, I was shown by an old dealer in Mossul one lamp such as I had looked for. I had been tracing it for nearly a year, always suffering disappointment, but always buoyed up to further endeavour by a growing hope that I was on the track.

"I do not know how I restrained myself when I realised that, at last, I was at least close to success. I was skilled, however, in the finesse of Eastern trade; and the Jew-Arab-Portugee trader met his match. I wanted to see all his stock before buying; and one by one he produced, amongst masses of rubbish, seven different lamps. Each of them had a distinguishing mark; and each and all was some form of the symbol of Hathor. I think I shook the imperturbability of my swarthy friend by the magnitude of my purchases; for in order to prevent him guessing what form of goods I sought, I nearly cleared out his shop. At the end he nearly wept, and said I had ruined him; for now he had nothing to sell. He would have torn his hair had he known what price I should ultimately have given for some of his stock, that perhaps he valued least.

"I parted with most of my merchandise at normal price as I hurried home. I did not dare to give it away, or even lose it, lest I should incur suspicion. My burden was far too precious to be risked by any foolishness now. I got on as fast as it is possible to travel in such countries; and arrived in London with only the lamps and certain portable curios and papyri which I had picked up on my travels.

"Now, Mr. Ross, you know all I know; and I leave it to your discretion how much, if any of it, you will tell Miss Trelawny."

As he finished a clear young voice said behind us:

"What about Miss Trelawny? She is here!"

We turned, startled; and looked at each other inquiringly. Miss Trelawny stood in the doorway. We did not know how long she had been present, or how much she had heard.

CHAPTER XIII

AWAKING FROM THE TRANCE

THE FIRST UNEXPECTED words may always startle a hearer; but when the shock is over, the listener's reason has asserted itself, and he can judge of the manner, as well as of the matter, of speech. Thus it was on this occasion. With intelligence now alert, I could not doubt of the simple sincerity of Margaret's next question.

"What have you two men been talking about all this time, Mr. Ross? I suppose, Mr. Corbeck has been telling you all his adventures in finding the lamps. I hope you will tell me too, some day, Mr. Corbeck; but that must not be till my poor Father is better. He would like, I am sure, to tell me all about these things himself; or to be present when I heard them." She glanced sharply from one to the other. "Oh, that was what you were saying as I came in? All right! I shall wait; but I hope it won't be long. The continuance of Father's condition is, I feel, breaking me down. A little while ago I felt that my nerves were giving out; so I determined to go out for a walk in the Park. I am sure it will do me good. I want you, if you will, Mr. Ross, to be with Father whilst I am away. I shall feel secure then."

I rose with alacrity, rejoicing that the poor girl was going out, even for half an hour. She was looking terribly wearied and haggard; and the sight of her pale cheeks made my heart ache. I went to the sick-room; and sat down in my usual place. Mrs. Grant was then on duty; we had not found it necessary to have more than one person in the room during the day. When I came in, she took occasion to go about some household duty. The blinds were up, but the north aspect of the room softened the hot glare of the sunlight without.

I sat for a long time thinking over all that Mr. Corbeck had told me; and weaving its wonders into the tissue of strange things which had come to pass since I had entered the house. At times I was inclined to doubt; to doubt everything and every one; to doubt even the evidences of my own five senses. The warnings of the skilled detective kept coming back to my mind. He had put down Mr. Corbeck as a clever liar, and a confederate of Miss Trelawny. Of Margaret! That settled it! Face to face with such a proposition as that, doubt vanished. Each time when her image, her name, the merest thought of her, came before my mind, each event stood out stark as a living fact. My life upon her faith!

I was recalled from my reverie, which was fast becoming a dream of love, in a startling manner. A voice came from the bed; a deep, strong, masterful voice. The first note of it called up like a clarion my eyes and my ears. The sick man was awake and speaking!

"Who are you? What are you doing here?"

Whatever ideas any of us had ever formed of his waking, I am quite sure that none of us expected to see him start up all awake and full master of himself. I was so surprised that I answered almost mechanically:

"Ross is my name. I have been watching by you!" He looked surprised for an instant, and then I could see that his habit of judging for himself came into play.

"Watching by me! How do you mean? Why watching by me?" His eye had now lit on his heavily bandaged wrist. He went on in a different tone; less aggressive, more genial, as of one accepting facts:

"Are you a doctor?" I felt myself almost smiling as I answered; the relief from the long pressure of anxiety regarding his life was beginning to tell:

"No, sir!"

"Then why are you here? If you are not a doctor, what are you?" His tone was again more dictatorial. Thought is quick; the whole train of reasoning on which my answer must be based flooded through my brain before the words could leave my lips. Margaret! I must think of Margaret! This was her father, who as yet knew nothing of me; even of my very existence. He would be naturally curious, if not anxious, to know why I amongst men had been chosen as his daughter's friend on the occasion of his illness. Fathers are naturally a little jealous in such matters as a daughter's choice, and in the undeclared state of my love for Margaret I must do nothing which could ultimately embarrass her.

"I am a Barrister. It is not, however, in that capacity I am here; but simply as a friend of your daughter. It was probably her knowledge of my being a lawyer which first determined her to ask me to come when she thought you had been murdered. Afterwards she was good enough to consider me to be a friend, and to allow me to remain in accordance with your expressed wish that someone should remain to watch."

Mr. Trelawny was manifestly a man of quick thought, and of few words. He gazed at me keenly as I spoke, and his piercing eyes seemed to read my thought. To my relief he said no more on the subject just then, seeming to accept my words in simple faith. There was evidently in his own mind some cause for the acceptance deeper than my own knowledge. His eyes flashed, and there was an unconscious movement of the mouth—it could hardly be called a twitch—which betokened satisfaction. He was following out some train of reasoning in his own mind. Suddenly he said:

"She thought I had been murdered! Was that last night?"

"No! four days ago." He seemed surprised. Whilst he had been speaking the first time he had sat up in bed; now he made a movement as though he would jump out. With an effort, however, he restrained himself; leaning back on his pillows he said quietly:

"Tell me all about it! All you know! Every detail! Omit nothing! But stay; first lock the door! I want to know, before I see anyone, exactly how things stand."

Somehow his last words made my heart leap. "Anyone!" He evidently accepted me, then, as an exception. In my present state of feeling for his daughter, this was a comforting thought. I felt exultant as I went over to the door and softly turned the key. When I came back I found him sitting up again. He said:

"Go on!"

Accordingly, I told him every detail, even of the slightest which I could remember, of what had happened from the moment of my arrival at the house. Of course I said nothing of my feeling towards Margaret, and spoke only concerning those things already within his own knowledge. With regard to Corbeck, I simply said that he had brought back some lamps of which he had been in quest. Then I proceeded to tell him fully of their loss, and of their re-discovery in the house.

He listened with a self-control which, under the circumstances, was to me little less than marvellous. It was impassiveness, for at times his eyes would flash or blaze, and the strong fingers of his uninjured hand would grip the sheet, pulling it into far-extending wrinkles. This was most noticeable when I told him of the return of Corbeck, and the finding of the lamps in the boudoir. At times he spoke, but only a few words, and as if unconsciously in emotional comment. The mysterious parts, those which had most puzzled us, seemed to have no special interest for him; he seemed to know them already. The utmost concern he showed was when I told him of Daw's shooting. His muttered comment: "stupid ass!" together with a quick glance across the room at the injured cabinet, marked the measure of his disgust. As I told him of his daughter's harrowing anxiety for him, of her unending care and devotion, of the tender love which she had shown, he seemed much moved. There was a sort of veiled surprise in his unconscious whisper:

"Margaret! Margaret!"

When I had finished my narration, bringing matters up to the moment when Miss Trelawny had gone out for her walk—I thought of her as "Miss Trelawny," not as "Margaret" now, in the presence of her father—he remained silent for quite a long time. It was probably two or three minutes; but it seemed interminable. All at once he turned and said to me briskly:

"Now tell me all about yourself!" This was something of a floorer; I felt myself grow red-hot. Mr. Trelawny's eyes were upon me; they were now calm and inquiring, but never ceasing in their soul-searching scrutiny. There was just a suspicion of a smile on the mouth which, though it added to my embarrassment, gave me a certain measure of relief. I was, however, face to face with difficulty; and the habit of my life stood me in good stead. I looked him straight in the eyes as I spoke:

"My name, as I told you, is Ross, Malcolm Ross. I am by profession a Barrister. I was made a Q.C. in the last year of the Queen's reign. I have been fairly successful in my work." To my relief he said:

"Yes, I know. I have always heard well of you! Where and when did you meet Margaret?"

"First at the Hay's in Belgrave Square, ten days ago. Then at a picnic up the river with Lady Strathconnell. We went from Windsor to Cookham. Mar—Miss Trelawny was in my boat. I scull a little, and I had my own boat at Windsor. We had a good deal of conversation—naturally."

"Naturally!" there was just a suspicion of something sardonic in the tone of acquiescence; but there was no other intimation of his feeling. I began to think that as I was in the presence of a strong man, I should show something of my own strength. My friends, and sometimes my opponents, say that I am a strong man. In my present circumstances, not to be absolutely truthful would be to be weak. So I stood up to the difficulty before me; always bearing in mind, however, that my words might affect Margaret's happiness through her love for her father. I went on:

"In conversation at a place and time and amid surroundings so pleasing, and in a solitude inviting to confidence, I got a glimpse of her inner life. Such a glimpse as a man of my years and experience may get from a young girl!" The father's face grew graver as I went on; but he said nothing. I was committed now to a definite line of speech, and went on with such mastery of my mind as I could exercise. The occasion might be fraught with serious consequences to me too.

"I could not but see that there was over her spirit a sense of loneliness which was habitual to her. I thought I understood it; I am myself an only child. I ventured to encourage her to speak to me freely; and was happy enough to succeed. A sort of confidence became established between us." There was something in the father's face which made me add hurriedly:

"Nothing was said by her, sir, as you can well imagine, which was not right and proper. She only told me in the impulsive way of one longing to give voice to thoughts long carefully concealed, of her yearning to be closer to the father whom she loved; more en rapport with him; more in his confidence; closer within the circle of his sympathies. Oh, believe me, sir, that it was all good! All that a father's heart could hope or wish for! It was all loyal! That she spoke it to me was perhaps because I was almost a stranger with whom there was no previous barrier to confidence."

Here I paused. It was hard to go on; and I feared lest I might, in my zeal, do Margaret a disservice. The relief of the strain came from her father.

"And you?"

"Sir, Miss Trelawny is very sweet and beautiful! She is young; and her mind is like crystal! Her sympathy is a joy! I am not an old man, and my affections were not engaged. They never had been till then.

I hope I may say as much, even to a father!" My eyes involuntarily dropped. When I raised them again Mr. Trelawny was still gazing at me keenly. All the kindliness of his nature seemed to wreath itself in a smile as he held out his hand and said:

"Malcolm Ross, I have always heard of you as a fearless and honourable gentleman. I am glad my girl has such a friend! Go on!"

My heart leaped. The first step to the winning of Margaret's father was gained. I dare say I was somewhat more effusive in my words and my manner as I went on. I certainly felt that way.

"One thing we gain as we grow older: to use our age judiciously! I have had much experience. I have fought for it and worked for it all my life; and I felt that I was justified in using it. I ventured to ask Miss Trelawny to count on me as a friend; to let me serve her should occasion arise. She promised me that she would. I had little idea that my chance of serving her should come so soon or in such a way; but that very night you were stricken down. In her desolation and anxiety she sent for me!" I paused. He continued to look at me as I went on:

"When your letter of instructions was found, I offered my services. They were accepted, as you know."

"And these days, how did they pass for you?" The question startled me. There was in it something of Margaret's own voice and manner; something so greatly resembling her lighter moments that it brought out all the masculinity in me. I felt more sure of my ground now as I said:

"These days, sir, despite all their harrowing anxiety, despite all the pain they held for the girl whom I grew to love more and more with each passing hour, have been the happiest of my life!" He kept silence for a long time; so long that, as I waited for him to speak, with my heart beating, I began to wonder if my frankness had been too effusive. At last he said:

"I suppose it is hard to say so much vicariously. Her poor mother should have heard you; it would have made her heart glad!" Then a shadow swept across his face; and he went on more hurriedly.

"But are you quite sure of all this?"

"I know my own heart, sir; or, at least, I think I do!"

"No! no!" he answered, "I don't mean you. That is all right! But you spoke of my girl's affection for me . . . and yet . . . ! And yet she has been living here, in my house, a whole year. . . Still, she spoke to you of her loneliness—her desolation. I never—it grieves me to say it, but it is true—I never saw sign of such affection towards myself in all the year! . . ." His voice trembled away into sad, reminiscent introspection.

"Then, sir," I said, "I have been privileged to see more in a few days than you in her whole lifetime!" My words seemed to call him up from himself; and I thought that it was with pleasure as well as surprise that he said:

"I had no idea of it. I thought that she was indifferent to me. That what seemed like the neglect of her youth was revenging itself on me. That she was cold of heart. . . . It is a joy unspeakable to me that her mother's daughter loves me too!" Unconsciously he sank back upon his pillow, lost in memories of the past.

How he must have loved her mother! It was the love of her mother's child, rather than the love of his own daughter, that appealed to him. My heart went out to him in a great wave of sympathy and kindliness. I began to understand. To understand the passion of these two great, silent, reserved natures, that successfully concealed the burning hunger for the other's love! It did not surprise me when presently he murmured to himself:

"Margaret, my child! Tender, and thoughtful, and strong, and true, and brave! Like her dear mother! like her dear mother!"

And then to the very depths of my heart I rejoiced that I had spoken so frankly.

Presently Mr. Trelawny said:

"Four days! The sixteenth! Then this is the twentieth of July?" I nodded affirmation; he went on:

"So I have been lying in a trance for four days. It is not the first time. I was in a trance once under strange conditions for three days; and never even suspected it till I was told of the lapse of time. I shall tell you all about it some day, if you care to hear."

That made me thrill with pleasure. That he, Margaret's father, would so take me into his confidence made it possible. . . . The business-like, every-day alertness of his voice as he spoke next quite recalled me:

"I had better get up now. When Margaret comes in, tell her yourself that I am all right. It will avoid any shock! And will you tell Corbeck that I would like to see him as soon as I can. I want to see those lamps, and hear all about them!"

His attitude towards me filled me with delight. There was a possible father-in-law aspect that would have raised me from a death-bed. I was hurrying away to carry out his wishes; when, however, my hand was on the key of the door, his voice recalled me:

"Mr. Ross!"

I did not like to hear him say "Mr." After he knew of my friendship with his daughter he had called me Malcolm Ross; and this obvious return to formality not only pained, but filled me with apprehension. It must be something about Margaret. I thought of her as "Margaret" and not as "Miss Trelawny", now that there was danger of losing her. I know now what I felt then: that I was determined to fight for her rather than lose her. I came back, unconsciously holding myself erect. Mr. Trelawny, the keen observer of men, seemed to read my thought; his face, which was set in a new anxiety, relaxed as he said:

"Sit down a minute; it is better that we speak now than later. We are both men, and men of the world. All this about my daughter is very new to me, and very sudden; and I want to know exactly how and where I stand. Mind, I am making no objection; but as a father I have duties which are grave, and may prove to be painful. I—I"—he seemed slightly at a loss how to begin, and this gave me hope—"I suppose I am to take it, from what you have said to me of your feelings towards

my girl, that it is in your mind to be a suitor for her hand, later on?"
I answered at once:

"Absolutely! Firm and fixed; it was my intention the evening after
I had been with her on the river, to seek you, of course after a proper
and respectful interval, and to ask you if I might approach her on the
subject. Events forced me into closer relationship more quickly than
I had to hope would be possible; but that first purpose has remained
fresh in my heart, and has grown in intensity, and multiplied itself with
every hour which has passed since then." His face seemed to soften as
he looked at me; the memory of his own youth was coming back to him
instinctively. After a pause he said:

"I suppose I may take it, too, Malcolm Ross"—the return to the
familiarity of address swept through me with a glorious thrill—"that as
yet you have not made any protestation to my daughter?"

"Not in words, sir." The arriere pensee of my phrase struck me, not
by its own humour, but through the grave, kindly smile on the father's
face. There was a pleasant sarcasm in his comment:

"Not in words! That is dangerous! She might have doubted words,
or even disbelieved them."

I felt myself blushing to the roots of my hair as I went on:

"The duty of delicacy in her defenceless position; my respect for
her father—I did not know you then, sir, as yourself, but only as her
father—restrained me. But even had not these barriers existed, I should
not have dared in the presence of such grief and anxiety to have declared
myself. Mr. Trelawny, I assure you on my word of honour that your
daughter and I are as yet, on her part, but friends and nothing more!"
Once again he held out his hands, and we clasped each other warmly.
Then he said heartily:

"I am satisfied, Malcolm Ross. Of course, I take it that until I have
seen her and have given you permission, you will not make any declara-

tion to my daughter—in words," he added, with an indulgent smile. But his face became stern again as he went on:

"Time presses; and I have to think of some matters so urgent and so strange that I dare not lose an hour. Otherwise I should not have been prepared to enter, at so short a notice and to so new a friend, on the subject of my daughter's settlement in life, and of her future happiness." There was a dignity and a certain proudness in his manner which impressed me much.

"I shall respect your wishes, sir!" I said as I went back and opened the door. I heard him lock it behind me.

When I told Mr. Corbeck that Mr. Trelawny had quite recovered, he began to dance about like a wild man. But he suddenly stopped, and asked me to be careful not to draw any inferences, at all events at first, when in the future speaking of the finding of the lamps, or of the first visits to the tomb. This was in case Mr. Trelawny should speak to me on the subject; "as, of course, he will," he added, with a sidelong look at me which meant knowledge of the affairs of my heart. I agreed to this, feeling that it was quite right. I did not quite understand why; but I knew that Mr. Trelawny was a peculiar man. In no case could one make a mistake by being reticent. Reticence is a quality which a strong man always respects.

The manner in which the others of the house took the news of the recovery varied much. Mrs. Grant wept with emotion; then she hurried off to see if she could do anything personally, and to set the house in order for "Master", as she always called him. The Nurse's face fell: she was deprived of an interesting case. But the disappointment was only momentary; and she rejoiced that the trouble was over. She was ready to come to the patient the moment she should be wanted; but in the meantime she occupied herself in packing her portmanteau.

I took Sergeant Daw into the study, so that we should be alone when I told him the news. It surprised even his iron self-control when

I told him the method of the waking. I was myself surprised in turn by his first words:

"And how did he explain the first attack? He was unconscious when the second was made."

Up to that moment the nature of the attack, which was the cause of my coming to the house, had never even crossed my mind, except when I had simply narrated the various occurrences in sequence to Mr. Trelawny. The Detective did not seem to think much of my answer:

"Do you know, it never occurred to me to ask him!" The professional instinct was strong in the man, and seemed to supersede everything else.

"That is why so few cases are ever followed out," he said, "unless our people are in them. Your amateur detective neer hunts down to the death. As for ordinary people, the moment things begin to mend, and the strain of suspense is off them, they drop the matter in hand. It is like sea-sickness," he added philosophically after a pause; "the moment you touch the shore you never give it a thought, but run off to the buffet to feed! Well, Mr. Ross, I'm glad the case is over; for over it is, so far as I am concerned. I suppose that Mr. Trelawny knows his own business; and that now he is well again, he will take it up himself. Perhaps, however, he will not do anything. As he seemed to expect something to happen, but did not ask for protection from the police in any way, I take it that he don't want them to interfere with an eye to punishment. We'll be told officially, I suppose, that it was an accident, or sleep-walking, or something of the kind, to satisfy the conscience of our Record Department; and that will be the end. As for me, I tell you frankly, sir, that it will be the saving of me. I verily believe I was beginning to get dotty over it all. There were too many mysteries, that aren't in my line, for me to be really satisfied as to either facts or the causes of them. Now I'll be able to wash my hands of it, and get back to clean, wholesome, criminal work. Of course, sir, I'll be glad to know if you ever do light on a cause of any kind. And I'll be grateful if you can ever tell me how the man was dragged out of bed when the cat bit him, and who used the knife the second time. For master Silvio could never have done it by himself. But there! I keep thinking of it still. I must look out and keep a check on myself, or I shall think of it when I have to keep my mind on other things!"

When Margaret returned from her walk, I met her in the hall. She was still pale and sad; somehow, I had expected to see her radiant after her walk. The moment she saw me her eyes brightened, and she looked at me keenly.

"You have some good news for me?" she said. "Is Father better?"

"He is! Why did you think so?"

"I saw it in your face. I must go to him at once." She was hurrying away when I stopped her.

"He said he would send for you the moment he was dressed."

"He said he would send for me!" she repeated in amazement. "Then he is awake again, and conscious? I had no idea he was so well as that! O Malcolm!"

She sat down on the nearest chair and began to cry. I felt overcome myself. The sight of her joy and emotion, the mention of my own name in such a way and at such a time, the rush of glorious possibilities all coming together, quite unmanned me. She saw my emotion, and seemed to understand. She put out her hand. I held it hard, and kissed it. Such moments as these, the opportunities of lovers, are gifts of the gods! Up to this instant, though I knew I loved her, and though I believed she returned my affection, I had had only hope. Now, however, the self-surrender manifest in her willingness to let me squeeze her hand, the ardour of her pressure in return, and the glorious flush of love in her beautiful, deep, dark eyes as she lifted them to mine, were all the eloquences which the most impatient or exacting lover could expect or demand.

No word was spoken; none was needed. Even had I not been pledged to verbal silence, words would have been poor and dull to express what we felt. Hand in hand, like two little children, we went up the staircase and waited on the landing, till the summons from Mr. Trelawny should come.

I whispered in her ear—it was nicer than speaking aloud and at a greater distance—how her father had awakened, and what he had said; and all that had passed between us, except when she herself had been the subject of conversation.

Presently a bell rang from the room. Margaret slipped from me, and looked back with warning finger on lip. She went over to her father's door and knocked softly.

"Come in!" said the strong voice.

"It is I, Father!" The voice was tremulous with love and hope.

There was a quick step inside the room; the door was hurriedly thrown open, and in an instant Margaret, who had sprung forward, was clasped in her father's arms. There was little speech; only a few broken phrases.

"Father! Dear, dear Father!"

"My child! Margaret! My dear, dear child!"

"O Father, Father! At last! At last!"

Here the father and daughter went into the room together, and the door closed.

CHAPTER XIV

THE BIRTH-MARK

DURING MY WAITING for the summons to Mr. Trelawny's room, which I knew would come, the time was long and lonely. After the first few moments of emotional happiness at Margaret's joy, I somehow felt apart and alone; and for a little time the selfishness of a lover possessed me. But it was not for long. Margaret's happiness was all to me; and in the conscious sense of it I lost my baser self. Margaret's last words as the door closed on them gave the key to the whole situation, as it had been and as it was. These two proud, strong people, though father and daughter, had only come to know each other when the girl was grown up. Margaret's nature was of that kind which matures early.

The pride and strength of each, and the reticence which was their corollary, made a barrier at the beginning. Each had respected the other's reticence too much thereafter; and the misunderstanding grew to habit. And so these two loving hearts, each of which yearned for sympathy from the other, were kept apart. But now all was well, and in my heart of hearts I rejoiced that at last Margaret was happy. Whilst I was still musing on the subject, and dreaming dreams of a personal nature, the door was opened, and Mr. Trelawny beckoned to me.

"Come in, Mr. Ross!" he said cordially, but with a certain formality which I dreaded. I entered the room, and he closed the door again. He held out his hand, and I put mine in it. He did not let it go, but still held it as he drew me over toward his daughter. Margaret looked from me to him, and back again; and her eyes fell. When I was close to her,

Mr. Trelawny let go my hand, and, looking his daughter straight in the face, said:

"If things are as I fancy, we shall not have any secrets between us. Malcolm Ross knows so much of my affairs already, that I take it he must either let matters stop where they are and go away in silence, or else he must know more. Margaret! are you willing to let Mr. Ross see your wrist?"

She threw one swift look of appeal in his eyes; but even as she did so she seemed to make up her mind. Without a word she raised her right hand, so that the bracelet of spreading wings which covered the wrist fell back, leaving the flesh bare. Then an icy chill shot through me.

On her wrist was a thin red jagged line, from which seemed to hang red stains like drops of blood!

She stood there, a veritable figure of patient pride.

Oh! but she looked proud! Through all her sweetness, all her dignity, all her high-souled negation of self which I had known, and which never seemed more marked than now—through all the fire that seemed to shine from the dark depths of her eyes into my very soul, pride shone conspicuously. The pride that has faith; the pride that is born of conscious purity; the pride of a veritable queen of Old Time, when to be royal was to be the first and greatest and bravest in all high things. As we stood thus for some seconds, the deep, grave voice of her father seemed to sound a challenge in my ears:

"What do you say now?"

My answer was not in words. I caught Margaret's right hand in mine as it fell, and, holding it tight, whilst with the other I pushed back the golden cincture, stooped and kissed the wrist. As I looked up at her, but never letting go her hand, there was a look of joy on her face such as I dream of when I think of heaven. Then I faced her father.

"You have my answer, sir!" His strong face looked gravely sweet. He only said one word as he laid his hand on our clasped ones, whilst he bent over and kissed his daughter:

"Good!"

We were interrupted by a knock at the door. In answer to an impatient "Come in!" from Mr. Trelawny, Mr. Corbeck entered. When he saw us grouped he would have drawn back; but in an instant Mr. Trelawny had sprung forth and dragged him forward. As he shook him by both hands, he seemed a transformed man. All the enthusiasm of his youth, of which Mr. Corbeck had told us, seemed to have come back to him in an instant.

"So you have got the lamps!" he almost shouted. "My reasoning was right after all. Come to the library, where we will be alone, and tell me all about it! And while he does it, Ross," said he, turning to me, "do you, like a good fellow, get the key from the safe deposit, so that I may have a look at the lamps!"

Then the three of them, the daughter lovingly holding her father's arm, went into the library, whilst I hurried off to Chancery Lane.

When I returned with the key, I found them still engaged in the narrative; but Doctor Winchester, who had arrived soon after I left, was with them. Mr. Trelawny, on hearing from Margaret of his great attention and kindness, and how he had, under much pressure to the contrary, steadfastly obeyed his written wishes, had asked him to remain and listen. "It will interest you, perhaps," he said, "to learn the end of the story!"

We all had an early dinner together. We sat after it a good while, and then Mr. Trelawny said:

"Now, I think we had all better separate and go quietly to bed early. We may have much to talk about tomorrow; and tonight I want to think."

Doctor Winchester went away, taking, with a courteous for-ethought, Mr. Corbeck with him, and leaving me behind. When the others had gone Mr. Trelawny said:

"I think it will be well if you, too, will go home for tonight. I want to be quite alone with my daughter; there are many things I wish to speak of to her, and to her alone. Perhaps, even tomorrow, I will be able to tell you also of them; but in the meantime there will be less distraction to us both if we are alone in the house." I quite understood and sympathised with his feelings; but the experiences of the last few days were strong on me, and with some hesitation I said:

"But may it not be dangerous? If you knew as we do—" To my surprise Margaret interrupted me:

"There will be no danger, Malcolm. I shall be with Father!" As she spoke she clung to him in a protective way. I said no more, but stood up to go at once. Mr. Trelawny said heartily:

"Come as early as you please, Ross. Come to breakfast. After it, you and I will want to have a word together." He went out of the room quietly, leaving us together. I clasped and kissed Margaret's hands, which she held out to me, and then drew her close to me, and our lips met for the first time.

I did not sleep much that night. Happiness on the one side of my bed and Anxiety on the other kept sleep away. But if I had anxious care, I had also happiness which had not equal in my life—or ever can have. The night went by so quickly that the dawn seemed to rush on me, not stealing as is its wont.

Before nine o'clock I was at Kensington. All anxiety seemed to float away like a cloud as I met Margaret, and saw that already the pallor of her face had given to the rich bloom which I knew. She told me that her father had slept well, and that he would be with us soon.

"I do believe," she whispered, "that my dear and thoughtful Father has kept back on purpose, so that I might meet you first, and alone!"

After breakfast Mr. Trelawny took us into the study, saying as he passed in:

"I have asked Margaret to come too." When we were seated, he said gravely:

"I told you last night that we might have something to say to each other. I dare say that you may have thought that it was about Margaret and yourself. Isn't that so?"

"I thought so."

"Well, my boy, that is all right. Margaret and I have been talking, and I know her wishes." He held out his hand. When I wrung it, and had kissed Margaret, who drew her chair close to mine, so that we could hold hands as we listened, he went on, but with a certain hesitation—it could hardly be called nervousness—which was new to me.

"You know a good deal of my hunt after this mummy and her belongings; and I dare say you have guessed a good deal of my theories. But these at any rate I shall explain later, concisely and categorically, if it be necessary. What I want to consult you about now is this: Margaret and I disagree on one point. I am about to make an experiment; the experiment which is to crown all that I have devoted twenty years of research, and danger, and labour to prepare for. Through it we may learn things that have been hidden from the eyes and the knowledge of men for centuries; for scores of centuries. I do not want my daughter to be present; for I cannot blind myself to the fact that there may be danger in it—great danger, and of an unknown kind. I have, however, already faced very great dangers, and of an unknown kind; and so has that brave scholar who has helped me in the work. As to myself, I am willing to run any risk. For science, and history, and philosophy may benefit; and we may turn one old page of a wisdom unknown in this prosaic age. But for my daughter to run such a risk I am loth. Her young bright life is too precious to throw lightly away; now especially when she is on the very threshold of new happiness. I do not wish to see her life given, as her dear mother's was—"

He broke down for a moment, and covered his eyes with his hands. In an instant Margaret was beside him, clasping him close, and kissing him, and comforting him with loving words. Then, standing erect, with one hand on his head, she said:

"Father! mother did not bid you stay beside her, even when you wanted to go on that journey of unknown danger to Egypt; though that country was then upset from end to end with war and the dangers that follow war. You have told me how she left you free to go as you wished; though that she thought of danger for you and and feared it for you, is proved by this!" She held up her wrist with the scar that seemed to run blood. "Now, mother's daughter does as mother would have done herself!" Then she turned to me:

"Malcolm, you know I love you! But love is trust; and you must trust me in danger as well as in joy. You and I must stand beside Father in this unknown peril. Together we shall come through it; or together we shall fail; together we shall die. That is my wish; my first wish to my husband that is to be! Do you not think that, as a daughter, I am right? Tell my Father what you think!"

She looked like a Queen stooping to plead. My love for her grew and grew. I stood up beside her; and took her hand and said:

"Mr. Trelawny! in this Margaret and I are one!"

He took both our hands and held them hard. Presently he said with deep emotion:

"It is as her mother would have done!"

Mr. Corbeck and Doctor Winchester came exactly at the time appointed, and joined us in the library. Despite my great happiness I felt our meeting to be a very solemn function. For I could never forget the strange things that had been; and the idea of the strange things which might be, was with me like a cloud, pressing down on us all. From the gravity of my companions I gathered that each of them also was ruled by some such dominating thought.

Instinctively we gathered our chairs into a circle round Mr. Trelawny, who had taken the great armchair near the window. Margaret sat by him on his right, and I was next to her. Mr. Corbeck was on his left, with Doctor Winchester on the other side. After a few seconds of silence Mr. Trelawny said to Mr. Corbeck:

"You have told Doctor Winchester all up to the present, as we arranged?"

"Yes," he answered; so Mr. Trelawny said:

"And I have told Margaret, so we all know!" Then, turning to the Doctor, he asked:

"And am I to take it that you, knowing all as we know it who have followed the matter for years, wish to share in the experiment which we hope to make?" His answer was direct and uncompromising:

"Certainly! Why, when this matter was fresh to me, I offered to go on with it to the end. Now that it is of such strange interest, I would not miss it for anything which you could name. Be quite easy in your mind, Mr. Trelawny. I am a scientist and an investigator of phenomena. I have no one belonging to me or dependent on me. I am quite alone, and free to do what I like with my own—including my life!" Mr. Trelawny bowed gravely, and turning to Mr. Corbeck said:

"I have known your ideas for many years past, old friend; so I need ask you nothing. As to Margaret and Malcolm Ross, they have already told me their wishes in no uncertain way." He paused a few seconds, as though to put his thoughts or his words in order; then he began to explain his views and intentions. He spoke very carefully, seeming always to bear in mind that some of us who listened were ignorant of the very root and nature of some things touched upon, and explaining them to us as he went on:

"The experiment which is before us is to try whether or no there is any force, any reality, in the old Magic. There could not possibly be more favourable conditions for the test; and it is my own desire to do all that is possible to make the original design effective. That there is some such existing power I firmly believe. It might not be possible to create, or arrange, or organise such a power in our own time; but I take it that if in Old Time such a power existed, it may have some exceptional survival. After all, the Bible is not a myth; and we read there that the sun stood still at a man's command, and that an ass—not a human one—spoke. And if the Witch at Endor could call up to Saul the spirit of Samuel, why may not there have been others with equal powers; and why may not one among them survive? Indeed, we are told in the Book of Samuel that the Witch of Endor was only one of many, and her being consulted by Saul was a matter of chance. He only sought one among the many whom he had driven out of Israel; 'all those that had Familiar Spirits, and the Wizards.' This Egyptian Queen, Tera, who reigned nearly two thousand years before Saul, had a Familiar, and was a Wizard too. See how the priests of her time, and those after it tried to wipe out her name from the face of the earth, and put a curse over the very door of her tomb so that none might ever discover the lost name. Ay, and they succeeded so well that even Manetho, the historian of the Egyptian Kings, writing in the tenth century before Christ, with all the lore of the priesthood for forty centuries behind him, and with possibility of access to every existing record, could not even find her name. Did it strike any of you, in thinking of the late events, who or what her Familiar was?" There was an interruption, for Doctor Winchester struck one hand loudly on the other as he ejaculated:

"The cat! The mummy cat! I knew it!" Mr. Trelawny smiled over at him.

"You are right! There is every indication that the Familiar of the Wizard Queen was that cat which was mummied when she was, and was not only placed in her tomb, but was laid in the sarcophagus with her. That was what bit into my wrist, what cut me with sharp claws." He paused. Margaret's comment was a purely girlish one:

"Then my poor Silvio is acquitted! I am glad!" Her father stroked her hair and went on:

"This woman seems to have had an extraordinary foresight. Foresight far, far beyond her age and the philosophy of her time. She seems to have seen through the weakness of her own religion, and even prepared for emergence into a different world. All her aspirations were for the North, the point of the compass whence blew the cool invigorating breezes that make life a joy. From the first, her eyes seem to have been attracted to the seven stars of the Plough from the fact, as recorded in the hieroglyphics in her tomb, that at her birth a great aerolite fell, from whose heart was finally extracted that Jewel of Seven Stars which she regarded as the talisman of her life. It seems to have so far ruled her destiny that all her thought and care circled round it. The Magic Coffer, so wondrously wrought with seven sides, we learn from the same source, came from the aerolite. Seven was to her a magic number; and no wonder. With seven fingers on one hand, and seven toes on one foot. With a talisman of a rare ruby with seven stars in the same position as in that constellation which ruled her birth, each star of the seven having seven points—in itself a geological wonder—it would have been odd if she had not been attracted by it. Again, she was born, we learn in the Stele of her tomb, in the seventh month of the year—the month beginning with the Inundation of the Nile. Of which month the presiding Goddess was Hathor, the Goddess of her own house, of the Antefs of the Theban line—the Goddess who in various forms symbolises beauty, and pleasure, and resurrection. Again, in this seventh month—which, by later Egyptian astronomy began on Octorber 28th, and ran to the 27th of our November—on the seventh day the Pointer of the Plough just rises above the horizon of the sky at Thebes.

"In a marvellously strange way, therefore, are grouped into this woman's life these various things. The number seven; the Pole Star, with the constellation of seven stars; the God of the month, Hathor, who was her own particular God, the God of her family, the Antefs of the Theban Dynasty, whose Kings' symbol it was, and whose seven forms ruled love and the delights of life and resurrection. If ever there was ground for magic; for the power of symbolism carried into mystic use; for a belief in finites spirits in an age which knew not the Living God, it is here.

"Remember, too, that this woman was skilled in all the science of her time. Her wise and cautious father took care of that, knowing that by her own wisdom she must ultimately combat the intrigues of the Hierarchy. Bear in mind that in old Egypt the science of Astronomy began and was developed to an extraordinary height; and that Astrology followed Astronomy in its progress. And it is possible that in the later developments of science with regard to light rays, we may yet find that Astrology is on a scientific basis. Our next wave of scientific thought may deal with this. I shall have something special to call your minds to on this point presently. Bear in mind also that the Egyptians knew sciences, of which today, despite all our advantages, we are profoundly ignorant. Acoustics, for instance, an exact science with the builders of the temples of Karnak, of Luxor, of the Pyramids, is today a mystery to Bell, and Kelvin, and Edison, and Marconi. Again, these old miracle-workers probably understood some practical way of using other forces, and amongst them the forces of light that at present we do not dream of. But of this matter I shall speak later. That Magic Coffer of Queen Tera is probably a magic box in more ways than one. It may—possibly it does—contain forces that we wot not of. We cannot open it; it must be closed from within. How then was it closed? It is a coffer of solid stone, of amazing hardness, more like a jewel than an ordinary marble, with a lid equally solid; and yet all is so finely wrought that the finest tool made today cannot be inserted under the flange. How was it wrought to such perfection? How was the stone so chosen that those translucent patches match the relations of the seven stars of the constellation? How is it, or from what cause, that when the starlight shines on it, it glows from within—that when I fix the lamps in similar form the glow grows greater still; and yet the box is irresponsive to ordinary light however great? I tell you that that box hides some great mystery of science. We shall find that the light will open it in some way: either by striking on some substance, sensitive in a peculiar way to its effect, or in releasing some greater power. I only trust that in our ignorance we may not so bungle things as to do harm to its mechanism; and so deprive the knowledge of our time of a lesson handed down, as by a miracle, through nearly five thousand years.

"In another way, too, there may be hidden in that box secrets which, for good or ill, may enlighten the world. We know from their records, and inferentially also, that the Egyptians studied the properties of herbs and minerals for magic purposes—white magic as well as black. We know that some of the wizards of old could induce from sleep dreams of any given kind. That this purpose was mainly effected by hypnotism, which was another art or science of Old Nile, I have little doubt. But still, they must have had a mastery of drugs that is far beyond anything we know. With our own pharmacopoeia we can, to a certain extent, induce dreams. We may even differentiate between good and bad-dreams of pleasure, or disturbing and harrowing dreams. But these old practitioners seemed to have been able to command at will any form or colour of dreaming; could work round any given subject or thought in almost any was required. In that coffer, which you have seen, may rest a very armoury of dreams. Indeed, some of the forces that lie within it may have been already used in my household." Again there was an interruption from Doctor Winchester.

"But if in your case some of these imprisoned forces were used, what set them free at the opportune time, or how? Besides, you and Mr. Corbeck were once before put into a trance for three whole days, when you were in the Queen's tomb for the second time. And then, as I gathered from Mr. Corbeck's story, the coffer was not back in the tomb, though the mummy was. Surely in both these cases there must have been some active intelligence awake, and with some other power to wield." Mr. Trelawny's answer was equally to the point:

"There was some active intelligence awake. I am convinced of it. And it wielded a power which it never lacks. I believe that on both those occasions hypnotism was the power wielded."

"And wherein is that power contained? What view do you hold on the subject?" Doctor Winchester's voice vibrated with the intensity of his excitement as he leaned forward, breathing hard, and with eyes staring. Mr. Trelawny said solemnly:

"In the mummy of the Queen Tera! I was coming to that presently. Perhaps we had better wait till I clear the ground a little. What I hold is, that the preparation of that box was made for a special occasion; as indeed were all the preparations of the tomb and all belonging to it. Queen Tera did not trouble herself to guard against snakes and scorpions, in that rocky tomb cut in the sheer cliff face a hundred feet above the level of the valley, and fifty down from the summit. Her precautions were against the disturbances of human hands; against the jealousy and hatred of the priests, who, had they known of her real aims, would have tried to baffle them. From her point of view, she made all ready for the time of resurrection, whenever that might be. I gather from the symbolic pictures in the tomb that she so far differed from the belief of her time that she looked for a resurrection in the flesh. It was doubtless this that intensified the hatred of the priesthood, and gave them an acceptable cause for obliterating the very existence, present and future, of one who had outrage their theories and blasphemed their gods. All that she might require, either in the accomplishment of the resurrection or after it, were contained in that almost hermetically sealed suite of chambers in the rock. In the great sarcophagus, which as you know is of a size quite unusual even for kings, was the mummy

of her Familiar, the cat, which from its great size I take to be a sort
of tiger-cat. In the tomb, also in a strong receptacle, were the cano-
pic jars usually containing those internal organs which are separately
embalmed, but which in this case had no such contents. So that, I take
it, there was in her case a departure in embalming; and that the organs
were restored to the body, each in its proper place—if, indeed, they
had ever been removed. If this surmise be true, we shall find that the
brain of the Queen either was never extracted in the usual way, or, if so
taken out, that it was duly replaced, instead of being enclosed within
the mummy wrappings. Finally, in the sarcophagus there was the Magic Coffer on which her feet rested. Mark you also, the care taken in
the preservance of her power to control the elements. According to her
belief, the open hand outside the wrappings controlled the Air, and the
strange Jewel Stone with the shining stars controlled Fire. The symbolism inscribed on the soles of her feet gave sway over Land and Water.
About the Star Stone I shall tell you later; but whilst we are speaking
of the sarcophagus, mark how she guarded her secret in case of grave-
wrecking or intrusion. None could open her Magic Coffer without the
lamps, for we know now that ordinary light will not be effective. The
great lid of the sarcophagus was not sealed down as usual, because she
wished to control the air. But she hid the lamps, which in structure
belong to the Magic Coffer, in a place where none could find them,
except by following the secret guidance which she had prepared for
only the eyes of wisdom. And even here she had guarded against chance
discovery, by preparing a bolt of death for the unwary discoverer. To do
this she had applied the lesson of the tradition of the avenging guard
of the treasures of the pyramid, built by her great predecessor of the
Fourth Dynasty of the throne of Egypt.

"You have noted, I suppose, how there were, in the case of her
tomb, certain deviations from the usual rules. For instance, the shaft
of the Mummy Pit, which is usually filled up solid with stones and

rubbish, was left open. Why was this? I take it that she had made arrangements for leaving the tomb when, after her resurrection, she should be a new woman, with a different personality, and less inured to the hardships that in her first existence she had suffered. So far as we can judge of her intent, all things needful for her exit into the world had been thought of, even to the iron chain, described by Van Huyn, close to the door in the rock, by which she might be able to lower herself to the ground. That she expected a long period to elapse was shown in the choice of material. An ordinary rope would be rendered weaker or unsafe in process of time, but she imagined, and rightly, that the iron would endure.

"What her intentions were when once she trod the open earth afresh we do not know, and we never shall, unless her own dead lips can soften and speak."

CHAPTER XV

THE PURPOSE OF
QUEEN TERA

"NOW, AS TO the Star Jewel! This she manifestly regarded as the greatest of her treasures. On it she had engraven words which none of her time dared to speak.

"In the old Egyptian belief it was held that there were words, which, if used properly—for the method of speaking them was as important as the words themselves—could command the Lords of the Upper and the Lower Worlds. The 'hekau', or word of power, was all-important in certain ritual. On the Jewel of Seven Stars, which, as you know, is carved into the image of a scarab, are graven in hieroglyphic two such hekau, one above, the other underneath. But you will understand better when you see it! Wait here! Do not stir!"

As he spoke, he rose and left the room. A great fear for him came over me; but I was in some strange way relieved when I looked at Margaret. Whenever there had been any possibility of danger to her father, she had shown great fear for him; now she was calm and placid. I said nothing, but waited.

In two or three minutes, Mr. Trelawny returned. He held in his hand a little golden box. This, as he resumed his seat, he placed before him on the table. We all leaned forward as he opened it.

On a lining of white satin lay a wondrous ruby of immense size, almost as big as the top joint of Margaret's little finger. It was carven—it could not possibly have been its natural shape, but jewels do not show the working of the tool—into the shape of a scarab, with its wings folded, and its legs and feelers pressed back to its sides. Shining through its wondrous "pigeon's blood" colour were seven different stars, each of seven points, in such position that they reproduced exactly the figure of the Plough. There could be no possible mistake as to this in the mind of anyone who had ever noted the constellation. On it were some hieroglyphic figures, cut with the most exquisite precision, as I could see when it came to my turn to use the magnifying-glass, which Mr. Trelawny took from his pocket and handed to us.

When we all had seen it fully, Mr. Trelawny turned it over so that it rested on its back in a cavity made to hold it in the upper half of the box. The reverse was no less wonderful than the upper, being carved to resemble the under side of the beetle. It, too, had some hieroglyphic figures cut on it. Mr. Trelawny resumed his lecture as we all sat with our heads close to this wonderful jewel:

"As you see, there are two words, one on the top, the other underneath. The symbols on the top represent a single word, composed of one syllable prolonged, with its determinatives. You know, all of you, I suppose, that the Egyptian language was phonetic, and that the hieroglyphic symbol represented the sound. The first symbol here, the hoe, means 'mer', and the two pointed ellipses the prolongation of the final r: mer-r-r. The sitting figure with the hand to its face is what we call the 'determinative' of 'thought'; and the roll of papyrus that of 'abstraction'. Thus we get the word 'mer', love, in its abstract, general, and fullest sense. This is the hekau which can command the Upper World."

Margaret's face was a glory as she said in a deep, low, ringing tone:

"Oh, but it is true. How the old wonder-workers guessed at almighty Truth!" Then a hot blush swept her face, and her eyes fell. Her father smiled at her lovingly as he resumed:

"The symbolisation of the word on the reverse is simpler, though the meaning is more abstruse. The first symbol means 'men', 'abiding', and the second, 'ab', 'the heart'. So that we get 'abiding of heart', or in our own language 'patience'. And this is the hekau to control the Lower World!"

He closed the box, and motioning us to remain as we were, he went back to his room to replace the Jewel in the safe. When he had returned and resumed his seat, he went on:

"That Jewel, with its mystic words, and which Queen Tera held under her hand in the sarcophagus, was to be an important factor—probably the most important—in the working out of the act of her resurrection. From the first I seemed by a sort of instinct to realise this. I kept the Jewel within my great safe, whence none could extract it; not even Queen Tera herself with her astral body."

"Her 'astral body'? What is that, Father? What does that mean?" There was a keenness in Margaret's voice as she asked the question which surprised me a little; but Trelawny smiled a sort of indulgent parental smile, which came through his grim solemnity like sunshine through a rifted cloud, as he spoke:

"The astral body, which is a part of Buddhist belief, long subsequent to the time I speak of, and which is an accepted fact of modern mysticism, had its rise in Ancient Egypt; at least, so far as we know. It is that the gifted individual can at will, quick as thought itself, transfer his body whithersoever he chooses, by the dissolution and reincarnation of particles. In the ancient belief there were several parts of a human being. You may as well know them; so that you will understand matters relative to them or dependent on them as they occur.

"First there is the 'Ka', or 'Double', which, as Doctor Budge explains, may be defined as 'an abstract individuality of personality' which was imbued with all the characteristic attributes of the individual it represented, and possessed an absolutely independent existence. It was free to move from place to place on earth at will; and it could enter into heaven and hold converse with the gods. Then there was the 'Ba', or 'soul', which dwelt in the 'Ka', and had the power of becoming corporeal or incorporeal at will; 'it had both substance and form. . . . It had power to leave the tomb . . .It could revisit the body in the tomb . . . and could reincarnate it and hold converse with it.' Again there was the 'Khu', the 'spiritual intelligence', or spirit. It took the form of 'a shining, luminous, intangible shape of the body.'. . . Then, again, there was the 'Sekhem', or 'power' of a man, his strength or vital force personified. These were the 'Khaibit', or 'shadow', the 'Ren', or 'name', the 'Khat', or 'physical body', and 'Ab', the 'heart', in which life was seated, went to the full making up of a man.

"Thus you will see, that if this division of functions, spiritual and bodily, ethereal and corporeal, ideal and actual, be accepted as exact, there are all the possibilities and capabilities of corporeal transference, guided always by an unimprisonable will or intelligence." As he paused I murmured the lines from Shelley's "Prometheus Unbound":

"The Magnus Zoroaster . . . Met his own image walking in the garden.'"

Mr. Trelawny was not displeased. "Quite so!" he said, in his quiet way. "Shelley had a better conception of ancient beliefs than any of our poets." With a voice changed again he resumed his lecture, for so it was to some of us:

"There is another belief of the ancient Egyptian which you must bear in mind; that regarding the ushaptiu figures of Osiris, which were placed with the dead to its work in the Under World. The enlargement of this idea came to a belief that it was possible to transmit, by magical formulae, the soul and qualities of any living creature to a figure made in its image. This would give a terrible extension of power to one who held the gift of magic.

"It is from a union of these various beliefs, and their natural corollaries, that I have come to the conclusion that Queen Tera expected to be able to effect her own resurrection, when, and where, and how, she would. That she may have held before her a definite time for making her effort is not only possible but likely. I shall not stop now to explain it, but shall enter upon the subject later on. With a soul with the Gods, a spirit which could wander the earth at will, and a power of corporeal transference, or an astral body, there need be no bounds or limits to her ambition. The belief is forced upon us that for these forty or fifty centuries she lay dormant in her tomb-waiting. Waiting with that 'patience' which could rule the Gods of the Under World, for that 'love' which could command those of the Upper World. What she may have dreamt we know not; but her dream must have been broken when the Dutch explorer entered her sculptured cavern, and his follower violated the sacred privacy of her tomb by his rude outrage in the theft of her hand.

"That theft, with all that followed, proved to us one thing, however: that each part of her body, though separated from the rest, can be a central point or rallying place for the items or particles of her astral body. That hand in my room could ensure her instantaneous presence in the flesh, and its equally rapid dissolution.

"Now comes the crown of my argument. The purpose of the attack on me was to get the safe open, so that the sacred Jewel of Seven Stars could be extracted. That immense door of the safe could not keep out her astral body, which, or any part of it, could gather itself as well within as without the safe. And I doubt not that in the darkness of the night that mummied hand sought often the Talisman Jewel, and drew new inspiration from its touch. But despite all its power, the astral body could not remove the Jewel through the chinks of the safe. The Ruby is not astral; and it could only be moved in the ordinary way by the opening of the doors. To this end, the Queen used her astral body and

the fierce force of her Familiar, to bring to the keyhole of the safe the
master key which debarred her wish. For years I have suspected, nay,
have believed as much; and I, too, guarded myself against powers of
the Nether World. I, too, waited in patience till I should have gathered
together all the factors required for the opening of the Magic Coffer
and the resurrection of the mummied Queen!" He paused, and his
daughter's voice came out sweet and clear, and full of intense feeling:

"Father, in the Egyptian belief, was the power of resurrection of
a mummied body a general one, or was it limited? That is: could it
achieve resurrection many times in the course of ages; or only once,
and that one final?"

"There was but one resurrection," he answered. "There were some
who believed that this was to be a definite resurrection of the body into
the real world. But in the common belief, the Spirit found joy in the
Elysian Fields, where there was plenty of food and no fear of famine.
Where there was moisture and deep-rooted reeds, and all the joys that
are to be expected by the people of an arid land and burning clime."

Then Margaret spoke with an earnestness which showed the conviction of her inmost soul:

"To me, then, it is given to understand what was the dream of this
great and far-thinking and high-souled lady of old; the dream that held
her soul in patient waiting for its realisation through the passing of all
those tens of centuries. The dream of a love that might be; a love that
she felt she might, even under new conditions, herself evoke. The love
that is the dream of every woman's life; of the Old and of the New;
Pagan or Christian; under whatever sun; in whatever rank or calling;
however may have been the joy or pain of her life in other ways. Oh!
I know it! I know it! I am a woman, and I know a woman's heart. What
were the lack of food or the plenitude of it; what were feast or famine
to this woman, born in a palace, with the shadow of the Crown of the
Two Egypts on her brows! What were reedy morasses or the tinkle of

running water to her whose barges could sweep the great Nile from the mountains to the sea. What were petty joys and absence of petty fears to her, the raising of whose hand could hurl armies, or draw to the water-stairs of her palaces the commerce of the world! At whose word rose temples filled with all the artistic beauty of the Times of Old which it was her aim and pleasure to restore! Under whose guidance the solid rock yawned into the sepulchre that she designed!

"Surely, surely, such a one had nobler dreams! I can feel them in my heart; I can see them with my sleeping eyes!"

As she spoke she seemed to be inspired; and her eyes had a far-away look as though they saw something beyond mortal sight. And then the deep eyes filled up with unshed tears of great emotion. The very soul of the woman seemed to speak in her voice; whilst we who listened sat entranced.

"I can see her in her loneliness and in the silence of her mighty pride, dreaming her own dream of things far different from those around her. Of some other land, far, far away under the canopy of the silent night, lit by the cool, beautiful light of the stars. A land under that Northern star, whence blew the sweet winds that cooled the feverish desert air. A land of wholesome greenery, far, far away. Where were no scheming and malignant priesthood; whose ideas were to lead to power through gloomy temples and more gloomy caverns of the dead, through an endless ritual of death! A land where love was not base, but a divine possession of the soul! Where there might be some one kindred spirit which could speak to hers through mortal lips like her own; whose being could merge with hers in a sweet communion of soul to soul, even as their breaths could mingle in the ambient air! I know the feeling, for I have shared it myself. I may speak of it now, since the blessing has come into my own life. I may speak of it since it enables me to interpret the feelings, the very longing soul, of that sweet and lovely Queen, so different from her surroundings, so high above her time! Whose nature, put into a word, could control the forces of the Under World; and the name of whose aspiration, though but graven on a star-lit jewel, could command all the powers in the Pantheon of the High Gods.

"And in the realisation of that dream she will surely be content to rest!"

We men sat silent, as the young girl gave her powerful interpretation of the design or purpose of the woman of old. Her every word and tone carried with it the conviction of her own belief. The loftiness of her thoughts seemed to uplift us all as we listened. Her noble words, flowing in musical cadence and vibrant with internal force, seemed to issue from some great instrument of elemental power. Even her tone was new to us all; so that we listened as to some new and strange being from a new and strange world. Her father's face was full of delight. I knew now its cause. I understood the happiness that had come into his life, on his return to the world that he knew, from that prolonged sojourn in the world of dreams. To find in his daughter, whose nature he had never till now known, such a wealth of affection, such a splendour of spiritual insight, such a scholarly imagination, such . . . The rest of his feeling was of hope!

The two other men were silent unconsciously. One man had had his dreaming; for the other, his dreams were to come.

For myself, I was like one in a trance. Who was this new, radiant being who had won to existence out of the mist and darkness of our fears? Love has divine possibilities for the lover's heart! The wings of the soul may expand at any time from the shoulders of the loved one, who then may sweep into angel form. I knew that in my Margaret's nature were divine possibilities of many kinds. When under the shade of the overhanging willow-tree on the river, I had gazed into the depths of her beautiful eyes, I had thenceforth a strict belief in the manifold beauties and excellences of her nature; but this soaring and understanding spirit was, indeed, a revelation. My pride, like her father's, was outside myself; my joy and rapture were complete and supreme!

When we had all got back to earth again in our various ways, Mr. Trelawny, holding his daughter's hand in his, went on with his discourse:

"Now, as to the time at which Queen Tera intended her resurrection to take place! We are in contact with some of the higher astronomical calculations in connection with true orientation. As you know, the stars shift their relative positions in the heavens; but though the real distances traversed are beyond all ordinary comprehension, the effects as we see them are small. Nevertheless, they are susceptible of measurement, not by years, indeed, but by centuries. It was by this means that Sir John Herschel arrived at the date of the building of the Great Pyramid—a date fixed by the time necessary to change the star of the true north from Draconis to the Pole Star, and since then verified by later discoveries. From the above there can be no doubt whatever that astronomy was an exact science with the Egyptians at least a thousand years before the time of Queen Tera. Now, the stars that go to make up a constellation change in process of time their relative positions, and the Plough is a notable example. The changes in the position of stars in even forty centuries is so small as to be hardly noticeable by an eye not trained to minute observances, but they can be measured and verified. Did you, or any of you, notice how exactly the stars in the Ruby correspond to the position of the stars in the Plough; or how the same holds with regard to the translucent places in the Magic Coffer?"

We all assented. He went on:

"You are quite correct. They correspond exactly. And yet when Queen Tera was laid in her tomb, neither the stars in the Jewel nor the translucent places in the Coffer corresponded to the position of the stars in the Constellation as they then were!"

We looked at each other as he paused: a new light was breaking upon us. With a ring of mastery in his voice he went on:

"Do you not see the meaning of this? Does it not throw a light on the intention of the Queen? She, who was guided by augury, and magic, and superstition, naturally chose a time for her resurrection which seemed to have been pointed out by the High Gods themselves, who had sent their message on a thunderbolt from other worlds. When such a time was fixed by supernal wisdom, would it not be the height of human wisdom to avail itself of it? Thus it is"—here his voice deepened and trembled with the intensity of his feeling—"that to us and our time is given the opportunity of this wondrous peep into the old world, such as has been the privilege of none other of our time; which may never be again.

"From first to last the cryptic writing and symbolism of that wondrous tomb of that wondrous woman is full of guiding light; and the key of the many mysteries lies in that most wondrous Jewel which she held in her dead hand over the dead heart, which she hoped and believed would beat again in a newer and nobler world!

"There are only loose ends now to consider. Margaret has given us the true inwardness of the feeling of the other Queen!" He looked at her fondly, and stroked her hand as he said it. "For my own part I sincerely hope she is right; for in such case it will be a joy, I am sure, to all of us to assist at such a realisation of hope. But we must not go too fast, or believe too much in our present state of knowledge. The voice that we hearken for comes out of times strangely other than our own; when human life counted for little, and when the morality of the time made little account of the removing of obstacles in the way to achievement of desire. We must keep our eyes fixed on the scientific side, and wait for the developments on the psychic side.

"Now, as to this stone box, which we call the Magic Coffer. As I have said, I am convinced that it opens only in obedience to some principle of light, or the exercise of some of its forces at present unknown to us. There is here much ground for conjecture and for experiment; for as yet the scientists have not thoroughly differentiated the kinds, and powers, and degrees of light. Without analysing various rays we may,

I think, take it for granted that there are different qualities and powers of light; and this great field of scientific investigation is almost virgin soil. We know as yet so little of natural forces, that imagination need set no bounds to its flights in considering the possibilities of the future. Within but a few years we have made such discoveries as two centuries ago would have sent the discoverers to the flames. The liquefaction of oxygen; the existence of radium, of helium, of polonium, of argon; the different powers of Rontgen and Cathode and Bequerel rays. And as we may finally prove that there are different kinds and qualities of light, so we may find that combustion may have its own powers of differentiation; that there are qualities in some flames non-existent in others. It may be that some of the essential conditions of substance are continuous, even in the destruction of their bases. Last night I was thinking of this, and reasoning that as there are certain qualities in some oils which are not in others, so there may be certain similar or corresponding qualities or powers in the combinations of each. I suppose we have all noticed some time or other that the light of colza oil is not quite the same as that of paraffin, or that the flames of coal gas and whale oil are different. They find it so in the light-houses! All at once it occurred to me that there might be some special virtue in the oil which had been found in the jars when Queen Tera's tomb was opened. These had not been used to preserve the intestines as usual, so they must have been placed there for some other purpose. I remembered that in Van Huyn's narrative he had commented on the way the jars were sealed. This was lightly, though effectually; they could be opened without force. The jars were themselves preserved in a sarcophagus which, though of immense strength and hermetically sealed, could be opened easily. Accordingly, I went at once to examine the jars. A little—a very little of the oil still remained, but it had grown thick in the two and a half centuries in which the jars had been open. Still, it was not rancid; and on examining it I found it was cedar oil, and that it still exhaled something of its original aroma. This gave me the idea that it was to be used to fill the lamps. Whoever had placed the oil in the jars, and the jars in the sarcophagus, knew that there might be shrinkage in process of time, even in vases of alabaster, and fully allowed for it; for each of the jars would have filled the lamps half a dozen times. With part of the oil remaining I made some experiments, therefore, which may give useful results. You know, Doctor, that cedar oil, which was much used in the preparation and ceremonials of the Egyptian dead, has a certain refractive power which we do not find in other oils. For instance, we use it on the lenses of our microscopes to give additional clearness of vision. Last night I put some in one of the lamps, and placed it near a translucent part of the Magic Coffer. The effect was very great; the glow of light within was fuller and more intense than I could have imagined, where an electric light similarly placed had little, if any, effect. I should have tried others of the seven lamps, but that my supply of oil ran out. This, however, is on the road to rectification. I have sent for more cedar oil, and expect to have before long an ample supply. Whatever may happen from other causes, our experiment shall not, at all events, fail from this. We shall see! We shall see!"

Doctor Winchester had evidently been following the logical process of the other's mind, for his comment was:

"I do hope that when the light is effective in opening the box, the mechanism will not be impaired or destroyed."

His doubt as to this gave anxious thought to some of us.

CHAPTER XVI

POWERS—OLD AND NEW

THE TIME WORE away, wondrous slowly in some ways, wonderfully quickly in others. To-day, in the new-found joyous certainty of the return of my love, I should have liked to have had Margaret all to myself. But this day was not for love or for love-making. The shadow of fearful expectation was over it. The more I thought over the coming experiment, the more strange it all seemed; and the more foolish were we who were deliberately entering upon it. It was all so stupendous, so mysterious, so unnecessary! The issues were so vast; the danger so strange, so unknown. Even if it should be successful, what new difficulties would it not raise. What changes might happen, did men know that the portals of the House of Death were not in very truth eternally fixed; and that the Dead could come forth again! Could we realize what it was for us modern mortals to be arrayed against the Gods of Old, with their mysterious powers gotten from natural forces, or begotten of them when the world was young. When land and water were forming themselves from out the primeval slime. When the very air was purifying itself from elemental dross. When the "dragons of the prime" were changing their forms and their powers, made only to combat with geologic forces, to grow in accord with the new vegetable life which was springing up around them. When animals, when even man himself and man's advance were growths as natural as the planetary movements, growths as natural as the planetary movements, or the shining of the stars. Ay! and further back still, when as yet the Spirit which moved on the face of the waters had not spoken the words commanding to come into existence Light and the Life which followed it.

Nay, even beyond this was a still more overwhelming conjecture. The whole possibility of the Great Experiment to which we were now pledged was based on the reality of the existence of the Old Forces which seemed to be coming in contact with the New Civilization. That there were, and are, such cosmic forces we cannot doubt, and that the Intelligence, which is behind them, was and is. Were those primal and elemental forces controlled at any time by other than that Final Cause which Christendom holds as its very essence? If there were truth at all in the belief of Ancient Egypt then their Gods had real existence, real power, real force. Godhead is not a quality subject to the ills of mortals: as in its essence it is creative and recreative, it cannot die. Any belief to the contrary would be antagonistic to reason; for it would hold that a part is greater than the whole. If then the Old Gods held their forces, wherein was the supremacy of the new? Of course, if the Old Gods had lost their power, or if they never had any, the Experiment could not succeed. But if it should indeed succeed, or if there were a possibility of success, then we should be face to face with an inference so overwhelming that one hardly dared to follow it to its conclusion. This would be: that the struggle between Life and Death would no longer be a matter of the earth, earthy; that the war of supra-elemental forces would be moved from the tangible world of facts to the Mid-Region, wherever it may be, which is the home of the Gods. Did such a region exist? What was it that Milton saw with his blind eyes in the rays of poetic light falling between him and Heaven? Whence came that stupendous vision of the Evangelist which has for eighteen centuries held spell-bound the intelligence of Christendom? Was there room in the Universe for opposing Gods; or if such there were, would the stronger allow manifestations of power on the part of the opposing Force which would tend to the weakening of His own teaching and designs? Surely, surely if this supposition were correct there would be some strange and awful development—something unexpected and unpredictable—before the end should be allowed to come. . . !

The subject was too vast and, under the present conditions, too full of strange surmises. I dared not follow it! I set myself to wait in patience till the time should come.

Margaret remained divinely calm. I think I envied her, even whilst I admired and loved her for it. Mr. Trelawny was nervously anxious, as indeed were the other men. With him it took the form of movement; movement both of body and mind. In both respects he was restless, going from one place to another with or without a cause, or even a pretext; and changing from one subject of thought to another. Now and again he would show glimpses of the harrowing anxiety which filled him, by his manifest expectation of finding a similar condition in myself. He would be ever explaining things. And in his explanations I could see the way in which he was turning over in his mind all the phenomena; all the possible causes; all the possible results. Once, in the midst of a most learned dissertation on the growth of Egyptian Astrology, he broke out on a different subject, or rather a branch or corollary of the same:

"I do not see why starlight may not have some subtle quality of its own! We know that other lights have special forces. The Rontgen Ray is not the only discovery to be made in the world of light. Sunlight has its own forces, that are not given to other lights. It warms wine; it quickens fungoid growth. Men are often moonstruck. Why not, then, a more subtle, if less active or powerful, force in the light of the stars. It should be a pure light coming through such vastness of space, and may have a quality which a pure, unimpulsive force may have. The time may not be far off when Astrology shall be accepted on a scientific basis. In the recrudescence of the art, many new experiences will be brought to bear; many new phases of old wisdom will appear in the light of fresh discovery, and afford bases for new reasoning. Men may find that what seemed empiric deductions were in reality the results of a loftier intelligence and a learning greater than our own. We know already that the whole of the living world is full of microbes of varying powers and of methods of working quite antagonistic. We do not know yet whether they can lie latent until quickened by some ray of light as yet unidentified as a separate and peculiar force. As yet we know nothing of what goes to create or evoke the active spark of life. We have no knowledge of the methods of conception; of the laws which govern molecular or foetal growth, of the final influences which attend birth. Year by year, day by day, hour by hour, we are learning; but the end is far, far off. It seems to me that we are now in that stage of intellectual progress in which the rough machinery for making discovery is being invented. Later on, we shall have enough of first principles to help us in the development of equipment for the true study of the inwardness of things. Then we may perhaps arrive at the perfection of means to an end which the scholars of Old Nile achieved at a time when Methuselah was beginning to brag about the number of his years, perhaps even when the great grandchildren of Adam were coming to regard the old man as what our Transatlantic friends call a 'back number.' Is it possible, for instance, that the people who invented Astronomy did not finally use instruments of extraordinary precision; that applied optics was not a cult of some of the specialists in the Colleges of the Theban priesthood. The Egyptians were essentially specialists. It is true that, in so far as we can judge, the range of their study was limited to subjects connected with their aims of government on earth by controlling all that bore on the life to follow it. But can anyone imagine that by the eyes of men, unaided by lenses of wondrous excellence, Astronomy was brought to such a pitch that the true orientation of temples and pyramids and tombs followed for four thousand years the wanderings of the planetary systems in space. If an instance of their knowledge of microscopy is wanted let me hazard a conjecture. How was it that in their hieroglyphic writing they took as the symbol or determinative of 'flesh' the very form which the science of to-day, relying on the revelations of a microscope of a thousand powers, gives to protoplasm—that unit of living organism which has been differentiated as Flagellula. If they could make analysis like this, why may they not have gone further? In that wonderful atmosphere of theirs, where sunlight fierce and clear is perpetually co-existent with day, where the dryness of earth and air gives perfect refraction, why may they not have learned secrets of light hidden from us in the density of our northern mists? May it not have been possible that they learned to store light, just as we have learned to store electricity. Nay more, is it not even possible that they did so. They must have had some form of artificial light which they used in the construction and adornment of those vast caverns hewn in the solid rock which became whole ceme-teries of the dead. Why, some of these caverns, with their labyrinthine windings and endless passages and chambers, all sculptured and graven and painted with an elaboration of detail which absolutely bewilders one, must have taken years and years to complete. And yet in them is no mark of smoke, such as lamps or torches would have left behind them. Again, if they knew how to store light, is it not possible that they had learned to understand and separate its component elements? And if these men of old arrived at such a point, may not we too in the fullness of time? We shall see! We shall see!

"There is another matter, too, on which recent discoveries in science throw a light. It is only a glimmer at present; a glimmer sufficient to illuminate probabilities, rather than actualities, or even possibilities. The discoveries of the Curies and Laborde, of Sir William Crooks and Becquerel, may have far-reaching results on Egyptian investigation. This new metal, radium—or rather this old metal of which our know-ledge is new—may have been known to the ancients. Indeed it may have been used thousands of years ago in greater degree than seems possible to-day. As yet Egypt has not been named as a place where the discovery of pitchblende, in which only as far as is known yet radium is contained, may be made. And yet it is more than probable that radium exists in Egypt. That country has perhaps the greatest masses of granite to be found in the world; and pitchblende is found as a vein in granitic rocks. In no place, at no time, has granite ever been quarried in such proportions as in Egypt during the earlier dynasties. Who may say what great veins of pitchblende may not have been found in the gigantic operations of hewing out columns for the temples, or great stones for the pyramids. Why, veins of pitchblende, of a richness unknown in our recent mines in Cornwall, or Bohemia, or Saxony, or Hungary, or Turkey, or Colorado, may have been found by these old quarrymen of Aswan, or Turra, or Mokattam, or Elephantine.

"Beyond this again, it is possible that here and there amongst these vast granite quarries may have been found not merely veins but masses or pockets of pitchblende. In such case the power at the disposal of those who knew how to use it must have been wonderful. The learning of Egypt was kept amongst its priests, and in their vast colleges must have been men of great learning; men who knew well how to exercise to the best advantage, and in the direction they wished, the terrific forces at their command. And if pitchblende did and does exist in Egypt, do you not think that much of it must have been freed by the gradual attrition and wearing down of the granitic rocks? Time and weather bring in time all rocks to dust; the very sands of the desert, which in centuries have buried in this very land some of the greatest monuments of man's achievement, are the evidences of the fact. If, then, radium is divisible into such minute particles as the scientists tell us, it too must have been freed in time from its granite prison and left to work in the air. One might almost hazard a suggestion that the taking the scarab as the symbol of life may not have been without an empiric basis. Might it not be possible that Coprophagi have power or instinct to seize upon the minute particles of heat-giving, light-giving—perhaps life-giving—radium, and enclosing them with their ova in those globes of matter which they roll so assiduously, and from which they take their early name, Pilulariae. In the billions of tons of the desert waste there is surely mingled some proportion of each of the earths and rocks and metals of their zone; and, each to each, nature forms her living entities to flourish on those without life.

"Travellers tell us that glass left in tropic deserts changes colour, and darkens in the fierce sunlight, just as it does under the influence of the rays of radium. Does not this imply some sort of similarity between the two forces yet to be identified!"

These scientific, or quasi-scientific discussions soothed me. They took my mind from brooding on the mysteries of the occult, by attracting it to the wonders of nature.

CHAPTER XVII

THE CAVERN

IN THE EVENING Mr. Trelawny took again the whole party into the study. When we were all at attention he began to unfold his plans:

"I have come to the conclusion that for the proper carrying out of what we will call our Great Experiment we must have absolute and complete isolation. Isolation not merely for a day or two, but for as long as we may require. Here such a thing would be impossible; the needs and habits of a great city with its ingrained possibilities of interruption, would, or might, quite upset us. Telegrams, registered letters, or express messengers would alone be sufficient; but the great army of those who want to get something would make disaster certain. In addition, the occurrences of the last week have drawn police attention to this house. Even if special instructions to keep an eye on it have not been issued from Scotland Yard or the District Station, you may be sure that the individual policeman on his rounds will keep it well under observation. Besides, the servants who have discharged themselves will before long begin to talk. They must; for they have, for the sake of their own characters, to give some reason for the termination of a service which has I should say a position in the neighbourhood. The servants of the neighbours will begin to talk, and, perhaps the neighbours themselves. Then the active and intelligent Press will, with its usual zeal for the enlightenment of the public and its eye to increase of circulation, get hold of the matter. When the reporter is after us we shall not have much chance of privacy. Even if we were to bar ourselves in, we should not be free from interruption, possibly from intrusion. Either would ruin our plans, and so we must take measures to effect a retreat, carrying all our impedimenta with us. For this I am prepared. For a long time past I have foreseen such a possibility, and have made preparation for it. Of course, I had no foreknowledge of what has happened; but I knew something would, or might, happen. For more than two years past my house in Cornwall has been made ready to receive all the curios which are preserved here. When Corbeck went off on his search for the lamps I had the old house at Kyllion made ready; it is fitted with electric light all over, and all the appliances for manufacture of the light are complete. I had perhaps better tell you, for none of you, not even Margaret, knows anything of it, that the house is absolutely shut out from public access or even from view. It stands on a little rocky promontory behind a steep hill, and except from the sea cannot be seen. Of old it was fenced in by a high stone wall, for the house which it succeeded was built by an ancestor of mine in the days when a great house far away from a centre had to be prepared to defend itself. Here, then, is a place so well adapted to our needs that it might have been prepared on purpose. I shall explain it to you when we are all there. This will not be long, for already our movement is in train. I have sent word to Marvin to have all preparation for our transport ready. He is to have a special train, which is to run at night so as to avoid notice. Also a number of carts and stone-wagons, with sufficient men and appliances to take all our packing-cases to Paddington. We shall be away before the Argus-eyed Pressman is on the watch. We shall today begin our packing up; and I dare say that by tomorrow night we shall be ready. In the outhouses I have all the packing-cases which were used for bringing the things from Egypt, and I am satisfied that as they were sufficient for the journey across the desert and down the Nile to Alexandria and thence on to London, they will serve without fail between here and Kyllion. We four men, with Margaret to hand us such things as we may require, will be able to get the things packed safely; and the carrier's men will take them to the trucks.

"Today the servants go to Kyllion, and Mrs. Grant will make such arrangements as may be required. She will take a stock of necessaries with her, so that we will not attract local attention by our daily needs; and will keep us supplied with perishable food from London. Thanks to Margaret's wise and generous treatment of the servants who decided to remain, we have got a staff on which we can depend. They have been already cautioned to secrecy, so that we need not fear gossip from within. Indeed, as the servants will be in London after their preparations at Kyllion are complete, there will not be much subject for gossip, in detail at any rate.

"As, however, we should commence the immediate work of packing at once, we will leave over the after proceedings till later when we have leisure."

Accordingly we set about our work. Under Mr. Trelawny's guidance, and aided by the servants, we took from the outhouses great packing-cases. Some of these were of enormous strength, fortified by many thicknesses of wood, and by iron bands and rods with screw-ends and nuts. We placed them throughout the house, each close to the object which it was to contain. When this preliminary work had been effected, and there had been placed in each room and in the hall great masses of new hay, cotton-waste and paper, the servants were sent away. Then we set about packing.

No one, not accustomed to packing, could have the slightest idea of the amount of work involved in such a task as that in which in we were engaged. For my own part I had had a vague idea that there were a large number of Egyptian objects in Mr. Trelawny's house; but until I came to deal with them seriatim I had little idea of either their importance, the size of some of them, or of their endless number. Far into the night we worked. At times we used all the strength which we could muster on a single object; again we worked separately, but always under Mr. Trelawny's immediate direction. He himself, assisted by Margaret, kept an exact tall of each piece.

It was only when we sat down, utterly wearied, to a long-delayed supper that we began to realise that a large part of the work was done. Only a few of the packing-cases, however, were closed; for a vast amount of work still remained. We had finished some of the cases, each of which held only one of the great sarcophagi. The cases which held many objects could not be closed till all had been differentiated and packed.

I slept that night without movement or without dreams; and on our comparing notes in the morning, I found that each of the others had had the same experience.

By dinner-time next evening the whole work was complete, and all was ready for the carriers who were to come at midnight. A little before the appointed time we heard the rumble of carts; then we were shortly invaded by an army of workmen, who seemed by sheer force of numbers to move without effort, in an endless procession, all our prepared packages. A little over an hour sufficed them, and when the carts had rumbled away, we all got ready to follow them to Paddington. Silvio was of course to be taken as one of our party.

Before leaving we went in a body over the house, which looked desolate indeed. As the servants had all gone to Cornwall there had been no attempt at tidying-up; every room and passage in which we had worked, and all the stairways, were strewn with paper and waste, and marked with dirty feet.

The last thing which Mr. Trelawny did before coming away was to take from the great safe the Ruby with the Seven Stars. As he put it safely into his pocket-book, Margaret, who had all at once seemed to grow deadly tired and stood beside her father pale and rigid, suddenly became all aglow, as though the sight of the Jewel had inspired her. She smiled at her father approvingly as she said:

"You are right, Father. There will not be any more trouble tonight. She will not wreck your arrangements for any cause. I would stake my life upon it."

"She—or something—wrecked us in the desert when we had come from the tomb in the Valley of the Sorcerer!" was the grim comment of Corbeck, who was standing by. Margaret answered him like a flash:

"Ah! she was then near her tomb from which for thousands of years her body had not been moved. She must know that things are different now."

"How must she know?" asked Corbeck keenly.

"If she has that astral body that Father spoke of, surely she must know! How can she fail to, with an invisible presence and an intellect that can roam abroad even to the stars and the worlds beyond us!" She paused, and her father said solemnly:

"It is on that supposition that we are proceeding. We must have the courage of our convictions, and act on them—to the last!"

Margaret took his hand and held it in a dreamy kind of way as we filed out of the house. She was holding it still when he locked the hall door, and when we moved up the road to the gateway, whence we took a cab to Paddington.

When all the goods were loaded at the station, the whole of the workmen went on to the train; this took also some of the stone-wagons used for carrying the cases with the great sarcophagi. Ordinary carts and plenty of horses were to be found at Westerton, which was our station for Kyllion. Mr. Trelawny had ordered a sleeping-carriage for our party; as soon as the train had started we all turned into our cubicles.

That night I slept sound. There was over me a conviction of security which was absolute and supreme. Margaret's definite announcement: "There will not be any trouble tonight!" seemed to carry assurance with it. I did not question it; nor did anyone else. It was only afterwards that I began to think as to how she was so sure. The train was a slow one, stopping many times and for considerable intervals. As Mr. Trelawny did not wish to arrive at Westerton before dark, there was no need to hurry; and arrangements had been made to feed the workmen at certain places on the journey. We had our own hamper with us in the private car.

All that afternoon we talked over the Great Experiment, which seemed to have become a definite entity in our thoughts. Mr. Trelawny became more and more enthusiastic as the time wore on; hope was with him becoming certainty. Doctor Winchester seemed to become imbued with some of his spirit, though at times he would throw out some scientific fact which would either make an impasse to the other's line of argument, or would come as an arresting shock. Mr. Corbeck, on the other hand, seemed slightly antagonistic to the theory. It may have been that whilst the opinions of the others advanced, his own stood still; but the effect was an attitude which appeared negative, if not wholly one of negation.

As for Margaret, she seemed to be in some way overcome. Either it was some new phase of feeling with her, or else she was taking the issue more seriously than she had yet done. She was generally more or less distraite, as though sunk in a brown study; from this she would recover herself with a start. This was usually when there occurred some marked episode in the journey, such as stopping at a station, or when the thunderous rumble of crossing a viaduct woke the echoes of the hills or cliffs around us. On each such occasion she would plunge into the conversation, taking such a part in it as to show that, whatever had been her abstracted thought, her senses had taken in fully all that had gone on around her. Towards myself her manner was strange. Sometimes it was marked by a distance, half shy, half haughty, which was new to me. At other times there were moments of passion in look and gesture which almost made me dizzy with delight. Little, however, of a marked nature transpired during the journey. There was but one episode which had in it any element of alarm, but as we were all asleep at the time it did not disturb us. We only learned it from a communicative guard in the morning. Whilst running between Dawlish and Teignmouth the train was stopped by a warning given by someone who moved a torch to and fro right on the very track. The driver had found on pulling up that just ahead of the train a small landslip had taken place, some of the red earth from the high bank having fallen away. It did not however reach to the metals; and the driver had resumed his way, none too well pleased at the delay. To use his own words, the guard thought "there was too much bally caution on this 'ere line!'"

We arrived at Westerton about nine o'clock in the evening. Carts and horses were in waiting, and the work of unloading the train began at once. Our own party did not wait to see the work done, as it was in the hands of competent people. We took the carriage which was in waiting, and through the darkness of the night sped on to Kyllion.

We were all impressed by the house as it appeared in the bright moonlight. A great grey stone mansion of the Jacobean period; vast and spacious, standing high over the sea on the very verge of a high cliff. When we had swept round the curve of the avenue cut through the rock, and come out on the high plateau on which the house stood, the crash and murmur of waves breaking against rock far below us came with an invigorating breath of moist sea air. We understood then in an instant how well we were shut out from the world on that rocky shelf above the sea.

Within the house we found all ready. Mrs. Grant and her staff had worked well, and all was bright and fresh and clean. We took a brief survey of the chief rooms and then separated to have a wash and to change our clothes after our long journey of more than four-and-twenty hours.

We had supper in the great dining-room on the south side, the walls of which actually hung over the sea. The murmur came up muffled, but it never ceased. As the little promontory stood well out into the sea, the northern side of the house was open; and the due north was in no way shut out by the great mass of rock, which, reared high above us, shut out the rest of the world. Far off across the bay we could see the trembling lights of the castle, and here and there along the shore the faint light of a fisher's window. For the rest the sea was a dark blue plain with an occasional flicker of light as the gleam of starlight fell on the slope of a swelling wave.

When supper was over we all adjourned to the room which Mr. Trelawny had set aside as his study, his bedroom being close to it. As we entered, the first thing I noticed was a great safe, somewhat similar to that which stood in his room in London. When we were in the room Mr. Trelawny went over to the table, and, taking out his pocket-book, laid it on the table. As he did so he pressed down on it with the palm of his hand. A strange pallor came over his face. With fingers that trembled he opened the book, saying as he did so:

"Its bulk does not seem the same; I hope nothing has happened!"

All three of us men crowded round close. Margaret alone remained calm; she stood erect and silent, and still as a statue. She had a far-away look in her eyes, as though she did not either know or care what was going on around her.

With a despairing gesture Trelawny threw open the pouch of the pocket-book wherein he had placed the Jewel of Seven Stars. As he sank down on the chair which stood close to him, he said in a hoarse voice:

"My God! it is gone. Without it the Great Experiment can come to nothing!"

His words seemed to wake Margaret from her introspective mood. An agonised spasm swept her face; but almost on the instant she was calm. She almost smiled as she said:

"You may have left it in your room, Father. Perhaps it has fallen out of the pocket-book whilst you were changing." Without a word we all hurried into the next room through the open door between the study and the bedroom. And then a sudden calm fell on us like a cloud of fear.

There! on the table, lay the Jewel of Seven Stars, shining and spark-
ling with lurid light, as though each of the seven points of each the
seven stars gleamed through blood!

Timidly we each looked behind us, and then at each other. Margaret was now like the rest of us. She had lost her statuesque calm. All
the introspective rigidity had gone from her; and she clasped her hands
together till the knuckles were white.

Without a word Mr. Trelawny raised the Jewel, and hurried with it
into the next room. As quietly as he could he opened the door of the safe
with the key fastened to his wrist and placed the Jewel within. When the
heavy doors were closed and locked he seemed to breathe more freely.

Somehow this episode, though a disturbing one in many ways,
seemed to bring us back to our old selves. Since we had left London we
had all been overstrained; and this was a sort of relief. Another step in
our strange enterprise had been effected.

The change back was more marked in Margaret than in any of us.
Perhaps it was that she was a woman, whilst we were men; perhaps it was
that she was younger than the rest; perhaps both reasons were effective,
each in its own way. At any rate the change was there, and I was happier
than I had been through the long journey. All her buoyancy, her tenderness, her deep feeling seemed to shine forth once more; now and again
as her father's eyes rested on her, his face seemed to light up.

Whilst we waited for the carts to arrive, Mr. Trelawny took us
through the house, pointing out and explaining where the objects
which we had brought with us were to be placed. In one respect only
did he withhold confidence. The positions of all those things which had
connection with the Great Experiment were not indicated. The cases
containing them were to be left in the outer hall, for the present.

By the time we had made the survey, the carts began to arrive; and
the stir and bustle of the previous night were renewed. Mr. Trelawny
stood in the hall beside the massive ironbound door, and gave directions

as to the placing of each of the great packing-cases. Those containing
many items were placed in the inner hall where they were to be unpacked.

In an incredibly short time the whole consignment was delivered;
and the men departed with a douceur for each, given through their
foreman, which made them effusive in their thanks. Then we all went
to our own rooms. There was a strange confidence over us all. I do not
think that any one of us had a doubt as the the quiet passing of the
remainder of the night.

The faith was justified, for on our re-assembling in the morning we
found that all had slept well and peaceably.

During that day all the curios, except those required for the Great
Experiment, were put into the places designed for them. Then it was
arranged that all the servants should go back with Mrs. Grant to
London on the next morning.

When they had all gone Mr. Trelawny, having seen the doors locked,
took us into the study.

"Now," said he when we were seated, "I have a secret to impart;
but, according to an old promise which does not leave me free, I must
ask you each to give me a solemn promise not to reveal it. For three
hundred years at least such a promise has been exacted from everyone
to whom it was told, and more than once life and safety were secured
through loyal observance of the promise. Even as it is, I am breaking
the letter, if not the spirit of the tradition; for I should only tell it to the
immediate members of my family."

We all gave the promise required. Then he went on:

"There is a secret place in this house, a cave, natural originally but
finished by labour, underneath this house. I will not undertake to say
that it has always been used according to the law. During the Bloody
Assize more than a few Cornishmen found refuge in it; and later, and
earlier, it formed, I have no doubt whatever, a useful place for storing
contraband goods. 'Tre Pol and Pen', I suppose you know, have always

been smugglers; and their relations and friends and neighbours have not held back from the enterprise. For all such reasons a safe hiding-place was always considered a valuable possession; and as the heads of our House have always insisted on preserving the secret, I am in honour bound to it. Later on, if all be well, I shall of course tell you, Margaret, and you too, Ross, under the conditions that I am bound to make."

He rose up, and we all followed him. Leaving us in the outer hall, he went away alone for a few minutes; and returning, beckoned us to follow him.

In the inside hall we found a whole section of an outstanding angle moved away, and from the cavity saw a great hole dimly dark, and the beginning of a rough staircase cut in the rock. As it was not pitch dark there was manifestly some means of lighting it naturally, so without pause we followed our host as he descended. After some forty or fifty steps cut in a winding passage, we came to a great cave whose further end tapered away into blackness. It was a huge place, dimly lit by a few irregular slits of eccentric shape. Manifestly these were faults in the rock which would readily allow the windows be disguised. Close to each of them was a hanging shutter which could be easily swung across by means of a dangling rope. The sound of the ceaseless beat of the waves came up muffled from far below. Mr. Trelawny at once began to speak:

"This is the spot which I have chosen, as the best I know, for the scene of our Great Experiment. In a hundred different ways it fulfils the conditions which I am led to believe are primary with regard to success. Here, we are, and shall be, as isolated as Queen Tera herself would have been in her rocky tomb in the Valley of the Sorcerer, and still in a rocky cavern. For good or ill we must here stand by our chances, and abide by results. If we are successful we shall be able to let in on the world of modern science such a flood of light from the Old World as will change every condition of thought and experiment and practice. If we fail, then even the knowledge of our attempt will die with us. For this, and all else which may come, I believe we are prepared!" He paused. No one spoke, but we all bowed our heads gravely in acquiescence. He resumed, but with a certain hesitancy:

"It is not yet too late! If any of you have a doubt or misgiving, for God's sake speak it now! Whoever it may be, can go hence without let or hindrance. The rest of us can go on our way alone!"

Again he paused, and looked keenly at us in turn. We looked at each other; but no one quailed. For my own part, if I had had any doubt as to going on, the look on Margaret's face would have reassured me. It was fearless; it was intense; it was full of a divine calm.

Mr. Trelawny took a long breath, and in a more cheerful, as well as in a more decided tone, went on:

"As we are all of one mind, the sooner we get the necessary matters in train the better. Let me tell you that this place, like all the rest of the house, can be lit with electricity. We could not join the wires to the mains lest our secret should become known, but I have a cable here which we can attach in the hall and complete the circuit!" As he was speaking, he began to ascend the steps. From close to the entrance he took the end of a cable; this he drew forward and attached to a switch in the wall. Then, turning on a tap, he flooded the whole vault and staircase below with light. I could now see from the volume of light streaming up into the hallway that the hole beside the staircase went direct into the cave. Above it was a pulley and a mass of strong tackle with multiplying blocks of the Smeaton order. Mr. Trelawny, seeing me looking at this, said, correctly interpreting my thoughts:

"Yes! it is new. I hung it there myself on purpose. I knew we should have to lower great weights; and as I did not wish to take too many into my confidence, I arranged a tackle which I could work alone if necessary."

We set to work at once; and before nightfall had lowered, unhooked, and placed in the positions designated for each by Trelawny, all the great sarcophagi and all the curios and other matters which we had taken with us.

It was a strange and weird proceeding, the placing of those wonderful monuments of a bygone age in that green cavern, which represented in its cutting and purpose and up-to-date mechanism and electric lights both the old world and the new. But as time went on I grew more and more to recognise the wisdom and correctness of Mr. Trelawny's choice. I was much disturbed when Silvio, who had been brought into the cave in the arms of his mistress, and who was lying asleep on my coat which I had taken off, sprang up when the cat mummy had been unpacked, and flew at it with the same ferocity which he had previously exhibited. The incident showed Margaret in a new phase, and one which gave my heart a pang. She had been standing quite still at one side of the cave leaning on a sarcophagus, in one of those fits of abstraction which had of late come upon her; but on hearing the sound, and seeing Silvio's violent onslaught, she seemed to fall into a positive fury of passion. Her eyes blazed, and her mouth took a hard, cruel tension which was new to me. Instinctively she stepped towards Silvio as if to interfere in the attack. But I too had stepped forward; and as she caught my eye a strange spasm came upon her, and she stopped. Its intensity made me hold my breath; and I put up my hand to clear my eyes. When I had done this, she had on the instant recovered her calm, and there was a look of brief wonder on her face. With all her old grace and sweetness she swept over and lifted Silvio, just as she had done on former occasions, and held him in her arms, petting him and treating him as though he were a little child who had erred.

As I looked a strange fear came over me. The Margaret that I knew seemed to be changing; and in my inmost heart I prayed that the disturbing cause might soon come to an end. More than ever I longed at that moment that our terrible Experiment should come to a prosperous termination.

When all had been arranged in the room as Mr. Trelawny wished he turned to us, one after another, till he had concentrated the intelligence of us all upon him. Then he said:

"All is now ready in this place. We must only await the proper time to begin."

We were silent for a while. Doctor Winchester was the first to speak:

"What is the proper time? Have you any approximation, even if you are not satisfied as to the exact day?" He answered at once:

"After the most anxious thought I have fixed on July 31!"

"May I ask why that date?" He spoke his answer slowly:

"Queen Tera was ruled in great degree by mysticism, and there are so many evidences that she looked for resurrection that naturally she would choose a period ruled over by a God specialised to such a purpose. Now, the fourth month of the season of Inundation was ruled by Harmachis, this being the name for 'Ra', the Sun-God, at his rising in the morning, and therefore typifying the awakening or arising. This arising is manifestly to physical life, since it is of the mid-world of human daily life. Now as this month begins on our 25th July, the seventh day would be July 31st, for you may be sure that the mystic Queen would not have chosen any day but the seventh or some power of seven.

"I dare say that some of you have wondered why our preparations have been so deliberately undertaken. This is why! We must be ready in every possible way when the time comes; but there was no use in having to wait round for a needless number of days."

And so we waited only for the 31st of July, the next day but one, when the Great Experiment would be made.

CHAPTER XVIII

DOUBTS AND FEARS

WE LEARN OF great things by little experiences. The history of ages is but an indefinite repetition of the history of hours. The record of a soul is but a multiple of the story of a moment. The Recording Angel writes in the Great Book in no rainbow tints; his pen is dipped in no colours but light and darkness. For the eye of infinite wisdom there is no need of shading. All things, all thoughts, all emotions, all experiences, all doubts and hopes and fears, all intentions, all wishes seen down to the lower strata of their concrete and multitudinous elements, are finally resolved into direct opposites.

Did any human being wish for the epitome of a life wherein were gathered and grouped all the experiences that a child of Adam could have, the history, fully and frankly written, of my own mind during the next forty-eight hours would afford him all that could be wanted. And the Recorder could have wrought as usual in sunlight and shadow, which may be taken to represent the final expressions of Heaven and Hell. For in the highest Heaven is Faith; and Doubt hangs over the yawning blackness of Hell.

There were of course times of sunshine in those two days; moments when, in the realisation of Margaret's sweetness and her love for me, all doubts were dissipated like morning mist before the sun. But the balance of the time—and an overwhelming balance it was—gloom hung over me like a pall. The hour, in whose coming I had acquiesced, was approaching so quickly and was already so near that the sense of

finality was bearing upon me! The issue was perhaps life or death to any
of us; but for this we were all prepared. Margaret and I were one as to
the risk. The question of the moral aspect of the case, which involved
the religious belief in which I had been reared, was not one to trouble
me; for the issues, and the causes that lay behind them, were not within
my power even to comprehend. The doubt of the success of the Great
Experiment was such a doubt as exists in all enterprises which have
great possibilities. To me, whose life was passed in a series of intellectual struggles, this form of doubt was a stimulus, rather than deterrent.
What then was it that made for me a trouble, which became an anguish
when my thoughts dwelt long on it?

I was beginning to doubt Margaret!

What it was that I doubted I knew not. It was not her love, or her
honour, or her truth, or her kindness, or her zeal. What then was it?

It was herself!

Margaret was changing! At times during the past few days I had
hardly known her as the same girl whom I had met at the picnic, and
whose vigils I had shared in the sick-room of her father. Then, even in
her moments of greatest sorrow or fright or anxiety, she was all life and
thought and keenness. Now she was generally distraite, and at times
in a sort of negative condition as though her mind—her very being—
was not present. At such moments she would have full possession of
observation and memory. She would know and remember all that was
going on, and had gone on around her; but her coming back to her old
self had to me something the sensation of a new person coming into the
room. Up to the time of leaving London I had been content whenever
she was present. I had over me that delicious sense of security which
comes with the consciousness that love is mutual. But now doubt had
taken its place. I never knew whether the personality present was my
Margaret—the old Margaret whom I had loved at the first glance—
or the other new Margaret, whom I hardly understood, and whose

intellectual aloofness made an impalpable barrier between us. Sometimes she would become, as it were, awake all at once. At such times,
though she would say to me sweet and pleasant things which she had
often said before, she would seem most unlike herself. It was almost as
if she was speaking parrot-like or at dictation of one who could read
words or acts, but not thoughts. After one or two experiences of this
kind, my own doubting began to make a barrier; for I could not speak
with the ease and freedom which were usual to me. And so hour by
hour we drifted apart. Were it not for the few odd moments when the
old Margaret was back with me full of her charm I do not know what
would have happened. As it was, each such moment gave me a fresh
start and kept my love from changing.

I would have given the world for a confidant; but this was
impossible. How could I speak a doubt of Margaret to anyone, even
her father! How could I speak a doubt to Margaret, when Margaret
herself was the theme! I could only endure—and hope. And of the two
the endurance was the lesser pain.

I think that Margaret must have at times felt that there was some
cloud between us, for towards the end of the first day she began to shun
me a little; or perhaps it was that she had become more diffident than
usual about me. Hitherto she had sought every opportunity of being
with me, just as I had tried to be with her; so that now any avoidance,
one of the other, made a new pain to us both.

On this day the household seemed very still. Each one of us was
about his own work, or occupied with his own thoughts. We only met
at meal times; and then, though we talked, all seemed more or less
preoccupied. There was not in the house even the stir of the routine of
service. The precaution of Mr. Trelawny in having three rooms prepared
for each of us had rendered servants unnecessary. The dining-room
was solidly prepared with cooked provisions for several days. Towards
evening I went out by myself for a stroll. I had looked for Margaret to

ask her to come with me; but when I found her, she was in one of her apathetic moods, and the charm of her presence seemed lost to me. Angry with myself, but unable to quell my own spirit of discontent, I went out alone over the rocky headland.

On the cliff, with the wide expanse of wonderful sea before me, and no sound but the dash of waves below and the harsh screams of the seagulls above, my thoughts ran free. Do what I would, they returned continuously to one subject, the solving of the doubt that was upon me. Here in the solitude, amid the wide circle of Nature's force and strife, my mind began to work truly. Unconsciously I found myself asking a question which I would not allow myself to answer. At last the persistence of a mind working truly prevailed; I found myself face to face with my doubt. The habit of my life began to assert itself, and I analysed the evidence before me.

It was so startling that I had to force myself into obedience to logical effort. My starting-place was this: Margaret was changed—in what way, and by what means? Was it her character, or her mind, or her nature? for her physical appearance remained the same. I began to group all that I had ever heard of her, beginning at her birth.

It was strange at the very first. She had been, according to Corbeck's statement, born of a dead mother during the time that her father and his friend were in a trance in the tomb at Aswan. That trance was presumably effected by a woman; a woman mummied, yet preserving as we had every reason to believe from after experience, an astral body subject to a free will and an active intelligence. With that astral body, space ceased to exist. The vast distance between London and Aswan became as naught; and whatever power of necromancy the Sorceress had might have been exercised over the dead mother, and possibly the dead child.

The dead child! Was it possible that the child was dead and was made alive again? Whence then came the animating spirit—the soul? Logic was pointing the way to me now with a vengeance!

If the Egyptian belief was true for Egyptians, then the "Ka" of the dead Queen and her "Khu" could animate what she might choose. In such case Margaret would not be an individual at all, but simply a phase of Queen Tera herself; an astral body obedient to her will!

Here I revolted against logic. Every fibre of my being resented such a conclusion. How could I believe that there was no Margaret at all; but just an animated image, used by the Double of a woman of forty centuries ago to its own ends . . . ! Somehow, the outlook was brighter to me now, despite the new doubts.

At least I had Margaret!

Back swung the logical pendulum again. The child then was not dead. If so, had the Sorceress had anything to do with her birth at all? It was evident—so I took it again from Corbeck—that there was a strange likeness between Margaret and the pictures of Queen Tera. How could this be? It could not be any birth-mark reproducing what had been in the mother's mind; for Mrs. Trelawny had never seen the pictures. Nay, even her father had not seen them till he had found his way into the tomb only a few days before her birth. This phase I could not get rid of so easily as the last; the fibres of my being remained quiet. There remained to me the horror of doubt. And even then, so strange is the mind of man, Doubt itself took a concrete image; a vast and impenetrable gloom, through which flickered irregularly and spasmodically tiny points of evanescent light, which seemed to quicken the darkness into a positive existence.

The remaining possibility of relations between Margaret and the mummied Queen was, that in some occult way the Sorceress had power to change places with the other. This view of things could not be so lightly thrown aside. There were too many suspicious circumstances to warrant this, now that my attention was fixed on it and my intelligence recognised the possibility. Hereupon there began to come into my mind all the strange incomprehensible matters which had whirled through our lives in the last few days. At first they all crowded in upon me in a jumbled mass; but again the habit of mind of my working life prevailed, and they took order. I found it now easier to control myself; for there was something to grasp, some work to be done; though it was of a sorry kind, for it was or might be antagonistic to Margaret. But Margaret was herself at stake! I was thinking of her and fighting for her; and yet if I were to work in the dark, I might be even harmful to her. My first weapon in her defence was truth. I must know and understand; I might then be able to act. Certainly, I could not act beneficently without a just conception and recognition of the facts. Arranged in order these were as follows:

Firstly: the strange likeness of Queen Tera to Margaret who had been born in another country a thousand miles away, where her mother could not possibly have had even a passing knowledge of her appearance.

Secondly: the disappearance of Van Huyn's book when I had read up to the description of the Star Ruby.

Thirdly: the finding of the lamps in the boudoir. Tera with her astral body could have unlocked the door of Corbeck's room in the hotel, and have locked it again after her exit with the lamps. She could in the same way have opened the window, and put the lamps in the boudoir. It need not have been that Margaret in her own person should have had any hand in this; but—but it was at least strange.

Fourthly: here the suspicions of the Detective and the Doctor came back to me with renewed force, and with a larger understanding.

Fifthly: there were the occasions on which Margaret foretold with accuracy the coming occasions of quietude, as though she had some conviction or knowledge of the intentions of the astral-bodied Queen.

Sixthly: there was her suggestion of the finding of the Ruby which her father had lost. As I thought now afresh over this episode in the light of suspicion in which her own powers were involved, the only conclusion I could come to was—always supposing that the theory of the Queen's astral power was correct—that Queen Tera being anxious that all should go well in the movement from London to Kyllion had in her own way taken the Jewel from Mr. Trelawny's pocket-book, finding it of some use in her supernatural guardianship of the journey. Then in some mysterious way she had, through Margaret, made the suggestion of its loss and finding.

Seventhly, and lastly, was the strange dual existence which Margaret seemed of late to be leading; and which in some way seemed a consequence or corollary of all that had gone before.

The dual existence! This was indeed the conclusion which overcame all difficulties and reconciled opposites. If indeed Margaret were not in all ways a free agent, but could be compelled to speak or act as she might be instructed; or if her whole being could be changed for another without the possibility of any one noticing the doing of it, then all things were possible. All would depend on the spirit of the individuality by which she could be so compelled. If this individuality were just and kind and clean, all might be well. But if not! . . . . The thought was too awful for words. I ground my teeth with futile rage, as the ideas of horrible possibilities swept through me.

Up to this morning Margaret's lapses into her new self had been few and hardly noticeable, save when once or twice her attitude towards myself had been marked by a bearing strange to me. But today the contrary was the case; and the change presaged badly. It might be that that other individuality was of the lower, not of the better sort! Now that I thought of it I had reason to fear. In the history of the mummy, from the time of Van Huyn's breaking into the tomb, the record of deaths that we knew of, presumably effected by her will and agency, was a startling one. The Arab who had stolen the hand from the mummy; and the one who had taken it from his body. The Arab chief who had tried to steal the Jewel from Van Huyn, and whose throat bore the marks of seven fingers. The two men found dead on the first night of

Trelawny's taking away the sarcophagus; and the three on the return to the tomb. The Arab who had opened the secret serdab. Nine dead men, one of them slain manifestly by the Queen's own hand! And beyond this again the several savage attacks on Mr. Trelawny in his own room, in which, aided by her Familiar, she had tried to open the safe and to extract the Talisman jewel. His device of fastening the key to his wrist by a steel bangle, though successful in the end, had wellnigh cost him his life.

If then the Queen, intent on her resurrection under her own conditions had, so to speak, waded to it through blood, what might she not do were her purpose thwarted? What terrible step might she not take to effect her wishes? Nay, what were her wishes; what was her ultimate purpose? As yet we had had only Margaret's statement of them, given in all the glorious enthusiasm of her lofty soul. In her record there was no expression of love to be sought or found. All we knew for certain was that she had set before her the object of resurrection, and that in it the North which she had manifestly loved was to have a special part. But that the resurrection was to be accomplished in the lonely tomb in the Valley of the Sorcerer was apparent. All preparations had been carefully made for accomplishment from within, and for her ultimate exit in her new and living form. The sarcophagus was unlidded. The oil jars, though hermetically sealed, were to be easily opened by hand; and in them provision was made for shrinkage through a vast period of time. Even flint and steel were provided for the production of flame. The Mummy Pit was left open in violation of usage; and beside the stone door on the cliff side was fixed an imperishable chain by which she might in safety descend to earth. But as to what her after intentions were we had no clue. If it was that she meant to begin life again as a humble individual, there was something so noble in the thought that it even warmed my heart to her and turned my wishes to her success.

The very idea seemed to endorse Margaret's magnificent tribute to her purpose, and helped to calm my troubled spirit.

Then and there, with this feeling strong upon me, I determined to warn Margaret and her father of dire possibilities; and to await, as well content as I could in my ignorance, the development of things over which I had no power.

I returned to the house in a different frame of mind to that in which I had left it; and was enchanted to find Margaret—the old Margaret— waiting for me.

After dinner, when I was alone for a time with the father and daughter, I opened the subject, though with considerable hesitation:

"Would it not be well to take every possible precaution, in case the Queen may not wish what we are doing, with regard to what may occur before the Experiment; and at or after her waking, if it comes off?" Margaret's answer came back quickly; so quickly that I was convinced she must have had it ready for some one:

"But she does approve! Surely it cannot be otherwise. Father is doing, with all his brains and all his energy and all his great courage, just exactly what the great Queen had arranged!"

"But," I answered, "that can hardly be. All that she arranged was in a tomb high up in a rock, in a desert solitude, shut away from the world by every conceivable means. She seems to have depended on this isolation to insure against accident. Surely, here in another country and age, with quite different conditions, she may in her anxiety make mistakes and treat any of you—of us—as she did those others in times gone past. Nine men that we know of have been slain by her own hand or by her instigation. She can be remorseless if she will." It did not strike me till afterwards when I was thinking over this conversation, how thoroughly I had accepted the living and conscious condition of Queen Tera as a fact. Before I spoke, I had feared I might offend Mr. Trelawny; but to my pleasant surprise he smiled quite genially as he answered me:

"My dear fellow, in a way you are quite right. The Queen did undoubtedly intend isolation; and, all told, it would be best that her experiment should be made as she arranged it. But just think, that became impossible when once the Dutch explorer had broken into her tomb. That was not my doing. I am innocent of it, though it was the cause of my setting out to rediscover the sepulchre. Mind, I do not say for a moment that I would not have done just the same as Van Huyn. I went into the tomb from curiosity; and I took away what I did, being fired with the zeal of acquisitiveness which animates the collector. But, remember also, that at this time I did not know of the Queen's intention of resurrection; I had no idea of the completeness of her preparations. All that came long afterwards. But when it did come, I have done all that I could to carry out her wishes to the full. My only fear is that I may have misinterpreted some of her cryptic instructions, or have omitted or overlooked something. But of this I am certain; I have left undone nothing that I can imagine right to be done; and I have done nothing that I know of to clash with Queen Tera's arrangement. I want her Great Experiment to succeed. To this end I have not spared labour or time or money—or myself. I have endured hardship, and braved danger. All my brains; all my knowledge and learning, such as they are; all my endeavours such as they can be, have been, are, and shall be devoted to this end, till we either win or lose the great stake that we play for."

"The great stake?" I repeated; "the resurrection of the woman, and the woman's life? The proof that resurrection can be accomplished; by magical powers; by scientific knowledge; or by use of some force which at present the world does not know?"

Then Mr. Trelawny spoke out the hopes of his heart which up to now he had indicated rather than expressed. Once or twice I had heard Corbeck speak of the fiery energy of his youth; but, save for the noble words of Margaret when she had spoken of Queen Tera's hope—which coming from his daughter made possible a belief that her power was in some sense due to heredity—I had seen no marked sign of it. But now his words, sweeping before them like a torrent all antagonistic thought, gave me a new idea of the man.

"'A woman's life!' What is a woman's life in the scale with what we hope for! Why, we are risking already a woman's life; the dearest life to me in all the world, and that grows more dear with every hour that passes. We are risking as well the lives of four men; yours and my own, as well as those two others who have been won to our confidence. 'The proof that resurrection can be accomplished!' That is much. A marvellous thing in this age of science, and the scepticism that knowledge makes. But life and resurrection are themselves but items in what may be won by the accomplishment of this Great Experiment. Imagine what it will be for the world of thought—the true world of human progress—the veritable road to the Stars, the itur ad astra of the Ancients—if there can come back to us out of the unknown past one who can yield to us the lore stored in the great Library of Alexandria, and lost in its consuming flames. Not only history can be set right, and the teachings of science made veritable from their beginnings; but we can be placed on the road to the knowledge of lost arts, lost learning, lost sciences, so that our feet may tread on the indicated path to their ultimate and complete restoration. Why, this woman can tell us what the world was like before what is called 'the Flood'; can give us the origin of that vast astounding myth; can set the mind back to the consideration of things which to us now seem primeval, but which were old stories before the days of the Patriarchs. But this is not the end! No, not even the beginning! If the story of this woman be all that we think—which some of us most firmly believe; if her powers and the restoration of them prove to be what we expect, why, then we may yet achieve a knowledge beyond what our age has ever known—beyond what is believed today possible for the children of men. If indeed this resurrection can be accomplished, how can we doubt the old knowledge, the old magic, the old belief! And if this be so, we must take it that the 'Ka' of this great and learned Queen has won secrets of more than mortal worth from her surroundings amongst the stars. This woman in her life voluntarily went down living to the grave, and came back again, as we learn from the records in her tomb; she chose to die her mortal death whilst young, so that at her resurrection in another age, beyond a trance of countless magnitude, she might emerge from her tomb in all the fulness and splendour of her youth and power. Already we have evidence that though her body slept in patience through those many centuries, her intelligence never passed away, that her resolution never flagged, that her will remained supreme; and, most important of all, that her memory was unimpaired. Oh, what possibilities are there in the coming of such a being into our midst! One whose history began before the concrete teaching of our Bible; whose experiences were antecedent to the formulation of the Gods of Greece; who can link together the Old and the New, Earth and Heaven, and yield to the known worlds of thought and physical existence the mystery of the Unknown—of the Old World in its youth, and of Worlds beyond our ken!"

He paused, almost overcome. Margaret had taken his hand when he spoke of her being so dear to him, and held it hard. As he spoke she continued to hold it. But there came over her face that change which I had so often seen of late; that mysterious veiling of her own personality which gave me the subtle sense of separation from her. In his impassioned vehemence her father did not notice; but when he stopped she seemed all at once to be herself again. In her glorious eyes came the added brightness of unshed tears; and with a gesture of passionate love and admiration, she stooped and kissed her father's hand. Then, turning to me, she too spoke:

"Malcolm, you have spoken of the deaths that came from the poor Queen; or rather that justly came from meddling with her arrangements and thwarting her purpose. Do you not think that, in putting it as you have done, you have been unjust? Who would not have done just as she did? Remember she was fighting for her life! Ay, and for more than her life! For life, and love, and all the glorious possibilities of that dim future in the unknown world of the North which had such enchanting hopes for her! Do you not think that she, with all the learning of her time, and with all the great and resistless force of her mighty nature, had hopes of spreading in a wider way the lofty aspirations of her soul! That she hoped to bring to the conquering of unknown worlds, and using to the advantage of her people, all that she had won from sleep and death and time; all of which might and could have been frustrated by the ruthless hand of an assassin or a thief. Were it you, in such case would you not struggle by all means to achieve the object of your life and hope; whose possibilities grew and grew in the passing of those endless years? Can you think that that active brain was at rest during all those weary centuries, whilst her free soul was flitting from world to world amongst the boundless regions of the stars? Had these stars in their myriad and varied life no lessons for her; as they have had for us since we followed the glorious path which she and her people marked for us, when they sent their winged imaginations circling amongst the lamps of the night!"

Here she paused. She too was overcome, and the welling tears ran down her cheeks. I was myself more moved than I can say. This was indeed my Margaret; and in the consciousness of her presence my heart leapt. Out of my happiness came boldness, and I dared to say now what I had feared would be impossible: something which would call the attention of Mr. Trelawny to what I imagined was the dual existence of his daughter. As I took Margaret's hand in mine and kissed it, I said to her father:

"Why, sir! she couldn't speak more eloquently if the very spirit of Queen Tera was with her to animate her and suggest thoughts!"

Mr. Trelawny's answer simply overwhelmed me with surprise. It manifested to me that he too had gone through just such a process of thought as my own.

"And what if it was; if it is! I know well that the spirit of her mother is within her. If in addition there be the spirit of that great and wondrous Queen, then she would be no less dear to me, but doubly dear! Do not have fear for her, Malcolm Ross; at least have no more fear than you may have for the rest of us!" Margaret took up the theme, speaking so quickly that her words seemed a continuation of her father's, rather than an interruption of them.

"Have no special fear for me, Malcolm. Queen Tera knows, and will offer us no harm. I know it! I know it, as surely as I am lost in the depth of my own love for you!"

There was something in her voice so strange to me that I looked quickly into her eyes. They were bright as ever, but veiled to my seeing the inward thought behind them as are the eyes of a caged lion.

Then the two other men came in, and the subject changed.

CHAPTER XIX

THE LESSON OF THE "KA"

THAT NIGHT WE all went to bed early. The next night would be an anxious one, and Mr. Trelawny thought that we should all be fortified with what sleep we could get. The day, too, would be full of work. Everything in connection with the Great Experiment would have to be gone over, so that at the last we might not fail from any unthought-of flaw in our working. We made, of course, arrangements for summoning aid in case such should be needed; but I do not think that any of us had any real apprehension of danger. Certainly we had no fear of such danger from violence as we had had to guard against in London during Mr. Trelawny's long trance.

For my own part I felt a strange sense of relief in the matter. I had accepted Mr. Trelawny's reasoning that if the Queen were indeed such as we surmised—such as indeed we now took for granted—there would not be any opposition on her part; for we were carrying out her own wishes to the very last. So far I was at ease—far more at ease than earlier in the day I should have thought possible; but there were other sources of trouble which I could not blot out from my mind. Chief amongst them was Margaret's strange condition. If it was indeed that she had in her own person a dual existence, what might happen when the two existences became one? Again, and again, and again I turned this matter over in my mind, till I could have shrieked out in nervous anxiety. It was no consolation to me to remember that Margaret was herself satisfied, and her father acquiescent. Love is, after all, a selfish thing; and it throws a black shadow on anything between which and the light it stands. I seemed to hear the hands go round the dial of the clock; I saw darkness turn to gloom, and gloom to grey, and grey to light without pause or hindrance to the succession of my miserable feelings. At last, when it was decently possible without the fear of disturbing others, I got up. I crept along the passage to find if all was well with the others; for we had arranged that the door of each of our rooms should be left slightly open so that any sound of disturbance would be easily and distinctly heard.

One and all slept; I could hear the regular breathing of each, and my heart rejoiced that this miserable night of anxiety was safely passed. As I knelt in my own room in a burst of thankful prayer, I knew in the depths of my own heart the measure of my fear. I found my way out of the house, and went down to the water by the long stairway cut in the rock. A swim in the cool bright sea braced my nerves and made me my old self again.

As I came back to the top of the steps I could see the bright sunlight, rising from behind me, turning the rocks across the bay to glittering gold. And yet I felt somehow disturbed. It was all too bright; as it sometimes is before the coming of a storm. As I paused to watch it, I felt a soft hand on my shoulder; and, turning, found Margaret close to me; Margaret as bright and radiant as the morning glory of the sun! It was my own Margaret this time! My old Margaret, without alloy of any other; and I felt that, at least, this last and fatal day was well begun.

But alas! the joy did not last. When we got back to the house from a stroll around the cliffs, the same old routine of yesterday was resumed: gloom and anxiety, hope, high spirits, deep depression, and apathetic aloofness.

But it was to be a day of work; and we all braced ourselves to it with an energy which wrought its own salvation.

After breakfast we all adjourned to the cave, where Mr. Trelawny went over, point by point, the position of each item of our paraphernalia.

He explained as he went on why each piece was so placed. He had with him the great rools of paper with the measured plans and the signs and drawings which he had had made from his own and Corbeck's rough notes. As he had told us, these contained the whole of the hieroglyphics on walls and ceilings and floor of the tomb in the Valley of the Sorcerer. Even had not the measurements, made to scale, recorded the position of each piece of furniture, we could have eventually placed them by a study of the cryptic writings and symbols.

Mr. Trelawny explained to us certain other things, not laid down on the chart. Such as, for instance, that the hollowed part of the table was exactly fitted to the bottom of the Magic Coffer, which was therefore intended to be placed on it. The respective legs of this table were indicated by differently shaped uraei outlined on the floor, the head of each being extended in the direction of the similar uraeus twined round the leg. Also that the mummy, when laid on the raised portion in the bottom of the sarcophagus, seemingly made to fit the form, would lie head to the West and feet to the East, thus receiving the natural earth currents. "If this be intended," he said, "as I presume it is, I gather that the force to be used has something to do with magnetism or electricity, or both. It may be, of course, that some other force, such, for instance, as that emanating from radium, is to be employed. I have experimented with the latter, but only in such small quantity as I could obtain; but so far as I can ascertain the stone of the Coffer is absolutely impervious to its influence. There must be some such unsusceptible substances in nature. Radium does not seemingly manifest itself when distributed through pitchblende; and there are doubtless other such substances in which it can be imprisoned. Possibly these may belong to that class of "inert" elements discovered or isolated by Sir William Ramsay. It is therefore possible that in this Coffer, made from an aerolite and therefore perhaps containing some element unknown in our world, may be imprisoned some mighty power which is to be released on its opening."

This appeared to be an end of this branch of the subject; but as he still kept the fixed look of one who is engaged in a theme we all waited in silence. After a pause he went on:

"There is one thing which has up to now, I confess, puzzled me. It may not be of prime importance; but in a matter like this, where all is unknown, we must take it that everything is important. I cannot think that in a matter worked out with such extraordinary scrupulosity such a thing should be overlooked. As you may see by the ground-plan of the tomb the sarcophagus stands near the north wall, with the Magic Coffer to the south of it. The space covered by the former is left quite bare of symbol or ornamentation of any kind. At the first glance this would seem to imply that the drawings had been made after the sarcophagus had been put into its place. But a more minute examination will show that the symbolisation on the floor is so arranged that a definite effect is produced. See, here the writings run in correct order as though they had jumped across the gap. It is only from certain effects that it becomes clear that there is a meaning of some kind. What that meaning may be is what we want to know. Look at the top and bottom of the vacant space, which lies West and East corresponding to the head and foot of the sarcophagus. In both are duplications of the same symbolisation, but so arranged that the parts of each one of them are integral portions of some other writing running crosswise. It is only when we get a coup d'oeil from either the head or the foot that you recognise that there are symbolisations. See! they are in triplicate at the corners and the centre of both top and bottom. In every case there is a sun cut in half by the line of the sarcophagus, as by the horizon. Close behind each of these and faced away from it, as though in some way dependent on it, is the vase which in hieroglyphic writing symbolises the heart—'Ab' the Egyptians called it. Beyond each of these again is the figure of a pair of widespread arms turned upwards from the elbow; this is the determinative of the 'Ka' or 'Double'. But its relative position is different at top and bottom. At the head of the sarcophagus the top of the 'Ka' is turned towards the mouth of the vase, but at the foot the extended arms point away from it.

"The symbolisation seems to mean that during the passing of the Sun from West to East—from sunset to sunrise, or through the Under World, otherwise night—the Heart, which is material even in the tomb and cannot leave it, simply revolves, so that it can always rest on 'Ra' the Sun-God, the origin of all good; but that the Double, which represents the active principle, goes whither it will, the same by night as by day. If this be correct it is a warning—a caution—a reminder that the consciousness of the mummy does not rest but is to be reckoned with.

"Or it may be intended to convey that after the particular night of the resurrection, the 'Ka' would leave the heart altogether, thus typifying that in her resurrection the Queen would be restored to a lower and purely physical existence. In such case what would become of her memory and the experiences of her wide-wandering soul? The chiefest value of her resurrection would be lost to the world! This, however, does not alarm me. It is only guess-work after all, and is contradictory to the intellectual belief of the Egyptian theology, that the 'Ka' is an essential portion of humanity." He paused and we all waited. The silence was broken by Doctor Winchester:

"But would not all this imply that the Queen feared intrusion of her tomb?" Mr. Trelawny smiled as he answered:

"My dear sir, she was prepared for it. The grave robber is no modern application of endeavour; he was probably known in the Queen's own dynasty. Not only was she prepared for intrusion, but, as shown in several ways, she expected it. The hiding of the lamps in the serdab, and the institution of the avenging 'treasurer' shows that there was defence, positive as well as negative. Indeed, from the many indications afforded in the clues laid out with the most consummated thought, we may almost gather that she entertained it as a possibility that others—like ourselves, for instance—might in all seriousness undertake the work which she had made ready for her own hands when the time should have come. This very matter that I have been speaking of is an instance. The clue is intended for seeing eyes!"

Again we were silent. It was Margaret who spoke:

"Father, may I have that chart? I should like to study it during the day!"

"Certainly, my dear!" answered Mr. Trelawny heartily, as he handed it to her. He resumed his instructions in a different tone, a more matter-of- fact one suitable to a practical theme which had no mystery about it:

"I think you had better all understand the working of the electric light in case any sudden contingency should arise. I dare say you have noticed that we have a complete supply in every part of the house, so that there need not be a dark corner anywhere. This I had specially arranged. It is worked by a set of turbines moved by the flowing and ebbing tide, after the manner of the turbines at Niagara. I hope by this means to nullify accident and to have without fail a full supply ready at any time. Come with me and I will explain the system of circuits, and point out to you the taps and the fuses." I could not but notice, as we went with him all over the house, how absolutely complete the system was, and how he had guarded himself against any disaster that human thought could foresee.

But out of the very completeness came a fear! In such an enterprise as ours the bounds of human thought were but narrow. Beyond it lay the vast of Divine wisdom, and Divine power!

When we came back to the cave, Mr. Trelawny took up another theme:

"We have now to settle definitely the exact hour at which the Great Experiment is to be made. So far as science and mechanism go, if the preparations are complete, all hours are the same. But as we have to deal with preparations made by a woman of extraordinarily subtle mind, and who had full belief in magic and had a cryptic meaning in everything, we should place ourselves in her position before deciding. It is now manifest that the sunset has an important place in the arrangements. As those suns, cut so mathematically by the edge of the sarcophagus, were arranged of full design, we must take our cue from this. Again, we find all along that the number seven has had an important bearing on every phase of the Queen's thought and reasoning and action. The logical result is that the seventh hour after sunset was the time fixed on. This is borne out by the fact that on each of the occasions when action was taken in my house, this was the time chosen. As the sun sets tonight in Cornwall at eight, our hour is to be three in the morning!" He spoke in a matter-of-fact way, though with great gravity; but there was nothing of mystery in his word or manner. Still, we were all impressed to a remarkable degree. I could see this in the other men by the pallor that came on some of their faces, and by the stillness and unquestioning silence with which the decision was received. The only one who remained in any way at ease was Margaret, who had lapsed into one of her moods of abstraction, but who seemed to wake up to a note of gladness. Her father, who was watching her intently, smiled; her mood was to him a direct confirmation of his theory.

For myself I was almost overcome. The definite fixing of the hour seemed like the voice of Doom. When I think of it now, I can realise how a condemned man feels at his sentence, or at the sounding of the last hour he is to hear.

There could be no going back now! We were in the hands of God! The hands of God . . . ! And yet . . . . ! What other forces were arrayed? . . . What would become of us all, poor atoms of earthly dust whirled in the wind which comesth whence and goeth whither no man may know. It was not for myself . . . Margaret . . . !

I was recalled by Mr. Trelawny's firm voice:

"Now we shall see to the lamps and finish our preparations." Accordingly we set to work, and under his supervision made ready the Egyptian lamps, seeing that they were well filled with the cedar oil, and that the wicks were adjusted and in good order. We lighted and tested them one by one, and left them ready so that they would light at once and evenly. When this was done we had a general look round; and fixed all in readiness for our work at night.

All this had taken time, and we were I think all surprised when as we emerged from the cave we heard the great clock in the hall chime four.

We had a late lunch, a thing possible without trouble in the present state of our commissariat arrangements. Afte it, by Mr. Trelawny's advice, we separated; each to prepare in our own way for the strain of the coming night. Margaret looked pale and somewhat overwrought, so I advised her to lie down and try to sleep. She promised that she would. The abstraction which had been upon her fitfully all day lifted for the time; with all her old sweetness and loving delicacy she kissed me good-bye for the present! With the sense of happiness which this gave me I went out for a walk on the cliffs. I did not want to think; and I had an instinctive feeling that fresh air and God's sunlight, and the myriad beauties of the works of His hand would be the best preparation of fortitude for what was to come.

When I got back, all the party were assembling for a late tea. Coming fresh from the exhilaration of nature, it struck me as almost comic that we, who were nearing the end of so strange—almost monstrous—an undertaking, should be yet bound by the needs and habits of our lives.

All the men of the party were grave; the time of seclusion, even if it had given them rest, had also given opportunity for thought. Margaret was bright, almost buoyant; but I missed about her something of her usual spontaneity. Towards myself there was a shadowy air of reserve, which brought back something of my suspicion. When tea was over, she went out of the room; but returned in a minute with the roll of drawing which she had taken with her earlier in the day. Coming close to Mr. Trelawny, she said:

"Father, I have been carefully considering what you said today about the hidden meaning of those suns and hearts and 'Ka's', and I have been examining the drawings again."

"And with what result, my child?" asked Mr. Trelawny eagerly.

"There is another reading possible!"

"And that?" His voice was now tremulous with anxiety. Margaret spoke with a strange ring in her voice; a ring that cannot be, unless there is the consciousness of truth behind it:

"It means that at the sunset the 'Ka' is to enter the 'Ab'; and it is only at the sunrise that it will leave it!"

"Go on!" said her father hoarsely.

"It means that for this night the Queen's Double, which is otherwise free, will remain in her heart, which is mortal and cannot leave its prison-place in the mummy-shrouding. It means that when the sun has dropped into the sea, Queen Tera will cease to exist as a conscious power, till sunrise; unless the Great Experiment can recall her to waking life. It means that there will be nothing whatever for you or others to fear from her in such way as we have all cause to remember. Whatever change may come from the working of the Great Experiment, there can come none from the poor, helpless, dead woman who has waited all those centuries for this night; who has given up to the coming hour all the freedom of eternity, won in the old way, in hope of a new life in a new world such as she longed for . . . !" She stopped suddenly. As she had gone on speaking there had come with her words a strange pathetic, almost pleading, tone which touched me to the quick. As she stopped, I could see, before she turned away her head, that her eyes were full of tears.

For once the heart of her father did not respond to her feeling. He looked exultant, but with a grim masterfulness which reminded me of the set look of his stern face as he had lain in the trance. He did not offer any consolation to his daughter in her sympathetic pain. He only said:

"We may test the accuracy of your surmise, and of her feeling, when the time comes!" Having said so, he went up the stone stairway and into his own room. Margaret's face had a troubled look as she gazed after him.

Strangely enough her trouble did not as usual touch me to the quick.

When Mr. Trelawny had gone, silence reigned. I do not think that any of us wanted to talk. Presently Margaret went to her room, and I went out on the terrace over the sea. The fresh air and the beauty of all before helped to restore the good spirits which I had known earlier in the day. Presently I felt myself actually rejoicing in the belief that the danger which I had feared from the Queen's violence on the coming night was obviated. I believed in Margaret's belief so thoroughly that it did not occur to me to dispute her reasoning. In a lofty frame of mind, and with less anxiety than I had felt for days, I went to my room and lay down on the sofa.

I was awaked by Corbeck calling to me, hurriedly:

"Come down to the cave as quickly as you can. Mr. Trelawny wants to see us all there at once. Hurry!"

I jumped up and ran down to the cave. All were there except Margaret, who came immediately after me carrying Silvio in her arms. When the cat saw his old enemy he struggled to get down; but Margaret held him fast and soothed him. I looked at my watch. It was close to eight.

When Margaret was with us her father said directly, with a quiet insistence which was new to me:

"You believe, Margaret, that Queen Tera has voluntarily undertaken to give up her freedom for this night? To become a mummy and nothing more, till the Experiment has been completed? To be content that she shall be powerless under all and any circumstances until after all is over and the act of resurrection has been accomplished, or the effort has failed?" After a pause Margaret answered in a low voice:

"Yes!"

In the pause her whole being, appearance, expression, voice, manner had changed. Even Silvio noticed it, and with a violent effort wriggled away from her arms; she did not seem to notice the act. I expected that the cat, when he had achieved his freedom, would have attacked the mummy; but on this occasion he did not. He seemed too cowed to approach it. He shrunk away, and with a piteous "miaou" came over and rubbed himself against my ankles. I took him up in my arms, and he nestled there content. Mr. Trelawny spoke again:

"You are sure of what you say! You believe it with all your soul?" Margaret's face had lost the abstracted look; it now seemed illuminated with the devotion of one to whom is given to speak of great things. She answered in a voice which, though quiet, vibrated with conviction:

"I know it! My knowledge is beyond belief!" Mr. Trelawny spoke again:

"Then you are so sure, that were you Queen Tera herself, you would be willing to prove it in any way that I might suggest?"

"Yes, any way!" the answer rang out fearlessly. He spoke again, in a voice in which was no note of doubt:

"Even in the abandonment of your Familiar to death—to annihilation."

She paused, and I could see that she suffered—suffered horribly. There was in her eyes a hunted look, which no man can, unmoved, see in the eyes of his beloved. I was about to interrupt, when her father's eyes, glancing round with a fierce determination, met mine. I stood silent, almost spellbound; so also the other men. Something was going on before us which we did not understand!

With a few long strides Mr. Trelawny went to the west side of the cave and tore back the shutter which obscured the window. The cool air blew in, and the sunlight streamed over them both, for Margaret was now by his side. He pointed to where the sun was sinking into the sea in a halo of golden fire, and his face was as set as flint. In a voice whose absolute uncompromising hardness I shall hear in my ears at times till my dying day, he said:

"Choose! Speak! When the sun has dipped below the sea, it will be too late!" The glory of the dying sun seemed to light up Margaret's face, till it shone as if lit from within by a noble light, as she answered:

"Even that!"

Then stepping over to where the mummy cat stood on the little table, she placed her hand on it. She had now left the sunlight, and the shadows looked dark and deep over her. In a clear voice she said:

"Were I Tera, I would say 'Take all I have! This night is for the Gods alone!'"

As she spoke the sun dipped, and the cold shadow suddenly fell on us. We all stood still for a while. Silvio jumped from my arms and ran over to his mistress, rearing himself up against her dress as if asking to be lifted. He took no notice whatever of the mummy now.

Margaret was glorious with all her wonted sweetness as she said sadly:

"The sun is down, Father! Shall any of us see it again? The night of nights is come!"

CHAPTER XX

THE GREAT EXPERIMENT

IF ANY EVIDENCE had been wanted of how absolutely one and all of us had come to believe in the spiritual existence of the Egyptian Queen, it would have been found in the change which in a few minutes had been effected in us by the statement of voluntary negation made, we all believed, through Margaret. Despite the coming of the fearful ordeal, the sense of which it was impossible to forget, we looked and acted as though a great relief had come to us. We had indeed lived in such a state of terrorism during the days when Mr. Trelawny was lying in a trance that the feeling had bitten deeply into us. No one knows till he has experienced it, what it is to be in constant dread of some unknown danger which may come at any time and in any form.

The change was manifested in different ways, according to each nature. Margaret was sad. Doctor Winchester was in high spirits, and keenly observant; the process of thought which had served as an antidote to fear, being now relieved from this duty, added to his intellectual enthusiasm. Mr. Corbeck seemed to be in a retrospective rather than a speculative mood. I was myself rather inclined to be gay; the relief from certain anxiety regarding Margaret was sufficient for me for the time.

As to Mr. Trelawny he seemed less changed than any. Perhaps this was only natural, as he had had in his mind the intention for so many years of doing that in which we were tonight engaged, that any event connected with it could only seem to him as an episode, a step to the end. His was that commanding nature which looks so to the end of an undertaking that all else is of secondary importance. Even now, though his terrible sternness relaxed under the relief from the strain, he never flagged nor faltered for a moment in his purpose. He asked us men to come with him; and going to the hall we presently managed to lower into the cave an oak table, fairly long and not too wide, which stood against the wall in the hall. This we placed under the strong cluster of electric lights in the middle of the cave. Margaret looked on for a while; then all at once her face blanched, and in an agitated voice she said:

"What are you going to do, Father?"

"To unroll the mummy of the cat! Queen Tera will not need her Familiar tonight. If she should want him, it might be dangerous to us; so we shall make him safe. You are not alarmed, dear?"

"Oh no!" she answered quickly. "But I was thinking of my Silvio, and how I should feel if he had been the mummy that was to be unswathed!"

Mr. Trelawny got knives and scissors ready, and placed the cat on the table. It was a grim beginning to our work; and it made my heart sink when I thought of what might happen in that lonely house in the mid-gloom of the night. The sense of loneliness and isolation from the world was increased by the moaning of the wind which had now risen ominously, and by the beating of waves on the rocks below. But we had too grave a task before us to be swayed by external manifestations: the unrolling of the mummy began.

There was an incredible number of bandages; and the tearing sound—they being stuck fast to each other by bitumen and gums and spices—and the little cloud of red pungent dust that arose, pressed on the senses of all of us. As the last wrappings came away, we saw the animal seated before us. He was all hunkered up; his hair and teeth and claws were complete. The eyes were closed, but the eyelids had not the fierce look which I expected. The whiskers had been pressed down on the side of the face by the bandaging; but when the pressure was taken away they stood out, just as they would have done in life. He was a magnificent creature, a tiger-cat of great size. But as we looked at him, our first glance of admiration changed to one of fear, and a shudder ran through each one of us; for here was a confirmation of the fears which we had endured.

His mouth and his claws were smeared with the dry, red stains of recent blood!

Doctor Winchester was the first to recover; blood in itself had small disturbing quality for him. He had taken out his magnifying-glass and was examining the stains on the cat's mouth. Mr. Trelawny breathed loudly, as though a strain had been taken from him.

"It is as I expected," he said. "This promises well for what is to follow."

By this time Doctor Winchester was looking at the red stained paws. "As I expected!" he said. "He has seven claws, too!" Opening his pocket-book, he took out the piece of blotting-paper marked by Silvio's claws, on which was also marked in pencil a diagram of the cuts made on Mr. Trelawny's wrist. He placed the paper under the mummy cat's paw. The marks fitted exactly.

When we had carefully examined the cat, finding, however, nothing strange about it but its wonderful preservation, Mr. Trelawny lifted it from the table. Margaret started forward, crying out:

"Take care, Father! Take care! He may injure you!"

"Not now, my dear!" he answered as he moved towards the stairway. Her face fell. "Where are you going?" she asked in a faint voice.

"To the kitchen," he answered. "Fire will take away all danger for the future; even an astral body cannot materialise from ashes!" He signed to us to follow him. Margaret turned away with a sob. I went to her; but she motioned me back and whispered:

"No, no! Go with the others. Father may want you. Oh! it seems like murder! The poor Queen's pet . . . !" The tears were dropping from under the fingers that covered her eyes.

In the kitchen was a fire of wood ready laid. To this Mr. Trelawny applied a match; in a few seconds the kindling had caught and the flames leaped. When the fire was solidly ablaze, he threw the body of the cat into it. For a few seconds it lay a dark mass amidst the flames, and the room was rank with the smell of burning hair. Then the dry body caught fire too. The inflammable substances used in embalming became new fuel, and the flames roared. A few minutes of fierce conflagration; and then we breathed freely. Queen Tera's Familiar was no more!

When we went back to the cave we found Margaret sitting in the dark. She had switched off the electric light, and only a faint glow of the evening light came through the narrow openings. Her father went quickly over to her and put his arms round her in a loving protective way. She laid her head on his shoulder for a minute and seemed comforted. Presently she called to me:

"Malcolm, turn up the light!" I carried out her orders, and could see that, though she had been crying, her eyes were now dry. Her father saw it too and looked glad. He said to us in a grave tone:

"Now we had better prepare for our great work. It will not do to leave anything to the last!" Margaret must have had a suspicion of what was coming, for it was with a sinking voice that she asked:

"What are you going to do now?" Mr. Trelawny too must have had a suspicion of her feelings, for he answered in a low tone:

"To unroll the mummy of Queen Tera!" She came close to him and said pleadingly in a whisper:

"Father, you are not going to unswathe her! All you men . . . ! And in the glare of light!"

"But why not, my dear?"

"Just think, Father, a woman! All alone! In such a way! In such a place! Oh! it's cruel, cruel!" She was manifestly much overcome. Her cheeks were flaming red, and her eyes were full of indignant tears. Her father saw her distress; and, sympathising with it, began to comfort her. I was moving off; but he signed to me to stay. I took it that after the usual manner of men he wanted help on such an occasion, and man-like wished to throw on someone else the task of dealing with a woman in indignant distress. However, he began to appeal first to her reason:

"Not a woman, dear; a mummy! She has been dead nearly five thousand years!"

"What does that matter? Sex is not a matter of years! A woman is a woman, if she had been dead five thousand centuries! And you expect her to arise out of that long sleep! It could not be real death, if she is to rise out of it! You have led me to believe that she will come alive when the Coffer is opened!"

"I did, my dear; and I believe it! But if it isn't death that has been the matter with her all these years, it is something uncommonly like it. Then again, just think; it was men who embalmed her. They didn't have women's rights or lady doctors in ancient Egypt, my dear! And besides," he went on more freely, seeing that she was accepting his argument, if not yielding to it, "we men are accustomed to such things. Corbeck and I have unrolled a hundred mummies; and there were as many women as men amongst them. Doctor Winchester in his work has had to deal with women as well of men, till custom has made him think nothing of sex. Even Ross has in his work as a barrister . . ." He stopped suddenly.

"You were going to help too!" she said to me, with an indignant look.

I said nothing; I thought silence was best. Mr. Trelawny went on hurriedly; I could see that he was glad of interruption, for the part of his argument concerning a barrister's work was becoming decidedly weak:

"My child, you will be with us yourself. Would we do anything which would hurt or offend you? Come now! be reasonable! We are not at a pleasure party. We are all grave men, entering gravely on an experiment which may unfold the wisdom of old times, and enlarge human knowledge indefinitely; which may put the minds of men on new tracks of thought and research. An experiment," as he went on his voice deepened, "which may be fraught with death to any one of us—to us all! We know from what has been, that there are, or may be, vast and unknown dangers ahead of us, of which none in the house today may ever see the end. Take it, my child, that we are not acting lightly; but with all the gravity of deeply earnest men! Besides, my dear, whatever feelings you or any of us may have on the subject, it is necessary for the success of the experiment to unswathe her. I think that under any circumstances it would be necessary to remove the wrappings before she became again a live human being instead of a spiritualised corpse with an astral body. Were her original intention carried out, and did she come to new life within her mummy wrappings, it might be to exchange a coffin for a grave! She would die the death of the buried alive! But now, when she has voluntarily abandoned for the time her astral power, there can be no doubt on the subject."

Margaret's face cleared. "All right, Father!" she said as she kissed him. "But oh! it seems a horrible indignity to a Queen, and a woman."

I was moving away to the staircase when she called me:

"Where are you going?" I came back and took her hand and stroked it as I answered:

"I shall come back when the unrolling is over!" She looked at me long, and a faint suggestion of a smile came over her face as she said:

"Perhaps you had better stay, too! It may be useful to you in your work as a barrister!" She smiled out as she met my eyes: but in an instant she changed. Her face grew grave, and deadly white. In a far away voice she said:

"Father is right! It is a terrible occasion; we need all to be serious over it. But all the same—nay, for that very reason you had better stay, Malcolm! You may be glad, later on, that you were present tonight!"

My heart sank down, down, at her words; but I thought it better to say nothing. Fear was stalking openly enough amongst us already!

By this time Mr. Trelawny, assisted by Mr. Corbeck and Doctor Winchester, had raised the lid of the ironstone sarcophagus which contained the mummy of the Queen. It was a large one; but it was none too big. The mummy was both long and broad and high; and was of such weight that it was no easy task, even for the four of us, to lift it out. Under Mr. Trelawny's direction we laid it out on the table prepared for it.

Then, and then only, did the full horror of the whole thing burst upon me! There, in the full glare of the light, the whole material and sordid side of death seemed staringly real. The outer wrappings, torn and loosened by rude touch, and with the colour either darkened by dust or worn light by friction, seemed creased as by rough treatment; the jagged edges of the wrapping-cloths looked fringed; the painting was patchy, and the varnish chipped. The coverings were evidently many, for the bulk was great. But through all, showed that unhidable human figure, which seems to look more horrible when partially concealed than at any other time. What was before us was Death, and nothing else. All the romance and sentiment of fancy had disappeared. The two elder men, enthusiasts who had often done such work, were not disconcerted; and Doctor Winchester seemed to hold himself in a business-like attitude, as if before the operating-table. But I felt low-spirited, and miserable, and ashamed; and besides I was pained and alarmed by Margaret's ghastly pallor.

Then the work began. The unrolling of the mummy cat had prepared me somewhat for it; but this was so much larger, and so infinitely more elaborate, that it seemed a different thing. Moreover, in addition to the ever present sense of death and humanity, there was a feeling of something finer in all this. The cat had been embalmed with coarser materials; here, all, when once the outer coverings were removed, was more delicately done. It seemed as if only the finest gums and spices had been used in this embalming. But there were the same surroundings, the same attendant red dust and pungent presence of bitumen; there was the same sound of rending which marked the tearing away of the bandages. There were an enormous number of these, and their bulk when opened was great. As the men unrolled them, I grew more and more excited. I did not take a part in it myself; Margaret had looked at me gratefully as I drew back. We clasped hands, and held each other hard. As the unrolling went on, the wrappings became finer, and the smell less laden with bitumen, but more pungent. We all, I think, began to feel it as though it caught or touched us in some special way. This, however, did not interfere with the work; it went on uninterruptedly. Some of the inner wrappings bore symbols or pictures. These were done sometimes wholly in pale green colour, sometimes in many colours; but always with a prevalence of green. Now and again Mr. Trelawny or Mr. Corbeck would point out some special drawing before laying the bandage on the pile behind them, which kept growing to a monstrous height.

At last we knew that the wrappings were coming to an end. Already the proportions were reduced to those of a normal figure of the manifest height of the Queen, who was more than average height. And as the end drew nearer, so Margaret's pallor grew; and her heart beat more and more wildly, till her breast heaved in a way that frightened me.

Just as her father was taking away the last of the bandages, he happened to look up and caught the pained and anxious look of her pale face. He paused, and taking her concern to be as to the outrage on modesty, said in a comforting way:

"Do not be uneasy, dear! See! there is nothing to harm you. The Queen has on a robe.—Ay, and a royal robe, too!"

The wrapping was a wide piece the whole length of the body. It being removed, a profusely full robe of white linen had appeared, covering the body from the throat to the feet.

And such linen! We all bent over to look at it.

Margaret lost her concern, in her woman's interest in fine stuff. Then the rest of us looked with admiration; for surely such linen was never seen by the eyes of our age. It was as fine as the finest silk. But never was spun or woven silk which lay in such gracious folds, constrict though they were by the close wrappings of the mummy cloth, and fixed into hardness by the passing of thousands of years.

Round the neck it was delicately embroidered in pure gold with tiny sprays of sycamore; and round the feet, similarly worked, was an endless line of lotus plants of unequal height, and with all the graceful abandon of natural growth.

Across the body, but manifestly not surrounding it, was a girdle of jewels. A wondrous girdle, which shone and glowed with all the forms and phases and colours of the sky!

The buckle was a great yellow stone, round of outline, deep and curved, as if a yielding globe had been pressed down. It shone and glowed, as though a veritable sun lay within; the rays of its light seemed to strike out and illumine all round. Flanking it were two great moonstones of lesser size, whose glowing, beside the glory of the sunstone, was like the silvery sheen of moonlight.

And then on either side, linked by golden clasps of exquisite shape, was a line of flaming jewels, of which the colours seemed to glow. Each of these stones seemed to hold a living star, which twinkled in every phase of changing light.

Margaret raised her hands in ecstasy. She bent over to examine more closely; but suddenly drew back and stood fully erect at her grand height. She seemed to speak with the conviction of absolute knowledge as she said:

"That is no cerement! It was not meant for the clothing of death! It is a marriage robe!"

Mr. Trelawny leaned over and touched the linen robe. He lifted a fold at the neck, and I knew from the quick intake of his breath that something had surprised him. He lifted yet a little more; and then he, too, stood back and pointed, saying:

"Margaret is right! That dress is not intended to be worn by the dead! See! her figure is not robed in it. It is but laid upon her." He lifted the zone of jewels and handed it to Margaret. Then with both hands he raised the ample robe, and laid it across the arms which she extended in a natural impulse. Things of such beauty were too precious to be handled with any but the greatest care.

We all stood awed at the beauty of the figure which, save for the face cloth, now lay completely nude before us. Mr. Trelawny bent over, and with hands that trembled slightly, raised this linen cloth which was of the same fineness as the robe. As he stood back and the whole glorious beauty of the Queen was revealed, I felt a rush of shame sweep over me. It was not right that we should be there, gazing with irreverent eyes on such unclad beauty: it was indecent; it was almost sacrilegious! And yet the white wonder of that beautiful form was something to dream of. It was not like death at all; it was like a statue carven in ivory by the hand of a Praxiteles. There was nothing of that horrible shrinkage which death seems to effect in a moment. There was none of the wrinkled toughness which seems to be a leading characteristic of most mummies. There was not the shrunken attenuation of a body dried in the sand, as I had seen before in museums. All the pores of the body seemed to have been preserved in some wonderful way. The flesh was full and round, as in a living person; and the skin was as smooth as satin. The colour seemed extraordinary. It was like ivory, new ivory; except where the right arm, with shattered, bloodstained wrist and missing hand had lain bare to exposure in the sarcophagus for so many tens of centuries.

With a womanly impulse; with a mouth that drooped with pity, with eyes that flashed with anger, and cheeks that flamed, Margaret threw over the body the beautiful robe which lay across her arm. Only the face was then to be seen. This was more startling even than the body, for it seemed not dead, but alive. The eyelids were closed; but the long, black, curling lashes lay over on the cheeks. The nostrils, set in grave pride, seemed to have the repose which, when it is seen in life, is greater than the repose of death. The full, red lips, though the mouth was not open, showed the tiniest white line of pearly teeth within. Her hair, glorious in quantity and glossy black as the raven's wing, was piled in great masses over the white forehead, on which a few curling tresses strayed like tendrils. I was amazed at the likeness to Margaret, though I had had my mind prepared for this by Mr. Corbeck's quotation of her father's statement. This woman—I could not think of her as a mummy or a corpse—was the image of Margaret as my eyes had first lit on her. The likeness was increased by the jewelled ornament which she wore in her hair, the "Disk and Plumes", such as Margaret, too, had worn. It, too, was a glorious jewel; one noble pearl of moonlight lustre, flanked by carven pieces of moonstone.

Mr. Trelawny was overcome as he looked. He quite broke down; and when Margaret flew to him and held him close in her arms and comforted him, I heard him murmur brokenly:

"It looks as if you were dead, my child!"

There was a long silence. I could hear without the roar of the wind, which was now risen to a tempest, and the furious dashing of the waves far below. Mr. Trelawny's voice broke the spell:

"Later on we must try and find out the process of embalming. It is not like any that I know. There does not seem to have been any opening cut for the withdrawing of the viscera and organs, which apparently remain intact within the body. Then, again, there is no moisture in the flesh; but its place is supplied with something else, as though wax or stearine had been conveyed into the veins by some subtle process. I wonder could it be possible that at that time they could have used paraffin. It might have been, by some process that we know not, pumped into the veins, where it hardened!"

Margaret, having thrown a white sheet over the Queen's body, asked us to bring it to her own room, where we laid it on her bed. Then she sent us away, saying:

"Leave her alone with me. There are still many hours to pass, and I do not like to leave her lying there, all stark in the glare of light. This may be the Bridal she prepared for—the Bridal of Death; and at least she shall wear her pretty robes."

When presently she brought me back to her room, the dead Queen was dressed in the robe of fine linen with the embroidery of gold; and all her beautiful jewels were in place. Candles were lit around her, and white flowers lay upon her breast.

Hand in hand we stood looking at her for a while. Then with a sigh, Margaret covered her with one of her own snowy sheets. She turned away; and after softly closing the door of the room, went back with me to the others who had now come into the dining room. Here we all began to talk over the things that had been, and that were to be.

Now and again I could feel that one or other of us was forcing conversation, as if we were not sure of ourselves. The long wait was beginning to tell on our nerves. It was apparent to me that Mr. Trelawny had suffered in that strange trance more than we suspected, or than he cared to show. True, his will and his determination were as strong as ever; but the purely physical side of him had been weakened somewhat. It was indeed only natural that it should be. No man can go through a period of four days of absolute negation of life without being weakened by it somehow.

As the hours crept by, the time passed more and more slowly. The other men seemed to get unconsciously a little drowsy. I wondered if in the case of Mr. Trelawny and Mr. Corbeck, who had already been under the hypnotic influence of the Queen, the same dormance was manifesting itself. Doctor Winchester had periods of distraction which grew longer and more frequent as the time wore on.

As to Margaret, the suspense told on her exceedingly, as might have been expected in the case of a woman. She grew paler and paler still; till at last about midnight, I began to be seriously alarmed about her. I got her to come into the library with me, and tried to make her lie down on a sofa for a little while. As Mr. Trelawny had decided that the experiment was to be made exactly at the seventh hour after sunset, it would be as nearly as possible three o'clock in the morning when the great trial should be made. Even allowing a whole hour for the final preparations, we had still two hours of waiting to go through, and I promised faithfully to watch her and to awake her at any time she might name. She would not hear of it, however. She thanked me sweetly and smiled at me as she did so; but she assured me that she was not sleepy, and that she was quite able to bear up. That it was only the suspense and excitement of waiting that made her pale. I agreed perforce; but I kept her talking of many things in the library for more than an hour; so that at last, when she insisted on going back to her father's room I felt that I had at least done something to help her pass the time.

We found the three men sitting patiently in silence. With manlike fortitude they were content to be still when they felt they had done all in their power.

And so we waited.

The striking of two o'clock seemed to freshen us all up. Whatever shadows had been settling over us during the long hours preceding seemed to lift at once, and we all went about our separate duties alert and with alacrity. We looked first to the windows to see that they were closed; for now the storm raged so fiercely that we feared it might upset our plans which, after all, were based on perfect stillness. Then we got ready our respirators to put them on when the time should be close at hand. We had from the first arranged to use them, for we did not know whether some noxious fume might not come from the Magic Coffer when it should be opened. Somehow it never seemed to occur to any of us that there was any doubt as to its opening.

Then, under Margaret's guidance, we carried the body of Queen Tera, still clad in her Bridal robes, from her room into the cavern.

It was a strange sight, and a strange experience. The group of grave silent men carrying away from the lighted candles and the white flowers the white still figure, which looked like an ivory statue when through our moving the robe fell back.

We laid her in the sarcophagus, and placed the severed hand in its true position on her breast. Under it was laid the Jewel of Seven Stars, which Mr. Trelawny had taken from the safe. It seemed to flash and blaze as he put it in its place. The glare of the electric lights shone cold on the great sarcophagus fixed ready for the final experiment—the Great Experiment, consequent on the researches during a lifetime of these two travelled scholars. Again, the startling likeness between Margaret and the mummy, intensified by her own extraordinary pallor, heightened the strangeness of it all.

When all was finally fixed, three-quarters of an hour had gone; for we were deliberate in all our doings. Margaret beckoned me, and I went with her to her room. There she did a thing which moved me strangely, and brought home to me keenly the desperate nature of the enterprise on which we were embarked. One by one, she blew out the candles carefully, and placed them back in their usual places. When she had finished she said to me:

"They are done with! Whatever comes—Life or Death—there will be no purpose in their using now!"

We returned to the cavern with a strange thrill as of finality. There was to be no going back now!

We put on our respirators, and took our places as had been arranged. I was to stand by the taps of the electric lights, ready to turn them off or on as Mr. Trelawny should direct. His last caution to me to carry out his instructions exactly was almost like a menace; for he warned me that death to any or all of us might come from any error or neglect on my part. Margaret and Doctor Winchester were to stand between the sarcophagus and the wall, so that they would not be between the mummy and the Magic Coffer. They were to note accurately all that should happen with regard to the Queen.

Mr. Trelawny and Mr. Corbeck were to see the lamps lighted: and then to take their places, the former at the foot, the latter at the head, of the sarcophagus.

When the hands of the clock were close to the hour, they stood ready with their lit tapers, like gunners in old days with their linstocks.

For the few minutes that followed, the passing of time was a slow horror. Mr. Trelawny stood with his watch in his hand, ready to give the signal.

The time approached with inconceivable slowness; but at last came the whirring of wheels which warns that the hour is at hand. The striking of the silver bell of the clock seemed to smite on our hearts like the knell of doom. One! Two! Three!

The wicks of the lamps caught, and I turned out the electric light. In the dimness of the struggling lamps, and after the bright glow of the electric light, the room and all within it took weird shape, and everything seemed in an instant to change. We waited, with our hearts beating. I know mine did; and I fancied I could hear the pulsation of the others. Without, the storm raged; the shutters of the narrow windows shook and strained and rattled, as though something was striving for entrance.

The seconds seemed to pass with leaden wings; it was as though all the world were standing still. The figures of the others stood out dimly, Margaret's white dress alone showing clearly in the gloom. The thick respirators, which we all wore, added to the strange appearance. The thin light of the lamps, as the two men bent over the Coffer, showed

Mr. Trelawny's square jaw and strong mouth, and the brown, wrinkled face of Mr. Corbeck. Their eyes seemed to glare in the light. Across the room Doctor Winchester's eyes twinkled like stars, and Margaret's blazed like black suns.

Would the lamps never burn up!

It was only a few seconds in all till they did blaze up. A slow, steady light, growing more and more bright; and changing in colour from blue to crystal white. So they stayed for a couple of minutes, without any change in the Coffer being noticeable. At last there began to appear all over it a delicate glow. This grew and grew, till it became like a blazing jewel; and then like a living thing, whose essence was light. Mr. Trelawny and Mr. Corbeck moved silently to their places beside the sarcophagus.

We waited and waited, our hearts seeming to stand still.

All at once there was a sound like a tiny muffled explosion, and the cover of the Coffer lifted right up on a level plane a few inches; there was no mistaking anything now, for the whole cavern was full of light. Then the cover, staying fast at one side, rose slowly up on the other, as though yielding to some pressure of balance. I could not see what was within, for the risen cover stood between. The Coffer still continued to glow; from it began to steal a faint greenish vapour which floated in the direction of the sarcophagus as though impelled or drawn towards it. I could not smell it fully on account of the respirator; but, even through that, I was conscious of a strange, pungent odour. The vapour got somewhat denser after a few seconds, and began to pass directly into the open sarcophagus. It was evident now that the mummied body had some attraction for it; and also that it had some effect on the body, for the sarcophagus slowly became illumined as though the body had begun to glow. I could not see within from where I stood, but I gathered from the faces of all the four watchers that something strange was happening.

I longed to run over and take a look for myself; but I remembered Mr. Trelawny's solemn warning, and remained at my post.

The storm still thundered round the house, and I could feel the rock on which it was built tremble under the furious onslaught of the waves. The shutters strained as though the screaming wind without would in very anger have forced an entrance. In that dread hour of expectancy, when the forces of Life and Death were struggling for the mastery, imagination was awake. I almost fancied that the storm was a living thing, and animated with the wrath of the quick!

All at once the eager faces round the sarcophagus were bent forward. The look of speechless wonder in the eyes, lit by that super-natural glow from within the sarcophagus, had a more than mortal brilliance.

My own eyes were nearly blinded by the awful, paralysing light, so that I could hardly trust them. I saw something white rising up from the open sarcophagus. Something which appeared to my tortured eyes to be filmy, like a white mist. In the heart of this mist, which was cloudy and opaque like an opal, was something like a hand holding a fiery jewel flaming with many lights. As the fierce glow of the Coffer met this new living light, the green vapour floating between them seemed like a cascade of brilliant points—a miracle of light!

But at that very moment there came a change. The fierce storm, battling with the shutters of the narrow openings, won victory. With the sound of a pistol shot, one of the heavy shutters broke its fastening and was hurled on its hinges back against the wall. In rushed a fierce blast which blew the flames of the lamps to and fro, and drifted the green vapour from its course.

On the very instant came a change in the outcome from the Coffer. There was a moment's quick flame and a muffled explosion; and black smoke began to pour out. This got thicker and thicker with frightful rapidity, in volumes of ever-increasing density; till the whole cavern began to get obscure, and its outlines were lost. The screaming wind tore in and whirled it about. At a sign from Mr. Trelawny Mr. Corbeck went and closed the shutter and jammed it fast with a wedge.

I should have liked to help; but I had to wait directions from Mr. Trelawny, who inflexibly held his post at the head of the sarcophagus. I signed to him with my hand, but he motioned me back. Gradually the figures of all close to the sarcophagus became indistinct in the smoke which rolled round them in thick billowy clouds. Finally, I lost sight of them altogether. I had a terrible desire to rush over so as to be near Margaret; but again I restrained myself. If the Stygian gloom continued, light would be a necessity of safety; and I was the guardian of the light! My anguish of anxiety as I stood to my post was almost unendurable.

The Coffer was now but a dull colour; and the lamps were growing dim, as though they were being overpowered by the thick smoke. Absolute darkness would soon be upon us.

I waited and waited, expecting every instant to hear the command to turn up the light; but none came. I waited still, and looked with harrowing intensity at the rolling billows of smoke still pouring out of the casket whose glow was fading. The lamps sank down, and went out; one by one.

Finally, there was but one lamp alight, and that was dimly blue and flickering. I kept my eyes fixed towards Margaret, in the hope that I might see her in some lifting of the gloom; it was for her now that all my anxiety was claimed. I could just see her white frock beyond the dim outline of the sarcophagus.

Deeper and deeper grew the black mist, and its pungency began to assail my nostrils as well as my eyes. Now the volume of smoke coming from the Coffer seemed to lessen, and the smoke itself to be less dense. Across the room I saw a movement of something white where the sarcophagus was. There were several such movements. I could just catch the quick glint of white through the dense smoke in the fading light; for now even the last lamp began to flicker with the quick leaps before extinction.

Then the last glow disappeared. I felt that the time had come to speak; so I pulled off my respirator and called out:

"Shall I turn on the light?" There was no answer. Before the thick smoke choked me, I called again, but more loudly:

"Mr. Trelawny, shall I turn on the light? Answer me! If you do not forbid me, I shall turn it on!"

As there was no reply, I turned the tap. To my horror there was no response; something had gone wrong with the electric light! I moved, intending to run up the staircase to seek the cause, but I could now see nothing, all was pitch dark.

I groped my way across the room to where I thought Margaret was. As I went I stumbled across a body. I could feel by her dress that it was a woman. My heart sank; Margaret was unconscious, or perhaps dead. I lifted the body in my arms, and went straight forward till I touched a wall. Following it round I came to the stairway, and hurried up the steps with what haste I could make, hampered as I was with my dear burden. It may have been that hope lightened my task; but as I went the weight that I bore seemed to grow less as I ascended from the cavern.

I laid the body in the hall, and groped my way to Margaret's room, where I knew there were matches, and the candles which she had placed beside the Queen. I struck a match; and oh! it was good to see the light. I lit two candles, and taking one in each hand, hurried back to the hall where I had left, as I had supposed, Margaret.

Her body was not there. But on the spot where I had laid her was Queen Tera's Bridal robe, and surrounding it the girdle of wondrous gems. Where the heart had been, lay the Jewel of Seven Stars.

Sick at heart, and with a terror which has no name, I went down into the cavern. My two candles were like mere points of light in the black, impenetrable smoke. I put up again to my mouth the respirator which hung round my neck, and went to look for my companions.

I found them all where they had stood. They had sunk down on the floor, and were gazing upward with fixed eyes of unspeakable terror. Margaret had put her hands before her face, but the glassy stare of her eyes through her fingers was more terrible than an open glare.

I pulled back the shutters of all the windows to let in what air I could. The storm was dying away as quickly as it had risen, and now it only came in desultory puffs. It might well be quiescent; its work was done!

I did what I could for my companions; but there was nothing that could avail. There, in that lonely house, far away from aid of man, naught could avail.

It was merciful that I was spared the pain of hoping.

THE JEWEL OF SEVEN STARS, ALTERNATE ENDING (1912)

THE GREAT EXPERIMENT

IF ANY EVIDENCE had been wanted of how absolutely one and all of us had come to believe in the spiritual existence of the Egyptian Queen, it would have been found in the change which in a few minutes had been effected in us by the statement of voluntary negation made, we all believed, through Margaret. Despite the coming of the fearful ordeal, the sense of which it is impossible to forget, we looked and acted as though a great relief had come to us. We had indeed lived in such a state of terrorism during the days when Mr. Trelawny was lying in a trance that the feeling had bitten deeply into us. No one knows till he has experienced it, what it is to be in constant dread of some unknown danger which may come at any time and in any form.

The change was manifested in different ways, according to each nature. Margaret was sad. Doctor Winchester was in high spirits, and keenly observant; the process of thought which had served as an antidote to fear, being now relieved from this duty, added to his intellectual enthusiasm. Mr. Corbeck seemed to be in a retrospective rather than a speculative mood. I was myself rather inclined to be gay; the relief from certain anxiety regarding Margaret was sufficient for me for the time.

As to Mr. Trelawny he seemed less changed than any. Perhaps this was only natural, as he had had in his mind the intention for so many years of doing that in which we were tonight engaged, that any event connected with it could only seem to him as an episode, a step to the end. His was that commanding nature which looks so to the end of an undertaking that all else is of secondary importance. Even now, though his terrible sternness relaxed under the relief from the strain, he never flagged nor faltered for a moment in his purpose. He asked us men to come with him; and going to the hall we presently managed to lower into the cave an oak table, fairly long and not too wide, which stood against the wall in the hall. This we placed under the strong cluster of electric lights in the middle of the cave. Margaret looked on for a while; then all at once her face blanched, and in an agitated voice she said:

"What are you going to do, Father?"

"To unroll the mummy of the cat! Queen Tera will not need her Familiar tonight. If she should want him, it might be dangerous to us; so we shall make him safe. You are not alarmed, dear?"

"Oh no!" she answered quickly. "But I was thinking of my Silvio, and how I should feel if he had been the mummy that was to be unswathed!"

Mr. Trelawny got knives and scissors ready, and placed the cat on the table. It was a grim beginning to our work; and it made my heart sink when I thought of what might happen in that lonely house in the mid-gloom of the night. The sense of loneliness and isolation from the world was increased by the moaning of the wind which had now risen ominously, and by the beating of waves on the rocks below. But we had too grave a task before us to be swayed by external manifestations: the unrolling of the mummy began.

There was an incredible number of bandages; and the tearing sound— they being stuck fast to each other by bitumen and gums and spices—and the little cloud of red pungent dust that arose, pressed on the senses of all of us. As the last wrappings came away, we saw the animal seated before us. He was all hunkered up; his hair and teeth and claws were complete. The eyes were closed, but the eyelids had not the fierce look which I expected. The whiskers had been pressed down on the side of the face by the bandaging; but when the pressure was taken away they stood out, just as they would have done in life. He was a magnificent creature, a tiger-cat of great size. But as we looked at him, our first glance of admiration changed to one of fear, and a shudder ran through each one of us; for here was a confirmation of the fears which we had endured.

His mouth and his claws were smeared with the dry, red stains of recent blood!

Doctor Winchester was the first to recover; blood in itself had small disturbing quality for him. He had taken out his magnifying-glass and was examining the stains on the cat's mouth. Mr. Trelawny breathed loudly, as though a strain had been taken from him.

"It is as I expected," he said. "This promises well for what is to follow."

By this time Doctor Winchester was looking at the red stained paws. "As I expected!" he said. "He has seven claws, too!" Opening his pocket-book, he took out the piece of blotting-paper marked by Silvio's claws, on which was also marked in pencil a diagram of the cuts made on Mr. Trelawny's wrist. He placed the paper under the mummy cat's paw. The marks fitted exactly.

When we had carefully examined the cat, finding, however, nothing strange about it but its wonderful preservation, Mr. Trelawny lifted it from the table. Margaret started forward, crying out:

"Take care, Father! Take care! He may injure you!"

"Not now, my dear!" he answered as he moved towards the stairway. Her face fell. "Where are you going?" she asked in a faint voice.

"To the kitchen," he answered. "Fire will take away all danger for the future; even an astral body cannot materialise from ashes!" He signed to us to follow him. Margaret turned away with a sob. I went to her; but she motioned me back and whispered:

"No, no! Go with the others. Father may want you. Oh! it seems like murder! The poor Queen's pet . . . . !" The tears were dropping from under the fingers that covered her eyes.

In the kitchen was a fire of wood ready laid. To this Mr. Trelawny applied a match; in a few seconds the kindling had caught and the flames leaped. When the fire was solidly ablaze, he threw the body of the cat into it. For a few seconds it lay a dark mass amidst the flames, and the room was rank with the smell of burning hair. Then the dry body caught fire too. The inflammable substances used in embalming became new fuel, and the flames roared. A few minutes of fierce conflagration; and then we breathed freely. Queen Tera's Familiar was no more!

When we went back to the cave we found Margaret sitting in the dark. She had switched off the electric light, and only a faint glow of the evening light came through the narrow openings. Her father went quickly over to her and put his arms round her in a loving protective way. She laid her head on his shoulder for a minute and seemed comforted. Presently she called to me:

"Malcolm, turn up the light!" I carried out her orders, and could see that, though she had been crying, her eyes were now dry. Her father saw it too and looked glad. He said to us in a grave tone:

"Now we had better prepare for our great work. It will not do to leave anything to the last!" Margaret must have had a suspicion of what was coming, for it was with a sinking voice that she asked:

"What are you going to do now?" Mr. Trelawny too must have had a suspicion of her feelings, for he answered in a low tone:

"To unroll the mummy of Queen Tera!" She came close to him and said pleadingly in a whisper:

"Father, you are not going to unswathe her! All you men . . . ! And in the glare of light!"

"But why not, my dear?"

"Just think, Father, a woman! All alone! In such a way! In such a place! Oh! it's cruel, cruel!" She was manifestly much overcome. Her cheeks were flaming red, and her eyes were full of indignant tears. Her father saw her distress; and, sympathising with it, began to comfort her. I was moving off; but he signed to me to stay. I took it that after the usual manner of men he wanted help on such an occasion, and manlike wished to throw on someone else the task of dealing with a woman in indignant distress. However, he began to appeal first to her reason:

"Not a woman, dear; a mummy! She has been dead nearly five thousand years!"

"What does that matter? Sex is not a matter of years! A woman is a woman, if she had been dead five thousand centuries! And you expect her to arise out of that long sleep! It could not be real death, if she is to rise out of it! You have led me to believe that she will come alive when the Coffer is opened!"

"I did, my dear; and I believe it! But if it isn't death that has been the matter with her all these years, it is something uncommonly like it. Then again, just think; it was men who embalmed her. They didn't have women's rights or lady doctors in ancient Egypt, my dear! And besides," he went on more freely, seeing that she was accepting his argument, if not yielding to it, "we men are accustomed to such things. Corbeck and I have unrolled a hundred mummies; and there were as many women as men amongst them. Doctor Winchester in his work has had to deal with women as well of men, till custom has made him think nothing of sex. Even Ross has in his work as a barrister . . . " He stopped suddenly.

"You were going to help too!" she said to me, with an indignant look.

I said nothing; I thought silence was best. Mr. Trelawny went on hurriedly; I could see that he was glad of interruption, for the part of his argument concerning a barrister's work was becoming decidedly weak:

"My child, you will be with us yourself. Would we do anything which would hurt or offend you? Come now! be reasonable! We are not at a pleasure party. We are all grave men, entering gravely on an experiment which may unfold the wisdom of old times, and enlarge human knowledge indefinitely; which may put the minds of men on new tracks of thought and research. An experiment," as he went on his voice deepened, "which may be fraught with death to any one of us—to us all! We know from what has been, that there are, or may be, vast and unknown dangers ahead of us, of which none in the house today may ever see the end. Take it, my child, that we are not acting lightly; but with all the gravity of deeply earnest men! Besides, my dear, whatever feelings you or any of us may have on the subject, it is necessary for the success of the experiment to unswathe her. I think that under any circumstances it would be necessary to remove the wrappings before she became again a live human being instead of a spiritualised corpse with an astral body. Were her original intention carried out, and did she come to new life within her mummy wrappings, it might be to exchange a coffin for a grave! She would die the death of the buried alive! But now, when she has voluntarily abandoned for the time her astral power, there can be no doubt on the subject."

Margaret's face cleared. "All right, Father!" she said as she kissed him. "But oh! it seems a horrible indignity to a Queen, and a woman."

I was moving away to the staircase when she called me:

"Where are you going?" I came back and took her hand and stroked it as I answered:

"I shall come back when the unrolling is over!" She looked at me long, and a faint suggestion of a smile came over her face as she said:

"Perhaps you had better stay, too! It may be useful to you in your work as a barrister!" She smiled out as she met my eyes: but in an instant she changed. Her face grew grave, and deadly white. In a far away voice she said:

"Father is right! It is a terrible occasion; we need all to be serious over it. But all the same—nay, for that very reason you had better stay, Malcolm! You may be glad, later on, that you were present tonight!"

My heart sank down, down, at her words; but I thought it better to say nothing. Fear was stalking openly enough amongst us already!

By this time Mr. Trelawny, assisted by Mr. Corbeck and Doctor Winchester, had raised the lid of the ironstone sarcophagus which contained the mummy of the Queen. It was a large one; but it was none too big. The mummy was both long and broad and high; and was of such weight that it was no easy task, even for the four of us, to lift it out. Under Mr. Trelawny's direction we laid it out on the table prepared for it.

Then, and then only, did the full horror of the whole thing burst upon me! There, in the full glare of the light, the whole material and sordid side of death seemed staringly real. The outer wrappings, torn and loosened by rude touch, and with the colour either darkened by dust or worn light by friction, seemed creased as by rough treatment; the jagged edges of the wrapping-cloths looked fringed; the painting was patchy, and the varnish chipped. The coverings were evidently many, for the bulk was great. But through all, showed that unhidable human figure, which seems to look more horrible when partially concealed than at any other time. What was before us was Death, and nothing else. All the romance and sentiment of fancy had disappeared. The two elder men, enthusiasts who had often done such work, were not disconcerted; and Doctor Winchester seemed to hold himself in a business-like attitude, as if before the operating-table. But I felt low-spirited, and miserable, and ashamed; and besides I was pained and alarmed by Margaret's ghastly pallor.

Then the work began. The unrolling of the mummy cat had prepared me somewhat for it; but this was so much larger, and so infinitely more elaborate, that it seemed a different thing. Moreover, in addition to the ever present sense of death and humanity, there was a feeling of something finer in all this. The cat had been embalmed with coarser materials; here, all, when once the outer coverings were removed, was more delicately done. It seemed as if only the finest gums and spices had been used in this embalming. But there were the same surroundings, the same attendant red dust and pungent presence of bitumen; there was the same sound of rending which marked the tearing away of the bandages. There were an enormous number of these, and their bulk when opened was great. As the men unrolled them, I grew more and more excited. I did not take a part in it myself; Margaret had looked at me gratefully as I drew back. We clasped hands, and held each other hard. As the unrolling went on, the wrappings became finer, and the smell less laden with bitumen, but more pungent. We all, I think, began to feel it as though it caught or touched us in some special way. This, however, did not interfere with the work; it went on uninterruptedly. Some of the inner wrappings bore symbols or pictures. These were done sometimes wholly in pale green colour, sometimes in many colours; but always with a prevalence of green. Now and again Mr. Trelawny or Mr. Corbeck would point out some special drawing before laying the bandage on the pile behind them, which kept growing to a monstrous height.

At last we knew that the wrappings were coming to an end. Already the proportions were reduced to those of a normal figure of the manifest height of the Queen, who was more than average height. And as the end drew nearer, so Margaret's pallor grew; and her heart beat more and more wildly, till her breast heaved in a way that frightened me.

Just as her father was taking away the last of the bandages, he happened to look up and caught the pained and anxious look of her pale face. He paused, and taking her concern to be as to the outrage on modesty, said in a comforting way:

"Do not be uneasy, dear! See! there is nothing to harm you. The Queen has on a robe.—Ay, and a royal robe, too!"

The wrapping was a wide piece the whole length of the body. It being removed, a profusely full robe of white linen had appeared, covering the body from the throat to the feet.

And such linen! We all bent over to look at it.

Margaret lost her concern, in her woman's interest in fine stuff. Then the rest of us looked with admiration; for surely such linen was never seen by the eyes of our age. It was as fine as the finest silk. But never was spun or woven silk which lay in such gracious folds, constrict though they were by the close wrappings of the mummy cloth, and fixed into hardness by the passing of thousands of years.

Round the neck it was delicately embroidered in pure gold with tiny sprays of sycamore; and round the feet, similarly worked, was an endless line of lotus plants of unequal height, and with all the graceful abandon of natural growth.

Across the body, but manifestly not surrounding it, was a girdle of jewels. A wondrous girdle, which shone and glowed with all the forms and phases and colours of the sky!

The buckle was a great yellow stone, round of outline, deep and curved, as if a yielding globe had been pressed down. It shone and glowed, as though a veritable sun lay within; the rays of its light seemed to strike out and illumine all round. Flanking it were two great moonstones of lesser size, whose glowing, beside the glory of the sunstone, was like the silvery sheen of moonlight.

And then on either side, linked by golden clasps of exquisite shape, was a line of flaming jewels, of which the colours seemed to glow. Each of these stones seemed to hold a living star, which twinkled in every phase of changing light.

Margaret raised her hands in ecstasy. She bent over to examine more closely; but suddenly drew back and stood fully erect at her grand height. She seemed to speak with the conviction of absolute knowledge as she said:

"That is no cerement! It was not meant for the clothing of death! It is a marriage robe!"

Mr. Trelawny leaned over and touched the linen robe. He lifted a fold at the neck, and I knew from the quick intake of his breath that something had surprised him. He lifted yet a little more; and then he, too, stood back and pointed, saying:

"Margaret is right! That dress is not intended to be worn by the dead! See! her figure is not robed in it. It is but laid upon her." He lifted the zone of jewels and handed it to Margaret. Then with both hands he raised the ample robe, and laid it across the arms which she extended in a natural impulse. Things of such beauty were too precious to be handled with any but the greatest care.

We all stood awed at the beauty of the figure which, save for the face cloth, now lay completely nude before us. Mr. Trelawny bent over, and with hands that trembled slightly, raised this linen cloth which was of the same fineness as the robe. As he stood back and the whole glorious beauty of the Queen was revealed, I felt a rush of shame sweep over me. It was not right that we should be there, gazing with irreverent eyes on such unclad beauty: it was indecent; it was almost sacrilegious! And yet the white wonder of that beautiful form was something to dream of. It was not like death at all; it was like a statue carven in ivory by the hand of a Praxiteles. There was nothing of that horrible shrinkage which death seems to effect in a moment. There was none of the wrinkled toughness which seems to be a leading characteristic of most mummies. There was not the shrunken attenuation of a body dried in the sand, as I had seen before in museums. All the pores of the body seemed to have been preserved in some wonderful way. The flesh was full and round, as in a living person; and the skin was as smooth as satin. The colour seemed extraordinary. It was like ivory, new ivory; except where the right arm, with shattered, bloodstained wrist and missing hand had lain bare to exposure in the sarcophagus for so many tens of centuries.

With a womanly impulse; with a mouth that drooped with pity, with eyes that flashed with anger, and cheeks that flamed, Margaret threw over the body the beautiful robe which lay across her arm. Only the face was then to be seen. This was more startling even than the body, for it seemed not dead, but alive. The eyelids were closed; but the long, black, curling lashes lay over on the cheeks. The nostrils, set in grave pride, seemed to have the repose which, when it is seen in life, is greater than the repose of death. The full, red lips, though the mouth was not open, showed the tiniest white line of pearly teeth within. Her hair, glorious in quantity and glossy black as the raven's wing, was piled in great masses over the white forehead, on which a few curling tresses strayed like tendrils. I was amazed at the likeness to Margaret, though I had had my mind prepared for this by Mr. Corbeck's quotation of her father's statement. This woman—I could not think of her as a mummy or a corpse—was the image of Margaret as my eyes had first lit on her. The likeness was increased by the jewelled ornament which she wore in her hair, the "Disk and Plumes", such as Margaret, too, had worn. It, too, was a glorious jewel; one noble pearl of moonlight lustre, flanked by carven pieces of moonstone.

Mr. Trelawny was overcome as he looked. He quite broke down; and when Margaret flew to him and held him close in her arms and comforted him, I heard him murmur brokenly:

"It looks as if you were dead, my child!"

There was a long silence. I could hear without the roar of the wind, which was now risen to a tempest, and the furious dashing of the waves far below. Mr. Trelawny's voice broke the spell:

"Later on we must try and find out the process of embalming. It is not like any that I know. There does not seem to have been any opening cut for the withdrawing of the viscera and organs, which apparently remain intact within the body. Then, again, there is no moisture in the flesh; but its place is supplied with something else, as though wax or stearine had been conveyed into the veins by some subtle process. I wonder could it be possible that at that time they could have used paraffin. It might have been, by some process that we know not, pumped into the veins, where it hardened!"

Margaret, having thrown a white sheet over the Queen's body, asked us to bring it to her own room, where we laid it on her bed. Then she sent us away, saying:

"Leave her alone with me. There are still many hours to pass, and I do not like to leave her lying there, all stark in the glare of light. This may be the Bridal she prepared for–the Bridal of Death; and at least she shall wear her pretty robes."

When presently she brought me back to her room, the dead Queen was dressed in the robe of fine linen with the embroidery of gold; and all her beautiful jewels were in place. Candles were lit around her, and white flowers lay upon her breast.

Hand in hand we stood looking at her for a while. Then with a sigh, Margaret covered her with one of her own snowy sheets. She turned away; and after softly closing the door of the room, went back with me to the others who had now come into the dining room. Here we all began to talk over the things that had been, and that were to be.

Now and again I could feel that one or other of us was forcing conversation, as if we were not sure of ourselves. The long wait was beginning to tell on our nerves. It was apparent to me that Mr. Trelawny had suffered in that strange trance more than we suspected, or than he cared to show. True, his will and his determination were as strong as ever; but the purely physical side of him had been weakened somewhat. It was indeed only natural that it should be. No man can go through a period of four days of absolute negation of life without being weakened by it somehow.

As the hours crept by, the time passed more and more slowly. The other men seemed to get unconsciously a little drowsy. I wondered if in the case of Mr. Trelawny and Mr. Corbeck, who had already been under the hypnotic influence of the Queen, the same dormance was manifesting itself. Doctor Winchester had periods of distraction which grew longer and more frequent as the time wore on.

As to Margaret, the suspense told on her exceedingly, as might have been expected in the case of a woman. She grew paler and paler still; till at last about midnight, I began to be seriously alarmed about her. I got her to come into the library with me, and tried to make her lie down on a sofa for a little while. As Mr. Trelawny had decided that the experiment was to be made exactly at the seventh hour after sunset, it would be as nearly as possible three o'clock in the morning when the great trial should be made. Even allowing a whole hour for the final preparations, we had still two hours of waiting to go through, and I promised faithfully to watch her and to awake her at any time she might name. She would not hear of it, however. She thanked me sweetly and smiled at me as she did so; but she assured me that she was not sleepy, and that she was quite able to bear up. That it was only the suspense and excitement of waiting that made her pale. I agreed perforce; but I kept her talking of many things in the library for more than an hour; so that at last, when she insisted on going back to her father's room I felt that I had at least done something to help her pass the time.

We found the three men sitting patiently in silence. With manlike fortitude they were content to be still when they felt they had done all in their power. And so we waited.

The striking of two o'clock seemed to freshen us all up. Whatever shadows had been settling over us during the long hours preceding seemed to lift at once; and we went about our separate duties alert and with alacrity. We looked first to the windows to see that they were closed, and we got ready our respirators to put them on when the time should be close at hand. We had from the first arranged to use them for we did not know whether some noxious fume might not come from the Magic Coffer when it should be opened. Somehow, it never seemed to occur to any of us that there was any doubt as to its opening.

Then, under Margaret's guidance, we carried the mummied body of Queen Tera from her room into her father's, and laid it on a couch. We put the sheet lightly over it, so that if she should wake she could at once slip from under it. The severed hand was placed in its true position on her breast, and under it the Jewel of Seven Stars which Mr. Trelawny had taken from the great safe. It seemed to flash and blaze as he put it in its place.

It was a strange sight, and a strange experience. The group of grave silent men carried the white still figure, which looked like an ivory statue when through our moving the sheet fell back, away from the lighted candles and the white flowers. We placed it on the couch in that other room, where the blaze of the electric lights shone on the great sarcophagus fixed in the middle of the room ready for the final experiment, the great experiment consequent on the researches during a lifetime of these two travelled scholars. Again, the startling likeness between Margaret and the mummy, intensified by her own extraordinary pallor, heightened the strangeness of it all. When all was finally fixed three-quarters of an hour had gone, for we were deliberate in all our doings. Margaret beckoned me, and I went out with her to bring in Silvio. He came to her purring. She took him up and handed him to me; and then did a thing which moved me strangely and brought home to me keenly the desperate nature of the enterprise on which we were embarked. One by one, she blew out the candles carefully and placed them back in their usual places. When she had finished she said to me:

"They are done with now. Whatever comes—life or death—there will be no purpose in their using now." Then taking Silvio into her arms, and pressing him close to her bosom where he purred loudly, we went back to the room. I closed the door carefully behind me, feeling as I did so a strange thrill as of finality. There was to be no going back now. Then we put on our respirators, and took our places as had been arranged. I was to stand by the taps of the electric lights beside the door, ready to turn them off or on as Mr. Trelawny should direct. Doctor Winchester was to stand behind the couch so that he should not be between the mummy and the sarcophagus; he was to watch carefully what should take place with regard to the Queen. Margaret was to be beside him; she held Silvio ready to place him upon the couch or beside it when she might think right. Mr. Trelawny and Mr. Corbeck were to attend to the lighting of the lamps. When the hands of the clock were close to the hour, they stood ready with their linstocks.

The striking of the silver bell of the clock seemed to smite on our hearts like a knell of doom. One! Two! Three!

Before the third stroke the wicks of the lamps had caught, and I had turned out the electric light. In the dimness of the struggling lamps, and after the bright glow of the electric light, the room and all within it took weird shapes, and all seemed in an instant to change. We waited with our hearts beating. I know mine did, and I fancied I could hear the pulsation of the others.

The seconds seemed to pass with leaden wings. It were as though all the world were standing still. The figures of the others stood out dimly, Margaret's white dress alone showing clearly in the gloom. The thick respirators which we all wore added to the strange appearance. The thin light of the lamps showed Mr. Trelawny's square jaw and strong mouth and the brown shaven face of Mr. Corbeck. Their eyes seemed to glare in the light. Across the room Doctor Winchester's eyes twinkled like stars, and Margaret's blazed like black suns. Silvio's eyes were like emeralds.

Would the lamps never burn up!

It was only a few seconds in all till they did blaze up. A slow, steady light, growing more and more bright, and changing in colour from blue to crystal white. So they stayed for a couple of minutes without change in the coffer; till at last there began to appear all over it a delicate glow. This grew and grew, till it became like a blazing jewel, and then like a living thing whose essence of life was light. We waited and waited, our hearts seeming to stand still.

All at once there was a sound like a tiny muffled explosion and the cover lifted right up on a level plane a few inches; there was no mistaking anything now, for the whole room was full of a blaze of light. Then the cover, staying fast at one side rose slowly up on the other, as though yielding to some pressure of balance. The coffer still conti-nued to glow; from it began to steal a faint greenish smoke. I could not smell it fully on account of the respirator; but, even through that, I was conscious of a strange pungent odour. Then this smoke began to grow thicker, and to roll out in volumes of ever increasing density till the whole room began to get obscure. I had a terrible desire to rush over to Margaret, whom I saw through the smoke still standing erect behind the couch. Then, as I looked, I saw Doctor Winchester sink down. He was not unconscious; for he waved his hand back and forward, as though to forbid any one to come to him. At this time the figures of Mr. Trelawny and Mr. Corbeck were becoming indistinct in the smoke which rolled round them in thick billowy clouds. Finally I lost sight of them altogether. The coffer still continued to glow; but the lamps began to grow dim. At first I thought that their light was being overpowered by the thick black smoke; but presently I saw that they were, one by one, burning out. They must have burned quickly to produce such fierce and vivid flames.

I waited and waited, expecting every instant to hear the command to turn up the light; but none came. I waited still, and looked with harrowing intensity at the rolling billows of smoke still pouring out of the glowing casket, whilst the lamps sank down and went out one by one.

Finally there was but one lamp alight, and that was dimly blue and flickering. The only effective light in the room was from the glowing casket. I kept my eyes fixed toward Margaret; it was for her now that all my anxiety was claimed. I could just see her white frock beyond the still white shrouded figure on the couch. Silvio was troubled; his piteous mewing was the only sound in the room. Deeper and denser grew the black mist and its pungency began to assail my nostrils as well as my eyes. Now the volume of smoke coming from the coffer seemed to lessen, and the smoke itself to be less dense. Across the room I saw something white move where the couch was. There were several movements. I could just catch the quick glint of white through the dense smoke in the fading light; for now the glow of the coffer began quickly to subside. I could still hear Silvio, but his mewing came from close under; a moment later I could feel him piteously crouching on my foot.

Then the last spark of light disappeared, and through the Egyptian darkness I could see the faint line of white around the window blinds. I felt that the time had come to speak; so I pulled off my respirator and called out:

"Shall I turn up the light?" There was no answer; so before the thick smoke choked me, I called again but more loudly:

"Mr. Trelawny, shall I turn up the light?" He did not answer; but from across the room I heard Margaret's voice, sounding as sweet and clear as a bell:

"Yes, Malcolm!" I turned the tap and the lamps flashed out. But they were only dim points of light in the midst of that murky ball of smoke. In that thick atmosphere there was little possibility of illumination. I ran across to Margaret, guided by her white dress, and caught hold of her and held her hand. She recognised my anxiety and said at once:

"I am all right."

"Thank God!" I said. "How are the others? Quick, let us open all the windows and get rid of this smoke!" To my surprise, she answered in a sleepy way:

"They will be all right. They won't get any harm." I did not stop to inquire how or on what ground she formed such an opinion, but threw up the lower sashes of all the windows, and pulled down the upper. Then I threw open the door.

A few seconds made a perceptible change as the thick, black smoke began to roll out of the windows. Then the lights began to grow into strength and I could see the room. All the men were overcome. Beside the couch Doctor Winchester lay on his back as though he had sunk down and rolled over; and on the farther side of the sarcophagus, where they had stood, lay Mr. Trelawny and Mr. Corbeck. It was a relief to me to see that, though they were unconscious, all three were breathing heavily as though in a stupor. Margaret still stood behind the couch. She seemed at first to be in a partially dazed condition; but every instant appeared to get more command of herself. She stepped forward and helped me to raise her father and drag him close to a window. Together we placed the others similarly, and she flew down to the dining-room and returned with a decanter of brandy. This we proceeded to administer to them all in turn. It was not many minutes after we had opened the windows when all three were struggling back to consciousness. During this time my entire thoughts and efforts had been concentrated on their restoration; but now that this strain was off, I looked round the room to see what had been the effect of the experiment. The thick smoke had nearly cleared away; but the room was still misty and was full of a strange pungent acrid odour.

The great sarcophagus was just as it had been. The coffer was open, and in it, scattered through certain divisions or partitions wrought in its own substance, was a scattering of black ashes. Over all, sarcophagus, coffer and, indeed, all in the room, was a sort of black film of greasy soot. I went over to the couch. The white sheet still lay over part of it; but it had been thrown back, as might be when one is stepping out of bed.

But there was no sign of Queen Tera! I took Margaret by the hand and led her over. She reluctantly left her father to whom she was administering, but she came docilely enough. I whispered to her as I held her hand:

"What has become of the Queen? Tell me! You were close at hand, and must have seen if anything happened!" She answered me very softly:

"There was nothing that I could see. Until the smoke grew too dense I kept my eyes on the couch, but there was no change. Then, when all grew so dark that I could not see, I thought I heard a movement close to me. It might have been Doctor Winchester who had sunk down overcome; but I could not be sure. I thought that it might be the Queen waking, so I put down poor Silvio. I did not see what became of him; but I felt as if he had deserted me when I heard him mewing over by the door. I hope he is not offended with me!" As if in answer, Silvio came running into the room and reared himself against her dress, pulling it as though clamouring to be taken up. She stooped down and took him up and began to pet and comfort him.

I went over and examined the couch and all around it most carefully. When Mr. Trelawny and Mr. Corbeck recovered sufficiently, which they did quickly, though Doctor Winchester took longer to come round, we went over it afresh. But all we could find was a sort of ridge of impalpable dust, which gave out a strange dead odour. On the couch lay the jewel of the disk and plumes which the Queen had worn in her hair, and the Star Jewel which had words to command the Gods.

Other than this we never got clue to what had happened. There was just one thing which confirmed our idea of the physical annihilation of the mummy. In the sarcophagus in the hall, where we had placed the mummy of the cat, was a small patch of similar dust.

In the autumn Margaret and I were married. On the occasion she wore the mummy robe and zone and the jewel which Queen Tera had worn in her hair. On her breast, set in a ring of gold make like a twisted lotus stalk, she wore the strange Jewel of Seven Stars which held words to command the God of all the worlds. At the marriage the sunlight streaming through the chancel windows fell on it, and it seemed to glow like a living thing.

The graven words may have been of efficacy; for Margaret holds to them, and there is no other life in all the world so happy as my own.

We often think of the great Queen, and we talk of her freely. Once, when I said with a sigh that I was sorry she could not have waked into a new life in a new world, my wife, putting both her hands in mine and looking into my eyes with that far-away eloquent dreamy look which sometimes comes into her own, said lovingly:

"Do not grieve for her! Who knows, but she may have found the joy she sought? Love and patience are all that make for happiness in this world; or in the world of the past or of the future; of the living or the dead. She dreamed her dream; and that is all that any of us can ask!"

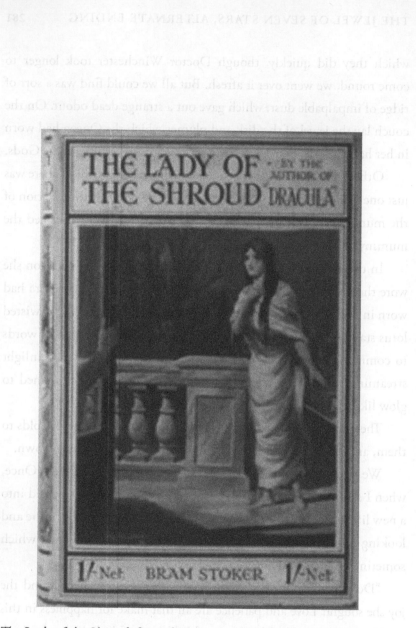

The Lady of the Shroud, first edition cover, Heinemann, London, 1909

INTRODUCTION

THE LADY OF THE SHROUD
(1909)

BRAM STOKER'S PENULTIMATE novel is perhaps the most obscure of the author's supernatural tales.

The Lady of the Shroud first appeared from William Heinemann in 1909, and the publisher also issued a "colonial" edition around the same time.

As with the author's *Dracula*—with which it shares a number of minor plot points and its European location—*The Lady of the Shroud* is an epistolary novel set in a fictional Balkan country, the Land of the Blue Mountains. The book starts with the appearance in the middle of the night of a mysterious woman in a floating coffin, but the story's Gothic trappings (including the apparent vampire, a psychic aunt, and a marriage in a subterranean crypt) are soon left behind.

Because the book also deals with the application of modern technology and radium-powered air flight, it has been labeled as early science fiction by some critics.

Not only may Stoker have been influenced by H.G. Wells's *The War in the Air,* which was serialized in a magazine in 1908 before being published in book form that same year, but he also consulted travel writer Archibald Ross Colquhoun's *The Whirlpool of Europe: Austria-Hungary and the Habsburgs* (1907) for background on the politics of the Balkans.

Although critical reaction was mixed, a contemporary reviewer for *The Bookman* considered the novel amongst the author's best work, and the book had gone through twenty printings by the mid-1930s.

Unfortunately, when the novel was issued in paperback in Britain in the early 1960s, the publisher omitted the last quarter of the book in an apparent attempt to focus on the story's supernatural elements.

As also happened with Stoker's final novel, *The Lair of the White Worm*, the book did not appear in America until 1966, when it was published as a Paperback Library Gothic.

S.J.

THE LADY OF THE SHROUD

Table of Contents

THE LADY OF THE SHROUD (1909)

From "The Journal Of Occultism"

Mid-January, 1907.

A STRANGE STORY comes from the Adriatic. It appears that on the night of the 9th, as the Italia Steamship Company's vessel "Victorine" was passing a little before midnight the point known as "the Spear of Ivan," on the coast of the Blue Mountains, the attention of the Captain, then on the bridge, was called by the look-out man to a tiny floating light close inshore. It is the custom of some South-going ships to run close to the Spear of Ivan in fine weather, as the water is deep, and there is no settled current; also there are no outlying rocks. Indeed, some years ago the local steamers had become accustomed to hug the shore here so closely that an intimation was sent from Lloyd's that any mischance under the circumstances would not be included in ordinary sea risks. Captain Mirolani is one of those who insist on a wholesome distance from the promontory being kept; but on his attention having been called to the circumstance reported, he thought it well to investigate it, as it might be some case of personal distress. Accordingly, he had the engines slowed down, and edged cautiously in towards shore. He was joined on the bridge by two of his officers, Signori Falamano and Destilia, and by one passenger on board, Mr. Peter Caulfield, whose reports of Spiritual Phenomena in remote places are well known to the readers of "The Journal of Occultism." The following account of the strange occurrence written by him, and attested by the signatures of Captain Mirolani and the other gentleman named, has been sent to us.

" . . . It was eleven minutes before twelve midnight on Saturday, the 9th day of January, 1907, when I saw the strange sight off the headland known as the Spear of Ivan on the coast of the Land of the Blue Mountains. It was a fine night, and I stood right on the bows of the ship, where there was nothing to obstruct my view. We were some distance from the Spear of Ivan, passing from northern to southern point of the wide bay into which it projects. Captain Mirolani, the Master, is a very careful seaman, and gives on his journeys a wide berth to the bay which is tabooed by Lloyd's. But when he saw in the moonlight, though far off, a tiny white figure of a woman drifting on some strange current in a small boat, on the prow of which rested a faint light (to me it looked like a corpse-candle!), he thought it might be some person in distress, and began to cautiously edge towards it. Two of his officers were with him on the bridge—Signori Falamano and Destilia. All these three, as well as myself, saw It. The rest of the crew and passengers were below. As we got close the true inwardness of It became apparent to me; but the mariners did not seem to realize till the very last. This is, after all, not strange, for none of them had either knowledge or experience in Occult matters, whereas for over thirty years I have made a special study of this subject, and have gone to and fro over the earth investigating to the nth all records of Spiritual Phenomena. As I could see from their movements that the officers did not comprehend that which was so apparent to myself, I took care not to enlighten them, lest such should result in the changing of the vessel's course before I should be near enough to make accurate observation. All turned out as I wished—at least, nearly so—as shall be seen. Being in the bow, I had, of course, a better view than from the bridge. Presently I made out that the boat, which had all along seemed to be of a queer shape, was none other than a Coffin, and that the woman standing up in it was clothed in a shroud. Her back was towards us, and she had evidently not heard our approach. As we were creeping along slowly, the engines were almost noiseless, and there was hardly a ripple as our fore-foot cut the dark water. Suddenly there was a wild cry from the bridge—Italians are certainly very excitable; hoarse commands were given to the Quartermaster at the wheel; the engine-room bell clanged. On the instant, as it seemed, the ship's head began to swing round to starboard; full steam ahead was in action, and before one could understand, the Apparition was fading in the distance. The last thing I saw was the flash of a white face with dark, burning eyes as the figure sank down into the coffin—just as mist or smoke disappears under a breeze."

BOOK I:
THE WILL OF ROGER MELTON
The Reading of the Will of Roger Melton and All That Followed

RECORD MADE BY Ernest Roger Halbard Melton, law-student of the Inner Temple, eldest son of Ernest Halbard Melton, eldest son of Ernest Melton, elder brother of the said Roger Melton and his next of kin.

I consider it at least useful—perhaps necessary—to have a complete and accurate record of all pertaining to the Will of my late grand-uncle Roger Melton.

To which end let me put down the various members of his family, and explain some of their occupations and idiosyncrasies. My father, Ernest Halbard Melton, was the only son of Ernest Melton, eldest son of Sir Geoffrey Halbard Melton of Humcroft, in the shire of Salop, a Justice of the Peace, and at one time Sheriff. My great-grandfather,

Sir Geoffrey, had inherited a small estate from his father, Roger Melton. In his time, by the way, the name was spelled Milton; but my great-grandfather changed the spelling to the later form, as he was a practical man not given to sentiment, and feared lest he should in the public eye be confused with others belonging to the family of a Radical person called Milton, who wrote poetry and was some sort of official in the time of Cromwell, whilst we are Conservatives. The same practical spirit which originated the change in the spelling of the family name inclined him to go into business. So he became, whilst still young, a tanner and leather-dresser. He utilized for the purpose the ponds and streams, and also the oak-woods on his estate—Torraby in Suffolk. He made a fine business, and accumulated a considerable fortune, with a part of which he purchased the Shropshire estate, which he entailed, and to which I am therefore heir-apparent.

Sir Geoffrey had, in addition to my grandfather, three sons and a daughter, the latter being born twenty years after her youngest brother. These sons were: Geoffrey, who died without issue, having been killed in the Indian Mutiny at Meerut in 1857, at which he took up a sword, though a civilian, to fight for his life; Roger (to whom I shall refer presently); and John—the latter, like Geoffrey, dying unmarried. Out of Sir Geoffrey's family of five, therefore, only three have to be considered: My grandfather, who had three children, two of whom, a son and a daughter, died young, leaving only my father, Roger, and Patience. Patience, who was born in 1858, married an Irishman of the name of Sellenger—which was the usual way of pronouncing the name of St. Leger, or, as they spelled it, Sent Leger—restored by later generations to the still older form. He was a reckless, dare-devil sort of fellow, then a Captain in the Lancers, a man not without the quality of bravery—he won the Victoria Cross at the Battle of Amoaful in the Ashantee Campaign. But I fear he lacked the seriousness and steadfast strenuous purpose which my father always says marks the character of our own family. He ran through nearly all of his patrimony—never a very large one; and had it not been for my grand-aunt's little fortune, his days, had he lived, must have ended in comparative poverty. Comparative, not actual; for the Meltons, who are persons of considerable pride, would not have tolerated a poverty-stricken branch of the family. We don't think much of that lot—any of us.

Fortunately, my great-aunt Patience had only one child, and the premature decease of Captain St. Leger (as I prefer to call the name) did not allow of the possibility of her having more. She did not marry again, though my grandmother tried several times to arrange an alliance for her. She was, I am told, always a stiff, uppish person, who would not yield herself to the wisdom of her superiors. Her own child was a son, who seemed to take his character rather from his father's family than from my own. He was a wastrel and a rolling stone, always in scrapes at school, and always wanting to do ridiculous things. My father, as Head of the House and his own senior by eighteen years, tried often to admonish him; but his perversity of spirit and his truculence were such that he had to desist. Indeed, I have heard my father say that he sometimes threatened his life. A desperate character he was, and almost devoid of reverence. No one, not even my father, had any influence—good influence, of course, I mean—over him, except his mother, who was of my family; and also a woman who lived with her—a sort of governess—aunt, he called her. The way of it was this: Captain St. Leger had a younger brother, who made an improvident marriage with a Scotch girl when they were both very young. They had nothing to live on except what the reckless Lancer gave them, for he had next to nothing himself, and she was "bare"—which is, I understand, the indelicate Scottish way of expressing lack of fortune. She was, however, I understand, of an old and somewhat good family, though broken in fortune—to use an expression which, however, could hardly be used precisely in regard to a family or a person who never had fortune to be broken in! It was so far well that the MacKelpies—that was the maiden name of Mrs. St. Leger—were reputable—so far as fighting was concerned. It would have been too humiliating to have allied to our family, even on the distaff side, a family both poor and of no account. Fighting alone does not make a family, I think. Soldiers are not everything, though they think they are. We have had in our family men who fought; but I never heard of any of them who fought because they *wanted* to. Mrs. St. Leger had a sister; fortunately there were only those two children in the family, or else they would all have had to be supported by the money of my family.

Mr. St. Leger, who was only a subaltern, was killed at Maiwand; and his wife was left a beggar. Fortunately, however, she died—her sister spread a story that it was from the shock and grief—before the child which she expected was born. This all happened when my cousin—or, rather, my father's cousin, my first-cousin-once-removed, to be accurate—was still a very small child. His mother then sent for Miss MacKelpie, her brother-in-law's sister-in-law, to come and live with her, which she did—beggars can't be choosers; and she helped to bring up young St. Leger.

I remember once my father giving me a sovereign for making a witty remark about her. I was quite a boy then, not more than thirteen; but our family were always clever from the very beginning of life, and father was telling me about the St. Leger family. My family hadn't, of course, seen anything of them since Captain St. Leger died—the circle to which we belong don't care for poor relations—and was explaining where Miss MacKelpie came in. She must have been a sort of nursery governess, for Mrs. St. Leger once told him that she helped her to educate the child.

"Then, father," I said, "if she helped to educate the child she ought to have been called Miss MacSkelpie!"

When my first-cousin-once-removed, Rupert, was twelve years old, his mother died, and he was in the dolefuls about it for more than a year. Miss MacKelpie kept on living with him all the same. Catch her quitting! That sort don't go into the poor-house when they can keep out! My father, being Head of the Family, was, of course, one of the trustees, and his uncle Roger, brother of the testator, another. The third was General MacKelpie, a poverty-stricken Scotch laird who had a lot of valueless land at Croom, in Ross-shire. I remember father gave me a new ten-pound note when I interrupted him whilst he was telling me of the incident of young St. Leger's improvidence by remarking that he was in error as to the land. From what I had heard of MacKelpie's estate, it was productive of one thing; when he asked me "What?" I answered "Mortgages!" Father, I knew, had bought, not long before, a lot of them at what a college friend of mine from Chicago used to call "cut-throat" price. When I remonstrated with my father for buying them at all, and so injuring the family estate which I was to inherit, he gave me an answer, the astuteness of which I have never forgotten.

"I did it so that I might keep my hand on the bold General, in case he should ever prove troublesome. And if the worst should ever come to the worst, Croom is a good country for grouse and stags!" My father can see as far as most men!

When my cousin—I shall call him cousin henceforth in this record, lest it might seem to any unkind person who might hereafter read it that I wished to taunt Rupert St. Leger with his somewhat obscure position, in reiterating his real distance in kinship with my family—when my cousin, Rupert St. Leger, wished to commit a certain idiotic act of financial folly, he approached my father on the subject, arriving at our estate, Humcroft, at an inconvenient time, without permission, not having had even the decent courtesy to say he was coming. I was then a little chap of six years old, but I could not help noticing his mean appearance. He was all dusty and dishevelled. When my father saw him—I came into the study with him—he said in a horrified voice:

"Good God!" He was further shocked when the boy brusquely acknowledged, in reply to my father's greeting, that he had travelled third class. Of course, none of my family ever go anything but first class; even the servants go second. My father was really angry when he said he had walked up from the station.

"A nice spectacle for my tenants and my tradesmen! To see my—my—a kinsman of my house, howsoever remote, trudging like a tramp on the road to my estate! Why, my avenue is two miles and a perch! No wonder you are filthy and insolent!" Rupert—really, I cannot call him cousin here—was exceedingly impertinent to my father.

"I walked, sir, because I had no money; but I assure you I did not mean to be insolent. I simply came here because I wished to ask your advice and assistance, not because you are an important person, and have a long avenue—as I know to my cost—but simply because you are one of my trustees."

"*Your* trustees, sirrah!" said my father, interrupting him. "Your trustees?"

"I beg your pardon, sir," he said, quite quietly. "I meant the trustees of my dear mother's will."

"And what, may I ask you," said father, "do you want in the way of advice from one of the trustees of your dear mother's will?" Rupert got very red, and was going to say something rude—I knew it from his look—but he stopped, and said in the same gentle way:

"I want your advice, sir, as to the best way of doing something which I wish to do, and, as I am under age, cannot do myself. It must be done through the trustees of my mother's will."

"And the assistance for which you wish?" said father, putting his hand in his pocket. I know what that action means when I am talking to him.

"The assistance I want," said Rupert, getting redder than ever, "is from my—the trustee also. To carry out what I want to do."

"And what may that be?" asked my father. "I would like, sir, to make over to my Aunt Janet—" My father interrupted him by asking—he had evidently remembered my jest:

"Miss MacSkelpie?" Rupert got still redder, and I turned away; I didn't quite wish that he should see me laughing. He went on quietly:

"*Mackelpie*, sir! Miss Janet MacKelpie, my aunt, who has always been so kind to me, and whom my mother loved—I want to have made over to her the money which my dear mother left to me." Father doubtless wished to have the matter take a less serious turn, for Rupert's eyes were all shiny with tears which had not fallen; so after a little pause he said, with indignation, which I knew was simulated:

"Have you forgotten your mother so soon, Rupert, that you wish to give away the very last gift which she bestowed on you?" Rupert was sitting, but he jumped up and stood opposite my father with his fist clenched. He was quite pale now, and his eyes looked so fierce that I thought he would do my father an injury. He spoke in a voice which did not seem like his own, it was so strong and deep.

"Sir!" he roared out. I suppose, if I was a writer, which, thank God, I am not—I have no need to follow a menial occupation—I would call it "thundered." "Thundered" is a longer word than "roared," and would, of course, help to gain the penny which a writer gets for a line. Father got pale too, and stood quite still. Rupert looked at him steadily for quite half a minute—it seemed longer at the time—and suddenly smiled and said, as he sat down again:

"Sorry. But, of course, you don't understand such things." Then he went on talking before father had time to say a word.

"Let us get back to business. As you do not seem to follow me, let me explain that it is *because* I do not forget that I wish to do this.

I remember my dear mother's wish to make Aunt Janet happy, and would like to do as she did."

"*Aunt* Janet?" said father, very properly sneering at his ignorance. "She is not your aunt. Why, even her sister, who was married to your uncle, was only your aunt by courtesy." I could not help feeling that Rupert meant to be rude to my father, though his words were quite polite. If I had been as much bigger than him as he was than me, I should have flown at him; but he was a very big boy for his age. I am myself rather thin. Mother says thinness is an "appanage of birth."

"My Aunt Janet, sir, is an aunt by love. Courtesy is a small word to use in connection with such devotion as she has given to us. But I needn't trouble you with such things, sir. I take it that my relations on the side of my own house do not affect you. I am a Sent Leger!" Father looked quite taken aback. He sat quite still before he spoke.

"Well, Mr. St. Leger, I shall think over the matter for a while, and shall presently let you know my decision. In the meantime, would you like something to eat? I take it that as you must have started very early, you have not had any breakfast?" Rupert smiled quite genially:

"That is true, sir. I haven't broken bread since dinner last night, and I am ravenously hungry." Father rang the bell, and told the footman who answered it to send the housekeeper. When she came, father said to her:

"Mrs. Martindale, take this boy to your room and give him some breakfast." Rupert stood very still for some seconds. His face had got red again after his paleness. Then he bowed to my father, and followed Mrs. Martindale, who had moved to the door.

Nearly an hour afterwards my father sent a servant to tell him to come to the study. My mother was there, too, and I had gone back with her. The man came back and said:

"Mrs. Martindale, sir, wishes to know, with her respectful service, if she may have a word with you." Before father could reply mother told him to bring her. The housekeeper could not have been far off—that kind are generally near a keyhole—for she came at once. When she came in, she stood at the door curtseying and looking pale. Father said:

"Well?"

"I thought, sir and ma'am, that I had better come and tell you about Master Sent Leger. I would have come at once, but I feared to disturb you."

"Well?" Father had a stern way with servants. When I'm head of the family I'll tread them under my feet. That's the way to get real devotion from servants!

"If you please, sir, I took the young gentleman into my room and ordered a nice breakfast for him, for I could see he was half famished— a growing boy like him, and so tall! Presently it came along. It was a good breakfast, too! The very smell of it made even me hungry. There were eggs and frizzled ham, and grilled kidneys, and coffee, and buttered toast, and bloater-paste—"

"That will do as to the menu," said mother. "Go on!"

"When it was all ready, and the maid had gone, I put a chair to the table and said, 'Now, sir, your breakfast is ready!' He stood up and said, 'Thank you, madam; you are very kind!' and he bowed to me quite nicely, just as if I was a lady, ma'am!"

"Go on," said mother.

"Then, sir, he held out his hand and said, 'Good-bye, and thank you,' and he took up his cap.

"'But aren't you going to have any breakfast, sir?' I says.

"'No, thank you, madam,' he said; 'I couldn't eat here . . . in this house, I mean!' Well, ma'am, he looked so lonely that I felt my heart melting, and I ventured to ask him if there was any mortal thing I could do for him. 'Do tell me, dear,' I ventured to say. 'I am an old woman, and you, sir, are only a boy, though it's a fine man you will be—like your dear, splendid father, which I remember so well, and gentle like your poor dear mother.'

"You're a dear!' he says; and with that I took up his hand and kissed it, for I remember his poor dear mother so well, that was dead only a year. Well, with that he turned his head away, and when I took him by the shoulders and turned him round—he is only a young boy, ma'am, for all he is so big—I saw that the tears were rolling down his cheeks. With that I laid his head on my breast—I've had children of my own, ma'am, as you know, though they're all gone. He came willing enough, and sobbed for a little bit. Then he straightened himself up, and I stood respectfully beside him.

"'Tell Mr. Melton,' he said, 'that I shall not trouble him about the trustee business.'

"'But won't you tell him yourself, sir, when you see him?' I says.

"'I shall not see him again,' he says; 'I am going back now!'

"Well, ma'am, I knew he'd had no breakfast, though he was hungry, and that he would walk as he come, so I ventured to say: 'If you won't take it a liberty, sir, may I do anything to make your going easier? Have you sufficient money, sir? If not, may I give, or lend, you some? I shall be very proud if you will allow me to.'

"'Yes,' he says quite hearty. 'If you will, you might lend me a shilling, as I have no money. I shall not forget it.' He said, as he took the coin: 'I shall return the amount, though I never can the kindness. I shall keep the coin.' He took the shilling, sir—he wouldn't take any more—and then he said good-bye. At the door he turned and walked back to me, and put his arms round me like a real boy does, and gave me a hug, and says he:

"'Thank you a thousand times, Mrs. Martindale, for your good-ness to me, for your sympathy, and for the way you have spoken of my father and mother. You have seen me cry, Mrs. Martindale,' he said; 'I don't often cry: the last time was when I came back to the lonely house after my poor dear was laid to rest. But you nor any other shall ever see a tear of mine again.' And with that he straightened out his big back and held up his fine proud head, and walked out. I saw him from the window striding down the avenue. My! but he is a proud boy, sir—an honour to your family, sir, say I respectfully. And there, the proud child has gone away hungry, and he won't, I know, ever use that shilling to buy food!"

Father was not going to have that, you know, so he said to her:

"He does not belong to my family, I would have you to know. True, he is allied to us through the female side; but we do not count him or his in my family." He turned away and began to read a book. It was a decided snub to her.

But mother had a word to say before Mrs. Martindale was done with. Mother has a pride of her own, and doesn't brook insolence from inferiors; and the housekeeper's conduct seemed to be rather presuming. Mother, of course, isn't quite our class, though her folk are quite worthy and enormously rich. She is one of the Dalmallingtons, the salt people, one of whom got a peerage when the Conservatives went out. She said to the housekeeper:

"I think, Mrs. Martindale, that I shall not require your services after this day month! And as I don't keep servants in my employment when I dismiss them, here is your month's wages due on the 25th of this month, and another month in lieu of notice. Sign this receipt." She was writing a receipt as she spoke. The other signed it without a word, and handed it to her. She seemed quite flabbergasted. Mother got up and sailed—that is the way that mother moves when she is in a wax—out of the room.

Lest I should forget it, let me say here that the dismissed housekeeper was engaged the very next day by the Countess of Salop. I may say in explanation that the Earl of Salop, K.G., who is Lord-Lieutenant of the County, is jealous of father's position and his growing influence. Father is going to contest the next election on the Conservative side, and is sure to be made a Baronet before long.

Letter from Major-General Sir Colin Alexander MacKelpie, V.C., K.C.B., of Croom, Ross, N.B., to Rupert Sent Leger, Esq., 14, Newland Park, Dulwich, London, S.E.

July 4, 1892.

MY DEAR GODSON,

I am truly sorry I am unable to agree with your request that I should acquiesce in your desire to transfer to Miss Janet MacKelpie the property bequeathed to you by your mother, of which property I am a trustee. Let me say at once that, had it been possible to me to do so, I should have held it a privilege to further such a wish—not because the beneficiare whom you would create is a near kinswoman of my own. That, in truth, is my real difficulty. I have undertaken a trust made by an honourable lady on behalf of her only son—son of a man of stainless honour, and a dear friend of my own, and whose son has a rich heritage of honour from both parents, and who will, I am sure, like to look back on his whole life as worthy of his parents, and of those whom his parents trusted. You will see, I am sure, that whatsoever I might grant regarding anyone else, my hands are tied in this matter.

And now let me say, my dear boy, that your letter has given me the most intense pleasure. It is an unspeakable delight to me to find in the son of your father—a man whom I loved, and a boy whom I love—the same generosity of spirit which endeared your father to all his comrades, old as well as young. Come what may, I shall always be proud of you; and if the sword of an old soldier—it is all I have—can ever serve you in any way, it and its master's life are, and shall be, whilst life remains to him, yours.

It grieves me to think that Janet cannot, through my act, be given that ease and tranquillity of spirit which come from competence. But, my dear Rupert, you will be of full age in seven years more. Then, if you are in the same mind—and I am sure you will not change—you, being your own master, can do freely as you will. In the meantime, to secure, so far as I can, my dear Janet against any malign stroke of fortune, I have given orders to my factor to remit semi-annually to Janet one full half of such income as may be derived in any form from my estate of Croom. It is, I am sorry to say, heavily mortgaged; but of such as is—or may be, free from such charge as the mortgage entails—something at least will, I trust, remain to her. And, my dear boy, I can frankly say that it is to me a real pleasure that you and I can be linked in one more bond in this association of purpose. I have always held you in my heart as though you were my own son. Let me tell you now that you have acted as I should have liked a son of my own, had I been blessed with one, to have acted. God bless you, my dear.

Yours ever,

COLIN ALEX. MACKELPIE.

Letter from Roger Melton, of Openshaw Grange, to Rupert Sent Leger, Esq., 14, Newland Park, Dulwich, London, S.E.

July 1, 1892.

MY DEAR NEPHEW,

Your letter of the 30th ult. received. Have carefully considered matter stated, and have come to the conclusion that my duty as a trustee would not allow me to give full consent, as you wish. Let me explain. The testator, in making her will, intended that such fortune as she had at disposal should be used to supply to you her son such benefits as its annual product should procure. To this end, and to provide against wastefulness or foolishness on your part, or, indeed, against any generosity, howsoever worthy, which might impoverish you and so defeat her benevolent intentions regarding your education, comfort, and future good, she did not place the estate directly in your hands, leaving you to do as you might feel inclined about it. But, on the contrary, she entrusted the corpus of it in the hands of men whom she believed should be resolute enough and strong enough to carry out her intent, even against any cajolements or pressure which might be employed to the contrary. It being her intention, then, that such trustees as she appointed would use for your benefit the interest accruing annually from the capital at command, *and that only* (as specifically directed in the will), so that on your arriving at full age the capital entrusted to us should be handed over to you intact, I find a hard-and-fast duty in the matter of adhering exactly to the directions given. I have no doubt that my co-trustees regard the matter in exactly the same light. Under the circumstances, therefore, we, the trustees, have not only a single and united duty towards you as the object of the testator's wishes, but towards each other as regards the manner of the carrying out of that duty. I take it, therefore, that it would not be consonant with the spirit of the trust or of our own ideas in accepting it that any of us should take a course pleasant to himself which would or might involve a stern opposition on the part of other of the co-trustees. We have each of us to do the unpleasant part of this duty without fear or favour. You understand, of course, that the time which must elapse before you come into absolute possession of your estate is a limited one. As by the terms of the will we are to hand over our trust when you have reached the age of twenty-one, there are only seven years to expire. But till then, though I should gladly meet your wishes if I could, I must adhere to the duty which I have undertaken. At the expiration of that period you will be quite free to divest yourself of your estate without protest or comment of any man.

Having now expressed as clearly as I can the limitations by which I am bound with regard to the corpus of your estate, let me say that in any other way which is in my power or discretion I shall be most happy to see your wishes carried out so far as rests with me. Indeed, I shall undertake to use what influence I may possess with my co-trustees to induce them to take a similar view of your wishes. In my own thinking you are quite free to use your own property in your own way. But as, until you shall have attained your majority, you have only life-user in your mother's bequest, you are only at liberty to deal with the annual increment. On our part as trustees we have a first charge on that increment to be used for purposes of your maintenance, clothes, and education. As to what may remain over each half-year, you will be free to deal with it as you choose. On receiving from you a written authorization to your trustees, if you desire the whole sum or any part of it to be paid over to Miss Janet MacKelpie, I shall see that it is effected. Believe me, that our duty is to protect the corpus of the estate, and to this end we may not act on any instruction to imperil it. But there our warranty stops. We can deal during our trusteeship with the corpus only. Further, lest there should arise any error on your part, we can deal with any general instruction for only so long as it may remain unrevoked. You are, and must be, free to alter your instructions or authorizations at any time. Thus your latest document must be used for our guidance.

As to the general principle involved in your wish I make no comment. You are at liberty to deal with your own how you will. I quite understand that your impulse is a generous one, and I fully believe that it is in consonance with what had always been the wishes of my sister. Had she been happily alive and had to give judgment of your intent, I am convinced that she would have approved. Therefore, my dear nephew, should you so wish, I shall be happy for her sake as well as your own to pay over on your account (as a confidential matter between you and me), but from my own pocket, a sum equal to that which you wish transferred to Miss Janet MacKelpie. On hearing from you I shall know how to act in the matter. With all good wishes,

Believe me to be,

                                        Your affectionate uncle,
                                        ROGER MELTON.

TO RUPERT SENT LEGER, ESQ.
Letter from Rupert Sent Leger to Roger Melton,
                                                July 5, 1892.

MY DEAR UNCLE,

Thank you heartily for your kind letter. I quite understand, and now see that I should not have asked you as a trustee, such a thing. I see your duty clearly, and agree with your view of it. I enclose a letter directed to my trustees, asking them to pay over annually till further direction to Miss Janet MacKelpie at this address whatever sum may remain over from the interest of my mother's bequest after deduction of such expenses as you may deem fit for my maintenance, clothing, and education, together with a sum of one pound sterling per month, which was the amount my dear mother always gave me for my personal use—"pocket-money," she called it.

With regard to your most kind and generous offer to give to my dear Aunt Janet the sum which I would have given myself, had such been in my power, I thank you most truly and sincerely, both for my dear aunt (to whom, of course, I shall not mention the matter unless you specially authorize me) and myself. But, indeed, I think it will be better not to offer it. Aunt Janet is very proud, and would not accept any benefit. With me, of course, it is different, for since I was a wee child she has been like another mother to me, and I love her very much. Since my mother died—and she, of course, was all-in-all to me—there has been no other. And in such a love as ours pride has no place. Thank you again, dear uncle, and God bless you.

                                        Your loving nephew,
                                        RUPERT SENT LEGER.

ERNEST ROGER HALBARD MELTON'S RECORD—
Continued,

And now *re* the remaining one of Sir Geoffrey's children, Roger. He was the third child and third son, the only daughter, Patience, having been born twenty years after the last of the four sons. Concerning Roger, I shall put down all I have heard of him from my father and grandfather. From my grand-aunt I heard nothing, I was a very small kid when she died; but I remember seeing her, but only once. A very tall, handsome woman of a little over thirty, with very dark hair and light-coloured eyes. I think they were either grey or blue, but I can't remember which. She looked very proud and haughty, but I am bound to say that she was very nice to me. I remember feeling very jealous of Rupert because his mother looked so distinguished. Rupert was eight years older than me, and I was afraid he would beat me if I said anything he did not like. So I was silent except when I forgot to be, and Rupert said very unkindly, and I think very unfairly, that I was "A sulky little beast." I haven't forgot that, and I don't mean to. However, it doesn't matter much what he said or thought. There he is—if he is at all—where no one can find him, with no money or nothing, for what little he had he settled when he came of age, on the MacSkel-pie. He wanted to give it to her when his mother died, but father, who was a trustee, refused; and Uncle Roger, as I call him, who is another, thought the trustees had no power to allow Rupert to throw away his matrimony, as I called it, making a joke to father when he called it patrimony. Old Sir Colin MacSkelpie, who is the third, said he couldn't take any part in such a permission, as the MacSkelpie was his niece. He is a rude old man, that. I remember when, not remembering his relationship, I spoke of the MacSkelpie, he caught me a clip on the ear that sent me across the room. His Scotch is very broad. I can hear him say, "Hae some attempt at even Soothern manners, and dinna misca' yer betters, ye young puddock, or I'll wring yer snoot!"

Father was, I could see, very much offended, but he didn't say anything. He remembered, I think, that the General is a V.C. man, and was fond of fighting duels. But to show that the fault was not his, *he* wrung *my* ear—and the same ear too! I suppose he thought that was justice! But it's only right to say that he made up for it afterwards. When the General had gone he gave me a five-pound note.

I don't think Uncle Roger was very pleased with the way Rupert behaved about the legacy, for I don't think he ever saw him from that day to this. Perhaps, of course, it was because Rupert ran away shortly afterwards; but I shall tell about that when I come to him. After all, why should my uncle bother about him? He is not a Melton at all, and I am to be Head of the House—of course, when the Lord thinks right to take father to Himself! Uncle Roger has tons of money, and he never married, so if he wants to leave it in the right direction he needn't have any trouble. He made his money in what he calls "the Eastern Trade." This, so far as I can gather, takes in the Levant and all east of it. I know he has what they call in trade "houses" in all sorts of places—Turkey, and Greece, and all round them, Morocco, Egypt, and Southern Russia, and the Holy Land; then on to Persia, India, and all round it; the Chersonese, China, Japan, and the Pacific Islands. It is not to be expected that we landowners can know much about trade, but my uncle covers—or alas! I must say "covered"—a lot of ground, I can tell you. Uncle Roger was a very grim sort of man, and only that I was brought up to try and be kind to him I shouldn't ever have dared to speak to him. But when was a child father and mother—especially mother—forced me to go and see him and be affectionate to him. He wasn't ever even civil to me, that I can remember—grumpy old bear! But, then, he never saw Rupert at all, so that I take it Master R--- is out of the running altogether for testamentary honours. The last time I saw him myself he was distinctly rude. He treated me as a boy, though I was getting on for eighteen years of age. I came into his office without knocking; and without looking up from his desk, where he was writing, he said: "Get out! Why do you venture to disturb me when I'm busy? Get out, and be damned to you!" I waited where I was, ready to transfix him with my eye when he should look up, for I cannot forget that when my father dies I shall be Head of my House. But when he did there was no transfixing possible. He said quite coolly:

"Oh, it's you, is it? I thought it was one of my office boys. Sit down, if you want to see me, and wait till I am ready." So I sat down and waited. Father always said that I should try to conciliate and please my uncle. Father is a very shrewd man, and Uncle Roger is a very rich one.

But I don't think Uncle R--- is as shrewd as he thinks he is. He sometimes makes awful mistakes in business. For instance, some years ago he bought an enormous estate on the Adriatic, in the country they call the "Land of Blue Mountains." At least, he says he bought it. He told father so in confidence. But he didn't show any title-deeds, and I'm greatly afraid he was "had." A bad job for me that he was, for father believes he paid an enormous sum for it, and as I am his natural heir, it reduces his available estate to so much less.

And now about Rupert. As I have said, he ran away when he was about fourteen, and we did not hear about him for years. When we— or, rather, my father—did hear of him, it was no good that he heard. He had gone as a cabin-boy on a sailing ship round the Horn. Then he joined an exploring party through the centre of Patagonia, and then another up in Alaska, and a third to the Aleutian Islands. After that he went through Central America, and then to Western Africa, the Pacific Islands, India, and a lot of places. We all know the wisdom of the adage that "A rolling stone gathers no moss"; and certainly, if there be any value in moss, Cousin Rupert will die a poor man. Indeed, nothing will stand his idiotic, boastful wastefulness. Look at the way in which, when he came of age, he made over all his mother's little for- tune to the MacSkelpie! I am sure that, though Uncle Roger made no comment to my father, who, as Head of our House, should, of course, have been informed, he was not pleased. My mother, who has a good fortune in her own right, and has had the sense to keep it in her own control—as I am to inherit it, and it is not in the entail, I am therefore quite impartial—I can approve of her spirited conduct in the matter. We never did think much of Rupert, anyhow; but now, since he is in the way to be a pauper, and therefore a dangerous nuisance, we look on him as quite an outsider. We know what he really is. For my own part, I loathe and despise him. Just now we are irritated with him, for we are all kept on tenterhooks regarding my dear Uncle Roger's Will. For Mr. Trent, the attorney who regulated my dear uncle's affairs and has possession of the Will, says it is necessary to know where every possible beneficiary is to be found before making the Will public, so we all have to wait. It is especially hard on me, who am the natural heir. It is very thoughtless indeed of Rupert to keep away like that. I wrote to old MacSkelpie about it, but he didn't seem to understand or to be at all anxious—he is not the heir! He said that probably Rupert Sent Leger—he, too, keeps to the old spelling—did not know of his uncle's death, or he would have taken steps to relieve our anxiety. Our anxiety, forsooth! We are not anxious; we only wish to *know*. And if we—and especially me—who have all the annoyance of thinking of the detestable and unfair death-duties, are anxious, we should be so. Well, anyhow, he'll get a properly bitter disappointment and set down when he does turn up and discovers that he is a pauper without hope!

To-day we (father and I) had letters from Mr. Trent, telling us that the whereabouts of "Mr. Rupert Sent Leger" had been discovered, and that a letter disclosing the fact of poor Uncle Roger's death had been sent to him. He was at Titicaca when last heard of. So goodness only knows when he may get the letter, which "asks him to come home at once, but only gives to him such information about the Will as has already been given to every member of the testator's family." And that is nil. I dare say we shall be kept waiting for months before we get hold of the estate which is ours. It is too bad!

Letter from Edward Bingham Trent to Ernest Roger Halbard Melton.

176, *LINCOLN'S INN FIELDS,*

December 28, 1906.

DEAR SIR,

I am glad to be able to inform you that I have just heard by letter from Mr. Rupert St. Leger that he intended leaving Rio de Janeiro by the S.S. Amazon, of the Royal Mail Company, on December 15. He further stated that he would cable just before leaving Rio de Janeiro, to say on what day the ship was expected to arrive in London. As all the others possibly interested in the Will of the late Roger Melton, and whose names are given to me in his instructions regarding the reading of the Will, have been advised, and have expressed their intention of being present at that event on being apprised of the time and place, I now beg to inform you that by cable message received the date scheduled for arrival at the Port of London was January 1 prox. I therefore beg to notify you, subject to postponement due to the non-arrival of the Amazon, the reading of the Will of the late Roger Melton, Esq., will take place in my office on Thursday, January 3 prox., at eleven o'clock a.m.

I have the honour to be, sir,

Yours faithfully,

EDWARD BINGHAM TRENT.

TO ERNEST ROGER HALBARD MELTON, ESQ.,

HUMCROFT, SALOP.

Cable: *Rupert Sent Leger to Edward Bingham Trent. Amazon* arrives London January 1. SENT LEGER.

Telegram (per Lloyd's): Rupert Sent Leger to Edward Bingham Trent.

THE LIZARD,

December 31.

Amazon arrives London to-morrow morning. All well.—LEGER.

Telegram: Edward Bingham Trent to Ernest Roger Halbard Mellon.

Rupert Sent Leger arrived. Reading Will takes place as arranged.—TRENT.

ERNEST ROGER HALBARD MELTON'S RECORD.

January 4, 1907.

The reading of Uncle Roger's Will is over. Father got a duplicate of Mr. Trent's letter to me, and of the cable and two telegrams
pasted into this Record. We both waited patiently till the third—
that is, we did not say anything. The only impatient member of
our family was my mother. She *did* say things, and if old Trent had
been here his ears would have been red. She said what ridiculous
nonsense it was delaying the reading of the Will, and keeping the
Heir waiting for the arrival of an obscure person who wasn't even
a member of the family, in as much as he didn't bear the name. I
don't think it's quite respectful to one who is some day to be Head
of the House! I thought father was weakening in his patience when
he said: "True, my dear—true!" and got up and left the room. Some
time afterwards when I passed the library I heard him walking up
and down.

Father and I went up to town on the afternoon of Wednesday,
January 2. We stayed, of course, at Claridge's, where we always stay
when we go to town. Mother wanted to come, too, but father thought
it better not. She would not agree to stay at home till we both promised
to send her separate telegrams after the reading.

At five minutes to eleven we entered Mr. Trent's office. Father
would not go a moment earlier, as he said it was bad form to seem eager
at any time, but most of all at the reading of a will. It was a rotten grind,

for we had to be walking all over the neighbourhood for half an hour before it was time, not to be too early.

When we went into the room we found there General Sir Colin MacKelpie and a big man, very bronzed, whom I took to be Rupert St. Leger—not a very creditable connection to look at, I thought! He and old MacKelpie took care to be in time! Rather low, I thought it. Mr. St. Leger was reading a letter. He had evidently come in but lately, for though he seemed to be eager about it, he was only at the first page, and I could see that there were many sheets. He did not look up when we came in, or till he had finished the letter; and you may be sure that neither I nor my father (who, as Head of the House, should have had more respect from him) took the trouble to go to him. After all, he is a pauper and a wastrel, and he has not the honour of bearing our Name. The General, however, came forward and greeted us both cordially. He evidently had forgotten—or pretended to have—the discourteous way he once treated me, for he spoke to me quite in a friendly way—I thought more warmly than he did to father. I was pleased to be spoken to so nicely, for, after all, whatever his manners may be, he is a distinguished man—has won the V.C. and a Baronetcy. He got the latter not long ago, after the Frontier War in India. I was not, however, led away into cordiality myself. I had not forgotten his rudeness, and I thought that he might be sucking up to me. I knew that when I had my dear Uncle Roger's many millions I should be a rather important person; and, of course, he knew it too. So I got even with him for his former impudence. When he held out his hand I put one finger in it, and said, "How do?" He got very red and turned away. Father and he had ended by glaring at each other, so neither of us was sorry to be done with him. All the time Mr. St. Leger did not seem to see or hear anything, but went on reading his letter. I thought the old MacSkelpie was going to bring him into the matter between us, for as he turned away I heard him say something under his breath. It sounded like "Help!" but Mr. S—did not hear. He certainly no notice of it.

As the MacS—and Mr. S—sat quite silent, neither looking at us, and as father was sitting on the other side of the room with his chin in his hand, and as I wanted to show that I was indifferent to the two S's, I took out this notebook, and went on with the Record, bringing it up to this moment.

THE RECORD—Continued.

When I had finished writing I looked over at Rupert.

When he saw us, he jumped up and went over to father and shook his hand quite warmly. Father took him very coolly. Rupert, however, did not seem to see it, but came towards me heartily. I happened to be doing something else at the moment, and at first I did not see his hand; but just as I was looking at it the clock struck eleven. Whilst it was striking Mr. Trent came into the room. Close behind him came his clerk, carrying a locked tin box. There were two other men also. He bowed to us all in turn, beginning with me. I was standing opposite the door; the others were scattered about. Father sat still, but Sir Colin and Mr. St. Leger rose. Mr. Trent not did shake hands with any of us—not even me. Nothing but his respectful bow. That is the etiquette for an attorney, I understand, on such formal occasions.

He sat down at the end of the big table in the centre of the room, and asked us to sit round. Father, of course, as Head of the Family, took the seat at his right hand. Sir Colin and St. Leger went to the other side, the former taking the seat next to the attorney. The General knows, of course, that a Baronet takes precedence at a ceremony. I may be a Baronet some day myself, and have to know these things.

The clerk took the key which his master handed to him, opened the tin box, and took from it a bundle of papers tied with red tape. This he placed before the attorney, and put the empty box behind him on the floor. Then he and the other man sat at the far end of the table; the latter took out a big notebook and several pencils, and put them before him. He was evidently a shorthand-writer. Mr. Trent removed the tape from the bundle of papers, which he placed a little distance in front of him. He took a sealed envelope from the top, broke the seal, opened the envelope, and from it took a parchment, in the folds of which were some sealed envelopes, which he laid in a heap in front of the other paper. Then he unfolded the parchment, and laid it before him with the outside page up. He fixed his glasses, and said:

"Gentlemen, the sealed envelope which you have seen me open is endorsed 'My Last Will and Testament—ROGER MELTON, June, 1906.' This document"—holding it up—"is as follows:

"'I Roger Melton of Openshaw Grange in the County of Dorset; of number one hundred and twenty-three Berkeley Square London; and of the Castle of Vissarion in the Land of the Blue Mountains, being of sound mind do make this my Last Will and Testament on this day Monday the eleventh day of the month of June in the year of Our Lord one thousand nine hundred and six at the office of my old friend and Attorney Edward Bingham Trent in number one hundred and seventy-six Lincoln's Inn Fields London hereby revoking all other wills that I may have formerly made and giving this as my sole and last Will making dispositions of my property as follows:

"'1. To my kinsman and nephew Ernest Halbard Melton Esquire, justice of the Peace, Humcroft the County of Salop, for his sole use and benefit the sum of twenty thousand pounds sterling free of all Duties Taxes and charges whatever to be paid out of my Five per centum Bonds of the City of Montreal, Canada.

"'2. To my respected friend and colleague as co-trustee to the Will of my late sister Patience late widow of the late Captain Rupert Sent Leger who predeceased her, Major-General Sir Colin Alexander

MacKelpie, Baronet, holder of the Victoria Cross, Knight Commander of the Order of the Bath, of Croom in the county of Ross Scotland a sum of Twenty thousand pounds sterling free of all Taxes and charges whatsoever; to be paid out of my Five per centum Bonds of the City of Toronto, Canada.

"'3. To Miss Janet MacKelpie presently residing at Croom in the County of Ross Scotland the sum of Twenty thousand pounds sterling free of all Duties Taxes and Charges whatsoever, to be paid out of my Five per centum Bonds of the London County Council.

"'4. To the various persons charities and Trustees named in the schedule attached to this Will and marked A. the various sums mentioned therein, all free of Duties and Taxes and charges whatsoever.'"

Here Mr. Trent read out the list here following, and announced for our immediate understanding of the situation the total amount as two hundred and fifty thousand pounds. Many of the beneficiaries were old friends, comrades, dependents, and servants, some of them being left quite large sums of money and specific objects, such as curios and pictures.

"'5. To my kinsman and nephew Ernest Roger Halbard Melton presently living in the house of his father at Humcroft Salop the sum of Ten thousand pounds sterling.

"'6. To my old and valued friend Edward Bingham Trent of one hundred and seventy-six Lincoln's Inn Fields sum of Twenty thousand pounds sterling free from all Duties Taxes and Charges whatsoever to be paid out of my Five per centum Bonds of the city of Manchester England.

"'7. To my dear nephew Rupert Sent Leger only son of my dear sister Patience Melton by her marriage with Captain Rupert Sent Leger the sum of one thousand pounds sterling. I also bequeath to the said Rupert Sent Leger a further sum conditional upon his acceptance of the terms of a letter addressed to him marked B, and left in the custody of the above Edward Bingham Trent and which letter is an integral part of this my Will. In case of the non-acceptance of the conditions of such letter, I devise and bequeath the whole of the sums and properties reserved therein to the executors herein appointed Colin Alexander MacKelpie and Edward Bingham Trent in trust to distribute the same in accordance with the terms of the letter in the present custody of Edward Bingham Trent marked C, and now deposited sealed with my seal in the sealed envelope containing my last Will to be kept in the custody of the said Edward Bingham Trent and which said letter C is also an integral part of my Will. And in case any doubt should arise as to my ultimate intention as to the disposal of my property the above-mentioned Executors are to have full power to arrange and dispose all such matters as may seem best to them without further appeal. And if any beneficiary under this Will shall challenge the same or any part of it, or dispute the validity thereof, he shall forfeit to the general estate the bequest made herein to him, and any such bequest shall cease and be void to all intents and purposes whatsoever.

"'8. For proper compliance with laws and duties connected with testamentary proceedings and to keep my secret trusts secret I direct my Executors to pay all Death, Estate, Settlement, Legacy, Succession, or other duties charges impositions and assessments whatever on the residue of my estate beyond the bequests already named, at the scale charged in the case of most distant relatives or strangers in blood.

"'9. I hereby appoint as my Executors Major-General Sir Colin Alexander MacKelpie, Baronet, of Croom in the County of Ross, and Edward Bingham Trent Attorney at Law of one hundred and seventy-six Lincoln's Inn Fields London West Central with full power to exercise their discretion in any circumstance which may arise in the carrying out my wishes as expressed in this Will. As reward for their services in this capacity as Executors they are to receive each out of the general estate a sum of one hundred thousand pounds sterling free of all Duties and impositions whatsoever.

"'12. The two Memoranda contained in the letters marked B and C are Integral Parts of this my Last Will are ultimately at the Probate of the Will to be taken as Clauses 10 and 11 of it. The envelopes are marked B and C on both envelope and contents and the contents of each is headed thus: B to be read as Clause 10 of my Will and the other C to be read as Clause 11 of my Will.

"'13. Should either of the above-mentioned Executors die before the completion of the above year and a half from the date of the Reading of my Will or before the Conditions rehearsed in Letter C the remaining Executor shall have all and several the Rights and Duties entrusted by my Will to both. And if both Executors should die then the matter of interpretation and execution of all matters in connection with this my Last Will shall rest with the Lord Chancellor of England for the time being or with whomsoever he may appoint for the purpose.

"'This my Last Will is given by me on the first day of January in the year of Our Lord one thousand nine hundred and seven.

"'ROGER MELTON.'

"We Andrew Rossiter and John Colson here in the presence of each other and of the Testator have seen the Testator Roger Melton sign and seal this document. In witness thereof we hereby set our names

"ANDREW ROSSITER clerk of 9 Primrose Avenue London W.C.

"JOHN COLSON caretaker of 176 Lincoln's Inn Fields and Verger of St. Tabitha's Church Clerkenwell London.'"

When Mr. Trent had finished the reading he put all the papers together, and tied them up in a bundle again with the red tape. Holding the bundle in his hand, he stood up, saying as he did so:

"That is all, gentlemen, unless any of you wish to ask me any questions; in which case I shall answer, of course, to the best of my power. I shall ask you, Sir Colin, to remain with me, as we have to deal with some matters, or to arrange a time when we may meet to do so. And you also, Mr. Sent Leger, as there is this letter to submit to you. It is necessary that you should open it in the presence of the executors, but there is no necessity that anyone else should be present."

The first to speak was my father. Of course, as a county gentleman of position and estate, who is sometimes asked to take the chair at Sessions—of course, when there is not anyone with a title present—he found himself under the duty of expressing himself first. Old MacKelpie has superior rank; but this was a family affair, in which my father is Head of the House, whilst old MacKelpie is only an outsider brought into it—and then only to the distaff side, by the wife of a younger brother of the man who married into our family. Father spoke with the same look on his face as when he asks important questions of witnesses at Quarter Sessions.

"I should like some points elucidated." The attorney bowed (he gets his 120 thou', any way, so he can afford to be oily—suave, I suppose he would call it); so father looked at a slip of paper in his hand and asked:

"How much is the amount of the whole estate?"

The attorney answered quickly, and I thought rather rudely. He was red in the face, and didn't bow this time; I suppose a man of his class hasn't more than a very limited stock of manners:

"That, sir, I am not at liberty to tell you. And I may say that I would not if I could."

"Is it a million?" said father again. He was angry this time, and even redder than the old attorney. The attorney said in answer, very quietly this time:

"Ah, that's cross-examining. Let me say, sir, that no one can know that until the accountants to be appointed for the purpose have examined the affairs of the testator up to date."

Mr. Rupert St. Leger, who was looking all this time angrier than even the attorney or my father—though at what he had to be angry about I can't imagine—struck his fist on the table and rose up as if to speak, but as he caught sight of both old MacKelpie and the attorney he sat down again. *Mem.*—Those three seem to agree too well. I must keep a sharp eye on them. I didn't think of this part any more at the time, for father asked another question which interested me much:

"May I ask why the other matters of the Will are not shown to us?" The attorney wiped his spectacles carefully with a big silk bandanna handkerchief before he answered:

"Simply because each of the two letters marked 'B' and 'C' is enclosed with instructions regarding their opening and the keeping secret of their contents. I shall call your attention to the fact that both envelopes are sealed, and that the testator and both witnesses have signed their names across the flap of each envelope. I shall read them. The letter marked 'B,' directed to 'Rupert Sent Leger,' is thus endorsed:

"'This letter is to be given to Rupert Sent Leger by the Trustees and is to be opened by him in their presence. He is to take such copy or make such notes as he may wish and is then to hand the letter with envelope to the Executors who are at once to read it, each of them being entitled to make copy or notes if desirous of so doing. The letter is then to be replaced in its envelope and letter and envelope are to be placed in another envelope to be endorsed on outside as to its contents and to be signed across the flap by both the Executors and by the said Rupert Sent Leger.

"'(Signed) ROGER MELTON 1/6/'06.

'The letter marked 'C,' directed to 'Edward Bingham Trent,' is thus endorsed:

"'This letter directed to Edward Bingham Trent is to be kept by him unopened for a term of two years after the reading of my Last Will unless said period is earlier terminated by either the acceptance or refusal of Rupert Sent Leger to accept the conditions mentioned in my letter to him marked 'B' which he is to receive and read in the presence of my Executors at the same meeting as but subsequent to the Reading of the clauses (except those to be ultimately numbers ten and eleven) of my Last Will. This letter contains instructions as to what both the Executors and the said Rupert Sent Leger are to do when such acceptance or refusal of the said Rupert Sent Leger has been made known, or if he omit or refuse to make any such acceptance or refusal, at the end of two years next after my decease.

"'(Signed) ROGER MELTON 1/6/'06.'"

When the attorney had finished reading the last letter he put it carefully in his pocket. Then he took the other letter in his hand, and stood up. "Mr. Rupert Sent Leger," he said, "please to open this letter, and in such a way that all present may see that the memorandum at top of the contents is given as—

"'B. To be read as clause ten of my Will.'"

St. Leger rolled up his sleeves and cuffs just as if he was going to perform some sort of prestidigitation—it was very theatrical and ridiculous—then, his wrists being quite bare, he opened the envelope and took out the letter. We all saw it quite well. It was folded with the first page outward, and on the top was written a line just as the attorney said. In obedience to a request from the attorney, he laid both letter and envelope on the table in front of him. The clerk then rose up, and, after handing a piece of paper to the attorney, went back to his seat. Mr. Trent, having written something on the paper, asked us all who were present, even the clerk and the shorthand man, to look at the memorandum on the letter and what was written on the envelope, and to sign the paper, which ran:

"We the signatories of this paper hereby declare that we have seen the sealed letter marked B and enclosed in the Will of Roger Melton opened in the presence of us all including Mr. Edward Bingham Trent and Sir Colin Alexander MacKelpie and we declare that the paper there in contained was headed 'B. To be read as clause ten of my Will' and that there were no other contents in the envelope. In attestation of which we in the presence of each other append our signatures."

The attorney motioned to my father to begin. Father is a cautious man, and he asked for a magnifying-glass, which was shortly brought to him by a clerk for whom the clerk in the room called. Father examined the envelope all over very carefully, and also the memorandum at top of the paper. Then, without a word, he signed the paper. Father is a just man. Then we all signed. The attorney folded the paper and put it in an envelope. Before closing it he passed it round, and we all saw that it had not been tampered with. Father took it out and read it, and then put it back. Then the attorney asked us all to sign it across the flap, which we did. Then he put the sealing-wax on it and asked father to seal it with his own seal. He did so. Then he and MacKelpie sealed it also with their own seals, Then he put it in another envelope, which he sealed himself, and he and MacKelpie signed it across the flap.

Then father stood up, and so did I. So did the two men—the clerk and the shorthand writer. Father did not say a word till we got out into the street. We walked along, and presently we passed an open gate into the fields. He turned back, saying to me:

"Come in here. There is no one about, and we can be quiet. I want to speak to you." When we sat down on a seat with none other near it, father said:

"You are a student of the law. What does all that mean?" I thought it a good occasion for an epigram, so I said one word:

"Bilk!"

"H'm!" said father; "that is so far as you and I are concerned. You with a beggarly ten thousand, and I with twenty. But what is, or will be, the effect of those secret trusts?"

"Oh, that," I said, "will, I dare say, be all right. Uncle Roger evidently did not intend the older generation to benefit too much by his death. But he only gave Rupert St. Leger one thousand pounds, whilst he gave me ten. That looks as if he had more regard for the direct line. Of course—" Father interrupted me:

"But what was the meaning of a further sum?"

"I don't know, father. There was evidently some condition which he was to fulfil; but he evidently didn't expect that he would. Why, otherwise, did he leave a second trust to Mr. Trent?"

"True!" said father. Then he went on: "I wonder why he left those enormous sums to Trent and old MacKelpie. They seem out of all proportion as executors' fees, unless—"

"Unless what, father?"

"Unless the fortune he has left is an enormous one. That is why I asked."

"And that," I laughed, "is why he refused to answer."

"Why, Ernest, it must run into big figures."

"Right-ho, father. The death-duties will be annoying. What a beastly swindle the death-duties are! Why, I shall suffer even on your own little estate . . . ."

"That will do!" he said curtly. Father is so ridiculously touchy. One would think he expects to live for ever. Presently he spoke again:

"I wonder what are the conditions of that trust. They are as important—almost—as the amount of the bequest—whatever it is. By the way, there seems to be no mention in the will of a residuary legatee. Ernest, my boy, we may have to fight over that."

"How do you make that out, father?" I asked. He had been very rude over the matter of the death-duties of his own estate, though it is entailed and I *must* inherit. So I determined to let him see that I know a good deal more than he does—of law, at any rate. "I fear that when we come to look into it closely that dog won't fight. In the first place, that may be all arranged in the letter to St. Leger, which is a part of the Will. And if that letter should be inoperative by his refusal of the conditions (whatever they may be), then the letter to the attorney begins to work. What it is we don't know, and perhaps even he doesn't—I looked at it as well as I could—and we law men are trained to observationn. But even if the instructions mentioned as being in Letter C fail, then the corpus of the Will gives full power to Trent to act just as he darn pleases. He can give the whole thing to himself if he likes, and no one can say a word. In fact, he is himself the final court of appeal."

"H'm!" said father to himself. "It is a queer kind of will, I take it, that can override the Court of Chancery. We shall perhaps have to try it before we are done with this!" With that he rose, and we walked home together—without saying another word.

My mother was very inquisitive about the whole thing—women always are. Father and I between us told her all it was necessary for her to know. I think we were both afraid that, woman-like, she would make trouble for us by saying or doing something injudicious. Indeed, she manifested such hostility towards Rupert St. Leger that it is quite on the cards that she may try to injure him in some way. So when father said that he would have to go out shortly again, as he wished to consult his solicitor, I jumped up and said I would go with him, as I, too, should take advice as to how I stood in the matter.

The Contents of Letter marked "B" attached as an Integral Part to the Last Will of Roger Melton.

June 11, 1907.

"This letter an integral part of my Last Will regards the entire residue of my estate beyond the specific bequests made in the body of my Will. It is to appoint as Residuary Legatee of such Will—in case he may accept in due form the Conditions herein laid down—my dear Nephew Rupert Sent Leger only son of my sister Patience Melton now deceased by her marriage with Captain Rupert Sent Leger also now deceased. On his acceptance of the Conditions and the fulfilment of the first of them the Entire residue of my estate after payments of all specific Legacies and of all my debts and other obligations is to become his absolute property to be dealt with or disposed of as he may desire. The following are the conditions.

"1. He is to accept provisionally by letter addressed to my Executors a sum of nine hundred and ninety-nine thousand pounds sterling free of all Duties Taxes or other imposts. This he will hold for a period of six months from the date of the Reading of my Last Will and have user of the accruements thereto calculated at the rate of ten per centum per annum which amount he shall under no circumstances be required to replace. At the end of said six months he must express in writing directed to the Executors of my Will his acceptance or refusal of the other conditions herein to follow. But if he may so choose he shall be free to declare in writing to the Executors within one week from the time of the Reading of the Will his wish to accept or to withdraw altogether from the responsibility of this Trust. In case of withdrawal he is to retain absolutely and for his own use the above-mentioned sum of nine hundred and ninety-nine thousand pounds sterling free of all Duties Taxes and imposts whatsoever making with the specific bequest of one thousand pounds a clear sum of one million pounds sterling free of all imposts. And he will from the moment of the delivery of such written withdrawal cease to have any right or interest whatsoever in the further disposition of my estate under this instrument. Should such written withdrawal be received by my Executors they shall have possession of such residue of my estate as shall remain after the payment of the above sum of nine hundred and ninety-nine thousand pounds sterling and the payment of all Duties Taxes assessments or Imposts as may be entailed by law by its conveyance to the said Rupert Sent Leger and these my Executors shall hold the same for the further disposal of it according to the instructions given in the letter marked C and which is also an integral part of my Last Will and Testament.

"2. If at or before the expiration of the six months above-mentioned the said Rupert Sent Leger shall have accepted the further conditions herein stated, he is to have user of the entire income produced by such residue of my estate the said income being paid to him Quarterly on the usual Quarter Days by the aforesaid Executors to wit Major General Sir Colin Alexander MacKelpie Bart. and Edward Bingham Trent to be used by him in accordance with the terms and conditions here in after mentioned.

"3. The said Rupert Sent Leger is to reside for a period of at least six months to begin not later than three months from the reading of my Will in the Castle of Vissarion in the Land of the Blue Mountains. And if he fulfil the Conditions imposed on him and shall thereby become possessed of the residue of my estate he is to continue to reside there in part for a period of one year. He is not to change his British Nationality except by a formal consent of the Privy Council of Great Britain.

"At the end of a year and a half from the Reading of my Will he is to report in person to my Executors of the expenditure of amounts paid or due by him in the carrying out of the Trust and if they are satisfied that same are in general accord with the conditions named in above-mentioned letter marked C and which is an integral part of my

Will they are to record their approval on such Will which can then go for final Probate and Taxation. On the Completion of which the said Rupert Sent Leger shall become possessed absolutely and without further act or need of the entire residue of my estate. In witness whereof, etc.

"(Signed) ROGER MELTON."

This document is attested by the witnesses to the Will on the same date.

(Personal and Confidential.)

MEMORANDA MADE BY EDWARD BINGHAM TRENT IN CONNECTION WITH THE WILL OF ROGER MELTON.

January 3, 1907.

The interests and issues of all concerned in the Will and estate of the late Roger Melton of Openshaw Grange are so vast that in case any litigation should take place regarding the same, I, as the solicitor, having the carriage of the testator's wishes, think it well to make certain memoranda of events, conversations, etc., not covered by documentary evidence. I make the first memorandum immediately after the event, whilst every detail of act and conversation is still fresh in my mind. I shall also try to make such comments thereon as may serve to refresh my memory hereafter, and which in case of my death may perhaps afford as opinions contemporaneously recorded some guiding light to other or others who may later on have to continue and complete the tasks entrusted to me.

I.

CONCERNING THE READING OF THE WILL OF ROGER MELTON.

When, beginning at 11 o'clock a.m. on this the forenoon of Thursday, the 3rd day of January, 1907, I opened the Will and read it in full, except the clauses contained in the letters marked "B" and "C"; there were present in addition to myself, the following:

1. Ernest Halbard Melton, J.P., nephew of the testator.

2. Ernest Roger Halbard Melton, son of the above.

3. Rupert Sent Leger, nephew of the testator.

4. Major-General Sir Colin Alexander MacKelpie, Bart., co-executor with myself of the Will.

5. Andrew Rossiter, my clerk, one of the witnesses of the testator's Will.

6. Alfred Nugent, stenographer (of Messrs. Castle's office, 21, Bream's Buildings, W.C.).

When the Will had been read, Mr. E. H. Melton asked the value of the estate left by the testator, which query I did not feel empowered or otherwise able to answer; and a further query, as to why those present were not shown the secret clauses of the Will. I answered by reading the instructions endorsed on the envelopes of the two letters marked "B" and "C," which were sufficiently explanatory.

But, lest any question should hereafter arise as to the fact that the memoranda in letters marked "B" and "C," which were to be read as clauses 10 and 11 of the Will, I caused Rupert Sent Leger to open the envelope marked "B" in the presence of all in the room. These all signed a paper which I had already prepared, to the effect that they had seen the envelope opened, and that the memorandum marked "B. To be read as clause ten of my Will," was contained in the envelope, of which it was to be the sole contents. Mr. Ernest Halbard Melton, J.P., before signing, carefully examined with a magnifying-glass, for which he had asked, both the envelope and the heading of the memorandum enclosed in the letter. He was about to turn the folded paper which was lying on the table over, by which he might have been able to read the matter of the memorandum had he so desired. I at once advised

him that the memorandum he was to sign dealt only with the heading
of the page, and not with the matter. He looked very angry, but said
nothing, and after a second scrutiny signed. I put the memorandum
in an envelope, which we all signed across the flap. Before signing,
Mr Ernest Halbard Melton took out the paper and verified it. I then
asked him to close it, which he did, and when the sealing-wax was on
it he sealed it with his own seal. Sir Colin A. MacKelpie and I also
appended our own seals. I put the envelope in another, which I sealed
with my own seal, and my co-executor and I signed it across the flap
and added the date. I took charge of this. When the others present
had taken their departure, my co-executor and I, together with Mr.
Rupert Sent Leger, who had remained at my request, went into my
private room.

Here Mr. Rupert Sent Leger read the memorandum marked "B,"
which is to be read as clause 10 of the Will. He is evidently a man
of considerable nerve, for his face was quite impassive as he read the
document, which conveyed to him (subject to the conditions laid
down) a fortune which has no equal in amount in Europe, even, so
far as I know, amongst the crowned heads. When he had read it over a
second time he stood up and said:

"I wish I had known my uncle better. He must have had the heart
of a king. I never heard of such generosity as he has shown me. Mr.
Trent, I see, from the conditions of this memorandum, or codicil,
or whatever it is, that I am to declare within a week as to whether I
accept the conditions imposed on me. Now, I want you to tell me this:
must I wait a week to declare?" In answer, I told him that the testator's
intention was manifestly to see that he had full time to consider fully
every point before making formal decision and declaration. But, in
answer to the specific question, I could answer that he might make
declaration when he would, provided it was *within*, or rather not after,
the week named. I added:

"But I strongly advise you not to act hurriedly. So enormous a sum is involved that you may be sure that all possible efforts will be made by someone or other to dispossess you of your inheritance, and it will be well that everything shall be done, not only in perfect order, but with such manifest care and deliberation that there can be no question as to your intention."

"Thank you, sir," he answered; "I shall do as you shall kindly advise me in this as in other things. But I may tell you now—and you, too, my dear Sir Colin—that I not only accept my Uncle Roger's conditions in this, but that when the time comes in the other matters I shall accept every condition that he had in his mind—and that I may know of—in everything." He looked exceedingly in earnest, and it gave me much pleasure to see and hear him. It was just what a young man should do who had been so generously treated. As the time had now come, I gave him the bulky letter addressed to him, marked "D" which I had in my safe. As I fulfilled my obligation in the matter, I said:

"You need not read the letter here. You can take it away with you, and read it by yourself at leisure. It is your own property, without any obligation whatever attached to it. By the way, perhaps it would be well if you knew. I have a copy sealed up in an envelope, and endorsed, 'To be opened if occasion should arise,' but not otherwise. Will you see me to-morrow, or, better still, dine with me alone here to-night? I should like to have a talk with you, and you may wish to ask me some questions." He answered me cordially. I actually felt touched by the way he said good-bye before he went away. Sir Colin MacKelpie went with him, as Sent Leger was to drop him at the Reform.

Letter from Roger Melton to Rupert Sent Leger, endorsed "D. re Rupert Sent Leger. To be given to him by Edward Bingham Trent if and as soon as he has declared (formally or informally) his intention of accepting the conditions named in Letter B., forming Clause 10 in my Will. R. M., 1/1/'07.

"Mem.—Copy (sealed) left in custody of E. B. Trent, to be opened if necessary, as directed."

June 11, 1906.

My Dear Nephew,

When (if ever) you receive this you will know that (with the exception of some definite bequests) I have left to you, under certain conditions, the entire bulk of my fortune—a fortune so great that by its aid as a help, a man of courage and ability may carve out for himself a name and place in history. The specific conditions contained in Clause 10 of my Will have to be observed, for such I deem to be of service to your own fortune; but herein I give my advice, which you are at liberty to follow or not as you will, and my wishes, which I shall try to explain fully and clearly, so that you may be in possession of my views in case you should desire to carry them out, or, at least, to so endeavour that the results I hope for may be ultimately achieved. First let me explain—for your understanding and your guidance—that the power, or perhaps it had better be called the pressure, behind the accumulation of my fortune has been ambition. In obedience to its compulsion, I toiled early and late until I had so arranged matters that, subject to broad supervision, my ideas could be carried out by men whom I had selected and tested, and not found wanting. This was for years to the satisfaction, and ultimately to the accumulation by these men of fortune commensurate in some measure to their own worth and their importance to my designs. Thus I had accumulated, whilst still a young man, a considerable fortune. This I have for over forty years used sparingly as regards my personal needs, daringly with regard to speculative investments. With the latter I took such very great care, studying the conditions surrounding them so thoroughly, that even now my schedule of bad debts or unsuccessful investments is almost a blank.

Perhaps by such means things flourished with me, and wealth piled in so fast that at times I could hardly use it to advantage. This was all done as the forerunner of ambition, but I was over fifty years of age when the horizon of ambition itself opened up to me. I speak thus freely, my dear Rupert, as when you read it I shall have passed away, and not ambition nor the fear of misunderstanding, nor even of scorn can touch me. My ventures in commerce and finance covered not only the Far East, but every foot of the way to it, so that the Mediterranean and all its opening seas were familiar to me. In my journeyings up and down the Adriatic I was always struck by the great beauty and seeming richness—native richness—of the Land of the Blue Mountains. At last Chance took me into that delectable region. When the "Balkan Struggle" of '90 was on, one of the great Voivodes came to me in secret to arrange a large loan for national purposes. It was known in financial circles of both Europe and Asia that I took an active part in the *haute politique* of national treasuries, and the Voivode Vissarion came to me as to one able and willing to carry out his wishes. After confidential pour-parlers, he explained to me that his nation was in the throes of a great crisis. As you perhaps know, the gallant little Nation in the Land of the Blue Mountains has had a strange history. For more than a thousand years—ever since its settlement after the disaster of Rossoro—it had maintained its national independence under several forms of Government. At first it had a King whose successors became so despotic that they were dethroned. Then it was governed by its Voivodes, with the combining influence of a Vladika somewhat similar in power and function to the Prince-Bishops of Montenegro; afterwards by a Prince; or, as at present, by an irregular elective Council, influenced in a modified form by the Vladika, who was then supposed to exercise a purely spiritual function. Such a Council in a small, poor nation did not have sufficient funds for armaments, which were not immediately and imperatively necessary; and therefore the Voivode Vissarion, who had vast estates in his own possession, and who was the present representative a family which of old had been leaders in the land, found it a duty to do on his own account that which the State could not do. For security as to the loan which he wished to get, and which was indeed a vast one, he offered to sell me his whole estate if I would secure to him a right to repurchase it within a given time (a time which I may say has some time ago expired). He made it a condition that the sale and agreement should remain a strict secret between us, as a widespread knowledge that his estate had changed hands would in all probability result in my death and his own at the hands of the mountaineers, who are beyond everything loyal, and were jealous to the last degree. An attack by Turkey was feared, and new armaments were required; and the patriotic Voivode was sacrificing his own great fortune for the public good. What a sacrifice this was he well knew, for in all discussions regarding a possible change in the Constitution of the Blue Mountains it was always taken for granted that if the principles of the Constitution should change to a more personal rule, his own family should be regarded as the Most Noble. It had ever been on the side of freedom in olden time; before the establishment of the Council, or even during the rule of the Voivodes, the Vissarion had every now and again stood out against the King or challenged the Princedom. The very name stood for freedom, for nationality, against foreign oppression; and the bold mountaineers were devoted to it, as in other free countries men follow the flag.

Such loyalty was a power and a help in the land, for it knew danger in every form; and anything which aided the cohesion of its integers was a natural asset. On every side other powers, great and small, pressed the land, anxious to acquire its suzerainty by any means—fraud or force. Greece, Turkey, Austria, Russia, Italy, France, had all tried in vain. Russia, often hurled back, was waiting an opportunity to attack.

Austria and Greece, although united by no common purpose or design, were ready to throw in their forces with whomsoever might seem most likely to be victor. Other Balkan States, too, were not lacking in desire to add the little territory of the Blue Mountains to their more ample possessions. Albania, Dalmatia, Herzegovina, Servia, Bulgaria, looked with lustful eyes on the land, which was in itself a vast natural fortress, having close under its shelter perhaps the finest harbour between Gibraltar and the Dardanelles.

But the fierce, hardy mountaineers were unconquerable. For centuries they had fought, with a fervour and fury that nothing could withstand or abate, attacks on their independence. Time after time, century after century, they had opposed with dauntless front invading armies sent against them. This unquenchable fire of freedom had had its effect. One and all, the great Powers knew that to conquer that little nation would be no mean task, but rather that of a tireless giant. Over and over again had they fought with units against hundreds, never ceasing until they had either wiped out their foes entirely or seen them retreat across the frontier in diminished numbers.

For many years past, however, the Land of the Blue Mountains had remained unassailable, for all the Powers and States had feared lest the others should unite against the one who should begin the attack.

At the time I speak of there was a feeling throughout the Blue Mountains—and, indeed, elsewhere—that Turkey was preparing for a war of offence. The objective of her attack was not known anywhere, but here there was evidence that the Turkish "Bureau of Spies" was in active exercise towards their sturdy little neighbour. To prepare for this, the Voivode Peter Vissarion approached me in order to obtain the necessary "sinews of war."

The situation was complicated by the fact that the Elective Council was at present largely held together by the old Greek Church, which was the religion of the people, and which had had since the beginning its destinies linked in a large degree with theirs. Thus it was possible that if a war should break out, it might easily become—whatever might have been its cause or beginnings—a war of creeds. This in the Balkans must be largely one of races, the end of which no mind could diagnose or even guess at.

I had now for some time had knowledge of the country and its people, and had come to love them both. The nobility of Vissarion's self-sacrifice at once appealed to me, and I felt that I, too, should like to have a hand in the upholding of such a land and such a people. They both deserved freedom. When Vissarion handed me the completed deed of sale I was going to tear it up; but he somehow recognized my intention, and forestalled it. He held up his hand arrestingly as he said:

"I recognize your purpose, and, believe me, I honour you for it from the very depths of my soul. But, my friend, it must not be. Our mountaineers are proud beyond belief. Though they would allow me— who am one of themselves, and whose fathers have been in some way leaders and spokesmen amongst them for many centuries—to do all that is in my power to do—and what, each and all, they would be glad to do were the call to them—they would not accept aid from one outside themselves. My good friend, they would resent it, and might show to you, who wish us all so well, active hostility, which might end in danger, or even death. That was why, my friend, I asked to put a clause in our agreement, that I might have right to repurchase my estate, regarding which you would fain act so generously."

Thus it is, my dear nephew Rupert, only son of my dear sister, that I hereby charge you solemnly as you value me—as you value yourself—as you value honour, that, should it ever become known that that noble Voivode, Peter Vissarion, imperilled himself for his country's good, and if it be of danger or evil repute to him that even for such a purpose he sold his heritage, you shall at once and to the knowledge of the mountaineers—though not necessarily to others—reconvey to him or his heirs the freehold that he was willing to part with—and that he has *de facto* parted with by the effluxion of the time during which his right of repurchase existed. This is a secret trust and duty which is between thee and me alone in the first instance; a duty which I have undertaken on behalf of my heirs, and which must be carried out, at whatsoever cost may ensue. You must not take it that it is from any mistrust of you or belief that you will fail that I have taken another measure to insure that this my cherished idea is borne out. Indeed, it is that the law may, in case of need—for no man can know what may happen after his own hand be taken from the plough—be complied with, that I have in another letter written for the guidance of others, directed that in case of any failure to carry out this trust—death or other—the direction become a clause or codicil to my Will. But in the meantime I wish that this be kept a secret between us two. To show you the full extent of my confidence, let me here tell you that the letter alluded to above is marked "C," and directed to my solicitor and co-executor, Edward Bingham Trent, which is finally to be regarded as clause eleven of my Will. To which end he has my instructions and also a copy of this letter, which is, in case of need, and that only, to be opened, and is to be a guide to my wishes as to the carrying out by you of the conditions on which you inherit.

And now, my dear nephew, let me change to another subject more dear to me—yourself. When you read this I shall have passed away, so that I need not be hampered now by that reserve which I feel has grown upon me through a long and self-contained life. Your mother was very dear to me. As you know, she was twenty years younger than her youngest brother, who was two years younger than me. So we were all young men when she was a baby, and, I need not say, a pet amongst us—almost like our own child to each of us, as well as our sister. You knew her sweetness and high quality, so I need say nothing of these; but I should like you to understand that she was very dear to me. When she and your father came to know and love each other I was far away, opening up a new branch of business in the interior of China, and it was not for several months that I got home news. When I first heard of him they had already been married. I was delighted to find that they were very happy. They needed nothing that I could give. When he died so suddenly I tried to comfort her, and all I had was at her disposal, did she want it. She was a proud woman—though not with me. She had come to understand that, though I seemed cold and hard (and perhaps was so generally), I was not so to her. But she would not have help of any kind. When I pressed her, she told me that she had enough for your keep and education and her own sustenance for the time she must still live; that your father and she had agreed that you should be brought up to a healthy and strenuous life rather than to one of luxury; and she thought that it would be better for the development of your character that you should learn to be self-reliant and to be content with what your dear father had left you. She had always been a wise and thoughtful girl, and now all her wisdom and thought were for you, your father's and her child. When she spoke of you and your future, she said many things which I thought memorable. One of them I remember to this day. It was apropos of my saying that there is a danger of its own kind in extreme poverty. A young man might know too much want. She answered me: "True! That is so! But there is a danger that overrides it;" and after a time went on:

"It is better not to know wants than not to know want!" I tell you, boy, that is a great truth, and I hope you will remember it for yourself as well as a part of the wisdom of your mother. And here let me say something else which is a sort of corollary of that wise utterance:

I dare say you thought me very hard and unsympathetic that time I would not, as one of your trustees, agree to your transferring your little fortune to Miss MacKelpie. I dare say you bear a grudge towards me about it up to this day. Well, if you have any of that remaining, put it aside when you know the truth. That request of yours was an unspeakable delight to me. It was like your mother coming back from the dead. That little letter of yours made me wish for the first time that I had a son—and that he should be like you. I fell into a sort of reverie, thinking if I were yet too old to marry, so that a son might be with me in my declining years—if such were to ever be for me. But I concluded that this might not be. There was no woman whom I knew or had ever met with that I could love as your mother loved your father and as he loved her. So I resigned myself to my fate. I must go my lonely road on to the end. And then came a ray of light into my darkness: there was you. Though you might not feel like a son to me—I could not expect it when the memory of that sweet relationship was more worthily filled. But I could feel like a father to you. Nothing could prevent that or interfere with it, for I would keep it as my secret in the very holy of holies of my heart, where had been for thirty years the image of a sweet little child—your mother. My boy, when in your future life you shall have happiness and honour and power, I hope you will sometimes give a thought to the lonely old man whose later years your very existence seemed to brighten.

The thought of your mother recalled me to my duty. I had under-taken for her a sacred task: to carry out her wishes regarding her son. I knew how she would have acted. It might—would—have been to her a struggle of inclination and duty; and duty would have won. And so I carried out my duty, though I tell you it was a harsh and bitter task to me at the time. But I may tell you that I have since been glad when I think of the result. I tried, as you may perhaps remember, to carry out your wishes in another way, but your letter put the difficulty of doing so so clearly before me that I had to give it up. And let me tell you that that letter endeared you to me more than ever.

I need not tell you that thenceforth I followed your life very closely. When you ran away to sea, I used in secret every part of the mechanism of commerce to find out what had become of you. Then, until you had reached your majority, I had a constant watch kept upon you—not to interfere with you in any way, but so that I might be able to find you should need arise. When in due course I heard of your first act on coming of age I was satisfied. I had to know of the carrying out of your original intention towards Janet MacKelpie, for the securities had to be transferred.

From that time on I watched—of course through other eyes—your chief doings. It would have been a pleasure to me to have been able to help in carrying out any hope or ambition of yours, but I realized that in the years intervening between your coming of age and the present moment you were fulfilling your ideas and ambitions in your own way, and, as I shall try to explain to you presently, my ambitions also. You were of so adventurous a nature that even my own widely-spread machinery of acquiring information—what I may call my private "intelligence department"—was inadequate. My machinery was fairly adequate for the East—in great part, at all events. But you went North and South, and West also, and, in addition, you essayed realms where commerce and purely real affairs have no foothold—worlds of thought, of spiritual import, of psychic phenomena—speaking generally, of mysteries. As now and again I was baffled in my inquiries, I had to enlarge my mechanism, and to this end started—not in my own name, of course—some new magazines devoted to certain branches of inquiry and adventure. Should you ever care to know more of these things, Mr. Trent, in whose name the stock is left, will be delighted to give you all details. Indeed, these stocks, like all else I have, shall be yours when the time comes, if you care to ask for them. By means of *The Journal of Adventure, The Magazine of Mystery, Occultism, Balloon and Aeroplane, The Submarine, Jungle and Pampas, The Ghost World, The*

Explorer, Forest and Island, Ocean and Creek, I was often kept informed when I should otherwise have been ignorant of your whereabouts and designs. For instance, when you had disappeared into the Forest of the Incas, I got the first whisper of your strange adventures and discoveries in the buried cities of Eudori from a correspondent of *The Journal of Adventure* long before the details given in *The Times* of the rock-temple of the primeval savages, where only remained the little dragon serpents, whose giant ancestors were rudely sculptured on the sacrificial altar. I well remember how I thrilled at even that meagre account of your going in alone into that veritable hell. It was from *Occultism* that I learned how you had made a stay alone in the haunted catacombs of Elora, in the far recesses of the Himalayas, and of the fearful experiences which, when you came out shuddering and ghastly, overcame to almost epileptic fear those who had banded themselves together to go as far as the rock-cut approach to the hidden temple.

All such things I read with rejoicing. You were shaping yourself for a wider and loftier adventure, which would crown more worthily your matured manhood. When I read of you in a description of Mihask, in Madagascar, and the devil-worship there rarely held, I felt I had only to wait for your home-coming in order to broach the enterprise I had so long contemplated. This was what I read:

"He is a man to whom no adventure is too wild or too daring. His reckless bravery is a byword amongst many savage peoples and amongst many others not savages, whose fears are not of material things, but of the world of mysteries in and beyond the grave. He dares not only wild animals and savage men; but has tackled African magic and Indian mysticism. The Psychical Research Society has long exploited his deeds of valiance, and looked upon him as perhaps their most trusted agent or source of discovery. He is in the very prime of life, of almost giant stature and strength, trained to the use of all arms of all countries, inured to every kind of hardship, subtle-minded and resourceful, understanding human nature from its elemental form up. To say that he is fearless would be inadequate. In a word, he is a man whose strength and daring fit him for any enterprise of any kind. He would dare and do anything in the world or out of it, on the earth or under it, in the sea or—in the air, fearing nothing material or unseen, not man or ghost, nor God nor Devil."

If you ever care to think of it, I carried that cutting in my pocketbook from that hour I read it till now.

Remember, again, I say, that I never interfered in the slightest way in any of your adventures. I wanted you to "dree your own weird," as the Scotch say; and I wanted to know of it—that was all. Now, as I hold you fully equipped for greater enterprise, I want to set your feet on the road and to provide you with the most potent weapon—beyond personal qualities—for the winning of great honour—a gain, my dear nephew, which, I am right sure, does and will appeal to you as it has ever done to me. I have worked for it for more than fifty years; but now that the time has come when the torch is slipping from my old hands, I look to you, my dearest kinsman, to lift it and carry it on.

The little nation of the Blue Mountains has from the first appealed to me. It is poor and proud and brave. Its people are well worth winning, and I would advise you to throw in your lot with them. You may find them hard to win, for when peoples, like individuals, are poor and proud, these qualities are apt to react on each other to an endless degree. These men are untamable, and no one can ever succeed with them unless he is with them in all-in-all, and is a leader recognized. But if you can win them they are loyal to death. If you are ambitious—and I know you are—there may be a field for you in such a country. With your qualifications, fortified by the fortune which I am happy enough to be able to leave you, you may dare much and go far. Should I be alive when you return from your exploration in Northern South America, I may have the happiness of helping you to this or any other ambition, and I shall deem it a privilege to share it with you; but time is going on. I am in my seventy-second year . . . the years of man are three-score and ten—I suppose you understand; I do . . . Let me point out this: For ambitious projects the great nationalities are impossible to a stranger—and in our own we are limited by loyalty (and common-sense). It is only in a small nation that great ambitions can be achieved. If you share my own views and wishes, the Blue Mountains is your ground. I hoped at one time that I might yet become a Voivode—even a great one. But age has dulled my personal ambitions as it has cramped my powers. I no longer dream of such honour for myself, though I do look on it as a possibility for you if you care for it. Through my Will you will have a great position and a great estate, and though you may have to yield up the latter in accordance with my wish, as already expressed in this letter, the very doing so will give you an even greater hold than this possession in the hearts of the mountaineers, should they ever come to know it. Should it be that at the time you inherit from me the Voivode Vissarion should not be alive, it may serve or aid you to know that in such case you would be absolved from any conditions of mine, though I trust you would in that, as in all other matters, hold obligation enforced by your own honour as to my wishes. Therefore the matter stands thus: If Vissarion lives, you will relinquish the estates. Should such not be the case, you will act as you believe that I would wish you to. In either case the mountaineers should not know from you in any way of the secret contracts between Vissarion and myself. Enlightenment of the many should (if ever) come from others than yourself. And unless such take place, you would leave the estates without any *quid pro quo* whatever. This you need not mind, for the fortune you will inherit will leave you free and able to purchase other estates in the Blue Mountains or elsewhere that you may select in the world.

If others attack, attack them, and quicker and harder than they can, if such be a possibility. Should it ever be that you inherit the Castle of Vissarion on the Spear of Ivan, remember that I had it secretly fortified and armed against attack. There are not only massive grilles, but doors of chilled bronze where such be needed. My adherent Rooke, who has faithfully served me for nearly forty years, and has gone on my behalf on many perilous expeditions, will, I trust, serve you in the same way. Treat him well for my sake, if not for your own. I have left him provision for a life of ease; but he would rather take a part in dangerous enterprises. He is silent as the grave and as bold as a lion. He knows every detail of the fortification and of the secret means of defence. A word in your ear—he was once a pirate. He was then in his extreme youth, and long since changed his ways in this respect; but from this fact you can understand his nature. You will find him useful should occasion ever arise. Should you accept the conditions of my letter, you are to make the Blue Mountains—in part, at least—your home, living there a part of the year, if only for a week, as in England men of many estates share the time amongst them. To this you are not bound, and no one shall have power to compel you or interfere with you. I only express a hope. But one thing I do more than hope—I desire, if you will honour my wishes, that, come what may, you are to keep your British nationality, unless by special arrangement with and consent of the Privy Council. Such arrangement to be formally made by my friend, Edward Bingham Trent, or whomsoever he may appoint by deed or will to act in the matter, and made in such a way that no act save that alone of Parliament in all its estates, and endorsed by the King, may or can prevail against it.

My last word to you is, Be bold and honest, and fear not. Most things—even kingship—*somewhere* may now and again be won by the sword. A brave heart and a strong arm may go far. But whatever is so won cannot be held merely by the sword. Justice alone can hold in the long run. Where men trust they will follow, and the rank and file of people want to follow, not to lead. If it be your fortune to lead, be bold. Be wary, if you will; exercise any other faculties that may aid or guard. Shrink from nothing. Avoid nothing that is honourable in itself. Take responsibility when such presents itself. What others shrink from, accept. That is to be great in what world, little or big, you move. Fear nothing, no matter of what kind danger may be or whence it come. The only real way to meet danger is to despise it—except with your brains. Meet it in the gate, not the hall.

My kinsman, the name of my race and your own, worthily mingled in your own person, now rests with you!

Letter from Rupert Sent Leger, 32 Bodmin Street, Victoria, S.W., to Miss Janet MacKelpie, Croom, Ross-shire.

January 3, 1907.

MY DEAREST AUNT JANET,

You will, I know, be rejoiced to hear of the great good-fortune which has come to me through the Will of Uncle Roger. Perhaps Sir Colin will have written to you, as he is one of the executors, and there is a bequest to you, so I must not spoil his pleasure of telling you of that part himself. Unfortunately, I am not free to speak fully of my own legacy yet, but I want you to know that at worst I am to receive an amount many times more than I ever dreamt of possessing through any possible stroke of fortune. So soon as I can leave London—where, of course, I must remain until things are settled—I am coming up to Croom to see you, and I hope I shall by then be able to let you know so much that you will be able to guess at the extraordinary change that has come to my circumstances. It is all like an impossible dream: there is nothing like it in the "Arabian Nights." However, the details must wait, I am pledged to secrecy for the present. And you must be pledged too. You won't mind, dear, will you? What I want to do at present is merely to tell you of my own good-fortune, and that I shall be going presently to live for a while at Vissarion. Won't you come with me, Aunt Janet? We shall talk more of this when I come to Croom; but I want you to keep the subject in your mind.

Your loving

RUPERT.

From Rupert Sent Leger's Journal.

January 4, 1907.

Things have been humming about me so fast that I have had hardly time to think. But some of the things have been so important, and have so changed my entire outlook on life, that it may be well to keep some personal record of them. I may some day want to remember some detail—perhaps the sequence of events, or something like that—and it may be useful. It ought to be, if there is any justice in things, for it will be an awful swot to write it when I have so many things to think of now. Aunt Janet, I suppose, will like to keep it locked up for me, as she does with all my journals and papers. That is one good thing about Aunt Janet amongst many: she has no curiosity, or else she has some other quality which keeps her from prying as other women would. It would seem that she has not so much as opened the cover of one of my journals ever in her life, and that she would not without my permission. So this can in time go to her also.

I dined last night with Mr. Trent, by his special desire. The dinner was in his own rooms. Dinner sent in from the hotel. He would not have any waiters at all, but made them send in the dinner all at once, and we helped ourselves. As we were quite alone, we could talk freely, and we got over a lot of ground while we were dining. He began to tell me about Uncle Roger. I was glad of that, for, of course, I wanted to know all I could of him, and the fact was I had seen very little of him.

Of course, when I was a small kid he was often in our house, for he was very fond of mother, and she of him. But I fancy that a small boy was rather a nuisance to him. And then I was at school, and he was away in the East. And then poor mother died while he was living in the Blue Mountains, and I never saw him again. When I wrote to him about Aunt Janet he answered me very kindly but he was so very just in the matter that I got afraid of him. And after that I ran away, and have been roaming ever since; so there was never a chance of our meeting. But that letter of his has opened my eyes. To think of him following me that way all over the world, waiting to hold out a helping hand if I should want it, I only wish I had known, or even suspected, the sort of man he was, and how he cared for me, and I would sometimes have come back to see him, if I had to come half round the world. Well, all I can do now is to carry out his wishes; that will be my expiation for my neglect. He knew what he wanted exactly, and I suppose I shall come in time to know it all and understand it, too.

I was thinking something like this when Mr. Trent began to talk, so that all he said fitted exactly into my own thought. The two men were evidently great friends—I should have gathered that, anyhow, from the Will—and the letters—so I was not surprised when Mr. Trent told me that they had been to school together, Uncle Roger being a senior when he was a junior; and had then and ever after shared each other's confidence. Mr. Trent, I gathered, had from the very first been in love with my mother, even when she was a little girl; but he was poor and shy, and did not like to speak. When he had made up his mind to do so, he found that she had by then met my father, and could not help seeing that they loved each other. So he was silent. He told me he had never said a word about it to anyone—not even to my Uncle Roger, though he knew from one thing and another, though he never spoke of it, that he would like it. I could not help seeing that the dear old man regarded me in a sort of parental way—I have heard of such romantic attachments being transferred to the later generation. I was not displeased with it; on the contrary, I liked him better for it. I love my mother so much—I always think of her in the present—that I cannot think of her as dead. There is a tie between anyone else who loved her and myself. I tried to let Mr. Trent see that I liked him, and it pleased him so much that I could see his liking for me growing greater. Before we parted he told me that he was going to give up business. He must have understood how disappointed I was—for how could I ever get along at all without him?—for he said, as he laid a hand quite affectionately, I thought—on my shoulder:

"I shall have one client, though, whose business I always hope to keep, and for whom I shall be always whilst I live glad to act—if he will have me." I did not care to speak as I took his hand. He squeezed mine, too, and said very earnestly:

"I served your uncle's interests to the very best of my ability for nearly fifty years. He had full confidence in me, and I was proud of his trust. I can honestly say, Rupert—you won't mind me using that familiarity, will you?—that, though the interests which I guarded were so vast that without abusing my trust I could often have used my knowledge to my personal advantage, I never once, in little matters or big, abused that trust—no, not even rubbed the bloom off it. And now that he has remembered me in his Will so generously that I need work no more, it will be a very genuine pleasure and pride to me to carry out as well as I can the wishes that I partly knew, and now realize more fully towards you, his nephew."

In the long chat which we had, and which lasted till midnight, he told me many very interesting things about Uncle Roger. When, in the course of conversation, he mentioned that the fortune Uncle Roger left must be well over a hundred millions, I was so surprised that I said out loud—I did not mean to ask a question:

"How on earth could a man beginning with nothing realize such a gigantic fortune?"

"By all honest ways," he answered, "and his clever human insight. He knew one half of the world, and so kept abreast of all public and national movements that he knew the critical moment to advance money required. He was always generous, and always on the side of freedom. There are nations at this moment only now entering on the consolidation of their liberty, who owe all to him, who knew when and how to help. No wonder that in some lands they will drink to his memory on great occasions as they used to drink his health."

"As you and I shall do now, sir!" I said, as I filled my glass and stood up. We drank it in bumpers. We did not say a word, either of us; but the old gentleman held out his hand, and I took it. And so, holding hands, we drank in silence. It made me feel quite choky; and I could see that he, too, was moved.

From E. B. Trent's Memoranda.

January 4, 1907.

I asked Mr. Rupert Sent Leger to dine with me at my office alone, as I wished to have a chat with him. To-morrow Sir Colin and I will have a formal meeting with him for the settlement of affairs, but I thought it best to have an informal talk with him alone first, as I wished to tell him certain matters which will make our meeting to-morrow more productive of utility, as he can now have more full understanding of the subjects which we have to discuss. Sir Colin is all that can be in manhood, and I could wish no better colleague in the executorship of this phenomenal Will; but he has not had the privilege of a lifelong friendship with the testator as I have had. And as Rupert Sent Leger had to learn intimate details regarding his uncle, I could best make my confidences alone. To-morrow we shall have plenty of formality. I was delighted with Rupert. He is just what I could have wished his mother's boy to be—or a son of my own to be, had I had the good-fortune to have been a father. But this is not for me. I remember long, long ago reading a passage in Lamb's Essays which hangs in my mind: "The children of Alice call Bartrum father." Some of my old friends would laugh to see *me* write this, but these memoranda are for my eyes alone, and no one shall see them till after my death, unless by my own permission. The boy takes some qualities after his father; he has a daring that is disturbing to an old dryasdust lawyer like me. But somehow I like him more than I ever liked anyone—any man—in my life—more even than his uncle, my old friend, Roger Melton; and Lord knows I had much cause to like him. I have more than ever now. It was quite delightful to see the way the young adventurer was touched by his uncle's thought of him. He is a truly gallant fellow, but venturesome exploits have not affected the goodness of heart. It is a pleasure to me to think that Roger and Colin came together apropos of the boy's thoughtful generosity towards Miss MacKelpie. The old soldier will be a good friend to him, or I am much mistaken. With an old lawyer like me, and an old soldier like him, and a real old gentlewoman like Miss MacKelpie, who loves the very ground he walks on, to look after him, together with all his own fine qualities and his marvellous experience of the world, and the gigantic wealth that will surely be his, that young man will go far.

Letter from Rupert Sent Leger to Miss Janet MacKelpie, Croom.

January 5, 1907.

MY DEAREST AUNT JANET,

It is all over—the first stage of it; and that is as far as I can get at present. I shall have to wait for a few days—or it may be weeks—in London for the doing of certain things now necessitated by my acceptance of Uncle Roger's bequest. But as soon as I can, dear, I shall come down to Croom and spend with you as many days as possible. I shall then tell you all I am at liberty to tell, and I shall thank you personally for your consent to come with me to Vissarion. Oh, how I wish my dear mother had lived to be with us! It would have made her happy, I know, to have come; and then we three who shared together the old dear, hard days would have shared in the same way the new splendour. I would try to show all my love and gratitude to you both . . . You must take the whole burden of it now, dear, for you and I are alone. No, not alone, as we used to be, for I have now two old friends who are already dear to me. One is so to you already. Sir Colin is simply splendid, and so, in his own way, is Mr. Trent. I am lucky, Aunt Janet, to have two such men to think of affairs for me. Am I not? I shall send you a wire as soon as ever I can see my way to get through my work; and I want you to think over all the things you ever wished for in your life, so that I may—if there is any mortal way of doing so—get them for you. You will not stand in the way of my having this great pleasure, will you, dear? Good-bye.

Your loving
RUPERT.

E. B. Trent's Memoranda.

January 6, 1907.

The formal meeting of Sir Colin and myself with Rupert Sent Leger went off quite satisfactorily. From what he had said yesterday, and again last night, I had almost come to expect an unreserved acceptance of everything stated or implied in Roger Melton's Will; but when we had sat round the table—this appeared, by the way, to be a formality for which we were all prepared, for we sat down as if by instinct—the very first words he said were:

"As I suppose I must go through this formality, I may as well say at once that I accept every possible condition which was in the mind of Uncle Roger; and to this end I am prepared to sign, seal, and deliver—or whatever is the ritual—whatever document you, sir"—turning to me—"may think necessary or advisable, and of which you both approve." He stood up and walked about the room for a few moments, Sir Colin and I sitting quite still, silent. He came back to his seat, and after a few seconds of nervousness—a rare thing with him, I fancy—said: "I hope you both understand—of course, I know you do; I only speak because this is an occasion for formality—that I am willing to accept, and at once! I do so, believe me, not to get possession of this vast fortune, but because of him who has given it. The man who was fond of me, and who trusted me, and yet had strength to keep his own feelings in check—who followed me in spirit to far lands and desperate adventures, and who, though he might be across the world from me, was ready to put out a hand to save or help me, was no common man; and his care of my mother's son meant no common love for my dear mother. And so she and I together accept his trust, come of it what may. I have been thinking it over all night, and all the time I could not get out of the idea that mother was somewhere near me. The only thought that could debar me from doing as I wished to do—and intend to do—would be that she would not approve. Now that I am satisfied she would approve, I accept. Whatever may result or happen, I shall go on following the course that he has set for me. So help me, God!" Sir Colin stood up, and I must say a more martial figure I never saw. He was in full uniform, for he was going on to the King's levee after our business. He drew his sword from the scabbard and laid it naked on the table before Rupert, and said:

"You are going, sir, into a strange and danger country—I have been reading about it since we met—and you will be largely alone amongst fierce mountaineers who resent the very presence of a stranger, and to whom you are, and must be, one. If you should ever be in any trouble and want a man to stand back to back with you, I hope you will give me the honour!" As he said this pointed to his sword. Rupert and I were also standing now—one cannot sit down in the presence of such an act as that. "You are, I am proud to say, allied with my family: and I only wish to God it was closer to myself." Rupert took him by the hand and bent his head before him as answered:

"The honour is mine, Sir Colin; and no greater can come to any man than that which you have just done me. The best way I can show how I value it will be to call on you if I am ever in such a tight place. By Jove, sir, this is history repeating itself. Aunt Janet used to tell me when I was a youngster how MacKelpie of Croom laid his sword before Prince Charlie. I hope I may tell her of this; it would make her so proud and happy. Don't imagine, sir, that I am thinking myself a Charles Edward. It is only that Aunt Janet is so good to me that I might well think I was."

Sir Colin bowed grandly:

"Rupert Sent Leger, my dear niece is a woman of great discretion and discernment. And, moreover, I am thinking she has in her some of the gift of Second Sight that has been a heritage of our blood. And I am one with my niece—in everything!" The whole thing was quite regal in manner; it seemed to take me back to the days of the Pretender.

It was not, however, a time for sentiment, but for action—we had met regarding the future, not the past; so I produced the short document I had already prepared. On the strength of his steadfast declaration that he would accept the terms of the Will and the secret letters, I had got ready a formal acceptance. When I had once again formally asked Mr. Sent Leger's wishes, and he had declared his wish to accept, I got in a couple of my clerks as witnesses.

Then, having again asked him in their presence if it was his wish to declare acceptance of the conditions, the document was signed and witnessed, Sir Colin and I both appending our signatures to the Attestation.

And so the first stage of Rupert Sent Leger's inheritance is completed. The next step will not have to be undertaken on my part until the expiration of six months from his entry on his estate at Vissarion. As he announces his intention of going within a fortnight, this will mean practically a little over six months from now.

BOOK II: VISSARION

Letter from Rupert Sent Leger, Castle of Vissarion, the Spear of Ivan, Land of the Blue Mountains, to Miss Janet MacKelpie, Croom Castle, Ross-shire, N.B.

January 23, 1907.

MY DEAREST AUNT JANET,

As you see, I am here at last. Having got my formal duty done, as you made me promise—my letters reporting arrival to Sir Colin and Mr. Trent are lying sealed in front of me ready to post (for nothing shall go before yours)—I am free to speak to you.

This is a most lovely place, and I hope you will like it. I am quite sure you will. We passed it in the steamer coming from Trieste to Durazzo. I knew the locality from the chart, and it was pointed out to me by one of the officers with whom I had become quite friendly, and who kindly showed me interesting places whenever we got within sight of shore. The Spear of Ivan, on which the Castle stands, is a headland running well out into the sea. It is quite a peculiar place— a sort of headland on a headland, jutting out into a deep, wide bay, so that, though it is a promontory, it is as far away from the traffic of coast life as anything you can conceive. The main promontory is the end of a range of mountains, and looms up vast, towering over everything, a mass of sapphire blue. I can well understand how the country came to be called the "Land of the Blue Mountains," for it is all mountains, and they are all blue! The coast-line is magnificent— what is called "iron-bound"—being all rocky; sometimes great frowning precipices; sometimes jutting spurs of rock; again little rocky islets, now and again clad with trees and verdure, at other places stark and bare. Elsewhere are little rocky bays and indentations—always rock, and often with long, interesting caves. Some of the shores of the bays are sandy, or else ridges of beautiful pebbles, where the waves make endless murmur.

But of all the places I have seen—in this land or any other—the most absolutely beautiful is Vissarion. It stands at the ultimate point of the promontory—I mean the little, or, rather, lesser promontory—that continues on the spur of the mountain range. For the lesser promontory or extension of the mountain is in reality vast; the lowest bit of cliff along the sea-front is not less than a couple of hundred feet high. That point of rock is really very peculiar. I think Dame Nature must, in the early days of her housekeeping—or, rather, house-*building*— have intended to give her little child, man, a rudimentary lesson in self-protection. It is just a natural bastion such as a titanic Vauban might have designed in primeval times. So far as the Castle is concerned, it is alone visible from the sea. Any enemy approaching could see only that frowning wall of black rock, of vast height and perpendicular steepness. Even the old fortifications which crown it are not built, but cut in the solid rock. A long narrow creek of very deep water, walled in by high, steep cliffs, runs in behind the Castle, bending north and west, making safe and secret anchorage. Into the creek falls over a precipice a mountain-stream, which never fails in volume of water. On the western shore of that creek is the Castle, a huge pile of buildings of every style of architecture, from the Twelfth century to where such things seemed to stop in this dear old-world land—about the time of Queen Elizabeth. So it is pretty picturesque. I can tell you. When we got the first glimpse of the place from the steamer the officer, with whom I was on the bridge, pointed towards it and said:

"That is where we saw the dead woman floating in a coffin." That was rather interesting, so I asked him all about it. He took from his pocket-book a cutting from an Italian paper, which he handed to me. As I can read and speak Italian fairly well, it was all right; but as you, my dear Aunt Janet, are not skilled in languages, and as I doubt if there is any assistance of the kind to be had at Croom, I do not send it. But as I have heard that the item has been produced in the last number of *The Journal of Occultism,* you will be easily able to get it. As he handed me the cutting he said: "I am Destilia!" His story was so strange that I asked him a good many questions about it. He answered me quite frankly on every point, but always adhering stoutly to the main point—namely, that it was no phantom or mirage, no dream or imperfect vision in a fog. "We were four in all who saw it," he said—"three from the bridge and the Englishman, Caulfield—from the bows—whose account exactly agreed with what we saw. Captain Mirolani and Falamano and I were all awake and in good trim. We looked with our night-glasses, which are more than usually powerful. You know, we need good glasses for the east shore of the Adriatic and for among the islands to the south. There was a full moon and a brilliant light. Of course we were a little way off, for though the Spear of Ivan is in deep water, one has to be careful of currents, for it is in just such places that the dangerous currents run." The agent of Lloyd's told me only a few weeks ago that it was only after a prolonged investigation of the tidal and sea currents that the house decided to except from ordinary sea risks losses due to a too close course by the Spear of Ivan. When I tried to get a little more definite account of the coffin-boat and the dead lady that is given in *The Journal of Occultism* he simply shrugged his shoulders. "Signor, it is all," he said. "That Englishman wrote everything after endless questioning."

So you see, my dear, that our new home is not without superstitious interests of its own. It is rather a nice idea, is it not, to have a dead woman cruising round our promontory in a coffin? I doubt if even at Croom you can beat that. "Makes the place kind of homey," as an American would say. When you come, Aunt Janet, you will not feel lonesome, at any rate, and it will save us the trouble of importing some of your Highland ghosts to make you feel at home in the new land. I don't know, but we might ask the stiff to come to tea with us. Of course, it would be a late tea. Somewhere between midnight and cock-crow would be about the etiquette of the thing, I fancy!

But I must tell you all the realities of the Castle and around it. So I will write again within a day or two, and try to let you know enough to prepare you for coming here. Till then adieu, my dear.

Your loving

RUPERT.

From Rupert Sent Leger, Vissarion, to Janet MacKelpie, Croom.

January 25, 1907.

I hope I did not frighten you, dear Aunt Janet, by the yarn of the lady in the coffin. But I know you are not afraid; you have told me too many weird stories for me to dread that. Besides, you have Second Sight—latent, at all events. However, there won't be any more ghosts, or about ghosts, in this letter. I want to tell you all about our new home. I am so glad you are coming out so soon; I am beginning to feel so lonesome—I walk about sometimes aimlessly, and find my thoughts drifting in such an odd way. If I didn't know better, I might begin to think I was in love! There is no one here to be in love with; so make your mind easy, Aunt Janet. Not that you would be unhappy, I know, dear, if I *did* fall in love. I suppose I must marry some day. It is a duty now, I know, when there is such an estate as Uncle Roger has left me. And I know this: I shall never marry any woman unless I love her. And I am right sure that if I do love her you will love her, too, Aunt Janet!

Won't you, dear? It wouldn't be half a delight if you didn't. It won't if you don't. There, now!

But before I begin to describe Vissarion I shall throw a sop to you as a chatelaine; that may give you patience to read the rest. The Castle needs a lot of things to make it comfortable—as you would consider it. In fact, it is absolutely destitute of everything of a domestic nature. Uncle Roger had it vetted on the defence side, and so far it could stand a siege. But it couldn't cook a dinner or go through a spring-cleaning! As you know, I am not much up in domestic matters, and so I cannot give you details; but you may take it that it wants everything. I don't mean furniture, or silver, or even gold-plate, or works of art, for it is full of the most magnificent old things that you can imagine. I think Uncle Roger must have been a collector, and gathered a lot of good things in all sorts of places, stored them for years, and then sent them here. But as to glass, china, delft, all sorts of crockery, linen, household applian-ces and machinery, cooking utensils—except of the simplest—there are none. I don't think Uncle Roger could have lived here more than on a temporary picnic. So far as I only am concerned, I am all right; a gridiron and a saucepan are all *I* want—and I can use them myself. But, dear Aunt Janet, I don't want you to pig it. I would like you to have everything you can imagine, and all of the very best. Cost doesn't count now for us, thanks to Uncle Roger; and so I want you to order all. I know you, dear—being a woman—won't object to shopping. But it will have to be wholesale. This is an enormous place, and will swallow up all you can buy—like a quicksand. Do as you like about choosing, but get all the help you can. Don't be afraid of getting too much. You can't, or of being idle when you are here. I assure you that when you come there will be so much to do and so many things to think of that you will want to get away from it all. And, besides, Aunt Janet, I hope you won't be too long. Indeed, I don't wish to be selfish, but your boy is lonely, and wants you. And when you get here you will be an *empress*. I don't altogether like doing so, lest I should offend a millionairess like you; but it may facilitate matters, and the way's of commerce are strict, though devious. So I send you a cheque for 1,000 pounds for the little things: and a letter to the bank to honour your own cheques for any amount I have got.

I think, by the way, I should, if I were you, take or send out a few servants—not too many at first, only just enough to attend on our two selves. You can arrange to send for any more you may want later. Engage them, and arrange for their being paid—when they are in our service we must treat them well—and then they can be at our call as you find that we want them. I think you should secure, say, fifty or a hundred—'tis an awfu' big place, Aunt Janet! And in the same way will you secure—and, of course, arrange for pay similarly—a hundred men, exclusive of any servants you think it well to have. I should like the General, if he can give the time, to choose or pass them. I want clansmen that I can depend on, if need be. We are going to live in a country which is at present strange to us, and it is well to look things in the face. I know Sir Colin will only have men who are a credit to Scotland and to Ross and to Croom—men who will impress the Blue Mountaineers. I know they will take them to their hearts—certainly if any of them are bachelors the girls will! Forgive me! But if we are to settle here, our followers will probably want to settle also. Moreover, the Blue Mountaineers may want followers also! And will want them to settle, too, and have successors!

Now for the description of the place. Well, I simply can't just now. It is all so wonderful and so beautiful. The Castle—I have written so much already about other things that I really must keep the Castle for another letter! Love to Sir Colin if he is at Croom. And oh, dear Aunt Janet, how I wish that my dear mother was coming out! It all seems so dark and empty without her. How she would have enjoyed it! How proud she would have been! And, my dear, if she could be with us again, how grateful she would have been to you for all you have

done for her boy! As I am, believe me, most truly and sincerely and
affectionately grateful.

Your loving

RUPERT.

Rupert Sent Leger, Vissarion, to Janet MacKelpie, Croom.

January 26, 1907.

MY DEAR AUNT JANET,

Please read this as if it was a part of the letter I wrote yesterday.

The Castle itself is so vast that I really can't describe it in detail.
So I am waiting till you come; and then you and I will go over it
together and learn all that we can about it. We shall take Rooke with
us, and, as he is supposed to know every part of it, from the keep to
the torture-chamber, we can spend a few days over it. Of course, I
have been over most of it, since I came—that, is, I went at various
times to see different portions—the battlements, the bastions, the
old guard-room, the hall, the chapel, the walls, the roof. And I have
been through some of the network of rock passages. Uncle Roger
must have spent a mint of money on it, so far as I can see; and
though I am not a soldier, I have been in so many places fortified in
different ways that I am not entirely ignorant of the subject. He has
restored it in such an up-to-date way that it is practically impregnable to anything under big guns or a siege-train. He has gone so
far as to have certain outworks and the keep covered with armoured
plating of what looks like harveyized steel. You will wonder when
you see it. But as yet I really know only a few rooms, and am familiar with only one—my own room. The drawing-room—not the
great hall, which is a vast place; the library—a magnificent one,
but in sad disorder—we must get a librarian some day to put it in
trim; and the drawing-room and boudoir and bedroom suite which
I have selected for you, are all fine. But my own room is what suits

me best, though I do not think you would care for it for yourself.
If you do, you shall have it. It was Uncle Roger's own room when
he stayed here; living in it for a few days served to give me more
insight to his character—or rather to his mind—than I could have
otherwise had. It is just the kind of place I like myself; so, naturally,
I understand the other chap who liked it too. It is a fine big room,
not quite within the Castle, but an outlying part of it. It is not de-
tached, or anything of that sort, but is a sort of garden-room built
on to it. There seems to have been always some sort of place where it
is, for the passages and openings inside seem to accept or recognize
it. It can be shut off if necessary—it would be in case of attack—by
a great slab of steel, just like the door of a safe, which slides from inside the wall, and can be operated from either inside or outside—if
you know how. That is from my room or from within the keep. The
mechanism is a secret, and no one but Rooke and I know it. The
room opens out through a great French window—the French window is modern, I take it, and was arranged by or for Uncle Roger;
I think there must have been always a large opening there, for centuries at least—which opens on a wide terrace or balcony of white
marble, extending right and left. From this a white marble stair
lies straight in front of the window, and leads down to the garden.
The balcony and staircase are quite ancient—of old Italian work,
beautifully carved, and, of course, weather-worn through centuries.
There is just that little tinging of green here and there which makes
all outdoor marble so charming. It is hard to believe at times that it
is a part of a fortified castle, it is so elegant and free and open. The
first glance of it would make a burglar's heart glad. He would say to
himself: "Here is the sort of crib I like when I'm on the job. You can
just walk in and out as you choose." But, Aunt Janet, old Roger was
cuter than any burglar. He had the place so guarded that the burglar
would have been a baffled burglar. There are two steel shields which

can slide out from the wall and lock into the other side right across the whole big window. One is a grille of steel bands that open out into diamond-shaped lozenges. Nothing bigger than a kitten could get through; and yet you can see the garden and the mountains and the whole view—much the same as you ladies can see through your veils. The other is a great sheet of steel, which slides out in a similar way in different grooves. It is not, of course, so heavy and strong as the safe-door which covers the little opening in the main wall, but Rooke tells me it is proof against the heaviest rifle-ball.

Having told you this, I must tell you, too, Aunt Janet, lest you should be made anxious by the *arriere-pensee* of all these warlike measures of defence, that I always sleep at night with one of these iron screens across the window. Of course, when I am awake I leave it open. As yet I have tried only, but not used, the grille; and I don't think I shall ever use anything else, for it is a perfect guard. If it should be tampered with from outside it would sound an alarm at the head of the bed, and the pressing of a button would roll out the solid steel screen in front of it. As a matter of fact, I have been so used to the open that I don't feel comfortable shut in. I only close windows against cold or rain. The weather here is delightful—as yet, at all events—but they tell me that the rainy season will be on us before very long.

I think you will like my den, aunty dear, though it will doubtless be a worry to you to see it so untidy. But that can't be helped. I must be untidy *somewhere;* and it is best in my own den!

Again I find my letter so long that I must cut it off now and go on again to-night. So this must go as it stands. I shall not cause you to wait to hear all I can tell you about our new home.

Your loving
RUPERT.

From Rupert Sent Leger, Vissarion, to Janet MacKelpie, Croom.

January 29, 1907.

MY DEAR AUNT JANET,

My den looks out, as I told you in my last letter, on the garden, or, to speak more accurately, on *one* of the gardens, for there are acres of them. This is the old one, which must be almost as old as the Castle itself, for it was within the defences in the old days of bows. The wall that surrounds the inner portion of it has long ago been levelled, but sufficient remains at either end where it joined the outer defences to show the long casemates for the bowmen to shoot through and the raised stone gallery where they stood. It is just the same kind of building as the stone-work of the sentry's walk on the roof and of the great old guard-room under it.

But whatever the garden may have been, and no matter how it was guarded, it is a most lovely place. There are whole sections of garden here of various styles—Greek, Italian, French, German, Dutch, British, Spanish, African, Moorish—all the older nationalities. I am going to have a new one laid out for you—a Japanese garden. I have sent to the great gardener of Japan, Minaro, to make the plans for it, and to come over with workmen to carry it out. He is to bring trees and shrubs and flowers and stone-work, and everything that can be required; and you shall superintend the finishing, if not the doing, of it yourself. We have such a fine head of water here, and the climate is, they tell me, usually so lovely that we can do anything in the gardening way. If it should ever turn out that the climate does not suit, we shall put a great high glass roof over it, and *make* a suitable climate.

This garden in front of my room is the old Italian garden. It must have been done with extraordinary taste and care, for there is not a bit of it which is not rarely beautiful. Sir Thomas Browne himself, for all his Quincunx, would have been delighted with it, and have found material for another "Garden of Cyrus." It is so big that there are endless "episodes" of garden beauty I think all Italy must have been ransacked in old times for garden stone-work of exceptional beauty;

and these treasures have been put together by some master-hand. Even the formal borders of the walks are of old porous stone, which takes the weather-staining so beautifully, and are carved in endless variety. Now that the gardens have been so long neglected or left in abeyance, the green staining has become perfect. Though the stone-work is itself intact, it has all the picturesque effect of the wear and ruin wrought by many centuries. I am having it kept for you just as it is, except that I have had the weeds and undergrowth cleared away so that its beauties might be visible.

But it is not merely the architect work of the garden that is so beautiful, nor is the assembling there of the manifold wealth of floral beauty—there is the beauty that Nature creates by the hand of her servant, Time. You see, Aunt Janet, how the beautiful garden inspires a danger-hardened old tramp like me to high-grade sentiments of poetic fancy! Not only have limestone and sandstone, and even marble, grown green in time, but even the shrubs planted and then neglected have developed new kinds of beauty of their own. In some far-distant time some master-gardener of the Vissarions has tried to realize an idea—that of tiny plants that would grow just a little higher than the flowers, so that the effect of an uneven floral surface would be achieved without any hiding of anything in the garden seen from anywhere. This is only my reading of what has been from the effect of what is! In the long period of neglect the shrubs have outlived the flowers. Nature has been doing her own work all the time in enforcing the survival of the fittest. The shrubs have grown and grown, and have overtopped flower and weed, according to their inherent varieties of stature; to the effect that now you see irregularly scattered through the garden quite a number—for it is a big place—of vegetable products which from a landscape standpoint have something of the general effect of statues without the cramping feeling of detail. Whoever it was that laid out that part of the garden or made the choice of items, must have taken pains to get strange specimens, for all those taller shrubs are in special colours, mostly yellow or white—white cypress, white holly, yellow yew, grey-golden box, silver juniper, variegated maple, spiraea, and numbers of dwarf shrubs whose names I don't know. I only know that when the moon shines—and this, my dear Aunt Janet, is the very land of moonlight itself!—they all look ghastly pale. The effect is weird to the last degree, and I am sure that you will enjoy it. For myself, as you know, uncanny things hold no fear. I suppose it is that I have been up against so many different kinds of fears, or, rather, of things which for most people have terrors of their own, that I have come to have a contempt—not an active contempt, you know, but a tolerative contempt—for the whole family of them. And you, too, will enjoy yourself here famously, I know. You'll have to collect all the stories of such matters in our new world and make a new book of facts for the Psychical Research Society. It will be nice to see your own name on a title-page, won't it, Aunt Janet?

From Rupert Sent Leger, Vissarion, to Janet MacKelpie, Croom.

January 30, 1907.

MY DEAR AUNT JANET,

I stopped writing last night—do you know why? Because I wanted to write more! This sounds a paradox, but it is true. The fact is that, as I go on telling you of this delightful place, I keep finding out new beauties myself. Broadly speaking, it *is all* beautiful. In the long view or the little view—as the telescope or the microscope directs—it is all the same. Your eye can turn on nothing that does not entrance you. I was yesterday roaming about the upper part of time Castle, and came across some delightful nooks, which at once I became fond of, and already like them as if I had known them all my life. I felt at first a sense of greediness when I had appropriated to myself several rooms in different places—I who have never in my life had more than one room which I could call my own—and that only for a time! But when I slept on it the feeling changed, and its aspect is now not half bad. It is now under another classification—under a much more important label—*proprietorship.* If I were writing philosophy, I should here put in a cynical remark:

"Selfishness is an appanage of poverty. It might appear in the stud-book as by 'Morals' out of 'Wants.'"

I have now three bedrooms arranged as my own particular dens. One of the other two was also a choice of Uncle Roger's. It is at the top of one of the towers to the extreme east, and from it I can catch the first ray of light over the mountains. I slept in it last night, and when I woke, as in my travelling I was accustomed to do, at dawn, I saw from my bed through an open window—a small window, for it is in a fortress tower—the whole great expanse to the east. Not far off, and springing from the summit of a great ruin, where long ago a seed had fallen, rose a great silver-birch, and the half-transparent, drooping branches and hanging clusters of leaf broke the outline of the grey hills beyond, for the hills were, for a wonder, grey instead of blue. There was a mackerel sky, with the clouds dropping on the mountain-tops till you could hardly say which was which. It was a mackerel sky of a very bold and extraordinary kind—not a dish of mackerel, but a world of mackerel! The mountains are certainly most lovely. In this clear air they usually seem close at hand. It was only this morning, with the faint glimpse of the dawn whilst the night clouds were still unpierced by the sunlight, that I seemed to realize their greatness. I have seen the same enlightening effect of aerial perspective a few times before—in Colorado, in Upper India, in Thibet, and in the uplands amongst the Andes.

There is certainly something in looking at things from above which tends to raise one's own self-esteem. From the height, inequalities simply disappear. This I have often felt on a big scale when ballooning, or, better still, from an aeroplane. Even here from the tower the outlook is somehow quite different from below. One realizes the place and all around it, not in detail, but as a whole. I shall certainly sleep up here occasionally, when you have come and we have settled down to our life as it is to be. I shall live in my own room downstairs, where I can have the intimacy of the garden. But I shall appreciate it all the more from now and again losing the sense of intimacy for a while, and surveying it without the sense of one's own self-importance.

I hope you have started on that matter of the servants. For myself, I don't care a button whether or not there are any servants at all; but I know well that you won't come till you have made your arrangements regarding them! Another thing, Aunt Janet. You must not be killed with work here, and it is all so vast . . . . Why can't you get some sort of secretary who will write your letters and do all that sort of thing for you? I know you won't have a man secretary; but there are lots of women now who can write shorthand and typewrite. You could doubtless get one in the clan—someone with a desire to better herself. I know you would make her happy here. If she is not too young, all the better; she will have learned to hold her tongue and mind her own business, and not be too inquisitive. That would be a nuisance when we are finding our way about in a new country and trying to reconcile all sorts of opposites in a whole new country with new people, whom at first we shan't understand, and who certainly won't understand us; where every man carries a gun with as little thought of it as he has of buttons! Good-bye for a while.

Your loving
RUPERT.

From Rupert Sent Leger, Vissarion, to Janet MacKelpie, Croom.
February 3, 1907.

I am back in my own room again. Already it seems to me that to get here again is like coming home. I have been going about for the last few days amongst the mountaineers and trying to make their acquaintance. It is a tough job; and I can see that there will be nothing but to stick to it. They are in reality the most primitive people I ever met—the most fixed to their own ideas, which belong to centuries back. I can understand now what people were like in England—not in Queen Elizabeth's time, for that was civilized time, but in the time of Coeur-de-Lion, or even earlier—and all the time with the most absolute mastery of weapons of precision. Every man carries a rifle—and knows how to use it, too. I do believe they would rather go without their clothes than their guns if they had to choose between them. They also carry a handjar, which used to be their national weapon. It is a sort of heavy, straight cutlass, and they are so expert with it as well as so strong that it is as facile in the hands of a Blue Mountaineer as is a foil in the hands of a Persian *maitre d'armes*. They are so proud and reserved that they make one feel quite small, and an "outsider" as well. I can see quite well that they rather resent my being here at all. It is not personal, for when alone with me they are genial, almost brotherly; but the moment a few of them get together they are like a sort of jury, with me as the criminal before them. It is an odd situation, and quite new to me. I am pretty well accustomed to all sorts of people, from cannibals to Mahatmas, but I'm blessed if I ever struck such a type as this—so proud, so haughty, so reserved, so distant, so absolutely fearless, so honourable, so hospitable. Uncle Roger's head was level when he chose them out as a people to live amongst. Do you know, Aunt Janet, I can't help feeling that they are very much like your own Highlanders—only more so. I'm sure of one thing: that in the end we shall get on capitally together. But it will be a slow job, and will need a lot of patience. I have a feeling in my bones that when they know me better they will be very loyal and very true; and I am not a hair's-breadth afraid of them or anything they shall or might do. That is, of course, if I live long enough for them to have time to know

me. Anything may happen with such an indomitable, proud people
to whom pride is more than victuals. After all, it only needs one man
out of a crowd to have a wrong idea or to make a mistake as to one's
motive—and there you are. But it will be all right that way, I am sure.
I am come here to stay, as Uncle Roger wished. And stay I shall even
if it has to be in a little bed of my own beyond the garden—seven feet
odd long, and not too narrow—or else a stone-box of equal propor-
tioons in the vaults of St. Sava's Church across the Creek—the old
burial-place of the Vissarions and other noble people for a good many
centuries back . . .

I have been reading over this letter, dear Aunt Janet, and I am afraid the record is rather an alarming one. But don't you go building
up superstitious horrors or fears on it. Honestly, I am only joking
about death—a thing to which I have been rather prone for a good
many years back. Not in very good taste, I suppose, but certainly
very useful when the old man with the black wings goes flying about
you day and night in strange places, sometimes visible and at others invisible. But you can always hear wings, especially in the dark,
when you cannot see them. *You* know that, Aunt Janet, who come
of a race of warriors, and who have special sight behind or through
the black curtain.

Honestly, I am in no whit afraid of the Blue Mountaineers, nor have
I a doubt of them. I love them already for their splendid qualities, and I
am prepared to love them for themselves. I feel, too, that they will love
me (and incidentally they are sure to love you). I have a sort of undercurrent of thought that there is something in their minds concerning
me—something not painful, but disturbing; something that has a base
in the past; something that has hope in it and possible pride, and not a
little respect. As yet they can have had no opportunity of forming such
impression from seeing me or from any thing I have done. Of course, it
may be that, although they are fine, tall, stalwart men, I am still a head

and shoulders over the tallest of them that I have yet seen. I catch their eyes looking up at me as though they were measuring me, even when they are keeping away from me, or, rather, keeping me from them at arm's length. I suppose I shall understand what it all means some day. In the meantime there is nothing to do but to go on my own way—which is Uncle Roger's—and wait and be patient and just. I have learned the value of that, any way, in my life amongst strange peoples. Good-night.

Your loving
RUPERT.

From Rupert Sent Leger, Vissarion, to Janet MacKelpie, Croom.
February 24, 1907.

MY DEAR AUNT JANET,

I am more than rejoiced to hear that you are coming here so soon. This isolation is, I think, getting on my nerves. I thought for a while last night that I was getting on, but the reaction came all too soon. I was in my room in the east turret, the room on the *corbeille,* and saw here and there men passing silently and swiftly between the trees as though in secret. By-and-by I located their meeting-place, which was in a hollow in the midst of the wood just outside the "natural" garden, as the map or plan of the castle calls it. I stalked that place for all I was worth, and suddenly walked straight into the midst of them. There were perhaps two or three hundred gathered, about the very finest lot of men I ever saw in my life. It was in its way quite an experience, and one not likely to be repeated, for, as I told you, in this country every man carries a rifle, and knows how to use it. I do not think I have seen a single man (or married man either) without his rifle since I came here. I wonder if they take them with them to bed! Well, the instant after I stood amongst them every rifle in the place was aimed straight at me. Don't be alarmed, Aunt Janet; they did not fire at me. If they had I should not be writing to you now. I should be in that little bit of real estate or the stone box, and about as full of lead as I could hold. Ordinarily, I take it, they would have fired on the instant; that is the etiquette here. But this time they—all separately but all together—made a new rule. No one said a word or, so far as I could see, made a movement. Here came in my own experience. I had been more than once in a tight place of something of the same kind, so I simply behaved in the most natural way I could. I felt conscious—it was all in a flash, remember—that if I showed fear or cause for fear, or even acknowledged danger by so much as even holding up my hands, I should have drawn all the fire. They all remained stock-still, as though they had been turned into stone, for several seconds. Then a queer kind of look flashed round them like wind over corn—something like the surprise one shows unconsciously on waking in a strange place. A second after they each dropped the rifle to the hollow of his arm and stood ready for anything. It was all as regular and quick and simultaneous as a salute at St. James's Palace.

Happily I had no arms of any kind with me, so that there could be no complication. I am rather a quick hand myself when there is any shooting to be done. However, there was no trouble here, but the contrary; the Blue Mountaineers—it sounds like a new sort of Bond Street band, doesn't it?—treated me in quite a different way than they did when I first met them. They were amazingly civil, almost deferential. But, all time same, they were more distant than ever, and all the time I was there I could get not a whit closer to them. They seemed in a sort of way to be afraid or in awe of me. No doubt that will soon pass away, and when we know one another better we shall become close friends. They are too fine fellows not to be worth a little waiting for. (That sentence, by the way, is a pretty bad sentence! In old days you would have slippered me for it!) Your journey is all arranged, and I hope you will be comfortable. Rooke will meet you at Liverpool Street and look after everything.

I shan't write again, but when we meet at Fiume I shall begin to tell you all the rest. Till then, good-bye. A good journey to you, and a happy meeting to us both.

RUPERT.

Letter from Janet MacKelpie, Vissarion, to Sir Colin MacKelpie, United Service Club, London.

February 28, 1907.

DEAREST UNCLE,

I had a very comfortable journey all across Europe. Rupert wrote to me some time ago to say that when I got to Vissarion I should be an Empress, and he certainly took care that on the way here I should be treated like one. Rooke, who seems a wonderful old man, was in the next compartment to that reserved for me. At Harwich he had everything arranged perfectly, and so right on to Fiume. Everywhere there were attentive officials waiting. I had a carriage all to myself, which I joined at Antwerp—a whole carriage with a suite of rooms, dining-room, drawing-room, bedroom, even bath-room. There was a cook with a kitchen of his own on board, a real chef like a French nobleman in disguise. There were also a waiter and a servant-maid. My own maid Maggie was quite awed at first. We were as far as Cologne before she summoned up courage to order them about. Whenever we stopped Rooke was on the platform with local officials, and kept the door of my carriage like a sentry on duty.

At Fiume, when the train slowed down, I saw Rupert waiting on the platform. He looked magnificent, towering over everybody there like a giant. He is in perfect health, and seemed glad to see me. He took me off at once on an automobile to a quay where an electric launch was waiting. This took us on board a beautiful big steam-yacht, which was waiting with full steam up and—how he got there I don't know— Rooke waiting at the gangway.

I had another suite all to myself. Rupert and I had dinner together—I think the finest dinner I ever sat down to. This was very nice of Rupert, for it was all for me. He himself only ate a piece of steak and drank a glass of water. I went to bed early, for, despite the luxury of the journey, I was very tired.

I awoke in the grey of the morning, and came on deck. We were close to the coast. Rupert was on the bridge with the Captain, and Rooke was acting as pilot. When Rupert saw me, he ran down the ladder and took me up on the bridge. He left me there while he ran down again and brought me up a lovely fur cloak which I had never seen. He put it on me and kissed me. He is the tenderest-hearted boy in the world, as well as the best and bravest! He made me take his arm whilst he pointed out Vissarion, towards which we were steering. It is the most lovely place I ever saw. I won't stop to describe it now, for it will be better that you see it for yourself and enjoy it all fresh as I did.

The Castle is an immense place. You had better ship off, as soon as all is ready here and you can arrange it, the servants whom I engaged; and I am not sure that we shall not want as many more. There has hardly been a mop or broom on the place for centuries, and I doubt if it ever had a thorough good cleaning all over since it was built. And, do you know, Uncle, that it might be well to double that little army of yours that you are arranging for Rupert? Indeed, the boy told me himself that he was going to write to you about it. I think old Lachlan and his wife, Sandy's Mary, had better be in charge of the maids when they come over. A lot of lassies like yon will be iller to keep together than a flock of sheep. So it will be wise to have authority over them, especially as none of them speaks a word of foreign tongues. Rooke— you saw him at the station at Liverpool Street—will, if he be available, go over to bring the whole body here. He has offered to do it if I should wish. And, by the way, I think it will be well, when the time comes for their departure, if not only the lassies, but Lachlan and Sandy's Mary, too, will call him *Mister* Rooke. He is a very important person indeed here. He is, in fact, a sort of Master of the Castle, and though he is very self-suppressing, is a man of rarely fine qualities. Also it will be well to keep authority. When your clansmen come over, he will have charge of them, too. Dear me! I find I have written such a long letter, I must stop and get to work. I shall write again.

Your very affectionate
JANET.

From the Same to the Same.

March 3, 1907.

DEAREST UNCLE,

All goes well here, and as there is no news, I only write because you are a dear, and I want to thank you for all the trouble you have taken for me—and for Rupert. I think we had better wait awhile before bringing out the servants. Rooke is away on some business for Rupert, and will not be back for some time; Rupert thinks it may be a couple of months. There is no one else that he could send to take charge of the party from home, and I don't like the idea of all those lassies coming out without an escort. Even Lachlan and Sandy's Mary are ignorant of foreign languages and foreign ways. But as soon as Rooke returns we can have them all out. I dare say you will have some of your clansmen ready by then, and I think the poor girls, who may feel a bit strange in a new country like this, where the ways are so different from ours, will feel easier when they know that there are some of their own mankind near them. Perhaps it might be well that those of them who are engaged to each other—I know there are some—should marry before they come out here. It will be more convenient in many ways, and will save lodgment, and, besides, these Blue Mountaineers are very handsome men. Good-night.

JANET.

Sir Colin MacKelpie, Croom, to Janet MacKelpie, Vissarion.

March 9, 1907.

MY DEAR JANET,

I have duly received both your letters, and am delighted to find you are so well pleased with your new home. It must certainly be a very lovely and unique place, and I am myself longing to see it. I came up here three days ago, and am, as usual, feeling all the better for a breath of my native air. Time goes on, my dear, and I am beginning to feel not so young as I was. Tell Rupert that the men are all fit, and longing to get out to him. They are certainly a fine lot of men. I don't think I ever saw a finer. I have had them drilled and trained as soldiers, and, in addition, have had them taught a lot of trades just as they selected themselves. So he shall have nigh him men who can turn their hands to anything—not, of course, that they all know every trade, but amongst them there is someone who can do whatever may be required. There are blacksmiths, carpenters, farriers, saddle-makers, gardeners, plumbers, cutlers, gunsmiths, so, as they all are farmers by origin and sportsmen by practice, they will make a rare household body of men. They are nearly all first-class shots, and I am having them practise with revolvers. They are being taught fencing and broadsword and ju-jitsu; I have organized them in military form, with their own sergeants and corporals. This morning I had an inspection, and I assure you, my dear, they could give points to the Household troop in matters of drill. I tell you I am proud of my clansmen!

I think you are quite wise about waiting to bring out the lassies, and wiser still about the marrying. I dare say there will be more marrying when they all get settled in a foreign country. I shall be glad of it, for as Rupert is going to settle there, it will be good for him to have round him a little colony of his own people. And it will be good for them, too, for I know he will be good to them—as you will, my dear. The hills are barren here, and life is hard, and each year there is more and more demand for crofts, and sooner or later our people must thin out. And mayhap our little settlement of MacKelpie clan away beyond the frontiers of the Empire may be some service to the nation and the King. But this is a dream! I see that here I am beginning to realise in myself one part of Isaiah's prophecy:

"Your young men shall see visions, and your old men shall dream dreams."

By the way, my dear, talking about dreams, I am sending you out some boxes of books which were in your rooms. They are nearly all on odd subjects that *we* understand—Second Sight, Ghosts, Dreams (that was what brought the matter to my mind just now), superstitions, Vampires, Wehr-Wolves, and all such uncanny folk and things. I looked over some of these books, and found your marks and underlining and comments, so I fancy you will miss them in your new home. You will, I am sure, feel more at ease with such old friends close to you. I have taken the names and sent the list to London, so that when you pay me a visit again you will be at home in all ways. If you come to me altogether, you will be more welcome still—if possible. But I am sure that Rupert, who I know loves you very much, will try to make you so happy that you will not want to leave him. So I will have to come out often to see you both, even at the cost of leaving Croom for so long. Strange, is it not? that now, when, through Roger Melton's more than kind remembrance of me, I am able to go where I will and do what I will, I want more and more to remain at home by my own ingle. I don't think that anyone but you or Rupert could get me away from it. I am working very hard at my little regiment, as I call it. They are simply fine, and will, I am sure, do us credit. The uniforms are all made, and well made, too. There is not a man of them that does not look like an officer. I tell you, Janet, that when we turn out the Vissarion Guard we shall feel proud of them. I dare say that a couple of months will do all that can be done here. I shall come out with them myself. Rupert writes me that he thinks it will be more comfortable to come out direct in a ship of our own. So when I go up to London in a few weeks' time I shall see about chartering a suitable vessel. It will certainly save a lot of trouble to us and anxiety to our people. Would it not be well when I am getting the ship, if I charter one big enough to take out all your lassies, too? It is not as if they were strangers. After all, my dear, soldiers are soldiers and lassies are lassies. But these are all kinsfolk, as well as clansmen and clanswomen, and I, their Chief, shall be there. Let me know your views and wishes in this respect. Mr. Trent, whom I saw before leaving London, asked me to "convey to you his most respectful remembrances"—these were his very words, and here they are. Trent is a nice fellow, and I like him. He has promised to pay me a visit here before the month is up, and I look forward to our both enjoying ourselves.

Good-bye, my dear, and the Lord watch over you and our dear boy.

Your affectionate Uncle,
COLIN ALEXANDER MACKELPIE.

BOOK III: THE COMING OF THE LADY

RUPERT SENT LEGER'S JOURNAL.

April 3, 1907.

I HAVE WAITED till now—well into midday—before beginning to set down the details of the strange episode of last night. I have spoken with persons whom I know to be of normal type. I have breakfasted, as usual heartily, and have every reason to consider myself in perfect health and sanity. So that the record following may be regarded as not only true in substance, but exact as to details. I have investigated and reported on too many cases for the Psychical Research Society to be ignorant of the necessity for absolute accuracy in such matters of even the minutest detail.

Yesterday was Tuesday, the second day of April, 1907. I passed a day of interest, with its fair amount of work of varying kinds. Aunt Janet and I lunched together, had a stroll round the gardens after tea— especially examining the site for the new Japanese garden, which we shall call "Janet's Garden." We went in mackintoshes, for the rainy season is in its full, the only sign of its not being a repetition of the Deluge being that breaks in the continuance are beginning. They are short at present but will doubtless enlarge themselves as the season comes towards an end. We dined together at seven. After dinner I had a cigar, and then joined Aunt Janet for an hour in her drawing-room. I left her at half-past ten, when I went to my own room and wrote some letters. At ten minutes past eleven I wound my watch, so I know the time accurately. Having prepared for bed, I drew back the heavy curtain in front of my window, which opens on the marble steps into the Italian garden. I had put out my light before drawing back the curtain, for I wanted to have a look at the scene before turning in. Aunt Janet has always had an old-fashioned idea of the need (or propriety, I hardly know which) of keeping windows closed and curtains drawn. I am gradually getting her to leave my room alone in this respect, but at present the change is in its fitful stage, and of course I must not hurry matters or be too persistent, as it would hurt her feelings. This night was one of those under the old regime. It was a delight to look out, for the scene was perfect of its own kind. The long spell of rain—the ceaseless downpour which had for the time flooded everywhere—had passed, and water in abnormal places rather trickled than ran. We were now beginning to be in the sloppy rather than the deluged stage. There was plenty of light to see by, for the moon had begun to show out fitfully through the masses of flying clouds. The uncertain light made weird shadows with the shrubs and statues in the garden. The long straight walk which leads from the marble steps is strewn with fine sand white from the quartz strand in the nook to the south of the Castle. Tall shrubs of white holly, yew, juniper, cypress, and variegated maple and spiraea, which stood at intervals along the walk and its branches, appeared ghost-like in the fitful moonlight. The many vases and statues and urns, always like phantoms in a half-light, were more than ever weird. Last night the moonlight was unusually effective, and showed not only the gardens down to the defending wall, but the deep gloom of the great forest-trees beyond; and beyond that, again, to where the mountain chain began, the forest running up their silvered slopes flamelike in form, deviated here and there by great crags and the outcropping rocky sinews of the vast mountains.

Whilst I was looking at this lovely prospect, I thought I saw something white flit, like a modified white flash, at odd moments from one to another of the shrubs or statues—anything which would afford cover from observation. At first I was not sure whether I really saw anything or did not. This was in itself a little disturbing to me, for I have been so long trained to minute observation of facts surrounding me, on which often depend not only my own life, but the lives of others, that I have become accustomed to trust my eyes; and anything creating the faintest doubt in this respect is a cause of more or less anxiety to me. Now, however, that my attention was called to myself, I looked more keenly, and in a very short time was satisfied that something was moving—something clad in white. It was natural enough that my thoughts should tend towards something uncanny—the belief that this place is haunted, conveyed in a thousand ways of speech and inference. Aunt Janet's eerie beliefs, fortified by her books on occult subjects—and of late, in our isolation from the rest of the world, the subject of daily conversations—helped to this end. No wonder, then, that, fully awake and with senses all on edge, I waited for some further manifestation from this ghostly visitor— as in my mind I took it to be. It must surely be a ghost or spiritual manifestation of some kind which moved in this silent way. In order to see and hear better, I softly moved back the folding grille, opened the French window, and stepped out, bare-footed and pyjama-clad as I was, on the marble terrace. How cold the wet marble was! How heavy smelled the rain-laden garden! It was as though the night and the damp, and even the moonlight, were drawing the aroma from all the flowers that blossomed. The whole night seemed to exhale heavy, half-intoxicating odours! I stood at the head of the marble steps, and all immediately before me was ghostly in the extreme—the white marble terrace and steps, the white walks of quartz-sand glistening under the fitful moonlight; the shrubs of white or pale green or yellow,—all looking dim and ghostly in the glamorous light; the white statues and vases. And amongst them, still flitting noiselessly, that mysterious elusive figure which I could not say was based on fact or imagination. I held my breath, listening intently for every sound; but sound there was none, save those of the night and its denizens. Owls hooted in the forest; bats, taking advantage of the cessation of the rain, flitted about silently, like shadows in the air. But there was no more sign of moving ghost or phantom, or whatever I had seen might have been—if, indeed, there had been anything except imagination.

So, after waiting awhile, I returned to my room, closed the window, drew the grille across again, and dragged the heavy curtain before the opening; then, having extinguished my candles, went to bed in the dark. In a few minutes I must have been asleep.

"What was that?" I almost heard the words of my own thought as I sat up in bed wide awake. To memory rather than present hearing the disturbing sound had seemed like the faint tapping at the window. For some seconds I listened, mechanically but intently, with bated breath and that quick beating of the heart which in a timorous person speaks for fear, and for expectation in another. In the stillness the sound came again—this time a very, very faint but unmistakable tapping at the glass door.

I jumped up, drew back the curtain, and for a moment stood appalled.

There, outside on the balcony, in the now brilliant moonlight, stood a woman, wrapped in white grave-clothes saturated with water, which dripped on the marble floor, making a pool which trickled slowly down the wet steps. Attitude and dress and circumstance all conveyed the idea that, though she moved and spoke, she was not quick, but dead. She was young and very beautiful, but pale, like the grey pallor of death. Through the still white of her face, which made her look as cold as the wet marble she stood on, her dark eyes seemed to gleam with a strange but enticing lustre. Even in the unsearching moonlight, which is after all rather deceptive than illuminative, I could not but notice one rare quality of her eyes. Each had some quality of refraction which made it look as though it contained a star. At every movement she made, the stars exhibited new beauties, of more rare and radiant force. She looked at me imploringly as the heavy curtain rolled back, and in eloquent gestures implored me to admit her. Instinctively I obeyed; I rolled back the steel grille, and threw open the French window. I noticed that she shivered and trembled as the glass door fell open. Indeed, she seemed so overcome with cold as to seem almost unable to move. In the sense of her helplessness all idea of the strangeness of the situation entirely disappeared. It was not as if my first idea of death taken from her cerements was negatived. It was simply that I did not think of it at all; I was content to accept things as they were—she was a woman, and in some dreadful trouble; that was enough.

I am thus particular about my own emotions, as I may have to refer to them again in matters of comprehension or comparison. The whole thing is so vastly strange and abnormal that the least thing may afterwards give some guiding light or clue to something otherwise not understandable. I have always found that in recondite matters first impressions are of more real value than later conclusions. We humans place far too little reliance on instinct as against reason; and yet instinct is the great gift of Nature to all animals for their protection and the fulfilment of their functions generally.

When I stepped out on the balcony, not thinking of my costume, I found that the woman was benumbed and hardly able to move. Even when I asked her to enter, and supplemented my words with gestures in case she should not understand my language, she stood stock-still, only rocking slightly to and fro as though she had just strength enough left to balance herself on her feet. I was afraid, from the condition in which she was, that she might drop down dead at any moment. So I took her by the hand to lead her in. But she seemed too weak to even make the attempt. When I pulled her slightly forward, thinking to help her, she tottered, and would have fallen had I not caught her in my arms. Then, half lifting her, I moved her forwards. Her feet, relieved of her weight, now seemed able to make the necessary effort; and so, I almost carrying her, we moved into the room. She was at the very end of her strength; I had to lift her over the sill. In obedience to her motion, I closed the French window and bolted it. I supposed the warmth of the room—though cool, it was warmer than the damp air without—affected her quickly, for on the instant she seemed to begin to recover herself. In a few seconds, as though she had reacquired her strength, she herself pulled the heavy curtain across the window. This left us in darkness, through which I heard her say in English:

"Light. Get a light!"

I found matches, and at once lit a candle. As the wick flared, she moved over to the door of the room, and tried if the lock and bolt were fastened. Satisfied as to this, she moved towards me, her wet shroud leaving a trail of moisture on the green carpet. By this time the wax of the candle had melted sufficiently to let me see her clearly. She was shaking and quivering as though in an ague; she drew the wet shroud around her piteously. Instinctively I spoke:

"Can I do anything for you?"

She answered, still in English, and in a voice of thrilling, almost piercing sweetness, which seemed somehow to go straight to my heart, and affected me strangely: "Give me warmth."

I hurried to the fireplace. It was empty; there was no fire laid. I turned to her, and said:

"Wait just a few minutes here. I shall call someone, and get help—and fire."

Her voice seemed to ring with intensity as she answered without a pause:

"No, no! Rather would I be"—here she hesitated for an instant, but as she caught sight of her cerements went on hurriedly—"as I am. I trust you—not others; and you must not betray my trust." Almost instantly she fell into a frightful fit of shivering, drawing again her death-clothes close to her, so piteously that it wrung my heart. I suppose I am a practical man. At any rate, I am accustomed to action. I took from its place beside my bed a thick Jaeger dressing-gown of dark brown—it was, of course, of extra length—and held it out to her as I said:

"Put that on. It is the only warm thing here which would be suitable. Stay; you must remove that wet—wet"—I stumbled about for a word that would not be offensive—"that frock—dress—costume— whatever it is." I pointed to where, in the corner of the room, stood a chintz-covered folding-screen which fences in my cold sponge bath, which is laid ready for me overnight, as I am an early riser.

She bowed gravely, and taking the dressing-gown in a long, white, finely-shaped hand, bore it behind the screen. There was a slight rustle, and then a hollow "flop" as the wet garment fell on the floor; more rustling and rubbing, and a minute later she emerged wrapped from head to foot in the long Jaeger garment, which trailed on the floor behind her, though she was a tall woman. She was still shivering painfully, however. I took a flask of brandy and a glass from a cupboard, and offered her some; but with a motion of her hand she refused it, though she moaned grievously.

"Oh, I am so cold—so cold!" Her teeth were chattering. I was pained at her sad condition, and said despairingly, for I was at my wits' end to know what to do:

"Tell me anything that I can do to help you, and I will do it. I may not call help; there is no fire—nothing to make it with; you will not take some brandy. What on earth can I do to give you warmth?"

Her answer certainly surprised me when it came, though it was practical enough—so practical that I should not have dared to say it. She looked me straight in the face for a few seconds before speaking.

Then, with an air of girlish innocence which disarmed suspicion and convinced me at once of her simple faith, she said in a voice that at once thrilled me and evoked all my pity:

"Let me rest for a while, and cover me up with rugs. That may give me warmth. I am dying of cold. And I have a deadly fear upon me—a deadly fear. Sit by me, and let me hold your hand. You are big and strong, and you look brave. It will reassure me. I am not myself a coward, but to-night fear has got me by the throat. I can hardly breathe. Do let me stay till I am warm. If you only knew what I have gone through, and have to go through still, I am sure you would pity me and help me."

To say that I was astonished would be a mild description of my feelings. I was not shocked. The life which I have led was not one which makes for prudery. To travel in strange places amongst strange peoples with strange views of their own is to have odd experiences and peculiar adventures now and again; a man without human passions is not the type necessary for an adventurous life, such as I myself have had. But even a man of passions and experiences can, when he respects a woman, be shocked—even prudish—where his own opinion of her is concerned. Such must bring to her guarding any generosity which he has, and any self-restraint also. Even should she place herself in a doubtful position, her honour calls to his honour. This is a call which may not be—*must* not be—unanswered. Even passion must pause for at least a while at sound of such a trumpet-call.

This woman I did respect—much respect. Her youth and beauty; her manifest ignorance of evil; her superb disdain of convention, which could only come through hereditary dignity; her terrible fear and suffering—for there must be more in her unhappy condition than meets the eye—would all demand respect, even if one did not hasten to yield it. Nevertheless, I thought it necessary to enter a protest against her embarrassing suggestion. I certainly did feel a fool when making it, also a cad. I can truly say it was made only for her good, and out of the best of me, such as I am. I felt impossibly awkward; and stuttered and stumbled before I spoke:

"But surely—the convenances! Your being here alone at night! Mrs. Grundy—convention—the—"

She interrupted me with an incomparable dignity—a dignity which had the effect of shutting me up like a clasp-knife and making me feel a decided inferior—and a poor show at that. There was such a gracious simplicity and honesty in it, too, such self-respecting knowledge of herself and her position, that I could be neither angry nor hurt. I could only feel ashamed of myself, and of my own littleness of mind and morals. She seemed in her icy coldness—now spiritual as well as bodily—like an incarnate figure of Pride as she answered:

"What are convenances or conventions to me! If you only knew where I have come from—the existence (if it can be called so) which I have had—the loneliness—the horror! And besides, it is for me to *make* conventions, not to yield my personal freedom of action to them. Even as I am—even here and in this garb—I am above convention. Convenances do not trouble me or hamper me. That, at least, I have won by what I have gone through, even if it had never come to me through any other way. Let me stay." She said the last words, in spite of all her pride, appealingly. But still, there was a note of high pride in all this—in all she said and did, in her attitude and movement, in the tones of her voice, in the loftiness of her carriage and the steadfast look of her open, starlit eyes. Altogether, there was something so rarely lofty in herself and all that clad her that, face to face with it and with her, my feeble attempt at moral precaution seemed puny, ridiculous, and out of place. Without a word in the doing, I took from an old chiffonier chest an armful of blankets, several of which I threw over her as she lay, for in the meantime, having replaced the coverlet, she had lain down at length on the bed. I took a chair, and sat down beside her. When she stretched out her hand from beneath the pile of wraps, I took it in mine, saying:

"Get warm and rest. Sleep if you can. You need not fear; I shall guard you with my life."

She looked at me gratefully, her starry eyes taking a new light more full of illumination than was afforded by the wax candle, which was shaded from her by my body . . . She was horribly cold, and her teeth chattered so violently that I feared lest she should have incurred some dangerous evil from her wetting and the cold that followed it. I felt, however, so awkward that I could find no words to express my fears; moreover, I hardly dared say anything at all regarding herself after the haughty way in which she had received my well-meant protest. Manifestly I was but to her as a sort of refuge and provider of heat, altogether impersonal, and not to be regarded in any degree as an individual. In these humiliating circumstances what could I do but sit quiet—and wait developments?

Little by little the fierce chattering of her teeth began to abate as the warmth of her surroundings stole through her. I also felt, even in this strangely awakening position, the influence of the quiet; and sleep began to steal over me. Several times I tried to fend it off, but, as I could not make any overt movement without alarming my strange and beautiful companion, I had to yield myself to drowsiness. I was still in such an overwhelming stupor of surprise that I could not even think freely. There was nothing for me but to control myself and wait. Before I could well fix my thoughts I was asleep.

I was recalled to consciousness by hearing, even through the pall of sleep that bound me, the crowing of a cock in some of the out-offices of the castle. At the same instant the figure, lying deathly still but for the gentle heaving of her bosom, began to struggle wildly. The sound had won through the gates of her sleep also. With a swift, gliding motion she slipped from the bed to the floor, saying in a fierce whisper as she pulled herself up to her full height:

"Let me out! I must go! I must go!"

By this time I was fully awake, and the whole position of things came to me in an instant which I shall never—can never—forget: the dim light of the candle, now nearly burned down to the socket, all the dimmer from the fact that the first grey gleam of morning was stealing in round the edges of the heavy curtain; the tall, slim figure in the brown dressing-gown whose over-length trailed on the floor, the black hair showing glossy in the light, and increasing by contrast the marble whiteness of the face, in which the black eyes sent through their stars fiery gleams. She appeared quite in a frenzy of haste; her eagerness was simply irresistible.

I was so stupefied with amazement, as well as with sleep, that I did not attempt to stop her, but began instinctively to help her by furthering her wishes. As she ran behind the screen, and, as far as sound could inform me,—began frantically to disrobe herself of the warm dressing-gown and to don again the ice-cold wet shroud, I pulled back the curtain from the window, and drew the bolt of the glass door. As I did so she was already behind me, shivering. As I threw open the door she glided out with a swift silent movement, but trembling in an agonized way. As she passed me, she murmured in a low voice, which was almost lost in the chattering of her teeth:

"Oh, thank you—thank you a thousand times! But I must go. I *must!* I *must!* I shall come again, and try to show my gratitude. Do not condemn me as ungrateful—till then." And she was gone.

I watched her pass the length of the white path, flitting from shrub to shrub or statue as she had come. In the cold grey light of the unde-veloped dawn she seemed even more ghostly than she had done in the black shadow of the night.

When she disappeared from sight in the shadow of the wood, I stood on the terrace for a long time watching, in case I should be afforded another glimpse of her, for there was now no doubt in my mind that she had for me some strange attraction. I felt even then that the look in those glorious starry eyes would be with me always so long as I might live. There was some fascination which went deeper than my eyes or my flesh or my heart—down deep into the very depths of my soul. My mind was all in a whirl, so that I could hardly think coherently. It all was like a dream; the reality seemed far away. It was not possible to doubt that the phantom figure which had been so close to me during the dark hours of the night was actual flesh and blood. Yet she was so cold, so cold! Altogether I could not fix my mind to either proposition: that it was a living woman who had held my hand, or a dead body reanimated for the time or the occasion in some strange manner.

The difficulty was too great for me to make up my mind upon it, even had I wanted to. But, in any case, I did not want to. This would, no doubt, come in time. But till then I wished to dream on, as anyone does in a dream which can still be blissful though there be pauses of pain, or ghastliness, or doubt, or terror.

So I closed the window and drew the curtain again, feeling for the first time the cold in which I had stood on the wet marble floor of the terrace when my bare feet began to get warm on the soft carpet. To get rid of the chill feeling I got into the bed on which *she* had lain, and as the warmth restored me tried to think coherently. For a short while I was going over the facts of the night—or what seemed as facts to my remembrance. But as I continued to think, the possibilities of any result seemed to get less, and I found myself vainly trying to reconcile with the logic of life the grim episode of the night. The effort proved to be too much for such concentration as was left to me; moreover, interrupted sleep was clamant, and would not be denied. What I dreamt of—if I dreamt at all—I know not. I only know that I was ready for waking when the time came. It came with a violent knocking at my door. I sprang from bed, fully awake in a second, drew the bolt, and slipped back to bed. With a hurried "May I come in?" Aunt Janet entered. She seemed relieved when she saw me, and gave without my asking an explanation of her perturbation:

"Oh, laddie, I hae been so uneasy aboot ye all the nicht. I hae had dreams an' veesions an' a' sorts o' uncanny fancies. I fear that—" She was by now drawing back the curtain, and as her eyes took in the marks of wet all over the floor the current of her thoughts changed:

"Why, laddie, whativer hae ye been doin' wi' yer baith? Oh, the mess ye hae made! 'Tis sinful to gie sic trouble an' waste . . ." And so she went on. I was glad to hear the tirade, which was only what a good housewife, outraged in her sentiments of order, would have made. I listened in patience—with pleasure when I thought of what she would have thought (and said) had she known the real facts. I was well pleased to have got off so easily.

RUPERT'S JOURNAL—*Continued.*

April 10, 1907.

For some days after what I call "the episode" I was in a strange condition of mind. I did not take anyone—not even Aunt Janet—into confidence. Even she dear, and open-hearted and liberal-minded as she is, might not have understood well enough to be just and tolerant; and I did not care to hear any adverse comment on my strange visitor. Somehow I could not bear the thought of anyone finding fault with her or in her, though, strangely enough, I was eternally defending her to myself; for, despite my wishes, embarrassing thoughts *would* come again and again, and again in all sorts and variants of queries difficult to answer. I found myself defending her, sometimes as a woman hard pressed by spiritual fear and physical suffering, sometimes as not being amenable to laws that govern the Living. Indeed, I could not make up my mind whether I looked on her as a living human being or as one with some strange existence in another world, and having only a chance foothold in our own. In such doubt imagination began to work, and thoughts of evil, of danger, of doubt, even of fear, began to crowd on me with such persistence and in such varied forms that I found my instinct of reticence growing into a settled purpose. The value of this instinctive precaution was promptly shown by Aunt Janet's state of mind, with consequent revelation of it. She became full of gloomy prognostications and what I thought were morbid fears. For the first time in my life I discovered that Aunt Janet had nerves! I had long had a secret belief that she was gifted, to some degree at any rate, with Second Sight, which quality, or whatever it is, skilled in the powers if not the lore of superstition, manages to keep at stretch not only the mind of its immediate pathic, but of others relevant to it. Perhaps this natural quality had received a fresh impetus from the arrival of some cases of her books sent on by Sir Colin. She appeared to read and reread these works, which were chiefly on occult subjects, day and night, except when she was imparting to me choice excerpts of the most baleful and fearsome kind. Indeed, before a week was over I found myself to be an expert in the history of the cult, as well as in its manifestations, which latter I had been versed in for a good many years.

The result of all this was that it set me brooding. Such, at least, I gathered was the fact when Aunt Janet took me to task for it. She always speaks out according to her convictions, so that her thinking I brooded was to me a proof that I did; and after a personal examination I came—reluctantly—to the conclusion that she was right, so far, at any rate, as my outer conduct was concerned. The state of mind I was in, however, kept me from making any acknowledgment of it—the real cause of my keeping so much to myself and of being so *distrait*. And so I went on, torturing myself as before with introspective questioning; and she, with her mind set on my actions, and endeavouring to find a cause for them, continued and expounded her beliefs and fears.

Her nightly chats with me when we were alone after dinner— for I had come to avoid her questioning at other times—kept my imagination at high pressure. Despite myself, I could not but find new cause for concern in the perennial founts of her superstition. I had thought, years ago, that I had then sounded the depths of this branch of psychicism; but this new phase of thought, founded on the really deep hold which the existence of my beautiful visitor and her sad and dreadful circumstances had taken upon me, brought me a new concern in the matter of self-importance. I came to think that I must reconstruct my self-values, and begin a fresh understanding of ethical beliefs. Do what I would, my mind would keep turning on the uncanny subjects brought before it. I began to apply them one by one to my own late experience, and unconsciously to try to fit them in turn to the present case.

The effect of this brooding was that I was, despite my own will, struck by the similarity of circumstances bearing on my visitor, and the conditions apportioned by tradition and superstition to such strange survivals from earlier ages as these partial existences which are rather Undead than Living—still walking the earth, though claimed by the world of the Dead. Amongst them are the Vampire, or the Wehr-Wolf. To this class also might belong in a measure the Doppelganger—one of whose dual existences commonly belongs to the actual world around it. So, too, the denizens of the world of Astralism. In any of these named worlds there is a material presence—which must be created, if only for a single or periodic purpose. It matters not whether a material presence already created can be receptive of a disembodied soul, or a soul unattached can have a body built up for it or around it; or, again, whether the body of a dead person can be made seeming quick

through some diabolic influence manifested in the present, or an inheritance or result of some baleful use of malefic power in the past.
The result is the same in each case, though the ways be widely different: a soul and a body which are not in unity but brought together
for strange purposes through stranger means and by powers still more
strange.

Through much thought and a process of exclusions the eerie form
which seemed to be most in correspondence with my adventure, and
most suitable to my fascinating visitor, appeared to be the Vampire.
Doppelganger, Astral creations, and all such-like, did not comply with
the conditions of my night experience. The Wehr-Wolf is but a variant
of the Vampire, and so needed not to be classed or examined at all.
Then it was that, thus focussed, the Lady of the Shroud (for so I came to
hold her in my mind) began to assume a new force. Aunt Janet's library
afforded me clues which I followed with avidity. In my secret heart I
hated the quest, and did not wish to go on with it. But in this I was not
my own master. Do what I would—brush away doubts never so often,
new doubts and imaginings came in their stead. The circumstance
almost repeated the parable of the Seven Devils who took the place of
the exorcised one. Doubts I could stand. Imaginings I could stand. But
doubts and imaginings together made a force so fell that I was driven
to accept any reading of the mystery which might presumably afford a
foothold for satisfying thought. And so I came to accept tentatively the
Vampire theory—accept it, at least, so far as to examine it as judicially
as was given me to do. As the days wore on, so the conviction grew.
The more I read on the subject, the more directly the evidences pointed
towards this view. The more I thought, the more obstinate became the
conviction. I ransacked Aunt Janet's volumes again and again to find
anything to the contrary; but in vain. Again, no matter how obstinate
were my convictions at any given time, unsettlement came with fresh

thinking over the argument, so that I was kept in a harassing state of uncertainty.

Briefly, the evidence in favour of accord between the facts of the case and the Vampire theory were:

Her coming was at night—the time the Vampire is according to the theory, free to move at will.

She wore her shroud—a necessity of coming fresh from grave or tomb; for there is nothing occult about clothing which is not subject to astral or other influences.

She had to be helped into my room—in strict accordance with what one sceptical critic of occultism has called "the Vampire etiquette."

She made violent haste in getting away at cock-crow.

She seemed preternaturally cold; her sleep was almost abnormal in intensity, and yet the sound of the cock-crowing came through it.

These things showed her to be subject to *some* laws, though not in exact accord within those which govern human beings. Under the stress of such circumstances as she must have gone through, her vitality seemed more than human—the quality of vitality which could outlive ordinary burial. Again, such purpose as she had shown in donning, under stress of some compelling direction, her ice-cold wet shroud, and, wrapt in it, going out again into the night, was hardly normal for a woman.

But if so, and if she was indeed a Vampire, might not whatever it may be that holds such beings in thrall be by some means or other exorcised? To find the means must be my next task. I am actually pining to see her again. Never before have I been stirred to my depths by anyone. Come it from Heaven or Hell, from the Earth or the Grave, it does not matter; I shall make it my task to win her back to life and peace. If she be indeed a Vampire, the task may be hard and long; if she be not so, and if it be merely that circumstances have so gathered round her as to produce that impression, the task may be simpler and the result more sweet. No, not more sweet; for what can be more sweet than to restore the lost or seemingly lost soul of the woman you love! There, the truth is out at last! I suppose that I have fallen in love with her. If so, it is too late for me to fight against it. I can only wait with what patience I can till I see her again. But to that end I can do nothing. I know absolutely nothing about her—not even her name. Patience!

RUPERT'S JOURNAL—*Continued.*

April 16, 1907.

The only relief I have had from the haunting anxiety regarding the Lady of the Shroud has been in the troubled state of my adopted country. There has evidently been something up which I have not been allowed to know. The mountaineers are troubled and restless; are wandering about, singly and in parties, and holding meetings in strange places. This is what I gather used to be in old days when intrigues were on foot with Turks, Greeks, Austrians, Italians, Russians. This concerns me vitally, for my mind has long been made up to share the fortunes of the Land of the Blue Mountains. For good or ill I mean to stay here: *J'y suis, j'y reste.* I share henceforth the lot of the Blue Mountaineers; and not Turkey, nor Greece, nor Austria, nor Italy, nor Russia—no, not France nor Germany either; not man nor God nor Devil shall drive me from my purpose. With these patriots I throw in my lot! My only difficulty seemed at first to be with the men themselves. They are so proud that at the beginning I feared they would not even accord me the honour of being one of them! However, things always move on somehow, no matter what difficulties there be at the beginning. Never mind! When one looks back at an accomplished fact the beginning is not to be seen—and if it were it would not matter. It is not of any account, anyhow.

I heard that there was going to be a great meeting near here yesterday afternoon, and I attended it. I think it was a success. If such is any proof, I felt elated as well as satisfied when I came away. Aunt Janet's Second Sight on the subject was comforting, though grim, and in a measure disconcerting. When I was saying good-night she asked me to bend down my head. As I did so, she laid her hands on it and passed them all over it. I heard her say to herself:

"Strange! There's nothing there; yet I could have sworn I saw it!" I asked her to explain, but she would not. For once she was a little obstinate, and refused point blank to even talk of the subject. She was not worried nor unhappy; so I had no cause for concern. I said nothing, but I shall wait and see. Most mysteries become plain or disappear altogether in time. But about the meeting—lest I forget!

When I joined the mountaineers who had assembled, I really think they were glad to see me; though some of them seemed adverse, and others did not seem over well satisfied. However, absolute unity is very seldom to be found. Indeed, it is almost impossible; and in a free community is not altogether to be desired. When it is apparent, the gathering lacks that sense of individual feeling which makes for the real consensus of opinion—which is the real unity of purpose. The meeting was at first, therefore, a little cold and distant. But presently it began to thaw, and after some fiery harangues I was asked to speak. Happily, I had begun to learn the Balkan language as soon as ever Uncle Roger's wishes had been made known to me, and as I have some facility of tongues and a great deal of experience, I soon began to know something of it. Indeed, when I had been here a few weeks, with opportunity of speaking daily with the people themselves, and learned to understand the intonations and vocal inflexions, I felt quite easy in speaking it. I understood every word which had up to then been spoken at the meeting, and when I spoke myself I felt that they understood. That is an experience which every speaker has in a certain way and up to a certain point. He knows by some kind of instinct if his hearers are with him; if they respond, they must certainly have understood. Last night this was marked. I felt it every instant I was talking and when I came to realize that the men were in strict accord with my general views, I took them into confidence with regard to my own personal purpose. It was the beginning of a mutual trust; so for peroration I told them that I had come to the conclusion that what they wanted most for their own protection and the security and consolidation of their nation was arms—arms of the very latest pattern. Here they interrupted me with wild cheers, which so strung me up that I went farther than I intended, and made a daring venture. "Ay," I repeated, "the security and consolidation of your country—of *our* country, for I have come to live amongst you. Here is my home whilst I live. I am with you heart and soul. I shall live with you, fight shoulder to shoulder with you, and, if need be, shall die with you!" Here the shouting was terrific, and the younger men raised their guns to fire a salute in Blue Mountain fashion. But on the instant the Vladika[1] held up his hands and motioned them to desist. In the immediate silence he spoke, sharply at first, but later ascending to a high pitch of single-minded, lofty eloquence. His words rang in my ears long after the meeting was over and other thoughts had come between them and the present.

"Silence!" he thundered. "Make no echoes in the forest or through the hills at this dire time of stress and threatened danger to our land. Bethink ye of this meeting, held here and in secret, in order that no whisper of it may be heard afar. Have ye all, brave men of the Blue Mountains, come hither through the forest like shadows that some of you, thoughtless, may enlighten your enemies as to our secret purpose? The thunder of your guns would doubtless sound well in the ears of those who wish us ill and try to work us wrong. Fellow-countrymen, know ye not that the Turk is awake once more for our harming? The Bureau of Spies has risen from the torpor which came on it when the purpose against our Teuta roused our mountains to such anger that the frontiers blazed with passion, and were swept with fire and sword.

Moreover, there is a traitor somewhere in the land, or else incautious carelessness has served the same base purpose. Something of our needs—our doing, whose secret we have tried to hide, has gone out. The myrmidons of the Turk are close on our borders, and it may be that some of them have passed our guards and are amidst us unknown. So it behoves us doubly to be discreet. Believe me that I share with you, my brothers, our love for the gallant Englishman who has come amongst us to share our sorrows and ambitions—and I trust it may be our joys. We are all united in the wish to do him honour—though not in the way by which danger might be carried on the wings of love. My brothers, our newest brother comes to us from the Great Nation which amongst the nations has been our only friend, and which has ere now helped us in our direst need—that mighty Britain whose hand has ever been raised in the cause of freedom. We of the Blue Mountains know her best as she stands with sword in hand face to face with our foes. And this, her son and now our brother, brings further to our need the hand of a giant and the heart of a lion. Later on, when danger does not ring us round, when silence is no longer our outer guard; we shall bid him welcome in true fashion of our land. But till then he will believe— for he is great-hearted—that our love and thanks and welcome are not to be measured by sound. When the time comes, then shall be sound in his honour—not of rifles alone, but bells and cannon and the mighty voice of a free people shouting as one. But now we must be wise and silent, for the Turk is once again at our gates. Alas! the cause of his for- mer coming may not be, for she whose beauty and nobility and whose place in our nation and in our hearts tempted him to fraud and vio- lence is not with us to share even our anxiety."

Here his voice broke, and there arose from all a deep wailing sound, which rose and rose till the woods around us seemed broken by a mighty and long-sustained sob. The orator saw that his purpose was accomplished, and with a short sentence finished his harangue: "But the need of our nation still remains!" Then, with an eloquent gesture to me to proceed, he merged in the crowd and disappeared.

How could I even attempt to follow such a speaker with any hope of success? I simply told them what I had already done in the way of help, saying:

"As you needed arms, I have got them. My agent sends me word through the code between us that he has procured for me—for us—fifty thousand of the newest-pattern rifles, the French Ingis-Malbron, which has surpassed all others, and sufficient ammunition to last for a year of war. The first section is in hand, and will soon be ready for consignment. There are other war materials, too, which, when they arrive, will enable every man and woman—even the children—of our land to take a part in its defence should such be needed. My brothers, I am with you in all things, for good or ill!"

It made me very proud to hear the mighty shout which arose. I had felt exalted before, but now this personal development almost unmanned me. I was glad of the long-sustained applause to recover my self-control.

I was quite satisfied that the meeting did not want to hear any other speaker, for they began to melt away without any formal notification having been given. I doubt if there will be another meeting soon again. The weather has begun to break, and we are in for another spell of rain. It is disagreeable, of course; but it has its own charm. It was during a spell of wet weather that the Lady of the Shroud came to me. Perhaps the rain may bring her again. I hope so, with all my soul.

RUPERT'S JOURNAL—*Continued*.

April 23, 1907.

The rain has continued for four whole days and nights, and the low-lying ground is like a quagmire in places. In the sunlight the whole mountains glisten with running streams and falling water. I feel a strange kind of elation, but from no visible cause. Aunt Janet rather queered it by telling me, as she said good-night, to be very careful of myself, as she had seen in a dream last night a figure in a shroud. I fear she was not pleased that I did not take it with all the seriousness that she did. I would not wound her for the world if I could help it, but the idea of a shroud gets too near the bone to be safe, and I had to fend her off at all hazards. So when I doubted if the Fates regarded the visionary shroud as of necessity appertaining to me, she said, in a way that was, for her, almost sharp:

"Take care, laddie. 'Tis ill jesting wi' the powers o' time Unknown."

Perhaps it was that her talk put the subject in my mind. The woman needed no such aid; she was always there; but when I locked myself into my room that night, I half expected to find her in the room. I was not sleepy, so I took a book of Aunt Janet's and began to read. The title was "On the Powers and Qualities of Disembodied Spirits." "Your grammar," said I to the author, "is hardly attractive, but I may learn something which might apply to her. I shall read your book." Before settling down to it, however, I thought I would have a look at the garden. Since the night of the visit the garden seemed to have a new attractiveness for me: a night seldom passed without my having a last look at it before turning in. So I drew the great curtain and looked out.

The scene was beautiful, but almost entirely desolate. All was ghastly in the raw, hard gleams of moonlight coming fitfully through the masses of flying cloud. The wind was rising, and the air was damp and cold. I looked round the room instinctively, and noticed that the fire was laid ready for lighting, and that there were small-cut logs of wood piled beside the hearth. Ever since that night I have had a fire laid ready. I was tempted to light it, but as I never have a fire unless I sleep in the open, I hesitated to begin. I went back to the window, and, opening the catch, stepped out on the terrace. As I looked down the white walk and let my eyes range over the expanse of the garden, where everything glistened as the moonlight caught the wet, I half expected to see some white figure flitting amongst the shrubs and statues. The whole scene of the former visit came back to me so vividly that I could hardly believe that any time had passed since then. It was the same scene, and again late in the evening. Life in Vissarion was primitive, and early hours prevailed—though not so late as on that night.

As I looked I thought I caught a glimpse of something white far away. It was only a ray of moonlight coming through the rugged edge of a cloud. But all the same it set me in a strange state of perturbation. Somehow I seemed to lose sight of my own identity. It was as though I was hypnotized by the situation or by memory, or perhaps by some occult force. Without thinking of what I was doing, or being conscious of any reason for it, I crossed the room and set light to the fire. Then I blew out the candle and came to the window again. I never thought it might be a foolish thing to do—to stand at a window with a light behind me in this country, where every man carries a gun with him always. I was in my evening clothes, too, with my breast well marked by a white shirt. I opened the window and stepped out on the terrace. There I stood for many minutes, thinking. All the time my eyes kept ranging over the garden. Once I thought I saw a white figure moving, but it was not followed up, so, becoming conscious that it was again beginning to rain, I stepped back into the room, shut the window, and drew the curtain. Then I realized the comforting appearance of the fire, and went over and stood before it.

Hark! Once more there was a gentle tapping at the window. I rushed over to it and drew the curtain.

There, out on the rain-beaten terrace, stood the white shrouded figure, more desolate-appearing than ever. Ghastly pale she looked, as before, but her eyes had an eager look which was new. I took it that she was attracted by the fire, which was by now well ablaze, and was throwing up jets of flame as the dry logs crackled. The leaping flames threw fitful light across the room, and every gleam threw the white-clad figure into prominence, showing the gleam of the black eyes, and fixing the stars that lay in them.

Without a word I threw open the window, and, taking the white hand extended to me, drew into the room the Lady of the Shroud.

As she entered and felt the warmth of the blazing fire, a glad look spread over her face. She made a movement as if to run to it. But she drew back an instant after, looking round with instinctive caution. She closed the window and bolted it, touched the lever which spread the grille across the opening, and pulled close the curtain behind it. Then she went swiftly to the door and tried if it was locked. Satisfied as to this, she came quickly over to the fire, and, kneeling before it, stretched out her numbed hands to the blaze. Almost on the instant her wet shroud began to steam. I stood wondering. The precautions of secrecy in the midst of her suffering—for that she did suffer was only too painfully manifest—must have presupposed some danger. Then and there my mind was made up that there should no harm assail her that I by any means could fend off. Still, the present must be attended to; pneumonia and other ills stalked behind such a chill as must infallibly come on her unless precautions were taken. I took again the dressing-gown which she had worn before and handed it to her, motioning as I did so towards the screen which had made a dressing-room for her on the former occasion. To my surprise she hesitated. I waited. She waited, too, and then laid down the dressing-gown on the edge of the stone fender. So I spoke:

"Won't you change as you did before? Your—your frock can then be dried. Do! It will be so much safer for you to be dry clad when you resume your own dress."

"How can I whilst you are here?"

Her words made me stare, so different were they from her acts of the other visit. I simply bowed—speech on such a subject would be at least inadequate—and walked over to the window. Passing behind the curtain, I opened the window. Before stepping out on to the terrace, I looked into the room and said:

"Take your own time. There is no hurry. I dare say you will find there all you may want. I shall remain on the terrace until you summon me." With that I went out on the terrace, drawing close the glass door behind me.

I stood looking out on the dreary scene for what seemed a very short time, my mind in a whirl. There came a rustle from within, and I saw a dark brown figure steal round the edge of the curtain. A white hand was raised, and beckoned me to come in. I entered, bolting the window behind me. She had passed across the room, and was again kneeling before the fire with her hands outstretched. The shroud was laid in partially opened folds on one side of the hearth, and was steaming heavily. I brought over some cushions and pillows, and made a little pile of them beside her.

"Sit there," I said, "and rest quietly in the heat." It may have been the effect of the glowing heat, but there was a rich colour in her face as she looked at me with shining eyes. Without a word, but with a courteous little bow, she sat down at once. I put a thick rug across her shoulders, and sat down myself on a stool a couple of feet away.

For fully five or six minutes we sat in silence. At last, turning her head towards me she said in a sweet, low voice:

"I had intended coming earlier on purpose to thank you for your very sweet and gracious courtesy to me, but circumstances were such that I could not leave my—my"—she hesitated before saying—"my abode. I am not free, as you and others are, to do what I will. My existence is sadly cold and stern, and full of horrors that appal. But I *do* thank you. For myself I am not sorry for the delay, for every hour shows me more clearly how good and understanding and sympathetic you have been to me. I only hope that some day you may realize how kind you have been, and how much I appreciate it."

"I am only too glad to be of any service," I said, feebly I felt, as I held out my hand. She did not seem to see it. Her eyes were now on the fire, and a warm blush dyed forehead and cheek and neck. The reproof was so gentle that no one could have been offended. It was evident that she was something coy and reticent, and would not allow me to come at present more close to her, even to the touching of her hand. But that her heart was not in the denial was also evident in the glance from her glorious dark starry eyes. These glances—veritable lightning flashes coming through her pronounced reserve—finished entirely any wavering there might be in my own purpose. I was aware now to the full that my heart was quite subjugated. I knew that I was in love— veritably so much in love as to feel that without this woman, be she what she might, by my side my future must be absolutely barren.

It was presently apparent that she did not mean to stay as long on this occasion as on the last. When the castle clock struck midnight she suddenly sprang to her feet with a bound, saying:

"I must go! There is midnight!" I rose at once, the intensity of her speech having instantly obliterated the sleep which, under the influence of rest and warmth, was creeping upon me. Once more she was in a frenzy of haste, so I hurried towards the window, but as I looked back saw her, despite her haste, still standing. I motioned towards the screen, and slipping behind the curtain, opened the window and went out on the terrace. As I was disappearing behind the curtain I saw her with the tail of my eye lifting the shroud, now dry, from the hearth.

She was out through the window in an incredibly short time, now clothed once more in that dreadful wrapping. As she sped past me barefooted on the wet, chilly marble which made her shudder, she whispered:

"Thank you again. You *are* good to me. You can understand."

Once again I stood on the terrace, saw her melt like a shadow down the steps, and disappear behind the nearest shrub. Thence she flitted away from point to point with exceeding haste. The moonlight had now disappeared behind heavy banks of cloud, so there was little light to see by. I could just distinguish a pale gleam here and there as she wended her secret way.

For a long time I stood there alone thinking, as I watched the course she had taken, and wondering where might be her ultimate destination. As she had spoken of her "abode," I knew there was some definitive objective of her flight.

It was no use wondering. I was so entirely ignorant of her surroundings that I had not even a starting-place for speculation. So I went in, leaving the window open. It seemed that this being so made one barrier the less between us. I gathered the cushions and rugs from before the fire, which was no longer leaping, but burning with a steady glow, and put them back in their places. Aunt Janet might come in the morning, as she had done before, and I did not wish to set her thinking. She is much too clever a person to have treading on the heels of a mystery—especially one in which my own affections are engaged. I wonder what she would have said had she seen me kiss the cushion on which my beautiful guest's head had rested?

When I was in bed, and in the dark save for the fading glow of the fire, my thoughts became fixed that whether she came from Earth or Heaven or Hell, my lovely visitor was already more to me than aught else in the world. This time she had, on going, said no word of returning. I had been so much taken up with her presence, and so upset by her abrupt departure, that I had omitted to ask her. And so I am driven, as before, to accept the chance of her returning—a chance which I fear I am or may be unable to control.

Surely enough Aunt Janet did come in the morning, early. I was still asleep when she knocked at my door. With that purely physical subconsciousness which comes with habit I must have realized the cause of the sound, for I woke fully conscious of the fact that Aunt Janet had knocked and was waiting to come in. I jumped from bed, and back again when I had unlocked the door. When Aunt Janet came in she noticed the cold of the room.

"Save us, laddie, but ye'll get your death o' cold in this room." Then, as she looked round and noticed the ashes of the extinct fire in the grate:

"Eh, but ye're no that daft after a'; ye've had the sense to light yer fire. Glad I am that we had the fire laid and a wheen o' dry logs ready to yer hand." She evidently felt the cold air coming from the window, for she went over and drew the curtain. When she saw the open window, she raised her hands in a sort of dismay, which to me, knowing how little base for concern could be within her knowledge, was comic. Hurriedly she shut the window, and then, coming close over to my bed, said:

"Yon has been a fearsome nicht again, laddie, for yer poor auld aunty."

"Dreaming again, Aunt Janet?" I asked—rather flippantly as it seemed to me. She shook her head:

"Not so, Rupert, unless it be that the Lord gies us in dreams what we in our spiritual darkness think are veesions." I roused up at this. When Aunt Janet calls me Rupert, as she always used to do in my dear mother's time, things are serious with her. As I was back in childhood now, recalled by her word, I thought the best thing I could do to cheer her would be to bring her back there too—if I could. So I patted the edge of the bed as I used to do when I was a wee kiddie and wanted her to comfort me, and said:

"Sit down, Aunt Janet, and tell me." She yielded at once, and the look of the happy old days grew over her face as though there had come a gleam of sunshine. She sat down, and I put out my hands as I used to do, and took her hand between them. There was a tear in her eye as she raised my hand and kissed it as in old times. But for the infinite pathos of it, it would have been comic:

Aunt Janet, old and grey-haired, but still retaining her girlish slimness of figure, petite, dainty as a Dresden figure, her face lined with the care of years, but softened and ennobled by the unselfishness of those years, holding up my big hand, which would outweigh her whole arm; sitting dainty as a pretty old fairy beside a recumbent giant—for my bulk never seems so great as when I am near this real little good fairy of my life—seven feet beside four feet seven.

So she began as of old, as though she were about to soothe a frightened child with a fairy tale:

"Twas a veesion, I think, though a dream it may hae been. But whichever or whatever it was, it concerned my little boy, who has grown to be a big giant, so much that I woke all of a tremble. Laddie dear, I thought that I saw ye being married." This gave me an opening, though a small one, for comforting her, so I took it at once:

"Why, dear, there isn't anything to alarm you in that, is there? It was only the other day when you spoke to me about the need of my getting married, if it was only that you might have children of your boy playing around your knees as their father used to do when he was a helpless wee child himself."

"That is so, laddie," she answered gravely. "But your weddin' was none so merry as I fain would see. True, you seemed to lo'e her wi' all yer hairt. Yer eyes shone that bright that ye might ha' set her afire, for all her black locks and her winsome face. But, laddie, that was not all—no, not though her black een, that had the licht o' all the stars o' nicht in them, shone in yours as though a hairt o' love an' passion, too, dwelt in them. I saw ye join hands, an' heard a strange voice that talked stranger still, but I saw none ither. Your eyes an' her eyes, an' your hand an' hers, were all I saw. For all else was dim, and the darkness was close around ye twa. And when the benison was spoken—I knew that by the voices that sang, and by the gladness of her een, as well as by the pride and glory of yours—the licht began to glow a wee more, an' I could see yer bride. She was in a veil o' wondrous fine lace. And there were orange-flowers in her hair, though there were twigs, too, and there was a crown o' flowers on head wi' a golden band round it. And the heathen candles that stood on the table wi' the Book had some strange effect, for the reflex o' it hung in the air o'er her head like the shadow of a crown. There was a gold ring on her finger and a silver one on yours." Here she paused and trembled, so that, hoping to dispel her fears, I said, as like as I could to the way I used to when I was a child:

"Go on, Aunt Janet."

She did not seem to recognize consciously the likeness between past and present; but the effect was there, for she went on more like her old self, though there was a prophetic gravity in her voice, more marked than I had ever heard from her:

"All this I've told ye was well; but, oh, laddie, there was a dreadful lack o' livin' joy such as I should expect from the woman whom my boy had chosen for his wife—and at the marriage coupling, too! And no wonder, when all is said; for though the marriage veil o' love was fine, an' the garland o' flowers was fresh-gathered, underneath them a' was nane ither than a ghastly shroud. As I looked in my veesion—or maybe dream—I expectit to see the worms crawl round the flagstane at her feet. If 'twas not Death, laddie dear, that stood by ye, it was the shadow o' Death that made the darkness round ye, that neither the light o' candles nor the smoke o' heathen incense could pierce. Oh, laddie, laddie, wae is me that I hae seen sic a veesion—waking or sleeping, it matters not! I was sair distressed—so sair that I woke wi' a shriek on my lips and bathed in cold sweat. I would hae come doon to ye to see if you were hearty or no—or even to listen at your door for any sound o' yer being quick, but that I feared to alarm ye till morn should come. I've counted the hours and the minutes since midnight, when I saw the veesion, till I came hither just the now."

"Quite right, Aunt Janet," I said, "and I thank you for your kind thought for me in the matter, now and always." Then I went on, for I wanted to take precautions against the possibility of her discovery of my secret. I could not bear to think that she might run my precious secret to earth in any well-meant piece of bungling. That would be to me disaster unbearable. She might frighten away altogether my beautiful visitor, even whose name or origin I did not know, and I might never see her again:

"You must never do that, Aunt Janet. You and I are too good friends to have sense of distrust or annoyance come between us—which would surely happen if I had to keep thinking that you or anyone else might be watching me."

RUPERT'S JOURNAL—*Continued*.

April 27, 1907.

After a spell of loneliness which has seemed endless I have something to write. When the void in my heart was becoming the receptacle for many devils of suspicion and distrust I set myself a task which might, I thought, keep my thoughts in part, at any rate, occupied—to explore minutely the neighbourhood round the Castle. This might, I hoped, serve as an anodyne to my pain of loneliness, which grew more acute as the days, the hours, wore on, even if it should not ultimately afford me some clue to the whereabouts of the woman whom I had now grown to love so madly.

My exploration soon took a systematic form, as I intended that it should be exhaustive. I would take every day a separate line of advance from the Castle, beginning at the south and working round by the east to the north. The first day only took me to the edge of the creek, which I crossed in a boat, and landed at the base of the cliff opposite. I found the cliffs alone worth a visit. Here and there were openings to caves which I made up my mind to explore later. I managed to climb up the cliff at a spot less beetling than the rest, and continued my journey. It was, though very beautiful, not a specially interesting place. I explored that spoke of the wheel of which Vissarion was the hub, and got back just in time for dinner.

The next day I took a course slightly more to the eastward. I had no difficulty in keeping a straight path, for, once I had rowed across the creek, the old church of St. Sava rose before me in stately gloom. This was the spot where many generations of the noblest of the Land of the Blue Mountains had from time immemorial been laid to rest, amongst them the Vissarions. Again, I found the opposite cliffs pierced here and there with caves, some with wide openings,—others the openings of which were partly above and partly below water. I could, however, find no means of climbing the cliff at this part, and had to make a long detour, following up the line of the creek till further on I found a piece of beach from which ascent was possible. Here I ascended, and found that I was on a line between the Castle and the southern side of the mountains. I saw the church of St. Sava away to my right, and not far from the edge of the cliff. I made my way to it at once, for as yet I had never been near it. Hitherto my excursions had been limited to the Castle and its many gardens and surroundings. It was of a style with which I was not familiar—with four wings to the points of the compass. The great doorway, set in a magnificent frontage of carved stone of manifestly ancient date, faced west, so that, when one entered, he went east. To my surprise—for somehow I expected the contrary—I found the door open. Not wide open, but what is called ajar—manifestly not locked or barred, but not sufficiently open for one to look in. I entered, and after passing through a wide vestibule, more like a section of a corridor than an ostensible entrance, made my way through a spacious doorway into the body of the church. The church itself was almost circular, the openings of the four naves being spacious enough to give the appearance of the interior as a whole, being a huge cross. It was strangely dim, for the window openings were small and high-set, and were, moreover, filled with green or blue glass, each window having a colour to itself. The glass was very old, being of the thirteenth or fourteenth century. Such appointments as there were—for it had a general air of desolation—were of great beauty and richness,—especially so to be in a place—even a church—where the door lay open, and no one was to be seen. It was strangely silent even for an old church on a lonesome headland. There reigned a dismal solemnity which seemed to chill me, accustomed as I have been to strange and weird places. It seemed abandoned, though it had not that air of having been neglected which is so often to be noticed in old churches. There was none of the everlasting accumulation of dust which prevails in places of higher cultivation and larger and more strenuous work.

In the church itself or its appending chambers I could find no clue or suggestion which could guide me in any way in my search for the Lady of the Shroud. Monuments there were in profusion—statues, tablets, and all the customary memorials of the dead. The families and dates represented were simply bewildering. Often the name of Vissarion was given, and the inscription which it held I read through carefully, looking to find some enlightenment of any kind. But all in vain: there was nothing to see in the church itself. So I determined to visit the crypt. I had no lantern or candle with me, so had to go back to the Castle to secure one.

It was strange, coming in from the sunlight, here overwhelming to one so recently accustomed to northern skies, to note the slender gleam of the lantern which I carried, and which I had lit inside the door. At my first entry to the church my mind had been so much taken up with the strangeness of the place, together with the intensity of wish for some sort of clue, that I had really no opportunity of examining detail. But now detail became necessary, as I had to find the entrance to the crypt. My puny light could not dissipate the semi-Cimmerian gloom of the vast edifice; I had to throw the feeble gleam into one after another of the dark corners.

At last I found, behind the great screen, a narrow stone staircase which seemed to wind down into the rock. It was not in any way secret, but being in the narrow space behind the great screen, was not visible except when close to it. I knew I was now close to my objective, and began to descend. Accustomed though I have been to all sorts of mysteries and dangers, I felt awed and almost overwhelmed by a sense of loneliness and desolation as I descended the ancient winding steps. These were many in number, roughly hewn of old in the solid rock on which the church was built.

I met a fresh surprise in finding that the door of the crypt was open. After all, this was different from the church-door being open; for in many places it is a custom to allow all comers at all times to find rest and comfort in the sacred place. But I did expect that at least the final resting-place of the historic dead would be held safe against casual intrusion. Even I, on a quest which was very near my heart, paused with an almost overwhelming sense of decorum before passing through that open door. The crypt was a huge place, strangely lofty for a vault. From its formation, however, I soon came to the conclusion that it was originally a natural cavern altered to its present purpose by the hand of man. I could hear somewhere near the sound of running water, but I could not locate it. Now and again at irregular intervals there was a prolonged booming, which could only come from a wave breaking in a confined place. The recollection then came to me of the proximity of the church to the top of the beetling cliff, and of the half-sunk cavern entrances which pierced it.

With the gleam of my lamp to guide me, I went through and round the whole place. There were many massive tombs, mostly rough-hewn from great slabs or blocks of stone. Some of them were marble, and the cutting of all was ancient. So large and heavy were some of them that it was a wonder to me how they could ever have been brought to this place, to which the only entrance was seemingly the narrow, tortuous stairway by which I had come. At last I saw near one end of the crypt a great chain hanging. Turning the light upward, I found that it depended from a ring set over a wide opening, evidently made artificially. It must have been through this opening that the great sarcophagi had been lowered.

Directly underneath the hanging chain, which did not come closer to the ground than some eight or ten feet, was a huge tomb in the shape of a rectangular coffer or sarcophagus. It was open, save for a huge sheet of thick glass which rested above it on two thick balks of dark oak, cut to exceeding smoothness, which lay across it, one at either end. On the far side from where I stood each of these was joined to another oak plank, also cut smooth, which sloped gently to the rocky floor. Should it be necessary to open the tomb, the glass could be made to slide along the supports and descend by the sloping planks.

Naturally curious to know what might be within such a strange receptacle, I raised the lantern, depressing its lens so that the light might fall within.

Then I started back with a cry, the lantern slipping from my nerveless hand and falling with a ringing sound on the great sheet of thick glass.

Within, pillowed on soft cushions, and covered with a mantle woven of white natural fleece sprigged with tiny sprays of pine wrought in gold, lay the body of a woman—none other than my beautiful visitor. She was marble white, and her long black eyelashes lay on her white cheeks as though she slept.

Without a word or a sound, save the sounds made by my hurrying feet on the stone flooring, I fled up the steep steps, and through the dim expanse of the church, out into the bright sunlight. I found that I had mechanically raised the fallen lamp, and had taken it with me in my flight.

My feet naturally turned towards home. It was all instinctive. The new horror had—for the time, at any rate—drowned my mind in its mystery, deeper than the deepest depths of thought or imagination.

BOOK IV: UNDER THE FLAGSTAFF

RUPERT'S JOURNAL—Continued

May 1, 1907.

FOR SOME DAYS after the last adventure I was in truth in a half-dazed condition, unable to think sensibly, hardly coherently. Indeed, it was as much as I could do to preserve something of my habitual appearance and manner. However, my first test happily came soon, and when I was once through it I reacquired sufficient self-confidence to go through with my purpose. Gradually the original phase of stupefaction passed, and I was able to look the situation in the face. I knew the worst now, at any rate; and when the lowest point has been reached things must begin to mend. Still, I was wofully sensitive regarding anything which might affect my Lady of the Shroud, or even my opinion of her. I even began to dread Aunt Janet's Second-Sight visions or dreams. These had a fatal habit of coming so near to fact that they always made for a danger of discovery. I had to realize now that the Lady of the Shroud might indeed be a Vampire—one of that horrid race that survives death and carries on a life-in-death existence eternally and only for evil. Indeed, I began to *expect* that Aunt Janet would ere long have some prophetic insight to the matter. She had been so wonderfully correct in her prophetic surmises with regard to both the visits to my room that it was hardly possible that she could fail to take cognizance of this last development.

But my dread was not justified; at any rate, I had no reason to suspect that by any force or exercise of her occult gift she might cause me concern by the discovery of my secret. Only once did I feel that actual danger in that respect was close to me. That was when she came early one morning and rapped at my door. When I called out, "Who is that? What is it?" she said in an agitated way:

"Thank God, laddie, you are all right! Go to sleep again."

Later on, when we met at breakfast, she explained that she had had a nightmare in the grey of the morning. She thought she had seen me in the crypt of a great church close beside a stone coffin; and, knowing that such was an ominous subject to dream about, came as soon as she dared to see if I was all right. Her mind was evidently set on death and burial, for she went on:

"By the way, Rupert, I am told that the great church on time top of the cliff across the creek is St. Sava's, where the great people of the country used to be buried. I want you to take me there some day. We shall go over it, and look at the tombs and monuments together. I really think I should be afraid to go alone, but it will be all right if you are with me." This was getting really dangerous, so I turned it aside:

"Really, Aunt Janet, I'm afraid it won't do. If you go off to weird old churches, and fill yourself up with a fresh supply of horrors, I don't know what will happen. You'll be dreaming dreadful things about me every night and neither you nor I shall get any sleep." It went to my heart to oppose her in any wish; and also this kind of chaffy opposition might pain her. But I had no alternative; the matter was too serious to be allowed to proceed. Should Aunt Janet go to the church, she would surely want to visit the crypt. Should she do so, and there notice the glass-covered tomb—as she could not help doing—the Lord only knew what would happen. She had already Second-Sighted a woman being married to me, and before I myself knew that I had such a hope. What might she not reveal did she know where the woman came from? It may have been that her power of Second Sight had to rest on some basis of knowledge or belief, and that her vision was but some intuitive percep- tion of my own subjective thought. But whatever it was it should be stopped—at all hazards.

This whole episode set me thinking introspectively, and led me gradually but imperatively to self-analysis—not of powers, but of motives. I found myself before long examining myself as to what were my real intentions. I thought at first that this intellectual process was an exercise of pure reason; but soon discarded this as inadequate— even impossible. Reason is a cold manifestation; this feeling which swayed and dominated me is none other than passion, which is quick, hot, and insistent.

As for myself, the self-analysis could lead to but one result—the expression to myself of the reality and definiteness of an already-formed though unconscious intention. I wished to do the woman good—to serve her in some way—to secure her some benefit by any means, no matter how difficult, which might be within my power. I knew that I loved her—loved her most truly and fervently; there was no need for self-analysis to tell me that. And, moreover, no self-analysis, or any other mental process that I knew of, could help my one doubt: whether she was an ordinary woman (or an extraordinary woman, for the matter of that) in some sore and terrible straits; or else one who lay under some dreadful condition, only partially alive, and not mistress of herself or her acts. Whichever her condition might be, there was in my own feeling a superfluity of affection for her. The self-analysis taught me one thing, at any rate—that I had for her, to start with, an infinite pity which had softened towards her my whole being, and had already mastered merely selfish desire. Out of it I began to find excuses for her every act. In the doing so I knew now, though perhaps I did not at the time the process was going on, that my view in its true inwardness was of her as a living woman—the woman I loved.

In the forming of our ideas there are different methods of work, as though the analogy with material life holds good. In the building of a house, for instance, there are many persons employed; men of different trades and occupations—architect, builder, masons, carpenters, plumbers, and a host of others—and all these with the officials of each guild or trade. So in the world of thought and feelings: knowledge and understanding come through various agents, each competent to its task.

How far pity reacted with love I knew not; I only knew that whatever her state might be, were she living or dead, I could find in my heart no blame for the Lady of the Shroud. It could not be that she was dead in the real conventional way; for, after all, the Dead do not walk the earth in corporal substance, even if there be spirits which take the corporal form. This woman was of actual form and weight. How could I doubt that, at all events—I, who had held her in my arms? Might it not be that she was not quite dead, and that it had been given to me to restore her to life again? Ah! that would be, indeed, a privilege well worth the giving my life to accomplish. That such a thing may be is possible. Surely the old myths were not absolute inventions; they must have had a basis somewhere in fact. May not the world-old story of Orpheus and Eurydice have been based on some deep-lying principle or power of human nature? There is not one of us but has wished at some time to bring back the dead. Ay, and who has not felt that in himself or herself was power in the deep love for our dead to make them quick again, did we but know the secret of how it was to be done?

For myself, I have seen such mysteries that I am open to conviction regarding things not yet explained. These have been, of course, amongst savages or those old-world people who have brought unchecked traditions and beliefs—ay, and powers too—down the ages from the dim days when the world was young; when forces were elemental, and Nature's handiwork was experimental rather than completed. Some of these wonders may have been older still than the accepted period of our own period of creation. May we not have to-day other wonders, different only in method, but not more susceptible of belief? Obi-ism and Fantee-ism have been exercised in my own presence, and their results proved by the evidence of my own eyes and other senses. So, too, have stranger rites, with the same object and the same success, in the far Pacific Islands. So, too, in India and China, in Thibet and in the Golden Chersonese. On all and each of these occasions there was, on my own part, enough belief to set in motion the powers of understanding; and there were no moral scruples to stand in the way of realization. Those whose lives are so spent that they achieve the reputation of not fearing man or God or devil are not deterred in their doing or thwarted from a set purpose by things which might deter others not so equipped for adventure. Whatever may be before them—pleasant or painful, bitter or sweet, arduous or facile, enjoyable or terrible, humorous or full of awe and horror—they must accept, taking them in the onward course as a good athlete takes hurdles in his stride. And there must be no hesitating, no looking back. If the explorer or the adventurer has scruples, he had better give up that special branch of effort and come himself to a more level walk in life. Neither must there be regrets. There is no need for such; savage life has this advantage: it begets a certain toleration not to be found in conventional existence.

RUPERT'S JOURNAL—*Continued*.

May 2, 1907.

I had heard long ago that Second Sight is a terrible gift, even to its possessor. I am now inclined not only to believe, but to understand it.

Aunt Janet has made such a practice of it of late that I go in constant dread of discovery of my secret. She seems to parallel me all the time, whatever I may do. It is like a sort of dual existence to her; for she is her dear old self all the time, and yet some other person with a sort of intellectual kit of telescope and notebook, which are eternally used on me. I know they are *for* me, too—for what she considers my good. But all the same it makes an embarrassment. Happily Second Sight cannot speak as clearly as it sees, or, rather, as it understands. For the translation of the vague beliefs which it inculcates is both nebulous and uncertain—a sort of Delphic oracle which always says things which no one can make out at the time, but which can be afterwards read in any one of several ways. This is all right, for in my case it is a kind of safety; but, then, Aunt Janet is a very clever woman, and some time she herself may be able to understand. Then she may begin to put two and two together. When she does that, it will not be long before she knows more than I do of the facts of the whole affair. And her reading of them and of the Lady of the Shroud, round whom they circle, may not be the same as mine. Well, that will be all right too. Aunt Janet loves me—God knows I have good reason to know that all through these years—and whatever view she may take, her acts will be all I could wish. But I shall come in for a good lot of scolding, I am sure. By the way, I ought to think of that; if Aunt Janet scolds me, it is a pretty good proof that I ought to be scolded. I wonder if I dare tell her all. No! It is too strange. She is only a woman, after all: and if she knew I loved . . . I wish I knew her name, and thought—as I might myself do, only that I resist it—that she is not alive at all. Well, what she would either think or do beats me. I suppose she would want to slipper me as she used to do when I was a wee kiddie—in a different way, of course.

May 3, 1907.

I really could not go on seriously last night. The idea of Aunt Janet giving me a licking as in the dear old days made me laugh so much that nothing in the world seemed serious then. Oh, Aunt Janet is all right whatever comes. That I am sure of, so I needn't worry over it. A good thing too; there will be plenty to worry about without that. I shall not check her telling me of her visions, however; I may learn something from them.

For the last four-and-twenty hours I have, whilst awake, been looking over Aunt Janet's books, of which I brought a wheen down here. Gee whizz! No wonder the old dear is superstitious, when she is filled up to the back teeth with that sort of stuff! There may be some truth in some of those yarns; those who wrote them may believe in them, or some of them, at all events. But as to coherence or logic, or any sort of reasonable or instructive deduction, they might as well have been written by so many hens! These occult book-makers seem to gather only a lot of bare, bald facts, which they put down in the most uninteresting way possible. They go by quantity only. One story of the kind, well examined and with logical comments, would be more convincing to a third party than a whole hecatomb of them.

RUPERT'S JOURNAL—_Continued._

May 4, 1907.

There is evidently something up in the country. The mountaineers are more uneasy than they have been as yet. There is constant going to and fro amongst them, mostly at night and in the grey of the morning. I spend many hours in my room in the eastern tower, from which I can watch the woods, and gather from signs the passing to and fro. But with all this activity no one has said to me a word on the subject. It is undoubtedly a disappointment to me. I had hoped that the mountaineers had come to trust me; that gathering at which they wanted to fire their guns for me gave me strong hopes. But now it is apparent that they do not trust me in full—as yet, at all events. Well, I must not complain. It is all only right and just. As yet I have done nothing to prove to them the love and devotion that I feel to the country. I know that such individuals as I have met trust me, and I believe like me. But the trust of a nation is different. That has to be won and tested; he who would win it must justify, and in a way that only troublous times can allow. No nation will—can—give full meed of honour to a stranger in times of peace. Why should it? I must not forget that I am here a stranger in the land, and that to the great mass of people even my name is unknown. Perhaps they will know me better when Rooke comes back with that store of arms and ammunition that he has bought, and the little warship he has got from South America. When they see that I hand over the whole lot to the nation without a string on them, they may begin to believe. In the meantime all I can do is to wait. It will all come right in time, I have no doubt. And if it doesn't come right, well, we can only die once!

Is that so? What about my Lady of the Shroud? I must not think of that or of her in this gallery. Love and war are separate, and may not mix—cannot mix, if it comes to that. I must be wise in the matter; and if I have got the hump in any degree whatever, must not show it.

But one thing is certain: something is up, and it must be the Turks. From what the Vladika said at that meeting they have some intention of an attack on the Blue Mountains. If that be so, we must be ready; and perhaps I can help there. The forces must be organized; we must have some method of communication. In this country, where are neither roads nor railways nor telegraphs, we must establish a signalling system of some sort. *That* I can begin at once. I can make a code, or adapt one that I have used elsewhere already. I shall rig up a semaphore on the top of the Castle which can be seen for an enormous distance around. I shall train a number of men to be facile in signalling. And then, should need come, I may be able to show the mountaineers that I am fit to live in their hearts . . .

And all this work may prove an anodyne to pain of another kind. It will help, at any rate, to keep my mind occupied whilst I am waiting for another visit from my Lady of the Shroud.

RUPERT'S JOURNAL—*Continued.*

May 18, 1907.

The two weeks that have passed have been busy, and may, as time goes on, prove eventful. I really think they have placed me in a different position with the Blue Mountaineers—certainly so far as those in this part of the country are concerned. They are no longer suspicious of me—which is much; though they have not yet received me into their confidence. I suppose this will come in time, but I must not try to hustle them. Already they are willing, so far as I can see, to use me to their own ends. They accepted the signalling idea very readily, and are quite willing to drill as much as I like. This can be (and I think is, in its way) a pleasure to them. They are born soldiers, every man of them; and practice together is only a realization of their own wishes and a further development of their powers. I think I can understand the trend of their thoughts, and what ideas of public policy lie behind them. In all that we have attempted together as yet they are themselves in absolute power. It rests with them to carry out any ideas I may suggest, so they do not fear any assumption of power or governance on my part. Thus, so long as they keep secret from me both their ideas of high policy and their immediate intentions, I am powerless to do them ill, and I *may* be of service should occasion arise. Well, all told, this is much. Already they accept me as an individual, not merely one of the mass. I am pretty sure that they are satisfied of my personal *bona fides*. It is policy and not mistrust that hedges me in. Well, policy is a matter of time. They are a splendid people, but if they knew a little more than they do they would understand that the wisest of all policies is trust—when it can be given. I must hold myself in check, and never be betrayed into a harsh thought towards them. Poor souls! with a thousand years behind them of Turkish aggression, strenuously attempted by both force and fraud, no wonder they are suspicious. Likewise every other nation with whom they have ever come in contact—except one, my own—has deceived or betrayed them. Anyhow, they are fine soldiers, and before long we shall have an army that cannot be ignored. If I can get so that they trust me, I shall ask Sir Colin to come out here. He would be a splendid head for their army. His great military knowledge and tactical skill would come in well. It makes me glow to think of what an army he would turn out of this splendid material, and one especially adapted for the style of fighting which would be necessary in this country.

If a mere amateur like myself, who has only had experience of organizing the wildest kind of savages, has been able to advance or compact their individual style of fighting into systematic effort, a great soldier like MacKelpie will bring them to perfection as a fighting machine. Our Highlanders, when they come out, will foregather with them, as mountaineers always do with each other. Then we shall have a force which can hold its own against any odds. I only hope that Rooke will be returning soon. I want to see those Ingis-Malbron rifles either safely stored in the Castle or, what is better, divided up amongst the mountaineers—a thing which will be done at the very earliest moment that I can accomplish it. I have a conviction that when these men have received their arms and ammunition from me they will understand me better, and not keep any secrets from me.

All this fortnight when I was not drilling or going about amongst the mountaineers, and teaching them the code which I have now got perfected, I was exploring the side of the mountain nearest to here. I could not bear to be still. It is torture to me to be idle in my present condition of mind regarding my Lady of the Shroud . . . Strange I do not mind mentioning the word to myself now. I used to at first; but that bitterness has all gone away.

RUPERT'S JOURNAL—*Continued.*

May 19, 1907.

I was so restless early this morning that before daylight I was out exploring on the mountain-side. By chance I came across a secret

place just as the day was breaking. Indeed, it was by the change of
light as the first sun-rays seemed to fall down the mountain-side that
my attention was called to an opening shown by a light behind it. It
was, indeed, a secret place—so secret that I thought at first I should
keep it to myself. In such a place as this either to hide in or to be
able to prevent anyone else hiding in might on occasion be an asset
of safety.

When, however, I saw indications rather than traces that someone
had already used it to camp in, I changed my mind, and thought
that whenever I should get an opportunity I would tell the Vladika
of it, as he is a man on whose discretion I can rely. If we ever have
a war here or any sort of invasion, it is just such places that may be
dangerous. Even in my own case it is much too near the Castle to be
neglected.

The indications were meagre—only where a fire had been on
a little shelf of rock; and it was not possible, through the results of
burning vegetation or scorched grass, to tell how long before the
fire had been alight. I could only guess. Perhaps the mountaineers
might be able to tell or even to guess better than I could. But I
am not so sure of this. I am a mountaineer myself, and with larger
and more varied experience than any of them. For myself, though
I could not be certain, I came to the conclusion that whoever had
used the place had done so not many days before. It could not
have been quite recently; but it may not have been very long ago.
Whoever had used it had covered up his tracks well. Even the ashes
had been carefully removed, and the place where they had lain was
cleaned or swept in some way, so that there was no trace on the
spot. I applied some of my West African experience, and looked
on the rough bark of the trees to leeward, to where the agitated
air, however directed, must have come, unless it was wanted to call
attention to the place by the scattered wood-ashes, however fine. I

found traces of it, but they were faint. There had not been rain for several days; so the dust must have been blown there since the rain had fallen, for it was still dry.

The place was a tiny gorge, with but one entrance, which was hidden behind a barren spur of rock—just a sort of long fissure, jagged and curving, in the rock, like a fault in the stratification. I could just struggle through it with considerable effort, holding my breath here and there, so as to reduce my depth of chest. Within it was tree-clad, and full of possibilities of concealment.

As I came away I marked well its direction and approaches, noting any guiding mark which might aid in finding it by day or night. I explored every foot of ground around it—in front, on each side, and above. But from nowhere could I see an indication of its existence. It was a veritable secret chamber wrought by the hand of Nature itself. I did not return home till I was familiar with every detail near and around it. This new knowledge added distinctly to my sense of security.

Later in the day I tried to find the Vladika or any mountaineer of importance, for I thought that such a hiding-place which had been used so recently might be dangerous, and especially at a time when, as I had learned at the meeting where they did *not* fire their guns that there may have been spies about or a traitor in the land.

Even before I came to my own room to-night I had fully made up my mind to go out early in the morning and find some proper person to whom to impart the information, so that a watch might be kept on the place. It is now getting on for midnight, and when I have had my usual last look at the garden I shall turn in. Aunt Janet was uneasy all day, and especially so this evening. I think it must have been my absence at the usual breakfast-hour which got on her nerves; and that unsatisfied mental or psychical irritation increased as the day wore on.

RUPERT'S JOURNAL—*Continued.*

May 20, 1907.

The clock on the mantelpiece in my room, which chimes on the notes of the clock at St. James's Palace, was striking midnight when I opened the glass door on the terrace. I had put out my lights before I drew the curtain, as I wished to see the full effect of the moonlight. Now that the rainy season is over, the moon is quite as beautiful as it was in the wet, and a great deal more comfortable. I was in evening dress, with a smoking-jacket in lieu of a coat, and I felt the air mild and mellow on the warm side, as I stood on the terrace.

But even in that bright moonlight the further corners of the great garden were full of mysterious shadows. I peered into them as well as I could—and my eyes are pretty good naturally, and are well trained. There was not the least movement. The air was as still as death, the foliage as still as though wrought in stone.

I looked for quite a long time in the hope of seeing something of my Lady. The quarters chimed several times, but I stood on unheeding. At last I thought I saw far off in the very corner of the old defending wall a flicker of white. It was but momentary, and could hardly have accounted in itself for the way my heart beat. I controlled myself, and stood as though I, too, were a graven image. I was rewarded by seeing presently another gleam of white. And then an unspeakable rapture stole over me as I realized that my Lady was coming as she had come before. I would have hurried out to meet her, but that I knew well that this would not be in accord with her wishes. So, thinking to please her, I drew back into the room. I was glad I had done so when, from the dark corner where I stood, I saw her steal up the marble steps and stand timidly looking in at the door. Then, after a long pause, came a whisper as faint and sweet as the music of a distant AEolian harp:

"Are you there? May I come in? Answer me! I am lonely and in fear!" For answer I emerged from my dim corner so swiftly that she was startled. I could hear from the quivering intake of her breath that she was striving—happily with success—to suppress a shriek.

"Come in," I said quietly. "I was waiting for you, for I felt that you would come. I only came in from the terrace when I saw you coming, lest you might fear that anyone might see us. That is not possible, but I thought you wished that I should be careful."

"I did—I do," she answered in a low, sweet voice, but very firmly. "But never avoid precaution. There is nothing that may not happen here. There may be eyes where we least expect—or suspect them." As she spoke the last words solemnly and in a low whisper, she was entering the room. I closed the glass door and bolted it, rolled back the steel grille, and pulled the heavy curtain. Then, when I had lit a candle, I went over and put a light to the fire. In a few seconds the dry wood had caught, and the flames were beginning to rise and crackle. She had not objected to my closing the window and drawing the curtain; neither did she make any comment on my lighting the fire. She simply acquiesced in it, as though it was now a matter of course. When I made the pile of cushions before it as on the occasion of her last visit, she sank down on them, and held out her white, trembling hands to the warmth.

She was different to-night from what she had been on either of the two former visits. From her present bearing I arrived at some gauge of her self-concern, her self-respect. Now that she was dry, and not over-mastered by wet and cold, a sweet and gracious dignity seemed to shine from her, enwrapping her, as it were, with a luminous veil. It was not that she was by this made or shown as cold or distant, or in any way harsh or forbidding. On the contrary, protected by this dignity, she seemed much more sweet and genial than before. It was as though she felt that she could afford to stoop now that her loftiness was realized— that her position was recognized and secure. If her inherent dignity made an impenetrable nimbus round her, this was against others; she herself was not bound by it, or to be bound. So marked was this, so entirely and sweetly womanly did she appear, that I caught myself wondering in flashes of thought, which came as sharp periods of doubting judgment between spells of unconscious fascination, how I had ever come to think she was aught but perfect woman. As she rested, half sitting and half lying on the pile of cushions, she was all grace, and beauty, and charm, and sweetness—the veritable perfect woman of the dreams of a man, be he young or old. To have such a woman sit by his hearth and hold her holy of holies in his heart might well be a rapture to any man. Even an hour of such entrancing joy might be well won by a lifetime of pain, by the balance of a long life sacrificed, by the extinction of life itself. Quick behind the record of such thoughts came the answer to the doubt they challenged: if it should turn out that she was not living at all, but one of the doomed and pitiful Un-Dead, then so much more on account of her very sweetness and beauty would be the winning of her back to Life and Heaven—even were it that she might find happiness in the heart and in the arms of another man.

Once, when I leaned over the hearth to put fresh logs on the fire, my face was so close to hers that I felt her breath on my cheek. It thrilled me to feel even the suggestion of that ineffable contact. Her breath was sweet—sweet as the breath of a calf, sweet as the whiff of a summer breeze across beds of mignonette. How could anyone believe for a moment that such sweet breath could come from the lips of the dead—the dead *in esse* or *in posse*—that corruption could send forth fragrance so sweet and pure? It was with satisfied happiness that, as I looked at her from my stool, I saw the dancing of the flames from the beech-logs reflected in her glorious black eyes, and the stars that were hidden in them shine out with new colours and new lustre as they gleamed, rising and falling like hopes and fears. As the light leaped, so did smiles of quiet happiness flit over her beautiful face, the merriment of the joyous flames being reflected in ever-changing dimples.

At first I was a little disconcerted whenever my eyes took note of her shroud, and there came a momentary regret that the weather had not been again bad, so that there might have been compulsion for her putting on another garment—anything lacking the loathsomeness of that pitiful wrapping. Little by little, however, this feeling disappeared, and I found no matter for even dissatisfaction in her wrapping. Indeed, my thoughts found inward voice before the subject was dismissed from my mind:

"One becomes accustomed to anything—even a shroud!" But the thought was followed by a submerging wave of pity that she should have had such a dreadful experience.

By-and-by we seemed both to forget everything—I know I did—except that we were man and woman, and close together. The strangeness of the situation and the circumstances did not seem of moment—not worth even a passing thought. We still sat apart and said little, if anything. I cannot recall a single word that either of us spoke whilst we sat before the fire, but other language than speech came into play; the eyes told their own story, as eyes can do, and more eloquently than lips whilst exercising their function of speech. Question and answer followed each other in this satisfying language, and with an unspeakable rapture I began to realize that my affection was returned. Under these circumstances it was unrealizable that there should be any incongruity in the whole affair. I was not myself in the mood of questioning. I was diffident with that diffidence which comes alone from true love, as though it were a necessary emanation from that delightful and overwhelming and commanding passion. In her presence there seemed to surge up within me that which forbade speech. Speech under present conditions would have seemed to me unnecessary, imperfect, and even vulgarly overt. She, too, was silent. But now that I am alone, and memory is alone with me, I am convinced that she also had been happy. No, not that exactly.

"Happiness" is not the word to describe either her feeling or my own. Happiness is more active, a more conscious enjoyment. We had been content. That expresses our condition perfectly; and now that I can analyze my own feeling, and understand what the word implies, I am satisfied of its accuracy. "Content" has both a positive and negative meaning or antecedent condition. It implies an absence of disturbing conditions as well as of wants; also it implies something positive which has been won or achieved, or which has accrued. In our state of mind—for though it may be presumption on my part, I am satisfied that our ideas were mutual—it meant that we had reached an understanding whence all that might come must be for good. God grant that it may be so!

As we sat silent, looking into each other's eyes, and whilst the stars in hers were now full of latent fire, perhaps from the reflection of the flames, she suddenly sprang to her feet, instinctively drawing the horrible shroud round her as she rose to her full height in a voice full of lingering emotion, as of one who is acting under spiritual compulsion rather than personal will, she said in a whisper:

"I must go at once. I feel the morning drawing nigh. I must be in my place when the light of day comes."

She was so earnest that I felt I must not oppose her wish; so I, too, sprang to my feet and ran towards the window. I pulled the curtain aside sufficiently far for me to press back the grille and reach the glass door, the latch of which I opened. I passed behind the curtain again, and held the edge of it back so that she could go through. For an instant she stopped as she broke the long silence:

"You are a true gentleman, and my friend. You understand all I wish. Out of the depth of my heart I thank you." She held out her beautiful high-bred hand. I took it in both mine as I fell on my knees, and raised it to my lips. Its touch made me quiver. She, too, trembled as she looked down at me with a glance which seemed to search my very soul. The stars in her eyes, now that the firelight was no longer on them, had gone back to their own mysterious silver. Then she drew her hand from mine very, very gently, as though it would fain linger; and she passed out behind the curtain with a gentle, sweet, dignified little bow which left me on my knees.

When I heard the glass door pulled-to gently behind her, I rose from my knees and hurried without the curtain, just in time to watch her pass down the steps. I wanted to see her as long as I could. The grey of morning was just beginning to war with the night gloom, and by the faint uncertain light I could see dimly the white figure flit between shrub and statue till finally it merged in the far darkness.

I stood for a long time on the terrace, sometimes looking into the darkness in front of me, in case I might be blessed with another glimpse of her; sometimes with my eyes closed, so that I might recall and hold in my mind her passage down the steps. For the first time since I had met her she had thrown back at me a glance as she stepped on the white path below the terrace. With the glamour over me of that look, which was all love and enticement, I could have dared all the powers that be.

When the grey dawn was becoming apparent through the lightening of the sky I returned to my room. In a dazed condition— half hypnotized by love—I went to bed, and in dreams continued to think, all happily, of my Lady of the Shroud.

RUPERT'S JOURNAL—*Continued.*

May 27, 1907.

A whole week has gone since I saw my Love! There it is; no doubt whatever is left in my mind about it now! Since I saw her my passion has grown and grown by leaps and bounds, as novelists put it. It has now become so vast as to overwhelm me, to wipe out all thought of doubt or difficulty. I suppose it must be what men suffered—suffering need not mean pain—under enchantments in old times. I am but as a straw whirled in the resistless eddies of a whirlpool. I feel that I *must* see her again, even if it be but in her tomb in the crypt. I must, I suppose, prepare myself for the venture, for many things have to be thought of. The visit must not be at night, for in such case I might miss her, did she come to me again here . . . .

The morning came and went, but my wish and intention still remained; and so in the full tide of noon, with the sun in all its fiery force, I set out for the old church of St. Sava. I carried with me a lantern with powerful lens. I had wrapped it up secretly, for I had a feeling that I should not like anyone to know that I had such a thing with me.

On this occasion I had no misgivings. On the former visit I had for a moment been overwhelmed at the unexpected sight of the body of the woman I thought I loved—I knew it now—lying in her tomb. But now I knew all, and it was to see this woman, though in her tomb, that I came.

When I had lit my lantern, which I did as soon as I had pushed open the great door, which was once again unlocked, I turned my steps to the steps of the crypt, which lay behind the richly carven wood screen. This I could see, with the better light, was a noble piece of work of priceless beauty and worth. I tried to keep my heart in full courage with thoughts of my Lady, and of the sweetness and dignity of our last meeting; but, despite all, it sank down, down, and turned to water as I passed with uncertain feet down the narrow, tortuous steps. My concern, I am now convinced, was not for myself, but that she whom I adored should have to endure such a fearful place. As anodyne to my own pain I thought what it would be, and how I should feel, when I should have won for her a way out of that horror, at any rate. This thought reassured me somewhat, and restored my courage. It was in something of the same fashion which has hitherto carried me out of tight places as well as into them that at last I pushed open the low, narrow door at the foot of the rock-hewn staircase and entered the crypt.

Without delay I made my way to the glass-covered tomb set beneath the hanging chain. I could see by the flashing of the light around me that my hand which held the lantern trembled. With a great effort I steadied myself, and raising the lantern, turned its light down into the sarcophagus.

Once again the fallen lantern rang on the tingling glass, and I stood alone in the darkness, for an instant almost paralyzed with surprised disappointment.

The tomb was empty! Even the trappings of the dead had been removed.

I knew not what happened till I found myself groping my way up the winding stair. Here, in comparison with the solid darkness of the crypt, it seemed almost light. The dim expanse of the church sent a few straggling rays down the vaulted steps, and as I could see, be it never so dimly, I felt I was not in absolute darkness. With the light came a sense of power and fresh courage, and I groped my way back into the crypt again. There, by now and again lighting matches, I found my way to the tomb and recovered my lantern. Then I took my way slowly—for I wished to prove, if not my own courage, at least such vestiges of self-respect as the venture had left me—through the church, where I extinguished my lantern, and out through the great door into the open sunlight. I seemed to have heard, both in the darkness of the crypt and through the dimness of the church, mysterious sounds as of whispers and suppressed breathing; but the memory of these did not count for much when once I was free. I was only satisfied of my own consciousness and identity when I found myself on the broad rock terrace in front of the church, with the fierce sunlight beating on my upturned face, and, looking downward, saw far below me the rippled blue of the open sea.

RUPERT'S JOURNAL—*Continued.*

Another week has elapsed—a week full of movement of many
kinds and in many ways—but as yet I have had no tale or tidings
of my Lady of the Shroud. I have not had an opportunity of going
again in daylight to St. Sava's as I should have liked to have done. I
felt that I must not go at night. The night is her time of freedom, and
it must be kept for her—or else I may miss her, or perhaps never see
her again.

The days have been full of national movement. The mountaineers
have evidently been organizing themselves, for some reason which I
cannot quite understand, and which they have hesitated to make known
to me. I have taken care not to manifest any curiosity, whatever I may
have felt. This would certainly arouse suspicion, and might ultimately
cause disaster to my hopes of aiding the nation in their struggle to
preserve their freedom.

These fierce mountaineers are strangely—almost unduly—suspicious,
and the only way to win their confidence is to begin the trusting. A young
American attaché of the Embassy at Vienna, who had made a journey
through the Land of the Blue Mountains, once put it to me in this form:
"Keep your head shut, and they'll open theirs. If you don't, they'll
open it for you—down to the chine!"

It was quite apparent to me that they were completing some fresh
arrangements for signalling with a code of their own. This was natural
enough, and in no way inconsistent with the measure of friendliness
already shown to me. Where there are neither telegraphs, railways, nor
roads, any effective form of communication must—can only be purely
personal. And so, if they wish to keep any secret amongst themselves,
they must preserve the secret of their code. I should have dearly liked
to learn their new code and their manner of using it, but as I want to
be a helpful friend to them—and as this implies not only trust, but the
appearance of it—I had to school myself to patience.

This attitude so far won their confidence that before we parted at our last meeting, after most solemn vows of faith and secrecy, they took me into the secret. This was, however, only to the extent of teaching me the code and method; they still withheld from me rigidly the fact or political secret, or whatever it was that was the mainspring of their united action.

When I got home I wrote down, whilst it was fresh in my memory, all they told me. This script I studied until I had it so thoroughly by heart that I *could* not forget it. Then I burned the paper. However, there is now one gain at least: with my semaphore I can send through the Blue Mountains from side to side, with expedition, secrecy, and exactness, a message comprehensible to all.

RUPERT'S JOURNAL—*Continued*.

June 6, 1907.

Last night I had a new experience of my Lady of the Shroud—in so far as form was concerned, at any rate. I was in bed, and just falling asleep, when I heard a queer kind of scratching at the glass door of the terrace. I listened acutely, my heart beating hard. The sound seemed to come from low down, close to the floor. I jumped out of bed, ran to the window, and, pulling aside the heavy curtains, looked out.

There, just inside the glass door, as though it had been pushed under the door, lay a paper closely folded in several laps. I picked it up and opened it. I was all in a tumult, for my heart told me whence it came. Inside was written in English, in a large, sprawling hand, such as might be from an English child of seven or eight:

"Meet me at the Flagstaff on the Rock!"

I knew the place, of course. On the farthermost point of the rock on which the Castle stands is set a high flagstaff, whereon in old time the banner of the Vissarion family flew. At some far-off time, when the Castle had been liable to attack, this point had been strongly fortified. Indeed, in the days when the bow was a martial weapon it must have been quite impregnable.

A covered gallery, with loopholes for arrows, had been cut in the solid rock, running right round the point, quite surrounding the flagstaff and the great boss of rock on whose centre it was reared. A narrow drawbridge of immense strength had connected—in peaceful times, and still remained—the outer point of rock with an entrance formed in the outer wall, and guarded with flanking towers and a portcullis. Its use was manifestly to guard against surprise. From this point only could be seen the line of the rocks all round the point. Thus, any secret attack by boats could be made impossible.

Having hurriedly dressed myself, and taking with me both hunting-knife and revolver, I went out on the terrace, taking the precaution, unusual to me, of drawing the grille behind me and locking it. Matters around the Castle are in far too disturbed a condition to allow the taking of any foolish chances, either in the way of being unarmed or of leaving the private entrance to the Castle open. I found my way through the rocky passage, and climbed by the Jacob's ladder fixed on the rock—a device of convenience in time of peace—to the foot of the flagstaff.

I was all on fire with expectation, and the time of going seemed exceeding long; so I was additionally disappointed by the contrast when I did not see my Lady there when I arrived. However, my heart beat freely again—perhaps more freely than ever—when I saw her crouching in the shadow of the Castle wall. From where she was she could not be seen from any point save that alone which I occupied; even from there it was only her white shroud that was conspicuous through the deep gloom of the shadow. The moonlight was so bright that the shadows were almost unnaturally black.

I rushed over towards her, and when close was about to say impulsively, "Why did you leave your tomb?" when it suddenly struck me that the question would be malapropos and embarrassing in many ways. So, better judgment prevailing, I said instead:

"It has been so long since I saw you! It has seemed an eternity to me!" Her answer came as quickly as even I could have wished; she spoke impulsively and without thought:

"It has been long to me too! Oh, so long! so long! I have asked you to come out here because I wanted to see you so much that I could not wait any longer. I have been heart-hungry for a sight of you!"

Her words, her eager attitude, the ineffable something which conveys the messages of the heart, the longing expression in her eyes as the full moonlight fell on her face, showing the stars as living gold—for in her eagerness she had stepped out towards me from the shadow—all set me on fire. Without a thought or a word—for it was Nature speaking in the language of Love, which is a silent tongue—I stepped towards her and took her in my arms. She yielded with that sweet unconsciousness which is the perfection of Love, as if it was in obedience to some command uttered before the beginning of the world. Probably without any conscious effort on either side—I know there was none on mine—our mouths met in the first kiss of love.

At the time nothing in the meeting struck me as out of the common. But later in the night, when I was alone and in darkness, whenever I thought of it all—its strangeness and its stranger rapture—I could not but be sensible of the bizarre conditions for a love meeting. The place lonely, the time night, the man young and strong, and full of life and hope and ambition; the woman, beautiful and ardent though she was, a woman seemingly dead, clothed in the shroud in which she had been wrapped when lying in her tomb in the crypt of the old church.

Whilst we were together, anyhow, there was little thought of the kind; no reasoning of any kind on my part. Love has its own laws and its own logic. Under the flagstaff, where the Vissarion banner was wont to flap in the breeze, she was in my arms; her sweet breath was on my face; her heart was beating against my own. What need was there for reason at all? *Inter arma silent leges*—the voice of reason is silent in the stress of passion. Dead she may be, or Un-dead—a Vampire with one foot in Hell and one on earth. But I love her; and come what may, here or hereafter, she is mine. As my mate, we shall fare along together, whatsoever the end may be, or wheresoever our path may lead. If she is indeed to be won from the nethermost Hell, then be mine the task!

But to go back to the record. When I had once started speaking to her in words of passion I could not stop. I did not want to—if I could; and she did not appear to wish it either. Can there be a woman—alive or dead—who would not want to hear the rapture of her lover expressed to her whilst she is enclosed in his arms?

There was no attempt at reticence on my part now; I took it for granted that she knew all that I surmised, and, as she made neither protest nor comment, that she accepted my belief as to her indeterminate existence. Sometimes her eyes would be closed, but even then the rapture of her face was almost beyond belief. Then, when the beautiful eyes would open and gaze on me, the stars that were in them would shine and scintillate as though they were formed of living fire. She said little, very little; but though the words were few, every syllable was fraught with love, and went straight to the very core of my heart.

By-and-by, when our transport had calmed to joy, I asked when I might next see her, and how and where I might find her when I should want to. She did not reply directly, but, holding me close in her arms, whispered in my ear with that breathless softness which is a lover's rapture of speech:

"I have come here under terrible difficulties, not only because I love you—and that would be enough—but because, as well as the joy of seeing you, I wanted to warn you."

"To warn me! Why?" I queried. Her reply came with a bashful hesitation, with something of a struggle in it, as of one who for some ulterior reason had to pick her words:

"There are difficulties and dangers ahead of you. You are beset with them; and they are all the greater because they are, of grim necessity, hidden from you. You cannot go anywhere, look in any direction, do anything, say anything, but it may be a signal for danger. My dear, it lurks everywhere—in the light as well as in the darkness; in the open as well as in the secret places; from friends as well as foes; when you are least prepared; when you may least expect it. Oh, I know it, and what it is to endure; for I share it for you—for your dear sake!"

"My darling!" was all I could say, as I drew her again closer to me and kissed her. After a bit she was calmer; seeing this, I came back to the subject that she had—in part, at all events—come to me to speak about:

"But if difficulty and danger hedge me in so everlastingly, and if I am to have no indication whatever of its kind or purpose, what can I do? God knows I would willingly guard myself—not on my own account, but for your dear sake. I have now a cause to live and be strong, and to keep all my faculties, since it may mean much to you. If you may not tell me details, may you not indicate to me some line of conduct, of action, that would be most in accord with your wishes— or, rather, with your idea of what would be best?"

She looked at me fixedly before speaking—a long, purposeful, loving look which no man born of woman could misunderstand. Then she spoke slowly, deliberately, emphatically:

"Be bold, and fear not. Be true to yourself, to me—it is the same thing. These are the best guards you can use. Your safety does not rest with me. Ah, I wish it did! I wish to God it did!" In my inner heart it thrilled me not merely to hear the expression of her wish, but to hear her use the name of God as she did. I understand now, in the calm of this place and with the sunlight before me, that my belief as to her being all woman—living woman—was not quite dead: but though at the moment my heart did not recognize the doubt, my brain did. And I made up my mind that we should not part this time until she knew that I had seen her, and where; but, despite my own thoughts, my outer ears listened greedily as she went on.

"As for me, you may not find *me*, but *I* shall find *you*, be sure! And now we must say 'Good-night,' my dear, my dear! Tell me once again that you love me, for it is a sweetness that one does not wish to forego— even one who wears such a garment as this—and rests where I must rest." As she spoke she held up part of her cerements for me to see. What could I do but take her once again in my arms and hold her close, close. God knows it was all in love; but it was passionate love which surged through my every vein as I strained her dear body to mine. But yet this embrace was not selfish; it was not all an expression of my own passion. It was based on pity—the pity which is twin-born with true love. Breathless from our kisses, when presently we released each other, she stood in a glorious rapture, like a white spirit in the moonlight, and as her lovely, starlit eyes seemed to devour me, she spoke in a languorous ecstasy:

"Oh, how you love me! how you love me! It is worth all I have gone through for this, even to wearing this terrible drapery." And again she pointed to her shroud.

Here was my chance to speak of what I knew, and I took it. "I know, I know. Moreover, I know that awful resting-place."

I was interrupted, cut short in the midst of my sentence, not by any word, but by the frightened look in her eyes and the fear-mastered way in which she shrank away from me. I suppose in reality she could not be paler than she looked when the colour-absorbing moonlight fell on her; but on the instant all semblance of living seemed to shrink and fall away, and she looked with eyes of dread as if in I some awful way held in thrall. But for the movement of the pitiful glance, she would have seemed of soulless marble, so deadly cold did she look.

The moments that dragged themselves out whilst I waited for her to speak seemed endless. At length her words came in an awed whisper, so faint that even in that stilly night I could hardly hear it:

"You know—you know my resting-place! How—when was that?" There was nothing to do now but to speak out the truth:

"I was in the crypt of St. Sava. It was all by accident. I was exploring all around the Castle, and I went there in my course. I found the winding stair in the rock behind the screen, and went down. Dear, I loved you well before that awful moment, but then, even as the lantern fell tingling on the glass, my love multiplied itself, with pity as a factor." She was silent for a few seconds. When she spoke, there was a new tone in her voice:

"But were you not shocked?"

"Of course I was," I answered on the spur of the moment, and I now think wisely. "Shocked is hardly the word. I was horrified beyond anything that words can convey that you—*you* should have to so endure! I did not like to return, for I feared lest my doing so might set some barrier between us. But in due time I did return on another day."

"Well?" Her voice was like sweet music.

"I had another shock that time, worse than before, for you were not there. Then indeed it was that I knew to myself how dear you were— how dear you are to me. Whilst I live, you—living or dead—shall always be in my heart." She breathed hard. The elation in her eyes made them outshine the moonlight, but she said no word. I went on:

"My dear, I had come into the crypt full of courage and hope, though I knew what dreadful sight should sear my eyes once again. But we little know what may be in store for us, no matter what we expect. I went out with a heart like water from that dreadful desolation."

"Oh, how you love me, dear!" Cheered by her words, and even more by her tone, I went on with renewed courage. There was no halting, no faltering in my intention now:

"You and I, my dear, were ordained for each other. I cannot help it that you had already suffered before I knew you. It may be that there may be for you still suffering that I may not prevent, endurance that I may not shorten; but what a man can do is yours. Not Hell itself will stop me, if it be possible that I may win through its torments with you in my arms!"

"Will nothing stop you, then?" Her question was breathed as softly as the strain of an AEolian harp.

"Nothing!" I said, and I heard my own teeth snap together. There was something speaking within me stronger than I had ever known myself to be. Again came a query, trembling, quavering, quivering, as though the issue was of more than life or death:

"Not this?" She held up a corner of the shroud, and as she saw my face and realized the answer before I spoke, went on: "With all it implies?"

"Not if it were wrought of the cerecloths of the damned!" There was a long pause. Her voice was more resolute when she spoke again. It rang. Moreover, there was in it a joyous note, as of one who feels new hope:

"But do you know what men say? Some of them, that I am dead and buried; others, that I am not only dead and buried, but that I am one of those unhappy beings that may not die the common death of man. Who live on a fearful life-in-death, whereby they are harmful to all. Those unhappy Un-dead whom men call Vampires—who live on the blood of the living, and bring eternal damnation as well as death with the poison of their dreadful kisses!"

"I know what men say sometimes," I answered. "But I know also what my own heart says; and I rather choose to obey its calling than all the voices of the living or the dead. Come what may, I am pledged to you. If it be that your old life has to be rewon for you out of the very jaws of Death and Hell, I shall keep the faith I have pledged, and that here I pledge again!" As I finished speaking I sank on my knees at her feet, and, putting my arms round her, drew her close to me. Her tears rained down on my face as she stroked my hair with her soft, strong hand and whispered to me:

"This is indeed to be one. What more holy marriage can God give to any of His creatures?" We were both silent for a time.

I think I was the first to recover my senses. That I did so was manifest by my asking her: "When may we meet again?"—a thing I had never remembered doing at any of our former partings. She answered with a rising and falling of the voice that was just above a whisper, as soft and cooing as the voice of a pigeon:

"That will be soon—as soon as I can manage it, be sure. My dear, my dear!" The last four words of endearment she spoke in a low but prolonged and piercing tone which made me thrill with delight.

"Give me some token," I said, "that I may have always close to me to ease my aching heart till we meet again, and ever after, for love's sake!" Her mind seemed to leap to understanding, and with a purpose all her own. Stooping for an instant, she tore off with swift, strong fingers a fragment of her shroud. This, having kissed it, she handed to me, whispering:

"It is time that we part. You must leave me now. Take this, and keep it for ever. I shall be less unhappy in my terrible loneliness whilst it lasts if I know that this my gift, which for good or ill is a part of me as you know me, is close to you. It may be, my very dear, that some day you may be glad and even proud of this hour, as I am." She kissed me as I took it.

"For life or death, I care not which, so long as I am with you!" I said, as I moved off. Descending the Jacob's ladder, I made my way down the rock-hewn passage.

The last thing I saw was the beautiful face of my Lady of the Shroud as she leaned over the edge of the opening. Her eyes were like glowing stars as her looks followed me. That look shall never fade from my memory.

After a few agitating moments of thought I half mechanically took my way down to the garden. Opening the grille, I entered my lonely room, which looked all the more lonely for the memory of the rapturous moments under the Flagstaff. I went to bed as one in a dream. There I lay till sunrise—awake and thinking.

BOOK V: A RITUAL AT MIDNIGHT

RUPERT'S JOURNAL—Continued

June 20, 1907.

THE TIME HAS gone as quickly as work can effect since I saw my Lady. As I told the mountaineers, Rooke, whom I had sent on the service, had made a contract for fifty thousand Ingis-Malbron rifles, and as many tons of ammunition as the French experts calculated to be a full supply for a year of warfare. I heard from him by our secret telegraph code that the order had been completed, and that the goods were already on the way. The morning after the meeting at the Flagstaff I had word that at night the vessel—one chartered by Rooke for the purpose—would arrive at Vissarion during the night. We were all expectation. I had always now in the Castle a signalling party, the signals being renewed as fast as the men were sufficiently expert to proceed with their practice alone or in groups. We hoped that every fighting-man in the country would in time become an expert signaller. Beyond these, again, we have always a few priests. The Church of the country is a militant

Church; its priests are soldiers, its Bishops commanders. But they all serve wherever the battle most needs them. Naturally they, as men of brains, are quicker at learning than the average mountaineers; with the result that they learnt the code and the signalling almost by instinct. We have now at least one such expert in each community of them, and shortly the priests alone will be able to signal, if need be, for the nation; thus releasing for active service the merely fighting-man. The men at present with me I took into confidence as to the vessel's arrival, and we were all ready for work when the man on the lookout at the Flagstaff sent word that a vessel without lights was creeping in towards shore. We all assembled on the rocky edge of the creek, and saw her steal up the creek and gain the shelter of the harbour. When this had been effected, we ran out the boom which protects the opening, and after that the great armoured sliding-gates which Uncle Roger had himself had made so as to protect the harbour in case of need.

We then came within and assisted in warping the steamer to the side of the dock.

Rooke looked fit, and was full of fire and vigour. His responsibility and the mere thought of warlike action seemed to have renewed his youth.

When we had arranged for the unloading of the cases of arms and ammunition, I took Rooke into the room which we call my "office," where he gave me an account of his doings. He had not only secured the rifles and the ammunition for them, but he had purchased from one of the small American Republics an armoured yacht which had been especially built for war service. He grew quite enthusiastic, even excited, as he told me of her:

"She is the last word in naval construction—a torpedo yacht. A small cruiser, with turbines up to date, oil-fuelled, and fully armed with the latest and most perfect weapons and explosives of all kinds. The fastest boat afloat to-day. Built by Thorneycroft, engined by

Parsons, armoured by Armstrong, armed by Crupp. If she ever comes into action, it will be bad for her opponent, for she need not fear to tackle anything less than a *Dreadnought*."

He also told me that from the same Government, whose nation had just established an unlooked-for peace, he had also purchased a whole park of artillery of the very latest patterns, and that for range and accuracy the guns were held to be supreme. These would follow before long, and with them their proper ammunition, with a shipload of the same to follow shortly after.

When he had told me all the rest of his news, and handed me the accounts, we went out to the dock to see the debarkation of the war material. Knowing that it was arriving, I had sent word in the afternoon to the mountaineers to tell them to come and remove it. They had answered the call, and it really seemed to me that the whole of the land must that night have been in motion.

They came as individuals, grouping themselves as they came within the defences of the Castle; some had gathered at fixed points on the way. They went secretly and in silence, stealing through the forests like ghosts, each party when it grouped taking the place of that which had gone on one of the routes radiating round Vissarion. Their coming and going was more than ghostly. It was, indeed, the outward manifestation of an inward spirit—a whole nation dominated by one common purpose.

The men in the steamer were nearly all engineers, mostly British, well conducted, and to be depended upon. Rooke had picked them separately, and in the doing had used well his great experience of both men and adventurous life. These men were to form part of the armoured yacht's crew when she should come into the Mediterranean waters. They and the priests and fighting-men in the Castle worked well together, and with a zeal that was beyond praise. The heavy cases seemed almost of their own accord to leave the holds, so fast came the procession of them along the gangways from deck to dock-wall. It was a part of my design that the arms should be placed in centres ready for local distribution. In such a country as this, without railways or even roads, the distribution of war material in any quantity is a great labour, for it has to be done individually, or at least from centres.

But of this work the great number of mountaineers who were arriving made little account. As fast as the ship's company, with the assistance of the priests and fighting-men, placed the cases on the quay, the engineers opened them and laid the contents ready for portage. The mountaineers seemed to come in a continuous stream; each in turn shouldered his burden and passed out, the captain of his section giving him as he passed his instruction where to go and in what route. The method had been already prepared in my office ready for such a distribution when the arms should arrive, and descriptions and quantities had been noted by the captains. The whole affair was treated by all as a matter of the utmost secrecy. Hardly a word was spoken beyond the necessary directions, and these were given in whispers. All night long the stream of men went and came, and towards dawn the bulk of the imported material was lessened by half. On the following night the remainder was removed, after my own men had stored in the Castle the rifles and ammunition reserved for its defence if necessary. It was advisable to keep a reserve supply in case it should ever be required. The following night Rooke went away secretly in the chartered vessel. He had to bring back with him the purchased cannon and heavy ammunition, which had been in the meantime stored on one of the Greek islands. The second morning, having had secret word that the steamer was on the way, I had given the signal for the assembling of the mountaineers.

A little after dark the vessel, showing no light, stole into the creek. The barrier gates were once again closed, and when a sufficient number of men had arrived to handle the guns, we began to unload. The actual deportation was easy enough, for the dock had all necessary appliances quite up to date, including a pair of shears for gun-lifting which could be raised into position in a very short time.

The guns were well furnished with tackle of all sorts, and before many hours had passed a little procession of them disappeared into the woods in ghostly silence. A number of men surrounded each, and they moved as well as if properly supplied with horses.

In the meantime, and for a week after the arrival of the guns, the drilling went on without pause. The gun-drill was wonderful. In the arduous work necessary for it the great strength and stamina of the mountaineers showed out wonderfully. They did not seem to know fatigue any more than they knew fear.

For a week this went on, till a perfect discipline and management was obtained. They did not practise the shooting, for this would have made secrecy impossible. It was reported all along the Turkish frontier that the Sultan's troops were being massed, and though this was not on a war footing, the movement was more or less dangerous. The reports of our own spies, although vague as to the purpose and extent of the movement, were definite as to something being on foot. And Turkey does not do something without a purpose that bodes ill to someone. Certainly the sound of cannon, which is a far-reaching sound, would have given them warning of our preparations, and would so have sadly minimized their effectiveness.

When the cannon had all been disposed of—except, of course, those destined for defence of the Castle or to be stored there—Rooke went away with the ship and crew. The ship he was to return to the owners; the men would be shipped on the war-yacht, of whose crew they would form a part. The rest of them had been carefully selected by Rooke himself, and were kept in secrecy at Cattaro, ready for service the moment required. They were all good men, and quite capable of whatever work they might be set to. So Rooke told me, and he ought to know. The experience of his young days as a private made him an expert in such a job.

RUPERT'S JOURNAL—*Continued.*

June 24, 1907.

Last night I got from my Lady a similar message to the last, and delivered in a similar way. This time, however, our meeting was to be on the leads of the Keep.

I dressed myself very carefully before going on this adventure, lest by any chance of household concern, any of the servants should see me; for if this should happen, Aunt Janet would be sure to hear of it, which would give rise to endless surmises and questionings—a thing I was far from desiring.

I confess that in thinking the matter over during the time I was making my hurried preparations I was at a loss to understand how any human body, even though it be of the dead, could go or be conveyed to such a place without some sort of assistance, or, at least, collusion, on the part of some of the inmates. At the visit to the Flagstaff circumstances were different. This spot was actually outside the Castle, and in order to reach it I myself had to leave the Castle privately, and from the garden ascend to the ramparts. But here was no such possibility. The Keep was an *imperium in imperio*. It stood within the Castle, though separated from it, and it had its own defences against intrusion. The roof of it was, so far as I knew, as little approachable as the magazine.

The difficulty did not, however, trouble me beyond a mere passing thought. In the joy of the coming meeting and the longing rapture at the mere thought of it, all difficulties disappeared. Love makes its own faith, and I never doubted that my Lady would be waiting for me at the place designated. When I had passed through the little arched passages, and up the doubly-grated stairways contrived in the massiveness of the walls, I let myself out on the leads. It was well that as yet the times were sufficiently peaceful not to necessitate guards or sentries at all such points.

There, in a dim corner where the moonlight and the passing clouds threw deep shadows, I saw her, clothed as ever in her shroud. Why, I know not. I felt somehow that the situation was even more serious than ever. But I was steeled to whatever might come. My mind had been already made up. To carry out my resolve to win the woman I loved I was ready to face death. But now, after we had for a few brief moments held each other in our arms, I was willing to accept death—or more than death. Now, more than before, was she sweet and dear to me. Whatever qualms there might have been at the beginning of our love-making, or during the progress of it, did not now exist. We had exchanged vows and confidences, and acknowledged our loves. What, then, could there be of distrust, or even doubt, that the present might not set at naught? But even had there been such doubts or qualms, they must have disappeared in the ardour of our mutual embrace. I was by now mad for her, and was content to be so mad. When she had breath to speak after the strictness of our embrace, she said:

"I have come to warn you to be more than ever careful." It was, I confess, a pang to me, who thought only of love, to hear that anything else should have been the initiative power of her coming, even though it had been her concern for my own safety. I could not but notice the bitter note of chagrin in my voice as I answered:

"It was for love's sake that *I* came." She, too, evidently felt the undercurrent of pain, for she said quickly:

"Ah, dearest, I, too, came for love's sake. It is because I love you that I am so anxious about you. What would the world—ay, or heaven—be to me without you?"

There was such earnest truth in her tone that the sense and realization of my own harshness smote me. In the presence of such love as this even a lover's selfishness must become abashed. I could not express myself in words, so simply raised her slim hand in mine and kissed it. As it lay warm in my own I could not but notice, as well as its fineness, its strength and the firmness of its clasp. Its warmth and fervour struck into my heart—and my brain. Thereupon I poured out to her once more my love for her, she listening all afire. When passion had had its say, the calmer emotions had opportunity of expression. When I was satisfied afresh of her affection, I began to value her care for my safety, and so I went back to the subject. Her very insistence, based on personal affection, gave me more solid ground for fear. In the moment of love transports I had forgotten, or did not think, of what wonderful power or knowledge she must have to be able to move in such strange ways as she did. Why, at this very moment she was within my own gates. Locks and bars, even the very seal of death itself, seemed unable to make for her a prison-house. With such freedom of action and movement, going when she would into secret places, what might she not know that was known to others? How could anyone keep secret from such an one even an ill intent? Such thoughts, such surmises, had often flashed through my mind in moments of excitement rather than of reflection, but never long enough to become fixed into belief. But yet the consequences, the convictions, of them were with me, though unconsciously, though the thoughts themselves were perhaps forgotten or withered before development.

"And you?" I asked her earnestly. "What about danger to you?" She smiled, her little pearl-white teeth gleaming in the moonlight, as she spoke:

"There is no danger for me. I am safe. I am the safest person, perhaps the only safe person, in all this land." The full significance of her words did not seem to come to me all at once. Some base for understanding such an assertion seemed to be wanting. It was not that

I did not trust or believe her, but that I thought she might be mistaken. I wanted to reassure myself, so in my distress I asked unthinkingly:

"How the safest? What is your protection?" For several moments that spun themselves out endlessly she looked me straight in the face, the stars in her eyes seeming to glow like fire; then, lowering her head, she took a fold of her shroud and held it up to me.

"This!"

The meaning was complete and understandable now. I could not speak at once for the wave of emotion which choked me. I dropped on my knees, and taking her in my arms, held her close to me. She saw that I was moved, and tenderly stroked my hair, and with delicate touch pressed down my head on her bosom, as a mother might have done to comfort a frightened child.

Presently we got back to the realities of life again. I murmured:

"Your safety, your life, your happiness are all-in-all to me. When will you let them be my care?" She trembled in my arms, nestling even closer to me. Her own arms seemed to quiver with delight as she said:

"Would you indeed like me to be always with you? To me it would be a happiness unspeakable; and to you, what would it be?"

I thought that she wished to hear me speak my love to her, and that, woman-like, she had led me to the utterance, and so I spoke again of the passion that now raged in me, she listening eagerly as we strained each other tight in our arms. At last there came a pause, a long, long pause, and our hearts beat consciously in unison as we stood together. Presently she said in a sweet, low, intense whisper, as soft as the sighing of summer wind:

"It shall be as you wish; but oh, my dear, you will have to first go through an ordeal which may try you terribly! Do not ask me anything! You must not ask, because I may not answer, and it would be pain to me to deny you anything. Marriage with such an one as I am has its own ritual, which may not be foregone. It may . . . " I broke passionately into her speaking:

"There is no ritual that I fear, so long as it be that it is for your good, and your lasting happiness. And if the end of it be that I may call you mine, there is no horror in life or death that I shall not gladly face. Dear, I ask you nothing. I am content to leave myself in your hands. You shall advise me when the time comes, and I shall be satisfied, content to obey. Content! It is but a poor word to express what I long for! I shall shirk nothing which may come to me from this or any other world, so long as it is to make you mine!" Once again her murmured happiness was music to my ears:

"Oh, how you love me! how you love me, dear, dear!" She took me in her arms, and for a few seconds we hung together. Suddenly she tore herself apart from me, and stood drawn up to the full height, with a dignity I cannot describe or express. Her voice had a new dominance, as with firm utterance and in staccato manner she said:

"Rupert Sent Leger, before we go a step further I must say something to you, ask you something, and I charge you, on your most sacred honour and belief, to answer me truly. Do you believe me to be one of those unhappy beings who may not die, but have to live in shameful existence between earth and the nether world, and whose hellish mission is to destroy, body and soul, those who love them till they fall to their level? You are a gentleman, and a brave one. I have found you fearless. Answer me in sternest truth, no matter what the issue may be!"

She stood there in the glamorous moonlight with a commanding dignity which seemed more than human. In that mystic light her white shroud seemed diaphanous, and she appeared like a spirit of power. What was I to say? How could I admit to such a being that I had actually had at moments, if not a belief, a passing doubt? It was a conviction with me that if I spoke wrongly I should lose her for ever. I was in a desperate strait. In such a case there is but one solid ground which one may rest on——the Truth.

I really felt I was between the devil and the deep sea. There was no avoiding the issue, and so, out of this all-embracing, all-compelling conviction of truth, I spoke.

For a fleeting moment I felt that my tone was truculent, and almost hesitated; but as I saw no anger or indignation on my Lady's face, but rather an eager approval, I was reassured. A woman, after all, is glad to see a man strong, for all belief in him must be based on that.

"I shall speak the truth. Remember that I have no wish to hurt your feelings, but as you conjure me by my honour, you must forgive me if I pain. It is true that I had at first——ay, and later, when I came to think matters over after you had gone, when reason came to the aid of impression——a passing belief that you are a Vampire. How can I fail to have, even now, though I love you with all my soul, though I have held you in my arms and kissed you on the mouth, a doubt, when all the evidences seem to point to one thing? Remember that I have only seen you at night, except that bitter moment when, in the broad noonday of the upper world, I saw you, clad as ever in a shroud, lying seemingly dead in a tomb in the crypt of St. Sava's Church . . . But let that pass. Such belief as I have is all in you. Be you woman or Vampire, it is all the same to me. It is *you* whom I love! Should it be that you are——you are not woman, which I cannot believe, then it will be my glory to break your fetters, to open your prison, and set you free. To that I consecrate my life." For a few seconds I stood silent, vibrating with the passion which had been awakened in me. She had by now lost the measure of her haughty isolation, and had softened into womanhood again. It was really like a realization of the old theme of Pygmalion's statue. It was with rather a pleading than a commanding voice that she said:

"And shall you always be true to me?"

"Always—so help me, God!" I answered, and I felt that there could be no lack of conviction in my voice.

Indeed, there was no cause for such lack. She also stood for a little while stone-still, and I was beginning to expand to the rapture which was in store for me when she should take me again in her arms.

But there was no such moment of softness. All at once she started as if she had suddenly wakened from a dream, and on the spur of the moment said:

"Now go, go!" I felt the conviction of necessity to obey, and turned at once. As I moved towards the door by which I had entered, I asked:

"When shall I see you again?"

"Soon!" came her answer. "I shall let you know soon—when and where. Oh, go, go!" She almost pushed me from her.

When I had passed through the low doorway and locked and barred it behind me, I felt a pang that I should have had to shut her out like that; but I feared lest there should arise some embarrassing suspicion if the door should be found open. Later came the comforting thought that, as she had got to the roof though the door had been shut, she would be able to get away by the same means. She had evidently knowledge of some secret way into the Castle. The alternative was that she must have some supernatural quality or faculty which gave her strange powers. I did not wish to pursue that train of thought, and so, after an effort, shut it out from my mind.

When I got back to my room I locked the door behind me, and went to sleep in the dark. I did not want light just then—could not bear it.

This morning I woke, a little later than usual, with a kind of apprehension which I could not at once understand. Presently, however, when my faculties became fully awake and in working order, I realized that I feared, half expected, that Aunt Janet would come to me in a worse state of alarm than ever apropos of some new Second-Sight experience of more than usual ferocity.

But, strange to say, I had no such visit. Later on in the morning, when, after breakfast, we walked together through the garden, I asked her how she had slept, and if she had dreamt. She answered me that she had slept without waking, and if she had had any dreams, they must have been pleasant ones, for she did not remember them. "And you know, Rupert," she added, "that if there be anything bad or fearsome or warning in dreams, I always remember them."

Later still, when I was by myself on the cliff beyond the creek, I could not help commenting on the absence of her power of Second Sight on the occasion. Surely, if ever there was a time when she might have had cause of apprehension, it might well have been when I asked the Lady whom she did not know to marry me—the Lady of whose identity I knew nothing, even whose name I did not know—whom I loved with all my heart and soul—my Lady of the Shroud.

I have lost faith in Second Sight.

RUPERT'S JOURNAL—*Continued.*

July 1, 1907.

Another week gone. I have waited patiently, and I am at last rewarded by another letter. I was preparing for bed a little while ago, when I heard the same mysterious sound at the door as on the last two occasions. I hurried to the glass door, and there found another close-folded letter. But I could see no sign of my Lady, or of any other living being. The letter, which was without direction, ran as follows:

"If you are still of the same mind, and feel no misgivings, meet me at the Church of St. Sava beyond the Creek to-morrow night at a quarter before midnight. If you come, come in secret, and, of course, alone. Do not come at all unless you are prepared for a terrible ordeal. But if you love me, and have neither doubts nor fears, come. Come!"

Needless to say, I did not sleep last night. I tried to, but without success. It was no morbid happiness that kept me awake, no doubting, no fear. I was simply overwhelmed with the idea of the coming rapture when I should call my Lady my very, very own. In this sea of happy expectation all lesser things were submerged. Even sleep, which is an imperative force with me, failed in its usual effectiveness, and I lay still, calm, content.

With the coming of the morning, however, restlessness began. I did not know what to do, how to restrain myself, where to look for an anodyne. Happily the latter came in the shape of Rooke, who turned up shortly after breakfast. He had a satisfactory tale to tell me of the armoured yacht, which had lain off Cattaro on the previous night, and to which he had brought his contingent of crew which had waited for her coming. He did not like to take the risk of going into any port with such a vessel, lest he might be detained or otherwise hampered by forms, and had gone out upon the open sea before daylight. There was on board the yacht a tiny torpedo-boat, for which provision was made both for hoisting on deck and housing there. This last would run into the creek at ten o'clock that evening, at which time it would be dark. The yacht would then run to near Otranto, to which she would send a boat to get any message I might send. This was to be in a code, which we arranged, and would convey instructions as to what night and approximate hour the yacht would come to the creek.

The day was well on before we had made certain arrangements for the future; and not till then did I feel again the pressure of my personal restlessness. Rooke, like a wise commander, took rest whilst he could. Well he knew that for a couple of days and nights at least there would be little, if any, sleep for him.

For myself, the habit of self-control stood to me, and I managed to get through the day somehow without exciting the attention of anyone else. The arrival of the torpedo-boat and the departure of Rooke made for me a welcome break in my uneasiness. An hour ago I said good-night to Aunt Janet, and shut myself up alone here. My watch is on the table before me, so that I may make sure of starting to the moment. I have allowed myself half an hour to reach St. Sava. My skiff is waiting, moored at the foot of the cliff on the hither side, where the zigzag comes close to the water. It is now ten minutes past eleven.

I shall add the odd five minutes to the time for my journey so as to make safe. I go unarmed and without a light.

I shall show no distrust of anyone or anything this night.

RUPERT'S JOURNAL—_Continued._

July 2, 1907.

When I was outside the church, I looked at my watch in the bright moonlight, and found I had one minute to wait. So I stood in the shadow of the doorway and looked out at the scene before me. Not a sign of life was visible around me, either on land or sea. On the broad plateau on which the church stands there was no movement of any kind. The wind, which had been pleasant in the noontide, had fallen completely, and not a leaf was stirring. I could see across the creek and note the hard line where the battlements of the Castle cut the sky, and where the keep towered above the line of black rock, which in the shadow of the land made an ebon frame for the picture. When I had seen the same view on former occasions, the line where the rock rose from the sea was a fringe of white foam. But then, in the daylight, the sea was sapphire blue; now it was an expanse of dark blue—so dark as to seem almost black. It had not even the relief of waves or ripples— simply a dark, cold, lifeless expanse, with no gleam of light anywhere, of lighthouse or ship; neither was there any special sound to be heard that one could distinguish—nothing but the distant hum of the my- riad voices of the dark mingling in one ceaseless inarticulate sound. It was well I had not time to dwell on it, or I might have reached some spiritually-disturbing melancholy.

Let me say here that ever since I had received my Lady's message concerning this visit to St. Sava's I had been all on fire—not, perhaps, at every moment consciously or actually so, but always, as it were, prepared to break out into flame. Did I want a simile, I might compare myself to a well-banked furnace, whose present function it is to contain heat rather than to create it; whose crust can at any moment be broken by a force external to itself, and burst into raging, all-compelling heat. No thought of fear really entered my mind. Every other emotion there was, coming and going as occasion excited or lulled, but not fear. Well I knew in the depths of my heart the purpose which that secret quest was to serve. I knew not only from my Lady's words, but from the teachings of my own senses and experiences, that some dreadful ordeal must take place before happiness of any kind could be won. And that ordeal, though method or detail was unknown to me, I was prepared to undertake. This was one of those occasions when a man must undertake, blindfold, ways that may lead to torture or death, or unknown terrors beyond. But, then, a man—if, indeed, he have the heart of a man—can always undertake; he can at least make the first step, though it may turn out that through the weakness of mortality he may be unable to fulfil his own intent, or justify his belief in his own powers. Such, I take it, was the intellectual attitude of the brave souls who of old faced the tortures of the Inquisition.

But though there was no immediate fear, there was a certain doubt. For doubt is one of those mental conditions whose calling we cannot control. The end of the doubting may not be a reality to us, or be accepted as a possibility. These things cannot forego the existence of the doubt. "For even if a man," says Victor Cousin, "doubt everything else, at least he cannot doubt that he doubts." The doubt had at times been on me that my Lady of the Shroud was a Vampire. Much that had happened seemed to point that way, and here, on the very threshold of the Unknown, when, through the door which I was pushing open, my eyes met only an expanse of absolute blackness, all doubts which had ever been seemed to surround me in a legion. I have heard that, when a man is drowning, there comes a time when his whole life passes in review during the space of time which cannot be computed as even a part of a second. So it was to me in the moment of my body passing into the church. In that moment came to my mind all that had been, which bore on the knowledge of my Lady; and the general tendency was to prove or convince that she was indeed a Vampire. Much that had happened, or become known to me, seemed to justify the resolving of doubt into belief. Even my own reading of the books in Aunt Janet's little library, and the dear lady's comments on them, mingled with her own uncanny beliefs, left little opening for doubt. My having to help my Lady over the threshold of my house on her first entry was in accord with Vampire tradition; so, too, her flying at cock-crow from the warmth in which she revelled on that strange first night of our meeting; so, too, her swift departure at midnight on the second. Into the same category came the facts of her constant wearing of her Shroud, even her pledging herself, and me also, on the fragment torn from it, which she had given to me as a souvenir; her lying still in the glass-covered tomb; her coming alone to the most secret places in a fortified Castle where every aperture was secured by unopened locks and bolts; her very movements, though all of grace, as she flitted noiselessly through the gloom of night.

All these things, and a thousand others of lesser import, seemed, for the moment, to have consolidated an initial belief. But then came the supreme recollections of how she had lain in my arms; of her kisses on my lips; of the beating of her heart against my own; of her sweet words of belief and faith breathed in my ear in intoxicating whispers; of . . . I paused. No! I could not accept belief as to her being other than a living woman of soul and sense, of flesh and blood, of all the sweet and passionate instincts of true and perfect womanhood.

And so, in spite of all—in spite of all beliefs, fixed or transitory, with a mind whirling amid contesting forces and compelling beliefs—I stepped into the church overwhelmed with that most receptive of atmospheres—doubt.

In one thing only was I fixed: here at least was no doubt or misgiving whatever. I intended to go through what I had undertaken. Moreover, I felt that I was strong enough to carry out my intention, whatever might be of the Unknown—however horrible, however terrible.

When I had entered the church and closed the heavy door behind me, the sense of darkness and loneliness in all their horror enfolded me round. The great church seemed a living mystery, and served as an almost terrible background to thoughts and remembrances of unutterable gloom. My adventurous life has had its own schooling to endurance and upholding one's courage in trying times; but it has its contra in fulness of memory.

I felt my way forward with both hands and feet. Every second seemed as if it had brought me at last to a darkness which was actually tangible. All at once, and with no heed of sequence or order, I was conscious of all around me, the knowledge or perception of which—or even speculation on the subject—had never entered my mind. They furnished the darkness with which I was encompassed with all the crowded phases of a dream. I knew that all around me were memorials of the dead—that in the Crypt deep-wrought in the rock below my feet lay the dead themselves. Some of them, perhaps—one of them I knew—had even passed the grim portals of time Unknown, and had, by some mysterious power or agency, come back again to material earth. There was no resting-place for thought when I knew that the very air which I breathed might be full of denizens of the spirit-world. In that impenetrable blackness was a world of imagining whose possibilities of horror were endless.

I almost fancied that I could see with mortal eyes down through that rocky floor to where, in the lonely Crypt, lay, in her tomb of massive stone and under that bewildering coverlet of glass, the woman whom I love. I could see her beautiful face, her long black lashes, her sweet mouth—which I had kissed—relaxed in the sleep of death. I could note the voluminous shroud—a piece of which as a precious souvenir lay even then so close to my heart—the snowy woollen coverlet wrought over in gold with sprigs of pine, the soft dent in the cushion on which her head must for so long have lain. I could see myself—within my eyes the memory of that first visit—coming once again with glad step to renew that dear sight—dear, though it scorched my eyes and harrowed my heart—and finding the greater sorrow, the greater desolation of the empty tomb!

There! I felt that I must think no more of that lest the thought should unnerve me when I should most want all my courage. That way madness lay! The darkness had already sufficient terrors of its own without bringing to it such grim remembrances and imaginings . . . And I had yet to go through some ordeal which, even to her who had passed and repassed the portals of death, was full of fear.

It was a merciful relief to me when, in groping my way forwards through the darkness, I struck against some portion of the furnishing of the church. Fortunately I was all strung up to tension, else I should never have been able to control instinctively, as I did, the shriek which was rising to my lips.

I would have given anything to have been able to light even a match. A single second of light would, I felt, have made me my own man again. But I knew that this would be against the implied condition of my being there at all, and might have had disastrous consequences to her whom I had come to save. It might even frustrate my scheme, and altogether destroy my opportunity. At that moment it was borne upon me more strongly than ever that this was not a mere fight for myself or my own selfish purposes—not merely an adventure or a struggle for only life and death against unknown difficulties and dangers. It was a fight on behalf of her I loved, not merely for her life, but perhaps even for her soul.

And yet this very thinking—understanding—created a new form of terror. For in that grim, shrouding darkness came memories of other moments of terrible stress.

Of wild, mystic rites held in the deep gloom of African forests, when, amid scenes of revolting horror, Obi and the devils of his kind seemed to reveal themselves to reckless worshippers, surfeited with horror, whose lives counted for naught; when even human sacrifice was an episode, and the reek of old deviltries and recent carnage tainted the air, till even I, who was, at the risk of my life, a privileged spectator who had come through dangers without end to behold the scene, rose and fled in horror.

Of scenes of mystery enacted in rock-cut temples beyond the Himalayas, whose fanatic priests, cold as death and as remorseless, in the reaction of their phrenzy of passion, foamed at the mouth and then sank into marble quiet, as with inner eyes they beheld the visions of the hellish powers which they had invoked.

Of wild, fantastic dances of the Devil-worshippers of Madagascar, where even the very semblance of humanity disappeared in the fantastic excesses of their orgies.

Of strange doings of gloom and mystery in the rock-perched monasteries of Thibet.

Of awful sacrifices, all to mystic ends, in the innermost recesses of Cathay.

Of weird movements with masses of poisonous snakes by the medicine-men of the Zuni and Mochi Indians in the far south-west of the Rockies, beyond the great plains.

Of secret gatherings in vast temples of old Mexico, and by dim altars of forgotten cities in the heart of great forests in South America.

Of rites of inconceivable horror in the fastnesses of Patagonia.

Of . . . Here I once more pulled myself up. Such thoughts were no kind of proper preparation for what I might have to endure. My work that night was to be based on love, on hope, on self-sacrifice for the woman who in all the world was the closest to my heart, whose future I was to share, whether that sharing might lead me to Hell or Heaven. The hand which undertook such a task must have no trembling.

Still, those horrible memories had, I am bound to say, a useful part in my preparation for the ordeal. They were of fact which I had seen, of which I had myself been in part a sharer, and which I had survived. With such experiences behind me, could there be aught before me more dreadful? . . .

Moreover, if the coming ordeal was of supernatural or superhuman order, could it transcend in living horror the vilest and most desperate acts of the basest men? . . .

With renewed courage I felt my way before me, till my sense of touch told me that I was at the screen behind which lay the stair to the Crypt. There I waited, silent, still.

My own part was done, so far as I knew how to do it. Beyond this, what was to come was, so far as I knew, beyond my own control. I had done what I could; the rest must come from others. I had exactly obeyed my instructions, fulfilled my warranty to the utmost in my knowledge and power. There was, therefore, left for me in the present nothing but to wait.

It is a peculiarity of absolute darkness that it creates its own reaction. The eye, wearied of the blackness, begins to imagine forms of light. How far this is effected by imagination pure and simple I know not. It may be that nerves have their own senses that bring thought to the depository common to all the human functions, but, whatever may be the mechanism or the objective, the darkness seems to people itself with luminous entities.

So was it with me as I stood lonely in the dark, silent church. Here and there seemed to flash tiny points of light.

In the same way the silence began to be broken now and again by strange muffled sounds—the suggestion of sounds rather than actual vibrations. These were all at first of the minor importance of movement—rustlings, creakings, faint stirrings, fainter breathings. Presently, when I had somewhat recovered from the sort of hypnotic trance to which the darkness and stillness had during the time of waiting reduced me, I looked around in wonder.

The phantoms of light and sound seemed to have become real. There were most certainly actual little points of light in places—not enough to see details by, but quite sufficient to relieve the utter gloom. I thought—though it may have been a mingling of recollection and imagination—that I could distinguish the outlines of the church; certainly the great altar-screen was dimly visible. Instinctively I looked up—and thrilled. There, hung high above me, was, surely enough, a great Greek Cross, outlined by tiny points of light.

I lost myself in wonder, and stood still, in a purely receptive mood, unantagonistic to aught, willing for whatever might come, ready for all things, in rather a negative than a positive mood—a mood which has an aspect of spiritual meekness. This is the true spirit of the neophyte, and, though I did not think of it at the time, the proper attitude for what is called by the Church in whose temple I stood a "neo-nymph."

As the light grew a little in power, though never increasing enough for distinctness, I saw dimly before me a table on which rested a great open book, whereon were laid two rings—one of sliver, the other of gold—and two crowns wrought of flowers, bound at the joining of their stems with tissue—one of gold, the other of silver. I do not know much of the ritual of the old Greek Church, which is the religion of the Blue Mountains, but the things which I saw before me could be none other than enlightening symbols. Instinctively I knew that I had been brought hither, though in this grim way, to be married. The very idea of it thrilled me to the heart's core. I thought the best thing I could do would be to stay quite still, and not show surprise at anything that might happen; but be sure I was all eyes and ears.

I peered anxiously around me in every direction, but I could see no sign of her whom I had come to meet.

Incidentally, however, I noticed that in the lighting, such as it was, there was no flame, no "living" light. Whatever light there was came muffled, as though through some green translucent stone. The whole effect was terribly weird and disconcerting.

Presently I started, as, seemingly out of the darkness beside me, a man's hand stretched out and took mine. Turning, I found close to me a tall man with shining black eyes and long black hair and beard. He was clad in some kind of gorgeous robe of cloth of gold, rich with variety of adornment. His head was covered with a high, over-hanging hat draped closely with a black scarf, the ends of which formed a long, hanging veil on either side. These veils, falling over the magnificent robes of cloth of gold, had an extraordinarily solemn effect.

I yielded myself to the guiding hand, and shortly found myself, so far as I could see, at one side of the sanctuary.

In the floor close to my feet was a yawning chasm, into which, from so high over my head that in the uncertain light I could not distinguish its origin, hung a chain. At the sight a strange wave of memory swept over me. I could not but remember the chain which hung over the glass-covered tomb in the Crypt, and I had an instinctive feeling that the grim chasm in the floor of the sanctuary was but the other side of the opening in the roof of the crypt from which the chain over the sarcophagus depended.

There was a creaking sound—the groaning of a windlass and the clanking of a chain. There was heavy breathing close to me somewhere.

I was so intent on what was going on that I did not see that one by one, seeming to grow out of the surrounding darkness, several black figures in monkish garb appeared with the silence of ghosts. Their faces were shrouded in black cowls, wherein were holes through which I could see dark gleaming eyes. My guide held me tightly by the hand. This gave me a feeling of security in the touch which helped to retain within my breast some semblance of calm.

The strain of the creaking windlass and the clanking chain continued for so long that the suspense became almost unendurable. At last there came into sight an iron ring, from which as a centre depended four lesser chains spreading wide. In a few seconds more I could see that these were fixed to the corners of the great stone tomb with the covering of glass, which was being dragged upward. As it arose it filled closely the whole aperture. When its bottom had reached the level of the floor it stopped, and remained rigid. There was no room for oscillation. It was at once surrounded by a number of black figures, who raised the glass covering and bore it away into the darkness. Then there stepped forward a very tall man, black-bearded, and with head-gear like my guide, but made in triple tiers, he also was gorgeously arrayed in flowing robes of cloth of gold richly embroidered. He raised his hand, and forthwith eight other black-clad figures stepped forward, and bending over the stone coffin, raised from it the rigid form of my Lady, still clad in her Shroud, and laid it gently on the floor of the sanctuary.

I felt it a grace that at that instant the dim lights seemed to grow less, and finally to disappear—all save the tiny points that marked the outline of the great Cross high overhead. These only gave light enough to accentuate the gloom. The hand that held mine now released it, and with a sigh I realized that I was alone. After a few moments more of the groaning of the winch and clanking of the chain there was a sharp sound of stone meeting stone; then there was silence. I listened acutely, but could not hear near me the slightest sound. Even the cautious, restrained breathing around me, of which up to then I had been conscious, had ceased. Not knowing, in the helplessness of my ignorance, what I should do, I remained as I was, still and silent, for a time that seemed endless. At last, overcome by some emotion which I could not at the moment understand, I slowly sank to my knees and bowed my head. Covering my face with my hands, I tried to recall the prayers of my youth. It was not, I am certain, that fear in any form had come upon me, or that I hesitated or faltered in my intention. That much I know now; I knew it even then. It was, I believe, that the prolonged impressive gloom and mystery had at last touched me to the quick. The bending of the knees was but symbolical of the bowing of the spirit to a higher Power. When I had realized that much, I felt more content than I had done since I had entered the church, and with the renewed consciousness of courage, took my hands from my face, and lifted again my bowed head.

Impulsively I sprang to my feet and stood erect—waiting. All seemed to have changed since I had dropped on my knees. The points of light about time church, which had been eclipsed, had come again, and were growing in power to a partial revealing of the dim expanse. Before me was the table with the open book, on which were laid the gold and silver rings and the two crowns of flowers. There were also two tall candles, with tiniest flames of blue—the only living light to be seen.

Out of the darkness stepped the same tall figure in the gorgeous robes and the triple hat. He led by the hand my Lady, still clad in her Shroud; but over it, descending from the crown of her head, was a veil of very old and magnificent lace of astonishing fineness. Even in that dim light I could note the exquisite beauty of the fabric. The veil was fastened with a bunch of tiny sprays of orange-blossom mingled with cypress and laurel—a strange combination. In her hand she carried a great bouquet of the same. Its sweet intoxicating odour floated up to my nostrils. It and the sentiment which its very presence evoked made me quiver.

Yielding to the guiding of the hand which held hers, she stood at my left side before the table. Her guide then took his place behind her. At either end of the table, to right and left of us, stood a long-bearded priest in splendid robes, and wearing the hat with depending veil of black. One of them, who seemed to be the more important of the two, and took the initiative, signed to us to put our right hands on the open book. My Lady, of course, understood the ritual, and knew the words which the priest was speaking, and of her own accord put out her hand. My guide at the same moment directed my hand to the same end. It thrilled me to touch my Lady's hand, even under such mysterious conditions.

After the priest had signed us each thrice on the forehead with the sign of the Cross, he gave to each of us a tiny lighted taper brought to him for the purpose. The lights were welcome, not so much for the solace of the added light, great as that was, but because it allowed us to see a little more of each other's faces. It was rapture to me to see the face of my Bride; and from the expression of her face I was assured that she felt as I did. It gave me an inexpressible pleasure when, as her eyes rested on me, there grew a faint blush over the grey pallor of her cheeks.

The priest then put in solemn voice to each of us in turn, beginning with me, the questions of consent which are common to all such rituals. I answered as well as I could, following the murmured words of my guide. My Lady answered out proudly in a voice which, though given softly, seemed to ring. It was a concern—even a grief—to me that I could not, in the priest's questioning, catch her name, of which, strangely enough,—I was ignorant. But, as I did not know the language, and as the phrases were not in accord literally with our own ritual, I could not make out which word was the name.

After some prayers and blessings, rhythmically spoken or sung by an invisible choir, the priest took the rings from the open book, and, after signing my forehead thrice with the gold one as he repeated the blessing in each case, placed it on my right hand; then he gave my Lady the silver one, with the same ritual thrice repeated. I suppose it was the blessing which is the effective point in making two into one.

After this, those who stood behind us exchanged our rings thrice, taking them from one finger and placing them on the other, so that at the end my wife wore the gold ring and I the silver one.

Then came a chant, during which the priest swung the censer himself, and my wife and I held our tapers. After that he blessed us, the responses coming from the voices of the unseen singers in the darkness.

After a long ritual of prayer and blessing, sung in triplicate, the priest took the crowns of flowers, and put one on the head of each, crowning me first, and with the crown tied with gold. Then he signed and blessed us each thrice. The guides, who stood behind us, exchanged our crowns thrice, as they had exchanged the rings; so that at the last, as I was glad to see, my wife wore the crown of gold, and I that of silver.

Then there came, if it is possible to describe such a thing, a hush over even that stillness, as though some form of added solemnity were to be gone through. I was not surprised, therefore, when the priest took in his hands the great golden chalice. Kneeling, my wife and I partook together thrice.

When we had risen from our knees and stood for a little while, the priest took my left hand in his right, and I, by direction of my guide, gave my right hand to my wife. And so in a line, the priest leading, we circled round the table in rhythmic measure. Those who supported us moved behind us, holding the crowns over our heads, and replacing them when we stopped.

After a hymn, sung through the darkness, the priest took off our crowns. This was evidently the conclusion of the ritual, for the priest placed us in each other's arms to embrace each other. Then he blessed us, who were now man and wife!

The lights went out at once, some as if extinguished, others slowly fading down to blackness.

Left in the dark, my wife and I sought each other's arms again, and stood together for a few moments heart to heart, tightly clasping each other, and kissed each other fervently.

Instinctively we turned to the door of the church, which was slightly open, so that we could see the moonlight stealing in through the aperture. With even steps, she holding me tightly by the left arm—which is the wife's arm, we passed through the old church and out into the free air.

Despite all that the gloom had brought me, it was sweet to be in the open air and together—this quite apart from our new relations to each other. The moon rode high, and the full light, coming after the dimness or darkness in the church, seemed as bright as day. I could now, for the first time, see my wife's face properly. The glamour of the moonlight may have served to enhance its ethereal beauty, but neither moonlight nor sunlight could do justice to that beauty in its living human splendour. As I gloried in her starry eyes I could think of nothing else; but when for a moment my eyes, roving round for the purpose of protection, caught sight of her whole figure, there was a pang to my heart. The brilliant moonlight showed every detail in terrible effect, and I could see that she wore only her Shroud. In the moment of darkness, after the last benediction, before she returned to my arms, she must have removed her bridal veil. This may, of course, have been in accordance with the established ritual of her church; but, all the same, my heart was sore. The glamour of calling her my very own was somewhat obscured by the bridal adornment being shorn. But it made no difference in her sweetness to me. Together we went along the path through the wood, she keeping equal step with me in wifely way.

When we had come through the trees near enough to see the roof of the Castle, now gilded with the moonlight, she stopped, and looking at me with eyes full of love, said:

"Here I must leave you!"

"What?" I was all aghast, and I felt that my chagrin was expressed in the tone of horrified surprise in my voice. She went on quickly:

"Alas! It is impossible that I should go farther—at present!"

"But what is to prevent you?" I queried. "You are now my wife. This is our wedding-night; and surely your place is with me!" The wail in her voice as she answered touched me to the quick:

"Oh, I know, I know! There is no dearer wish in my heart—there can be none—than to share my husband's home. Oh, my dear, my dear, if you only knew what it would be to me to be with you always! But indeed I may not—not yet! I am not free! If you but knew how much that which has happened to-night has cost me—or how much cost to others as well as to myself may be yet to come—you would understand. Rupert"—it was the first time she had ever addressed me by name, and naturally it thrilled me through and through—"Rupert, my husband, only that I trust you with all the faith which is in perfect love—mutual love, I dare not have done what I have done this night. But, dear, I know that you will bear me out; that your wife's honour is your honour, even as your honour is mine. My honour is given to this; and you can help me—the only help I can have at present—by trusting me. Be patient, my beloved, be patient! Oh, be patient for a little longer! It shall not be for long. So soon as ever my soul is freed I shall come to you, my husband; and we shall never part again. Be content for a while! Believe me that I love you with my very soul; and to keep away from your dear side is more bitter for me than even it can be for you! Think, my dear one, I am not as other women are, as some day you shall clearly understand. I am at the present, and shall be for a little longer, constrained by duties and obligations put upon me by others, and for others, and to which I am pledged by the most sacred promises—given not only by myself, but by others—and which I must not forgo. These forbid me to do as I wish. Oh, trust me, my beloved—my husband!"

She held out her hands appealingly. The moonlight, falling through the thinning forest, showed her white cerements. Then the recollection of all she must have suffered—the awful loneliness in that grim tomb in the Crypt, the despairing agony of one who is helpless against the unknown—swept over me in a wave of pity. What could I do but save her from further pain? And this could only be by showing her my faith and trust. If she was to go back to that dreadful charnel-house, she would at least take with her the remembrance that one who loved her and whom she loved—to whom she had been lately bound in the mystery of marriage—trusted her to the full. I loved her more than myself—more than my own soul; and I was moved by pity so great that all possible selfishness was merged in its depths. I bowed my head before her—my Lady and my Wife—as I said:

"So be it, my beloved. I trust you to the full, even as you trust me. And that has been proven this night, even to my own doubting heart. I shall wait; and as I know you wish it, I shall wait as patiently as I can. But till you come to me for good and all, let me see you or hear from you when you can. The time, dear wife, must go heavily with me as I think of you suffering and lonely. So be good to me, and let not too long a time elapse between my glimpses of hope. And, sweetheart, when you *do* come to me, it shall be for ever!" There was something in the intonation of the last sentence—I felt its sincerity myself—some implied yearning for a promise, that made her beautiful eyes swim. The glorious stars in them were blurred as she answered with a fervour which seemed to me as more than earthly:

"For ever! I swear it!"

With one long kiss, and a straining in each others arms, which left me tingling for long after we had lost sight of each other, we parted. I stood and watched her as her white figure, gliding through the deepening gloom, faded as the forest thickened. It surely was no optical delusion or a phantom of the mind that her shrouded arm was raised as though in blessing or farewell before the darkness swallowed her up.

BOOK VI: THE PURSUIT IN THE FOREST

RUPERT'S JOURNAL—*Continued.*

July 3, 1907.

THERE IS NO anodyne but work to pain of the heart; and my pain is all of the heart. I sometimes feel that it is rather hard that with so much to make me happy I cannot know happiness. How can I be happy when my wife, whom I fondly love, and who I know loves me, is suffering in horror and loneliness of a kind which is almost beyond human belief? However, what is my loss is my country's gain, for the Land of the Blue Mountains is my country now, despite the fact that I am still a loyal subject of good King Edward. Uncle Roger took care of that when he said I should have the consent of the Privy Council before I might be naturalized anywhere else.

When I got home yesterday morning I naturally could not sleep. The events of the night and the bitter disappointment that followed my exciting joy made such a thing impossible. When I drew the curtain over the window, the reflection of the sunrise was just beginning to tinge the high-sailing clouds in front of me. I laid down and tried to rest, but without avail. However, I schooled myself to lie still, and at last, if I did not sleep, was at least quiescent.

Disturbed by a gentle tap at the door, I sprang up at once and threw on a dressing gown. Outside, when I opened the door, was Aunt Janet. She was holding a lighted candle in her hand, for though it was getting light in the open, the passages were still dark. When she saw me she seemed to breathe more freely, and asked if she might come in.

Whilst she sat on the edge of my bed, in her old-time way, she said in a hushed voice:

"Oh, laddie, laddie, I trust yer burden is no too heavy to bear."

"My burden! What on earth do you mean, Aunt Janet?" I said in reply. I did not wish to commit myself by a definite answer, for it was evident that she had been dreaming or Second Sighting again. She replied with the grim seriousness usual to her when she touched on occult matters:

"I saw your hairt bleeding, laddie. I kent it was yours, though how I kent it I don't know. It lay on a stone floor in the dark, save for a dim blue light such as corpse-lights are. On it was placed a great book, and close around were scattered many strange things, amongst them two crowns o' flowers—the one bound wi' silver, the other wi' gold. There was also a golden cup, like a chalice, o'erturned. The red wine trickled from it an' mingled wi' yer hairt's bluid; for on the great book was some vast dim weight wrapped up in black, and on it stepped in turn many men all swathed in black. An' as the weight of each came on it the bluid gushed out afresh. And oh, yer puir hairt, my laddie, was quick and leaping, so that at every beat it raised the black-clad weight! An' yet that was not all, for hard by stood a tall imperial shape o' a woman, all arrayed in white, wi' a great veil o' finest lace worn o'er a shroud. An' she was whiter than the snow, an' fairer than the morn for beauty; though a dark woman she was, wi' hair like the raven, an' eyes black as the sea at nicht, an' there was stars in them. An' at each beat o' yer puir bleeding hairt she wrung her white hands, an' the manin' o' her sweet voice rent my hairt in twain. Oh, laddie, laddie! what does it mean?"

I managed to murmur: "I'm sure I don't know, Aunt Janet. I suppose it was all a dream!"

"A dream it was, my dear. A dream or a veesion, whilka matters nane, for a' such are warnin's sent frae God . . . " Suddenly she said in a different voice:

"Laddie, hae ye been fause to any lassie? I'm no blamin' ye. For ye men are different frae us women, an' yer regard on recht and wrang differs from oors. But oh, laddie, a woman's tears fa' heavy when her hairt is for sair wi' the yieldin' to fause words. 'Tis a heavy burden for ony man to carry wi' him as he goes, an' may well cause pain to ithers that he fain would spare." She stopped, and in dead silence waited for me to speak. I thought it would be best to set her poor loving heart at rest, and as I could not divulge my special secret, spoke in general terms:

"Aunt Janet, I am a man, and have led a man's life, such as it is. But I can tell you, who have always loved me and taught me to be true, that in all the world there is no woman who must weep for any falsity of mine. If close there be any who, sleeping or waking, in dreams or visions or in reality, weeps because of me, it is surely not for my doing, but because of something outside me. It may be that her heart is sore because I must suffer, as all men must in some degree; but she does not weep for or through any act of mine."

She sighed happily at my assurance, and looked up through her tears, for she was much moved; and after tenderly kissing my forehead and blessing me, stole away. She was more sweet and tender than I have words to say, and the only regret that I have in all that is gone is that I have not been able to bring my wife to her, and let her share in the love she has for me. But that, too, will come, please God!

In the morning I sent a message to Rooke at Otranto, instructing him by code to bring the yacht to Vissarion in the coming night.

All day I spent in going about amongst the mountaineers, drilling them and looking after their arms. I *could* not stay still. My only chance of peace was to work, my only chance of sleep to tire myself out. Unhappily, I am very strong, so even when I came home at dark I was quite fresh. However, I found a cable message from Rooke that the yacht would arrive at midnight.

There was no need to summon the mountaineers, as the men in the Castle would be sufficient to make preparations for the yacht's coming.

Later.

The yacht has come. At half-past eleven the lookout signalled that a steamer without lights was creeping in towards the Creek. I ran out to the Flagstaff, and saw her steal in like a ghost. She is painted a steely blue-grey, and it is almost impossible to see her at any distance. She certainly goes wonderfully. Although there was not enough throb from the engines to mar the absolute stillness, she came on at a fine speed, and within a few minutes was close to the boom. I had only time to run down to give orders to draw back the boom when she glided in and stopped dead at the harbour wall. Rooke steered her himself, and he says he never was on a boat that so well or so quickly answered her helm. She is certainly a beauty, and so far as I can see at night perfect in every detail. I promise myself a few pleasant hours over her in the daylight. The men seem a splendid lot.

But I do not feel sleepy; I despair of sleep to-night. But work demands that I be fit for whatever may come, and so I shall try to sleep—to rest, at any rate.

RUPERT'S JOURNAL—*Continued.*

July 4, 1907.

I was up with the first ray of sunrise, so by the time I had my bath and was dressed there was ample light. I went down to the dock at once, and spent the morning looking over the vessel, which fully justifies Rooke's enthusiasm about her. She is built on lovely lines, and I can quite understand that she is enormously fast. Her armour I can only take on the specifications, but her armament is really wonderful. And there are not only all the very newest devices of aggressive warfare—indeed, she has the newest up-to-date torpedoes and torpedo-guns—but also the old-fashioned rocket-tubes, which in certain occasions are so useful. She has electric guns and the latest Massillon water-guns, and Reinhardt electro-pneumatic "deliverers" for pyroxiline shells. She is even equipped with war-balloons easy of expansion, and with compressible Kitson aeroplanes. I don't suppose that there is anything quite like her in the world.

The crew are worthy of her. I can't imagine where Rooke picked up such a splendid lot of men. They are nearly all man-of-warsmen; of various nationalities, but mostly British. All young men—the oldest of them hasn't got into the forties—and, so far as I can learn, all experts of one kind or another in some special subject of warfare. It will go hard with me, but I shall keep them together.

How I got through the rest of the day I know not. I tried hard not to create any domestic trouble by my manner, lest Aunt Janet should, after her lurid dream or vision of last night, attach some new importance to it. I think I succeeded, for she did not, so far as I could tell, take any special notice of me. We parted as usual at half-past ten, and I came here and made this entry in my journal. I am more restless than ever to-night, and no wonder. I would give anything to be able to pay a visit to St. Sava's, and see my wife again—if it were only sleeping in her tomb. But I dare not do even that, lest she should come to see me here, and I should miss her. So I have done what I can. The glass door to the Terrace is open, so that she can enter at once if she comes. The fire is lit, and the room is warm. There is food ready in case she should care for it. I have plenty of light in the room, so that through the aperture where I have not fully drawn the curtain there may be light to guide her.

Oh, how the time drags! The clock has struck midnight. One, two! Thank goodness, it will shortly be dawn, and the activity of the day may begin! Work may again prove, in a way, to be an anodyne. In the meantime I must write on, lest despair overwhelm me.

Once during the night I thought I heard a footstep outside. I rushed to the window and looked out, but there was nothing to see, no sound to hear. That was a little after one o'clock. I feared to go outside, lest that should alarm her; so I came back to my table. I could not write, but I sat as if writing for a while. But I could not stand it, so rose and walked about the room. As I walked I felt that my Lady—it gives me a pang every time I remember that I do not know even her name—was not quite so far away from me. It made my heart beat to think that it might mean that she was coming to me. Could not I as well as Aunt Janet have a little Second Sight! I went towards the window, and, standing behind the curtain, listened. Far away I thought I heard a cry, and ran out on the Terrace; but there was no sound to be heard, and no sign of any living thing anywhere; so I took it for granted that it was the cry of some night bird, and came back to my room, and wrote at my journal till I was calm. I think my nerves must be getting out of order, when every sound of the night seems to have a special meaning for me.

RUPERT'S JOURNAL—*Continued.*

July 7, 1907.

When the grey of the morning came, I gave up hope of my wife appearing, and made up my mind that, so soon as I could get away without exciting Aunt Janet's attention, I would go to St. Sava's. I always eat a good breakfast, and did I forgo it altogether, it would be sure to excite her curiosity—a thing I do not wish at present. As there was still time to wait, I lay down on my bed as I was, and—such is the way of Fate—shortly fell asleep.

I was awakened by a terrific clattering at my door. When I opened it I found a little group of servants, very apologetic at awaking me without instructions. The chief of them explained that a young priest had come from the Vladika with a message so urgent that he insisted on seeing me immediately at all hazards. I came out at once, and found him in the hall of the Castle, standing before the great fire, which was always lit in the early morning. He had a letter in his hand, but before giving it to me he said:

"I am sent by the Vladika, who pressed on me that I was not to lose a single instant in seeing you; that time is of golden price—nay, beyond price. This letter, amongst other things, vouches for me. A terrible misfortune has occurred. The daughter of our leader has disappeared during last night—the same, he commanded me to remind you, that he spoke of at the meeting when he would not let the mountaineers fire their guns. No sign of her can be found, and it is believed that she has been carried off by the emissaries of the Sultan of Turkey, who once before brought our nations to the verge of war by demanding her as a wife. I was also to say that the Vladika Plamenac would have come himself, but that it was necessary that he should at once consult with the Archbishop, Stevan Palealogue, as to what step is best to take in this dire calamity. He has sent out a search-party under the Archimandrite of Spazac, Petrof Vlastimir, who is to come on here with any news he can get, as you have command of the signalling, and can best spread the news. He knows that you, Gospodar, are in your great heart one of our compatriots, and that you have already proved your friendship by many efforts to strengthen our hands for war. And as a great compatriot, he calls on you to aid us in our need." He then handed me the letter, and stood by respectfully whilst I broke the seal and read it. It was written in great haste, and signed by the Vladika.

"Come with us now in our nation's peril. Help us to rescue what we most adore, and henceforth we shall hold you in our hearts. You shall learn how the men of the Blue Mountains can love faith and valour. Come!"

This was a task indeed—a duty worthy of any man. It thrilled me to the core to know that the men of the Blue Mountains had called on me in their dire need. It woke all the fighting instinct of my Viking forbears, and I vowed in my heart that they should be satisfied with my work. I called to me the corps of signallers who were in the house, and led them to the Castle roof, taking with me the young messenger-priest.

"Come with me," I said to him, "and see how I answer the Vladika's command."

The National flag was run up—the established signal that the nation was in need. Instantly on every summit near and far was seen the flutter of an answering flag. Quickly followed the signal that commanded the call to arms.

One by one I gave the signallers orders in quick succession, for the plan of search unfolded itself to me as I went on. The arms of the semaphore whirled in a way that made the young priest stare. One by one, as they took their orders, the signallers seemed to catch fire. Instinctively they understood the plan, and worked like demigods. They knew that so widespread a movement had its best chance in rapidity and in unity of action.

From the forest which lay in sight of the Castle came a wild cheering, which seemed to interpret the former stillness of the hills. It was good to feel that those who saw the signals—types of many—were ready. I saw the look of expectation on the face of the messenger-priest, and rejoiced at the glow that came as I turned to him to speak. Of course, he wanted to know something of what

was going on. I saw the flashing of my own eyes reflected in his as
I spoke:

"Tell the Vladika that within a minute of his message being read the
Land of the Blue Mountains was awake. The mountaineers are already
marching, and before the sun is high there will be a line of guards within
hail of each other round the whole frontier—from Angusa to Ilsin; from
Ilsin to Bajana; from Bajana to Ispazar; from Ispazar to Volok; from
Volok to Tatra; from Tatra to Domitan; from Domitan to Gravaja; and
from Gravaja back to Angusa. The line is double. The old men keep
guard on the line, and the young men advance. These will close in at the
advancing line, so that nothing can escape them. They will cover mountain-top and forest depth, and will close in finally on the Castle here,
which they can behold from afar. My own yacht is here, and will sweep
the coast from end to end. It is the fastest boat afloat, and armed against
a squadron. Here will all signals come. In an hour where we stand will
be a signal bureau, where trained eyes will watch night and day till the
lost one has been found and the outrage has been avenged. The robbers
are even now within a ring of steel, and cannot escape."

The young priest, all on fire, sprang on the battlements and
shouted to the crowd, which was massing round the Castle in the gardens far below. The forest was giving up its units till they seemed like
the nucleus of an army. The men cheered lustily, till the sound swung
high up to us like the roaring of a winter sea. With bared heads they
were crying:

"God and the Blue Mountains! God and the Blue Mountains!"

I ran down to them as quickly as I could, and began to issue their
instructions. Within a time to be computed by minutes the whole
number, organized by sections, had started to scour the neighbouring
mountains. At first they had only understood the call to arms for
general safety. But when they learned that the daughter of a chief had
been captured, they simply went mad. From something which the

messenger first said, but which I could not catch or did not understand, the blow seemed to have for them some sort of personal significance which wrought them to a frenzy.

When the bulk of the men had disappeared, I took with me a few of my own men and several of the mountaineers whom I had asked to remain, and together we went to the hidden ravine which I knew. We found the place empty; but there were unmistakable signs that a party of men had been encamped there for several days. Some of our men, who were skilled in woodcraft and in signs generally, agreed that there must have been some twenty of them. As they could not find any trail either coming to or going from the place, they came to the conclusion that they must have come separately from different directions and gathered there, and that they must have departed in something of the same mysterious way.

However, this was, at any rate, some sort of a beginning, and the men separated, having agreed amongst themselves to make a wide cast round the place in the search for tracks. Whoever should find a trail was to follow with at least one comrade, and when there was any definite news, it was to be signalled to the Castle.

I myself returned at once, and set the signallers to work to spread amongst our own people such news as we had.

When presently such discoveries as had been made were signalled with flags to the Castle, it was found that the marauders had, in their flight, followed a strangely zigzag course. It was evident that, in trying to baffle pursuit, they had tried to avoid places which they thought might be dangerous to them. This may have been simply a method to disconcert pursuit. If so, it was, in a measure, excellent, for none of those immediately following could possibly tell in what direction they were heading. It was only when we worked the course on the great map in the signaller's room (which was the old guard room of the Castle) that we could get an inkling of the general direction of their flight. This gave added trouble to the pursuit; for the men who followed, being ignorant of their general intent, could not ever take chance to head them off, but had to be ready to follow in any or every direction. In this manner the pursuit was altogether a stern chase, and therefore bound to be a long one.

As at present we could not do anything till the intended route was more marked, I left the signalling corps to the task of receiving and giving information to the moving bands, so that, if occasion served, they might head off the marauders. I myself took Rooke, as captain of the yacht, and swept out of the creek. We ran up north to Dalairi, then down south to Olesso, and came back to Vissarion. We saw nothing suspicious except, far off to the extreme southward, one warship which flew no flag. Rooke, however, who seemed to know ships by instinct, said she was a Turk; so on our return we signalled along the whole shore to watch her. Rooke held *The Lady*—which was the name I had given the armoured yacht—in readiness to dart out in case anything suspicious was reported. He was not to stand on any ceremony, but if necessary to attack. We did not intend to lose a point in this desperate struggle which we had undertaken. We had placed in different likely spots a couple of our own men to look after the signalling.

When I got back I found that the route of the fugitives, who had now joined into one party, had been definitely ascertained. They had gone south, but manifestly taking alarm from the advancing line of guards, had headed up again to the north-east, where the country was broader and the mountains wilder and less inhabited.

Forthwith, leaving the signalling altogether in the hands of the fighting priests, I took a small chosen band of the mountaineers of our own district, and made, with all the speed we could, to cut across the track of the fugitives a little ahead of them. The Archimandrite (Abbot) of Spazac, who had just arrived, came with us. He is a splendid man—a real fighter as well as a holy cleric, as good with his handjar as with his Bible, and a runner to beat the band. The marauders were going at a fearful pace, considering that they were all afoot; so we had to go fast also! Amongst these mountains there is no other means of progressing. Our own men were so aflame with ardour that I could not but notice that they, more than any of the others whom I had seen, had some special cause for concern.

When I mentioned it to the Archimandrite, who moved by my side, he answered:

"All natural enough; they are not only fighting for their country, but for their own!" I did not quite understand his answer, and so began to ask him some questions, to the effect that I soon began to understand a good deal more than he did.

Letter from Archbishop Stevan Palealogue, Head of the Eastern Church of the Blue Mountains, to the Lady Janet MacKelpie, Vissarion.

Written July 9, 1907.

HONOURED LADY,

As you wish for an understanding regarding the late lamentable occurrence in which so much danger was incurred to this our Land of the Blue Mountains, and one dear to us, I send these words by request of the Gospodar Rupert, beloved of our mountaineers.

When the Voivode Peter Vissarion made his journey to the great nation to whom we looked in our hour of need, it was necessary that he should go in secret. The Turk was at our gates, and full of the malice of baffled greed. Already he had tried to arrange a marriage with the Voivodin, so that in time to come he, as her husband, might have established a claim to the inheritance of the land. Well he knew, as do all men, that the Blue Mountaineers owe allegiance to none that they themselves do not appoint to rulership. This has been the history in the past. But now and again an individual has arisen or come to the front adapted personally for such government as this land requires. And so the Lady Teuta, Voivodin of the Blue Mountains, was put for her proper guarding in the charge of myself as Head of the Eastern Church in the Land of the Blue Mountains, steps being taken in such wise that no capture of her could be effected by unscrupulous enemies of this our Land. This task and guardianship was gladly held as an honour by all concerned. For the Voivodin Teuta of Vissarion must be taken as representing in her own person the glory of the old Serb race, inasmuch as being the only child of the Voivode Vissarion, last male of his princely race—the race which ever, during the ten centuries of our history, unflinchingly gave life and all they held for the protection, safety, and well-being of the Land of the Blue Mountains. Never during those centuries had any one of the race been known to fail in patriotism, or to draw back from any loss or hardship enjoined by high duty or stress of need. Moreover, this was the race of that first Voivode Vissarion, of whom, in legend, it was prophesied that he—once known as "The Sword of Freedom," a giant amongst men—would some day, when the nation had need of him, come forth from his water-tomb in the lost Lake of Reo, and lead once more the men of the Blue Mountains to lasting victory. This noble race, then, had come to be known as the last hope of the Land. So that when the Voivode was away on his country's service, his daughter should be closely guarded. Soon after the Voivode had gone, it was reported that he might be long delayed in his diplomacies, and also in studying the system of Constitutional Monarchy, for which it had been hoped to exchange our imperfect political system. I may say *inter alia* that he was mentioned as to be the first king when the new constitution should have been arranged.

Then a great misfortune came on us; a terrible grief overshadowed the land. After a short illness, the Voivodin Teuta Vissarion died mysteriously of a mysterious ailment. The grief of the mountaineers was so great that it became necessary for the governing Council to warn them not to allow their sorrow to be seen. It was imperatively necessary that the fact of her death should be kept secret. For there were dangers and difficulties of several kinds. In the first place it was advisable that even her father should be kept in ignorance of his terrible loss. It was well known that he held her as the very core of his heart and that if he should hear of her death, he would be too much prostrated to be able to do the intricate and delicate work which he had undertaken. Nay, more: he would never remain afar off, under the sad circumstances, but would straightway return, so as to be in the land where she lay. Then suspicions would crop up, and the truth must shortly be known afield, with the inevitable result that the Land would become the very centre of a war of many nations.

In the second place, if the Turks were to know that the race of Vissarion was becoming extinct, this would encourage them to further aggression, which would become immediate should they find out that the Voivode was himself away. It was well known that they were already only suspending hostilities until a fitting opportunity should arise. Their desire for aggression had become acute after the refusal of the nation, and of the girl herself, that she should become a wife of the Sultan.

The dead girl had been buried in the Crypt of the church of St. Sava, and day after day and night after night, singly and in parties, the sorrowing mountaineers had come to pay devotion and reverence at her tomb. So many had wished to have a last glimpse of her face that the Vladika had, with my own consent as Archbishop, arranged for a glass cover to be put over the stone coffin wherein her body lay.

After a little time, however, there came a belief to all concerned in the guarding of the body—these, of course, being the priests of various degrees of dignity appointed to the task—that the Voivodin was not really dead, but only in a strangely-prolonged trance. Thereupon a new complication arose. Our mountaineers are, as perhaps you know, by nature deeply suspicious—a characteristic of all brave and self-sacrificing people who are jealous of their noble heritage. Having, as they believed, seen the girl dead, they might not be willing to accept the fact of her being alive. They might even imagine that there was on foot some deep, dark plot which was, or might be, a menace, now or hereafter, to their independence. In any case, there would be certain to be two parties on the subject, a dangerous and deplorable thing in the present condition of affairs.

As the trance, or catalepsy, whatever it was, continued for many days, there had been ample time for the leaders of the Council, the Vladika, the priesthood represented by the Archimandrite of Spazac, myself as Archbishop and guardian of the Voivodin in her father's absence, to consult as to a policy to be observed in case of the girl awaking. For in such case the difficulty of the situation would be multiplied indefinitely. In the secret chambers of St. Sava's we had many secret meetings, and were finally converging on agreement when the end of the trance came.

The girl awoke!

She was, of course, terribly frightened when she found herself in a tomb in the Crypt. It was truly fortunate that the great candles around her tomb had been kept lighted, for their light mitigated the horror of the place. Had she waked in darkness, her reason might have become unseated.

She was, however, a very noble girl; brave, with extraordinary will, and resolution, and self-command, and power of endurance. When she had been taken into one of the secret chambers of the church, where she was warmed and cared for, a hurried meeting was held by the Vladika, myself, and the chiefs of the National Council. Word had been at once sent to me of the joyful news of her recovery; and with the utmost haste I came, arriving in time to take a part in the Council.

At the meeting the Voivodin was herself present, and full confidence of the situation was made to her. She herself proposed that the belief in her death should be allowed to prevail until the return of her father, when all could be effectively made clear. To this end she undertook to submit to the terrific strain which such a proceeding would involve. At first we men could not believe that any woman could go through with such a task, and some of us did not hesitate to voice our doubts—our disbelief. But she stood to her guns, and actually down-faced us. At the last we, remembering things that had been done, though long ages ago, by others of her race, came to believe not merely in her self-belief and intention, but even in the feasibility of her plan. She took the most solemn oaths not to betray the secret under any possible stress.

The priesthood undertook through the Vladika and myself to further a ghostly belief amongst the mountaineers which would tend to prevent a too close or too persistent observation. The Vampire legend was spread as a protection against partial discovery by any mischance, and other weird beliefs were set afoot and fostered. Arrangements were made that only on certain days were the mountaineers to be admitted to the Crypt, she agreeing that for these occasions she was to take opiates or carry out any other aid to the preservation of the secret. She was willing, she impressed upon us, to make any personal sacrifice which might be deemed necessary for the carrying out her father's task for the good of the nation.

Of course, she had at first terrible frights lying alone in the horror of the Crypt. But after a time the terrors of the situation, if they did not cease, were mitigated. There are secret caverns off the Crypt, wherein in troublous times the priests and others of high place have found safe retreat. One of these was prepared for the Voivodin, and there she remained, except for such times as she was on show—and certain other times of which I shall tell you. Provision was made for the possibility of any accidental visit to the church. At such times, warned by an automatic signal from the opening door, she was to take her place in the tomb. The mechanism was so arranged that the means to replace the glass cover, and to take the opiate, were there ready to her hand. There was to be always a watch of priests at night in the church, to guard her from ghostly fears as well as from more physical dangers; and if she was actually in her tomb, it was to be visited at certain intervals. Even the draperies which covered her in the sarcophagus were rested on a bridge placed from side to side just above her, so as to hide the rising and falling of her bosom as she slept under the narcotic.

After a while the prolonged strain began to tell so much on her that it was decided that she should take now and again exercise out of doors. This was not difficult, for when the Vampire story which we had spread began to be widely known, her being seen would be accepted as a proof of its truth. Still, as there was a certain danger in her being seen at all, we thought it necessary to exact from her a solemn oath that so long as her sad task lasted she should under no circumstances ever wear any dress but her shroud—this being the only way to insure secrecy and to prevail against accident.

There is a secret way from the Crypt to a sea cavern, whose entrance is at high-tide under the water-line at the base of the cliff on which the church is built. A boat, shaped like a coffin, was provided for her; and in this she was accustomed to pass across the creek whenever she wished to make excursion. It was an excellent device, and most efficacious in disseminating the Vampire belief.

This state of things had now lasted from before the time when the Gospodar Rupert came to Vissarion up to the day of the arrival of the armoured yacht.

That night the priest on duty, on going his round of the Crypt just before dawn, found the tomb empty. He called the others, and they made full search. The boat was gone from the cavern, but on making search they found it on the farther side of the creek, close to the garden stairs. Beyond this they could discover nothing. She seemed to have disappeared without leaving a trace.

Straightway they went to the Vladika, and signalled to me by the fire-signal at the monastery at Astrag, where I then was. I took a band of mountaineers with me, and set out to scour the country. But before going I sent an urgent message to the Gospodar Rupert, asking him, who showed so much interest and love to our Land, to help us in our trouble. He, of course, knew nothing then of all have now told you. Nevertheless, he devoted himself whole-heartedly to our needs—as doubtless you know.

But the time had now come close when the Voivode Vissarion was about to return from his mission; and we of the council of his daughter's guardianship were beginning to arrange matters so that at his return the good news of her being still alive could be made public. With her father present to vouch for her, no question as to truth could arise.

But by some means the Turkish "Bureau of Spies" must have got knowledge of the fact already. To steal a dead body for the purpose of later establishing a fictitious claim would have been an enterprise even more desperate than that already undertaken. We inferred from many signs, made known to us in an investigation, that a daring party of the Sultan's emissaries had made a secret incursion with the object of kidnapping the Voivodin. They must have been bold of heart and strong of resource to enter the Land of the Blue Mountains on any errand, let alone such a desperate one as this. For centuries we have been teaching the Turk through bitter lessons that it is neither a safe task nor an easy one to make incursion here.

How they did it we know not—at present; but enter they did, and, after waiting in some secret hiding-place for a favourable opportunity, secured their prey. We know not even now whether they had found entrance to the Crypt and stole, as they thought, the dead body, or whether, by some dire mischance, they found her abroad— under her disguise as a ghost. At any rate, they had captured her, and through devious ways amongst the mountains were bearing her back to Turkey. It was manifest that when she was on Turkish soil the Sultan would force a marriage on her so as eventually to secure for himself or his successors as against all other nations a claim for the suzerainty or guardianship of the Blue Mountains.

Such was the state of affairs when the Gospodar Rupert threw himself into the pursuit with fiery zeal and the Berserk passion which he inherited from Viking ancestors, whence of old came "The Sword of Freedom" himself.

But at that very time was another possibility which the Gospodar was himself the first to realize. Failing the getting the Voivodin safe to Turkish soil, the ravishers might kill her! This would be entirely in accord with the base traditions and history of the Moslems. So, too, it would accord with Turkish customs and the Sultan's present desires. It would, in its way, benefit the ultimate strategetic ends of Turkey. For were once the Vissarion race at an end, the subjection of the Land of the Blue Mountains might, in their view, be an easier task than it had yet been found to be.

Such, illustrious lady, were the conditions of affairs when the Gospodar Rupert first drew his handjar for the Blue Mountains and what it held most dear.

PALEALOGUE,

Archbishop of the Eastern Church, in the Land of the Blue Mountains.
RUPERT'S JOURNAL—*Continued.*

July 8, 1907.

I wonder if ever in the long, strange history of the world had there come to any other such glad tidings as came to me—and even then rather inferentially than directly—from the Archimandrite's answers to my questioning. Happily I was able to restrain myself, or I should have created some strange confusion which might have evoked distrust, and would certainly have hampered us in our pursuit. For a little I could hardly accept the truth which wove itself through my brain as the true inwardness of each fact came home to me and took its place in the whole fabric. But even the most welcome truth has to be accepted some time by even a doubting heart. My heart, whatever it may have been, was not then a doubting heart, but a very, very grateful one. It was only the splendid magnitude of the truth which forbade its immediate acceptance. I could have shouted for joy, and only stilled myself by keeping my thoughts fixed on the danger which my wife was in. My wife! My wife! Not a Vampire; not a poor harassed creature doomed to terrible woe, but a splendid woman, brave beyond belief, patriotic in a way which has but few peers even in the wide history of bravery! I began to understand the true meaning of the strange occurrences that have come into my life. Even the origin and purpose of that first strange visit to my room became clear. No wonder that the girl could move about the Castle in so mysterious a manner. She had lived there all her life, and was familiar with the secret ways of entrance and exit. I had always believed that the place must have been honeycombed with secret passages. No wonder that she could find a way to the battlements, mysterious to everybody else. No wonder that she could meet me at the Flagstaff when she so desired.

To say that I was in a tumult would be to but faintly express my condition. I was rapt into a heaven of delight which had no measure in all my adventurous life—the lifting of the veil which showed that my wife—mine—won in all sincerity in the very teeth of appalling difficulties and dangers—was no Vampire, no corpse, no ghost or phantom, but a real woman of flesh and blood, of affection, and love, and passion. Now at last would my love be crowned indeed when, having rescued her from the marauders, I should bear her to my own home, where she would live and reign in peace and comfort and honour, and in love and wifely happiness if I could achieve such a blessing for her— and for myself.

But here a dreadful thought flashed across me, which in an instant turned my joy to despair, my throbbing heart to ice:

"As she is a real woman, she is in greater danger than ever in the hands of Turkish ruffians. To them a woman is in any case no more than a sheep; and if they cannot bring her to the harem of the Sultan, they may deem it the next wisest step to kill her. In that way, too, they might find a better chance of escape. Once rid of her the party could separate, and there might be a chance of some of them finding escape as individuals that would not exist for a party. But even if they did not kill her, to escape with her would be to condemn her to the worst fate of all the harem of the Turk! Lifelong misery and despair—however long that life might be—must be the lot of a Christian woman doomed to such a lot. And to her, just happily wedded, and after she had served her country in such a noble way as she had done, that dreadful life of shameful slavery would be a misery beyond belief.

"She must be rescued—and quickly! The marauders must be caught soon, and suddenly, so that they may have neither time nor opportunity to harm her, as they would be certain to do if they have warning of immediate danger.

"On! on!"

And "on" it was all through that terrible night as well as we could through the forest.

It was a race between the mountaineers and myself as to who should be first. I understood now the feeling that animated them, and which singled them out even from amongst their fiery comrades, when the danger of the Voivodin became known. These men were no mean contestants even in such a race, and, strong as I am, it took my utmost effort to keep ahead of them. They were keen as leopards, and as swift. Their lives had been spent among the mountains, and their hearts and souls on were in the chase. I doubt not that if the death of any one of us could have through any means effected my wife's release, we should, if necessary, have fought amongst ourselves for the honour.

From the nature of the work before us our party had to keep to the top of the hills. We had not only to keep observation on the flying party whom we followed, and to prevent them making discovery of us, but we had to be always in a position to receive and answer signals made to us from the Castle, or sent to us from other eminences.

Letter from Petrof Vlastimir, Archimandrite of Spazac, to the Lady Janet MacKelpie, of Vissarion.

Written July 8, 1907.

GREAT LADY,

I am asked to write by the Vladika, and have permission of the Archbishop. I have the honour of transmitting to you the record of the pursuit of the Turkish spies who carried off the Voivodin Teuta, of the noble House of Vissarion. The pursuit was undertaken by the Gospodar Rupert, who asked that I would come with his party, since what he was so good as to call my "great knowledge of the country and its people" might serve much. It is true that I have had much knowledge of the Land of the Blue Mountains and its people, amongst which and whom my whole life has been passed. But in such a cause no reason was required. There was not a man in the Blue Mountains who would not have given his life for the Voivodin Teuta, and when they heard that she had not been dead, as they thought, but only in a trance, and that it was she whom the marauders had carried off, they were in a frenzy. So why should I—to whom has been given the great trust of the Monastery of Spazac—hesitate at such a time? For myself, I wanted to hurry on, and to come at once to the fight with my country's foes; and well I knew that the Gospodar Rupert, with a lion's heart meet for his giant body, would press on with a matchless speed. We of the Blue Mountains do not lag when our foes are in front of us; most of all do we of the Eastern Church press on when the Crescent wars against the Cross!

We took with us no gear or hamper of any kind; no coverings except what we stood in; no food—nothing but our handjars and our rifles, with a sufficiency of ammunition. Before starting, the Gospodar gave hurried orders by signal from the Castle to have food and ammunition sent to us (as we might signal) by the nearest hamlet.

It was high noon when we started, only ten strong—for our leader would take none but approved runners who could shoot straight and use the handjar as it should be used. So as we went light, we expected to go fast. By this time we knew from the reports signalled to Vissarion that the enemies were chosen men of no despicable prowess.

The Keeper of the Green Flag of Islam is well served, and as though the Turk is an infidel and a dog, he is sometimes brave and strong. Indeed, except when he passes the confines of the Blue Mountains, he has been known to do stirring deeds. But as none who have dared to wander in amongst our hills ever return to their own land, we may not know of how they speak at home of their battles here. Still, these men were evidently not to be despised; and our Gospodar, who is a wise man as well as a valiant, warned us to be prudent, and not to despise our foes over much. We did as he counselled, and in proof we only took ten men, as we had only twenty against us. But then there was at stake much beyond life, and we took no risks. So, as the great clock at Vissarion clanged of noon, the eight fastest runners of the Blue Mountains, together with the Gospodar Rupert and myself, swept out on our journey. It had been signalled to us that the course which the marauders had as yet taken in their flight was a zigzag one, running eccentrically at all sorts of angles in all sorts of directions. But our leader had marked out a course where we might intercept our foes across the main line of their flight; and till we had reached that region we paused not a second, but went as fast as we could all night long. Indeed, it was amongst us a race as was the Olympic race of old Greece, each one vying with his fellows, though not in jealous emulation, but in high spirit, to best serve his country and the Voivodin Teuta. Foremost amongst us went the Gospodar, bearing himself as a Paladin of old, his mighty form pausing for no obstacle. Perpetually did he urge us on. He would not stop or pause for a moment, but often as he and I ran together—for, lady, in my youth I was the fleetest of all in the race, and even that now can head a battalion when duty calls—he would ask me certain questions as to the Lady Teuta and of the strange manner of her reputed death, as it was gradually unfolded in my answers to his questioning. And as each new phase of knowledge came to him, he would rush on as one possessed of fiends: whereat our mountaineers, who seem to respect even fiends for their thoroughness, would strive to keep pace with him till they too seemed worked into diabolic possession. And I myself, left alone in the calmness of sacerdotal office, forgot even that. With surging ears and eyes that saw blood, I rushed along with best of them.

Then truly the spirit of a great captain showed itself in the Gospodar, for when others were charged with fury he began to force himself into calm, so that out of his present self-command and the memory of his exalted position came a worthy strategy and thought for every contingency that might arise. So that when some new direction was required for our guidance, there was no hesitation in its coming. We, nine men of varying kinds, all felt that we had a master; and so, being willing to limit ourselves to strict obedience, we were free to use such thoughts as well as such powers as we had to the best advantage of the doing.

We came across the trail of the flying marauders on the second morning after the abduction, a little before noon. It was easy enough to see, for by this time the miscreants were all together, and our people, who were woodlanders, were able to tell much of the party that passed. These were evidently in a terrified hurry, for they had taken no precautions such as are necessary baffle pursuit, and all of which take time. Our foresters said that two went ahead and two behind. In the centre went the mass, moving close together, as though surrounding their prisoner. We caught not even a single glimpse her—could not have, they encompassed her so closely. But our foresters saw other than the mass; the ground that had been passed was before them. They knew that the prisoner had gone unwillingly—nay, more: one of them said as he rose from his knees, where he had been examining of the ground:

"The misbegotten dogs have been urging her on with their yataghans! There are drops of blood, though there are no blood-marks on her feet."

Whereupon the Gospodar flamed with passion. His teeth ground together, and with a deep-breathed "On, on!" he sprang off again, handjar in hand, on the track.

Before long we saw the party in the distance. They this were far below us in a deep valley, although the track of their going passed away to the right hand. They were making for the base of the great cliff, which rose before us all. Their reason was twofold, as we soon knew. Far off down the valley which they were crossing we saw signs of persons coming in haste, who must be of the search party coming from the north. Though the trees hid them, we could not mistake the signs. I was myself forester enough to have no doubt. Again, it was evident that the young Voivodin could travel no longer at the dreadful pace at which they had been going. Those blood-marks told their own tale! They meant to make a last stand here in case they should be discovered.

Then it was that he, who amongst us all had been most fierce and most bent on rapid pursuit, became the most calm. Raising his hand for silence—though, God knows, we were and had been silent enough during that long rush through the forest—he said, in a low, keen whisper which cut the silence like a knife:

"My friends, the time is come for action. God be thanked, who has now brought us face to face with our foes! But we must be careful here—not on our own account, for we wish nothing more than to rush on and conquer or die—but for the sake of her whom you love, and whom I, too, love. She is in danger from anything which may give warning to those fiends. If they know or even suspect for an instant that we are near, they will murder her . . . "

Here his voice broke for an instant with the extremity of his passion or the depth of his feeling—I hardly know which; I think both acted on him.

"We know from those blood-marks what they can do—even to her." His teeth ground together again, but he went on without stopping further:

"Let us arrange the battle. Though we are but little distance from them as the crow flies, the way is far to travel. There is, I can see, but one path down to the valley from this side. That they have gone by, and that they will sure to guard—to watch, at any rate. Let us divide, as to surround them. The cliff towards which they make runs far to the left without a break. That to the right we cannot see from this spot; but from the nature of the ground it is not unlikely that it turns round in this direction, making the hither end of the valley like a vast pocket or amphitheatre. As they have studied the ground in other places, they may have done so in this, and have come hither as to a known refuge. Let one man, a marksman, stay here."

As he spoke a man stepped to the front. He was, I knew, an excellent shot.

"Let two others go to the left and try to find a way down the cliff before us. When they have descended to the level of the valley— path or no path—let them advance cautiously and secretly, keeping their guns in readiness. But they must not fire till need. Remember, my brothers," he said, turning to those who stepped out a pace or two to the left, "that the first shot gives the warning which will be the signal for the Voivodin's death. These men will not hesitate. You must judge yourselves of the time to shoot. The others of us will move to the right and try to find a path on that side. If the valley be indeed a pocket between the cliffs, we must find a way down that is not a path!"

As he spoke thus there was a blaze in his eyes that betokened no good to aught that might stand in his way. I ran by his side as we moved to the right.

It was as he surmised about the cliff. When we got a little on our way we saw how the rocky formation trended to our right, till, finally, with a wide curve, it came round to the other side.

It was a fearful valley that, with its narrow girth and its towering walls that seemed to topple over. On the farther side from us the great trees that clothed the slope of the mountain over it grew down to the very edge of the rock, so that their spreading branches hung far over the chasm. And, so far as we could understand, the same condition existed on our own side. Below us the valley was dark even in the daylight. We could best tell the movement of the flying marauders by the flashes of the white shroud of their captive in the midst of them.

From where we were grouped, amid the great tree-trunks on the very brow of the cliff, we could, when our eyes were accustomed to the shadow, see them quite well. In great haste, and half dragging, half carrying the Voivodin, they crossed the open space and took refuge in a little grassy alcove surrounded, save for its tortuous entrance, by undergrowth. From the valley level it was manifestly impossible to see them, though we from our altitude could see over the stunted undergrowth. When within the glade, they took their hands from her. She, shuddering instinctively, withdrew to a remote corner of the dell.

And then, oh, shame on their manhood!—Turks and heathens though they were—we could see that they had submitted her to the indignity of gagging her and binding her hands!

Our Voivodin Teuta bound! To one and all of us it was like lashing us across the face. I heard the Gospodar's teeth grind again. But once more he schooled himself to calmness ere he said:

"It is, perhaps, as well, great though the indignity be. They are seeking their own doom, which is coming quickly . . . Moreover, they are thwarting their own base plans. Now that she is bound they will trust to their binding, so that they will delay their murderous alternative to the very last moment. Such is our chance of rescuing her alive!"

For a few moments he stood as still as a stone, as though revolving something in his mind whilst he watched. I could see that some grim resolution was forming in his mind, for his eyes ranged to the top of the trees above cliff, and down again, very slowly this time, as though measuring and studying the detail of what was in front of him. Then he spoke:

"They are in hopes that the other pursuing party may not come across them. To know that, they are waiting. If those others do not come up the valley, they will proceed on their way. They will return up the path the way they came. There we can wait them, charge into the middle of them when she is opposite, and cut down those around her. Then the others will open fire, and we shall be rid of them!

Whilst he was speaking, two of the men of our party, who I knew to be good sharpshooters, and who had just before lain on their faces and had steadied their rifles to shoot, rose to their feet.

"Command us, Gospodar!" they said simply, as they stood to attention. "Shall we go to the head of the ravine road and there take hiding?" He thought for perhaps a minute, whilst we all stood as silent as images. I could hear our hearts beating. Then he said:

"No, not yet. There is time for that yet. They will not—cannot stir or make plans in any way till they know whether the other party is coming towards them or not. From our height here we can see what course the others are taking long before those villains do. Then we can make our plans and be ready in time.

We waited many minutes, but could see no further signs the other pursuing party. These had evidently adopted greater caution in their movements as they came closer to where they expected to find the enemy. The marauders began to grow anxious. Even at our distance we could gather as much from their attitude and movements.

Presently, when the suspense of their ignorance grew too much for them, they drew to the entrance of the glade, which was the farthest place to which, without exposing themselves to anyone who might come to the valley, they could withdraw from their captive. Here they consulted together. We could follow from their gestures what they were saying, for as they did not wish their prisoner to hear, their gesticulation was enlightening to us as to each other. Our people, like all mountaineers, have good eyes, and the Gospodar is himself an eagle in this as in other ways. Three men stood back from the rest. They stacked their rifles so that they could seize them easily. Then they drew their scimitars, and stood ready, as though on guard.

These were evidently the appointed murderers. Well they knew their work; for though they stood in a desert place with none within long distance except the pursuing party, of whose approach they would have good notice, they stood so close to their prisoner that no marksman in the world—now or that ever had been; not William Tell himself—could have harmed any of them without at least endangering her. Two of them turned the Voivodin round so that her face was towards the precipice—in which position she could not see what was going on—whilst he who was evidently leader of the gang explained, in gesture, that the others were going to spy upon the pursuing party. When they had located them he, or one of his men, would come out of the opening of the wood wherein they had had evidence of them, and hold up his hand.

That was to be the signal for the cutting of the victim's throat—such being the chosen method (villainous even for heathen murderers) of her death. There was not one of our men who did not grind his teeth when we witnessed the grim action, only too expressive, of the Turk as he drew his right hand, clenched as though he held a yataghan in it, across his throat.

At the opening of the glade all the spying party halted whilst the leader appointed to each his place of entry of the wood, the front of which extended in an almost straight across the valley from cliff to cliff.

The men, stooping low when in the open, and taking instant advantage of every little obstacle on the ground, seemed to fade like spectres with incredible swiftness across the level mead, and were swallowed up in the wood.

When they had disappeared the Gospodar Rupert revealed to us the details of the plan of action which he had revolving in his mind. He motioned us to follow him: we threaded a way between the tree-trunks, keeping all the while on the very edge of the cliff, so that the space below was all visible to us. When we had got round the curve sufficiently to see the whole of the wood on the valley level, without losing sight of the Voivodin and her appointed assassins, we halted under his direction. There was an added advantage of this point over the other, for we could see directly the rising of the hill-road, up which farther side ran the continuation of the mountain path which the marauders had followed. It was somewhere on that path that the other pursuing party had hoped to intercept the fugitives. The Gospodar spoke quickly, though in a voice of command which true soldiers love to hear:

"Brothers, the time has come when we can strike a blow for Teuta and the Land. Do you two, marksmen, take position here facing the wood." The two men here lay down and got their rifles ready. "Divide the frontage of the wood between you; arrange between yourselves the limits of your positions. The very instant one of the marauders appears, cover him; drop him before he emerges from the wood. Even then still watch and treat similarly whoever else may take his place. Do this if they come singly till not a man is left. Remember, brothers, that brave hearts alone will not suffice at this grim crisis. In this hour the best safety of the Voivodin is in the calm spirit and the steady eye!" Then he turned to the rest of us, and spoke to me:

"Archimandrite of Plazac, you who are interpreter to God of the prayers of so many souls, my own hour has come. If I do not return, convey my love to my Aunt Janet—Miss MacKelpie, at Vissarion. There is but one thing left to us if we wish to save the Voivodin. Do you, when the time comes, take these men and join the watcher at the top of the ravine road. When the shots are fired, do you out handjar, and rush the ravine and across the valley. Brothers, you may be in time to avenge the Voivodin, if you cannot save her. For me there must be a quicker way, and to it I go. As there is not, and will not be, time to traverse the path, I must take a quicker way. Nature finds me a path that man has made it necessary for me to travel. See that giant beech-tree that towers above the glade where the Voivodin is held? There is my path! When you from here have marked the return of the spies, give me a signal with your hat—do not use a handkerchief, as others might see its white, and take warning. Then rush that ravine. I shall take that as the signal for my descent by the leafy road. If I can do naught else, I can crush the murderers with my falling weight, even if I have to kill

her too. At least we shall die together—and free. Lay us together in the
tomb at St. Sava's. Farewell, if it be the last!"

He threw down the scabbard in which he carried his handjar,
adjusted the naked weapon in his belt behind his back, and was
gone!

We who were not watching the wood kept our eyes fixed on
the great beech-tree, and with new interest noticed the long trailing
branches which hung low, and swayed even in the gentle breeze. For
a few minutes, which seemed amazingly long, we saw no sign of him.
Then, high up on one of the great branches which stood clear of obscuring leaves, we saw something crawling flat against the bark. He
was well out on the branch, hanging far over the precipice. He was
looking over at us, and I waved my hand so that he should know we
saw him. He was clad in green—his usual forest dress—so that there
was not any likelihood of any other eyes noticing him. I took off my
hat, and held it ready to signal with when the time should come. I
glanced down at the glade and saw the Voivodin standing, still safe,
with her guards so close to her as to touch. Then I, too, fixed my eyes
on the wood.

Suddenly the man standing beside me seized my arm and pointed.
I could just see through the trees, which were lower than elsewhere in
the front of the wood, a Turk moving stealthily; so I waved my hat. At
the same time a rifle underneath me cracked. A second or two later the
spy pitched forward on his face and lay still. At the same instant my
eyes sought the beech-tree, and I saw the close-lying figure raise itself
and slide forward to a joint of the branch. Then the Gospodar, as he
rose, hurled himself forward amid the mass of the trailing branches. He
dropped like a stone, and my heart sank.

But an instant later he seemed in poise. He had clutched the thin,
trailing branches as he fell; and as he sank a number of leaves which his
motion had torn off floated out round him.

Again the rifle below me cracked, and then again, and again, and again. The marauders had taken warning, and were coming out in mass. But my own eyes were fixed on the tree. Almost as a thunderbolt falls fell the giant body of the Gospodar, his size lost in the immensity of his surroundings. He fell in a series of jerks, as he kept clutching the trailing beech-branches whilst they lasted, and then other lesser verdure growing out from the fissures in the rock after the lengthening branches had with all their elasticity reached their last point.

At length—for though this all took place in a very few seconds the gravity of the crisis prolonged them immeasurably—there came a large space of rock some three times his own length. He did not pause, but swung himself to one side, so that he should fall close to the Voivodin and her guards. These men did not seem to notice, for their attention was fixed on the wood whence they expected their messenger to signal. But they raised their yataghans in readiness. The shots had alarmed them; and they meant to do the murder now—messenger or no messenger.

But though the men did not see the danger from above, the Voivodin did. She raised her eyes quickly at the first sound, and even from where we were, before we began to run towards the ravine path, I could see the triumphant look in her glorious eyes when she recognized the identity of the man who was seemingly coming straight down from Heaven itself to help her—as, indeed, she, and we too, can very well imagine that he did; for if ever heaven had a hand in a rescue on earth, it was now.

Even during the last drop from the rocky foliage the Gospodar kept his head. As he fell he pulled his handjar free, and almost as he was falling its sweep took off the head of one of the assassins. As he touched ground he stumbled for an instant, but it was towards his enemies.

Twice with lightning rapidity the handjar swept the air, and at each sweep a head rolled on the sward.

The Voivodin held up her tied hands. Again the handjar flashed, this time downwards, and the lady was free. Without an instant's pause the Gospodar tore off the gag, and with his left arm round her and handjar in right hand, stood face toward his living foes. The Voivodin stooped suddenly, and then, raising the yataghan which had fallen from the hand of one of the dead marauders, stood armed beside him.

The rifles were now cracking fast, as the marauders—those that were left of them—came rushing out into the open. But well the marksmen knew their work. Well they bore in mind the Gospodar's command regarding calmness. They kept picking off the foremost men only, so that the onward rush never seemed to get more forward.

As we rushed down the ravine we could see clearly all before us. But now, just as we were beginning to fear lest some mischance might allow some of them to reach the glade, there was another cause of surprise—of rejoicing.

From the face of the wood seemed to burst all at once a body of men, all wearing the national cap, so we knew them as our own. They were all armed with the handjar only, and they came like tigers. They swept on the rushing Turks as though, for all their swiftness, they were standing still—literally wiping them out as a child wipes a lesson from its slate.

A few seconds later these were followed by a tall figure with long hair and beard of black mingled with grey. Instinctively we all, as did those in the valley, shouted with joy. For this was the Vladika Milosh Plamenac himself.

I confess that, knowing what I knew, I was for a short space of time anxious lest, in the terrific excitement in which we were all lapped, someone might say or do something which might make for trouble later on. The Gospodar's splendid achievement, which was worthy of any hero of old romance, had set us all on fire. He himself must have been wrought to a high pitch of excitement to dare such an act; and it is not at such a time that discretion must be expected from any man. Most of all did I fear danger from the womanhood of the Voivodin. Had I not assisted at her marriage, I might not have understood then what it must have been to her to be saved from such a doom at such a time by such a man, who was so much to her, and in such a way. It would have been only natural if at such a moment of gratitude and triumph she had proclaimed the secret which we of the Council of the Nation and her father's Commissioners had so religiously kept. But none of us knew then either the Voivodin or the Gospodar Rupert as we do now. It was well that they were as they are, for the jealousy and suspicion of our mountaineers might, even at such a moment, and even whilst they throbbed at such a deed, have so manifested themselves as to have left a legacy of distrust. The Vladika and I, who of all (save the two immediately concerned) alone knew, looked at each other apprehensively. But at that instant the Voivodin, with a swift glance at her husband, laid a finger on her lip; and he, with quick understanding, gave assurance by a similar sign. Then she sank before him on one knee, and, raising his hand to her lips, kissed it, and spoke:

"Gospodar Rupert, I owe you all that a woman may owe, except to God. You have given me life and honour! I cannot thank you adequately for what you have done; my father will try to do so when he returns. But I am right sure that the men of the Blue Mountains, who so value honour, and freedom, and liberty, and bravery, will hold you in their hearts for ever!"

This was so sweetly spoken, with lips that trembled and eyes that swam in tears, so truly womanly and so in accord with the custom of our nation regarding the reverence that women owe to men, that the hearts of our mountaineers were touched to the quick. Their noble simplicity found expression in tears. But if the gallant Gospodar could have for a moment thought that so to weep was unmanly, his error would have had instant correction. When the Voivodin had risen to her feet, which she did with queenly dignity, the men around closed in on the Gospodar like a wave of the sea, and in a second held him above their heads, tossing on their lifted hands as if on stormy breakers. It was as though the old Vikings of whom we have heard, and whose blood flows in Rupert's veins, were choosing a chief in old fashion. I was myself glad that the men were so taken up with the Gospodar that they did not see the glory of the moment in the Voivodin's starry eyes; for else they might have guessed the secret. I knew from the Vladika's look that he shared my own satisfaction, even as he had shared my anxiety.

As the Gospodar Rupert was tossed high on the lifted hands of the mountaineers, their shouts rose to such a sudden volume that around us, as far as I could see, the frightened birds rose from the forest, and their noisy alarm swelled the tumult.

The Gospodar, ever thoughtful for others, was the first to calm himself.

"Come, brothers," he said, "let us gain the hilltop, where we can signal to the Castle. It is right that the whole nation should share in the glad tidings that the Voivodin Teuta of Vissarion is free. But before we go, let us remove the arms and clothing of these carrion marauders. We may have use for them later on."

The mountaineers set him down, gently enough. And he, taking the Voivodin by the hand, and calling the Vladika and myself close to them, led the way up the ravine path which the marauders had descended, and thence through the forest to the top of the hill that dominated the valley. Here we could, from an opening amongst the trees, catch a glimpse far off of the battlements of Vissarion. Forthwith the Gospodar signalled; and on the moment a reply of their awaiting was given. Then the Gospodar signalled the glad news. It was received with manifest rejoicing. We could not hear any sound so far away, but we could see the movement of lifted faces and waving hands, and knew that it was well. But an instant after came a calm so dread that we knew before the semaphore had begun to work that there was bad news in store for us. When the news did come, a bitter wailing arose amongst us; for the news that was signalled ran:

"The Voivode has been captured by the Turks on his return, and is held by them at Ilsin."

In an instant the temper of the mountaineers changed. It was as though by a flash summer had changed to winter, as though the yellow glory of the standing corn had been obliterated by the dreary waste of snow. Nay, more: it was as when one beholds the track of the whirlwind when the giants of the forest are levelled with the sward. For a few seconds there was silence; and then, with an angry roar, as when God speaks in the thunder, came the fierce determination of the men of the Blue Mountains:

"To Ilsin! To Ilsin!" and a stampede in the direction of the south began. For, Illustrious Lady, you, perhaps, who have been for so short a time at Vissarion, may not know that at the extreme southern point of the Land of the Blue Mountains lies the little port of Ilsin, which long ago we wrested from the Turk.

The stampede was checked by the command, "Halt!" spoken in a thunderous voice by the Gospodar. Instinctively all stopped. The Gospodar Rupert spoke again:

"Had we not better know a little more before we start on our journey? I shall get by semaphore what details are known. Do you all proceed in silence and as swiftly as possible. The Vladika and I will wait here till we have received the news and have sent some instructions, when we shall follow, and, if we can, overtake you. One thing: be absolutely silent on what has been. Be secret of every detail—even as to the rescue of the Voivodin—except what I send."

Without a word—thus showing immeasurable trust—the whole body—not a very large one, it is true—moved on, and the Gospodar began signalling. As I was myself expert in the code, I did not require any explanation, but followed question and answer on either side. The first words the Gospodar Rupert signalled were:

"Silence, absolute and profound, as to everything which has been." Then he asked for details of the capture of the Voivode. The answer ran:

"He was followed from Flushing, and his enemies advised by the spies all along the route. At Ragusa quite a number of strangers—travellers seemingly—went on board the packet. When he got out, the strangers debarked too, and evidently followed him, though, as yet, we have no details. He disappeared at Ilsin from the Hotel Reo, whither he had gone. All possible steps are being taken to trace his movements, and strictest silence and secrecy are observed."

His answer was:

"Good! Keep silent and secret. Am hurrying back. Signal request to Archbishop and all members of National Council to come to Gadaar with all speed. There the yacht will meet him. Tell Rooke take yacht all speed to Gadaar; there meet Archbishop and Council—give him list of names—and return full speed. Have ready plenty arms, six flying artillery. Two hundred men, provisions three days. Silence, silence. All depends on that. All to go on as usual at Castle, except to those in secret."

When the receipt of his message had been signalled, we three—for, of course, the Voivodin was with us; she had refused to leave the Gospodar—set out hot-foot after our comrades. But by the time we had descended the hill it was evident that the Voivodin could not keep up the terrific pace at which we were going. She struggled heroically, but the long journey she had already taken, and the hardship and anxiety she had suffered, had told on her. The Gospodar stopped, and said that it would be better that he should press on—it was, perhaps, her father's life—and said he would carry her.

"No, no!" she answered. "Go on! I shall follow with the Vladika. And then you can have things ready to get on soon after the Archbishop and Council arrive." They kissed each other after, on her part, a shy glance at me; and he went on the track of our comrades at a great pace. I could see him shortly after catch them up,—though they, too, were going fast. For a few minutes they ran together, he speaking—I could note it from the way they kept turning their heads towards him. Then he broke away from them hurriedly. He went like a stag breaking covert, and was soon out of sight. They halted a moment or two. Then some few ran on, and all the rest came back towards us. Quickly they improvised a litter with cords and branches, and insisted that the Voivodin should use it. In an incredibly short time we were under way again, and proceeding with great rapidity towards Vissarion. The men took it in turns to help with the litter; I had the honour of taking a hand in the work myself.

About a third of the way out from Vissarion a number of our people met us. They were fresh, and as they carried the litter, we who were relieved were free for speed. So we soon arrived at the Castle.

Here we found all humming like a hive of bees. The yacht, which Captain Rooke had kept fired ever since the pursuing party under the Gospodar had left Vissarion, was already away, and tearing up the coast at a fearful rate. The rifles and ammunition were stacked on the quay. The field-guns, too, were equipped, and the cases of ammunition ready to ship. The men, two hundred of them, were paraded in full kit, ready to start at a moment's notice. The provision for three days was all ready to put aboard, and barrels of fresh water to trundle aboard when the yacht should return. At one end of the quay, ready to lift on board, stood also the Gospodar's aeroplane, fully equipped, and ready, if need were, for immediate flight.

I was glad to see that the Voivodin seemed none the worse for her terrible experience. She still wore her shroud; but no one seemed to notice it as anything strange. The whisper had evidently gone round of what had been. But discretion ruled the day. She and the Gospodar met as two who had served and suffered in common; but I was glad to notice that both kept themselves under such control that none of those not already in the secret even suspected that there was any love between them, let alone marriage.

We all waited with what patience we could till word was signalled from the Castle tower that the yacht had appeared over the northern horizon, and was coming down fast, keeping inshore as she came.

When she arrived, we heard to our joy that all concerned had done their work well. The Archbishop was aboard, and of the National Council not one was missing. The Gospodar hurried them all into the great hall of the Castle, which had in the meantime been got ready. I, too, went with him, but the Voivodin remained without.

When all were seated, he rose and said:

"My Lord Archbishop, Vladika, and Lords of the Council all, I have dared to summon you in this way because time presses, and the life of one you all love—the Voivode Vissarion—is at stake. This audacious attempt of the Turk is the old aggression under a new form. It is a new and more daring step than ever to try to capture your chief and his daughter, the Voivodin, whom you love. Happily, the latter part of the scheme is frustrated. The Voivodin is safe and amongst us. But the Voivode is held prisoner—if, indeed, he be still alive. He must be somewhere near Ilsin—but where exactly we know not as yet. We have an expedition ready to start the moment we receive your sanction—your commands. We shall obey your wishes with our lives. But as the matter is instant, I would venture to ask one question, and one only: 'Shall we rescue the Voivode at any cost that may present itself?' I ask this, for the matter has now become an international one, and, if our enemies are as earnest as we are, the issue is war!

Having so spoken, and with a dignity and force which is inexpressible, he withdrew; and the Council, having appointed a scribe—the monk Cristoferos, whom I had suggested—began its work.

The Archbishop spoke:

"Lords of the Council of the Blue Mountains, I venture to ask you that the answer to the Gospodar Rupert be an instant 'Yes!' together with thanks and honour to that gallant Englisher, who has made our cause his own, and who has so valiantly rescued our beloved Voivodin from the ruthless hands of our enemies." Forthwith the oldest member of the Council—Nicolos of Volok—rose, and, after throwing a searching look round the faces of all, and seeing grave nods of assent—for not a word was spoken—said to him who held the door: "Summon the Gospodar Rupert forthwith!" When Rupert entered, he spoke to him:

"Gospodar Rupert, the Council of the Blue Mountains has only one answer to give: Proceed! Rescue the Voivode Vissarion, whatever the cost may be! You hold henceforth in your hand the handjar of our nation, as already, for what you have done in your valiant rescue of our beloved Voivodin, your breast holds the heart of our people. Proceed at once! We give you, I fear, little time; but we know that such is your own wish. Later, we shall issue formal authorization, so that if war may ensue, our allies may understand that you have acted for the nation, and also such letters credential as may be required by you in this exceptional service. These shall follow you within an hour. For our enemies we take no account. See, we draw the handjar that we offer you." As one man all in the hall drew their handjars, which flashed as a blaze of lightning.

There did not seem to be an instant's delay. The Council broke up, and its members, mingling with the people without, took active part in the preparations. Not many minutes had elapsed when the yacht, manned and armed and stored as arranged, was rushing out of the creek. On the bridge, beside Captain Rooke, stood the Gospodar Rupert and the still-shrouded form of the Voivodin Teuta. I myself was on the lower deck with the soldiers, explaining to certain of them the special duties which they might be called on to fulfil. I held the list which the Gospodar Rupert had prepared whilst we were waiting for the yacht to arrive from Gadaar.

PETROF VLASTIMIR.

FROM RUPERT'S JOURNAL—*Continued.*

July 9, 1907.

We went at a terrific pace down the coast, keeping well inshore so as to avoid, if possible, being seen from the south. Just north of Ilsin a rocky headland juts out, and that was our cover. On the north of the peninsula is a small land-locked bay, with deep water. It is large enough to take the yacht, though a much larger vessel could not safely enter. We ran in, and anchored close to the shore, which has a rocky frontage— a natural shelf of rock, which is practically the same as a quay. Here we met the men who had come from Ilsin and the neighbourhood in answer to our signalling earlier in the day. They gave us the latest information regarding the kidnapping of the Voivode, and informed us that every man in that section of the country was simply aflame about it. They assured us that we could rely on them, not merely to fight to the death, but to keep silence absolutely. Whilst the seamen, under the direction of Rooke, took the aeroplane on shore and found a suitable place for it, where it was hidden from casual view, but from which it could be easily launched, the Vladika and I—and, of course, my wife—were hearing such details as were known of the disappearance of her father.

It seems that he travelled secretly in order to avoid just such a possibility as has happened. No one knew of his coming till he came to Fiume, whence he sent a guarded message to the Archbishop, which the latter alone would understand. But this Turkish agents were evidently on his track all the time, and doubtless the Bureau of Spies was kept well advised. He landed at Ilsin from a coasting steamer from Ragusa to the Levant.

For two days before his coming there had been quite an unusual number of arrivals at the little port, at which arrivals are rare. And it turned out that the little hotel—the only fairly good one in Ilsin—was almost filled up. Indeed, only one room was left, which the Voivode took for the night. The innkeeper did not know the Voivode in his disguise, but suspected who it was from the description. He dined quietly, and went to bed. His room was at the back, on the ground-floor, looking out on the bank of the little River Silva, which here runs into the harbour. No disturbance was heard in the night. Late in the morning, when the elderly stranger had not made his appearance, inquiry was made at his door. He did not answer, so presently the landlord forced the door, and found the room empty. His luggage was seemingly intact, only the clothes which he had worn were gone. A strange thing was that, though the bed had been slept in and his clothes were gone, his night-clothes were not to be found, from which it was argued by the local authorities, when they came to make inquiry, that he had gone or been taken from the room in his night-gear, and that his clothes had been taken with him. There was evidently some grim suspicion on the part of the authorities, for they had commanded absolute silence on all in the house. When they came to make inquiry as to the other guests, it was found that one and all had gone in the course of the morning, after paying their bills. None of them had any heavy luggage, and there was nothing remaining by which they might be traced or which would afford any clue to their identity. The authorities, having sent a confidential report to the seat of government, continued their inquiries, and even now all available hands were at work on the investigation. When I had signalled to Vissarion, before my arrival there, word had been sent through the priesthood to enlist in the investigation the services of all good men, so that every foot of ground in that section of the Blue Mountains was being investigated.

The port-master was assured by his watchmen that no vessel, large or small, had heft the harbour during the night. The inference, therefore, was that the Voivode's captors had made inland with him—if, indeed, they were not already secreted in or near the town.

Whilst we were receiving the various reports, a hurried message came that it was now believed that the whole party were in the Silent Tower. This was a well-chosen place for such an enterprise. It was a massive tower of immense strength, built as a memorial—and also as a "keep"—after one of the massacres of the invading Turks.

It stood on the summit of a rocky knoll some ten miles inland from the Port of Ilsin. It was a place shunned as a rule, and the country all around it was so arid and desolate that there were no residents near it. As it was kept for state use, and might be serviceable in time of war, it was closed with massive iron doors, which were kept locked except upon certain occasions. The keys were at the seat of government at Plazac. If, therefore, it had been possible to the Turkish marauders to gain entrance and exit, it might be a difficult as well as a dangerous task to try to cut the Voivode out. His presence with them was a dangerous menace to any force attacking them, for they would hold his life as a threat.

I consulted with the Vladika at once as to what was best to be done. And we decided that, though we should put a cordon of guards around it at a safe distance to prevent them receiving warning, we should at present make no attack.

We made further inquiry as to whether there had been any vessel seen in the neighbourhood during the past few days, and were informed that once or twice a warship had been seen on the near side of the southern horizon. This was evidently the ship which Rooke had seen on his rush down the coast after the abduction of the Voivodin, and which he had identified as a Turkish vessel. The glimpses of her which had been had were all in full daylight—there was no proof that she had not stolen up during the night-time without lights. But the Vladika and I were satisfied that the Turkish vessel was watching—was in league with both parties of marauders—and was intended to take off any of the strangers, or their prey, who might reach Ilsin undetected. It was evidently with this view that the kidnappers of Teuta had, in the first instance, made with all speed for the south. It was only when disappointed there that they headed up north, seeking in desperation for some chance of crossing the border. That ring of steel had so far well served its purpose.

I sent for Rooke, and put the matter before him. He had thought it out for himself to the same end as we had. His deduction was:

"Let us keep the cordon, and watch for any signal from the Silent Tower. The Turks will tire before we shall. I undertake to watch the Turkish warship. During the night I shall run down south, without lights, and have a look at her, even if I have to wait till the grey of the dawn to do so. She may see us; but if she does I shall crawl away at such pace that she shall not get any idea of our speed. She will certainly come nearer before a day is over, for be sure the bureau of spies is kept advised, and they know that when the country is awake each day increases the hazard of them and their plans being discovered. From their caution I gather that they do not court discovery; and from that that they do not wish for an open declaration of war. If this be so, why should we not come out to them and force an issue if need be?"

When Teuta and I got a chance to be alone, we discussed the situation in every phase. The poor girl was in a dreadful state of anxiety regarding her father's safety. At first she was hardly able to speak, or even to think, coherently. Her utterance was choked, and her reasoning palsied with indignation. But presently the fighting blood of her race restored her faculties, and then her woman's quick wit was worth the reasoning of a camp full of men. Seeing that she was all on fire with the subject, I sat still and waited, taking care not to interrupt her. For quite a long time she sat still, whilst the coming night thickened. When she spoke, the whole plan of action, based on subtle thinking, had mapped itself out in her mind:

"We must act quickly. Every hour increases the risk to my father." Here her voice broke for an instant; but she recovered herself and went on:

"If you go to the ship, I must not go with you. It would not do for me to be seen. The Captain doubtless knows of both attempts: that to carry me off as well as that against my father. As yet he is in ignorance of what has happened. You and your party of brave, loyal men did their work so well that no news could go forth. So long, therefore, as the naval Captain is ignorant, he must delay till the last. But if he saw me he would know that *that* branch of the venture had miscarried. He would gather from our being here that we had news of my father's capture, and as he would know that the marauders would fail unless they were relieved by force, he would order the captive to be slain."

"Yes, dear, to-morrow you had, perhaps, better see the Captain, but to-night we must try to rescue my father. Here I think I see a way. You have your aeroplane. Please take me with you into the Silent Tower."

"Not for a world of chrysolite!" said I, horrified. She took my hand and held it tight whilst she went on:

"Dear, I know, I know! Be satisfied. But it is the only way. You can, I know, get there, and in the dark. But if you were to go in it, it would give warning to the enemies, and besides, my father would not understand. Remember, he does not know you; he has never seen you, and does not, I suppose, even know as yet of your existence. But he would know me at once, and in any dress. You can manage to lower me into the Tower by a rope from the aeroplane. The Turks as yet do not know of our pursuit, and doubtless rely, at all events in part, on the strength and security of the Tower. Therefore their guard will be less active than it would at first or later on. I shall post father in all details, and we shall be ready quickly. Now, dear, let us think out the scheme together. Let your man's wit and experience help my ignorance, and we shall save my father!"

How could I have resisted such pleading—even had it not seemed wise? But wise it was; and I, who knew what the aeroplane could do under my own guidance, saw at once the practicalities of the scheme. Of course there was a dreadful risk in case anything should go wrong. But we are at present living in a world of risks—and her father's life was at stake. So I took my dear wife in my arms, and told her that my mind was hers for this, as my soul and body already were. And I cheered her by saying that I thought it might be done.

I sent for Rooke, and told him of the new adventure, and he quite agreed with me in the wisdom of it. I then told him that he would have to go and interview the Captain of the Turkish warship in the morning, if I did not turn up. "I am going to see the Vladika," I said. "He will lead our own troops in the attack on the Silent Tower. But it will rest with you to deal with the warship. Ask the Captain to whom or what nation the ship belongs. He is sure to refuse to tell. In such case mention to him that if he flies no nation's flag, his vessel is a pirate ship, and that you, who are in command of the navy of the Blue Mountains, will deal with him as a pirate is dealt with—no quarter, no mercy. He will temporize, and perhaps try a bluff; but when things get serious with him he will land a force, or try to, and may even prepare to shell the town. He will threaten to, at any rate. In such case deal with him as you think best, or as near to it as you can." He answered:

"I shall carry out your wishes with my life. It is a righteous task. Not that anything of that sort would ever stand in my way. If he attacks our nation, either as a Turk or a pirate, I shall wipe him out. We shall see what our own little packet can do. Moreover, any of the marauders who have entered the Blue Mountains, from sea or otherwise, shall never get out by sea! I take it that we of my contingent shall cover the attacking party. It will be a sorry time for us all if that happens without our seeing you and the Voivodin; for in such case we shall understand the worst!" Iron as he was, the man trembled.

"That is so, Rooke," I said. "We are taking a desperate chance, we know. But the case is desperate! But we all have our duty to do, whatever happens. Ours and yours is stern; but when we have done it, the result will be that life will be easier for others—for those that are left."

Before he left, I asked him to send up to me three suits of the Masterman bullet-proof clothes of which we had a supply on the yacht.

"Two are for the Voivodin and myself," I said; "the third is for the Voivode to put on. The Voivodin will take it with her when she descends from the aeroplane into the Tower."

Whilst any daylight was left I went out to survey the ground. My wife wanted to come with me, but I would not let her. "No," said I; "you will have at the best a fearful tax on your strength and your nerves. You will want to be as fresh as is possible when you get on the aeroplane." Like a good wife, she obeyed, and lay down to rest in the little tent provided for her.

I took with me a local man who knew the ground, and who was trusted to be silent. We made a long detour when we had got as near the Silent Tower as we could without being noticed. I made notes from my compass as to directions, and took good notice of anything that could possibly serve as a landmark. By the time we got home I was pretty well satisfied that if all should go well I could easily sail over the Tower in the dark. Then I had a talk with my wife, and gave her full instructions:

"When we arrive over the Tower," I said, "I shall lower you with a long rope. You will have a parcel of food and spirit for your father in case he is fatigued or faint; and, of course, the bullet-proof suit, which he must put on at once. You will also have a short rope with a belt at either end—one for your father, the other for you. When I turn the aeroplane and come back again, you will have ready the ring which lies midway between the belts. This you will catch into the hook at the end of the lowered rope. When all is secure, and I have pulled you both up by the windlass so as to clear the top, I shall throw out ballast which we shall carry on purpose, and away we go! I am sorry it must be so uncomfortable for you both, but there is no other way. When we get well clear of the Tower, I shall take you both up on the platform. If necessary, I shall descend to do it—and then we shall steer for Ilsin."

"When all is safe, our men will attack the Tower. We must let them do it, for they expect it. A few men in the clothes and arms which we took from your captors will be pursued by some of ours. It is all arranged. They will ask the Turks to admit them, and if the latter have not learned of your father's escape, perhaps they will do so. Once in, our men will try to open the gate. The chances are against them, poor fellows! but they are all volunteers, and will die fighting. If they win out, great glory will be theirs."

"The moon does not rise to-night till just before midnight, so we have plenty of time. We shall start from here at ten. If all be well, I shall place you in the Tower with your father in less than a quarter-hour from that. A few minutes will suffice to clothe him in bullet-proof and get on his belt. I shall not be away from the Tower more than a very few minutes, and, please God, long before eleven we shall be safe. Then the Tower can be won in an attack by our mountaineers. Perhaps, when the guns are heard on the ship of war—for there is sure to be firing—the Captain may try to land a shore party. But Rooke will stand in the way, and if I know the man and *The Lady*, we shall not be troubled with many Turks to-night. By midnight you and your father can be on the way to Vissarion. I can interview the naval Captain in the morning."

My wife's marvellous courage and self-possession stood to her. At half an hour before the time fixed she was ready for our adventure. She had improved the scheme in one detail. She had put on her own belt and coiled the rope round her waist, so the only delay would be in bringing her father's belt. She would keep the bullet-proof dress intended to be his strapped in a packet on her back, so that if occasion should be favourable he would not want to put it on till he and she should have reached the platform of the aeroplane. In such case, I should not steer away from the Tower at all, but would pass slowly across it and take up the captive and his brave daughter before leaving. I had learned from local sources that the Tower was in several stories. Entrance was by the foot, where the great iron-clad door was; then came living-rooms and storage, and an open space at the top. This would probably be thought the best place for the prisoner, for it was deep-sunk within the massive walls, wherein was no loophole of any kind. This, if it should so happen, would be the disposition of things best for our plan. The guards would at this time be all inside the Tower—probably resting, most of them— so that it was possible that no one might notice the coming of the airship. I was afraid to think that all might turn out so well, for in such case our task would be a simple enough one, and would in all human probability be crowned with success.

At ten o'clock we started. Teuta did not show the smallest sign of fear or even uneasiness, though this was the first time she had even seen an aeroplane at work. She proved to be an admirable passenger for an airship. She stayed quite still, holding herself rigidly in the position arranged, by the cords which I had fixed for her.

When I had trued my course by the landmarks and with the compass lit by the Tiny my electric light in the dark box, I had time to look about me. All seemed quite dark wherever I looked—to land, or sea, or sky. But darkness is relative, and though each quarter and spot looked dark in turn, there was not such absolute darkness as a whole. I could tell the difference, for instance, between land and sea, no matter how far off we might be from either. Looking upward, the sky was dark; yet there was light enough to see, and even distinguish broad effects. I had no difficulty in distinguishing the Tower towards which we were moving, and that, after all, was the main thing. We drifted slowly, very slowly, as the air was still, and I only used the minimum pressure necessary for the engine. I think I now understood for the first time the extraordinary value of the engine with which my Kitson was equipped. It was noiseless, it was practically of no weight, and it allowed the machine to progress as easily as the old-fashioned balloon used to drift before a breeze. Teuta, who had naturally very fine sight, seemed to see even better than I did, for as we drew nearer to the Tower, and its round, open top began to articulate itself, she commenced to prepare for her part of the task. She it was who uncoiled the long drag-rope ready for her lowering. We were proceeding so gently that she as well as I had hopes that I might be able to actually balance the machine on the top of the curving wall—a thing manifestly impossible on a straight surface, though it might have been possible on an angle.

On we crept—on, and on! There was no sign of light about the Tower, and not the faintest sound to be heard till we were almost close to the line of the rising wall; then we heard a sound of something like mirth, but muffled by distance and thick walls. From it we took fresh heart, for it told us that our enemies were gathered in the lower chambers. If only the Voivode should be on the upper stage, all would be well.

Slowly, almost inch by inch, and with a suspense that was agonizing, we crossed some twenty or thirty feet above the top of the wall. I could see as we came near the jagged line of white patches where the heads of the massacred Turks placed there on spikes in old days seemed to give still their grim warning. Seeing that they made in themselves a difficulty of landing on the wall, I deflected the plane so that, as we crept over the wall, we might, if they became displaced, brush them to the outside of the wall. A few seconds more, and I was able to bring the machine to rest with the front of the platform jutting out beyond the Tower wall. Here I anchored her fore and aft with clamps which had been already prepared.

Whilst I was doing so Teuta had leaned over the inner edge of the platform, and whispered as softly as the sigh of a gentle breeze:

"Hist! hist!" The answer came in a similar sound from some twenty feet below us, and we knew that the prisoner was alone. Forthwith, having fixed the hook of the rope in the ring to which was attached her belt, I lowered my wife. Her father evidently knew her whisper, and was ready. The hollow Tower—a smooth cylinder within—sent up the voices from it faint as were the whispers:

"Father, it is I—Teuta!"

"My child, my brave daughter!"

"Quick, father; strap the belt round you. See that it is secure. We have to be lifted into the air if necessary. Hold together. It will be easier for Rupert to lift us to the airship."

"Rupert?"

"Yes; I shall explain later. Quick, quick! There is not a moment to lose. He is enormously strong, and can lift us together; but we must help him by being still, so he won't have to use the windlass, which might creak." As she spoke she jerked slightly at the rope, which was our preconcerted signal that I was to lift. I was afraid the windlass might creak, and her thoughtful hint decided me. I bent my back to the task, and in a few seconds they were on the platform on which they, at Teuta's suggestion, lay flat, one at each side of my seat, so as to keep the best balance possible.

I took off the clamps, lifted the bags of ballast to the top of the wall, so that there should be no sound of falling, and started the engine. The machine moved forward a few inches, so that it tilted towards the outside of the wall. I threw my weight on the front part of the platform, and we commenced our downward fall at a sharp angle. A second enlarged the angle, and without further ado we slid away into the darkness. Then, ascending as we went, when the engine began to work at its strength, we turned, and presently made straight for Ilsin.

The journey was short—not many minutes. It almost seemed as if no time whatever had elapsed till we saw below us the gleam of lights, and by them saw a great body of men gathered in military array. We slackened and descended. The crowd kept deathly silence, but when we were amongst them we needed no telling that it was not due to lack of heart or absence of joy. The pressure of their hands as they surrounded us, and the devotion with which they kissed the hands and feet of both the Voivode and his daughter, were evidence enough for me, even had I not had my own share of their grateful rejoicing.

In the midst of it all the low, stern voice of Rooke, who had burst a way to the front beside the Vladika, said:

"Now is the time to attack the Tower. Forward, brothers, but in silence. Let there not be a sound till you are near the gate; then play your little comedy of the escaping marauders. And 'twill be no comedy for them in the Tower. The yacht is all ready for the morning, Mr. Sent Leger, in case I do not come out of the scrimmage if the bluejackets arrive. In such case you will have to handle her yourself. God keep you, my Lady; and you, too, Voivode! Forward!"

In a ghostly silence the grim little army moved forwards. Rooke and the men with him disappeared into the darkness in the direction of the harbour of Ilsin.

FROM THE SCRIPT OF THE VOIVODE, PETER VISSARION,

July 7, 1907.

I had little idea, when I started on my homeward journey, that it would have such a strange termination. Even I, who ever since my boyhood have lived in a whirl of adventure, intrigue, or diplomacy—whichever it may be called—statecraft, and war, had reason to be surprised. I certainly thought that when I locked myself into my room in the hotel at Ilsin that I would have at last a spell, however short, of quiet. All the time of my prolonged negotiations with the various nationalities I had to be at tension; so, too, on my homeward journey, lest something at the last moment should happen adversely to my mission. But when I was safe on my own Land of the Blue Mountains, and laid my head on my pillow, where only friends could be around me, I thought I might forget care.

But to wake with a rude hand over my mouth, and to feel myself grasped tight by so many hands that I could not move a limb, was a dreadful shock. All after that was like a dreadful dream. I was rolled in a great rug so tightly that I could hardly breathe, let alone cry out. Lifted by many hands through the window, which I could hear was softly opened and shut for the purpose, and carried to a boat. Again lifted into some sort of litter, on which I was borne a long distance, but with considerable rapidity. Again lifted out and dragged through a doorway opened on purpose—I could hear the clang as it was shut behind me. Then the rug was removed, and I found myself, still in my night-gear, in the midst of a ring of men. There were two score of them, all Turks, all strong-looking, resolute men, armed to the teeth. My clothes, which had been taken from my room, were thrown down beside me, and I was told to dress. As the Turks were going from the room—shaped like a vault—where we then were, the last of them, who seemed to be some sort of officer, said:

"If you cry out or make any noise whatever whilst you are in this Tower, you shall die before your time!" Presently some food and water were brought me, and a couple of blankets. I wrapped myself up and slept till early in the morning. Breakfast was brought, and the same men filed in. In the presence of them all the same officer said:

"I have given instructions that if you make any noise or betray your presence to anyone outside this Tower, the nearest man is to restore you to immediate quiet with his yataghan. If you promise me that you will remain quiet whilst you are within the Tower, I can enlarge your liberties somewhat. Do you promise?" I promised as he wished; there was no need to make necessary any stricter measure of confinement. Any chance of escape lay in having the utmost freedom allowed to me. Although I had been taken away with such secrecy, I knew that before long there would be pursuit. So I waited with what patience I could. I was allowed to go on the upper platform—a consideration due, I am convinced, to my captors' wish for their own comfort rather than for mine.

It was not very cheering, for during the daytime I had satisfied myself that it would be quite impossible for even a younger and more active man than I am to climb the walls. They were built for prison purposes, and a cat could not find entry for its claws between the stones. I resigned myself to my fate as well as I could. Wrapping my blanket round me, I lay down and looked up at the sky. I wished to see it whilst I could. I was just dropping to sleep—the unutterable silence of the place broken only now and again by some remark by my captors in the rooms below me—when there was a strange appearance just over me—an appearance so strange that I sat up, and gazed with distended eyes.

Across the top of the tower, some height above, drifted, slowly and silently, a great platform. Although the night was dark, it was so much darker where I was within the hollow of the Tower that I could actually see what was above me. I knew it was an aeroplane—one of which I had seen in Washington. A man was seated in the centre, steering; and beside him was a silent figure of a woman all wrapped in white. It made my heart beat to see her, for she was figured something like my Teuta, but broader, less shapely. She leaned over, and a whispered "Ssh!" crept down to me. I answered in similar way. Whereupon she rose, and the man lowered her down into the Tower. Then I saw that it was my dear daughter who had come in this wonderful way to save me. With infinite haste she helped me to fasten round my waist a belt attached to a rope, which was coiled round her; and then the man, who was a giant in strength as well as stature, raised us both to the platform of the aeroplane, which he set in motion without an instant's delay.

Within a few seconds, and without any discovery being made of my escape, we were speeding towards the sea. The lights of Ilsin were in front of us. Before reaching the town, however, we descended in the midst of a little army of my own people, who were gathered ready to advance upon the Silent Tower, there to effect, if necessary, my rescue by force. Small chance would there have been of my life in case of such a struggle. Happily, however, the devotion and courage of my dear daughter and of her gallant companion prevented such a necessity. It was strange to me to find such joyous reception amongst my friends expressed in such a whispered silence. There was no time for comment or understanding or the asking of questions—I was fain to take things as they stood, and wait for fuller explanation.

This came later, when my daughter and I were able to converse alone.

When the expedition went out against the Silent Tower, Teuta and I went to her tent, and with us came her gigantic companion, who seemed not wearied, but almost overcome with sleep. When we came into the tent, over which at a little distance a cordon of our mountaineers stood on guard, he said to me:

"May I ask you, sir, to pardon me for a time, and allow the Voivodin to explain matters to you? She will, I know, so far assist me, for there is so much work still to be done before we are free of the present peril. For myself, I am almost overcome with sleep. For three nights I have had no sleep, but all during that time much labour and more anxiety. I could hold on longer; but at daybreak I must go out to the Turkish warship that lies in the offing. She is a Turk, though she does not confess to it; and she it is who has brought hither the marauders who captured both your daughter and yourself. It is needful that I go, for I hold a personal authority from the National Council to take whatever step may be necessary for our protection. And when I go I should be clear-headed, for war may rest on that meeting. I shall be in the adjoining tent, and shall come at once if I am summoned, in case you wish for me before dawn." Here my daughter struck in:

"Father, ask him to remain here. We shall not disturb him, I am sure, in our talking. And, moreover, if you knew how much I owe to him—to his own bravery and his strength—you would understand how much safer I feel when he is close to me, though we are surrounded by an army of our brave mountaineers."

"But, my daughter," I said, for I was as yet all in ignorance, "there are confidences between father and daughter which none other may share. Some of what has been I know, but I want to know all, and it might be better that no stranger—however valiant he may be, or no matter in what measure we are bound to him—should be present." To my astonishment, she who had always been amenable to my lightest wish actually argued with me:

"Father, there are other confidences which have to be respected in like wise. Bear with me, dear, till I have told you all, and I am right sure that you will agree with me. I ask it, father."

That settled the matter, and as I could see that the gallant gentleman who had rescued me was swaying on his feet as he waited respectfully, I said to him:

"Rest with us, sir. We shall watch over your sleep."

Then I had to help him, for almost on the instant he sank down, and I had to guide him to the rugs spread on the ground. In a few seconds he was in a deep sleep. As I stood looking at him, till I had realized that he was really asleep, I could not help marvelling at the bounty of Nature that could uphold even such a man as this to the last moment of work to be done, and then allow so swift a collapse when all was over, and he could rest peacefully.

He was certainly a splendid fellow. I think I never saw so fine a man physically in my life. And if the lesson of his physiognomy be true, he is as sterling inwardly as his external is fair. "Now," said I to Teuta, "we are to all intents quite alone. Tell me all that has been, so that I may understand."

Whereupon my daughter, making me sit down, knelt beside me, and told me from end to end the most marvellous story I had ever heard or read of. Something of it I had already known from the Archbishop Paleologue's later letters, but of all else I was ignorant. Far away in the great West beyond the Atlantic, and again on the fringe of the Eastern seas, I had been thrilled to my heart's core by the heroic devotion and fortitude of my daughter in yielding herself for her country's sake to that fearful ordeal of the Crypt; of the grief of the nation at her reported death, news of which was so mercifully and wisely withheld from me as long as possible; of the supernatural rumours that took root so deep; but no word or hint had come to me of a man who had come across the orbit of her life, much less of all that has resulted from it. Neither had I known of her being carried off, or of the thrice gallant rescue of her by Rupert. Little wonder that I thought so highly of him even at the first moment I had a clear view of him when he sank down to sleep before me. Why, the man must be a marvel. Even our mountaineers could not match such endurance as his. In the course of her narrative my daughter told me of how, being wearied with her long waiting in the tomb, and waking to find herself alone when the floods were out, and even the Crypt submerged, she sought safety and warmth elsewhere; and how she came to the Castle in the night, and found the strange man alone. I said: "That was dangerous, daughter, if not wrong. The man, brave and devoted as he is, must answer me—your father." At that she was greatly upset, and before going on with her narrative, drew me close in her arms, and whispered to me:

"Be gentle to me, father, for I have had much to bear. And be good to him, for he holds my heart in his breast!" I reassured her with a gentle pressure—there was no need to speak. She then went on to tell me about her marriage, and how her husband, who had fallen into the belief that she was a Vampire, had determined to give even his soul for her; and how she had on the night of the marriage left him and gone back to the tomb to play to the end the grim comedy which she had undertaken to perform till my return; and how, on the second night after her marriage, as she was in the garden of the Castle—going, as she shyly told me, to see if all was well with her husband—she was seized secretly, muffled up, bound, and carried off. Here she made a pause and a digression. Evidently some fear lest her husband and myself should quarrel assailed her, for she said:

"Do understand, father, that Rupert's marriage to me was in all ways regular, and quite in accord with our customs. Before we were married I told the Archbishop of my wish. He, as your representative during your absence, consented himself, and brought the matter to the notice of the Vladika and the Archimandrites. All these concurred, having exacted from me—very properly, I think—a sacred promise to adhere to my self-appointed task. The marriage itself was orthodox in all ways—though so far unusual that it was held at night, and in darkness, save for the lights appointed by the ritual. As to that, the Archbishop himself, or the Archimandrite of Spazac, who assisted him, or the Vladika, who acted as Paranymph, will, all or any of them, give you full details. Your representative made all inquiries as to Rupert Sent Leger, who lived in Vissarion, though he did not know who I was, or from his point of view who I had been. But I must tell you of my rescue."

And so she went on to tell me of that unavailing journey south by her captors; of their bafflement by the cordon which Rupert had established at the first word of danger to "the daughter of our leader," though he little knew who the "leader" was, or who was his "daughter"; of how the brutal marauders tortured her to speed with their daggers; and how her wounds left blood-marks on the ground as she passed along; then of the halt in the valley, when the marauders came to know that their road north was menaced, if not already blocked; of the choosing of the murderers, and their keeping ward over her whilst their companions went to survey the situation; and of her gallant rescue by that noble fellow, her husband—my son I shall call him henceforth, and thank God that I may have that happiness and that honour!

Then my daughter went on to tell me of the race back to Vissarion, when Rupert went ahead of all—as a leader should do; of the summoning of the Archbishop and the National Council; and of their placing the nation's handjar in Rupert's hand; of the journey to Ilsin, and the flight of my daughter—and my son—on the aeroplane.

The rest I knew.

As she finished, the sleeping man stirred and woke—broad awake in a second—sure sign of a man accustomed to campaign and adventure. At a glance he recalled everything that had been, and sprang to his feet. He stood respectfully before me for a few seconds before speaking. Then he said, with an open, engaging smile:

"I see, sir, you know all. Am I forgiven—for Teuta's sake as well as my own?" By this time I was also on my feet. A man like that walks straight into my heart. My daughter, too, had risen, and stood by my side. I put out my hand and grasped his, which seemed to leap to meet me—as only the hand of a swordsman can do.

"I am glad you are my son!" I said. It was all I could say, and I meant it and all it implied. We shook hands warmly. Teuta was pleased;

she kissed me, and then stood holding my arm with one hand, whilst she linked her other hand in the arm of her husband.

He summoned one of the sentries without, and told him to ask Captain Rooke to come to him. The latter had been ready for a call, and came at once. When through the open flap of the tent we saw him coming, Rupert—as I must call him now, because Teuta wishes it; and I like to do it myself—said:

"I must be off to board the Turkish vessel before it comes inshore. Good-bye, sir, in case we do not meet again." He said the last few words in so low a voice that I only could hear them. Then he kissed his wife, and told her he expected to be back in time for breakfast, and was gone. He met Rooke—I am hardly accustomed to call him Captain as yet, though, indeed, he well deserves it—at the edge of the cordon of sentries, and they went quickly together towards the port, where the yacht was lying with steam up.

BOOK VII: THE EMPIRE OF THE AIR
FROM THE REPORT OF CRISTOFEROS, WAR-SCRIBE TO THE NATIONAL COUNCIL.

July 7, 1907.

WHEN THE GOSPODAR Rupert and Captain Rooke came within hailing distance of the strange ship, the former hailed her, using one after another the languages of England, Germany, France, Russia, Turkey, Greece, Spain, Portugal, and another which I did not know; I think it must have been American. By this time the whole line of the bulwark was covered by a row of Turkish faces. When, in Turkish, the Gospodar asked for the Captain, the latter came to the gangway, which had been opened, and stood there. His uniform was that of the Turkish navy—of that I am prepared to swear—but he made signs of not understanding what had been said; whereupon the Gospodar spoke again, but in French this time. I append the exact conversation which took place, none other joining in it. I took down in shorthand the words of both as they were spoken:

THE GOSPODAR. "Are you the Captain of this ship?"

THE CAPTAIN. "I am."

GOSPODAR. "To what nationality do you belong?"

CAPTAIN. "It matters not. I am Captain of this ship."

GOSPODAR. "I alluded to your ship. What national flag is she under?"

CAPTAIN (*throwing his eye over the top-hamper*). "I do not see that any flag is flying."

GOSPODAR. "I take it that, as commander, you can allow me on board with my two companions?"

CAPTAIN. "I can, upon proper request being made!"

GOSPODAR (*taking off his cap*). "I ask your courtesy, Captain. I am the representative and accredited officer of the National Council of the Land of the Blue Mountains, in whose waters you now are; and on their account I ask for a formal interview on urgent matters."

The Turk, who was, I am bound to say, in manner most courteous as yet, gave some command to his officers, whereupon the companion-ladders and stage were lowered and the gangway manned, as is usual for the reception on a ship of war of an honoured guest.

CAPTAIN. "You are welcome, sir—you and your two companions—as you request."

The Gospodar bowed. Our companion-ladder was rigged on the instant, and a launch lowered. The Gospodar and Captain Rooke—taking me with them—entered, and rowed to the warship, where we were all honourably received. There were an immense number of men on board, soldiers as well as seamen. It looked more like a warlike expedition than a fighting-ship in time of peace. As we stepped on the deck, the seamen and marines, who were all armed as at drill, presented arms. The Gospodar went first towards the Captain, and Captain Rooke and I followed close behind him. The Gospodar spoke:

"I am Rupert Sent Leger, a subject of his Britannic Majesty, presently residing at Vissarion, in the Land of the Blue Mountains. I am at present empowered to act for the National Council in all matters. Here is my credential!" As he spoke he handed to the Captain a letter. It was written in five different languages—Balkan, Turkish, Greek, English, and French. The Captain read it carefully all through, forgetful for the moment that he had seemingly been unable to understand the Gospodar's question spoken in the Turkish tongue. Then he answered:

"I see the document is complete. May I ask on what subject you wish to see me?"

GOSPODAR. "You are here in a ship of war in Blue Mountain waters, yet you fly no flag of any nation. You have sent armed men ashore in your boats, thus committing an act of war. The National Council of the Land of the Blue Mountains requires to know what nation you serve, and why the obligations of international law are thus broken."

The Captain seemed to wait for further speech, but the Gospodar remained silent; whereupon the former spoke.

CAPTAIN. "I am responsible to my own—chiefs. I refuse to answer your question."

The Gospodar spoke at once in reply.

GOSPODAR. "Then, sir, you, as commander of a ship—and especially a ship of war—must know that in thus violating national and maritime laws you, and all on board this ship, are guilty of an act of piracy. This is not even piracy on the high seas. You are not merely within territorial waters, but you have invaded a national port. As you refuse to disclose the nationality of your ship, I accept, as you seem to do, your status as that of a pirate, and shall in due season act accordingly."

CAPTAIN (*with manifest hostility*). "I accept the responsibility of my own acts. Without admitting your contention, I tell you now that whatever action you take shall be at your own peril and that of your National Council. Moreover, I have reason to believe that my men who were sent ashore on special service have been beleaguered in a tower which can be seen from the ship. Before dawn this morning firing was heard from that direction, from which I gather that attack was made on them. They, being only a small party, may have been murdered. If such be so, I tell you that you and your miserable little nation, as you call it, shall pay such blood-money as you never thought of. I am responsible for this, and, by Allah! there shall be a great revenge. You have not in all your navy—if navy you have at all—power to cope with even one ship like this, which is but one of many. My guns shall be trained on Ilsin, to which end I have come inshore. You and your companions have free conduct back to port; such is due to the white flag which you fly. Fifteen minutes will bring you back whence you came. Go! And remember that whatever you may do amongst your mountain defiles, at sea you cannot even defend yourselves."

GOSPODAR (*slowly and in a ringing voice*). "The Land of the Blue Mountains has its own defences on sea and land. Its people know how to defend themselves."

CAPTAIN (*taking out his watch*). "It is now close on five bells. At the first stroke of six bells our guns shall open fire."

GOSPODAR (*calmly*). "It is my last duty to warn you, sir—and to warn all on this ship—that much may happen before even the first stroke of six bells. Be warned in time, and give over this piratical attack, the very threat of which may be the cause of much bloodshed."

CAPTAIN (*violently*). "Do you dare to threaten me, and, moreover, my ship's company? We are one, I tell you, in this ship; and the last man shall perish like the first ere this enterprise fail. Go!"

With a bow, the Gospodar turned and went down the ladder, we following him. In a couple of minutes the yacht was on her way to the port.

FROM RUPERT'S JOURNAL.

July 10, 1907.

When we turned shoreward after my stormy interview with the pirate Captain—I can call him nothing else at present, Rooke gave orders to a quartermaster on the bridge, and *The Lady* began to make to a little northward of Ilsin port. Rooke himself went aft to the wheelhouse, taking several men with him.

When we were quite near the rocks—the water is so deep here that there is no danger—we slowed down, merely drifting along southwards towards the port. I was myself on the bridge, and could see all over the decks. I could also see preparations going on upon the warship. Ports were opened, and the great guns on the turrets were lowered for action. When we were starboard broadside on to the warship, I saw the port side of the steering-house open, and Rooke's men sliding out what looked like a huge grey crab, which by tackle from within the wheelhouse was lowered softly into the sea. The position of the yacht hid the operation from sight of the warship. The doors were shut again, and the yacht's pace began to quicken. We ran into the port. I had a vague idea that Rooke had some desperate project on hand. Not for nothing had he kept the wheel-house locked on that mysterious crab.

All along the frontage was a great crowd of eager men. But they had considerately left the little mole at the southern entrance, whereon was a little tower, on whose round top a signal-gun was placed, free for my own use. When I was landed on this pier I went along to the end, and, climbing the narrow stair within, went out on the sloping roof. I stood up, for I was determined to show the Turks that I was not afraid for myself, as they would understand when the bombardment should begin. It was now but a very few minutes before the fatal hour—six bells. But all the same I was almost in a state of despair. It was terrible to think of all those poor souls in the town who had done nothing wrong, and who were to be wiped out in the coming blood-thirsty, wanton attack. I raised my glasses to see how preparations were going on upon the warship.

As I looked I had a momentary fear that my eyesight was giving way. At one moment I had the deck of the warship focussed with my glasses, and could see every detail as the gunners waited for the word to begin the bombardment with the great guns of the barbettes. The next I saw nothing but the empty sea. Then in another instant there was the ship as before, but the details were blurred. I steadied myself against the signal-gun, and looked again. Not more than two, or at the most three, seconds had elapsed. The ship was, for the moment, full in view.

As I looked, she gave a queer kind of quick shiver, prow and stern, and then sideways. It was for all the world like a rat shaken in the mouth of a skilled terrier. Then she remained still, the one placid thing to be seen, for all around her the sea seemed to shiver in little independent eddies, as when water is broken without a current to guide it.

I continued to look, and when the deck was, or seemed, quite still—for the shivering water round the ship kept catching my eyes through the outer rays of the lenses—I noticed that nothing was stirring. The men who had been at the guns were all lying down; the men in the fighting-tops had leaned forward or backward, and their arms hung down helplessly. Everywhere was desolation—in so far as life was concerned. Even a little brown bear, which had been seated on the cannon which was being put into range position, had jumped or fallen on deck, and lay there stretched out—and still. It was evident that some terrible shock had been given to the mighty war-vessel. Without a doubt or a thought why I did so, I turned my eyes towards where *The Lady* lay, port broadside now to the inside, in the harbour mouth. I had the key now to the mystery of Rooke's proceedings with the great grey crab.

As I looked I saw just outside the harbour a thin line of cleaving water. This became more marked each instant, till a steel disc with glass eyes that shone in the light of the sun rose above the water. It was about the size of a beehive, and was shaped like one. It made a straight line for the aft of the yacht. At the same moment, in obedience to some command, given so quietly that I did not hear it, the men went below—all save some few, who began to open out doors in the port side of the wheel-house. The tackle was run out through an opened gangway on that side, and a man stood on the great hook at the lower end, balancing himself by hanging on the chain. In a few seconds he came up again. The chain tightened and the great grey crab rose over the edge of the deck, and was drawn into the wheel-house, the doors of which were closed, shutting in a few only of the men.

I waited, quite quiet. After a space of a few minutes, Captain Rooke in his uniform walked out of the wheel-house. He entered a small boat, which had been in the meantime lowered for the purpose, and was rowed to the steps on the mole. Ascending these, he came directly towards the signal-tower. When he had ascended and stood beside me, he saluted.

"Well?" I asked.

"All well, sir," he answered. "We shan't have any more trouble with that lot, I think. You warned that pirate—I wish he had been in truth a clean, honest, straightforward pirate, instead of the measly Turkish swab he was—that something might occur before the first stroke of six bells. Well, something has occurred, and for him and all his crew that six bells will never sound. So the Lord fights for the Cross against the Crescent! Bismillah. Amen!" He said this in a manifestly formal way, as though declaiming a ritual. The next instant he went on in the thoroughly practical conventional way which was usual to him:

"May I ask a favour, Mr. Sent Leger?"

"A thousand, my dear Rooke," I said. "You can't ask me anything which I shall not freely grant. And I speak within my brief from the National Council. You have saved Ilsin this day, and the Council will thank you for it in due time."

"Me, sir?" he said, with a look of surprise on his face which seemed quite genuine. "If you think that, I am well out of it. I was afraid, when I woke, that you might court-martial me!"

"Court-martial you! What for?" I asked, surprised in my turn.

"For going to sleep on duty, sir! And the fact is, I was worn out in the attack on the Silent Tower last night, and when you had your interview with the pirate—all good pirates forgive me for the blasphe-my! Amen!—and I knew that everything was going smoothly, I went into the wheel-house and took forty winks." He said all this without moving so much as an eyelid, from which I gathered that he wished absolute silence to be observed on my part. Whilst I was revolving this in my mind he went on:

"Touching that request, sir. When I have left you and the Voivode—and the Voivodin, of course—at Vissarion, together with such others as you may choose to bring there with you, may I bring the yacht back here for a spell? I rather think that there is a good deal of cleaning up to be done, and the crew of *The Lady* with myself are the men to do it. We shall be back by nightfall at the creek."

"Do as you think best, Admiral Rooke," I said.

"Admiral?"

"Yes, Admiral. At present I can only say that tentatively, but by to-morrow I am sure the National Council will have confirmed it. I am afraid, old friend, that your squadron will be only your flagship for the present; but later we may do better."

"So long as I am Admiral, your honour, I shall have no other flagship than *The Lady*. I am not a young man, but, young or old, my pennon shall float over no other deck. Now, one other favour, Mr. Sent Leger? It is a corollary of the first, so I do not hesitate to ask. May I appoint Lieutenant Desmond, my present First Officer, to the command of the battleship? Of course, he will at first only command the prize crew; but in such case he will fairly expect the confirmation of his rank later. I had better, perhaps, tell you, sir, that he is a very capable seaman, learned in all the sciences that pertain to a battleship, and bred in the first navy in the world."

"By all means, Admiral. Your nomination shall, I think I may promise you, be confirmed."

Not another word we spoke. I returned with him in his boat to *The Lady*, which was brought to the dock wall, where we were received with tumultuous cheering.

I hurried off to my Wife and the Voivode. Rooke, calling Desmond to him, went on the bridge of *The Lady*, which turned, and went out at terrific speed to the battleship, which was already drifting up northward on the tide.

FROM THE REPORT OF CRISTOFEROS, SCRIBE OF THE NATIONAL COUNCIL OF THE LAND OF THE BLUE MOUNTAINS.

July 8, 1907.

The meeting of the National Council, July 6, was but a continuation of that held before the rescue of the Voivodin Vissarion, the members of the Council having been during the intervening night housed in the Castle of Vissarion. When, in the early morning, they met, all were jubilant; for late at night the fire-signal had flamed up from Ilsin with the glad news that the Voivode Peter Vissarion was safe, having been rescued with great daring on an aeroplane by his daughter and the Gospodar Rupert, as the people call him—Mister Rupert Sent Leger, as he is in his British name and degree.

Whilst the Council was sitting, word came that a great peril to the town of Ilsin had been averted. A war-vessel acknowledging to no nationality, and therefore to be deemed a pirate, had threatened to bombard the town; but just before the time fixed for the fulfilment of her threat, she was shaken to such an extent by some sub-aqueous means that, though she herself was seemingly uninjured, nothing was left alive on board. Thus the Lord preserves His own! The consideration of this, as well as the other incident, was postponed until the coming Voivode and the Gospodar Rupert, together with who were already on their way hither.

THE SAME (LATER IN THE SAME DAY).

The Council resumed its sitting at four o'clock. The Voivode Peter Vissarion and the Voivodin Teuta had arrived with the "Gospodar Rupert," as the mountaineers call him (Mr. Rupert Sent Leger) on the armoured yacht he calls *The Lady*. The National Council showed great pleasure when the Voivode entered the hall in which the Council met. He seemed much gratified by the reception given to him. Mr. Rupert Sent Leger, by the express desire of the Council, was asked to be present at the meeting. He took a seat at the bottom of the hall, and seemed to prefer to remain there, though asked by the President of the Council to sit at the top of the table with himself and the Voivode.

When the formalities of such Councils had been completed, the Voivode handed to the President a memorandum of his report on his secret mission to foreign Courts on behalf of the National Council. He then explained at length, for the benefit of the various members of the Council, the broad results of his mission. The result was, he said, absolutely satisfactory. Everywhere he had been received with distinguished courtesy, and given a sympathetic hearing. Several of the Powers consulted had made delay in giving final answers, but this, he explained, was necessarily due to new considerations arising from the international complications which were universally dealt with throughout the world as "the Balkan Crisis." In time, however (the Voivode went on), these matters became so far declared as to allow the waiting Powers to form definite judgment—which, of course, they did not declare to him—as to their own ultimate action. The final result—if at this initial stage such tentative setting forth of their own attitude in each case can be so named—was that he returned full of hope (founded, he might say, upon a justifiable personal belief) that the Great Powers throughout the world—North, South, East, and West—were in thorough sympathy with the Land of the Blue Mountains in its aspirations for the continuance of its freedom. "I also am honoured," he continued, "to bring to you, the Great Council of the nation, the assurance of protection against unworthy aggression on the part of neighbouring nations of present greater strength."

Whilst he was speaking, the Gospodar Rupert was writing a few words on a strip of paper, which he sent up to the President. When the Voivode had finished speaking, there was a prolonged silence. The President rose, and in a hush said that the Council would like to hear Mr. Rupert Sent Leger, who had a communication to make regarding certain recent events.

Mr. Rupert Sent Leger rose, and reported how, since he had been entrusted by the Council with the rescue of the Voivode Peter of Vissarion, he had, by aid of the Voivodin, effected the escape of the Voivode from the Silent Tower; also that, following this happy event, the mountaineers, who had made a great cordon round the Tower so soon as it was known that the Voivode had been imprisoned within it, had stormed it in the night. As a determined resistance was offered by the marauders, who had used it as a place of refuge, none of these escaped. He then went on to tell how he sought interview with the Captain of the strange warship, which, without flying any flag, invaded our waters. He asked the President to call on me to read the report of that meeting. This, in obedience to his direction, I did. The acquiescent murmuring of the Council showed how thoroughly they endorsed Mr. Sent Leger's words and acts.

When I resumed my seat, Mr. Sent Leger described how, just before the time fixed by the "pirate Captain"—so he designated him, as did every speaker thereafter—the warship met with some under-sea accident, which had a destructive effect on all on board her. Then he added certain words, which I give verbatim, as I am sure that others will some time wish to remember them in their exactness:

"By the way, President and Lords of the Council, I trust I may ask you to confirm Captain Rooke, of the armoured yacht *The Lady*, to be Admiral of the Squadron of the Land of the Blue Mountains, and also Captain (tentatively) Desmond, late First-Lieutenant of *The Lady*, to the command of the second warship of our fleet—the as yet unnamed vessel, whose former Captain threatened to bombard Ilsin. My Lords, Admiral Rooke has done great service to the Land of the Blue Mountains, and deserves well at your hands. You will have in him, I am sure, a great official. One who will till his last breath give you good and loyal service."

He had sat down, the President put to the Council resolutions, which were passed by acclamation. Admiral Rooke was given command of the navy, and Captain Desmond confirmed in his appointment to the captaincy of the new ship, which was, by a further resolution, named *The Gospodar Rupert*.

In thanking the Council for acceding to his request, and for the great honour done him in the naming of the ship, Mr. Sent Leger said:

"May I ask that the armoured yacht *The Lady* be accepted by you, the National Council, on behalf of the nation, as a gift on behalf of the cause of freedom from the Voivodin Teuta?"

In response to the mighty cheer of the Council with which the splendid gift was accepted the Gospodar Rupert—Mr. Sent Leger—bowed, and went quietly out of the room.

As no agenda of the meeting had been prepared, there was for a time, not silence, but much individual conversation. In the midst of it the Voivode rose up, whereupon there was a strict silence. All listened with an intensity of eagerness whilst he spoke.

"President and Lords of the Council, Archbishop, and Vladika, I should but ill show my respect did I hesitate to tell you at this the first opportunity I have had of certain matters personal primarily to myself, but which, in the progress of recent events, have come to impinge on the affairs of the nation. Until I have done so, I shall not feel that I have done a duty, long due to you or your predecessors in office, and which I hope you will allow me to say that I have only kept back for purposes of statecraft. May I ask that you will come back with me in memory to the year 1890, when our struggle against Ottoman aggression, later on so successfully brought to a close, was begun. We were then in a desperate condition. Our finances had run so low that we could not purchase even the bread which we required. Nay, more, we could not procure through the National Exchequer what we wanted more than bread— arms of modern effectiveness; for men may endure hunger and yet fight well, as the glorious past of our country has proved again and again and again. But when our foes are better armed than we are, the penalty is dreadful to a nation small as our own is in number, no matter how brave their hearts. In this strait I myself had to secretly raise a sufficient sum of money to procure the weapons we needed. To this end I sought the assistance of a great merchant-prince, to whom our nation as well as myself was known. He met me in the same generous spirit which he had shown to other struggling nationalities throughout a long and honourable career. When I pledged to him as security my own estates, he wished to tear up the bond, and only under pressure would he meet my wishes in this respect. Lords of the Council, it was his money, thus generously advanced, which procured for us the arms with which we hewed out our freedom.

"Not long ago that noble merchant—and here I trust you will pardon me that I am so moved as to perhaps appear to suffer in want of respect to this great Council—this noble merchant passed to his account—leaving to a near kinsman of his own the royal fortune which he had amassed. Only a few hours ago that worthy kinsman of the benefactor of our nation made it known to me that in his last will he had bequeathed to me, by secret trust, the whole of those estates which long ago I had forfeited by effluxion of time, inasmuch as I had been unable to fulfil the terms of my voluntary bond. It grieves me to think that I have had to keep you so long in ignorance of the good thought and wishes and acts of this great man.

"But it was by his wise counsel, fortified by my own judgment, that I was silent; for, indeed, I feared, as he did, lest in our troublous times some doubting spirit without our boundaries, or even within it, might mistrust the honesty of my purposes for public good, because I was no longer one whose whole fortune was invested within our confines. This prince-merchant, the great English Roger Melton—let his name be for ever graven on the hearts of our people!—kept silent during his own life, and enjoined on others to come after him to keep secret from the men of the Blue Mountains that secret loan made to me on their behalf, lest in their eyes I, who had striven to be their friend and helper, should suffer wrong repute. But, happily, he has left me free to clear myself in your eyes. Moreover, by arranging to have—under certain contingencies, which have come to pass—the estates which were originally my own retransferred to me, I have no longer the honour of having given what I could to the national cause. All such now belongs to him; for it was his money—and his only—which purchased our national armament.

"His worthy kinsman you already know, for he has not only been amongst you for many months, but has already done you good service in his own person. He it was who, as a mighty warrior, answered the summons of the Vladika when misfortune came upon my house in the capture by enemies of my dear daughter, the Voivodin Teuta, whom you hold in your hearts; who, with a chosen band of our brothers, pursued the marauders, and himself, by a deed of daring and prowess, of which poets shall hereafter sing, saved her, when hope itself seemed to be dead, from their ruthless hands, and brought her back to us; who administered condign punishment to the miscreants who had dared to so wrong her. He it was who later took me, your servant, out of the prison wherein another band of Turkish miscreants held me captive; rescued me, with the help of my dear daughter, whom he had already freed, whilst I had on my person the documents of international secrecy of which I have already advised you—rescued me whilst I had been as yet unsubjected to the indignity of search.

"Beyond this you know now that of which I was in partial ignorance: how he had, through the skill and devotion of your new Admiral, wrought destruction on a hecatomb of our malignant foes. You who have received for the nation the splendid gift of the little warship, which already represents a new era in naval armament, can understand the great-souled generosity of the man who has restored the vast possessions of my House. On our way hither from Ilsin, Rupert Sent Leger made known to me the terms of the trust of his noble uncle, Roger Melton, and—believe me that he did so generously, with a joy that transcended my own—restored to the last male of the Vissarion race the whole inheritance of a noble line.

"And now, my Lords of the Council, I come to another matter, in which I find myself in something of a difficulty, for I am aware that in certain ways you actually know more of it than even I myself do. It is regarding the marriage of my daughter to Rupert Sent Leger. It is known to me that the matter has been brought before you by the Archbishop, who, as guardian of my daughter during my absence on the service of the nation, wished to obtain your sanction, as till my return he held her safety in trust. This was so, not from any merit of mine, but because she, in her own person, had undertaken for the service of our nation a task of almost incredible difficulty. My Lords, were she child of another father, I should extol to the skies her bravery, her self-devotion, her loyalty to the land she loves. Why, then, should I hesitate to speak of her deeds in fitting terms, since it is my duty, my glory, to hold them in higher honour than can any in this land? I shall not shame her—or even myself—by being silent when such a duty urges me to speak, as Voivode, as trusted envoy of our nation, as father. Ages hence loyal men and women of our Land of the Blue Mountains will sing her deeds in song and tell them in story. Her name, Teuta, already sacred in these regions, where it was held by a great Queen, and honoured by all men, will hereafter be held as a symbol and type of woman's devotion. Oh, my Lords, we pass along the path of life, the best of us but a little time marching in the sunlight between gloom and gloom, and it is during that march that we must be judged for the future. This brave woman has won knightly spurs as well as any Paladin of old. So is it meet that ere she might mate with one worthy of her you, who hold in your hands the safety and honour of the State, should give your approval. To you was it given to sit in judgment on the worth of this gallant Englisher, now my son. You judged him then, before you had seen his valour, his strength, and skill exercised on behalf of a national cause. You judged wisely, oh, my brothers, and out of a grateful heart I thank you one and all for it. Well has he justified your trust by his later acts. When, in obedience to the summons of the Vladika, he put the nation in a blaze and ranged our boundaries with a ring of steel, he did so unknowing that what was dearest to him in the world was at stake. He saved my daughter's honour and happiness, and won her safety by an act of valour that outvies any told in history. He took my daughter with him to bring me out from the Silent Tower on the wings of the air, when earth had for me no possibility of freedom—I, that had even then in my possession the documents involving other nations which the Soldan would fain have purchased with the half of his empire.

"Henceforth to me, Lords of the Council, this brave man must ever be as a son of my heart, and I trust that in his name grandsons of my own may keep in bright honour the name which in glorious days of old my fathers made illustrious. Did I know how adequately to thank you for your interest in my child, I would yield up to you my very soul in thanks."

The speech of the Voivode was received with the honour of the Blue Mountains—the drawing and raising of handjars.

FROM RUPERT'S JOURNAL.

July 14, 1907.

For nearly a week we waited for some message from Constantinople, fully expecting either a declaration of war, or else some inquiry
so couched as to make war an inevitable result. The National Council
remained on at Vissarion as the guests of the Voivode, to whom, in
accordance with my uncle's will, I had prepared to re-transfer all his
estates. He was, by the way, unwilling at first to accept, and it was only
when I showed him Uncle Roger's letter, and made him read the Deed
of Transfer prepared in anticipation by Mr. Trent, that he allowed me
to persuade him. Finally he said:

"As you, my good friends, have so arranged, I must accept, be it
only in honour to the wishes of the dead. But remember, I only do so
but for the present, reserving to myself the freedom to withdraw later
if I so desire."

But Constantinople was silent. The whole nefarious scheme was
one of the "put-up jobs" which are part of the dirty work of a certain
order of statecraft—to be accepted if successful; to be denied in case
of failure.

The matter stood thus: Turkey had thrown the dice—and lost. Her
men were dead; her ship was forfeit. It was only some ten days after the
warship was left derelict with every living thing—that is, everything
that had been living—with its neck broken, as Rooke informed me,
when he brought the ship down the creek, and housed it in the dock
behind the armoured gates—that we saw an item in *The Roma* copied
from *The Constantinople Journal* of July 9:

"LOSS OF AN OTTOMAN IRONCLAD WITH ALL HANDS.

"News has been received at Constantinople of the total loss,
with all hands, of one of the newest and finest warships in the Turkish fleet—*The Mahmoud*, Captain Ali Ali—which foundered in a
storm on the night of July 5, some distance off Cabrera, in the Bale-
aric Isles. There were no survivors, and no wreckage was discovered
by the ships which went in relief—the *Pera* and the *Mustapha*—or

reported from anywhere along the shores of the islands, of which exhaustive search was made. *The Mahmoud* was double-manned, as she carried a full extra crew sent on an educational cruise on the most perfectly scientifically equipped warship on service in the Mediterranean waters."

When the Voivode and I talked over the matter, he said:

"After all, Turkey is a shrewd Power. She certainly seems to know when she is beaten, and does not intend to make a bad thing seem worse in the eyes of the world."

Well, 'tis a bad wind that blows good to nobody. As *The Mahmoud* was lost off the Balearics, it cannot have been her that put the marauders on shore and trained her big guns on Ilsin. We take it, therefore, that the latter must have been a pirate, and as we have taken her derelict in our waters, she is now ours in all ways. Anyhow, she is ours, and is the first ship of her class in the navy of the Blue Mountains. I am inclined to think that even if she was—or is still—a Turkish ship, Admiral Rooke would not be inclined to let her go. As for Captain Desmond, I think he would go straight out of his mind if such a thing was to be even suggested to him.

It will be a pity if we have any more trouble, for life here is very happy with us all now. The Voivode is, I think, like a man in a dream. Teuta is ideally happy, and the real affection which sprang up between them when she and Aunt Janet met is a joy to think of. I had posted Teuta about her, so that when they should meet my wife might not, by any inadvertence, receive or cause any pain. But the moment Teuta saw her she ran straight over to her and lifted her in her strong young arms, and, raising her up as one would lift a child, kissed her. Then, when she had put her sitting in the chair from which she had arisen when we entered the room, she knelt down before her, and put her face down in her lap. Aunt Janet's face was a study; I myself could hardly say whether at the first moment surprise or joy predominated. But there could be no doubt about it the instant after. She seemed to beam with happiness. When Teuta knelt to her, she could only say:

"My dear, my dear, I am glad! Rupert's wife, you and I must love each other very much." Seeing that they were laughing and crying in each other's arms, I thought it best to come away and leave them alone. And I didn't feel a bit lonely either when I was out of sight of them. I knew that where those two dear women were there was a place for my own heart.

When I came back, Teuta was sitting on Aunt Janet's knee. It seemed rather stupendous for the old lady, for Teuta is such a splendid creature that even when she sits on my own knee and I catch a glimpse of us in some mirror, I cannot but notice what a nobly-built girl she is.

My wife was jumping up as soon as I was seen, but Aunt Janet held her tight to her, and said:

"Don't stir, dear. It is such happiness to me to have you there. Rupert has always been my 'little boy,' and, in spite of all his being such a giant, he is so still. And so you, that he loves, must be my little girl—in spite of all your beauty and your strength—and sit on my knee, till you can place there a little one that shall be dear to us all, and that shall let me feel my youth again. When first I saw you I was surprised, for, somehow, though I had never seen you nor even heard of you, I seemed to know your face. Sit where you are, dear. It is only Rupert—and we both love him."

Teuta looked at me, flushing rosily; but she sat quiet, and drew the old lady's white head on her young breast.

JANET MACKELPIE'S NOTES.

July 8, 1907.

I used to think that whenever Rupert should get married or start on the way to it by getting engaged—I would meet his future wife with something of the same affection that I have always had for himself. But

I know now that what was really in my mind was jealousy, and that I was really fighting against my own instincts, and pretending to myself that I was not jealous. Had I ever had the faintest idea that she would be anything the least like Teuta, that sort of feeling should never have had even a foothold. No wonder my dear boy is in love with her, for, truth to tell, I am in love with her myself. I don't think I ever met a creature—a woman creature, of course, I mean—with so many splendid qualities. I almost fear to say it, lest it should seem to myself wrong; but I think she is as good as a woman as Rupert is as a man. And what more than that can I say? I thought I loved her and trusted her, and knew her all I could, until this morning.

I was in my own room, as it is still called. For, though Rupert tells me in confidence that under his uncle's will the whole estate of Vissarion, Castle and all, really belongs to the Voivode, and though the Voivode has been persuaded to accept the position, he (the Voivode) will not allow anything to be changed. He will not even hear a word of my going, or changing my room, or anything. And Rupert backs him up in it, and Teuta too. So what am I to do but let the dears have their way?

Well, this morning, when Rupert was with the Voivode at a meeting of the National Council in the Great Hall, Teuta came to me, and (after closing the door and bolting it, which surprised me a little) came and knelt down beside me, and put her face in my lap. I stroked her beautiful black hair, and said:

"What is it, Teuta darling? Is there any trouble? And why did you bolt the door? Has anything happened to Rupert?" When she looked up I saw that her beautiful black eyes, with the stars in them, were overflowing with tears not yet shed. But she smiled through them, and the tears did not fall. When I saw her smile my heart was eased, and I said without thinking: "Thank God, darling, Rupert is all right."

"I thank God, too, dear Aunt Janet!" she said softly; and I took her in my arms and laid her head on my breast.

"Go on, dear," I said; "tell me what it is that troubles you?" This time I saw the tears drop, as she lowered her head and hid her face from me.

"I'm afraid I have deceived you, Aunt Janet, and that you will not—cannot—forgive me."

"Lord save you, child!" I said, "there's nothing that you could do that I could not and would not forgive. Not that you would ever do anything base, for that is the only thing that is hard to forgive. Tell me now what troubles you."

She looked up in my eyes fearlessly, this time with only the signs of tears that had been, and said proudly:

"Nothing base, Aunt Janet. My father's daughter would not willingly be base. I do not think she could. Moreover, had I ever done anything base I should not be here, for—for—I should never have been Rupert's wife!"

"Then what is it? Tell your old Aunt Janet, dearie." She answered me with another question:

"Aunt Janet, do you know who I am, and how I first met Rupert?"

"You are the Voivodin Teuta Vissarion—the daughter of the Voivode—Or, rather, you were; you are now Mrs. Rupert Sent Leger. For he is still an Englishman, and a good subject of our noble King."

"Yes, Aunt Janet," she said, "I am that, and proud to be it—prouder than I would be were I my namesake, who was Queen in the old days. But how and where did I see Rupert first?" I did not know, and frankly told her so. So she answered her question herself:

"I saw him first in his own room at night." I knew in my heart that in whatever she did had been nothing wrong, so I sat silent waiting for her to go on:

"I was in danger, and in deadly fear. I was afraid I might die—not that I fear death—and I wanted help and warmth. I was not dressed as I am now!"

On the instant it came to me how I knew her face, even the first time I had seen it. I wished to help her out of the embarrassing part of her confidence, so I said:

"Dearie, I think I know. Tell me, child, will you put on the frock . . . the dress . . . costume you wore that night, and let me see you in it? It is not mere idle curiosity, my child, but something far, far above such idle folly."

"Wait for me a minute, Aunt Janet," she said, as she rose up; "I shall not be long." Then she left the room.

In a very few minutes she was back. Her appearance might have frightened some people, for she was clad only in a shroud. Her feet were bare, and she walked across the room with the gait of an empress, and stood before me with her eyes modestly cast down. But when presently she looked up and caught my eyes, a smile rippled over her face. She threw herself once more before me on her knees, and embraced me as she said:

"I was afraid I might frighten you, dear." I knew I could truthfully reassure her as to that, so I proceeded to do so:

"Do not worry yourself, my dear. I am not by nature timid. I come of a fighting stock which has sent out heroes, and I belong to a family wherein is the gift of Second Sight. Why should we fear? We know! Moreover, I saw you in that dress before. Teuta, I saw you and Rupert married!" This time she herself it was that seemed disconcerted.

"Saw us married! How on earth did you manage to be there?"

"I was not there. My Seeing was long before! Tell me, dear, what day, or rather what night, was it that you first saw Rupert?" She answered sadly:

"I do not know. Alas! I lost count of the days as I lay in the tomb in that dreary Crypt."

"Was your—your clothing wet that night?" I asked.

"Yes. I had to leave the Crypt, for a great flood was out, and the church was flooded. I had to seek help—warmth—for I feared I might die. Oh, I was not, as I have told you, afraid of death. But I had undertaken a terrible task to which I had pledged myself. It was for my father's sake, and the sake of the Land, and I felt that it was a part of my duty to live. And so I lived on, when death would have been relief. It was to tell you all about this that I came to your room to-day. But how did you see me—us—married?"

"Ah, my child!" I answered, "that was before the marriage took place. The morn after the night that you came in the wet, when, having been troubled in uncanny dreaming, I came to see if Rupert was a'richt, I lost remembrance o' my dreaming, for the floor was all wet, and that took off my attention. But later, the morn after Rupert used his fire in his room for the first time, I told him what I had dreamt; for, lassie, my dear, I saw ye as bride at that weddin' in fine lace o'er yer shrood, and orange-flowers and ithers in yer black hair; an' I saw the stars in yer bonny een—the een I love. But oh, my dear, when I saw the shrood, and kent what it might mean, I expeckit to see the worms crawl round yer feet. But do ye ask yer man to tell ye what I tell't him that morn. 'Twill interest ye to know how the hairt o' men can learn by dreams. Has he ever tellt ye aught o' this?"

"No, dear," she said simply. "I think that perhaps he was afraid that one or other of us, if not both, might be upset by it if he did. You see, he did not tell you anything at all of our meeting, though I am sure that he will be glad when he knows that we both know all about it, and have told each other everything."

That was very sweet of her, and very thoughtful in all ways, so I said that which I thought would please her best—that is, the truth:

"Ah, lassie, that is what a wife should be—what a wife should do. Rupert is blessed and happy to have his heart in your keeping."

I knew from the added warmth of her kiss what I had said had pleased her.

Letter from Ernest Roger Halbard Melton, Humcroft, Salop, to Rupert Sent Leger, Vissarion, Land of the Blue Mountains.

July 29, 1907.

MY DEAR COUSIN RUPERT,

We have heard such glowing accounts of Vissarion that I am coming out to see you. As you are yourself now a landowner, you will understand that my coming is not altogether a pleasure. Indeed, it is a duty first. When my father dies I shall be head of the family—the family of which Uncle Roger, to whom we were related, was a member. It is therefore meet and fitting that I should know something of our family branches and of their Seats. I am not giving you time for much warning, so am coming on immediately—in fact, I shall arrive almost as soon as this letter. But I want to catch you in the middle of your tricks. I hear that the Blue Mountaineer girls are peaches, so don't send them *all* away when you hear I'm coming!

Do send a yacht up to Fiume to meet me. I hear you have all sorts of craft at Vissarion. The MacSkelpie, I hear, said you received her as a Queen; so I hope you will do the decent by one of your own flesh and blood, and the future Head of the House at that. I shan't bring much of a retinue with me. *I* wasn't made a billionaire by old Roger, so can only take my modest "man Friday"—whose name is Jenkinson, and a Cockney at that. So don't have too much gold lace and diamond-hilted scimitars about, like a good chap, or else he'll want the very worst—his wyges ryzed. That old image Rooke that came over for Miss McS., and whom by chance I saw at the attorney man's, might pilot me down from Fiume. The old gentleman-by-Act-of-Parliament Mr. Bingham Trent (I suppose he has hyphened it by this time) told me that Miss

McS. said he "did her proud" when she went over under his charge. I shall be at Fiume on the evening of Wednesday, and shall stay at the Europa, which is, I am told, the least indecent hotel in the place. So you know where to find me, or any of your attendant demons can know, in case I am to suffer "substituted service."

Your affectionate Cousin,

ERNEST ROGER HALBARD MELTON.

Letter from Admiral Rooke to the Gospodar Rupert.

August 1, 1907.

SIR,

In obedience to your explicit direction that I should meet Mr. Ernest R. H. Melton at Fiume, and report to you exactly what occurred, "without keeping anything back,"—as you will remember you said, I beg to report.

I brought the steam-yacht *Trent* to Fiume, arriving there on the morning of Thursday. At 11.30 p.m. I went to meet the train from St. Peter, due 11.40. It was something late, arriving just as the clock was beginning to strike midnight. Mr. Melton was on board, and with him his valet Jenkinson. I am bound to say that he did not seem very pleased with his journey, and expressed much disappointment at not seeing Your Honour awaiting him. I explained, as you directed, that you had to attend with the Voivode Vissarion and the Vladika the National Council, which met at Plazac, or that otherwise you would have done yourself the pleasure of coming to meet him. I had, of course, reserved rooms (the Prince of Wales's suite), for him at the Re d'Ungheria, and had waiting the carriage which the proprietor had provided for the Prince of Wales when he stayed there. Mr. Melton took his valet with him (on the box-seat), and I followed in a *Stadtwagen* with the luggage. When I arrived, I found the *maitre d'hotel* in a stupor of concern. The English nobleman, he said, had found fault with everything, and used to him language to which he was not accustomed. I quieted him, telling him that the stranger was probably unused to foreign ways, and assuring him that Your Honour had every faith in him. He announced himself satisfied and happy at the assurance. But I noticed that he promptly put everything in the hands of the headwaiter, telling him to satisfy the milor at any cost, and then went away to some urgent business in Vienna. Clever man!

I took Mr. Melton's orders for our journey in the morning, and asked if there was anything for which he wished. He simply said to me:

"Everything is rotten. Go to hell, and shut the door after you!" His man, who seems a very decent little fellow, though he is as vain as a peacock, and speaks with a Cockney accent which is simply terrible, came down the passage after me, and explained "on his own," as he expressed it, that his master, "Mr. Ernest," was upset by the long journey, and that I was not to mind. I did not wish to make him uncomfortable, so I explained that I minded nothing except what Your Honour wished; that the steam-yacht would be ready at 7 a.m.; and that I should be waiting in the hotel from that time on till Mr. Melton cared to start, to bring him aboard.

In the morning I waited till the man Jenkinson came and told me that Mr. Ernest would start at ten. I asked if he would breakfast on board; he answered that he would take his *cafe-complet* at the hotel, but breakfast on board.

We left at ten, and took the electric pinnace out to the *Trent*, which lay, with steam up, in the roads. Breakfast was served on board, by his orders, and presently he came up on the bridge, where I was in command. He brought his man Jenkinson with him. Seeing me there, and not (I suppose) understanding that I was in command, he unceremoniously ordered me to go on the deck. Indeed, he named a place much lower. I made a sign of silence to the quartermaster at the wheel, who had released the spokes, and was going, I feared, to make some impertinent remark. Jenkinson joined me presently, and said, as some sort of explanation of his master's discourtesy (of which he was manifestly ashamed), if not as an amende:

"The governor is in a hell of a wax this morning."

When we got in sight of Meleda, Mr. Melton sent for me and asked me where we were to land. I told him that, unless he wished to the contrary, we were to run to Vissarion; but that my instructions were to land at whatever port he wished. Whereupon he told me that he wished to stay the night at some place where he might be able to see some "life." He was pleased to add something, which I presume he thought jocular, about my being able to "coach" him in such matters, as doubtless even "an old has-been like you" had still some sort of an eye for a pretty girl. I told him as respectfully as I could that I had no knowledge whatever on such subjects, which were possibly of some interest to younger men, but of none to me. He said no more; so after waiting for further orders, but without receiving any, I said:

"I suppose, sir, we shall run to Vissarion?"

"Run to the devil, if you like!" was his reply, as he turned away. When we arrived in the creek at Vissarion, he seemed much milder—less aggressive in his manner; but when he heard that you were detained at Plazac, he got rather "fresh"—I use the American term—again. I greatly feared there would be a serious misfortune before we got into the Castle, for on the dock was Julia, the wife of Michael, the Master of the Wine, who is, as you know, very beautiful. Mr. Melton seemed much taken with her; and she, being flattered by the attention of a strange gentleman and Your Honour's kinsman, put aside the stand-offishness of most of the Blue Mountain women. Whereupon Mr. Melton, forgetting himself, took her in his arms and kissed her. Instantly there was a hubbub. The mountaineers present drew their handjars, and almost on the instant sudden death appeared to be amongst us. Happily the men waited as Michael, who had just arrived on the quay-wall as the outrage took place,

ran forward, wheeling his handjar round his head, and manifestly intending to decapitate Mr. Melton. On the instant—I am sorry to say it, for
it created a terribly bad effect—Mr. Melton dropped on his knees in a
state of panic. There was just this good use in it—that there was a pause
of a few seconds. During that time the little Cockney valet, who has the
heart of a man in him, literally burst his way forward, and stood in front
of his master in boxing attitude, calling out:

"Ere, come on, the 'ole lot of ye! 'E ain't done no 'arm. He honly
kissed the gal, as any man would. If ye want to cut off somebody's
'ed, cut off mine. I ain't afride!" There was such genuine pluck in this,
and it formed so fine a contrast to the other's craven attitude (forgive
me, Your Honour; but you want the truth!), that I was glad he was an
Englishman, too. The mountaineers recognized his spirit, and saluted
with their handjars, even Michael amongst the number. Half turning
his head, the little man said in a fierce whisper:

"Buck up, guv'nor! Get up, or they'll slice ye! 'Ere's Mr. Rooke; 'e'll
see ye through it."

By this time the men were amenable to reason, and when I reminded
them that Mr. Melton was Your Honour's cousin, they put aside their
handjars and went about their work. I asked Mr. Melton to follow, and
led the way to the Castle.

When we got close to the great entrance within the walled
courtyard, we found a large number of the servants gathered, and with
them many of the mountaineers, who have kept an organized guard
all round the Castle ever since the abducting of the Voivodin. As both
Your Honour and the Voivode were away at Plazac, the guard had for
the time been doubled. When the steward came and stood in the doorway, the servants stood off somewhat, and the mountaineers drew back
to the farther sides and angles of the courtyard. The Voivodin had, of
course, been informed of the guest's (your cousin) coming, and came
to meet him in the old custom of the Blue Mountains. As Your Honour

only came to the Blue Mountains recently, and as no occasion has been since then of illustrating the custom since the Voivode was away, and the Voivodin then believed to be dead, perhaps I, who have lived here so long, may explain:

When to an old Blue Mountain house a guest comes whom it is wished to do honour, the Lady, as in the vernacular the mistress of the house is called, comes herself to meet the guest at the door—or, rather, *outside* the door—so that she can herself conduct him within. It is a pretty ceremony, and it is said that of old in kingly days the monarch always set much store by it. The custom is that, when she approaches the honoured guest (he need not be royal), she bends—or more properly kneels—before him and kisses his hand. It has been explained by historians that the symbolism is that the woman, showing obedience to her husband, as the married woman of the Blue Mountains always does, emphasizes that obedience to her husband's guest. The custom is always observed in its largest formality when a young wife receives for the first time a guest, and especially one whom her husband wishes to honour. The Voivodin was, of course, aware that Mr. Melton was your kinsman, and naturally wished to make the ceremony of honour as marked as possible, so as to show overtly her sense of her husband's worth.

When we came into the courtyard, I held back, of course, for the honour is entirely individual, and is never extended to any other, no matter how worthy he may be. Naturally Mr. Melton did not know the etiquette of the situation, and so for that is not to be blamed. He took his valet with him when, seeing someone coming to the door, he went forward. I thought he was going to rush to his welcomer. Such, though not in the ritual, would have been natural in a young kinsman wishing to do honour to the bride of his host, and would to anyone have been both understandable and forgivable. It did not occur to me at the time, but I have since thought that perhaps he had not then heard of Your Honour's marriage, which I trust you will, in justice to the young gentleman, bear in mind when considering the matter. Unhappily, however, he did not show any such eagerness. On the contrary, he seemed to make a point of showing indifference. It seemed to me myself that he, seeing somebody wishing to make much of him, took what he considered a safe opportunity of restoring to himself his own good opinion, which must have been considerably lowered in the episode of the Wine Master's wife.

The Voivodin, thinking, doubtless, Your Honour, to add a fresh lustre to her welcome, had donned the costume which all her nation has now come to love and to accept as a dress of ceremonial honour. She wore her shroud. It moved the hearts of all of us who looked on to see it, and we appreciated its being worn for such a cause. But Mr. Melton did not seem to care. As he had been approaching she had begun to kneel, and was already on her knees whilst he was several yards away. There he stopped and turned to speak to his valet, put a glass in his eye, and looked all round him and up and down—indeed, everywhere except at the Great Lady, who was on her knees before him, waiting to bid him welcome. I could see in the eyes of such of the mountaineers as were within my range of vision a growing animosity; so, hoping to keep down any such expression, which I knew would cause harm to Your Honour and the Voivodin, I looked all round them straight in their faces with a fixed frown, which, indeed, they seemed to understand, for they regained, and for the time maintained, their usual dignified calm. The Voivodin, may I say, bore the trial wonderfully. No human being could see that she was in any degree pained or even surprised. Mr. Melton stood looking round him so long that I had full time to regain my own attitude of calm. At last he seemed to come back to the knowledge that someone was waiting for him, and sauntered leisurely forward. There was so much insolence—mind you, not insolence that was intended to appear as such—in his movement that the mountaineers began to steal forward. When he was close up to the Voivodin, and she put out her hand to take his, he put forward *ONE FINGER!* I could hear the intake of the breath of the men, now close around, for I had moved forward, too. I thought it would be as well to be close to your guest, lest something should happen to him. The Voivodin still kept her splendid self-control. Raising the finger put forward by the guest with the same deference as though it had been the hand of a King, she bent her head down and kissed it. Her duty of courtesy now done, she was preparing to rise, when he put his hand into his pocket, and, pulling out a sovereign, offered it to her. His valet moved his hand forward, as if to pull back his arm, but it was too late. I am sure, Your Honour, that no affront was intended. He doubtless thought that he was doing a kindness of the sort usual in England when one "tips" a housekeeper. But all the same, to one in her position, it was an affront, an insult, open and unmistakable. So it was received by the mountaineers, whose handjars flashed out as one. For a second it was so received even by the Voivodin, who, with face flushing scarlet, and the stars in her eyes flaming red, sprang to her feet. But in that second she had regained herself, and to all appearances her righteous anger passed away. Stooping, she took the hand of her guest and raised it—you know how strong she is—and, holding it in hers, led him into the doorway, saying:

"You are welcome, kinsman of my husband, to the house of my father, which is presently my husband's also. Both are grieved that, duty having called them away for the time, they are unable to be here to help me to greet you."

I tell you, Your Honour, that it was a lesson in self-respect which anyone who saw it can never forget. As to me, it makes my flesh quiver, old as I am, with delight, and my heart leap.

May I, as a faithful servant who has had many years of experience, suggest that Your Honour should seem—for the present, at any rate—

not to know any of these things which I have reported, as you wished me to do. Be sure that the Voivodin will tell you her gracious self aught that she would wish you to know. And such reticence on your part must make for her happiness, even if it did not for your own.

So that you may know all, as you desired, and that you may have time to school yourself to whatever attitude you think best to adopt, I send this off to you at once by fleet messenger. Were the aeroplane here, I should take it myself. I leave here shortly to await the arrival of Sir Colin at Otranto.

Your Honour's faithful servant,
ROOKE.

JANET MACKELPIE'S NOTES.

August 9, 1907.

To me it seems very providential that Rupert was not at home when that dreadful young man Ernest Melton arrived, though it is possible that if Rupert had been present he would not have dared to conduct himself so badly. Of course, I heard all about it from the maids; Teuta never opened her lips to me on the subject. It was bad enough and stupid enough for him to try to kiss a decent young woman like Julia, who is really as good as gold and as modest as one of our own Highland lassies; but to think of him insulting Teuta! The little beast! One would think that a champion idiot out of an Equatorial asylum would know better! If Michael, the Wine Master, wanted to kill him, I wonder what my Rupert and hers would have done? I am truly thankful that he was not present. And I am thankful, too, that I was not present either, for I should have made an exhibition of myself, and Rupert would not have liked that. He—the little beast! might have seen from the very dress that the dear girl wore that there was something exceptional about her. But on one account I should have liked to see her. They tell me that she was, in her true dignity, like a Queen, and that her humility in receiving her husband's kinsman was a lesson to every woman in the Land. I must be careful not to let Rupert know that I have heard of the incident. Later on, when it is all blown over and the young man has been got safely away, I shall tell him of it. Mr. Rooke—Lord High Admiral Rooke, I should say—must be a really wonderful man to have so held himself in check; for, from what I have heard of him, he must in his younger days have been worse than Old Morgan of Panama. Mr. Ernest Roger Halbard Melton, of Humcroft, Salop, little knows how near he was to being "cleft to the chine" also.

Fortunately, I had heard of his meeting with Teuta before he came to see me, for I did not get back from my walk till after he had arrived. Teuta's noble example was before me, and I determined that I, too, would show good manners under any circumstances. But I didn't know how mean he is. Think of his saying to me that Rupert's position here must be a great source of pride to me, who had been his nursery governess. He said "nursemaid" first, but then stumbled in his words, seeming to remember something. I did not turn a hair, I am glad to say. It is a mercy Uncle Colin was not here, for I honestly believe that, if he had been, he would have done the "cleaving to the chine" himself. It has been a narrow escape for Master Ernest, for only this morning Rupert had a message, sent on from Gibraltar, saying that he was arriving with his clansmen, and that they would not be far behind his letter. He would call at Otranto in case someone should come across to pilot him to Vissarion. Uncle told me all about that young cad having offered him one finger in Mr. Trent's office, though, of course, he didn't let the cad see that he noticed it. I have no doubt that, when he does arrive, that young man, if he is here still, will find that he will have to behave himself, if it be only on Sir Colin's account alone.

THE SAME (LATER).

I had hardly finished writing when the lookout on the tower announced that the *Teuta*, as Rupert calls his aeroplane, was sighted crossing the mountains from Plazac. I hurried up to see him arrive, for I had not as yet seen him on his "aero." Mr. Ernest Melton came up, too. Teuta was, of course, before any of us. She seems to know by instinct when Rupert is coming.

It was certainly a wonderful sight to see the little aeroplane, with outspread wings like a bird in flight, come sailing high over the mountains. There was a head-wind, and they were beating against it; otherwise we should not have had time to get to the tower before the arrival.

When once the "aero" had begun to drop on the near side of the mountains, however, and had got a measure of shelter from them, her pace was extraordinary. We could not tell, of course, what sort of pace she came at from looking at herself. But we gathered some idea from the rate at which the mountains and hills seemed to slide away from under her. When she got over the foot-hills, which are about ten miles away, she came on at a swift glide that seemed to throw the distance behind her. When quite close, she rose up a little till she was something higher than the Tower, to which she came as straight as an arrow from the bow, and glided to her moorings, stopping dead as Rupert pulled a lever, which seemed to turn a barrier to the wind. The Voivode sat beside Rupert, but I must say that he seemed to hold on to the bar in front of him even more firmly than Rupert held to his steering-gear.

When they had alighted, Rupert greeted his cousin with the utmost kindness, and bade him welcome to Vissarion.

"I see," he said, "you have met Teuta. Now you may congratulate me, if you wish."

Mr. Melton made a long rodomontade about her beauty, but presently, stumbling about in his speech, said something regarding it being unlucky to appear in grave-clothes. Rupert laughed, and clapped him on the shoulder as he answered:

"That pattern of frock is likely to become a national dress for loyal women of the Blue Mountains. When you know something of what that dress means to us all at present you will understand. In the meantime, take it that there is not a soul in the nation that does not love it and honour her for wearing it." To which the cad replied:

"Oh, indeed! I thought it was some preparation for a fancy-dress ball." Rupert's comment on this ill-natured speech was (for him) quite grumpily given:

"I should not advise you to think such things whilst you are in this part of the world, Ernest. They bury men here for much less."

The cad seemed struck with something—either what Rupert had said or his manner of saying it—for he was silent for several seconds before he spoke.

"I'm very tired with that long journey, Rupert. Would you and Mrs. Sent Leger mind if I go to my own room and turn in? My man can ask for a cup of tea and a sandwich for me."

RUPERT'S JOURNAL.

August 10, 1907.

When Ernest said he wished to retire it was about the wisest thing he could have said or done, and it suited Teuta and me down to the ground. I could see that the dear girl was agitated about something, so thought it would be best for her to be quiet, and not worried with being civil to the Bounder. Though he is my cousin, I can't think of him as anything else. The Voivode and I had certain matters to attend to arising out of the meeting of the Council, and when we were through the night was closing in. When I saw Teuta in our own rooms she said at once:

"Do you mind, dear, if I stay with Aunt Janet to-night? She is very upset and nervous, and when I offered to come to her she clung to me and cried with relief."

So when I had had some supper, which I took with the Voivode, I came down to my old quarters in the Garden Room, and turned in early.

I was awakened a little before dawn by the coming of the fighting monk Theophrastos, a notable runner, who had an urgent message for me. This was the letter to me given to him by Rooke. He had been cautioned to give it into no other hand, but to find me wherever I might be, and convey it personally. When he had arrived at Plazac I had left on the aeroplane, so he had turned back to Vissarion.

When I read Rooke's report of Ernest Melton's abominable conduct I was more angry with him than I can say. Indeed, I did not think before that that I could be angry with him, for I have always despised him. But this was too much. However, I realized the wisdom of Rooke's advice, and went away by myself to get over my anger and reacquire my self-mastery. The aeroplane Teuta was still housed on the tower, so I went up alone and took it out.

When I had had a spin of about a hundred miles I felt better. The bracing of the wind and the quick, exhilarating motion restored me to myself, and I felt able to cope with Master Ernest, or whatever else chagrinable might come along, without giving myself away. As Teuta had thought it better to keep silence as to Ernest's affront, I felt I must not acknowledge it; but, all the same, I determined to get rid of him before the day was much older.

When I had had my breakfast I sent word to him by a servant that I was coming to his rooms, and followed not long behind the messenger.

He was in a suit of silk pyjamas, such as not even Solomon in all his glory was arrayed in. I closed the door behind me before I began to speak. He listened, at first amazed, then disconcerted, then angry, and then cowering down like a whipped hound. I felt that it was a case for speaking out. A bumptious ass like him, who deliberately insulted everyone he came across—for if all or any of his efforts in that way were due to mere elemental ignorance he was not fit to live, but should be silenced on sight as a modern Caliban—deserved neither pity nor mercy. To extend to him fine feeling, tolerance, and such-like gentlenesses would be to deprive the world of them without benefit to any. So well as I can remember, what I said was something like this:

"Ernest, as you say, you've got to go, and to go quick, you understand. I dare say you look on this as a land of barbarians, and think that any of your high-toned refinements are thrown away on people here. Well, perhaps it is so. Undoubtedly, the structure of the country is rough; the mountains may only represent the glacial epoch; but so far as I can gather from some of your exploits—for I have only learned a small part as yet—you represent a period a good deal farther back. You seem to have given our folk here an exhibition of the playfulness of the hooligan of the Saurian stage of development; but the Blue Mountains, rough as they are, have come up out of the primeval slime, and even now the people aim at better manners. They may be rough, primitive, barbarian, elemental, if you will, but they are not low down enough to tolerate either your ethics or your taste. My dear cousin, your life is not safe here! I am told that yesterday, only for the restraint exercised by certain offended mountaineers on other grounds than your own worth, you would have been abbreviated by the head. Another day of your fascinating presence would do away with this restraint, and then we should have a scandal. I am a new-comer here myself—too new a comer to be able to afford a scandal of that kind—and so I shall not delay your going. Believe me, my dear cousin, Ernest Roger Halbard Melton, of Humcroft, Salop, that I am inconsolable about your resolution of immediate departure, but I cannot shut my eyes to its wisdom. At present the matter is altogether amongst ourselves, and when you have gone—if it be immediately—silence will be observed on all hands for the sake of the house wherein you are a guest; but if there be time for scandal to spread, you will be made, whether you be alive or dead, a European laughing-stock. Accordingly, I have anticipated your wishes, and have ordered a fast steam yacht to take you to Ancona, or to whatever other port you may desire. The yacht will be under the command of Captain Desmond, of one of our battleships—a most determined officer, who will carry out any directions which may be given to him. This will insure your safety so far as Italian territory. Some of his officials will arrange a special carriage for you up to Flushing, and a cabin on the steamer to Queenboro'. A man of mine will travel on the train and steamer with you, and will see that whatever you may wish in the way of food or comfort will be provided. Of course, you understand, my dear cousin, that you are my guest until you arrive in London. I have not asked Rooke to accompany you, as when he went to meet you, it was a mistake. Indeed, there might have been a danger to you which I never contemplated—a quite unnecessary danger, I assure you. But happily Admiral Rooke, though a man of strong passions, has wonderful self-control."

"Admiral Rooke?" he queried. "Admiral?"

"Admiral, certainly," I replied, "but not an ordinary Admiral—one of many. He is *the* Admiral—the Lord High Admiral of the Land of the Blue Mountains, with sole control of its expanding navy. When such a man is treated as a valet, there may be . . . But why go into this? It is all over. I only mention it lest anything of a similar kind should occur with Captain Desmond, who is a younger man, and therefore with probably less self-repression."

I saw that he had learned his lesson, and so said no more on the subject.

There was another reason for his going which I did not speak of. Sir Colin MacKelpie was coming with his clansmen, and I knew he did not like Ernest Melton. I well remembered that episode of his offering one finger to the old gentleman in Mr. Trent's office, and, moreover, I had my suspicions that Aunt Janet's being upset was probably in some measure due to some rudeness of his that she did not wish to speak about. He is really an impossible young man, and is far better out of this country than in it. If he remained here, there would be some sort of a tragedy for certain.

I must say that it was with a feeling of considerable relief that I saw the yacht steam out of the creek, with Captain Desmond on the bridge and my cousin beside him.

Quite other were my feelings when, an hour after, *The Lady* came flying into the creek with the Lord High Admiral on the bridge, and beside him, more splendid and soldier-like than ever, Sir Colin MacKelpie. Mr. Bingham Trent was also on the bridge.

The General was full of enthusiasm regarding his regiment, for in all, those he brought with him and those finishing their training at home, the force is near the number of a full regiment. When we were alone he explained to me that all was arranged regarding the non-commissioned officers, but that he had held over the question of officers until we should have had a suitable opportunity of talking the matter over together. He explained to me his reasons, which were certainly simple and cogent. Officers, according to him, are a different class, and accustomed to a different standard altogether of life and living, of duties and pleasures. They are harder to deal with and more difficult to obtain. "There was no use," he said, "in getting a lot of failures, with old-crusted ways of their own importance. We must have young men for our purpose—that is, men not old, but with some experience—men, of course, who know how to behave themselves, or else, from what little I have seen of the Blue Mountaineers, they wouldn't last long here if they went on as some of them do elsewhere. I shall start things here as you wish me to, for I am here, my dear boy, to stay with you and Janet, and we shall, if it be given to us by the Almighty, help to build up together a new 'nation'—an ally of Britain, who will stand at least as an outpost of our own nation, and a guardian of our eastern road. When things are organized here on the military side, and are going strong, I shall, if you can spare me, run back to London for a few weeks. Whilst I am there I shall pick up a lot of the sort of officers we want. I know that there are loads of them to be had. I shall go slowly, however, and carefully, too, and every man I bring back will be recommended to me by some old soldier whom I know, and who knows the man he recommends, and has seen him work. We shall have, I dare say, an army for its size second to none in the world, and the day may come when your old country will be proud of your new one. Now I'm off to see that all is ready for my people—your people now."

I had had arrangements made for the comfort of the clansmen and the women, but I knew that the good old soldier would see for himself that his men were to be comfortable. It was not for nothing that he was—is—looked on as perhaps the General most beloved by his men in the whole British Army.

When he had gone, and I was alone, Mr. Trent, who had evidently been waiting for the opportunity, came to me. When we had spoken of my marriage and of Teuta, who seems to have made an immense impression on him, he said suddenly:

"I suppose we are quite alone, and that we shall not be interrupted?" I summoned the man outside—there is always a sentry on guard outside my door or near me, wherever I may be—and gave orders that I was not to be disturbed until I gave fresh orders. "If," I said, "there be anything pressing or important, let the Voivodin or Miss MacKelpie know. If either of them brings anyone to me, it will be all right."

When we were quite alone Mr. Trent took a slip of paper and some documents from the bag which was beside him. He then read out items from the slip, placing as he did so the documents so checked over before him.

1. New Will made on marriage, to be signed presently.
2. Copy of the Re-conveyance of Vissarion estates to Peter Vissarion, as directed by Will of Roger Melton.

3. Report of Correspondence with Privy Council, and proceedings following.

Taking up the last named, he untied the red tape, and, holding the bundle in his hand, went on:

"As you may, later on, wish to examine the details of the Proceedings, I have copied out the various letters, the originals of which are put safely away in my strong-room where, of course, they are always available in case you may want them. For your present information I shall give you a rough synopsis of the Proceedings, referring where advisable to this paper.

"On receipt of your letter of instructions regarding the Consent of the Privy Council to your changing your nationality in accordance with the terms of Roger Melton's Will, I put myself in communication with the Clerk of the Privy Council, informing him of your wish to be naturalized in due time to the Land of the Blue Mountains. After some letters between us, I got a summons to attend a meeting of the Council.

"I attended, as required, taking with me all necessary documents, and such as I conceived might be advisable to produce, if wanted.

"The Lord President informed me that the present meeting of the Council was specially summoned in obedience to the suggestion of the King, who had been consulted as to his personal wishes on the subject—should he have any. The President then proceeded to inform me officially that all Proceedings of the Privy Council were altogether confidential, and were not to be made public under any circumstances. He was gracious enough to add:

"'The circumstances of this case, however, are unique; and as you act for another, we have thought it advisable to enlarge your permission in the matter, so as to allow you to communicate freely with your principal. As that gentleman is settling himself in a part of the world which has been in the past, and may be again, united to this nation by some common interest, His Majesty wishes Mr. Sent Leger to feel assured of the good-will of Great Britain to the Land of the Blue Mountains, and even of his own personal satisfaction that a gentleman of so distinguished a lineage and such approved personal character is about to be—within his own scope—a connecting-link between the nations. To which end he has graciously announced that, should the Privy Council acquiesce in the request of Denaturalization, he will himself sign the Patent therefor.

"'The Privy Council has therefore held private session, at which the matter has been discussed in its many bearings; and it is content that the change can do no harm, but may be of some service to the two nations. We have, therefore, agreed to grant the prayer of the Applicant; and the officials of the Council have the matter of the form of Grant in hand. So you, sir, may rest satisfied that as soon as the formalities—which will, of course, require the formal signing of certain documents by the Applicant—can be complied with, the Grant and Patent will obtain.'"

Having made this statement in formal style, my old friend went on in more familiar way:

"And so, my dear Rupert, all is in hand; and before very long you will have the freedom required under the Will, and will be at liberty to take whatever steps may be necessary to be naturalized in your new country.

"I may tell you, by the way, that several members of the Council made very complimentary remarks regarding you. I am forbidden to give names, but I may tell you facts. One old Field-Marshal, whose name is familiar to the whole world, said that he had served in many places with your father, who was a very valiant soldier, and that he was glad that Great Britain was to have in the future the benefit of your father's son in a friendly land now beyond the outposts of our Empire, but which had been one with her in the past, and might be again.

"So much for the Privy Council. We can do no more at present until you sign and have attested the documents which I have brought with me.

"We can now formally complete the settlement of the Vissarion estates, which must be done whilst you are a British citizen. So, too, with the Will, the more formal and complete document, which is to take the place of that short one which you forwarded to me the day after your marriage. It may be, perhaps, necessary or advisable that, later on, when you are naturalized here, you shall make a new Will in strictest accordance with local law."

TEUTA SENT LEGER'S DIARY.

August 19, 1907.

We had a journey to-day that was simply glorious. We had been waiting to take it for more than a week. Rupert not only wanted the weather suitable, but he had to wait till the new aeroplane came home. It is more than twice as big as our biggest up to now. None of the others could take all the party which Rupert wanted to go. When he heard that the aero was coming from Whitby, where it was sent from Leeds, he directed by cable that it should be unshipped at Otranto, whence he took it here all by himself. I wanted to come with him, but he thought it better not. He says that Brindisi is too busy a place to keep anything quiet—if not secret—and he wants to be very dark indeed about this, as it is worked by the new radium engine. Ever since they found radium in our own hills he has been obsessed by the idea of an aerial navy for our protection. And after to-day's experiences I think he is right. As he wanted to survey the whole country at a glimpse, so that the general scheme of defence might be put in hand, we had to have an aero big enough to take the party as well as fast enough to do it rapidly, and all at once. We had, in addition to Rupert, my father, and myself, Sir

Colin and Lord High Admiral Rooke (I do like to give that splendid old fellow his full title!). The military and naval experts had with them scientific apparatus of various kinds, also cameras and range-finders, so that they could mark their maps as they required. Rupert, of course, drove, and I acted as his assistant. Father, who has not yet become accustomed to aerial travel, took a seat in the centre (which Rupert had thoughtfully prepared for him), where there is very little motion. I must say I was amazed to see the way that splendid old soldier Sir Colin bore himself. He had never been on an aeroplane before, but, all the same, he was as calm as if he was on a rock. Height or motion did not trouble him. Indeed, he seemed to *enjoy* himself all the time. The Admiral is himself almost an expert, but in any case I am sure he would have been unconcerned, just as he was in the *Crab* as Rupert has told me.

We left just after daylight, and ran down south. When we got to the east of Ilsin, we kept slightly within the border-line, and went north or east as it ran, making occasional loops inland over the mountains and back again. When we got up to our farthest point north, we began to go much slower. Sir Colin explained that for the rest all would be comparatively plain-sailing in the way of defence; but that as any foreign Power other than the Turk must attack from seaward, he would like to examine the seaboard very carefully in conjunction with the Admiral, whose advice as to sea defence would be invaluable.

Rupert was fine. No one could help admiring him as he sat working his lever and making the great machine obey every touch. He was wrapped up in his work. I don't believe that whilst he was working he ever thought of even me. He *is* splendid!

We got back just as the sun was dropping down over the Calabrian Mountains. It is quite wonderful how the horizon changes when you are sailing away up high on an aeroplane. Rupert is going to teach me how to manage one all by myself, and when I am fit he will give me one, which he is to have specially built for me.

I think I, too, have done some good work—at least, I have got some good ideas—from our journey to-day. Mine are not of war, but of peace, and I think I see a way by which we shall be able to develop our country in a wonderful way. I shall talk the idea over with Rupert to-night, when we are alone. In the meantime Sir Colin and Admiral Rooke will think their plans over individually, and to-morrow morning together. Then the next day they, too, are to go over their idea with Rupert and my father, and something may be decided then.

RUPERT'S JOURNAL—*Continued.*

August 21, 1907.

Our meeting on the subject of National Defence, held this afternoon, went off well. We were five in all, for with permission of the Voivode and the two fighting-men, naval and military, I brought Teuta with me. She sat beside me quite quietly, and never made a remark of any kind till the Defence business had been gone through. Both Sir Colin and Admiral Rooke were in perfect agreement as to the immediate steps to be taken for defence. In the first instance, the seaboard was to be properly fortified in the necessary places, and the navy largely strengthened. When we had got thus far I asked Rooke to tell of the navy increase already in hand. Whereupon he explained that, as we had found the small battleship *The Lady* of an excellent type for coast defence, acting only in home waters, and of a size to take cover where necessary at many places on our own shores, we had ordered nine others of the same pattern. Of these the first four were already in hand, and were proceeding with the greatest expedition. The General then supplemented this by saying that big guns could be used from points judiciously chosen on the seaboard, which was in all so short a length that no very great quantity of armament would be required.

"We can have," he said, "the biggest guns of the most perfect kind yet accomplished, and use them from land batteries of the most up-to-date pattern. The one serious proposition we have to deal with is the defence of the harbour—as yet quite undeveloped—which is known as the 'Blue Mouth.' Since our aerial journey I have been to it by sea with Admiral Rooke in *The Lady*, and then on land with the Vladika, who was born on its shores, and who knows every inch of it.

"It is worth fortifying—and fortifying well, for as a port it is peerless in Mediterranean seas. The navies of the world might ride in it, land-locked, and even hidden from view seawards. The mountains which enclose it are in themselves absolute protection. In addition, these can only be assailed from our own territory. Of course, Voivode, you understand when I say 'our' I mean the Land of the Blue Mountains, for whose safety and well-being I am alone concerned. Any ship anchoring in the roads of the Blue Mouth would have only one need—sufficient length of cable for its magnificent depth.

"When proper guns are properly placed on the steep cliffs to north and south of the entrance, and when the rock islet between has been armoured and armed as will be necessary, the Mouth will be impregnable. But we should not depend on the aiming of the entrance alone. At certain salient points—which I have marked upon this map—armour-plated sunken forts within earthworks should be established. There should be covering forts on the hillsides, and, of course, the final summits protected. Thus we could resist attack on any side or all sides—from sea or land. That port will yet mean the wealth as well as the strength of this nation, so it will be well to have it properly protected. This should be done soon, and the utmost secrecy observed in the doing of it, lest the so doing should become a matter of international concern."

Here Rooke smote the table hard.

"By God, that is true! It has been the dream of my own life for this many a year."

In the silence which followed the sweet, gentle voice of Teuta came clear as a bell:

"May I say a word? I am emboldened to, as Sir Colin has spoken so splendidly, and as the Lord High Admiral has not hesitated to mention his dreaming. I, too, have had a dream—a day-dream—which came in a flash, but no less a dream, for all that. It was when we hung on the aeroplane over the Blue Mouth. It seemed to me in an instant that I saw that beautiful spot as it will some time be—typical, as Sir Colin said, of the wealth as well as the strength of this nation; a mart for the world whence will come for barter some of the great wealth of the Blue Mountains. That wealth is as yet undeveloped. But the day is at hand when we may begin to use it, and through that very port. Our mountains and their valleys are clad with trees of splendid growth, virgin forests of priceless worth; hard woods of all kinds, which have no superior throughout the world. In the rocks, though hidden as yet, is vast mineral wealth of many kinds. I have been looking through the reports of the geological exports of the Commission of Investigation which my husband organized soon after he came to live here, and, according to them, our whole mountain ranges simply teem with vast quantities of minerals, almost more precious for industry than gold and silver are for commerce—though, indeed, gold is not altogether lacking as a mineral. When once our work on the harbour is done, and the place has been made secure against any attempt at foreign aggression, we must try to find a way to bring this wealth of woods and ores down to the sea.

"And then, perhaps, may begin the great prosperity of our Land, of which we have all dreamt."

She stopped, all vibrating, almost choked with emotion. We were all moved. For myself, I was thrilled to the core. Her enthusiasm was all-sweeping, and under its influence I found my own imagination expanding. Out of its experiences I spoke:

"And there is a way. I can see it. Whilst our dear Voivodin was speaking, the way seemed to clear. I saw at the back of the Blue Mouth, where it goes deepest into the heart of the cliffs, the opening of a great tunnel, which ran upward over a steep slope till it debouched on the first plateau beyond the range of the encompassing cliffs.

Thither came by various rails of steep gradient, by timber-shoots and cable-rails, by aerial cables and precipitating tubes, wealth from over ground and under it; for as our Land is all mountains, and as these tower up to the clouds, transport to the sea shall be easy and of little cost when once the machinery is established. As everything of much weight goes downward, the cars of the main tunnel of the port shall return upward without cost. We can have from the mountains a head of water under good control, which will allow of endless hydraulic power, so that the whole port and the mechanism of the town to which it will grow can be worked by it.

"This work can be put in hand at once. So soon as the place shall be perfectly surveyed and the engineering plans got ready, we can start on the main tunnel, working from the sea-level up, so that the cost of the transport of material will be almost nil. This work can go on whilst the forts are building; no time need be lost.

"Moreover, may I add a word on National Defence? We are, though old in honour, a young nation as to our place amongst Great Powers. And so we must show the courage and energy of a young nation. The Empire of the Air is not yet won. Why should not we make a bid for it? As our mountains are lofty, so shall we have initial power of attack or defence. We can have, in chosen spots amongst the clouds, depots of war aeroplanes, with which we can descend and smite our enemies quickly on land or sea. We shall hope to live for Peace; but woe to those who drive us to War!"

There is no doubt that the Vissarions are a warlike race. As I spoke, Teuta took one of my hands and held it hard. The old Voivode, his eyes blazing, rose and stood beside me and took the other. The two old fighting-men of the land and the sea stood up and saluted.

This was the beginning of what ultimately became "The National Committee of Defence and Development."

I had other, and perhaps greater, plans for the future in my mind; but the time had not come for their utterance.

To me it seems not only advisable, but necessary, that the utmost discretion be observed by all our little group, at all events for the present. There seems to be some new uneasiness in the Blue Mountains. There are constant meetings of members of the Council, but no formal meeting of the Council, as such, since the last one at which I was present. There is constant coming and going amongst the mountaineers, always in groups, small or large. Teuta and I, who have been about very much on the aeroplane, have both noticed it. But somehow we—that is, the Voivode and myself—are left out of everything; but we have not said as yet a word on the subject to any of the others. The Voivode notices, but he says nothing; so I am silent, and Teuta does whatever I ask. Sir Colin does not notice anything except the work he is engaged on—the planning the defences of the Blue Mouth. His old scientific training as an engineer, and his enormous experience of wars and sieges—for he was for nearly fifty years sent as military representative to all the great wars—seem to have become directed on that point. He is certainly planning it all out in a wonderful way. He consults Rooke almost hourly on the maritime side of the question. The Lord High Admiral has been a watcher all his life, and very few important points have ever escaped him, so that he can add greatly to the wisdom of the defensive construction. He notices, I think, that something is going on outside ourselves; but he keeps a resolute silence.

What the movement going on is I cannot guess. It is not like the uneasiness that went before the abduction of Teuta and the Voivode, but it is even more pronounced. That was an uneasiness founded on some suspicion. This is a positive thing, and has definite meaning—of some sort. We shall, I suppose, know all about it in good time. In the meantime we go on with our work. Happily the whole Blue Mouth and the mountains round it are on my own property, the portion acquired long ago by Uncle Roger, exclusive of the Vissarion estate. I asked the Voivode to allow me to transfer it to him, but he sternly refused and forbade me, quite peremptorily, to ever open the subject to him again. "You have done enough already," he said. "Were I to allow you to go further, I should feel mean. And I do not think you would like your wife's father to suffer that feeling after a long life, which he has tried to live in honour."

I bowed, and said no more. So there the matter rests, and I have to take my own course. I have had a survey made, and on the head of it the Tunnel to the harbour is begun.

BOOK VIII: THE FLASHING OF THE HANDJAR

PRIVATE MEMORANDUM OF THE MEETING OF VARIOUS MEMBERS OF THE NATIONAL COUNCIL, HELD AT THE STATE HOUSE OF THE BLUE MOUNTAINS AT PLAZAC ON MONDAY, AUGUST 26, 1907. *(Written by Cristoferos, Scribe of the Council, by instruction of those present.)*

WHEN THE PRIVATE meeting of various Members of the National Council had assembled in the Council Hall of the State House at Plazac, it was as a preliminary decided unanimously that now or hereafter no names of those present were to be mentioned, and that officials appointed for the purposes of this meeting should be designated by office only, the names of all being withheld.

The proceedings assumed the shape of a general conversation, quite informal, and therefore not to be recorded. The nett outcome was the unanimous expression of an opinion that the time, long contemplated by very many persons throughout the nation, had now come when the Constitution and machinery of the State should be changed; that the present form of ruling by an Irregular Council was not sufficient, and that a method more in accord with the spirit of the times should be adopted. To this end Constitutional Monarchy, such as that holding in Great Britain, seemed best adapted. Finally, it was decided that each Member of the Council should make a personal canvass of his district, talk over the matter with his electors, and bring back to another meeting—or, rather, as it was amended, to this meeting postponed for a week, until September 2nd—the opinions and wishes received. Before separating, the individual to be appointed King, in case the new idea should prove grateful to the nation, was discussed. The consensus of opinion was entirely to the effect that the Voivode Peter Vissarion should, if he would accept the high office, be appointed. It was urged that, as his daughter, the Voivodin Teuta, was now married to the Englishman, Rupert Sent Leger—called generally by the mountaineers "thee Gospodar Rupert"—a successor to follow the Voivode when God should call him would be at hand—a successor worthy in every way to succeed to so illustrious a post. It was urged by several speakers, with general acquiescence, that already Mr. Sent Leger's services to the State were such that he would be in himself a worthy person to begin the new Dynasty; but that, as he was now allied to the Voivode Peter Vissarion, it was becoming that the elder, born of the nation, should receive the first honour.

THE SAME—*Continued.*

The adjourned meeting of certain members of the National Council was resumed in the Hall of the State House at Plazac on Monday, September 2nd, 1907. By motion the same chairman was appointed, and the rule regarding the record renewed.

Reports were made by the various members of the Council in turn, according to the State Roll. Every district was represented. The reports were unanimously in favour of the New Constitution, and it was reported by each and all of the Councillors that the utmost enthusiasm marked in every case the suggestion of the Voivode Peter Vissarion as the first King to be crowned under the new Constitution, and that remainder should be settled on the Gospodar Rupert (the mountaineers would only receive his lawful name as an alternative; one and all said that he would be "Rupert" to them and to the nation—for ever).

The above matter having been satisfactorily settled, it was decided that a formal meeting of the National Council should be held at the State House, Plazac, in one week from to-day, and that the Voivode Peter Vissarion should be asked to be in the State

House in readiness to attend. It was also decided that instruction should be given to the High Court of National Law to prepare and have ready, in skeleton form, a rescript of the New Constitution to be adopted, the same to be founded on the Constitution and Procedure of Great Britain, so far as the same may be applicable to the traditional ideas of free Government in the Land of the Blue Mountains.

By unanimous vote this private and irregular meeting of "Various National Councillors" was then dissolved.

RECORD OF THE FIRST MEETING OF THE NATIONAL COUNCIL OF THE LAND OF THE BLUE MOUNTAINS, HELD AT PLAZAC ON MONDAY, SEPTEMBER 9TH, 1907, TO CONSIDER THE ADOPTION OF A NEW CONSTITUTION, AND TO GIVE PERMANENT EFFECT TO THE SAME IF, AND WHEN, DECIDED UPON. (*Kept by the Monk Cristoferos, Scribe to the National Council.*)

The adjourned meeting duly took place as arranged. There was a full attendance of Members of the Council, together with the Vladika, the Archbishop, the Archimandrites of Spazac, of Ispazar, of Domitan, and Astrag; the Chancellor; the Lord of the Exchequer; the President of the High Court of National Law; the President of the Council of Justice; and such other high officials as it is customary to summon to meetings of the National Council on occasions of great importance. The names of all present will be found in the full report, wherein are given the ipsissima verba of the various utterances made during the consideration of the questions discussed, the same having been taken down in shorthand by the humble scribe of this précis, which has been made for the convenience of Members of the Council and others.

The Voivode Peter Vissarion, obedient to the request of the Council, was in attendance at the State House, waiting in the "Chamber of the High Officers" until such time as he should be asked to come before the Council.

The President put before the National Council the matter of the new Constitution, outlining the headings of it as drawn up by the High Court of National Law, and the Constitution having been formally accepted *nem. con.* by the National Council on behalf of the people, he proposed that the Crown should be offered to the Voivode Peter Vissarion, with remainder to the "Gospodar Rupert" (legally, Rupert Sent Leger), husband of his only child, the Voivodin Teuta. This also was received with enthusiasm, and passed *nem. con.*

Thereupon the President of Council, the Archbishop, and the Vladika, acting together as a deputation, went to pray the attention of the Voivode Peter Vassarion.

When the Voivode entered, the whole Council and officials stood up, and for a few seconds waited in respectful silence with heads bowed down. Then, as if by a common impulse—for no word was spoken nor any signal given—they all drew their handjars, and stood to attention—with points raised and edges of the handjars to the front.

The Voivode stood very still. He seemed much moved, but controlled himself admirably. The only time when be seemed to lose his self-control was when, once again with a strange simultaneity, all present raised their handjars on high, and shouted: "Hail, Peter, King!" Then lowering their points till these almost touched the ground, they once again stood with bowed heads.

When he had quite mastered himself, the Voivode Peter Vissarion spoke:

"How can I, my brothers, sufficiently thank you, and, through you, the people of the Blue Mountains, for the honour done to me this day? In very truth it is not possible, and therefore I pray you to consider it as done, measuring my gratitude in the greatness of your own hearts. Such honour as you offer to me is not contemplated by any man in whose mind a wholesome sanity rules, nor is it even the dream of fervent imagination. So great is it, that I pray you, men with hearts and minds like my own, to extend to me, as a further measure of your generosity, a little time to think it over. I shall not want long, for even already, with the blaze of honour fresh upon me, I see the cool shadow of Duty, though his substance is yet hardly visible. Give me but an hour of solitude—an hour at most—if it do not prolong this your session unduly. It may be that a lesser time will serve, but in any case I promise you that, when I can see a just and fitting issue to my thought, I shall at once return."

The President of the Council looked around him, and, seeing everywhere the bowing heads of acquiescence, spoke with a reverent gravity:

"We shall wait in patience whatsoever time you will, and may the God who rules all worthy hearts guide you to His Will!"

And so in silence the Voivode passed out of the hall.

From my seat near a window I could watch him go, as with measured steps he passed up the hill which rises behind the State House, and disappeared into the shadow of the forest. Then my work claimed me, for I wished to record the proceedings so far whilst all was fresh in my mind. In silence, as of the dead, the Council waited, no man challenging opinion of his neighbour even by a glance.

Almost a full hour had elapsed when the Voivode came again to the Council, moving with slow and stately gravity, as has always been his wont since age began to hamper the movement which in youth had been so notable. The Members of the Council all stood up uncovered, and so remained while he made announcement of his conclusion. He spoke slowly; and as his answer was to be a valued record of this Land and its Race, I wrote down every word as uttered, leaving here and there space for description or comment, which spaces I have since then filled in.

"Lords of the National Council, Archbishop, Vladika, Lords of the Council of Justice and of National Law, Archimandrites, and my brothers all, I have, since I left you, held in the solitude of the forest counsel with myself—and with God; and He, in His gracious wisdom, has led my thinking to that conclusion which was from the first moment of knowledge of your intent presaged in my heart. Brothers, you know—or else a long life has been spent in vain—that my heart and mind are all for the nation—my experience, my life, my handjar. And when all is for her, why should I shrink to exercise on her behalf my riper judgment though the same should have to combat my own ambition? For ten centuries my race has not failed in its duty. Ages ago the men of that time trusted in the hands of my ancestors the Kingship, even as now you, their children, trust me. But to me it would be base to betray that trust, even by the smallest tittle. That would I do were I to take the honour of the crown which you have tendered to me, so long as there is another more worthy to wear it. Were there none other, I should place myself in your hands, and yield myself over to blind obedience of your desires. But such an one there is; dear to you already by his own deeds, now doubly dear to me, since he is my son by my daughter's love. He is young, whereas I am old. He is strong and brave and true; but my days of the usefulness of strength and bravery are over. For myself, I have long contemplated as the crown of my later years a quiet life in one of our monasteries, where I can still watch the whirl of the world around us on your behalf, and be a counsellor of younger men of more active minds. Brothers, we are entering on stirring times. I can see the signs of their coming all around us. North and South—the Old Order and the New, are about to clash, and we lie between the opposing forces. True it is that the Turk, after warring for a thousand years, is fading into insignificance. But from the North where conquests spring, have crept towards our Balkans the men of a mightier composite Power. Their march has been steady; and as they came, they fortified every step of the way. Now they are hard upon us, and are already beginning to swallow up the regions that we have helped to win from the dominion of Mahound. The Austrian is at our very gates. Beaten back by the Irredentists of Italy, she has so enmeshed herself with the Great Powers of Europe that she seems for the moment to be impregnable to a foe of our stature. There is but one hope for us—the uniting of the Balkan forces to turn a masterly front to North and West as well as to South and East. Is that a task for old hands to undertake? No; the hands must be young and supple; and the brain subtle, as well as the heart be strong, of whomsoever would dare such an accomplishment. Should I accept the crown, it would only postpone the doing of that which must ultimately be done. What avail would it be if, when the darkness closes over me, my daughter should be Queen Consort to the first King of a new dynasty? You know this man, and from your record I learn that you are already willing to have him as King to follow me. Why not begin with him? He comes of a great nation, wherein the principle of freedom is a vital principle that quickens all things. That nation has more than once shown to us its friendliness; and doubtless the very fact that an Englishman would become our King, and could carry into our Government the spirit and customs which have made his own country great, would do much to restore the old friendship, and even to create a new one, which would in times of trouble bring British fleets to our waters, and British bayonets to support our own handjars. It is within my own knowledge, though as yet unannounced to you, that Rupert Sent Leger has already obtained a patent, signed by the King of England himself, allowing him to be denaturalized in England, so that he can at once apply for naturalization here. I know also that he has brought hither a vast fortune, by aid of which he is beginning to strengthen our hands for war, in case that sad eventuality should arise. Witness his late ordering to be built nine other warships of the class that has already done such effective service in overthrowing the Turk—or the pirate, whichever he may have been. He has undertaken the defence of the Blue Mouth at his own cost in a way which will make it stronger than Gibraltar, and secure us against whatever use to which the Austrian may apply the vast forces already gathered in the Bocche di Cattaro. He is already founding aerial stations on our highest peaks for use of the war aeroplanes which are being built for him. It is such a man as this who makes a nation great; and right sure I am that in his hands this splendid land and our noble, freedom-loving people will flourish and become a power in the world. Then, brothers, let me, as one to whom this nation and its history and its future are dear, ask you to give to the husband of my daughter the honour which you would confer on me. For her I can speak as well as for myself. She shall suffer nothing in dignity either. Were I indeed King, she, as my daughter, would be a Princess of the world. As it will be, she shall be companion and Queen of a great King, and her race, which is mine, shall flourish in all the lustre of the new Dynasty.

"Therefore on all accounts, my brothers, for the sake of our dear Land of the Blue Mountains, make the Gospodar Rupert, who has so proved himself, your King. And make me happy in my retirement to the cloister."

When the Voivode ceased to speak, all still remained silent and standing. But there was no mistaking their acquiescence in his most generous prayer. The President of the Council well interpreted the general wish when he said:

"Lords of the National Council, Archbishop, Vladika, Lords of the Councils of Justice and National Law, Archimandrites, and all who are present, is it agreed that we prepare at leisure a fitting reply to the Voivode Peter of the historic House of Vissarion, stating our agreement with his wish?"

To which there was a unanimous answer:

"It is." He went on:

"Further. Shall we ask the Gospodar Rupert of the House of Sent Leger, allied through his marriage to the Voivodin Teuta, daughter and only child of the Voivode Peter of Vissarion, to come hither to-morrow? And that, when he is amongst us, we confer on him the Crown and Kingship of the Land of the Blue Mountains?"

Again came the answer: "It is."

But this time it rang out like the sound of a gigantic trumpet, and the handjars flashed.

Whereupon the session was adjourned for the space of a day.

THE SAME—*Continued.*

September 10, 1907.

When the National Council met to-day the Voivode Peter Vissarion sat with them, but well back, so that at first his presence was hardly noticeable. After the necessary preliminaries had been gone through, they requested the presence of the Gospodar Rupert—Mr. Rupert Sent Leger—who was reported as waiting in the "Chamber of the High Officers." He at once accompanied back to the Hall the deputation sent to conduct him. As he made his appearance in the doorway the Councillors stood up. There was a burst of enthusiasm, and the hand-jars flashed. For an instant he stood silent, with lifted hand, as though indicating that he wished to speak. So soon as this was recognized, silence fell on the assembly, and he spoke:

"I pray you, may the Voivodin Teuta of Vissarion, who has accompanied me hither, appear with me to hear your wishes?" There was an immediate and enthusiastic acquiescence, and, after bowing his thanks, he retired to conduct her.

Her appearance was received with an ovation similar to that given to Gospodar Rupert, to which she bowed with dignified sweet-ness. She, with her husband, was conducted to the top of the Hall by the President, who came down to escort them. In the meantime another chair had been placed beside that prepared for the Gospodar, and these two sat.

The President then made the formal statement conveying to the "Gospodar Rupert" the wishes of the Council, on behalf of the nation, to offer to him the Crown and Kingship of the Land of the Blue Mountains. The message was couched in almost the same words as had been used the previous day in making the offer to the Voivode Peter Vissarion, only differing to meet the special circumstances. The Gospodar Rupert listened in grave silence. The whole thing was manifestly quite new to him, but he preserved a self-control wonderful under the circumstances. When, having been made aware of the previous offer to the Voivode and the declared wish of the latter, he rose to speak, there was stillness in the Hall. He commenced with a few broken words of thanks; then he grew suddenly and strangely calm as he went on:

"But before I can even attempt to make a fitting reply, I should know if it is contemplated to join with me in this great honour my dear wife the Voivodin Teuta of Vissarion, who has so splendidly proved her worthiness to hold any place in the government of the Land. I fain would . . ."

He was interrupted by the Voivodin, who, standing up beside him and holding his left arm, said:

"Do not, President, and Lords all, think me wanting in that respect of a wife for husband which in the Blue Mountains we hold so dear, if I venture to interrupt my lord. I am here, not merely as a wife, but as Voivodin of Vissarion, and by the memory of all the noble women of that noble line I feel constrained to a great duty. We women of Vissarion, in all the history of centuries, have never put ourselves forward in rivalry of our lords. Well I know that my own dear lord will forgive me as wife if I err; but I speak to you, the Council of the nation, from another ground and with another tongue. My lord does not, I fear, know as you do, and as I do too, that of old, in the history of this Land, when Kingship was existent, that it was ruled by that law of masculine supremacy which, centuries after, became known as the *Lex Salica*. Lords of the Council of the Blue Mountains, I am a wife of the Blue Mountains—as a wife young as yet, but with the blood of forty generations of loyal women in my veins. And it would ill become me, whom my husband honours—wife to the man whom you would honour—to take a part in changing the ancient custom which has been held in honour for all the thousand years, which is the glory of Blue Mountain womanhood. What an example such would be in an age when self-seeking women of other nations seek to forget their womanhood in the struggle to vie in equality with men! Men of the Blue Mountains, I speak for our women when I say that we hold of greatest price the glory of our men. To be their companions is our happiness; to be their wives is the completion of our lives; to be mothers of their children is our share of the glory that is theirs.

"Therefore, I pray you, men of the Blue Mountains, let me but be as any other wife in our land, equal to them in domestic happiness, which is our woman's sphere; and if that priceless honour may be vouchsafed to me, and I be worthy and able to bear it, an exemplar of woman's rectitude." With a low, modest, graceful bow, she sat down.

There was no doubt as to the reception of her renunciation of Queenly dignity. There was more honour to her in the quick, fierce shout which arose, and the unanimous upward swing of the hand-jars, than in the wearing of any crown which could adorn the head of woman.

The spontaneous action of the Gospodar Rupert was another source of joy to all—a fitting corollary to what had gone before. He rose to his feet, and, taking his wife in his arms, kissed her before all.

Then they sat down, with their chairs close, bashfully holding hands like a pair of lovers.

Then Rupert arose—he is Rupert now; no lesser name is on the lips of his people henceforth. With an intense earnestness which seemed to glow in his face, he said simply:

"What can I say except that I am in all ways, now and for ever, obedient to your wishes?" Then, raising his handjar and holding it before him, he kissed the hilt, saying:

"Hereby I swear to be honest and just—to be, God helping me, such a King as you would wish—in so far as the strength is given me. Amen."

This ended the business of the Session, and the Council showed unmeasured delight. Again and again the handjars flashed, as the cheers rose "three times three" in British fashion.

When Rupert—I am told I must not write him down as "King Rupert" until after the formal crowning, which is ordained for Wednesday, October 16th,—and Teuta had withdrawn, the Voivode Peter Vissarion, the President and Council conferred in committee with the Presidents of the High Courts of National Law and of Justice as to the formalities to be observed in the crowning of the King, and of the formal notification to he given to foreign Powers. These proceedings kept them far into the night.

FROM *"The London Messenger."*

CORONATION FESTIVITIES OF THE BLUE MOUNTAINS.

(*From our Special Correspondent.*)

PLAZAC,
October 14, 1907.

As I sat down to a poorly-equipped luncheon-table on board the Austro-Orient liner *Franz Joseph*, I mourned in my heart (and I may say incidentally in other portions of my internal economy) the comfort and gastronomic luxury of the King and Emperor Hotel at Trieste. A brief comparison between the menus of to-day's lunch and yesterday's will afford to the reader a striking object-lesson:

Trieste.	Steamer.
Eggs a la cocotte.	Scrambled eggs on toast.
Stewed chicken, with paprika.	Cold chicken.
Devilled slices of Westphalian ham	Cold ham.
(boiled in wine).	Bismarck herrings.
Tunny fish, pickled.	Stewed apples.
Rice, burst in cream.	Swiss cheese.
Guava jelly.	

Consequence: Yesterday I was well and happy, and looked forward to a good night's sleep, which came off. To-day I am dull and heavy, also restless, and I am convinced that at sleeping-time my liver will have it all its own way.

The journey to Ragusa, and thence to Plazac, is writ large with a pigment of misery on at least one human heart. Let a silence fall upon it! In such wise only can Justice and Mercy join hands.

Plazac is a miserable place. There is not a decent hotel in it. It was perhaps on this account that the new King, Rupert, had erected for the alleged convenience of his guests of the Press a series of large temporary hotels, such as were in evidence at the St. Louis Exposition. Here each guest was given a room to himself, somewhat after the nature of the cribs in a Rowton house. From my first night in it I am able to speak from experience of the sufferings of a prisoner of the third class. I am, however, bound to say that the dining and reception rooms were, though uncomfortably plain, adequate for temporary use. Happily we shall not have to endure many more meals here, as to-morrow we all dine with the King in the State House; and as the cuisine is under the control of that *cordon bleu*, Gaston de Faux Pas, who so long controlled the gastronomic (we might almost say Gastonomic) destinies of the Rois des Diamants in the Place Vendóme, we may, I think, look forward to not going to bed hungry. Indeed, the anticipations formed from a survey of our meagre sleeping accommodation were not realized at dinnertime to-night. To our intense astonishment, an excellent dinner was served, though, to be sure, the cold dishes predominated (a thing I always find bad for one's liver). Just as we were finishing, the King (nominated) came amongst us in quite an informal way, and, having bidden us a hearty welcome, asked that we should drink a glass of wine together. This we did in an excellent (if rather sweet) glass of Cliquot '93. King Rupert (nominated) then asked us to resume our seats. He walked between the tables, now and again recognizing some journalistic friend whom he had met early in life in his days of adventure. The men spoken to seemed vastly pleased—with themselves probably. Pretty bad form of them, I call it! For myself, I was glad I had not previously met him in the same casual way, as it saved me from what I should have felt a humiliation—the being patronized in that public way by a prospective King who had not (in a Court sense) been born. The writer, who is by profession a barrister-at-law, is satisfied at being himself a county gentleman and heir to an historic estate in the ancient county of Salop, which can boast a larger population than the Land of the Blue Mountains.

EDITORIAL NOTE.—We must ask our readers to pardon the report in yesterday's paper sent from Plazac. The writer was not on our regular staff, but asked to be allowed to write the report, as he was a kinsman of King Rupert of the Blue Mountains, and would therefore be in a position to obtain special information and facilities of description "from inside," as he puts it. On reading the paper, we cabled his recall; we cabled also, in case he did not obey, to have his ejectment effected forthwith.

We have also cabled Mr. Mordred Booth, the well-known correspondent, who was, to our knowledge, in Plazac for his own purposes, to send us full (and proper) details. We take it our readers will prefer a graphic account of the ceremony to a farrago of cheap menus, comments on his own liver, and a belittling of an Englishman of such noble character and achievements that a rising nation has chosen him for their King, and one whom our own nation loves to honour. We shall not, of course, mention our abortive correspondent's name, unless compelled thereto by any future utterance of his.

FROM *"The London Messenger."*

THE CORONATION OF KING RUPERT OF THE BLUE MOUNTAINS.

(By our Special Correspondent, Mordred Booth.)

PLAZAC,

October 17, 1907.

Plazac does not boast of a cathedral or any church of sufficient dimensions for a coronation ceremony on an adequate scale. It was therefore decided by the National Council, with the consent of the King, that it should be held at the old church of St. Sava at Vissarion— the former home of the Queen. Accordingly, arrangements had been made to bring thither on the warships on the morning of the coronation the whole of the nation's guests. In St. Sava's the religious ceremony would take place, after which there would be a banquet in the Castle of Vissarion. The guests would then return on the warships to Plazac, where would be held what is called here the "National Coronation."

In the Land of the Blue Mountains it was customary in the old days, when there were Kings, to have two ceremonies—one carried out by the official head of the national Church, the Greek Church; the other by the people in a ritual adopted by themselves, on much the same basis as the Germanic Folk-Moot. The Blue Mountains is a nation of strangely loyal tendencies. What was a thousand years ago is to be to-day—so far, of course, as is possible under the altered condition of things.

The church of St. Sava is very old and very beautiful, built in the manner of old Greek churches, full of monuments of bygone worthies of the Blue Mountains. But, of course, neither it nor the ceremony held in it to-day can compare in splendour with certain other ceremonials—for instance, the coronation of the penultimate Czar in Moscow, of Alfonso XII. in Madrid, of Carlos I. in Lisbon.

The church was arranged much after the fashion of Westminster Abbey for the coronation of King Edward VII., though, of course, not so many persons present, nor so much individual splendour. Indeed, the number of those present, outside those officially concerned and the Press of the world, was very few.

The most striking figure present—next to King Rupert, who is seven feet high and a magnificent man—was the Queen Consort, Teuta. She sat in front of a small gallery erected for the purpose just opposite the throne. She is a strikingly beautiful woman, tall and finely-formed, with jet-black hair and eyes like black diamonds, but with the unique quality that there are stars in them which seem to take varied colour according to each strong emotion. But it was not even her beauty or the stars in her eyes which drew the first glance of all. These details showed on scrutiny, but from afar off the attractive point was her dress. Surely never before did woman, be she Queen or peasant, wear such a costume on a festive occasion.

She was dressed in a white *Shroud*, and in that only. I had heard something of the story which goes behind that strange costume, and shall later on send it to you. [2]

When the procession entered the church through the great western door, the national song of the Blue Mountains, "Guide our feet through darkness, O Jehovah," was sung by an unseen choir, in which the organ, supplemented by martial instruments, joined. The Archbishop was robed in readiness before the altar, and close around him stood the Archimandrites of the four great monasteries. The Vladika stood in front of the Members of the National Council. A little to one side of this body was a group of high officials, Presidents of the Councils of National Law and Justice, the Chancellor, etc.— all in splendid robes of great antiquity—the High Marshall of the Forces and the Lord high Admiral.

When all was ready for the ceremonial act of coronation, the Archbishop raised his hand, whereupon the music ceased. Turning around, so that he faced the Queen, who thereon stood up, the King drew his handjar and saluted her in Blue Mountain fashion—the point raised as high possible, and then dropped down till it almost touches the ground. Every man in the church, ecclesiastics and all, wear the handjar, and, following the King by the interval of a second, their weapons flashed out. There was something symbolic, as well as touching, in this truly royal salute, led by the King. His handjar is a mighty blade, and held high in the hands of a man of his stature, it overtowered everything in the church. It was an inspiriting sight. No one who saw will ever forget that noble flashing of blades in the thousand-year-old salute . . .

The coronation was short, simple, and impressive. Rupert knelt whilst the Archbishop, after a short, fervent prayer, placed on his head the bronze crown of the first King of the Blue Mountains, Peter. This was handed to him by the Vladika, to whom it was brought from the National Treasury by a procession of the high officers. A blessing of the new King and his Queen Teuta concluded the ceremony. Rupert's first act on rising from his knees was to draw his handjar and salute his people.

After the ceremony in St. Sava, the procession was reformed, and took its way to the Castle of Vissarion, which is some distance off across a picturesque creek, bounded on either side by noble cliffs of vast height. The King led the way, the Queen walking with him and holding his hand . . . The Castle of Vissarion is of great antiquity, and picturesque beyond belief. I am sending later on, as a special article, a description of it . . .

The "Coronation Feast," as it was called on the menu, was held in the Great Hall, which is of noble proportions. I enclose copy of the menu, as our readers may wish to know something of the details of such a feast in this part of the world.

One feature of the banquet was specially noticeable. As the National Officials were guests of the King and Queen, they were waited on and served by the King and Queen in person. The rest of the guests, including us of the Press, were served by the King's household, not the servants—none of that cult were visible—but by the ladies and gentlemen of the Court.

There was only one toast, and that was given by the King, all standing: "The Land of the Blue Mountains, and may we all do our duty to the Land we love!" Before drinking, his mighty handjar flashed out again, and in an instant every table at which the Blue Mountaineers sat was ringed with flashing steel. I may add parenthetically that the handjar is essentially the national weapon. I do not know if the Blue Mountaineers take it to bed with them, but they certainly wear it everywhere else. Its drawing seems to emphasize everything in national life . . .

We embarked again on the warships—one a huge, steel-plated Dreadnought, up to date in every particular, the other an armoured yacht most complete in every way, and of unique speed. The King and Queen, the Lords of the Council, together with the various high ecclesiastics and great officials, went on the yacht, which the Lord High Admiral, a man of remarkably masterful physiognomy, himself steered. The rest of those present at the Coronation came on the warship. The latter went fast, but the yacht showed her heels all the way. However, the King's party waited in the dock in the Blue Mouth. From this a new cable-line took us all to the State House at

Plazac. Here the procession was reformed, and wound its way to a bare hill in the immediate vicinity. The King and Queen—the King still wearing the ancient bronze crown with which the Archbishop had invested him at St. Sava's—the Archbishop, the Vladika, and the four Archimandrites stood together at the top of the hill, the King and Queen being, of course, in the front. A courteous young gentleman, to whom I had been accredited at the beginning of the day—all guests were so attended—explained to me that, as this was the national as opposed to the religious ceremony, the Vladika, who is the official representative of the laity, took command here. The ecclesiastics were put prominently forward, simply out of courtesy, in obedience to the wish of the people, by whom they were all greatly beloved.

Then commenced another unique ceremony, which, indeed, might well find a place in our Western countries. As far as ever we could see were masses of men roughly grouped, not in any uniform, but all in national costume, and armed only with the handjar. In the front of each of these groups or bodies stood the National Councillor for that district, distinguishable by his official robe and chain. There were in all seventeen of these bodies. These were unequal in numbers, some of them predominating enormously over others, as, indeed, might be expected in so mountainous a country. In all there were present, I was told, over a hundred thousand men. So far as I can judge from long experience of looking at great bodies of men, the estimate was a just one. I was a little surprised to see so many, for the population of the Blue Mountains is never accredited in books of geography as a large one. When I made inquiry as to how the frontier guard was being for the time maintained, I was told:

"By the women mainly. But, all the same, we have also a male guard which covers the whole frontier except that to seaward. Each man has with him six women, so that the whole line is unbroken. Moreover, sir, you must bear in mind that in the Blue Mountains our women are trained to arms as well as our men—ay, and they could give a good account of themselves, too, against any foe that should assail us. Our history shows what women can do in defence. I tell you, the Turkish population would be bigger to-day but for the women who on our frontier fought of old for defence of their homes!"

"No wonder this nation has kept her freedom for a thousand years!" I said.

At a signal given by the President of the National Council one of the Divisions moved forwards. It was not an ordinary movement, but an intense rush made with all the elan and vigour of hardy and highly-trained men. They came on, not merely at the double, but as if delivering an attack. Handjar in hand, they rushed forward. I can only compare their rush to an artillery charge or to an attack of massed cavalry battalions. It was my fortune to see the former at Magenta and the latter at Sadowa, so that I know what such illustration means. I may also say that I saw the relief column which Roberts organized rush through a town on its way to relieve Mafeking; and no one who had the delight of seeing that inspiring progress of a flying army on their way to relieve their comrades needs to be told what a rush of armed men can be. With speed which was simply desperate they ran up the hill, and, circling to the left, made a ring round the topmost plateau, where stood the King. When the ring was complete, the stream went on lapping round and round till the whole tally was exhausted. In the meantime another Division had followed, its leader joining close behind the end of the first. Then came another and another. An unbroken line circled and circled round the hill in seeming endless array, till the whole slopes were massed with moving men, dark in colour, and with countless glittering points everywhere. When the whole of the Divisions had thus surrounded the King, there was a moment's hush—a silence so still that it almost seemed as if Nature stood still also. We who looked on were almost afraid to breathe.

Then suddenly, without, so far as I could see, any fugleman or word of command, the handjars of all that mighty array of men flashed upward as one, and like thunder pealed the National cry:

"The Blue Mountains and Duty!"

After the cry there was a strange subsidence which made the onlooker rub his eyes. It seemed as though the whole mass of fighting men had partially sunk into the ground. Then the splendid truth burst upon us—the whole nation was kneeling at the feet of their chosen King, who stood upright.

Another moment of silence, as King Rupert, taking off his crown, held it up in his left hand, and, holding his great handjar high in his right, cried in a voice so strong that it came ringing over that serried mass like a trumpet:

"To Freedom of our Nation, and to Freedom within it, I dedicate these and myself. I swear!"

So saying, he, too, sank on his knees, whilst we all instinctively uncovered.

The silence which followed lasted several seconds; then, without a sign, as though one and all acted instinctively, the whole body stood up. Thereupon was executed a movement which, with all my experience of soldiers and war, I never saw equalled—not with the Russian Royal Guard saluting the Czar at his Coronation, not with an impi of Cetewayo's Zulus whirling through the opening of a kraal.

For a second or two the whole mass seemed to writhe or shudder, and then, lo! the whole District Divisions were massed again in completeness, its Councillors next the King, and the Divisions radiating outwards down the hill like wedges.

This completed the ceremony, and everything broke up into units. Later, I was told by my official friend that the King's last movement—the oath as he sank to his knees—was an innovation of his own. All I can say is, if, in the future, and for all time, it is not taken for a precedent, and made an important part of the Patriotic Coronation ceremony, the Blue Mountaineers will prove themselves to be a much more stupid people than they seem at present to be.

The conclusion of the Coronation festivities was a time of unalloyed joy. It was the banquet given to the King and Queen by the nation; the guests of the nation were included in the royal party. It was a unique ceremony. Fancy a picnic-party of a hundred thousand persons, nearly all men. There must have been made beforehand vast and elaborate preparations, ramifying through the whole nation. Each section had brought provisions sufficient for their own consumption in addition to several special dishes for the guest-tables; but the contribution of each section was not consumed by its own members.

It was evidently a part of the scheme that all should derive from a common stock, so that the feeling of brotherhood and common property should be preserved in this monumental fashion.

The guest-tables were the only tables to be seen. The bulk of the feasters sat on the ground. The tables were brought forward by the men themselves—no such thing as domestic service was known on this day—from a wood close at hand, where they and the chairs had been placed in readiness. The linen and crockery used had been sent for the purpose from the households of every town and village. The flowers were plucked in the mountains early that morning by the children, and the gold and silver plate used for adornment were supplied from the churches. Each dish at the guest-tables was served by the men of each section in turn.

Over the whole array seemed to be spread an atmosphere of joyousness, of peace, of brotherhood. It would be impossible to adequately describe that amazing scene, a whole nation of splendid men surrounding their new King and Queen, loving to honour and serve them. Scattered about through that vast crowd were groups of musicians, chosen from amongst themselves. The space covered by this titanic picnic was so vast that there were few spots from which you could hear music proceeding from different quarters.

After dinner we all sat and smoked; the music became rather vocal than instrumental—indeed, presently we did not hear the sound of any instrument at all. Only knowing a few words of Balkan, I could not follow the meanings of the songs, but I gathered that they were all legendary or historical. To those who could understand, as I was informed by my tutelary young friend, who stayed beside me the whole of this memorable day, we were listening to the history of the Land of the Blue Mountains in ballad form. Somewhere or other throughout that vast concourse each notable record of ten centuries was being told to eager ears.

It was now late in the day. Slowly the sun had been dropping down over the Calabrian Mountains, and the glamorous twilight was stealing over the immediate scene. No one seemed to notice the coming of the dark, which stole down on us with an unspeakable mystery. For long we sat still, the clatter of many tongues becoming stilled into the witchery of the scene. Lower the sun sank, till only the ruddiness of the afterglow lit the expanse with rosy light; then this failed in turn, and the night shut down quickly.

At last, when we could just discern the faces close to us, a simultaneous movement began. Lights began to flash out in places all over the hillside. At first these seemed as tiny as glow-worms seen in a summer wood, but by degrees they grew till the space was set with little circles of light. These in turn grew and grew in both number and strength. Flames began to leap out from piles of wood, torches were lighted and held high. Then the music began again, softly at first, but then louder as the musicians began to gather to the centre, where sat the King and Queen. The music was wild and semi-barbaric, but full of sweet melody. It somehow seemed to bring before us a distant past; one and all, according to the strength of our imagination and the volume of our knowledge, saw episodes and phases of bygone history come before us. There was a wonderful rhythmic, almost choric, force in the time kept, which made it almost impossible to sit still. It was an invitation to the dance such as I had never before heard in any nation or at any time. Then the lights began to gather round. Once more the mountaineers took something of the same formation as at the crowning. Where the royal party sat was a level mead, with crisp, short grass, and round it what one might well call the Ring of the Nation was formed.

The music grew louder. Each mountaineer who had not a lit torch already lighted one, and the whole rising hillside was a glory of light. The Queen rose, and the King an instant after. As they rose men stepped forward and carried away their chairs, or rather thrones. The Queen gave the King her hand—this is, it seems, the privilege of the wife as distinguished from any other woman. Their feet took the time of the music, and they moved into the centre of the ring.

That dance was another thing to remember, won from the haunting memories of that strange day. At first the King and Queen danced all alone. They began with stately movement, but as the music quickened their feet kept time, and the swing of their bodies with movements kept growing more and more ecstatic at every beat till, in true Balkan fashion, the dance became a very agony of passionate movement.

At this point the music slowed down again, and the mountaineers began to join in the dance. At first slowly, one by one, they joined in, the Vladika and the higher priests leading; then everywhere the whole vast crowd began to dance, till the earth around us seemed to shake. The lights quivered, flickered, blazed out again, and rose and fell as that hundred thousand men, each holding a torch, rose and fell with the rhythm of the dance. Quicker, quicker grew the music, faster grew the rushing and pounding of the feet, till the whole nation seemed now in an ecstasy.

I stood near the Vladika, and in the midst of this final wildness I saw him draw from his belt a short, thin flute; then he put it to his lips and blew a single note—a fierce, sharp note, which pierced the volume of sound more surely than would the thunder of a cannon-shot. On the instant everywhere each man put his torch under his foot.

There was complete and immediate darkness, for the fires, which had by now fallen low, had evidently been trodden out in the measure of the dance. The music still kept in its rhythmic beat, but slower than it had yet been. Little by little this beat was pointed and emphasized by the clapping of hands—at first only a few, but spreading till everyone present was beating hands to the slow music in the darkness. This lasted a little while, during which, looking round, I noticed a faint light beginning to steal up behind the hills. The moon was rising.

Again there came a note from the Vladika's flute—a single note, sweet and subtle, which I can only compare with a note from a nightingale, vastly increased in powers. It, too, won through the thunder of the hand-claps, and on the second the sound ceased. The sudden stillness, together with the darkness, was so impressive that we could almost hear our hearts beating. And then came through the darkness the most beautiful and impressive sound heard yet. That mighty concourse, without fugleman of any sort, began, in low, fervent voice, to sing the National Anthem. At first it was of so low tone as to convey the idea of a mighty assembly of violinists playing with the mutes on. But it gradually rose till the air above us seemed to throb and quiver. Each syllable—each word—spoken in unison by the vast throng was as clearly enunciated as though spoken by a single voice:

"Guide our feet through darkness, O Jehovah."

This anthem, sung out of full hearts, remains on our minds as the last perfection of a perfect day. For myself, I am not ashamed to own that it made me weep like a child. Indeed, I cannot write of it now as I would; it unmans me so!

* * *

In the early morning, whilst the mountains were still rather grey than blue, the cable-line took us to the Blue Mouth, where we embarked in the King's yacht, *The Lady*, which took us across the Adriatic at a pace which I had hitherto considered impossible. The King and Queen came to the landing to see us off. They stood together at the right-hand side of the red-carpeted gangway, and shook hands with each guest as he went on board. The instant the last passenger had stepped on deck the gangway was withdrawn. The Lord High Admiral, who stood on the bridge, raised his hand, and we swept towards the mouth of the gulf. Of course, all hats were off, and we cheered frantically. I can truly say that if King Rupert and Queen Teuta should ever wish to found in the Blue Mountains a colony of diplomatists and journalists, those who were their guests on this great occasion will volunteer to a man. I think old Hempetch, who is the doyen of English-speaking journalists, voiced our sentiments when he said:

"May God bless them and theirs with every grace and happiness, and send prosperity to the Land and the rule!" I think the King and Queen heard us cheer, they turned to look at our flying ship again.

BOOK IX: BALKA

RUPERT'S JOURNAL—Continued

(Longe Intervallo).

February 10, 1908.

IT IS SO long since I even thought of this journal that I hardly know where to begin. I always heard that a married man is a pretty busy man; but since I became one, though it is a new life to me, and of a happiness undreamt of, I *know* what that life is. But I had no idea that this King business was anything like what it is. Why, it never leaves me a moment at all to myself—or, what is worse, to Teuta. If people who condemn Kings had only a single month of my life in that capacity, they would form an opinion different from that which they hold. It might be useful to have a Professor of Kingship in the Anarchists' College—whenever it is founded!

Everything has gone on well with us, I am glad to say. Teuta is in splendid health, though she has—but only very lately—practically given up going on her own aeroplane. It was, I know, a great sacrifice to make, just as she had become an expert at it. They say here that she is one of the best drivers in the Blue Mountains—and that is in the world, for we have made that form of movement our own. Ever since we found the pitch-blende pockets in the Great Tunnel, and discovered the simple process of extracting the radium from it, we have gone on by leaps and bounds. When first Teuta told me she would "aero" no more for a while, I thought she was wise, and backed her up in it: for driving an aeroplane is trying work and hard on the nerves. I only learned then the reason for her caution—the usual one of a young wife. That was three months ago, and only this morning she told me she would not go sailing in the air, even with me, till she could do so "without risk"—she did not mean risk to herself. Aunt Janet knew what she meant, and counselled her strongly to stick to her resolution. So for the next few months I am to do my air-sailing alone.

The public works which we began immediately after the Coronation are going strong. We began at the very beginning on an elaborate system. The first thing was to adequately fortify the Blue Mouth. Whilst the fortifications were being constructed we kept all the warships in the gulf. But when the point of safety was reached, we made the ships do sentry-go along the coast, whilst we trained men for service at sea. It is our plan to take by degrees all the young men and teach them this wise, so that at the end the whole population shall be trained for sea as well as for land. And as we are teaching them the airship service, too, they will be at home in all the elements—except fire, of course, though if that should become a necessity, we shall tackle it too!

We started the Great Tunnel at the farthest inland point of the Blue Mouth, and ran it due east at an angle of 45 degrees, so that, when complete, it would go right through the first line of hills, coming out on the plateau Plazac. The plateau is not very wide—half a mile at most—and the second tunnel begins on the eastern side of it. This new tunnel is at a smaller angle, as it has to pierce the second hill—a mountain this time. When it comes out on the east side of that, it will tap the real productive belt. Here it is that our hardwood-trees are finest, and where the greatest mineral deposits are found. This plateau is of enormous length, and runs north arid south round the great bulk of the central mountain, so that in time, when we put up a circular railway, we can bring, at a merely nominal cost, all sorts of material up or down. It is on this level that we have built the great factories for war material. We are tunnelling into the mountains, where are the great deposits of coal. We run the trucks in and out on the level, and can get perfect ventilation with little cost or labour. Already we are mining all the coal which we consume within our own confines, and we can, if we wish, within a year export largely. The great slopes of these tunnels give us the necessary aid of specific gravity, and as we carry an endless water-supply in great tubes that way also, we can do whatever we wish by hydraulic power. As one by one the European and Asiatic nations began to reduce their war preparations, we took over their disbanded workmen though our agents, so that already we have a productive staff of skilled workmen larger than anywhere else in the world. I think myself that we were fortunate in being able to get ahead so fast with our preparations for war manufacture, for if some of the "Great Powers," as they call themselves, knew the measure of our present production, they would immediately try to take active measures against us. In such case we should have to fight them, which would delay us. But if we can have another year untroubled, we shall, so far as war material is concerned, be able to defy any nation in the world. And if the time may only come peacefully till we have our buildings and machinery complete, we can prepare war-stores and implements for the whole Balkan nations. And then—But that is a dream. We shall know in good time.

In the meantime all goes well. The cannon foundries are built and active. We are already beginning to turn out finished work. Of course, our first guns are not very large, but they are good. The big guns, and especially siege-guns, will come later. And when the great extensions are complete, and the boring and wire-winding machines are in working order, we can go merrily on. I suppose that by that time the whole of the upper plateau will be like a manufacturing town—at any rate, we have plenty of raw material to hand. The haematite mines seem to be inexhaustible, and as the raising of the ore is cheap and easy by means of our extraordinary water-power, and as coal comes down to the plateau by its own gravity on the cable-line, we have natural advantages which exist hardly anywhere else in the world—certainly not all together, as here. That bird's eye view of the Blue Mouth which we had from the aeroplane when Teuta saw that vision of the future has not been in vain. The aeroplane works are having a splendid output. The aeroplane is a large and visible product; there is no mistaking when it is there! We have already a large and respectable aerial fleet. The factories for explosives are, of course, far away in bare valleys, where accidental effects are minimized. So, too, are the radium works, wherein unknown dangers may lurk. The turbines in the tunnel give us all the power we want at present, and, later on, when the new tunnel, which we call the "water tunnel," which is already begun, is complete, the available power will be immense. All these works are bringing up our shipping, and we are in great hopes for the future.

So much for our material prosperity. But with it comes a larger life and greater hopes. The stress of organizing and founding these great works is practically over. As they are not only self-supporting, but largely productive, all anxiety in the way of national expenditure is minimized. And, more than all, I am able to give my unhampered attention to those matters of even more than national importance on which the ultimate development, if not the immediate strength, of our country must depend.

I am well into the subject of a great Balkan Federation. This, it turns out, has for long been the dream of Teuta's life, as also that of the present Archimandrite of Plazac, her father, who, since I last touched this journal, having taken on himself a Holy Life, was, by will of the Church, the Monks, and the People, appointed to that great office on the retirement of Petrof Vlastimir.

Such a Federation had long been in the air. For myself, I had seen its inevitableness from the first. The modern aggressions of the Dual Nation, interpreted by her past history with regard to Italy, pointed towards the necessity of such a protective measure. And now, when Servia and Bulgaria were used as blinds to cover her real movements to incorporate with herself as established the provinces, once Turkish, which had been entrusted to her temporary protection by the Treaty of Berlin; when it would seem that Montenegro was to be deprived for all time of the hope of regaining the Bocche di Cattaro, which she had a century ago won, and held at the point of the sword, until a Great Power had, under a wrong conviction, handed it over to her neighbouring Goliath; when the Sandjack of Novi-Bazar was threatened with the fate which seemed to have already overtaken Bosnia and Herzegovina; when gallant little Montenegro was already shut out from the sea by the octopus-like grip of Dalmatia crouching along her western shore; when Turkey was dwindling down to almost ineptitude; when Greece was almost a byword, and when Albania as a nation—though still nominally subject—was of such unimpaired virility that there were great possibilities of her future, it was imperative that something must happen if the Balkan race was not to be devoured piecemeal by her northern neighbours. To the end of ultimate protection I found most of them willing to make defensive alliance.

And as the true defence consists in judicious attack, I have no doubt that an alliance so based must ultimately become one for all purposes. Albania was the most difficult to win to the scheme, as her own complications with her suzerain, combined with the pride and suspiciousness of her people, made approach a matter of extreme caution. It was only possible when I could induce her rulers to see that, no matter how great her pride and valour, the magnitude of northern advance, if unchecked, must ultimately overwhelm her.

I own that this map-making was nervous work, for I could not shut my eyes to the fact that German lust of enlargement lay behind Austria's advance. At and before that time expansion was the dominant idea of the three Great Powers of Central Europe. Russia went eastward, hoping to gather to herself the rich north-eastern provinces of China, till ultimately she should dominate the whole of Northern Europe and Asia from the Gulf of Finland to the Yellow Sea. Germany wished to link the North Sea to the Mediterranean by her own territory, and thus stand as a flawless barrier across Europe from north to south.

When Nature should have terminated the headship of the Empire-Kingdom, she, as natural heir, would creep southward through the German-speaking provinces. Thus Austria, of course kept in ignorance of her neighbour's ultimate aims, had to extend towards the south. She had been barred in her western movement by the rise of the Irredentist party in Italy, and consequently had to withdraw behind the frontiers of Carinthia, Carniola, and Istria.

My own dream of the new map was to make "Balka"—the Balkan Federation—take in ultimately all south of a line drawn from the Isle of Serpents to Aquileia. There would—must—be difficulties in the carrying out of such a scheme. Of course, it involved Austria giving up Dalmatia, Istria, and Sclavonia, as well as a part of Croatia and the Hungarian Banat. On the contrary, she might look for centuries of peace in the south. But it would make for peace so strongly that each of the States impinging on it would find it worth while to make a considerable sacrifice to have it effected. To its own integers it would offer a lasting settlement of interests which at present conflicted, and a share in a new world-power. Each of these integers would be absolutely self-governing and independent, being only united for purposes of mutual good. I did not despair that even Turkey and Greece, recognizing that benefit and safety would ensue without the destruction or even minimizing of individuality, would, sooner or later, come into the Federation. The matter is already so far advanced that within a month the various rulers of the States involved are to have a secret and informal meeting. Doubtless some larger plan and further action will be then evolved. It will be an anxious time for all in this zone—and outside it—till this matter is all settled. In any case, the manufacture of war material will go on until it is settled, one way or another.

RUPERT'S JOURNAL—*Continued.*

March 6, 1908.

I breathe more freely. The meeting has taken place here at Vissarion. Nominal cause of meeting: a hunting-party in the Blue Mountains. Not any formal affair. Not a Chancellor or Secretary of State or Diplomatist of any sort present. All headquarters. It was, after all, a real hunting-party. Good sportsmen, plenty of game, lots of beaters, everything organized properly, and an effective tally of results. I think we all enjoyed ourselves in the matter of sport; and as the political result was absolute unanimity of purpose and intention, there could be no possible cause of complaint.

So it is all decided. Everything is pacific. There is not a suggestion even of war, revolt, or conflicting purpose of any kind. We all go on exactly as we are doing for another year, pursuing our own individual objects, just as at present. But we are all to see that in our own households order prevails. All that is supposed to be effective is to be kept in good working order, and whatever is, at present, not adequate to possibilities is to be made so. This is all simply protective and defensive. We understand each other. But if any hulking stranger should undertake to interfere in our domestic concerns, we shall all unite on the instant to keep things as we wish them to remain. We shall be ready. Alfred's maxim of Peace shall be once more exemplified. In the meantime the factories shall work overtime in our own mountains, and the output shall be for the general good of our special community—the bill to be settled afterwards amicably. There can hardly be any difference of opinion about that, as the others will be the consumers of our surplus products. We are the producers, who produce for ourselves first, and then for the limited market of those within the Ring. As we undertake to guard our own frontiers—sea and land—and are able to do so, the goods are to be warehoused in the Blue Mountains until required—if at all—for participation in the markets of the world, and especially in the European market. If all goes well and the markets are inactive, the goods shall be duly delivered to the purchasers as arranged.

So much for the purely mercantile aspect.

THE VOIVODIN JANET MACKELPIE'S NOTES.

May 21, 1908.

As Rupert began to neglect his Journal when he was made a King, so, too, I find in myself a tendency to leave writing to other people. But one thing I shall not be content to leave to others—little Rupert. The baby of Rupert and Teuta is much too precious a thing to be spoken of except with love, quite independent of the fact that he will be, in natural course, a King! So I have promised Teuta that whatever shall be put into this record of the first King of the Sent Leger Dynasty relating to His Royal Highness the Crown Prince shall only appear in either her hand or my own. And she has deputed the matter to me.

Our dear little Prince arrived punctually and in perfect condition. The angels that carried him evidently took the greatest care of him, and before they left him they gave him dower of all their best. He is a dear! Like both his father and his mother, and that says everything. My own private opinion is that he is a born King! He does not know what fear is, and he thinks more of everyone else than he does of his dear little self. And if those things do not show a truly royal nature, I do not know what does . . .

Teuta has read this. She held up a warning finger, and said:

"Aunt Janet dear, that is all true. He is a dear, and a King, and an angel! But we mustn't have too much about him just yet. This book is to be about Rupert. So our little man can only be what we shall call a corollary." And so it is.

I should mention here that the book is Teuta's idea. Before little Rupert came she controlled herself wonderfully, doing only what was thought best for her under the circumstances. As I could see that it would be a help for her to have some quiet occupation which would interest her without tiring her, I looked up (with his permission, of course) all Rupert's old letters and diaries, and journals and reports—all that I had kept for him during his absences on his adventures. At first I was a little afraid they might harm her, for at times she got so excited over some things that I had to caution her. Here again came in her wonderful self-control. I think the most soothing argument I used with her was to point out that the dear boy had come through all the dangers safely, and was actually with us, stronger and nobler than ever.

After we had read over together the whole matter several times—for it was practically new to me too, and I got nearly as excited as she was, though I have known him so much longer—we came to the conclusion that this particular volume would have to be of selected matter. There is enough of Rupert's work to make a lot of volumes and we have an ambitious literary project of some day publishing an *edition de luxe* of his whole collected works. It will be a rare showing amongst the works of Kings. But this is to be all about himself, so that in the future it may serve as a sort of backbone of his personal history.

By-and-by we came to a part when we had to ask him questions; and he was so interested in Teuta's work—he is really bound up body and soul in his beautiful wife, and no wonder—that we had to take him into full confidence. He promised he would help us all he could by giving us the use of his later journals, and such letters and papers as he had kept privately. He said he would make one condition—I use his own words: "As you two dear women are to be my editors, you must promise to put in everything exactly as I wrote it. It will not do to have any fake about this. I do not wish anything foolish or egotistical toned down out of affection for me. It was all written in sincerity, and if I had faults, they must not be hidden. If it is to be history, it must be true history, even if it gives you and me or any of us away."

So we promised.

He also said that, as Sir Edward Bingham Trent, Bart.—as he is now—was sure to have some matter which we should like, he would write and ask him to send such to us. He also said that Mr. Ernest Roger Halbard Melton, of Humcroft, Salop (he always gives this name and address in full, which is his way of showing contempt), would be sure to have some relevant matter, and that he would have him written to on the subject. This he did. The Chancellor wrote him in his most grandiloquent style. Mr. E. R. H. Melton, of H., S., replied by return post. His letter is a document which speaks for itself:

HUMCROFT, SALOP,
May 30, 1908.

MY DEAR COUSIN KING RUPERT,

I am honoured by the request made on your behalf by the Lord High Chancellor of your kingdom that I should make a literary contribution to the volume which my cousin, Queen Teuta, is, with the help of your former governess, Miss MacKelpie, compiling. I am willing to do so, as you naturally wish to have in that work some contemporary record made by the Head of the House of Melton, with which you are connected, though only on the distaff side. It is a natural ambition enough, even on the part of a barbarian—or perhaps semi-barbarian—King, and far be it from me, as Head of the House, to deny you such a coveted privilege. Perhaps you may not know that I am now Head of the House; my father died three days ago. I offered my mother the use of the Dower House—to the incumbency of which, indeed, she is entitled by her marriage settlement. But she preferred to go to live at her seat, Carfax, in Kent. She went this morning after the funeral. In letting you have the use of my manuscript I make only one stipulation, but that I expect to be rigidly adhered to. It is that all that I have written be put in the book *in extenso*. I do not wish any record of mine to be garbled to suit other ends than those ostensible, or whatever may be to the honour of myself or my House to be burked. I dare say you have noticed, my dear Rupert, that the compilers of family histories often, through jealousy, alter matter that they are allowed to use so as to suit their own purpose or minister to their own vanity. I think it right to tell you that I have had a certified copy made by Petter and Galpin, the law stationers, so that I shall be able to verify whether my stipulation has been honourably observed. I am having the book, which is naturally valuable, carefully packed, and shall have it forwarded to Sir Edward Bingham Trent, Baronet (which he now is—Heaven save the mark!), the Attorney. Please see that he returns it to me, and in proper order. He is not to publish for himself anything in it about him. A man of that class is apt to advertise the fact of anyone of distinction taking any notice of him. I would bring out the MS. to you myself, and stay for a while with you for some sport, only your lot—subjects I suppose you call them!—are such bounders that a gentleman's life is hardly safe amongst them. I never met anyone who had so poor an appreciation of a joke as they have. By the way, how is Teuta? She is one of them. I heard all about the hatching business. I hope the kid is all right. This is only a word in your ear, so don't get cocky, old son. I am open to a godfathership. Think of that, Hedda! Of course, if the other godfather and the godmother are up to the mark; I don't want to have to boost up the whole lot! Savvy? Kiss Teuta and the kid for me. I must have the boy over here for a bit later on—when he is presentable, and has learned not to be a nuisance. It will be good for him to see something of a real first-class English country house like Humcroft. To a person only accustomed to rough ways and meagre living its luxury will make a memory which will serve in time as an example to be aimed at. I shall write again soon. Don't hesitate to ask any favour which I may be able to confer on you. So long!

Your affectionate cousin,

ERNEST ROGER HALBARD MELTON.

Extract from Letter from E. Bingham Trent to Queen Teuta of the Blue Mountains.

. . . So I thought the best way to serve that appalling cad would be to take him at his word, and put in his literary contribution in full. I have had made and attested a copy of his "Record," as he calls it, so as to save you trouble. But I send the book itself, because I am afraid that unless you see his words in his own writing, you will not believe that he or anyone else ever penned seriously a document so incriminating. I am sure he must have forgotten what he had written, for even such a dull dog as he is could never have made public such a thing knowingly.

Such a nature has its revenges on itself. In this case the officers of revenge are his *ipsissima verba*.

RUPERT'S JOURNAL—*Continued.*

February 1, 1909.

All is now well in train. When the Czar of Russia, on being asked by the Sclavs (as was meet) to be the referee in the "Balkan Settlement," declined on the ground that he was himself by inference an interested party, it was unanimously agreed by the Balkan rulers that the Western King should be asked to arbitrate, as all concerned had perfect confidence in his wisdom, as well as his justice. To their wish he graciously assented. The matter has now been for more than six months in his hands, and he has taken endless trouble to obtain full information. He has now informed us through his Chancellor that his decision is almost ready, and will be communicated as soon as possible.

We have another hunting-party at Vissarion next week. Teuta is looking forward to it with extraordinary interest. She hopes then to present to our brothers of the Balkans our little son, and she is eager to know if they endorse her mother-approval of him.

RUPERT'S JOURNAL—*Continued.*

April 15, 1909.

The arbitrator's decision has been communicated to us through the Chancellor of the Western King, who brought it to us himself as a special act of friendliness. It met with the enthusiastic approval of all. The Premier remained with us during the progress of the hunting-party, which was one of the most joyous occasions ever known. We are all of good heart, for the future of the Balkan races is now assured. The strife—internal and external—of a thousand years has ceased, and we look with hope for a long and happy time. The Chancellor brought messages of grace and courtliness and friendliness to all. And when I, as spokesman of the party, asked him if we might convey a request of His Majesty that he would honour us by attending the ceremony of making known formally the Balkan Settlement, he answered that the King had authorized him to say that he would, if such were wished by us, gladly come; and that if he should come, he would attend with a fleet as an escort. The Chancellor also told me from himself that it might be possible to have other nationalities represented on such a great occasion by Ambassadors and even fleets, though the monarchs themselves might not be able to attend. He hinted that it might be well if I put the matter in train. (He evidently took it for granted that, though I was only one of several, the matter rested with me—possibly he chose me as the one to whom to make the confidence, as I was born a stranger.) As we talked it over, he grew more enthusiastic, and finally said that, as the King was taking the lead, doubtless all the nations of the earth friendly to him would like to take a part in the ceremony. So it is likely to turn out practically an international ceremony of a unique kind. Teuta will love it, and we shall all do what we can.

JANET MACKELPIE'S NOTES.

June 1, 1909.

Our dear Teuta is full of the forthcoming celebration of the Balkan Federation, which is to take place this day month, although I must say, for myself, that the ceremony is attaining to such dimensions that I am beginning to have a sort of vague fear of some kind. It almost seems uncanny. Rupert is working unceasingly—has been for some time. For weeks past he seems to have been out day and night on his aeroplane, going through and round over the country arranging matters, and seeing for himself that what has been arranged is being done. Uncle Colin is always about, too, and so is Admiral Rooke. But now Teuta is beginning to go with Rupert. That girl is simply fearless—just like Rupert. And they both seem anxious that little Rupert shall be the same. Indeed, he is the same. A few mornings ago Rupert and Teuta were about to start just after dawn from the top of the Castle. Little Rupert was there—he is always awake early and as bright as a bee. I was holding him in my arms, and when his mother leant over to kiss him good-bye, he held out his arms to her in a way that said as plainly as if he had spoken, "Take me with you."

She looked appealingly at Rupert, who nodded, and said: "All right. Take him, darling. He will have to learn some day, and the sooner the better." The baby, looking eagerly from one to the other with the same questioning in his eyes as there is sometimes in the eyes of a kitten or a puppy—but, of course, with an eager soul behind it—saw that he was going, and almost leaped into his mother's arms. I think she had expected him to come, for she took a little leather dress from Margareta, his nurse, and, flushing with pride, began to wrap him in it. When Teuta, holding him in her arms, stepped on the aeroplane, and took her place in the centre behind Rupert, the young men of the Crown Prince's Guard raised a cheer, amid which Rupert pulled the levers, and they glided off into the dawn.

The Crown Prince's Guard was established by the mountaineers themselves the day of his birth. Ten of the biggest and most powerful and cleverest young men of the nation were chosen, and were sworn in with a very impressive ceremony to guard the young Prince. They were to so arrange and order themselves and matters generally that two at least of them should always have him, or the place in which he was, within their sight. They all vowed that the last of their lives should go before harm came to him. Of course, Teuta understood, and so did Rupert. And these young men are the persons most privileged in the whole Castle. They are dear boys, every one of them, and we are all fond of them and respect them. They simply idolize the baby.

Ever since that morning little Rupert has, unless it is at a time appointed for his sleeping, gone in his mother's arms. I think in any other place there would be some State remonstrance at the whole royal family being at once and together in a dangerous position, but in the Blue Mountains danger and fear are not thought of—indeed, they can hardly be in their terminology. And I really think the child enjoys it even more than his parents. He is just like a little bird that has found the use of his wings. Bless him!

I find that even I have to study Court ritual a little. So many nationalities are to be represented at the ceremony of the "Balkan Settlement," and so many Kings and Princes and notabilities of all kinds are coming, that we must all take care not to make any mistakes. The Press alone would drive anyone silly. Rupert and Teuta come and sit with me sometimes in the evening when we are all too tired to work, and they rest themselves by talking matters over. Rupert says that there will be over five hundred reporters, and that the applications for permission are coming in so fast that there may be a thousand when the day comes. Last night he stopped in the middle of speaking of it, and said:

"I have an inspiration! Fancy a thousand journalists,—each wanting to get ahead of the rest, and all willing to invoke the Powers of Evil for exclusive information! The only man to look after this department is Rooke. He knows how to deal with men, and as we have already a large staff to look after the journalistic guests, he can be at the head, and appoint his own deputies to act for him. Somewhere and sometime the keeping the peace will be a matter of nerve and resolution, and Rooke is the man for the job."

We were all concerned about one thing, naturally important in the eyes of a woman: What robes was Teuta to wear? In the old days, when there were Kings and Queens, they doubtless wore something gorgeous or impressive; but whatever it was that they wore has gone to dust centuries ago, and there were no illustrated papers in those primitive days. Teuta was talking to me eagerly, with her dear beautiful brows all wrinkled, when Rupert, who was reading a bulky document of some kind, looked up and said:

"Of course, darling, you will wear your Shroud?"

"Capital!" she said, clapping her hands like a joyous child. "The very thing, and our people will like it."

I own that for a moment I was dismayed. It was a horrible test of a woman's love and devotion. At a time when she was entertaining Kings and notabilities in her own house—and be sure they would all be decked in their finery—to have to appear in such a garment! A plain thing with nothing even pretty, let alone gorgeous, about it! I expressed my views to Rupert, for I feared that Teuta might be disappointed, though she might not care to say so; but before he could say a word Teuta answered:

"Oh, thank you so much, dear! I should love that above everything, but I did not like to suggest it, lest you should think me arrogant or presuming; for, indeed, Rupert, I am very proud of it, and of the way our people look on it."

"Why not?" said Rupert, in his direct way. "It is a thing for us all to be proud of; the nation has already adopted it as a national emblem—our emblem of courage and devotion and patriotism, which will always, I hope, be treasured beyond price by the men and women of our Dynasty, the Nation, that is—of the Nation that is to be."

Later on in the evening we had a strange endorsement of the national will. A "People's Deputation" of mountaineers, without any official notice or introduction, arrived at the Castle late in the evening in the manner established by Rupert's "Proclamation of Freedom," wherein all citizens were entitled to send a deputation to the King, at will and in private, on any subject of State importance. This deputation was composed of seventeen men, one selected from each political section, so that the body as a whole represented the entire nation. They were of all sorts of social rank and all degrees of fortune, but they were mainly "of the people." They spoke hesitatingly—possibly because Teuta, or even because I, was present—but with a manifest earnestness. They made but one request—that the Queen should, on the great occasion of the Balkan Federation, wear as robes of State the Shroud that they loved to see her in. The spokesman, addressing the Queen, said in tones of rugged eloquence:

"This is a matter, Your Majesty, that the women naturally have a say in, so we have, of course, consulted them. They have discussed the matter by themselves, and then with us, and they are agreed without a flaw that it will be good for the Nation and for Womankind that you do this thing. You have shown to them, and to the world at large, what women should do, what they can do, and they want to make, in memory of your great act, the Shroud a garment of pride and honour for women who have deserved well of their country. In the future it can be a garment to be worn only by privileged women who have earned the right. But they hope, and we hope with them, that on this occasion of our Nation taking the lead before the eyes of the world, all our women may wear it on that day as a means of showing overtly their willingness to do their duty, even to the death. And so"—here he turned to the King—"Rupert, we trust that Her Majesty Queen Teuta will understand that in doing as the women of the Blue Mountains wish, she will bind afresh to the Queen the loyal devotion which she won from them as Voivodin. Henceforth and for all time the Shroud shall be a dress of honour in our Land."

Teuta looked all ablaze with love and pride and devotion. Stars in her eyes shone like white fire as she assured them of the granting of their request. She finished her little speech:

"I feared that if I carried out my own wish, it might look arrogant, but Rupert has expressed the same wish, and now I feel that I am free to wear that dress which brought me to you and to Rupert"—here she beamed on him, and took his hand—"fortified as I am by your wishes and the command of my lord the King."

Rupert took her in his arms and kissed her fondly before them all, saying:

"Tell your wives, my brothers, and the rest of the Blue Mountain women, that that is the answer of the husband who loves and honours his wife. All the world shall see at the ceremony of the Federation of Balka that we men love and honour the women who are loyal and can die for duty. And, men of the Blue Mountains, some day before long we shall organize that great idea, and make it a permanent thing—that the Order of the Shroud is the highest guerdon that a noble-hearted woman can wear."

Teuta disappeared for a few moments, and came back with the Crown Prince in her arms. Everyone present asked to be allowed to kiss him, which they did kneeling.

THE FEDERATION BALKA.

By the Correspondents of "Free America."

The Editors of *Free America* have thought it well to put in consecutive order the reports and descriptions of their Special Correspondents, of whom there were present no less than eight. Not a word they wrote is omitted, but the various parts of their reports are placed in different order, so that, whilst nothing which any of them recorded is left out, the reader may be able to follow the proceedings from the various points of view of the writers who had the most favourable opportunity of moment. In so large an assemblage of journalists—there were present over a thousand—they could not all be present in one place; so our men, in consultation amongst themselves, arranged to scatter, so as to cover the whole proceeding from the various "coigns of vantage," using their skill and experience in selecting these points. One was situated on the summit of the steel-clad tower in the entrance to the Blue Mouth; another on the "Press-boat," which was moored alongside King Rupert's armoured yacht, *The Lady*, whereon were gathered the various Kings and rulers of the Balkan States, all of whom were in the Federation; another was in a swift torpedo-boat, with a roving commission to cruise round the harbour as desired; another took his place on the top of the great mountain which overlooks Plazac, and so had a bird's-eye view of the whole scene of operations; two others were on the forts to right and left of the Blue Mouth; another was posted at the entrance to the Great Tunnel which runs from the water level right up through the mountains to the plateau, where the mines and factories are situate; another had the privilege of a place on an aeroplane, which went everywhere and saw everything. This aeroplane was driven by an old Special Correspondent of *Free America*, who had been a chum of our Special in the Japanese and Russian War, and who has taken service on the Blue Mountain *Official Gazette*.

PLAZAC,

June 30, 1909.

Two days before the time appointed for the ceremony the guests of the Land of the Blue Mountains began to arrive. The earlier comers were mostly the journalists who had come from almost over the whole inhabited world. King Rupert, who does things well, had made a camp for their exclusive use. There was a separate tent for each—of course, a small one, as there were over a thousand journalists—but there were big tents for general use scattered about—refectories, reading and writing rooms, a library, idle rooms for rest, etc. In the rooms for reading and writing, which were the work-rooms for general use, were newspapers, the latest attainable from all over the world, Blue-Books, guides, directories, and all such aids to work as forethought could arrange. There was for this special service a body of some hundreds of capable servants in special dress and bearing identification numbers—in fact, King Rupert "did us fine," to use a slang phrase of pregnant meaning.

There were other camps for special service, all of them well arranged, and with plenty of facility for transport. Each of the Federating Monarchs had a camp of his own, in which he had erected a magnificent pavilion. For the Western King, who had acted as Arbitrator in the matter of the Federation, a veritable palace had been built by King Rupert—a sort of Aladdin's palace it must have been, for only a few weeks ago the place it occupied was, I was told, only primeval wilderness. King Rupert and his Queen, Teuta, had a pavilion like the rest of the Federators of Balka, but infinitely more modest, both in size and adornments.

Everywhere were guards of the Blue Mountains, armed only with the "handjar," which is the national weapon. They wore the national dress, but so arranged in colour and accoutrement that the general air of uniformity took the place of a rigid uniform. There must have been at least seventy or eighty thousand of them.

The first day was one of investigation of details by the visitors. During the second day the retinues of the great Federators came. Some of these retinues were vast. For instance, the Soldan (though only just become a Federator) sent of one kind or another more than a thousand men. A brave show they made, for they are fine men, and drilled to perfection. As they swaggered along, singly or in mass, with their gay jackets and baggy trousers, their helmets surmounted by the golden crescent, they looked a foe not to be despised. Landreck Martin, the Nestor of journalists, said to me, as we stood together looking at them:

"To-day we witness a new departure in Blue Mountain history. This is the first occasion for a thousand years that so large a Turkish body has entered the Blue Mountains with a reasonable prospect of ever getting out again."

July 1, 1909.

To-day, the day appointed for the ceremony, was auspiciously fine, even for the Blue Mountains, where at this time of year the weather is nearly always fine. They are early folk in the Blue Mountains, but to-day things began to hum before daybreak. There were bugle-calls all over the place—everything here is arranged by calls of musical instruments—trumpets, or bugles, or drums (if, indeed, the drum can be called a musical instrument)—or by lights, if it be after dark. We journalists were all ready; coffee and bread-and-butter had been thoughtfully served early in our sleeping-tents, and an elaborate breakfast was going on all the time in the refectory pavilions. We had a preliminary look round, and then there was a sort of general pause for breakfast. We took advantage of it, and attacked the sumptuous—indeed, memorable—meal which was served for us.

The ceremony was to commence at noon, but at ten o'clock the whole place was astir—not merely beginning to move, but actually moving; everybody taking their places for the great ceremony. As noon drew near, the excitement was intense and prolonged. One by one the various signatories to the Federation began to assemble. They all came by sea; such of them as had sea-boards of their own having their fleets around them. Such as had no fleets of their own were attended by at least one of the Blue Mountain ironclads. And I am bound to say that I never in my life saw more dangerous craft than these little warships of King Rupert of the Blue Mountains. As they entered the Blue Mouth each ship took her appointed station, those which carried the signatories being close together in an isolated group in a little bay almost surrounded by high cliffs in the farthest recesses of the mighty harbour. King Rupert's armoured yacht all the time lay close inshore, hard by the mouth of the Great Tunnel which runs straight into the mountain from a wide plateau, partly natural rock, partly built up with mighty blocks of stone. Here it is, I am told, that the inland products are brought down to the modern town of Plazac. Just as the clocks were chiming the half-hour before noon this yacht glided out into the expanse of the "Mouth." Behind her came twelve great barges, royally decked, and draped each in the colour of the signatory nation. On each of these the ruler entered with his guard, and was carried to Rupert's yacht, he going on the bridge, whilst his suite remained on the lower deck. In the meantime whole fleets had been appearing on the southern horizon; the nations were sending their maritime quota to the christening of "Balka"! In such wonderful order as can only be seen with squadrons of fighting ships, the mighty throng swept into the Blue Mouth, and took up their stations in groups. The only arma-ment of a Great Power now missing was that of the Western King. But there was time. Indeed, as the crowd everywhere began to look at their watches a long line of ships began to spread up northward from the Italian coast. They came at great speed—nearly twenty knots. It was a really wonderful sight—fifty of the finest ships in the world; the very latest expression of naval giants, each seemingly typical of its class—Dreadnoughts, cruisers, destroyers. They came in a wedge, with the King's yacht flying the Royal Standard the apex. Every ship of the squadron bore a red ensign long enough to float from the masthead to the water. From the armoured tower in the waterway one could see the myriad of faces—white stars on both land and sea—for the great har-bour was now alive with ships and each and all of them alive with men.

Suddenly, without any direct cause, the white masses became eclipsed—everyone had turned round, and was loookinng the other way. I looked across the bay and up the mountain behind—a mighty mountain, whose slopes run up to the very sky, ridge after ridge seeming like itself a mountain. Far away on the very top the standard of the Blue Mountains was run up on a mighty Flagstaff which seemed like a shaft of light. It was two hundred feet high, and painted white, and as at the distance the steel stays were invisible, it towered up in lonely grandeur. At its foot was a dark mass grouped behind a white space, which I could not make out till I used my field-glasses.

Then I knew it was King Rupert and the Queen in the midst of a group of mountaineers. They were on the aero station behind the platform of the aero, which seemed to shine—shine, not glitter—as though it were overlaid with plates of gold.

Again the faces looked west. The Western Squadron was drawing near to the entrance of the Blue Mouth. On the bridge of the yacht stood the Western King in uniform of an Admiral, and by him his Queen in a dress of royal purple, splendid with gold. Another glance at the mountain-top showed that it had seemed to become alive. A whole park of artillery seemed to have suddenly sprung to life, round each its crew ready for action. Amongst the group at the foot of the Flagstaff we could distinguish King Rupert; his vast height and bulk stood out from and above all round him. Close to him was a patch of white, which we understood to be Queen Teuta, whom the Blue Mountaineers simply adore.

By this time the armoured yacht, bearing all the signatories to "Balka" (excepting King Rupert), had moved out towards the entrance, and lay still and silent, waiting the coming of the Royal Arbitrator, whose whole squadron simultaneously slowed down, and hardly drifted in the seething water of their backing engines.

When the flag which was in the yacht's prow was almost opposite the armoured fort, the Western King held up a roll of vellum handed to him by one of his officers. We onlookers held our breath, for in an instant was such a scene as we can never hope to see again.

At the raising of the Western King's hand, a gun was fired away on the top of the mountain where rose the mighty Flagstaff with the standard of the Blue Mountains. Then came the thunder of salute from the guns, bright flashes and reports, which echoed down the hillsides in never-ending sequence. At the first gun, by some trick of signalling, the flag of the Federated "Balka" floated out from the top of the Flagstaff, which had been mysteriously raised, and flew above that of the Blue Mountains.

At the same moment the figures of Rupert and Teuta sank; they were taking their places on the aeroplane. An instant after, like a great golden bird, it seemed to shoot out into the air, and then, dipping its head, dropped downward at an obtuse angle. We could see the King and Queen from time waist upwards—the King in Blue Mountain dress of green; the Queen, wrapped in her white Shroud, holding her baby on her breast. When far out from the mountain-top and over the Blue Mouth, the wings and tail of the great bird-like machine went up, and the aero dropped like a stone, till it was only some few hundred feet over the water. Then the wings and tail went down, but with diminishing speed. Below the expanse of the plane the King and Queen were now seen seated together on the tiny steering platform, which seemed to have been lowered; she sat behind her husband, after the manner of matrons of the Blue Mountains. That coming of that aeroplane was the most striking episode of all this wonderful day.

After floating for a few seconds, the engines began to work, whilst the planes moved back to their normal with beautiful simultaneity. There was a golden aero finding its safety in gliding movement. At the same time the steering platform was rising, so that once more the occupants were not far below, but above the plane. They were now only about a hundred feet above the water, moving from the far end of the Blue Mouth towards the entrance in the open space between the two lines of the fighting ships of the various nationalities, all of which had by now their yards manned—a manoeuvre which had begun at the firing of the first gun on the mountain-top. As the aero passed along, all the seamen began to cheer—a cheering which they kept up till the King and Queen had come so close to the Western King's vessel that the two Kings and Queens could greet each other. The wind was now beginning to blow westward from the mountain-top, and it took the sounds towards the armoured fort, so that at moments we could distinguish the cheers of the various nationalities, amongst which, more keen than the others, came the soft "Ban Zai!" of the Japanese.

King Rupert, holding his steering levers, sat like a man of marble. Behind him his beautiful wife, clad in her Shroud, and holding in her arms the young Crown Prince, seemed like a veritable statue.

The aero, guided by Rupert's unerring hand, lit softly on the after-deck of the Western King's yacht; and King Rupert, stepping on deck, lifted from her seat Queen Teuta with her baby in her arms. It was only when the Blue Mountain King stood amongst other men that one could realize his enormous stature. He stood literally head and shoulders over every other man present.

Whilst the aeroplane was giving up its burden, the Western King and his Queen were descending from the bridge. The host and hostess, hand in hand—after their usual fashion, as it seems—hurried forward to greet their guests. The meeting was touching in its simplicity. The two monarchs shook hands, and their consorts, representatives of the foremost types of national beauty of the North and South, instinctively drew close and kissed each other. Then the hostess Queen, moving towards the Western King, kneeled before him with the gracious obeisance of a Blue Mountain hostess, and kissed his hand.

Her words of greeting were:

"You are welcome, sire, to the Blue Mountains. We are grateful to you for all you have done for Balka, and to you and Her Majesty for giving us the honour of your presence."

The King seemed moved. Accustomed as he was to the ritual of great occasions, the warmth and sincerity, together with the gracious humility of this old Eastern custom, touched him, monarch though he was of a great land and many races in the Far East. Impulsively he broke through Court ritual, and did a thing which, I have since been told, won for him for ever a holy place in the warm hearts of the Blue Mountaineers. Sinking on his knee before the beautiful shroud-clad Queen, he raised her hand and kissed it. The act was seen by all in and around the Blue Mouth, and a mighty cheering rose, which seemed to rise and swell as it ran far and wide up the hillsides, till it faded away on the far-off mountain-top, where rose majestically the mighty Flagstaff bearing the standard of the Balkan Federation.

For myself, I can never forget that wonderful scene of a nation's enthusiasm, and the core of it is engraven on my memory. That spotless deck, typical of all that is perfect in naval use; the King and Queen of the greatest nation of the earth[3] received by the newest King and Queen—a King and Queen who won empire for themselves, so that the former subject of another King received him as a brother-monarch on a history-making occasion, when a new world-power was, under his tutelage, springing into existence. The fair Northern Queen in the arms of the dark Southern Queen with the starry eyes. The simple splendour of Northern dress arrayed against that of almost peasant plainness of the giant King of the South. But all were eclipsed—even the thousand years of royal lineage of the Western King, Rupert's natural dower of stature, and the other Queen's bearing of royal dignity and sweetness—by the elemental simplicity of Teuta's Shroud. Not one of all that mighty throng but knew something of her wonderful story; and not one but felt glad and proud that such a noble woman had won an empire through her own bravery, even in the jaws of the grave.

The armoured yacht, with the remainder of the signatories to the Balkan Federation, drew close, and the rulers stepped on board to greet the Western King, the Arbitrator, Rupert leaving his task as personal host and joining them. He took his part modestly in the rear of the group, and made a fresh obeisance in his new capacity.

Presently another warship, *The Balka*, drew close. It contained the ambassadors of Foreign Powers, and the Chancellors and high officials of the Balkan nations. It was followed by a fleet of warships, each one representing a Balkan Power. The great Western fleet lay at their moorings, but with the exception of manning their yards, took no immediate part in the proceedings.

On the deck of the new-comer the Balkan monarchs took their places, the officials of each State grading themselves behind their monarch. The Ambassadors formed a foremost group by themselves.

Last came the Western King, quite alone (save for the two Queens), bearing in his hand the vellum scroll, the record of his arbitration. This he proceeded to read, a polyglot copy of it having been already supplied to every Monarch, Ambassador, and official present. It was a long statement, but the occasion was so stupendous—so intense—that the time flew by quickly. The cheering had ceased the moment the Arbitrator opened the scroll, and a veritable silence of the grave abounded.

When the reading was concluded Rupert raised his hand, and on the instant came a terrific salvo of cannon-shots from not only the ships in the port, but seemingly all up and over the hillsides away to the very summit.

When the cheering which followed the salute had somewhat toned down, those on board talked together, and presentations were made. Then the barges took the whole company to the armour-clad fort in the entrance-way to the Blue Mouth. Here, in front, had been arranged for the occasion, platforms for the starting of aeroplanes. Behind them were the various thrones of state for the Western King and Queen, and the various rulers of "Balka"—as the new and completed Balkan Federation had become—*de jure* as well as *de facto*. Behind were seats for the rest of the company. All was a blaze of crimson and gold. We of the Press were all expectant, for some ceremony had manifestly been arranged, but of all details of it we had been kept in ignorance. So far as I could tell from the faces, those present were at best but partially informed. They were certainly ignorant of all details, and even of the entire programme of the day. There is a certain kind of expectation which is not concerned in the mere execution of fore-ordered things.

The aero on which the King and Queen had come down from the mountain now arrived on the platform in the charge of a tall young mountaineer, who stepped from the steering-platform at once. King Rupert, having handed his Queen (who still carried her baby) into her seat, took his place, and pulled a lever. The aero went forward, and seemed to fall head foremost off the fort. It was but a dip, however, such as a skilful diver takes from a height into shallow water, for the plane made an upward curve, and in a few seconds was skimming upwards towards the Flagstaff. Despite the wind, it arrived there in an incredibly short time. Immediately after his flight another aero, a big one this time, glided to the platform. To this immediately stepped a body of ten tall, fine-looking young men. The driver pulled his levers, and the plane glided out on the track of the King. The Western King, who was noticing, said to the Lord High Admiral, who had been himself in command of the ship of war, and now stood close behind him:

"Who are those men, Admiral?"

"The Guard of the Crown Prince, Your Majesty. They are appointed by the Nation."

"Tell me, Admiral, have they any special duties?"

"Yes, Your Majesty," came the answer: "to die, if need be, for the young Prince!"

"Quite right! That is fine service. But how if any of them should die?"

"Your Majesty, if one of them should die, there are ten thousand eager to take his place."

"Fine, fine! It is good to have even one man eager to give his life for duty. But ten thousand! That is what makes a nation!"

When King Rupert reached the platform by the Flagstaff, the Royal Standard of the Blue Mountains was hauled up under it. Rupert stood up and raised his hand. In a second a cannon beside him was fired; then, quick as thought, others were fired in sequence, as though by one prolonged lightning-flash. The roar was incessant, but getting less in detonating sound as the distance and the hills subdued it. But in the general silence which prevailed round us we could hear the sound as though passing in a distant circle, till finally the line which had gone northward came back by the south, stopping at the last gun to south'ard of the Flagstaff.

"What was that wonderful circle?" asked the King of the Lord High Admiral.

"That, Your Majesty, is the line of the frontier of the Blue Mountains. Rupert has ten thousand cannon in line."

"And who fires them? I thought all the army must be here."

"The women, Your Majesty. They are on frontier duty to-day, so that the men can come here."

Just at that moment one of the Crown Prince's Guards brought to the side of the King's aero something like a rubber ball on the end of a string. The Queen held it out to the baby in her arms, who grabbed at it. The guard drew back. Pressing that ball must have given some signal, for on the instant a cannon, elevated to perpendicular, was fired. A shell went straight up an enormous distance. The shell burst, and sent out both a light so bright that it could be seen in the daylight, and a red smoke, which might have been seen from the heights of the Calabrian Mountains over in Italy.

As the shell burst, the King's aero seemed once more to spring from the platform out into mid-air, dipped as before, and glided out over the Blue Mouth with a rapidity which, to look at, took one's breath away.

As it came, followed by the aero of the Crown Prince's Guard and a group of other aeros, the whole mountain-sides seemed to become alive. From everywhere, right away up to the farthest visible mountain-tops, darted aeroplanes, till a host of them were rushing with dreadful speed in the wake of the King. The King turned to Queen Teuta, and evidently said something, for she beckoned to the Captain of the Crown Prince's Guard, who was steering the plane. He swerved away to the right, and instead of following above the open track between the lines of warships, went high over the outer line. One of those on board began to drop something, which, fluttering down, landed on every occasion on the bridge of the ship high over which they then were.

The Western King said again to the Gospodar Rooke (the Lord High Admiral):

"It must need some skill to drop a letter with such accuracy."

With imperturbable face the Admiral replied:

"It is easier to drop bombs, Your Majesty."

The flight of aeroplanes was a memorable sight. It helped to make history. Henceforth no nation with an eye for either defence or attack can hope for success without the mastery of the air.

In the meantime—and after that time, too—God help the nation that attacks "Balka" or any part of it, so long as Rupert and Teuta live in the hearts of that people, and bind them into an irresistible unity.

Footnotes

[1] Vladika, a high functionary in the Land of the Blue Mountains. He is a sort of official descendant of the old Prince-Bishops who used at one time to govern the State. In process of time the system has changed, but the function—shorn of its personal dominance—remains. The nation is at present governed by the Council. The Church (which is, of course, the Eastern Church) is represented by the Archbishop, who controls the whole spiritual functions and organization. The connecting-link between them—they being quite independent organizations—is the Vladika, who is *ex officio* a member of the National Council. By custom he does not vote, but is looked on as an independent adviser who is in the confidence of both sides of national control.

[2] EDITORIAL NOTE—We shall, in our issue of Saturday week, give a full record of the romantic story of Queen Teuta and her Shroud, written by Mr. Mordred Booth, and illustrated by our special artist, Mr. Neillison Browne, who is Mr. Booth's artistic collaborateur in the account of King Rupert's Coronation.

[3] Greatest *Kingdom—Editor Free America.*

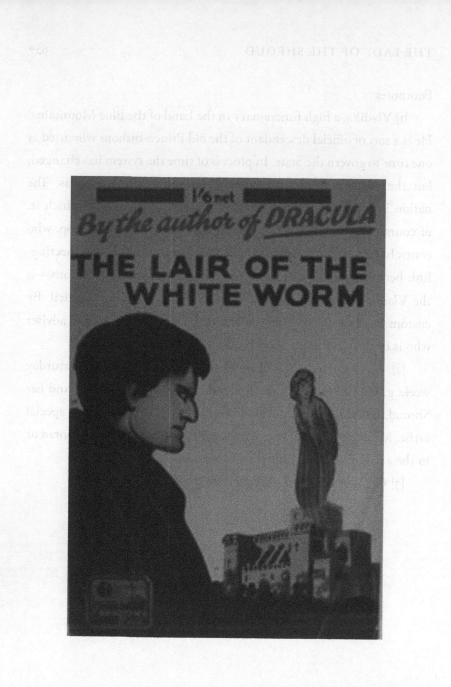

The Lair of the White Worm, first edition cover, Rider, London, 1911

INTRODUCTION

THE LAIR OF THE WHITE WORM (1911)

BRAM STOKER'S TWELFTH and final novel, *The Lair of the White Worm*, was originally published in November 1911 by William Rider and Son Ltd. of London. It contained six color illustrations by the author's friend Pamela Colman Smith ("Pixie"), a member of the Hermetic Order of the Golden Dawn and the designer of the famous 1909 Waite-Smith deck of *Tarot Cards*.

Written between March and June 1911, when Stoker was in declining health, the almost hallucinatory plot involves the legend of a primeval snake-like creature that emerges from a pit beneath the Yorkshire home of the novel's aristocratic vampire-like villainess.

In 1925 *The Lair of the White Worm* was reissued in a heavily edited and rewritten cheap edition, with more than one hundred pages deleted and the original forty chapters reduced down to just twenty-eight. This resulted in some critics complaining that Stoker's ending was too abrupt.

Despite his eleven other novels, Stoker would forever be known as "the author of *Dracula*," and the publicity for his final book inevitably referenced his most famous work: Dracula—*if you enjoyed this book or the play you will enjoy reading Bram Stoker's Eerie Novel* The Lair of the White Worm.

The novel finally saw print in America in 1966 as a Paperback Library Gothic under the title *The Garden of Evil*.

In 1988, maverick filmmaker Ken Russell loosely adapted Stoker's novel into a contemporary black comedy. Amanda Donohoe starred as the seductive snake woman, while a pre-stardom Hugh Grant turned up as the upper-class hero.

Although *The Lair of the White Worm* is the most "pulpy" of the writer's macabre novels, along with *Dracula*, *The Jewel of Seven Stars*, and *The Lady of the Shroud*, it forms a cornerstone not only to Bram Stoker's relatively limited career as an author of the supernatural, but also to the development of the modern horror story during the late nineteenth and early twentieth centuries.

S.J.

THE LAIR OF THE WHITE WORM
(1911)

Table of Contents

CHAPTER I

ADAM SALTON ARRIVES

ADAM SALTON SAUNTERED into the Empire Club, Sydney, and found awaiting him a letter from his grand-uncle. He had first heard from the old gentleman less than a year before, when Richard Salton had claimed kinship, stating that he had been unable to write earlier, as he had found it very difficult to trace his grand-nephew's address. Adam was delighted and replied cordially; he had often heard his father speak of the older branch of the family with whom his people had long lost touch. Some interesting correspondence had ensued. Adam eagerly opened the letter which had only just arrived, and conveyed a cordial invitation to stop with his grand-uncle at Lesser Hill, for as long a time as he could spare.

"Indeed," Richard Salton went on, "I am in hopes that you will make your permanent home here. You see, my dear boy, you and I are all that remain of our race, and it is but fitting that you should succeed me when the time comes. In this year of grace, 1860, I am close on eighty years of age, and though we have been a long-lived race, the span of life cannot be prolonged beyond reasonable bounds. I am prepared to like you, and to make your home with me as happy as you could wish. So do come at once on receipt of this, and find the welcome I am waiting to give you. I send, in case such may make matters easy for you, a banker's draft for £200. Come soon, so that we may both of us enjoy many happy days together. If you are able to give me the pleasure of seeing you, send me as soon as you can a letter telling me when to expect you. Then when you arrive at Plymouth or Southampton or whatever port you are bound for, wait on board, and I will meet you at the earliest hour possible."

Old Mr. Salton was delighted when Adam's reply arrived and sent a groom hot-foot to his crony, Sir Nathaniel de Salis, to inform him that his grand-nephew was due at Southampton on the twelfth of June.

Mr. Salton gave instructions to have ready a carriage early on the important day, to start for Stafford, where he would catch the 11.40 a.m. train. He would stay that night with his grand-nephew, either on the ship, which would be a new experience for him, or, if his guest should prefer it, at a hotel. In either case they would start in the early morning for home. He had given instructions to his bailiff to send the postillion carriage on to Southampton, to be ready for their journey home, and to arrange for relays of his own horses to be sent on at once. He intended that his grand-nephew, who had been all his life in Australia, should see something of rural England on the drive. He had plenty of young horses of his own breeding and breaking, and could depend on a journey memorable to the young man. The luggage would be sent on by rail to Stafford, where one of his carts would meet it. Mr. Salton, during the journey to Southampton, often wondered if his grand-nephew was as much excited as he was at the idea of meeting so near a relation for the first time; and it was with an effort that he controlled himself. The endless railway lines and switches round the Southampton Docks fired his anxiety afresh.

As the train drew up on the dockside, he was getting his hand traps together, when the carriage door was wrenched open and a young man jumped in.

"How are you, uncle? I recognised you from the photo you sent me! I wanted to meet you as soon as I could, but everything is so strange to me that I didn't quite know what to do. However, here I am. I am glad to see you, sir. I have been dreaming of this happiness for thousands of miles; now I find that the reality beats all the dreaming!" As he spoke the old man and the young one were heartily wringing each other's hands.

The meeting so auspiciously begun proceeded well. Adam, seeing that the old man was interested in the novelty of the ship, suggested that he should stay the night on board, and that he would himself be ready to start at any hour and go anywhere that the other suggested. This affectionate willingness to fall in with his own plans quite won the old man's heart. He warmly accepted the invitation, and at once they became not only on terms of affectionate relationship, but almost like old friends. The heart of the old man, which had been empty for so long, found a new delight. The young man found, on landing in the old country, a welcome and a surrounding in full harmony with all his dreams throughout his wanderings and solitude, and the promise of a fresh and adventurous life. It was not long before the old man accepted him to full relationship by calling him by his Christian name. After a long talk on affairs of interest, they retired to the cabin, which the elder was to share. Richard Salton put his hands affectionately on the boy's shoulders—though Adam was in his twenty-seventh year, he was a boy, and always would be, to his grand-uncle.

"I am so glad to find you as you are, my dear boy—just such a young man as I had always hoped for as a son, in the days when I still had such hopes. However, that is all past. But thank God there is a new life to begin for both of us. To you must be the larger part—but there is still time for some of it to be shared in common. I have waited till we should have seen each other to enter upon the subject; for I thought it better not to tie up your young life to my old one till we should have sufficient personal knowledge to justify such a venture. Now I can, so far as I am concerned, enter into it freely, since from the moment my eyes rested on you I saw my son—as he shall be, God willing—if he chooses such a course himself."

"Indeed I do, sir—with all my heart!"

"Thank you, Adam, for that." The old, man's eyes filled and his voice trembled. Then, after a long silence between them, he went on: "When I heard you were coming I made my will. It was well that your interests should be protected from that moment on. Here is the deed—keep it, Adam. All I have shall belong to you; and if love and good wishes, or the memory of them, can make life sweeter, yours shall be a happy one. Now, my dear boy, let us turn in. We start early in the morning and have a long drive before us. I hope you don't mind driving? I was going to have the old travelling carriage in which my grandfather, your great-grand-uncle, went to Court when William IV. was king. It is all right—they built well in those days—and it has been kept in perfect order. But I think I have done better: I have sent the carriage in which I travel myself. The horses are of my own breeding, and relays of them shall take us all the way. I hope you like horses? They have long been one of my greatest interests in life."

"I love them, sir, and I am happy to say I have many of my own. My father gave me a horse farm for myself when I was eighteen. I devoted myself to it, and it has gone on. Before I came away, my steward gave me a memorandum that we have in my own place more than a thousand, nearly all good."

"I am glad, my boy. Another link between us."

"Just fancy what a delight it will be, sir, to see so much of England—and with you!"

"Thank you again, my boy. I will tell you all about your future home and its surroundings as we go. We shall travel in old-fashioned state, I tell you. My grandfather always drove four-in-hand; and so shall we."

"Oh, thanks, sir, thanks. May I take the ribbons sometimes?"

"Whenever you choose, Adam. The team is your own. Every horse we use to-day is to be your own."

"You are too generous, uncle!"

"Not at all. Only an old man's selfish pleasure. It is not every day that an heir to the old home comes back. And—oh, by the way . . . No, we had better turn in now—I shall tell you the rest in the morning."

CHAPTER II

THE CASWALLS OF CASTRA REGIS

MR. SALTON HAD all his life been an early riser, and necessarily an early waker. But early as he woke on the next morning—and although there was an excuse for not prolonging sleep in the constant whirr and rattle of the "donkey" engine winches of the great ship—he met the eyes of Adam fixed on him from his berth. His grand-nephew had given him the sofa, occupying the lower berth himself. The old man, despite his great strength and normal activity, was somewhat tired by his long journey of the day before, and the prolonged and exciting interview which followed it. So he was glad to lie still and rest his body, whilst his mind was actively exercised in taking in all he could of his strange surroundings. Adam, too, after the pastoral habit to which he had been bred, woke with the dawn, and was ready to enter on the experiences of the new day whenever it might suit his elder companion. It was little wonder, then, that, so soon as each realised the other's readiness, they simultaneously jumped up and began to dress. The steward had by previous instructions early breakfast prepared, and it was not long before they went down the gangway on shore in search of the carriage.

They found Mr. Salton's bailiff looking out for them on the dock, and he brought them at once to where the carriage was waiting in the street. Richard Salton pointed out with pride to his young companion the suitability of the vehicle for every need of travel. To it were harnessed four useful horses, with a postillion to each pair.

"See," said the old man proudly, "how it has all the luxuries of useful travel—silence and isolation as well as speed. There is nothing to obstruct the view of those travelling and no one to overhear what they may say. I have used that trap for a quarter of a century, and I never saw one more suitable for travel. You shall test it shortly. We are going to drive through the heart of England; and as we go I'll tell you what I was speaking of last night. Our route is to be by Salisbury, Bath, Bristol, Cheltenham, Worcester, Stafford; and so home."

Adam remained silent a few minutes, during which he seemed all eyes, for he perpetually ranged the whole circle of the horizon.

"Has our journey to-day, sir," he asked, "any special relation to what you said last night that you wanted to tell me?"

"Not directly; but indirectly, everything."

"Won't you tell me now—I see we cannot be overheard—and if anything strikes you as we go along, just run it in. I shall understand."

So old Salton spoke:

"To begin at the beginning, Adam. That lecture of yours on 'The Romans in Britain,' a report of which you posted to me, set me thinking—in addition to telling me your tastes. I wrote to you at once and asked you to come home, for it struck me that if you were fond of historical research—as seemed a fact—this was exactly the place for you, in addition to its being the home of your own forbears. If you could learn so much of the British Romans so far away in New South Wales, where there cannot be even a tradition of them, what might you not make of the same amount of study on the very spot. Where we are going is in the real heart of the old kingdom of Mercia, where there are traces of all the various nationalities which made up the conglomerate which became Britain."

"I rather gathered that you had some more definite—more personal reason for my hurrying. After all, history can keep—except in the making!"

"Quite right, my boy. I had a reason such as you very wisely guessed. I was anxious for you to be here when a rather important phase of our local history occurred."

"What is that, if I may ask, sir?"

"Certainly. The principal landowner of our part of the county is on his way home, and there will be a great home-coming, which you may care to see. The fact is, for more than a century the various owners in the succession here, with the exception of a short time, have lived abroad."

"How is that, sir, if I may ask?"

"The great house and estate in our part of the world is Castra Regis, the family seat of the Caswall family. The last owner who lived here was Edgar Caswall, grandfather of the man who is coming here—and he was the only one who stayed even a short time. This man's grandfather, also named Edgar—they keep the tradition of the family Christian name—quarrelled with his family and went to live abroad, not keeping up any intercourse, good or bad, with his relatives, although this particular Edgar, as I told you, did visit his family estate, yet his son was born and lived and died abroad, while his grandson, the latest inheritor, was also born and lived abroad till he was over thirty—his present age. This was the second line of absentees. The great estate of Castra Regis has had no knowledge of its owner for five generations—covering more than a hundred and twenty years. It has been well administered, however, and no tenant or other connected with it has had anything of which to complain. All the same, there has been much natural anxiety to see the new owner, and we are all excited about the event of his coming. Even I am, though I own my own estate, which, though adjacent, is quite apart from Castra Regis.—Here we are now in new ground for you. That is the spire of Salisbury Cathedral, and when we leave that we shall be getting close to the old Roman county, and you will naturally want your eyes. So we shall shortly have to keep our minds on old Mercia. However, you need not be disappointed. My old friend, Sir Nathaniel de Salis, who, like myself, is a free-holder near Castra Regis—his estate, Doom Tower, is over the border of Derbyshire, on the Peak—is coming to stay with me for the festivities to welcome Edgar Caswall. He is just the sort of man you will like. He is devoted to history, and is President of the Mercian Archaeological Society. He knows more of our own part of the country, with its history and its people, than anyone else. I expect he will have arrived before us, and we three can have a long chat after dinner. He is also our local geologist and natural historian. So you and he will have many interests in common. Amongst other things he has a special knowledge of the Peak and its caverns, and knows all the old legends of prehistoric times."

They spent the night at Cheltenham, and on the following morning resumed their journey to Stafford. Adam's eyes were in constant employment, and it was not till Salton declared that they had now entered on the last stage of their journey, that he referred to Sir Nathaniel's coming.

As the dusk was closing down, they drove on to Lesser Hill, Mr. Salton's house. It was now too dark to see any details of their surroundings. Adam could just see that it was on the top of a hill, not quite so high as that which was covered by the Castle, on whose tower flew the flag, and which was all ablaze with moving lights, manifestly used in the preparations for the festivities on the morrow. So Adam deferred his curiosity till daylight. His grand-uncle was met at the door by a fine old man, who greeted him warmly.

"I came over early as you wished. I suppose this is your grand-nephew—I am glad to meet you, Mr. Adam Salton. I am Nathaniel de Salis, and your uncle is one of my oldest friends."

Adam, from the moment of their eyes meeting, felt as if they were already friends. The meeting was a new note of welcome to those that had already sounded in his ears.

The cordiality with which Sir Nathaniel and Adam met, made the imparting of information easy. Sir Nathaniel was a clever man of the world, who had travelled much, and within a certain area studied deeply. He was a brilliant conversationalist, as was to be expected from a successful diplomatist, even under unstimulating conditions. But he had been touched and to a certain extent fired by the younger man's evident admiration and willingness to learn from him. Accordingly the conversation, which began on the most friendly basis, soon warmed to an interest above proof, as the old man spoke of it next day to Richard Salton. He knew already that his old friend wanted his grand-nephew to learn all he could of the subject in hand, and so had during his journey from the Peak put his thoughts in sequence for narration and explanation. Accordingly, Adam had only to listen and he must learn much that he wanted to know. When dinner was over and the servants had withdrawn, leaving the three men at their wine, Sir Nathaniel began.

"I gather from your uncle—by the way, I suppose we had better speak of you as uncle and nephew, instead of going into exact relationship? In fact, your uncle is so old and dear a friend, that, with your permission, I shall drop formality with you altogether and speak of you and to you as Adam, as though you were his son."

"I should like," answered the young man, "nothing better!"

The answer warmed the hearts of both the old men, but, with the usual avoidance of Englishmen of emotional subjects personal to themselves, they instinctively returned to the previous question. Sir Nathaniel took the lead.

"I understand, Adam, that your uncle has posted you regarding the relationships of the Caswall family?"

"Partly, sir; but I understood that I was to hear minuter details from you—if you would be so good."

"I shall be delighted to tell you anything so far as my knowledge goes. Well, the first Caswall in our immediate record is an Edgar, head of the family and owner of the estate, who came into his kingdom just about the time that George III. did. He had one son of about twenty-four. There was a violent quarrel between the two. No one of this generation has any idea of the cause; but, considering the family characteristics, we may take it for granted that though it was deep and violent, it was on the surface trivial.

"The result of the quarrel was that the son left the house without a reconciliation or without even telling his father where he was going. He never came back again. A few years after, he died, without having in the meantime exchanged a word or a letter with his father. He married abroad and left one son, who seems to have been brought up in ignorance of all belonging to him. The gulf between them appears to have been unbridgable; for in time this son married and in turn had a son, but neither joy nor sorrow brought the sundered together. Under such conditions no *rapprochement* was to be looked for, and an utter indifference, founded at best on ignorance, took the place of family affection—even on community of interests. It was only due to the watchfulness of the lawyers that the birth of this new heir was ever made known. He actually spent a few months in the ancestral home.

"After this the family interest merely rested on heirship of the estate. As no other children have been born to any of the newer generations in the intervening years, all hopes of heritage are now centred in the grandson of this man.

"Now, it will be well for you to bear in mind the prevailing characteristics of this race. These were well preserved and unchanging; one and all they are the same: cold, selfish, dominant, reckless of consequences in pursuit of their own will. It was not that they did not keep faith, though that was a matter which gave them little concern, but that they took care to think beforehand of what they should do in order to gain their own ends. If they should make a mistake, someone else should bear the burthen of it. This was so perpetually recurrent that it seemed to be a part of a fixed policy. It was no wonder that, whatever changes took place, they were always ensured in their own possessions. They were absolutely cold and hard by nature. Not one of them—so far as we have any knowledge—was ever known to be touched by the softer sentiments, to swerve from his purpose, or hold his hand in obedience to the dictates of his heart. The pictures and effigies of them all show their adherence to the early Roman type. Their eyes were full; their hair, of raven blackness, grew thick and close and curly. Their figures were massive and typical of strength.

"The thick black hair, growing low down on the neck, told of vast physical strength and endurance. But the most remarkable characteristic is the eyes. Black, piercing, almost unendurable, they seem to contain in themselves a remarkable will power which there is no gainsaying. It is a power that is partly racial and partly individual: a power impregnated with some mysterious quality, partly hypnotic, partly mesmeric, which seems to take away from eyes that meet them all power of resistance— nay, all power of wishing to resist. With eyes like those, set in that all-commanding face, one would need to be strong indeed to think of resisting the inflexible will that lay behind.

"You may think, Adam, that all this is imagination on my part, especially as I have never seen any of them. So it is, but imagination based on deep study. I have made use of all I know or can surmise logically regarding this strange race. With such strange compelling qualities, is it any wonder that there is abroad an idea that in the race there is some demoniac possession, which tends to a more definite belief that certain individuals have in the past sold themselves to the Devil?

"But I think we had better go to bed now. We have a lot to get through to-morrow, and I want you to have your brain clear, and all your susceptibilities fresh. Moreover, I want you to come with me for an early walk, during which we may notice, whilst the matter is fresh in our minds, the peculiar disposition of this place—not merely your grand-uncle's estate, but the lie of the country around it. There are many things on which we may seek—and perhaps find—enlightenment. The more we know at the start, the more things which may come into our view will develop themselves."

CHAPTER III

DIANA'S GROVE

CURIOSITY TOOK ADAM Salton out of bed in the early morning, but when he had dressed and gone downstairs; he found that, early as he was, Sir Nathaniel was ahead of him. The old gentleman was quite prepared for a long walk, and they started at once.

Sir Nathaniel, without speaking, led the way to the east, down the hill. When they had descended and risen again, they found themselves on the eastern brink of a steep hill. It was of lesser height than that on which the Castle was situated; but it was so placed that it commanded the various hills that crowned the ridge. All along the ridge the rock cropped out, bare and bleak, but broken in rough natural castellation. The form of the ridge was a segment of a circle, with the higher points inland to the west. In the centre rose the Castle, on the highest point of all. Between the various rocky excrescences were groups of trees of various sizes and heights, amongst some of which were what, in the early morning light, looked like ruins. These—whatever they were—were of massive grey stone, probably limestone rudely cut—if indeed they were not shaped naturally. The fall of the ground was steep all along the ridge, so steep that here and there both trees and rocks and buildings seemed to overhang the plain far below, through which ran many streams.

Sir Nathaniel stopped and looked around, as though to lose nothing of the effect. The sun had climbed the eastern sky and was making all details clear. He pointed with a sweeping gesture, as though calling Adam's attention to the extent of the view. Having done so, he covered the ground more slowly, as though inviting attention to detail. Adam was a willing and attentive pupil, and followed his motions exactly, missing—or trying to miss—nothing.

"I have brought you here, Adam, because it seems to me that this is the spot on which to begin our investigations. You have now in front of you almost the whole of the ancient kingdom of Mercia. In fact, we see the whole of it except that furthest part, which is covered by the Welsh Marches and those parts which are hidden from where we stand by the high ground of the immediate west. We can see—theoretically—the whole of the eastern bound of the kingdom, which ran south from the Humber to the Wash. I want you to bear in mind the trend of the ground, for some time, sooner or later, we shall do well to have it in our mind's eye when we are considering the ancient traditions and superstitions, and are trying to find the *rationale* of them. Each legend, each superstition which we receive, will help in the understanding and possible elucidation of the others. And as all such have a local basis, we can come closer to the truth—or the probability—by knowing the local conditions as we go along. It will help us to bring to our aid such geological truth as we may have between us. For instance, the building materials used in various ages can afford their own lessons to understanding eyes. The very heights and shapes and materials of these hills—nay, even of the wide plain that lies between us and the sea—have in themselves the materials of enlightening books."

"For instance, sir?" said Adam, venturing a question.

"Well, look at those hills which surround the main one where the site for the Castle was wisely chosen—on the highest ground. Take the others. There is something ostensible in each of them, and in all probability something unseen and unproved, but to be imagined, also."

"For instance?" continued Adam.

"Let us take them *seriatim*. That to the east, where the trees are, lower down—that was once the location of a Roman temple, possibly founded on a pre-existing Druidical one. Its name implies the former, and the grove of ancient oaks suggests the latter."

"Please explain."

"The old name translated means 'Diana's Grove.' Then the next one higher than it, but just beyond it, is called '*Mercy*'—in all probability a corruption or familiarisation of the word *Mercia*, with a Roman pun included. We learn from early manuscripts that the place was called *Vilula Misericordiae*. It was originally a nunnery, founded by Queen Bertha, but done away with by King Penda, the reactionary to Paganism after St. Augustine. Then comes your uncle's place—Lesser Hill. Though it is so close to the Castle, it is not connected with it. It is a freehold, and, so far as we know, of equal age. It has always belonged to your family."

"Then there only remains the Castle!"

"That is all; but its history contains the histories of all the others— in fact, the whole history of early England." Sir Nathaniel, seeing the expectant look on Adam's face, went on:

"The history of the Castle has no beginning so far as we know. The furthest records or surmises or inferences simply accept it as existing. Some of these—guesses, let us call them—seem to show that there was some sort of structure there when the Romans came, therefore it must have been a place of importance in Druid times—if indeed that was the beginning. Naturally the Romans accepted it, as they did everything of the kind that was, or might be, useful. The change is shown or inferred in the name Castra. It was the highest protected ground, and so naturally became the most important of their camps. A study of the map will show you that it must have been a most important centre. It both protected the advances already made to the north, and helped to dominate the sea coast. It sheltered the western marches, beyond which lay savage Wales—and danger. It provided a means of getting to the Severn, round which lay the great Roman roads then coming into existence, and made possible the great waterway to the heart of England—through the Severn and its tributaries. It brought the east and the west together by the swiftest and easiest ways known to those times. And, finally, it provided means of descent on London and all the expanse of country watered by the Thames.

"With such a centre, already known and organised, we can easily see that each fresh wave of invasion—the Angles, the Saxons, the Danes, and the Normans—found it a desirable possession and so ensured its upholding. In the earlier centuries it was merely a vantage ground. But when the victorious Romans brought with them the heavy solid fortifications impregnable to the weapons of the time, its commanding position alone ensured its adequate building and equipment. Then it was that the fortified camp of the Caesars developed into the castle of the king. As we are as yet ignorant of the names of the first kings of Mercia, no historian has been able to guess which of them made it his ultimate defence; and I suppose we shall never know now. In process of time, as the arts of war developed, it increased in size and strength, and although recorded details are lacking, the history is written not merely in the stone of its building, but is inferred in the changes of structure. Then the sweeping changes which followed the Norman Conquest wiped out all lesser records than its own. To-day we must accept it as one of the earliest castles of the Conquest, probably not later than the time of Henry I. Roman and Norman were both wise in their retention of places of approved strength or utility. So it was that these surrounding heights, already established and to a certain extent proved, were retained. Indeed, such characteristics as already pertained to them were preserved, and to-day afford to us lessons regarding things which have themselves long since passed away.

"So much for the fortified heights; but the hollows too have their own story. But how the time passes! We must hurry home, or your uncle will wonder what has become of us."

He started with long steps towards Lesser Hill, and Adam was soon furtively running in order to keep up with him.

CHAPTER IV

THE LADY ARABELLA MARCH

"NOW, THERE IS no hurry, but so soon as you are both ready we shall start," Mr. Salton said when breakfast had begun. "I want to take you first to see a remarkable relic of Mercia, and then we'll go to Liverpool through what is called 'The Great Vale of Cheshire.' You may be disappointed, but take care not to prepare your mind"—this to Adam—"for anything stupendous or heroic. You would not think the place a vale at all, unless you were told so beforehand, and had confidence in the veracity of the teller. We should get to the Landing Stage in time to meet the *West African*, and catch Mr. Caswall as he comes ashore. We want to do him honour—and, besides, it will be more pleasant to have the introductions over before we go to his *fête* at the Castle."

The carriage was ready, the same as had been used the previous day, but there were different horses—magnificent animals, and keen for work. Breakfast was soon over, and they shortly took their places. The postillions had their orders, and were quickly on their way at an exhilarating pace.

Presently, in obedience to Mr. Salton's signal, the carriage drew up opposite a great heap of stones by the wayside.

"Here, Adam," he said, "is something that you of all men should not pass by unnoticed. That heap of stones brings us at once to the dawn of the Anglian kingdom. It was begun more than a thousand years ago—in the latter part of the seventh century—in memory of a murder. Wulfere, King of Mercia, nephew of Penda, here murdered his two sons for embracing Christianity. As was the custom of the time, each passer-by added a stone to the memorial heap. Penda represented heathen reaction after St. Augustine's mission. Sir Nathaniel can tell you as much as you want about this, and put you, if you wish, on the track of such accurate knowledge as there is."

Whilst they were looking at the heap of stones, they noticed that another carriage had drawn up beside them, and the passenger—there was only one—was regarding them curiously. The carriage was an old heavy travelling one, with arms blazoned on it gorgeously. The men took off their hats, as the occupant, a lady, addressed them.

"How do you do, Sir Nathaniel? How do you do, Mr. Salton? I hope you have not met with any accident. Look at me!"

As she spoke she pointed to where one of the heavy springs was broken across, the broken metal showing bright. Adam spoke up at once:

"Oh, that can soon be put right."

"Soon? There is no one near who can mend a break like that."

"I can."

"You!" She looked incredulously at the dapper young gentleman who spoke. "You—why, it's a workman's job."

"All right, I am a workman—though that is not the only sort of work I do. I am an Australian, and, as we have to move about fast, we are all trained to farriery and such mechanics as come into travel—I am quite at your service."

"I hardly know how to thank you for your kindness, of which I gladly avail myself. I don't know what else I can do, as I wish to meet Mr. Caswall of Castra Regis, who arrives home from Africa to-day. It is a notable home-coming; all the countryside want to do him honour." She looked at the old men and quickly made up her mind as to the identity of the stranger. "You must be Mr. Adam Salton of Lesser Hill. I am Lady Arabella March of Diana's Grove." As she spoke she turned slightly to Mr. Salton, who took the hint and made a formal introduction.

So soon as this was done, Adam took some tools from his uncle's carriage, and at once began work on the broken spring. He was an expert workman, and the breach was soon made good. Adam was gathering the tools which he had been using—which, after the manner of all workmen, had been scattered about—when he noticed that several black snakes had crawled out from the heap of stones and were gathering round him. This naturally occupied his mind, and he was not thinking of anything else when he noticed Lady Arabella, who had opened the door of the carriage, slip from it with a quick gliding motion. She was already among the snakes when he called out to warn her. But there seemed to be no need of warning. The snakes had turned and were wriggling back to the mound as quickly as they could. He laughed to himself behind his teeth as he whispered, "No need to fear there. They seem much more afraid of her than she of them." All the same he began to beat on the ground with a stick which was lying close to him, with the instinct of one used to such vermin. In an instant he was alone beside the mound with Lady Arabella, who appeared quite unconcerned at the incident. Then he took a long look at her, and her dress alone was sufficient to attract attention. She was clad in some kind of soft white stuff, which clung close to her form, showing to the full every movement of her sinuous figure. She wore a close-fitting cap of some fine fur of dazzling white. Coiled round her white throat was a large necklace of emeralds, whose profusion of colour dazzled when the sun shone on them. Her voice was peculiar, very low and sweet, and so soft that the dominant note was of sibilation. Her hands, too, were peculiar—long, flexible, white, with a strange movement as of waving gently to and fro.

She appeared quite at ease, and, after thanking Adam, said that if any of his uncle's party were going to Liverpool she would be most happy to join forces.

"Whilst you are staying here, Mr. Salton, you must look on the grounds of Diana's Grove as your own, so that you may come and go just as you do in Lesser Hill. There are some fine views, and not a few natural curiosities which are sure to interest you, if you are a student of natural history—specially of an earlier kind, when the world was younger."

The heartiness with which she spoke, and the warmth of her words—not of her manner, which was cold and distant—made him suspicious. In the meantime both his uncle and Sir Nathaniel had thanked her for the invitation—of which, however, they said they were unable to avail themselves. Adam had a suspicion that, though she answered regretfully, she was in reality relieved. When he had got into the carriage with the two old men, and they had driven off, he was not surprised when Sir Nathaniel spoke.

"I could not but feel that she was glad to be rid of us. She can play her game better alone!"

"What is her game?" asked Adam unthinkingly.

"All the county knows it, my boy. Caswall is a very rich man. Her husband was rich when she married him—or seemed to be. When he committed suicide, it was found that he had nothing left, and the estate was mortgaged up to the hilt. Her only hope is in a rich marriage. I suppose I need not draw any conclusion; you can do that as well as I can."

Adam remained silent nearly all the time they were travelling through the alleged Vale of Cheshire. He thought much during that journey and came to several conclusions, though his lips were unmoved. One of these conclusions was that he would be very careful about paying any attention to Lady Arabella. He was himself a rich man, how rich not even his uncle had the least idea, and would have been surprised had he known.

The remainder of the journey was uneventful, and upon arrival at Liverpool they went aboard the *West African*, which had just come to the landing-stage. There his uncle introduced himself to Mr. Caswall, and followed this up by introducing Sir Nathaniel and then Adam. The new-comer received them graciously, and said what a pleasure it was to be coming home after so long an absence of his family from their old seat. Adam was pleased at the warmth of the reception; but he could not avoid a feeling of repugnance at the man's face. He was trying hard to overcome this when a diversion was caused by the arrival of Lady Arabella. The diversion was welcome to all; the two Saltons and Sir Nathaniel were shocked at Caswall's face—so hard, so ruthless, so selfish, so dominant. "God help any," was the common thought, "who is under the domination of such a man!"

Presently his African servant approached him, and at once their thoughts changed to a larger toleration. Caswall looked indeed a savage—but a cultured savage. In him were traces of the softening civilisation of ages—of some of the higher instincts and education of man, no matter how rudimentary these might be. But the face of Oolanga, as his master called him, was unreformed, unsoftened savage, and inherent in it were all the hideous possibilities of a lost, devil-ridden child of the forest and the swamp—the lowest of all created things that could be regarded as in some form ostensibly human. Lady Arabella and Oolanga arrived almost simultaneously, and Adam was surprised to notice what effect their appearance had on each other. The woman seemed as if she would not—could not—condescend to exhibit any concern or interest in such a creature. On the other hand, the negro's bearing was such as in itself to justify her pride. He treated her not merely as a slave treats his master, but as a worshipper would treat a deity. He knelt before her with his hands out-stretched and his forehead in the dust. So long as she remained he did not move; it was only when she went over to Caswall that he relaxed his attitude of devotion and stood by respectfully.

Adam spoke to his own man, Davenport, who was standing by, having arrived with the bailiff of Lesser Hill, who had followed

Mr. Salton in a pony trap. As he spoke, he pointed to an attentive ship's steward, and presently the two men were conversing.

"I think we ought to be moving," Mr. Salton said to Adam. "I have some things to do in Liverpool, and I am sure that both Mr. Caswall and Lady Arabella would like to get under weigh for Castra Regis."

"I too, sir, would like to do something," replied Adam. "I want to find out where Ross, the animal merchant, lives—I want to take a small animal home with me, if you don't mind. He is only a little thing, and will be no trouble."

"Of course not, my boy. What kind of animal is it that you want?"

"A mongoose."

"A mongoose! What on earth do you want it for?"

"To kill snakes."

"Good!" The old man remembered the mound of stones. No explanation was needed.

When Ross heard what was wanted, he asked:

"Do you want something special, or will an ordinary mongoose do?"

"Well, of course I want a good one. But I see no need for anything special. It is for ordinary use."

"I can let you have a choice of ordinary ones. I only asked, because I have in stock a very special one which I got lately from Nepaul. He has a record of his own. He killed a king cobra that had been seen in the Rajah's garden. But I don't suppose we have any snakes of the kind in this cold climate—I daresay an ordinary one will do."

When Adam got back to the carriage, carefully carrying the box with the mongoose, Sir Nathaniel said: "Hullo! what have you got there?"

"A mongoose."

"What for?"

"To kill snakes!"

Sir Nathaniel laughed.

"I heard Lady Arabella's invitation to you to come to Diana's Grove."

"Well, what on earth has that got to do with it?"

"Nothing directly that I know of. But we shall see." Adam waited, and the old man went on: "Have you by any chance heard the other name which was given long ago to that place."

"No, sir."

"It was called—Look here, this subject wants a lot of talking over. Suppose we wait till we are alone and have lots of time before us."

"All right, sir." Adam was filled with curiosity, but he thought it better not to hurry matters. All would come in good time. Then the three men returned home, leaving Mr. Caswall to spend the night in Liverpool.

The following day the Lesser Hill party set out for Castra Regis, and for the time Adam thought no more of Diana's Grove or of what mysteries it had contained—or might still contain.

The guests were crowding in, and special places were marked for important people. Adam, seeing so many persons of varied degree, looked round for Lady Arabella, but could not locate her. It was only when he saw the old-fashioned travelling carriage approach and heard the sound of cheering which went with it, that he realised that Edgar Caswall had arrived. Then, on looking more closely, he saw that Lady Arabella, dressed as he had seen her last, was seated beside him. When the carriage drew up at the great flight of steps, the host jumped down and gave her his hand.

It was evident to all that she was the chief guest at the festivities. It was not long before the seats on the daïs were filled, while the tenants and guests of lesser importance had occupied all the coigns of vantage not reserved. The order of the day had been carefully arranged by a committee. There were some speeches, happily neither many nor long; and then festivities were suspended till the time for feasting arrived. In the interval Caswall walked among his guests, speaking to all in a friendly manner and expressing a general welcome. The other guests came down from the daïs and followed his example, so there was unceremonious meeting and greeting between gentle and simple.

Adam Salton naturally followed with his eyes all that went on within their scope, taking note of all who seemed to afford any interest. He was young and a man and a stranger from a far distance; so on all these accounts he naturally took stock rather of the women than of the men, and of these, those who were young and attractive. There were lots of pretty girls among the crowd, and Adam, who was a handsome young man and well set up, got his full share of admiring glances. These did not concern him much, and he remained unmoved until there came along a group of three, by their dress and bearing, of the farmer class. One was a sturdy old man; the other two were good-looking girls, one of a little over twenty, the other not quite so old. So soon as Adam's eyes met those of the younger girl, who stood nearest to him, some sort of electricity flashed—that divine spark which begins by recognition, and ends in obedience. Men call it "Love."

Both his companions noticed how much Adam was taken by the pretty girl, and spoke of her to him in a way which made his heart warm to them.

"Did you notice that party that passed? The old man is Michael Watford, one of the tenants of Mr. Caswall. He occupies Mercy Farm, which Sir Nathaniel pointed out to you to-day. The girls are his grand-daughters, the elder, Lilla, being the only child of his elder son, who died when she was less than a year old. His wife died on the same day. She is a good girl—as good as she is pretty. The other is her first cousin, the daughter of Watford's second son. He went for a soldier when he was just over twenty, and was drafted abroad. He was not a good correspondent, though he was a good enough son. A few letters came, and then his father heard from the colonel of his regiment that he had been killed by dacoits in Burmah. He heard from the same source that his boy had been married to a Burmese, and that there was a daughter only a year old. Watford had the child brought home, and she grew up beside Lilla. The only thing that they heard of her birth was that her name was Mimi. The two children adored each other, and do to this day. Strange how different they are! Lilla all fair, like the old Saxon stock from which she is sprung; Mimi showing a trace of her mother's race. Lilla is as gentle as a dove, but Mimi's black eyes can glow whenever she is upset. The only thing that upsets her is when anything happens to injure or threaten or annoy Lilla. Then her eyes glow as do the eyes of a bird when her young are menaced."

CHAPTER V

THE WHITE WORM

MR. SALTON INTRODUCED Adam to Mr. Watford and his grand-daughters, and they all moved on together. Of course neighbours in the position of the Watfords knew all about Adam Salton, his relationship, circumstances, and prospects. So it would have been strange indeed if both girls did not dream of possibilities of the future. In agricultural England, eligible men of any class are rare. This particular man was specially eligible, for he did not belong to a class in which barriers of caste were strong. So when it began to be noticed that he walked beside Mimi Watford and seemed to desire her society, all their friends endeavoured to give the promising affair a helping hand. When the gongs sounded for the banquet, he went with her into the tent where her grandfather had seats. Mr. Salton and Sir Nathaniel noticed that the young man did not come to claim his appointed place at the daïs table; but they understood and made no remark, or indeed did not seem to notice his absence.

Lady Arabella sat as before at Edgar Caswall's right hand. She was certainly a striking and unusual woman, and to all it seemed fitting from her rank and personal qualities that she should be the chosen partner of the heir on his first appearance. Of course nothing was said openly by those of her own class who were present; but words were not necessary when so much could be expressed by nods and smiles. It seemed to be an accepted thing that at last there was to be a mistress of Castra Regis, and that she was present amongst them. There were not lacking some who, whilst admitting all her charm and beauty, placed her in the second rank, Lilla Watford being marked as first. There was sufficient divergence of type, as well as of individual beauty, to allow of fair comment; Lady Arabella represented the aristocratic type, and Lilla that of the commonalty.

When the dusk began to thicken, Mr. Salton and Sir Nathaniel walked home—the trap had been sent away early in the day—leaving Adam to follow in his own time. He came in earlier than was expected, and seemed upset about something. Neither of the elders made any comment. They all lit cigarettes, and, as dinner-time was close at hand, went to their rooms to get ready.

Adam had evidently been thinking in the interval. He joined the others in the drawing-room, looking ruffled and impatient—a condition of things seen for the first time. The others, with the patience—or the experience—of age, trusted to time to unfold and explain things. They had not long to wait. After sitting down and standing up several times, Adam suddenly burst out.

"That fellow seems to think he owns the earth. Can't he let people alone! He seems to think that he has only to throw his handkerchief to any woman, and be her master."

This outburst was in itself enlightening. Only thwarted affection in some guise could produce this feeling in an amiable young man. Sir Nathaniel, as an old diplomatist, had a way of understanding, as if by foreknowledge, the true inwardness of things, and asked suddenly, but in a matter-of-fact, indifferent voice:

"Was he after Lilla?"

"Yes, and the fellow didn't lose any time either. Almost as soon as they met, he began to butter her up, and tell her how beautiful she was. Why, before he left her side, he had asked himself to tea to-morrow at Mercy Farm. Stupid ass! He might see that the girl isn't his sort! I never saw anything like it. It was just like a hawk and a pigeon."

As he spoke, Sir Nathaniel turned and looked at Mr. Salton—a keen look which implied a full understanding.

"Tell us all about it, Adam. There are still a few minutes before dinner, and we shall all have better appetites when we have come to some conclusion on this matter."

"There is nothing to tell, sir; that is the worst of it. I am bound to say that there was not a word said that a human being could object to. He was very civil, and all that was proper—just what a landlord might be to a tenant's daughter . . . Yet—yet—well, I don't know how it was, but it made my blood boil."

"How did the hawk and the pigeon come in?" Sir Nathaniel's voice was soft and soothing, nothing of contradiction or overdone curiosity in it—a tone eminently suited to win confidence.

"I can hardly explain. I can only say that he looked like a hawk and she like a dove—and, now that I think of it, that is what they each did look like; and do look like in their normal condition."

"That is so!" came the soft voice of Sir Nathaniel.

Adam went on:

"Perhaps that early Roman look of his set me off. But I wanted to protect her; she seemed in danger."

"She seems in danger, in a way, from all you young men. I couldn't help noticing the way that even you looked—as if you wished to absorb her!"

"I hope both you young men will keep your heads cool," put in Mr. Salton. "You know, Adam, it won't do to have any quarrel between you, especially so soon after his home-coming and your arrival here. We must think of the feelings and happiness of our neighbours; mustn't we?"

"I hope so, sir. I assure you that, whatever may happen, or even threaten, I shall obey your wishes in this as in all things."

"Hush!" whispered Sir Nathaniel, who heard the servants in the passage bringing dinner.

After dinner, over the walnuts and the wine, Sir Nathaniel returned to the subject of the local legends.

"It will perhaps be a less dangerous topic for us to discuss than more recent ones."

"All right, sir," said Adam heartily. "I think you may depend on me now with regard to any topic. I can even discuss Mr. Caswall. Indeed, I may meet him to-morrow. He is going, as I said, to call at Mercy Farm at three o'clock—but I have an appointment at two."

"I notice," said Mr. Salton, "that you do not lose any time."

The two old men once more looked at each other steadily. Then, lest the mood of his listener should change with delay, Sir Nathaniel began at once:

"I don't propose to tell you all the legends of Mercia, or even to make a selection of them. It will be better, I think, for our purpose if we consider a few facts—recorded or unrecorded—about this neigh-bourhood. I think we might begin with Diana's Grove. It has roots in the different epochs of our history, and each has its special crop of legend. The Druid and the Roman are too far off for matters of detail; but it seems to me the Saxon and the Angles are near enough to yield material for legendary lore. We find that this particular place had another name besides Diana's Grove. This was manifestly of Roman origin, or of Grecian accepted as Roman. The other is more pregnant of adventure and romance than the Roman name. In Mercian tongue it was 'The Lair of the White Worm.' This needs a word of explanation at the beginning.

"In the dawn of the language, the word 'worm' had a somewhat different meaning from that in use to-day. It was an adaptation of the Anglo-Saxon 'wyrm,' meaning a dragon or snake; or from the Gothic 'waurms,' a serpent; or the Icelandic 'ormur,' or the German 'wurm.' We gather that it conveyed originally an idea of size and power, not as now in the diminutive of both these meanings. Here legendary history helps us. We have the well-known legend of the 'Worm Well' of Lambton Castle, and that of the 'Laidly Worm of Spindleston

Heugh' near Bamborough. In both these legends the 'worm' was a monster of vast size and power—a veritable dragon or serpent, such as legend attributes to vast fens or quags where there was illimitable room for expansion. A glance at a geological map will show that whatever truth there may have been of the actuality of such monsters in the early geologic periods, at least there was plenty of possibility. In England there were originally vast plains where the plentiful supply of water could gather. The streams were deep and slow, and there were holes of abysmal depth, where any kind and size of antediluvian monster could find a habitat. In places, which now we can see from our windows, were mud-holes a hundred or more feet deep. Who can tell us when the age of the monsters which flourished in slime came to an end? There must have been places and conditions which made for greater longevity, greater size, greater strength than was usual. Such over-lappings may have come down even to our earlier centuries. Nay, are there not now creatures of a vastness of bulk regarded by the generality of men as impossible? Even in our own day there are seen the traces of animals, if not the animals themselves, of stupendous size—veritable survivals from earlier ages, preserved by some special qualities in their habitats. I remember meeting a distinguished man in India, who had the reputation of being a great shikaree, who told me that the greatest temptation he had ever had in his life was to shoot a giant snake which he had come across in the Terai of Upper India. He was on a tiger-shooting expedition, and as his elephant was crossing a nullah, it squealed. He looked down from his howdah and saw that the elephant had stepped across the body of a snake which was dragging itself through the jungle. 'So far as I could see,' he said, 'it must have been eighty or one hundred feet in length. Fully forty or fifty feet was on each side of the track, and though the weight which it dragged had thinned it, it was as thick round as a man's body. I suppose you know that when you are after tiger, it is a point of honour not to shoot at anything else, as life may depend on it. I could easily have spined this monster, but I felt that I must not—so, with regret, I had to let it go.'

"Just imagine such a monster anywhere in this country, and at once we could get a sort of idea of the 'worms,' which possibly did frequent the great morasses which spread round the mouths of many of the great European rivers."

"I haven't the least doubt, sir, that there may have been such monsters as you have spoken of still existing at a much later period than is generally accepted," replied Adam. "Also, if there were such things, that this was the very place for them. I have tried to think over the matter since you pointed out the configuration of the ground. But it seems to me that there is a hiatus somewhere. Are there not mechanical difficulties?"

"In what way?"

"Well, our antique monster must have been mighty heavy, and the distances he had to travel were long and the ways difficult. From where we are now sitting down to the level of the mud-holes is a distance of several hundred feet—I am leaving out of consideration altogether any lateral distance. Is it possible that there was a way by which a monster could travel up and down, and yet no chance recorder have ever seen him? Of course we have the legends; but is not some more exact evidence necessary in a scientific investigation?"

"My dear Adam, all you say is perfectly right, and, were we starting on such an investigation, we could not do better than follow your reasoning. But, my dear boy, you must remember that all this took place thousands of years ago. You must remember, too, that all records of the kind that would help us are lacking. Also, that the places to be considered were desert, so far as human habitation or population are considered. In the vast desolation of such a place as complied with the necessary conditions, there must have been such profusion of natural growth as would bar the progress of men formed as we are. The lair of such a monster would not have been disturbed for hundreds—or thousands—of years. Moreover, these creatures must have occupied places quite inaccessible to man. A snake who could make himself comfortable in a quagmire, a hundred feet deep, would be protected on the outskirts by such stupendous morasses as now no longer exist, or which, if they exist anywhere at all, can be on very few places on the earth's surface. Far be it from me to say that in more elemental times such things could not have been. The condition belongs to the geologic age—the great birth and growth of the world, when natural forces ran riot, when the struggle for existence was so savage that no vitality which was not founded in a gigantic form could have even a possibility of survival. That such a time existed, we have evidences in geology, but there only; we can never expect proofs such as this age demands. We can only imagine or surmise such things—or such conditions and such forces as overcame them."

CHAPTER VI

HAWK AND PIGEON

AT BREAKFAST-TIME NEXT morning Sir Nathaniel and Mr. Salton were seated when Adam came hurriedly into the room.

"Any news?" asked his uncle mechanically.

"Four."

"Four what?" asked Sir Nathaniel.

"Snakes," said Adam, helping himself to a grilled kidney.

"Four snakes. I don't understand."

"Mongoose," said Adam, and then added explanatorily: "I was out with the mongoose just after three."

"Four snakes in one morning! Why, I didn't know there were so many on the Brow"—the local name for the western cliff. "I hope that wasn't the consequence of our talk of last night?"

"It was, sir. But not directly."

"But, God bless my soul, you didn't expect to get a snake like the Lambton worm, did you? Why, a mongoose, to tackle a monster like that—if there were one—would have to be bigger than a haystack."

"These were ordinary snakes, about as big as a walking-stick."

"Well, it's pleasant to be rid of them, big or little. That is a good mongoose, I am sure; he'll clear out all such vermin round here," said Mr. Salton.

Adam went quietly on with his breakfast. Killing a few snakes in a morning was no new experience to him. He left the room the moment breakfast was finished and went to the study that his uncle had arranged for him. Both Sir Nathaniel and Mr. Salton took it that he wanted to be by himself, so as to avoid any questioning or talk of the visit that he was to make that afternoon. They saw nothing further of him till about half-an-hour before dinner-time. Then he came quietly into the smoking-room, where Mr. Salton and Sir Nathaniel were sitting together, ready dressed.

"I suppose there is no use waiting. We had better get it over at once," remarked Adam.

His uncle, thinking to make things easier for him, said: "Get what over?"

There was a sign of shyness about him at this. He stammered a little at first, but his voice became more even as he went on.

"My visit to Mercy Farm."

Mr. Salton waited eagerly. The old diplomatist simply smiled.

"I suppose you both know that I was much interested yesterday in the Watfords?" There was no denial or fending off the question. Both the old men smiled acquiescence. Adam went on: "I meant you to see it—both of you. You, uncle, because you are my uncle and the nearest of my own kin, and, moreover, you couldn't have been more kind to me or made me more welcome if you had been my own father." Mr. Salton said nothing. He simply held out his hand, and the other took it and held it for a few seconds. "And you, sir, because you have shown me something of the same affection which in my wildest dreams of home I had no right to expect." He stopped for an instant, much moved.

Sir Nathaniel answered softly, laying his hand on the youth's shoulder.

"You are right, my boy; quite right. That is the proper way to look at it. And I may tell you that we old men, who have no children of our own, feel our hearts growing warm when we hear words like those."

Then Adam hurried on, speaking with a rush, as if he wanted to come to the crucial point.

"Mr. Watford had not come in, but Lilla and Mimi were at home, and they made me feel very welcome. They have all a great regard for my uncle. I am glad of that any way, for I like them all—much. We were having tea, when Mr. Caswall came to the door, attended by the negro. Lilla opened the door herself. The window of the living-room at the farm is a large one, and from within you cannot help seeing anyone coming. Mr. Caswall said he had ventured to call, as he wished to make the acquaintance of all his tenants, in a less formal way, and more individually, than had been possible to him on the previous day. The girls made him welcome—they are very sweet girls those, sir; someone will be very happy some day there—with either of them."

"And that man may be you, Adam," said Mr. Salton heartily.

A sad look came over the young man's eyes, and the fire his uncle had seen there died out. Likewise the timbre left his voice, making it sound lonely.

"Such might crown my life. But that happiness, I fear, is not for me—or not without pain and loss and woe."

"Well, it's early days yet!" cried Sir Nathaniel heartily.

The young man turned on him his eyes, which had now grown excessively sad.

"Yesterday—a few hours ago—that remark would have given me new hope—new courage; but since then I have learned too much."

The old man, skilled in the human heart, did not attempt to argue in such a matter.

"Too early to give in, my boy."

"I am not of a giving-in kind," replied the young man earnestly. "But, after all, it is wise to realise a truth. And when a man, though he is young, feels as I do—as I have felt ever since yesterday, when I first saw Mimi's eyes—his heart jumps. He does not need to learn things. He knows."

There was silence in the room, during which the twilight stole on imperceptibly. It was Adam who again broke the silence.

"Do you know, uncle, if we have any second sight in our family?"

"No, not that I ever heard about. Why?"

"Because," he answered slowly, "I have a conviction which seems to answer all the conditions of second sight."

"And then?" asked the old man, much perturbed.

"And then the usual inevitable. What in the Hebrides and other places, where the Sight is a cult—a belief—is called 'the doom'—the court from which there is no appeal. I have often heard of second sight—we have many western Scots in Australia; but I have realised more of its true inwardness in an instant of this afternoon than I did in the whole of my life previously—a granite wall stretching up to the very heavens, so high and so dark that the eye of God Himself cannot see beyond. Well, if the Doom must come, it must. That is all."

The voice of Sir Nathaniel broke in, smooth and sweet and grave.

"Can there not be a fight for it? There can for most things."

"For most things, yes, but for the Doom, no. What a man can do I shall do. There will be—must be—a fight. When and where and how I know not, but a fight there will be. But, after all, what is a man in such a case?"

"Adam, there are three of us." Salton looked at his old friend as he spoke, and that old friend's eyes blazed.

"Ay, three of us," he said, and his voice rang.

There was again a pause, and Sir Nathaniel endeavoured to get back to less emotional and more neutral ground.

"Tell us of the rest of the meeting. Remember we are all pledged to this. It is a fight à l'outrance, and we can afford to throw away or forgo no chance."

"We shall throw away or lose nothing that we can help. We fight to win, and the stake is a life—perhaps more than one—we shall see." Then he went on in a conversational tone, such as he had used when he spoke of the coming to the farm of Edgar Caswall: "When

Mr. Caswall came in, the negro went a short distance away and there remained. It gave me the idea that he expected to be called, and intended to remain in sight, or within hail. Then Mimi got another cup and made fresh tea, and we all went on together."

"Was there anything uncommon—were you all quite friendly?" asked Sir Nathaniel quietly.

"Quite friendly. There was nothing that I could notice out of the common—except," he went on, with a slight hardening of the voice, "except that he kept his eyes fixed on Lilla, in a way which was quite intolerable to any man who might hold her dear."

"Now, in what way did he look?" asked Sir Nathaniel.

"There was nothing in itself offensive; but no one could help noticing it."

"You did. Miss Watford herself, who was the victim, and Mr. Caswall, who was the offender, are out of range as witnesses. Was there anyone else who noticed?"

"Mimi did. Her face flamed with anger as she saw the look."

"What kind of look was it? Over-ardent or too admiring, or what? Was it the look of a lover, or one who fain would be? You understand?"

"Yes, sir, I quite understand. Anything of that sort I should of course notice. It would be part of my preparation for keeping my self-control—to which I am pledged."

"If it were not amatory, was it threatening? Where was the offence?"

Adam smiled kindly at the old man.

"It was not amatory. Even if it was, such was to be expected. I should be the last man in the world to object, since I am myself an offender in that respect. Moreover, not only have I been taught to fight fair, but by nature I believe I am just. I would be as tolerant of and as liberal to a rival as I should expect him to be to me. No, the look I mean was nothing of that kind. And so long as it did not lack proper respect, I should not of my own part condescend to notice it. Did you ever study the eyes of a hound?"

"At rest?"

"No, when he is following his instincts! Or, better still," Adam went on, "the eyes of a bird of prey when he is following his instincts. Not when he is swooping, but merely when he is watching his quarry?"

"No," said Sir Nathaniel, "I don't know that I ever did. Why, may I ask?"

"That was the look. Certainly not amatory or anything of that kind—yet it was, it struck me, more dangerous, if not so deadly as an actual threatening."

Again there was a silence, which Sir Nathaniel broke as he stood up:

"I think it would be well if we all thought over this by ourselves. Then we can renew the subject."

CHAPTER VII

OOLANGA

MR. SALTON HAD an appointment for six o'clock at Liverpool. When he had driven off, Sir Nathaniel took Adam by the arm.

"May I come with you for a while to your study? I want to speak to you privately without your uncle knowing about it, or even what the subject is. You don't mind, do you? It is not idle curiosity. No, no. It is on the subject to which we are all committed."

"Is it necessary to keep my uncle in the dark about it? He might be offended."

"It is not necessary; but it is advisable. It is for his sake that I asked. My friend is an old man, and it might concern him unduly—even alarm him. I promise you there shall be nothing that could cause him anxiety in our silence, or at which he could take umbrage."

"Go on, sir!" said Adam simply.

"You see, your uncle is now an old man. I know it, for we were boys together. He has led an uneventful and somewhat self-contained life, so that any such condition of things as has now arisen is apt to perplex him from its very strangeness. In fact, any new matter is trying to old people. It has its own disturbances and its own anxieties, and neither of these things are good for lives that should be restful. Your uncle is a strong man, with a very happy and placid nature. Given health and ordinary conditions of life, there is no reason why he should not live to be a hundred. You and I, therefore, who both love him, though in different ways, should make it our business to protect him from all disturbing influences. I am sure you will agree with me that any labour to this end would be well spent. All right, my boy! I see your answer in your eyes; so we need say no more of that. And now," here his voice changed, "tell me all that took place at that interview. There are strange things in front of us—how strange we cannot at present even guess. Doubtless some of the difficult things to understand which lie behind the veil will in time be shown to us to see and to understand. In the meantime, all we can do is to work patiently, fearlessly, and unselfishly, to an end that we think is right. You had got so far as where Lilla opened the door to Mr. Caswall and the negro. You also observed that Mimi was disturbed in her mind at the way Mr. Caswall looked at her cousin."

"Certainly—though 'disturbed' is a poor way of expressing her objection."

"Can you remember well enough to describe Caswall's eyes, and how Lilla looked, and what Mimi said and did? Also Oolanga, Caswall's West African servant."

"I'll do what I can, sir. All the time Mr. Caswall was staring, he kept his eyes fixed and motionless—but not as if he was in a trance. His forehead was wrinkled up, as it is when one is trying to see through or into something. At the best of times his face has not a gentle expression; but when it was screwed up like that it was almost diabolical. It frightened poor Lilla so that she trembled, and after a bit got so pale that I thought she had fainted. However, she held up and tried to stare back, but in a feeble kind of way. Then Mimi came close and held her hand. That braced her up, and—still, never ceasing her return stare—she got colour again and seemed more like herself."

"Did he stare too?"

"More than ever. The weaker Lilla seemed, the stronger he became, just as if he were feeding on her strength. All at once she turned round, threw up her hands, and fell down in a faint. I could not see what else happened just then, for Mimi had thrown herself on her knees beside her and hid her from me. Then there was something like a black shadow between us, and there was the nigger, looking more like a malignant devil than ever. I am not usually a patient man, and the sight of that ugly devil is enough to make one's blood boil. When he saw my face, he seemed to realise danger—immediate danger—and slunk out of the room as noiselessly as if he had been blown out. I learned one thing, however—he is an enemy, if ever a man had one."

"That still leaves us three to two!" put in Sir Nathaniel.

"Then Caswall slunk out, much as the nigger had done. When he had gone, Lilla recovered at once."

"Now," said Sir Nathaniel, anxious to restore peace, "have you found out anything yet regarding the negro? I am anxious to be posted regarding him. I fear there will be, or may be, grave trouble with him."

"Yes, sir, I've heard a good deal about him—of course it is not official; but hearsay must guide us at first. You know my man Davenport— private secretary, confidential man of business, and general factotum. He is devoted to me, and has my full confidence. I asked him to stay on board the West African and have a good look round, and find out what he could about Mr. Caswall. Naturally, he was struck with the aboriginal savage. He found one of the ship's stewards, who had been on the regular voyages to South Africa. He knew Oolanga and had made a study of him. He is a man who gets on well with niggers, and they open their hearts to him. It seems that this Oolanga is quite a great person in the nigger world of the African West Coast. He has the two things which men of his own colour respect: he can make them afraid, and he is lavish with money. I don't know whose money—but that does not matter. They are always ready to trumpet his greatness. Evil greatness it is—but neither does that matter. Briefly, this is his history. He was originally a witch-finder—about as low an occupation as exists amongst aboriginal savages. Then he got up in the world and became an Obi-man, which gives an opportunity to wealth via blackmail. Finally, he reached the highest honour in hellish service. He became a user of Voodoo, which seems to be a service of the utmost baseness and cruelty. I was told some of his deeds of cruelty, which are simply sickening. They made me long for an opportunity of helping to drive him back to hell. You might think to look at him that you could measure in some way the extent of his vileness; but it would be a vain hope. Monsters such as he is belong to an earlier and more rudimentary stage of barbarism. He is in his way a clever fellow—for a nigger; but is none the less dangerous or the less hateful for that. The men in the ship told me that he was a collector: some of them had seen his collections. Such collections! All that was potent for evil in bird or beast, or even in fish. Beaks that could break and rend and tear—all the birds represented were of a predatory kind. Even the fishes are those which are born to destroy, to wound, to torture. The collection, I assure you, was an object lesson in human malignity. This being has enough evil in his face to frighten even a strong man. It is little wonder that the sight of it put that poor girl into a dead faint!"

Nothing more could be done at the moment, so they separated.

Adam was up in the early morning and took a smart walk round the Brow. As he was passing Diana's Grove, he looked in on the short avenue of trees, and noticed the snakes killed on the previous morning by the mongoose. They all lay in a row, straight and rigid, as if they had been placed by hands. Their skins seemed damp and sticky, and they were covered all over with ants and other insects. They looked loathsome, so after a glance, he passed on.

A little later, when his steps took him, naturally enough, past the entrance to Mercy Farm, he was passed by the negro, moving quickly under the trees wherever there was shadow. Laid across one extended arm, looking like dirty towels across a rail, he had the horrid-looking snakes. He did not seem to see Adam. No one was to be seen at Mercy except a few workmen in the farmyard, so, after waiting on the chance of seeing Mimi, Adam began to go slowly home.

Once more he was passed on the way. This time it was by Lady Arabella, walking hurriedly and so furiously angry that she did not recognise him, even to the extent of acknowledging his bow.

When Adam got back to Lesser Hill, he went to the coach-house where the box with the mongoose was kept, and took it with him, intending to finish at the Mound of Stone what he had begun the previous morning with regard to the extermination. He found that the snakes were even more easily attacked than on the previous day; no less than six were killed in the first half-hour. As no more appeared, he took it for granted that the morning's work was over, and went towards home. The mongoose had by this time become accustomed to him, and was willing to let himself be handled freely. Adam lifted him up and put him on his shoulder and walked on. Presently he saw a lady advancing towards him, and recognised Lady Arabella.

Hitherto the mongoose had been quiet, like a playful affectionate kitten; but when the two got close, Adam was horrified to see the mongoose, in a state of the wildest fury, with every hair standing on end, jump from his shoulder and run towards Lady Arabella. It looked so furious and so intent on attack that he called a warning.

"Look out—look out! The animal is furious and means to attack."

Lady Arabella looked more than ever disdainful and was passing on; the mongoose jumped at her in a furious attack. Adam rushed forward with his stick, the only weapon he had. But just as he got within striking distance, the lady drew out a revolver and shot the animal, breaking his backbone. Not satisfied with this, she poured shot after shot into him till the magazine was exhausted. There was no coolness or hauteur about her now; she seemed more furious even than the animal, her face transformed with hate, and as determined to kill as he had appeared to be. Adam, not knowing exactly what to do, lifted his hat in apology and hurried on to Lesser Hill.

CHAPTER VIII

SURVIVALS

AT BREAKFAST SIR Nathaniel noticed that Adam was put out about something, but he said nothing. The lesson of silence is better remembered in age than in youth. When they were both in the study, where Sir Nathaniel followed him, Adam at once began to tell his companion of what had happened. Sir Nathaniel looked graver and graver as the narration proceeded, and when Adam had stopped he remained silent for several minutes, before speaking.

"This is very grave. I have not formed any opinion yet; but it seems to me at first impression that this is worse than anything I had expected."

"Why, sir?" said Adam. "Is the killing of a mongoose—no matter by whom—so serious a thing as all that?"

His companion smoked on quietly for quite another few minutes before he spoke.

"When I have properly thought it over I may moderate my opinion, but in the meantime it seems to me that there is something dreadful behind all this—something that may affect all our lives—that may mean the issue of life or death to any of us."

Adam sat up quickly.

"Do tell me, sir, what is in your mind—if, of course, you have no objection, or do not think it better to withhold it."

"I have no objection, Adam—in fact, if I had, I should have to overcome it. I fear there can be no more reserved thoughts between us."

"Indeed, sir, that sounds serious, worse than serious!"

"Adam, I greatly fear that the time has come for us—for you and me, at all events—to speak out plainly to one another. Does not there seem something very mysterious about this?"

"I have thought so, sir, all along. The only difficulty one has is what one is to think and where to begin."

"Let us begin with what you have told me. First take the conduct of the mongoose. He was quiet, even friendly and affectionate with you. He only attacked the snakes, which is, after all, his business in life."

"That is so!"

"Then we must try to find some reason why he attacked Lady Arabella."

"May it not be that a mongoose may have merely the instinct to attack, that nature does not allow or provide him with the fine reasoning powers to discriminate who he is to attack?"

"Of course that may be so. But, on the other hand, should we not satisfy ourselves why he does wish to attack anything? If for centuries, this particular animal is known to attack only one kind of other animal, are we not justified in assuming that when one of them attacks a hitherto unclassed animal, he recognises in that animal some quality which it has in common with the hereditary enemy?"

"That is a good argument, sir," Adam went on, "but a dangerous one. If we followed it out, it would lead us to believe that Lady Arabella is a snake."

"We must be sure, before going to such an end, that there is no point as yet unconsidered which would account for the unknown thing which puzzles us."

"In what way?"

"Well, suppose the instinct works on some physical basis—for instance, smell. If there were anything in recent juxtaposition to the attacked which would carry the scent, surely that would supply the missing cause."

"Of course!" Adam spoke with conviction.

"Now, from what you tell me, the negro had just come from the direction of Diana's Grove, carrying the dead snakes which the mongoose had killed the previous morning. Might not the scent have been carried that way?"

"Of course it might, and probably was. I never thought of that. Is there any possible way of guessing approximately how long a scent will remain? You see, this is a natural scent, and may derive from a place where it has been effective for thousands of years. Then, does a scent of any kind carry with it any form or quality of another kind, either good or evil? I ask you because one ancient name of the house lived in by the lady who was attacked by the mongoose was 'The Lair of the White Worm.' If any of these things be so, our difficulties have multiplied indefinitely. They may even change in kind. We may get into moral entanglements; before we know it, we may be in the midst of a struggle between good and evil."

Sir Nathaniel smiled gravely.

"With regard to the first question—so far as I know, there are no fixed periods for which a scent may be active—I think we may take it that that period does not run into thousands of years. As to whether any moral change accompanies a physical one, I can only say that I have met no proof of the fact. At the same time, we must remember that 'good' and 'evil' are terms so wide as to take in the whole scheme of creation, and all that is implied by them and by their mutual action and reaction. Generally, I would say that in the scheme of a First Cause anything is possible. So long as the inherent forces or tendencies of any one thing are veiled from us we must expect mystery."

"There is one other question on which I should like to ask your opinion. Suppose that there are any permanent forces appertaining to the past, what we may call 'survivals,' do these belong to good as well as to evil? For instance, if the scent of the primaeval monster can so remain in proportion to the original strength, can the same be true of things of good import?"

Sir Nathaniel thought for a while before he answered.

"We must be careful not to confuse the physical and the moral. I can see that already you have switched on the moral entirely, so perhaps we had better follow it up first. On the side of the moral, we have certain justification for belief in the utterances of revealed religion. For instance, 'the effectual fervent prayer of a righteous man availeth much' is altogether for good. We have nothing of a similar kind on the side of evil. But if we accept this dictum we need have no more fear of 'mysteries': these become thenceforth merely obstacles."

Adam suddenly changed to another phase of the subject.

"And now, sir, may I turn for a few minutes to purely practical things, or rather to matters of historical fact?"

Sir Nathaniel bowed acquiescence.

"We have already spoken of the history, so far as it is known, of some of the places round us—'Castra Regis,' 'Diana's Grove,' and 'The Lair of the White Worm.' I would like to ask if there is anything not necessarily of evil import about any of the places?"

"Which?" asked Sir Nathaniel shrewdly.

"Well, for instance, this house and Mercy Farm?"

"Here we turn," said Sir Nathaniel, "to the other side, the light side of things. Let us take Mercy Farm first. When Augustine was sent by Pope Gregory to Christianise England, in the time of the Romans, he was received and protected by Ethelbert, King of Kent, whose wife, daughter of Charibert, King of Paris, was a Christian, and did much for Augustine. She founded a nunnery in memory of Columba, which was named *Sedes misericordioe*, the House of Mercy, and, as the region was Mercian, the two names became involved. As Columba is the Latin for dove, the dove became a sort of signification of the nunnery. She seized on the idea and made the newly-founded nunnery a house of doves. Someone sent her a freshly-discovered dove, a sort of carrier, but which had in the white feathers of its head and neck the form of a religious cowl. The nunnery flourished for more than a century, when, in the time of Penda, who was the reactionary of heathendom, it fell into decay. In the meantime the doves, protected by religious feeling, had increased mightily, and were known in all Catholic communities. When King Offa ruled in Mercia, about a hundred and fifty years later, he restored Christianity, and under its protection the nunnery of St. Columba was restored and its doves flourished again. In process of time this religious house again fell into desuetude; but before it disappeared it had achieved a great name for good works, and in especial for the piety of its members. If deeds and prayers and hopes and earnest thinking leave anywhere any moral effect, Mercy Farm and all around it have almost the right to be considered holy ground."

"Thank you, sir," said Adam earnestly, and was silent. Sir Nathaniel understood.

After lunch that day, Adam casually asked Sir Nathaniel to come for a walk with him. The keen-witted old diplomatist guessed that there must be some motive behind the suggestion, and he at once agreed.

As soon as they were free from observation, Adam began.

"I am afraid, sir, that there is more going on in this neighbourhood than most people imagine. I was out this morning, and on the edge of the small wood, I came upon the body of a child by the roadside. At first, I thought she was dead, and while examining her, I noticed on her neck some marks that looked like those of teeth."

"Some wild dog, perhaps?" put in Sir Nathaniel.

"Possibly, sir, though I think not—but listen to the rest of my news. I glanced around, and to my surprise, I noticed something white moving among the trees. I placed the child down carefully, and followed, but I could not find any further traces. So I returned to the child and resumed my examination, and, to my delight, I discovered that she was still alive. I chafed her hands and gradually she revived, but to my disappointment she remembered nothing—except that something had crept up quietly from behind, and had gripped her round the throat. Then, apparently, she fainted."

"Gripped her round the throat! Then it cannot have been a dog."

"No, sir, that is my difficulty, and explains why I brought you out here, where we cannot possibly be overheard. You have noticed, of course, the peculiar sinuous way in which Lady Arabella moves—well, I feel certain that the white thing that I saw in the wood was the mistress of Diana's Grove!"

"Good God, boy, be careful what you say."

"Yes, sir, I fully realise the gravity of my accusation, but I feel convinced that the marks on the child's throat were human—and made by a woman."

Adam's companion remained silent for some time, deep in thought.

"Adam, my boy," he said at last, "this matter appears to me to be far more serious even than you think. It forces me to break confidence with my old friend, your uncle—but, in order to spare him, I must do so. For some time now, things have been happening in this district that have been worrying him dreadfully—several people have disappeared, without leaving the slightest trace; a dead child was found by the roadside, with no visible or ascertainable cause of death—sheep and other animals have been found in the fields, bleeding from open wounds. There have been other matters—many of them apparently trivial in themselves. Some sinister influence has been at work, and I admit that I have suspected Lady Arabella—that is why I questioned you so closely about the mongoose and its strange attack upon Lady Arabella. You will think it strange that I should suspect the mistress of Diana's Grove, a beautiful woman of aristocratic birth. Let me explain—the family seat is near my own place, Doom Tower, and at one time I knew the family well. When still a young girl, Lady Arabella wandered into a small wood near her home, and did not return. She was found unconscious and in a high fever—the doctor said that she had received a poisonous bite, and the girl being at a delicate and critical age, the result was serious—so much so that she was not expected to recover. A great London physician came down but could do nothing—indeed, he said that the girl would not survive the night. All hope had been abandoned, when, to everyone's surprise, Lady Arabella made a sudden and startling recovery. Within a couple of days she was going about as usual! But to the horror of her people, she developed a terrible craving for cruelty, maiming and injuring birds and small animals—even killing them. This was put down to a nervous disturbance due to her age, and it was hoped that her marriage to Captain March would put this right. However, it was not a happy marriage, and eventually her husband was found shot through the head. I have always suspected suicide, though no pistol was found near the body. He may have discovered something—God knows what!—so possibly Lady Arabella may herself have killed him. Putting together many small matters that have come to my knowledge, I have come to the conclusion that the foul White Worm obtained control of her body, just as her soul was leaving its earthly tenement—that would explain the sudden revival of energy, the strange and inexplicable craving for maiming and killing, as well as many other matters with which I need not trouble you now, Adam. As I said just now, God alone knows what poor Captain March discovered—it must have been something too ghastly for human endurance, if my theory is correct that the once beautiful human body of Lady Arabella is under the control of this ghastly White Worm."

Adam nodded.

"But what can we do, sir—it seems a most difficult problem."

"We can do nothing, my boy—that is the important part of it. It would be impossible to take action—all we can do is to keep careful watch, especially as regards Lady Arabella, and be ready to act, promptly and decisively, if the opportunity occurs."

Adam agreed, and the two men returned to Lesser Hill.

CHAPTER IX

SMELLING DEATH

ADAM SALTON, THOUGH he talked little, did not let the grass grow under his feet in any matter which he had undertaken, or in which he was interested. He had agreed with Sir Nathaniel that they should not do anything with regard to the mystery of Lady Arabella's fear of the mongoose, but he steadily pursued his course in being *prepared* to act whenever the opportunity might come. He was in his own mind perpetually casting about for information or clues which might lead to possible lines of action. Baffled by the killing of the mongoose, he looked around for another line to follow. He was fascinated by the idea of there being a mysterious link between the woman and the animal, but he was already preparing a second string to his bow. His new idea was to use the faculties of Oolanga, so far as he could, in the service of discovery. His first move was to send Davenport to Liverpool to try to find the steward of the *West African*, who had told him about Oolanga, and if possible secure any further information, and then try to induce (by bribery or other means) the nigger to come to the Brow. So soon as he himself could have speech of the Voodoo-man he would be able to learn from him something useful. Davenport was successful in his missions, for he had to get another mongoose, and he was able to tell Adam that he had seen the steward, who told him much that he wanted to know, and had also arranged for Oolanga to come to Lesser Hill the following day. At this point Adam saw his way sufficiently clear to admit Davenport to some extent into his confidence. He had come to the conclusion that it would be better—certainly at first—

not himself to appear in the matter, with which Davenport was fully competent to deal. It would be time for himself to take a personal part when matters had advanced a little further.

If what the nigger said was in any wise true, the man had a rare gift which might be useful in the quest they were after. He could, as it were, "smell death." If any one was dead, if any one had died, or if a place had been used in connection with death, he seemed to know the broad fact by intuition. Adam made up his mind that to test this faculty with regard to several places would be his first task. Naturally he was anxious, and the time passed slowly. The only comfort was the arrival the next morning of a strong packing case, locked, from Ross, the key being in the custody of Davenport. In the case were two smaller boxes, both locked. One of them contained a mongoose to replace that killed by Lady Arabella; the other was the special mongoose which had already killed the king-cobra in Nepaul. When both the animals had been safely put under lock and key, he felt that he might breathe more freely. No one was allowed to know the secret of their existence in the house, except himself and Davenport. He arranged that Davenport should take Oolanga round the neighbourhood for a walk, stopping at each of the places which he designated. Having gone all along the Brow, he was to return the same way and induce him to touch on the same subjects in talking with Adam, who was to meet them as if by chance at the farthest part—that beyond Mercy Farm.

The incidents of the day proved much as Adam expected. At Mercy Farm, at Diana's Grove, at Castra Regis, and a few other spots, the negro stopped and, opening his wide nostrils as if to sniff boldly, said that he smelled death. It was not always in the same form. At Mercy Farm he said there were many small deaths. At Diana's Grove his bearing was different. There was a distinct sense of enjoyment about him, especially when he spoke of many great deaths. Here, too, he sniffed in a strange way, like a bloodhound at check, and looked puzzled. He said no word in either praise or disparagement, but in the centre of the Grove, where, hidden amongst ancient oak stumps, was a block of granite slightly hollowed on the top, he bent low and placed his forehead on the ground. This was the only place where he showed distinct reverence. At the Castle, though he spoke of much death, he showed no sign of respect.

There was evidently something about Diana's Grove which both interested and baffled him. Before leaving, he moved all over the place unsatisfied, and in one spot, close to the edge of the Brow, where there was a deep hollow, he appeared to be afraid. After returning several times to this place, he suddenly turned and ran in a panic of fear to the higher ground, crossing as he did so the outcropping rock. Then he seemed to breathe more freely, and recovered some of his jaunty impudence.

All this seemed to satisfy Adam's expectations. He went back to Lesser Hill with a serene and settled calm upon him. Sir Nathaniel followed him into his study.

"By the way, I forgot to ask you details about one thing. When that extraordinary staring episode of Mr. Caswall went on, how did Lilla take it—how did she bear herself?"

"She looked frightened, and trembled just as I have seen a pigeon with a hawk, or a bird with a serpent."

"Thanks. It is just as I expected. There have been circumstances in the Caswall family which lead one to believe that they have had from the earliest times some extraordinary mesmeric or hypnotic faculty. Indeed, a skilled eye could read so much in their physiognomy. That shot of yours, whether by instinct or intention, of the hawk and the pigeon was peculiarly apposite. I think we may settle on that as a fixed trait to be accepted throughout our investigation."

When dusk had fallen, Adam took the new mongoose—not the one from Nepaul—and, carrying the box slung over his shoulder, strolled towards Diana's Grove. Close to the gateway he met Lady Arabella, clad as usual in tightly fitting white, which showed off her slim figure.

To his intense astonishment the mongoose allowed her to pet him, take him up in her arms and fondle him. As she was going in his direction, they walked on together.

Round the roadway between the entrances of Diana's Grove and Lesser Hill were many trees, with not much foliage except at the top. In the dusk this place was shadowy, and the view was hampered by the clustering trunks. In the uncertain, tremulous light which fell through the tree-tops, it was hard to distinguish anything clearly, and at last, somehow, he lost sight of her altogether, and turned back on his track to find her. Presently he came across her close to her own gate. She was leaning over the paling of split oak branches which formed the paling of the avenue. He could not see the mongoose, so he asked her where it had gone.

"He slipt out of my arms while I was petting him," she answered, "and disappeared under the hedges."

They found him at a place where the avenue widened so as to let carriages pass each other. The little creature seemed quite changed. He had been ebulliently active; now he was dull and spiritless—seemed to be dazed. He allowed himself to be lifted by either of the pair; but when he was alone with Lady Arabella he kept looking round him in a strange way, as though trying to escape. When they had come out on the roadway Adam held the mongoose tight to him, and, lifting his hat to his companion, moved quickly towards Lesser Hill; he and Lady Arabella lost sight of each other in the thickening gloom.

When Adam got home, he put the mongoose in his box, and locked the door of the room. The other mongoose—the one from Nepaul—was safely locked in his own box, but he lay quiet and did not stir. When he got to his study Sir Nathaniel came in, shutting the door behind him.

"I have come," he said, "while we have an opportunity of being alone, to tell you something of the Caswall family which I think will interest you. There is, or used to be, a belief in this part of the world that the Caswall family had some strange power of making the wills of other persons subservient to their own. There are many allusions to the subject in memoirs and other unimportant works, but I only know of one where the subject is spoken of definitely. It is *Mercia and its Worthies*, written by Ezra Toms more than a hundred years ago. The author goes into the question of the close association of the then Edgar Caswall with Mesmer in Paris. He speaks of Caswall being a pupil and the fellow worker of Mesmer, and states that though, when the latter left France, he took away with him a vast quantity of philosophical and electric instruments, he was never known to use them again. He once made it known to a friend that he had given them to his old pupil. The term he used was odd, for it was 'bequeathed,' but no such bequest of Mesmer was ever made known. At any rate the instruments were missing, and never turned up."

A servant came into the room to tell Adam that there was some strange noise coming from the locked room into which he had gone when he came in. He hurried off to the place at once, Sir Nathaniel going with him. Having locked the door behind them, Adam opened the packing-case where the boxes of the two mongooses were locked up. There was no sound from one of them, but from the other a queer restless struggling. Having opened both boxes, he found that the noise was from the Nepaul animal, which, however, became quiet at once. In the other box the new mongoose lay dead, with every appearance of having been strangled!

CHAPTER X

THE KITE

ON THE FOLLOWING day, a little after four o'clock, Adam set out for Mercy.

He was home just as the clocks were striking six. He was pale and upset, but otherwise looked strong and alert. The old man summed up his appearance and manner thus: "Braced up for battle."

"Now!" said Sir Nathaniel, and settled down to listen, looking at Adam steadily and listening attentively that he might miss nothing—even the inflection of a word.

"I found Lilla and Mimi at home. Watford had been detained by business on the farm. Miss Watford received me as kindly as before; Mimi, too, seemed glad to see me. Mr. Caswall came so soon after I arrived, that he, or someone on his behalf, must have been watching for me. He was followed closely by the negro, who was puffing hard as if he had been running—so it was probably he who watched. Mr. Caswall was very cool and collected, but there was a more than usually iron look about his face that I did not like. However, we got on very well. He talked pleasantly on all sorts of questions. The nigger waited a while and then disappeared as on the other occasion. Mr. Caswall's eyes were as usual fixed on Lilla. True, they seemed to be very deep and earnest, but there was no offence in them. Had it not been for the drawing down of the brows and the stern set of the jaws, I should not at first have noticed anything. But the stare, when presently it began, increased in intensity. I could see that Lilla began to suffer from nervousness, as on the first occasion; but she carried herself bravely.

However, the more nervous she grew, the harder Mr. Caswall stared. It was evident to me that he had come prepared for some sort of mesmeric or hypnotic battle. After a while he began to throw glances round him and then raised his hand, without letting either Lilla or Mimi see the action. It was evidently intended to give some sign to the negro, for he came, in his usual stealthy way, quietly in by the hall door, which was open. Then Mr. Caswall's efforts at staring became intensified, and poor Lilla's nervousness grew greater. Mimi, seeing that her cousin was distressed, came close to her, as if to comfort or strengthen her with the consciousness of her presence. This evidently made a difficulty for Mr. Caswall, for his efforts, without appearing to get feebler, seemed less effective. This continued for a little while, to the gain of both Lilla and Mimi. Then there was a diversion. Without word or apology the door opened, and Lady Arabella March entered the room. I had seen her coming through the great window. Without a word she crossed the room and stood beside Mr. Caswall. It really was very like a fight of a peculiar kind; and the longer it was sustained the more earnest— the fiercer—it grew. That combination of forces—the over-lord, the white woman, and the black man—would have cost some—probably all of them—their lives in the Southern States of America. To us it was simply horrible. But all that you can understand. This time, to go on in sporting phrase, it was understood by all to be a 'fight to a finish,' and the mixed group did not slacken a moment or relax their efforts. On Lilla the strain began to tell disastrously. She grew pale—a patchy pallor, which meant that her nerves were out of order. She trembled like an aspen, and though she struggled bravely, I noticed that her legs would hardly support her. A dozen times she seemed about to collapse in a faint, but each time, on catching sight of Mimi's eyes, she made a fresh struggle and pulled through.

"By now Mr. Caswall's face had lost its appearance of passivity. His eyes glowed with a fiery light. He was still the old Roman in inflexibility of purpose; but grafted on to the Roman was a new Berserker fury. His companions in the baleful work seemed to have taken on something of his feeling. Lady Arabella looked like a soulless, pitiless being, not human, unless it revived old legends of transformed human beings who had lost their humanity in some transformation or in the sweep of natural savagery. As for the negro—well, I can only say that it was solely due to the self-restraint which you impressed on me that I did not wipe him out as he stood—without warning, without fair play—without a single one of the graces of life and death. Lilla was silent in the helpless concentration of deadly fear; Mimi was all resolve and self-forgetfulness, so intent on the soul-struggle in which she was engaged that there was no possibility of any other thought. As for myself, the bonds of will which held me inactive seemed like bands of steel which numbed all my faculties, except sight and hearing. We seemed fixed in an *impasse*. Something must happen, though the power of guessing was inactive. As in a dream, I saw Mimi's hand move restlessly, as if groping for something. Mechanically it touched that of Lilla, and in that instant she was transformed. It was as if youth and strength entered afresh into something already dead to sensibility and intention. As if by inspiration, she grasped the other's band with a force which blenched the knuckles. Her face suddenly flamed, as if some divine light shone through it. Her form expanded till it stood out majestically. Lifting her right hand, she stepped forward towards Caswall, and with a bold sweep of her arm seemed to drive some strange force towards him. Again and again was the gesture repeated, the man falling back from her at each movement. Towards the door he retreated, she following. There was a sound as of the cooing sob of doves, which seemed to multiply and intensify with each second. The sound from the unseen source rose and rose as he retreated, till finally it swelled out in a triumphant peal, as she with a fierce sweep of her arm, seemed to hurl something at her foe, and he, moving his hands blindly before his face, appeared to be swept through the doorway and out into the open sunlight.

"All at once my own faculties were fully restored; I could see and hear everything, and be fully conscious of what was going on. Even the figures of the baleful group were there, though dimly seen as through a veil—a shadowy veil. I saw Lilla sink down in a swoon, and Mimi throw up her arms in a gesture of triumph. As I saw her through the great window, the sunshine flooded the landscape, which, however, was momentarily becoming eclipsed by an onrush of a myriad birds."

By the next morning, daylight showed the actual danger which threatened. From every part of the eastern counties reports were received concerning the enormous immigration of birds. Experts were sending—on their own account, on behalf of learned societies, and through local and imperial governing bodies—reports dealing with the matter, and suggesting remedies.

The reports closer to home were even more disturbing. All day long it would seem that the birds were coming thicker from all quarters. Doubtless many were going as well as coming, but the mass seemed never to get less. Each bird seemed to sound some note of fear or anger or seeking, and the whirring of wings never ceased nor lessened. The air was full of a muttered throb. No window or barrier could shut out the sound, till the ears of any listener became dulled by the ceaseless murmur. So monotonous it was, so cheerless, so disheartening, so melancholy, that all longed, but in vain, for any variety, no matter how terrible it might be.

The second morning the reports from all the districts round were more alarming than ever. Farmers began to dread the coming of winter as they saw the dwindling of the timely fruitfulness of the earth. And as yet it was only a warning of evil, not the evil accomplished; the ground began to look bare whenever some passing sound temporarily frightened the birds.

Edgar Caswall tortured his brain for a long time unavailingly, to think of some means of getting rid of what he, as well as his neighbours, had come to regard as a plague of birds. At last he recalled a circumstance which promised a solution of the difficulty. The experience was of some years ago in China, far up-country, towards the head-waters of the Yang-tze-kiang, where the smaller tributaries spread out in a sort of natural irrigation scheme to supply the wilderness of paddy-fields. It was at the time of the ripening rice, and the myriads of birds which came to feed on the coming crop was a serious menace, not only to the district, but to the country at large. The farmers, who were more or less afflicted with the same trouble every season, knew how to deal with it. They made a vast kite, which they caused to be flown over the centre spot of the incursion. The kite was shaped like a great hawk; and the moment it rose into the air the birds began to cower and seek protection—and then to disappear. So long as that kite was flying overhead the birds lay low and the crop was saved. Accordingly Caswall ordered his men to construct an immense kite, adhering as well as they could to the lines of a hawk. Then he and his men, with a sufficiency of cord, began to fly it high overhead. The experience of China was repeated. The moment the kite rose, the birds hid or sought shelter. The following morning, the kite was still flying high, no bird was to be seen as far as the eye could reach from Castra Regis. But there followed in turn what proved even a worse evil. All the birds were cowed; their sounds stopped. Neither song nor chirp was heard—silence seemed to have taken the place of the normal voices of bird life. But that was not all. The silence spread to all animals.

The fear and restraint which brooded amongst the denizens of the air began to affect all life. Not only did the birds cease song or chirp, but the lowing of the cattle ceased in the fields and the varied sounds of life died away. In place of these things was only a soundless gloom, more dreadful, more disheartening, more soul-killing than any concourse of sounds, no matter how full of fear and dread. Pious individuals put up constant prayers for relief from the intolerable solitude. After a little there were signs of universal depression which those who ran might read. One and all, the faces of men and women seemed bereft of vitality, of interest, of thought, and, most of all, of hope. Men seemed to have lost the power of expression of their thoughts. The soundless air seemed to have the same effect as the universal darkness when men gnawed their tongues with pain.

From this infliction of silence there was no relief. Everything was affected; gloom was the predominant note. Joy appeared to have passed away as a factor of life, and this creative impulse had nothing to take its place. That giant spot in high air was a plague of evil influence. It seemed like a new misanthropic belief which had fallen on human beings, carrying with it the negation of all hope.

After a few days, men began to grow desperate; their very words as well as their senses seemed to be in chains. Edgar Caswall again tortured his brain to find any antidote or palliative of this greater evil than before. He would gladly have destroyed the kite, or caused its flying to cease; but the instant it was pulled down, the birds rose up in even greater numbers; all those who depended in any way on agriculture sent pitiful protests to Castra Regis.

It was strange indeed what influence that weird kite seemed to exercise. Even human beings were affected by it, as if both it and they were realities. As for the people at Mercy Farm, it was like a taste of actual death. Lilla felt it most. If she had been indeed a real dove, with a real kite hanging over her in the air, she could not have been more frightened or more affected by the terror this created.

Of course, some of those already drawn into the vortex noticed the effect on individuals. Those who were interested took care to compare their information. Strangely enough, as it seemed to the others, the person who took the ghastly silence least to heart was the negro. By nature he was not sensitive to, or afflicted by, nerves. This alone would not have produced the seeming indifference, so they set their minds to discover the real cause. Adam came quickly to the conclusion that there was for him some compensation that the others did not share; and he soon believed that that compensation was in one form or another the enjoyment of the sufferings of others. Thus the black had a never-failing source of amusement.

Lady Arabella's cold nature rendered her immune to anything in the way of pain or trouble concerning others. Edgar Caswall was far too haughty a person, and too stern of nature, to concern himself about poor or helpless people, much less the lower order of mere animals. Mr. Watford, Mr. Salton, and Sir Nathaniel were all concerned in the issue, partly from kindness of heart—for none of them could see suffering, even of wild birds, unmoved—and partly on account of their property, which had to be protected, or ruin would stare them in the face before long.

Lilla suffered acutely. As time went on, her face became pinched, and her eyes dull with watching and crying. Mimi suffered too on account of her cousin's suffering. But as she could do nothing, she resolutely made up her mind to self-restraint and patience. Adam's frequent visits comforted her.

CHAPTER XI

MESMER'S CHEST

AFTER A COUPLE of weeks had passed, the kite seemed to give Edgar Caswall a new zest for life. He was never tired of looking at its movements. He had a comfortable armchair put out on the tower, wherein he sat sometimes all day long, watching as though the kite was a new toy and he a child lately come into possession of it. He did not seem to have lost interest in Lilla, for he still paid an occasional visit at Mercy Farm.

Indeed, his feeling towards her, whatever it had been at first, had now so far changed that it had become a distinct affection of a purely animal kind. Indeed, it seemed as though the man's nature had become corrupted, and that all the baser and more selfish and more reckless qualities had become more conspicuous. There was not so much sternness apparent in his nature, because there was less self-restraint. Determination had become indifference.

The visible change in Edgar was that he grew morbid, sad, silent; the neighbours thought he was going mad. He became absorbed in the kite, and watched it not only by day, but often all night long. It became an obsession to him.

Caswall took a personal interest in the keeping of the great kite flying. He had a vast coil of cord efficient for the purpose, which worked on a roller fixed on the parapet of the tower. There was a winch for the pulling in of the slack; the outgoing line being controlled by a racket. There was invariably one man at least, day and night, on the tower to attend to it. At such an elevation there was always a strong wind, and at times the kite rose to an enormous height, as well as travelling for great distances laterally. In fact, the kite became, in a short time, one of the curiosities of Castra Regis and all around it. Edgar began to attribute to it, in his own mind, almost human qualities. It became to him a separate entity, with a mind and a soul of its own. Being idle-handed all day, he began to apply to what he considered the service of the kite some of his spare time, and found a new pleasure—a new object in life—in the old schoolboy game of sending up "runners" to the kite. The way this is done is to get round pieces of paper so cut that there is a hole in the centre, through which the string of the kite passes. The natural action of the wind-pressure takes the paper along the string, and so up to the kite itself, no matter how high or how far it may have gone.

In the early days of this amusement Edgar Caswall spent hours. Hundreds of such messengers flew along the string, until soon he bethought him of writing messages on these papers so that he could make known his ideas to the kite. It may be that his brain gave way under the opportunities given by his illusion of the entity of the toy and its power of separate thought. From sending messages he came to making direct speech to the kite—without, however, ceasing to send the runners. Doubtless, the height of the tower, seated as it was on the hill-top, the rushing of the ceaseless wind, the hypnotic effect of the lofty altitude of the speck in the sky at which he gazed, and the rushing of the paper messengers up the string till sight of them was lost in distance, all helped to further affect his brain, undoubtedly giving way under the strain of beliefs and circumstances which were at once stimulating to the imagination, occupative of his mind, and absorbing.

The next step of intellectual decline was to bring to bear on the main idea of the conscious identity of the kite all sorts of subjects which had imaginative force or tendency of their own. He had, in Castra Regis, a large collection of curious and interesting things formed in the past by his forebears, of similar tastes to his own. There were all sorts of strange anthropological specimens, both old and new, which had been collected through various travels in strange places: ancient Egyptian relics from tombs and mummies; curios from Australia, New Zealand, and the South Seas; idols and images—from Tartar ikons to ancient Egyptian, Persian, and Indian objects of worship; objects of death and torture of American Indians; and, above all, a vast collection of lethal weapons of every kind and from every place—Chinese "high pinders," double knives, Afghan double-edged scimitars made to cut a body in two, heavy knives from all the Eastern countries, ghost daggers from Thibet, the terrible kukri of the Ghourka and other hill tribes of India, assassins' weapons from Italy and Spain, even the knife which was formerly carried by the slave-drivers of the Mississippi region. Death and pain of every kind were fully represented in that gruesome collection.

That it had a fascination for Oolanga goes without saying. He was never tired of visiting the museum in the tower, and spent endless hours in inspecting the exhibits, till he was thoroughly familiar with every detail of all of them. He asked permission to clean and polish and sharpen them—a favour which was readily granted. In addition to the above objects, there were many things of a kind to awaken human fear. Stuffed serpents of the most objectionable and horrid kind; giant insects from the tropics, fearsome in every detail; fishes and crustaceans covered with weird spikes; dried octopuses of great size. Other things, too, there were, not less deadly though seemingly innocuous—dried fungi, traps intended for birds, beasts, fishes, reptiles, and insects; machines which could produce pain of any kind and degree, and the only mercy of which was the power of producing speedy death.

Caswall, who had never before seen any of these things, except those which he had collected himself, found a constant amusement and interest in them. He studied them, their uses, their mechanism—where there was such—and their places of origin, until he had an ample and real knowledge of all concerning them. Many were secret and intricate, but he never rested till he found out all the secrets. When once he had become interested in strange objects, and the way to use them, he began to explore various likely places for similar finds. He began to inquire of his household where strange lumber was kept. Several of the men spoke of old Simon Chester as one who knew everything in and about the house. Accordingly, he sent for the old man, who came at once. He was very old, nearly ninety years of age, and very infirm. He had been born in the Castle, and had served its succession of masters—present or absent—ever since. When Edgar began to question him on the subject regarding which he had sent for him, old Simon exhibited much perturbation. In fact, he became so frightened that his master, fully believing that he was concealing something, ordered him to tell at once what remained unseen, and where it was hidden away. Face to face with discovery of his secret, the old man, in a pitiable state of concern, spoke out even more fully than Mr. Caswall had expected.

"Indeed, indeed, sir, everything is here in the tower that has ever been put away in my time except—except—" here he began to shake and tremble it—"except the chest which Mr. Edgar—he who was Mr. Edgar when I first took service—brought back from France, after he had been with Dr. Mesmer. The trunk has been kept in my room for safety; but I shall send it down here now."

"What is in it?" asked Edgar sharply.

"That I do not know. Moreover, it is a peculiar trunk, without any visible means of opening."

"Is there no lock?"

"I suppose so, sir; but I do not know. There is no keyhole."

"Send it here; and then come to me yourself."

The trunk, a heavy one with steel bands round it, but no lock or keyhole, was carried in by two men. Shortly afterwards old Simon attended his master. When he came into the room, Mr. Caswall himself went and closed the door; then he asked:

"How do you open it?"

"I do not know, sir."

"Do you mean to say that you never opened it?"

"Most certainly I say so, your honour. How could I? It was entrusted to me with the other things by my master. To open it would have been a breach of trust."

Caswall sneered.

"Quite remarkable! Leave it with me. Close the door behind you. Stay—did no one ever tell you about it—say anything regarding it—make any remark?"

Old Simon turned pale, and put his trembling hands together.

"Oh, sir, I entreat you not to touch it. That trunk probably contains secrets which Dr. Mesmer told my master. Told them to his ruin!"

"How do you mean? What ruin?"

"Sir, he it was who, men said, sold his soul to the Evil One; I had thought that that time and the evil of it had all passed away."

"That will do. Go away; but remain in your own room, or within call. I may want you."

The old man bowed deeply and went out trembling, but without speaking a word.

CHAPTER XII

THE CHEST OPENED

LEFT ALONE IN the turret-room, Edgar Caswall carefully locked the door and hung a handkerchief over the keyhole. Next, he inspected the windows, and saw that they were not overlooked from any angle of the main building. Then he carefully examined the trunk, going over it with a magnifying glass. He found it intact: the steel bands were flawless; the whole trunk was compact. After sitting opposite to it for some time, and the shades of evening beginning to melt into darkness, he gave up the task and went to his bedroom, after locking the door of the turret-room behind him and taking away the key.

He woke in the morning at daylight, and resumed his patient but unavailing study of the metal trunk. This he continued during the whole day with the same result—humiliating disappointment, which overwrought his nerves and made his head ache. The result of the long strain was seen later in the afternoon, when he sat locked within the turret-room before the still baffling trunk, distrait, listless and yet agitated, sunk in a settled gloom. As the dusk was falling he told the steward to send him two men, strong ones. These he ordered to take the trunk to his bedroom. In that room he then sat on into the night, without pausing even to take any food. His mind was in a whirl, a fever of excitement. The result was that when, late in the night, he locked himself in his room his brain was full of odd fancies; he was on the high road to mental disturbance. He lay down on his bed in the dark, still brooding over the mystery of the closed trunk.

Gradually he yielded to the influences of silence and darkness. After lying there quietly for some time, his mind became active again. But this time there were round him no disturbing influences; his brain was active and able to work freely and to deal with memory. A thousand forgotten—or only half-known—incidents, fragments of conversations or theories long ago guessed at and long forgotten, crowded on his mind. He seemed to hear again around him the legions of whirring wings to which he had been so lately accustomed. Even to himself he knew that that was an effort of imagination founded on imperfect memory. But he was content that imagination should work, for out of it might come some solution of the mystery which surrounded him. And in this frame of mind, sleep made another and more successful essay. This time he enjoyed peaceful slumber, restful alike to his wearied body and his overwrought brain.

In his sleep he arose, and, as if in obedience to some influence beyond and greater than himself, lifted the great trunk and set it on a strong table at one side of the room, from which he had previously removed a quantity of books. To do this, he had to use an amount of strength which was, he knew, far beyond him in his normal state. As it was, it seemed easy enough; everything yielded before his touch. Then he became conscious that somehow—how, he never could remember— the chest was open. He unlocked his door, and, taking the chest on his shoulder, carried it up to the turret-room, the door of which also he unlocked. Even at the time he was amazed at his own strength, and wondered whence it had come. His mind, lost in conjecture, was too far off to realise more immediate things. He knew that the chest was enormously heavy. He seemed, in a sort of vision which lit up the absolute blackness around, to see the two sturdy servant men staggering under its great weight. He locked himself again in the turret-room, and laid the opened chest on a table, and in the darkness began to unpack it, laying out the contents, which were mainly of metal and glass—great pieces in strange forms—on another table. He was conscious of being still asleep, and of acting rather in obedience to some unseen and unknown command than in accordance with any reasonable plan, to be followed by results which he understood. This phase completed, he proceeded to arrange in order the component parts of some large instruments, formed mostly of glass. His fingers seemed to have acquired a new and exquisite subtlety and even a volition of their own. Then weariness of brain came upon him; his head sank down on his breast, and little by little everything became wrapped in gloom.

He awoke in the early morning in his bedroom, and looked around him, now clear-headed, in amazement. In its usual place on the strong table stood the great steel-hooped chest without lock or key. But it was now locked. He arose quietly and stole to the turret-room. There everything was as it had been on the previous evening. He looked out of the window where high in air flew, as usual, the giant kite. He unlocked the wicket gate of the turret stair and went out on the roof. Close to him was the great coil of cord on its reel. It was humming in the morning breeze, and when he touched the string it sent a quick thrill through hand and arm. There was no sign anywhere that there had been any disturbance or displacement of anything during the night.

Utterly bewildered, he sat down in his room to think. Now for the first time he *felt* that he was asleep and dreaming. Presently he fell asleep again, and slept for a long time. He awoke hungry and made a hearty meal. Then towards evening, having locked himself in, he fell asleep again. When he woke he was in darkness, and was quite at sea as to his whereabouts. He began feeling about the dark room, and was recalled to the consequences of his position by the breaking of a large piece of glass. Having obtained a light, he discovered this to be a glass wheel, part of an elaborate piece of mechanism which he must in his sleep have taken from the chest, which was now opened. He had once again opened it whilst asleep, but he had no recollection of the circumstances.

THE LAIR OF THE WHITE WORM

Caswall came to the conclusion that there had been some sort of dual action of his mind, which might lead to some catastrophe or some discovery of his secret plans; so he resolved to forgo for a while the pleasure of making discoveries regarding the chest. To this end, he applied himself to quite another matter—an investigation of the other treasures and rare objects in his collections. He went amongst them in simple, idle curiosity, his main object being to discover some strange item which he might use for experiment with the kite. He had already resolved to try some runners other than those made of paper. He had a vague idea that with such a force as the great kite straining at its leash, this might be used to lift to the altitude of the kite itself heavier articles. His first experiment with articles of little but increasing weight was eminently successful. So he added by degrees more and more weight, until he found out that the lifting power of the kite was considerable. He then determined to take a step further, and send to the kite some of the articles which lay in the steel-hooped chest. The last time he had opened it in sleep, it had not been shut again, and he had inserted a wedge so that he could open it at will. He made examination of the contents, but came to the conclusion that the glass objects were unsuitable. They were too light for testing weight, and they were so frail as to be dangerous to send to such a height.

So he looked around for something more solid with which to experiment. His eye caught sight of an object which at once attracted him. This was a small copy of one of the ancient Egyptian gods—that of Bes, who represented the destructive power of nature. It was so bizarre and mysterious as to commend itself to his mad humour. In lifting it from the cabinet, he was struck by its great weight in proportion to its size. He made accurate examination of it by the aid of some instruments, and came to the conclusion that it was carved from a lump of lodestone. He remembered that he had read somewhere of an ancient Egyptian god cut from a similar substance, and, thinking it over, he came to the conclusion that he must have read it in Sir Thomas Brown's *Popular Errors*, a book of the seventeenth century. He got the book from the library, and looked out the passage:

"A great example we have from the observation of our learned friend Mr. Graves, in an AEgyptian idol cut out of Loadstone and found among the Mummies; which still retains its attraction, though probably taken out of the mine about two thousand years ago."

The strangeness of the figure, and its being so close akin to his own nature, attracted him. He made from thin wood a large circular runner, and in front of it placed the weighty god, sending it up to the flying kite along the throbbing cord.

CHAPTER XIII

OOLANGA'S HALLUCINATIONS

DURING THE LAST few days Lady Arabella had been getting exceedingly impatient. Her debts, always pressing, were growing to an embarrassing amount. The only hope she had of comfort in life was a good marriage; but the good marriage on which she had fixed her eye did not seem to move quickly enough—indeed, it did not seem to move at all—in the right direction. Edgar Caswall was not an ardent wooer. From the very first he seemed *difficile*, but he had been keeping to his own room ever since his struggle with Mimi Watford. On that occasion Lady Arabella had shown him in an unmistakable way what her feelings were; indeed, she had made it known to him, in a more overt way than pride should allow, that she wished to help and support him. The moment when she had gone across the room to stand beside him in his mesmeric struggle, had been the very limit of her voluntary action. It was quite bitter enough, she felt, that he did not come to her, but now that she had made that advance, she felt that any withdrawal on his part would, to a woman of her class, be nothing less than a flaming insult. Had she not classed herself with his nigger servant, an unreformed savage? Had she not shown her preference for him at the festival of his home-coming? Had she not . . . Lady Arabella was cold-blooded, and she was prepared to go through all that might be necessary of indifference, and even insult, to become chatelaine of Castra Regis. In the meantime, she would show no hurry—she must wait. She might, in an unostentatious way, come to him again. She knew him now, and could make a keen guess at his desires with regard to Lilla Watford. With that secret in her possession, she could bring pressure to bear on Caswall which would make it no easy matter for him to evade her. The great difficulty was how to get near him. He was shut up within his Castle, and guarded by a defence of convention which she could not pass without danger of ill repute to herself. Over this question she thought and thought for days and nights. At last she decided that the only way would be to go to him openly at Castra Regis. Her rank and position would make such a thing possible, if carefully done. She could explain matters afterwards if necessary. Then when they were alone, she would use her arts and her experience to make him commit himself. After all, he was only a man, with a man's dislike of difficult or awkward situations. She felt quite sufficient confidence in her own womanhood to carry her through any difficulty which might arise.

From Diana's Grove she heard each day the luncheon-gong from Castra Regis sound, and knew the hour when the servants would be in the back of the house. She would enter the house at that hour, and, pretending that she could not make anyone hear her, would seek him in his own rooms. The tower was, she knew, away from all the usual sounds of the house, and moreover she knew that the servants had strict orders not to interrupt him when he was in the turret chamber. She had found out, partly by the aid of an opera-glass and partly by judicious questioning, that several times lately a heavy chest had been carried to and from his room, and that it rested in the room each night. She was, therefore, confident that he had some important work on hand which would keep him busy for long spells.

Meanwhile, another member of the household at Castra Regis had schemes which he thought were working to fruition. A man in the position of a servant has plenty of opportunity of watching his betters and forming opinions regarding them. Oolanga was in his way a clever, unscrupulous rogue, and he felt that with things moving round him in this great household there should be opportunities of self-advancement. Being unscrupulous and stealthy—and a savage—he looked to dishonest means. He saw plainly enough that Lady Arabella was making a dead set at his master, and he was watchful of the slightest sign of anything which might enhance this knowledge. Like the other men in the house, he knew of the carrying to and fro of the great chest, and had got it into his head that the care exercised in its porterage indicated that it was full of treasure. He was for ever lurking around the turret-rooms on the chance of making some useful discovery. But he was as cautious as he was stealthy, and took care that no one else watched him.

It was thus that the negro became aware of Lady Arabella's venture into the house, as she thought, unseen. He took more care than ever, since he was watching another, that the positions were not reversed. More than ever he kept his eyes and ears open and his mouth shut. Seeing Lady Arabella gliding up the stairs towards his master's room, he took it for granted that she was there for no good, and doubled his watching intentness and caution.

Oolanga was disappointed, but he dared not exhibit any feeling lest it should betray that he was hiding. Therefore he slunk downstairs again noiselessly, and waited for a more favourable opportunity of furthering his plans. It must be borne in mind that he thought that the heavy trunk was full of valuables, and that he believed that Lady Arabella had come to try to steal it. His purpose of using for his own advantage the combination of these two ideas was seen later in the day. Oolanga secretly followed her home. He was an expert at this game, and succeeded admirably on this occasion. He watched her enter the private gate of Diana's Grove, and then, taking a roundabout course and keeping out of her sight, he at last overtook her in a thick part of the Grove where no one could see the meeting.

Lady Arabella was much surprised. She had not seen the negro for several days, and had almost forgotten his existence. Oolanga would have been startled had he known and been capable of understanding the real value placed on him, his beauty, his worthiness, by other persons, and compared it with the value in these matters in which he held himself. Doubtless Oolanga had his dreams like other men. In such cases he saw himself as a young sun-god, as beautiful as the eye of dusky or even white womanhood had ever dwelt upon. He would have been filled with all noble and captivating qualities—or those regarded as such in West Africa. Women would have loved him, and would have told him so in the overt and fervid manner usual in affairs of the heart in the shadowy depths of the forest of the Gold Coast.

Oolanga came close behind Lady Arabella, and in a hushed voice, suitable to the importance of his task, and in deference to the respect he had for her and the place, began to unfold the story of his love. Lady Arabella was not usually a humorous person, but no man or woman of the white race could have checked the laughter which rose spontaneously to her lips. The circumstances were too grotesque, the contrast too violent, for subdued mirth. The man a debased specimen of one of the most primitive races of the earth, and of an ugliness which was simply devilish; the woman of high degree, beautiful, accomplished. She thought that her first moment's consideration of the outrage— it was nothing less in her eyes—had given her the full material for thought. But every instant after threw new and varied lights on the affront. Her indignation was too great for passion; only irony or satire would meet the situation. Her cold, cruel nature helped, and she did not shrink to subject this ignorant savage to the merciless fire-lash of her scorn.

Oolanga was dimly conscious that he was being flouted; but his anger was no less keen because of the measure of his ignorance. So he gave way to it, as does a tortured beast. He ground his great teeth together, raved, stamped, and swore in barbarous tongues and with barbarous imagery. Even Lady Arabella felt that it was well she was within reach of help, or he might have offered her brutal violence—even have killed her.

"Am I to understand," she said with cold disdain, so much more effective to wound than hot passion, "that you are offering me your love? Your—love?"

For reply he nodded his head. The scorn of her voice, in a sort of baleful hiss, sounded—and felt—like the lash of a whip.

"And you dared! you—a savage—a slave—the basest thing in the world of vermin! Take care! I don't value your worthless life more than I do that of a rat or a spider. Don't let me ever see your hideous face here again, or I shall rid the earth of you."

As she was speaking, she had taken out her revolver and was pointing it at him. In the immediate presence of death his impudence forsook him, and he made a weak effort to justify himself. His speech was short, consisting of single words. To Lady Arabella it sounded mere gibberish, but it was in his own dialect, and meant love, marriage, wife. From the intonation of the words, she guessed, with her woman's quick intuition, at their meaning; but she quite failed to follow, when, becoming more pressing, he continued to urge his suit in a mixture of the grossest animal passion and ridiculous threats. He warned her that he knew she had tried to steal his master's treasure, and that he had caught her in the act. But if she would be his, he would share the treasure with her, and they could live in luxury in the African forests. But if she refused, he would tell his master, who would flog and torture her and then give her to the police, who would kill her.

CHAPTER XIV

BATTLE RENEWED

THE CONSEQUENCES OF that meeting in the dusk of Diana's Grove were acute and far-reaching, and not only to the two engaged in it. From Oolanga, this might have been expected by anyone who knew the character of the tropical African savage. To such, there are two passions that are inexhaustible and insatiable—vanity and that which they are pleased to call love. Oolanga left the Grove with an absorbing hatred in his heart. His lust and greed were afire, while his vanity had been wounded to the core. Lady Arabella's icy nature was not so deeply stirred, though she was in a seething passion. More than ever she was set upon bringing Edgar Caswall to her feet. The obstacles she had encountered, the insults she had endured, were only as fuel to the purpose of revenge which consumed her.

As she sought her own rooms in Diana's Grove, she went over the whole subject again and again, always finding in the face of Lilla Watford a key to a problem which puzzled her—the problem of a way to turn Caswall's powers—his very existence—to aid her purpose.

When in her boudoir, she wrote a note, taking so much trouble over it that she destroyed, and rewrote, till her dainty waste-basket was half-full of torn sheets of notepaper. When quite satisfied, she copied out the last sheet afresh, and then carefully burned all the spoiled fragments. She put the copied note in an emblazoned envelope, and directed it to Edgar Caswall at Castra Regis. This she sent off by one of her grooms. The letter ran:

"DEAR MR. CASWALL,

"I want to have a chat with you on a subject in which I believe you are interested. Will you kindly call for me one day after lunch—say at three or four o'clock, and we can walk a little way together. Only as far as Mercy Farm, where I want to see Lilla and Mimi Watford. We can take a cup of tea at the Farm. Do not bring your African servant with you, as I am afraid his face frightens the girls. After all, he is not pretty, is he? I have an idea you will be pleased with your visit this time.

"Yours sincerely,

"ARABELLA MARCH."

At half-past three next day, Edgar Caswall called at Diana's Grove. Lady Arabella met him on the roadway outside the gate. She wished to take the servants into her confidence as little as possible. She turned when she saw him coming, and walked beside him towards Mercy Farm, keeping step with him as they walked. When they got near Mercy, she turned and looked around her, expecting to see Oolanga or some sign of him. He was, however, not visible. He had received from his master peremptory orders to keep out of sight—an order for which the African scored a new offence up against her. They found Lilla and Mimi at home and seemingly glad to see them, though both the girls were surprised at the visit coming so soon after the other.

The proceedings were a repetition of the battle of souls of the former visit. On this occasion, however, Edgar Caswall had only the presence of Lady Arabella to support him—Oolanga being absent; but Mimi lacked the support of Adam Salton, which had been of such effective service before. This time the struggle for supremacy of will was longer and more determined. Caswall felt that if he could not achieve supremacy he had better give up the idea, so all his pride was enlisted against Mimi. When they had been waiting for the door to be opened, Lady

Arabella, believing in a sudden attack, had said to him in a low voice, which somehow carried conviction:

"This time you should win. Mimi is, after all, only a woman. Show her no mercy. That is weakness. Fight her, beat her, trample on her—kill her if need be. She stands in your way, and I hate her. Never take your eyes off her. Never mind Lilla—she is afraid of you. You are already her master. Mimi will try to make you look at her cousin. There lies defeat. Let nothing take your attention from Mimi, and you will win. If she is overcoming you, take my hand and hold it hard whilst you are looking into her eyes. If she is too strong for you, I shall interfere. I'll make a diversion, and under cover of it you must retire unbeaten, even if not victorious. Hush! they are coming."

The two girls came to the door together. Strange sounds were coming up over the Brow from the west. It was the rustling and crackling of the dry reeds and rushes from the low lands. The season had been an unusually dry one. Also the strong east wind was helping forward enormous flocks of birds, most of them pigeons with white cowls. Not only were their wings whirring, but their cooing was plainly audible. From such a multitude of birds the mass of sound, individually small, assumed the volume of a storm. Surprised at the influx of birds, to which they had been strangers so long, they all looked towards Castra Regis, from whose high tower the great kite had been flying as usual. But even as they looked, the cord broke, and the great kite fell headlong in a series of sweeping dives. Its own weight, and the aerial force opposed to it, which caused it to rise, combined with the strong easterly breeze, had been too much for the great length of cord holding it.

Somehow, the mishap to the kite gave new hope to Mimi. It was as though the side issues had been shorn away, so that the main struggle was thenceforth on simpler lines. She had a feeling in her heart, as though some religious chord had been newly touched. It may, of course, have been that with the renewal of the bird voices a fresh courage, a fresh belief in the good issue of the struggle came too. In the misery of silence, from which they had all suffered for so long, any new train of thought was almost bound to be a boon. As the inrush of birds continued, their wings beating against the crackling rushes, Lady Arabella grew pale, and almost fainted.

"What is that?" she asked suddenly.

To Mimi, born and bred in Siam, the sound was strangely like an exaggeration of the sound produced by a snake-charmer.

Edgar Caswall was the first to recover from the interruption of the falling kite. After a few minutes he seemed to have quite recovered his *sang froid*, and was able to use his brains to the end which he had in view. Mimi too quickly recovered herself, but from a different cause. With her it was a deep religious conviction that the struggle round her was of the powers of Good and Evil, and that Good was triumphing. The very appearance of the snowy birds, with the cowls of Saint Columba, heightened the impression. With this conviction strong upon her, she continued the strange battle with fresh vigour. She seemed to tower over Caswall, and he to give back before her oncoming. Once again her vigorous passes drove him to the door. He was just going out backward when Lady Arabella, who had been gazing at him with fixed eyes, caught his hand and tried to stop his movement. She was, however, unable to do any good, and so, holding hands, they passed out together. As they did so, the strange music which had so alarmed Lady Arabella suddenly stopped. Instinctively they all looked towards the tower of Castra Regis, and saw that the workmen had refixed the kite, which had risen again and was beginning to float out to its former station.

As they were looking, the door opened and Michael Watford came into the room. By that time all had recovered their self-possession, and there was nothing out of the common to attract his attention. As he came in, seeing inquiring looks all around him, he said:

"The new influx of birds is only the annual migration of pigeons from Africa. I am told that it will soon be over."

The second victory of Mimi Watford made Edgar Caswall more moody than ever. He felt thrown back on himself, and this, added to his absorbing interest in the hope of a victory of his mesmeric powers, became a deep and settled purpose of revenge. The chief object of his animosity was, of course, Mimi, whose will had overcome his, but it was obscured in greater or lesser degree by all who had opposed him. Lilla was next to Mimi in his hate—Lilla, the harmless, tender-hearted, sweet-natured girl, whose heart was so full of love for all things that in it was no room for the passions of ordinary life—whose nature resembled those doves of St. Columba, whose colour she wore, whose appearance she reflected. Adam Salton came next—after a gap; for against him Caswall had no direct animosity. He regarded him as an interference, a difficulty to be got rid of or destroyed. The young Australian had been so discreet that the most he had against him was his knowledge of what had been. Caswall did not understand him, and to such a nature as his, ignorance was a cause of alarm, of dread.

Caswall resumed his habit of watching the great kite straining at its cord, varying his vigils in this way by a further examination of the mysterious treasures of his house, especially Mesmer's chest. He sat much on the roof of the tower, brooding over his thwarted passion. The vast extent of his possessions, visible to him at that altitude, might, one would have thought, have restored some of his complacency. But the very extent of his ownership, thus perpetually brought before him, created a fresh sense of grievance. How was it, he thought, that with so much at command that others wished for, he could not achieve the dearest wishes of his heart?

In this state of intellectual and moral depravity, he found a solace in the renewal of his experiments with the mechanical powers of the kite. For a couple of weeks he did not see Lady Arabella, who was always on the watch for a chance of meeting him; neither did he see the Watford girls, who studiously kept out of his way. Adam Salton simply marked time, keeping ready to deal with anything that might affect his friends. He called at the farm and heard from Mimi of the last battle of wills, but it had only one consequence. He got from Ross several more mongooses, including a second king-cobra-killer, which he generally carried with him in its box whenever he walked out.

Mr. Caswall's experiments with the kite went on successfully. Each day he tried the lifting of greater weight, and it seemed almost as if the machine had a sentience of its own, which was increasing with the obstacles placed before it. All this time the kite hung in the sky at an enormous height. The wind was steadily from the north, so the trend of the kite was to the south. All day long, runners of increasing magnitude were sent up. These were only of paper or thin cardboard, or leather, or other flexible materials. The great height at which the kite hung made a great concave curve in the string, so that as the runners went up they made a flapping sound. If one laid a finger on the string, the sound answered to the flapping of the runner in a sort of hollow intermittent murmur. Edgar Caswall, who was now wholly obsessed by the kite and all belonging to it, found a distinct resemblance between that intermittent rumble and the snake-charming music produced by the pigeons flying through the dry reeds.

One day he made a discovery in Mesmer's chest which he thought he would utilise with regard to the runners. This was a great length of wire, "fine as human hair," coiled round a finely made wheel, which ran to a wondrous distance freely, and as lightly. He tried this on runners, and found it work admirably. Whether the runner was alone, or carried something much more weighty than itself, it worked equally well. Also it was strong enough and light enough to draw back the runner without undue strain. He tried this a good many times successfully, but it was now growing dusk and he found some difficulty in keeping the runner in sight. So he looked for something heavy enough to keep it still. He placed the Egyptian image of Bes on the fine wire, which crossed the wooden ledge which protected it. Then, the darkness growing, he went indoors and forgot all about it.

He had a strange feeling of uneasiness that night—not sleeplessness, for he seemed conscious of being asleep. At daylight he rose, and as usual looked out for the kite. He did not see it in its usual position in the sky, so looked round the points of the compass. He was more than astonished when presently he saw the missing kite struggling as usual against the controlling cord. But it had gone to the further side of the tower, and now hung and strained *against the wind* to the north. He thought it so strange that he determined to investigate the phenomenon, and to say nothing about it in the meantime.

In his many travels, Edgar Caswall had been accustomed to use the sextant, and was now an expert in the matter. By the aid of this and other instruments, he was able to fix the position of the kite and the point over which it hung. He was startled to find that exactly under it—so far as he could ascertain—was Diana's Grove. He had an inclination to take Lady Arabella into his confidence in the matter, but he thought better of it and wisely refrained. For some reason which he did not try to explain to himself, he was glad of his silence, when, on the following morning, he found, on looking out, that the point over which the kite then hovered was Mercy Farm. When he had verified this with his instruments, he sat before the window of the tower, looking out and thinking. The new locality was more to his liking than the other; but the why of it puzzled him, all the same. He spent the rest of the day in the turret-room, which he did not leave all day. It seemed to him that he was now drawn by forces which he could not control—of which, indeed, he had no knowledge—in directions which he did not understand, and which were without his own volition. In sheer helpless inability to think the problem out satisfactorily, he called up a servant and told him to tell Oolanga that he wanted to see him at once in the turret-room. The answer came back that the African had not been seen since the previous evening.

Caswall was now so irritable that even this small thing upset him. As he was distrait and wanted to talk to somebody, he sent for Simon Chester, who came at once, breathless with hurrying and upset by the unexpected summons. Caswall bade him sit down, and when the old man was in a less uneasy frame of mind, he again asked him if he had ever seen what was in Mesmer's chest or heard it spoken about.

Chester admitted that he had once, in the time of "the then Mr. Edgar," seen the chest open, which, knowing something of its history and guessing more, so upset him that he had fainted. When he recovered, the chest was closed. From that time the then Mr. Edgar had never spoken about it again.

When Caswall asked him to describe what he had seen when the chest was open, he got very agitated, and, despite all his efforts to remain calm, he suddenly went off into a faint. Caswall summoned servants, who applied the usual remedies. Still the old man did not recover. After the lapse of a considerable time, the doctor who had been summoned made his appearance. A glance was sufficient for him to make up his mind. Still, he knelt down by the old man, and made a careful examination. Then he rose to his feet, and in a hushed voice said:

"I grieve to say, sir, that he has passed away."

CHAPTER XV

ON THE TRACK

THOSE WHO HAD seen Edgar Caswall familiarly since his arrival, and had already estimated his cold-blooded nature at something of its true value, were surprised that he took so to heart the death of old Chester. The fact was that not one of them had guessed correctly at his character. They thought, naturally enough, that the concern which he felt was that of a master for a faithful old servant of his family. They little thought that it was merely the selfish expression of his disappointment, that he had thus lost the only remaining clue to an interesting piece of family history—one which was now and would be for ever wrapped in mystery. Caswall knew enough about the life of his ancestor in Paris to wish to know more fully and more thoroughly all that had been. The period covered by that ancestor's life in Paris was one inviting every form of curiosity.

Lady Arabella, who had her own game to play, saw in the *métier* of sympathetic friend, a series of meetings with the man she wanted to secure. She made the first use of the opportunity the day after old Chester's death; indeed, as soon as the news had filtered in through the back door of Diana's Grove. At that meeting, she played her part so well that even Caswall's cold nature was impressed.

Oolanga was the only one who did not credit her with at least some sense of fine feeling in the matter. In emotional, as in other matters, Oolanga was distinctly a utilitarian, and as he could not understand anyone feeling grief except for his own suffering, pain, or for the loss of money, he could not understand anyone simulating such an emotion except for show intended to deceive. He thought that she had come to Castra Regis again for the opportunity of stealing something, and was determined that on this occasion the chance of pressing his advantage over her should not pass. He felt, therefore, that the occasion was one for extra carefulness in the watching of all that went on. Ever since he had come to the conclusion that Lady Arabella was trying to steal the treasure-chest, he suspected nearly everyone of the same design, and made it a point to watch all suspicious persons and places. As Adam was engaged on his own researches regarding Lady Arabella, it was only natural that there should be some crossing of each other's tracks. This is what did actually happen.

Adam had gone for an early morning survey of the place in which he was interested, taking with him the mongoose in its box. He arrived at the gate of Diana's Grove just as Lady Arabella was preparing to set out for Castra Regis on what she considered her mission of comfort. Seeing Adam from her window going through the shadows of the trees round the gate, she thought that he must be engaged on some purpose similar to her own. So, quickly making her toilet, she quietly left the house, and, taking advantage of every shadow and substance which could hide her, followed him on his walk.

Oolanga, the experienced tracker, followed her, but succeeded in hiding his movements better than she did. He saw that Adam had on his shoulder a mysterious box, which he took to contain something valuable. Seeing that Lady Arabella was secretly following Adam, he was confirmed in this idea. His mind—such as it was—was fixed on her trying to steal, and he credited her at once with making use of this new opportunity.

In his walk, Adam went into the grounds of Castra Regis, and Oolanga saw her follow him with great secrecy. He feared to go closer, as now on both sides of him were enemies who might make discovery. When he realised that Lady Arabella was bound for the Castle, he devoted himself to following her with singleness of purpose. He therefore missed seeing that Adam branched off the track and returned to the high road.

That night Edgar Caswall had slept badly. The tragic occurrence of the day was on his mind, and he kept waking and thinking of it. After an early breakfast, he sat at the open window watching the kite and thinking of many things. From his room he could see all round the neighbourhood, but the two places that interested him most were Mercy Farm and Diana's Grove. At first the movements about those spots were of a humble kind—those that belong to domestic service or agricultural needs—the opening of doors and windows, the sweeping and brushing, and generally the restoration of habitual order.

From his high window—whose height made it a screen from the observation of others—he saw the chain of watchers move into his own grounds, and then presently break up—Adam Salton going one way, and Lady Arabella, followed by the nigger, another. Then Oolanga disappeared amongst the trees; but Caswall could see that he was still watching. Lady Arabella, after looking around her, slipped in by the open door, and he could, of course, see her no longer.

Presently, however, he heard a light tap at his door, then the door opened slowly, and he could see the flash of Lady Arabella's white dress through the opening.

CHAPTER XVI

A VISIT OF SYMPATHY

CASWALL WAS GENUINELY surprised when he saw Lady Arabella, though he need not have been, after what had already occurred in the same way. The look of surprise on his face was so much greater than Lady Arabella had expected—though she thought she was prepared to meet anything that might occur—that she stood still, in sheer amazement. Cold-blooded as she was and ready for all social emergencies, she was nonplussed how to go on. She was plucky, however, and began to speak at once, although she had not the slightest idea what she was going to say.

"I came to offer you my very warm sympathy with the grief you have so lately experienced."

"My grief? I'm afraid I must be very dull; but I really do not understand."

Already she felt at a disadvantage, and hesitated.

"I mean about the old man who died so suddenly—your old . . . retainer."

Caswall's face relaxed something of its puzzled concentration.

"Oh, he was only a servant; and he had over-stayed his three-score and ten years by something like twenty years. He must have been ninety!"

"Still, as an old servant . . ."

Caswall's words were not so cold as their inflection.

"I never interfere with servants. He was kept on here merely because he had been so long on the premises. I suppose the steward thought it might make him unpopular if the old fellow had been dismissed."

How on earth was she to proceed on such a task as hers if this was the utmost geniality she could expect? So she at once tried another tack—this time a personal one.

"I am sorry I disturbed you. I am really not unconventional—though certainly no slave to convention. Still there are limits . . . it is bad enough to intrude in this way, and I do not know what you can say or think of the time selected, for the intrusion."

After all, Edgar Caswall was a gentleman by custom and habit, so he rose to the occasion.

"I can only say, Lady Arabella, that you are always welcome at any time you may deign to honour my house with your presence."

She smiled at him sweetly.

"Thank you *so* much. You *do* put one at ease. My breach of convention makes me glad rather than sorry. I feel that I can open my heart to you about anything."

Forthwith she proceeded to tell him about Oolanga and his strange suspicions of her honesty. Caswall laughed and made her explain all the details. His final comment was enlightening.

"Let me give you a word of advice: If you have the slightest fault to find with that infernal nigger, shoot him at sight. A swelled-headed nigger, with a bee in his bonnet, is one of the worst difficulties in the world to deal with. So better make a clean job of it, and wipe him out at once!"

"But what about the law, Mr. Caswall?"

"Oh, the law doesn't concern itself much about dead niggers. A few more or less do not matter. To my mind it's rather a relief!"

"I'm afraid of you," was her only comment, made with a sweet smile and in a soft voice.

"All right," he said, "let us leave it at that. Anyhow, we shall be rid of one of them!"

"I don't love niggers any more than you do," she replied, "and I suppose one mustn't be too particular where that sort of cleaning up is concerned." Then she changed in voice and manner, and asked genially: "And now tell me, am I forgiven?"

"You are, dear lady—if there is anything to forgive."

As he spoke, seeing that she had moved to go, he came to the door with her, and in the most natural way accompanied her downstairs. He passed through the hall with her and down the avenue. As he went back to the house, she smiled to herself.

"Well, that is all right. I don't think the morning has been altogether thrown away."

And she walked slowly back to Diana's Grove.

Adam Salton followed the line of the Brow, and refreshed his memory as to the various localities. He got home to Lesser Hill just as Sir Nathaniel was beginning lunch. Mr. Salton had gone to Walsall to keep an early appointment; so he was all alone. When the meal was over—seeing in Adam's face that he had something to speak about—he followed into the study and shut the door.

When the two men had lighted their pipes, Sir Nathaniel began.

"I have remembered an interesting fact about Diana's Grove—there is, I have long understood, some strange mystery about that house. It may be of some interest, or it may be trivial, in such a tangled skein as we are trying to unravel."

"Please tell me all you know' or suspect. To begin, then, of what sort is the mystery—physical, mental, moral, historical, scientific, occult? Any kind of hint will help me."

"Quite right. I shall try to tell you what I think; but I have not put my thoughts on the subject in sequence, so you must forgive me if due order is not observed in my narration. I suppose you have seen the house at Diana's Grove?"

"The outside of it; but I have that in my mind's eye, and I can fit into my memory whatever you may mention."

"The house is very old—probably the first house of some sort that stood there was in the time of the Romans. This was probably renewed—perhaps several times at later periods. The house stands, or, rather, used to stand here when Mercia was a kingdom—I do not suppose that the basement can be later than the Norman Conquest. Some years ago, when I was President of the Mercian Archaeological Society, I went all over it very carefully. This was when it was purchased by Captain March. The house had then been done up, so as to be suitable for the bride. The basement is very strong,—almost as strong and as heavy as if it had been intended as a fortress. There are a whole series of rooms deep underground. One of them in particular struck me. The room itself is of considerable size, but the masonry is more than massive. In the middle of the room is a sunk well, built up to floor level and evidently going deep underground. There is no windlass nor any trace of there ever having been any—no rope—nothing. Now, we know that the Romans had wells of immense depth, from which the water was lifted by the 'old rag rope'; that at Woodhull used to be nearly a thousand feet. Here, then, we have simply an enormously deep well-hole. The door of the room was massive, and was fastened with a lock nearly a foot square. It was evidently intended for some kind of protection to someone or something; but no one in those days had ever heard of anyone having been allowed even to see the room. All this is *à propos* of a suggestion on my part that the well-hole was a way by which the White Worm (whatever it was) went and came. At that time I would have had a search made—even excavation if necessary—at my own expense, but all suggestions were met with a prompt and explicit negative. So, of course, I took no further step in the matter. Then it died out of recollection—even of mine."

"Do you remember, sir," asked Adam, "what was the appearance of the room where the well-hole was? Was there furniture—in fact, any sort of thing in the room?"

"The only thing I remember was a sort of green light—very clouded, very dim—which came up from the well. Not a fixed light, but intermittent and irregular—quite unlike anything I had ever seen."

"Do you remember how you got into the well-room? Was there a separate door from outside, or was there any interior room or passage which opened into it?"

"I think there must have been some room with a way into it. I remember going up some steep steps; they must have been worn smooth by long use or something of the kind, for I could hardly keep my feet as I went up. Once I stumbled and nearly fell into the well-hole."

"Was there anything strange about the place—any queer smell, for instance?"

"Queer smell—yes! Like bilge or a rank swamp. It was distinctly nauseating; when I came out I felt as if I had just been going to be sick. I shall try back on my visit and see if I can recall any more of what I saw or felt."

"Then perhaps, sir, later in the day you will tell me anything you may chance to recollect."

"I shall be delighted, Adam. If your uncle has not returned by then, I'll join you in the study after dinner, and we can resume this interesting chat."

CHAPTER XVII

THE MYSTERY OF
"THE GROVE"

THAT AFTERNOON ADAM decided to do a little exploring. As he passed through the wood outside the gate of Diana's Grove, he thought he saw the African's face for an instant. So he went deeper into the undergrowth, and followed along parallel to the avenue to the house. He was glad that there was no workman or servant about, for he did not care that any of Lady Arabella's people should find him wandering about her grounds. Taking advantage of the denseness of the trees, he came close to the house and skirted round it. He was repaid for his trouble, for on the far side of the house, close to where the rocky frontage of the cliff fell away, he saw Oolanga crouched behind the irregular trunk of a great oak. The man was so intent on watching someone, or something, that he did not guard against being himself watched. This suited Adam, for he could thus make scrutiny at will.

The thick wood, though the trees were mostly of small girth, threw a heavy shadow, so that the steep declension, in front of which grew the tree behind which the African lurked, was almost in darkness. Adam drew as close as he could, and was amazed to see a patch of light on the ground before him; when he realised what it was, he was determined, more than ever to follow on his quest. The nigger had a dark lantern in his hand, and was throwing the light down the steep incline. The glare showed a series of stone steps, which ended in a low-lying heavy iron door fixed against the side of the house. All the strange things he had heard from Sir Nathaniel, and all those, little and big, which he had himself noticed, crowded into his mind in a chaotic way. Instinctively he took refuge behind a thick oak stem, and set himself down, to watch what might occur.

After a short time it became apparent that the African was trying to find out what was behind the heavy door. There was no way of looking in, for the door fitted tight into the massive stone slabs. The only opportunity for the entrance of light was through a small hole between the great stones above the door. This hole was too high up to look through from the ground level. Oolanga, having tried standing tiptoe on the highest point near, and holding the lantern as high as he could, threw the light round the edges of the door to see if he could find anywhere a hole or a flaw in the metal through which he could obtain a glimpse. Foiled in this, he brought from the shrubbery a plank, which he leant against the top of the door and then climbed up with great dexterity. This did not bring him near enough to the window-hole to look in, or even to throw the light of the lantern through it, so he climbed down and carried the plank back to the place from which he had got it. Then he concealed himself near the iron door and waited, manifestly with the intent of remaining there till someone came near. Presently Lady Arabella, moving noiselessly through the shade, approached the door. When he saw her close enough to touch it, Oolanga stepped forward from his concealment, and spoke in a whisper, which through the gloom sounded like a hiss.

"I want to see you, missy—soon and secret."

"What do you want?"

"You know well, missy; I told you already."

She turned on him with blazing eyes, the green tint in them glowing like emeralds.

"Come, none of that. If there is anything sensible which you wish to say to me, you can see me here, just where we are, at seven o'clock."

He made no reply in words, but, putting the backs of his hands together, bent lower and lower till his forehead touched the earth. Then he rose and went slowly away.

Adam Salton, from his hiding-place, saw and wondered. In a few minutes he moved from his place and went home to Lesser Hill, fully determined that seven o'clock would find him in some hidden place behind Diana's Grove.

At a little before seven Adam stole softly out of the house and took the back-way to the rear of Diana's Grove. The place seemed silent and deserted, so he took the opportunity of concealing himself near the spot whence he had seen Oolanga trying to investigate whatever was concealed behind the iron door. He waited, perfectly still, and at last saw a gleam of white passing soundlessly through the undergrowth. He was not surprised when he recognised the colour of Lady Arabella's dress. She came close and waited, with her face to the iron door. From some place of concealment near at hand Oolanga appeared, and came close to her. Adam noticed, with surprised amusement, that over his shoulder was the box with the mongoose. Of course the African did not know that he was seen by anyone, least of all by the man whose property he had with him.

Silent-footed as he was, Lady Arabella heard him coming, and turned to meet him. It was somewhat hard to see in the gloom, for, as usual, he was all in black, only his collar and cuffs showing white. Lady Arabella opened the conversation which ensued between the two.

"What do you want? To rob me, or murder me?"

"No, to lub you!"

This frightened her a little, and she tried to change the tone.

"Is that a coffin you have with you? If so, you are wasting your time. It would not hold me."

When a nigger suspects he is being laughed at, all the ferocity of his nature comes to the front; and this man was of the lowest kind.

"Dis ain't no coffin for nobody. Dis box is for you. Somefin you lub. Me give him to you!"

Still anxious to keep off the subject of affection, on which she believed him to have become crazed, she made another effort to keep his mind elsewhere.

"Is this why you want to see me?" He nodded. "Then come round to the other door. But be quiet. I have no desire to be seen so close to my own house in conversation with a—a—a nigger like you!"

She had chosen the word deliberately. She wished to meet his passion with another kind. Such would, at all events, help to keep him quiet. In the deep gloom she could not see the anger which suffused his face. Rolling eyeballs and grinding teeth are, however, sufficient signs of anger to be decipherable in the dark. She moved round the corner of the house to her right. Oolanga was following her, when she stopped him by raising her hand.

"No, not that door," she said; "that is not for niggers. The other door will do well enough for you!"

Lady Arabella took in her hand a small key which hung at the end of her watch-chain, and moved to a small door, low down, round the corner, and a little downhill from the edge of the Brow. Oolanga, in obedience to her gesture, went back to the iron door. Adam looked carefully at the mongoose box as the African went by, and was glad to see that it was intact. Unconsciously, as he looked, he fingered the key that was in his waistcoat pocket. When Oolanga was out of sight, Adam hurried after Lady Arabella.

CHAPTER XVIII

EXIT OOLANGA

THE WOMAN TURNED sharply as Adam touched her shoulder.

"One moment whilst we are alone. You had better not trust that nigger!" he whispered.

Her answer was crisp and concise:

"I don't."

"Forewarned is forearmed. Tell me if you will—it is for your own protection. Why do you mistrust him?"

"My friend, you have no idea of that man's impudence. Would you believe that he wants me to marry him?"

"No!" said Adam incredulously, amused in spite of himself.

"Yes, and wanted to bribe me to do it by sharing a chest of treasure—at least, he thought it was—stolen from Mr. Caswall. Why do you distrust him, Mr. Salton?"

"Did you notice that box he had slung on his shoulder? That belongs to me. I left it in the gun-room when I went to lunch. He must have crept in and stolen it. Doubtless he thinks that it, too, is full of treasure."

"He does!"

"How on earth do you know?" asked Adam.

"A little while ago he offered to give it to me—another bribe to accept him. Faugh! I am ashamed to tell you such a thing. The beast!"

Whilst they had been speaking, she had opened the door, a narrow iron one, well hung, for it opened easily and closed tightly without any creaking or sound of any kind. Within all was dark; but she entered as freely and with as little misgiving or restraint as if it had been broad daylight. For Adam, there was just sufficient green light from somewhere for him to see that there was a broad flight of heavy stone steps leading upward; but Lady Arabella, after shutting the door behind her, when it closed tightly without a clang, tripped up the steps lightly and swiftly. For an instant all was dark, but there came again the faint green light which enabled him to see the outlines of things. Another iron door, narrow like the first and fairly high, led into another large room, the walls of which were of massive stones, so closely joined together as to exhibit only one smooth surface. This presented the appearance of having at one time been polished. On the far side, also smooth like the walls, was the reverse of a wide, but not high, iron door. Here there was a little more light, for the high-up aperture over the door opened to the air.

Lady Arabella took from her girdle another small key, which she inserted in a keyhole in the centre of a massive lock. The great bolt seemed wonderfully hung, for the moment the small key was turned, the bolts of the great lock moved noiselessly and the iron doors swung open. On the stone steps outside stood Oolanga, with the mongoose box slung over his shoulder. Lady Arabella stood a little on one side, and the African, accepting the movement as an invitation, entered in an obsequious way. The moment, however, that he was inside, he gave a quick look around him.

"Much death here—big death. Many deaths. Good, good!"

He sniffed round as if he was enjoying the scent. The matter and manner of his speech were so revolting that instinctively Adam's hand wandered to his revolver, and, with his finger on the trigger, he rested satisfied that he was ready for any emergency.

There was certainly opportunity for the nigger's enjoyment, for the open well-hole was almost under his nose, sending up such a stench as almost made Adam sick, though Lady Arabella seemed not to mind it at all. It was like nothing that Adam had ever met with. He compared it with all the noxious experiences he had ever had—the drainage of war hospitals, of slaughter-houses, the refuse of dissecting rooms. None of these was like it, though it had something of them all, with, added, the sourness of chemical waste and the poisonous effluvium of the bilge of a water-logged ship whereon a multitude of rats had been drowned.

Then, quite unexpectedly, the negro noticed the presence of a third person—Adam Salton! He pulled out a pistol and shot at him, happily missing. Adam was himself usually a quick shot, but this time his mind had been on something else and he was not ready. However, he was quick to carry out an intention, and he was not a coward. In another moment both men were in grips. Beside them was the dark well-hole, with that horrid effluvium stealing up from its mysterious depths.

Adam and Oolanga both had pistols; Lady Arabella, who had not one, was probably the most ready of them all in the theory of shooting, but that being impossible, she made her effort in another way. Gliding forward, she tried to seize the African; but he eluded her grasp, just missing, in doing so, falling into the mysterious hole. As he swayed back to firm foothold, he turned his own gun on her and shot. Instinctively Adam leaped at his assailant; clutching at each other, they tottered on the very brink.

Lady Arabella's anger, now fully awake, was all for Oolanga. She moved towards him with her hands extended, and had just seized him when the catch of the locked box—due to some movement from within—flew open, and the king-cobra-killer flew at her with a venomous fury impossible to describe. As it seized her throat, she caught hold of it, and, with a fury superior to its own, tore it in two just as if it had been a sheet of paper. The strength used for such an act must have been terrific. In an instant, it seemed to spout blood and entrails, and was hurled into the well-hole. In another instant she had seized Oolanga, and with a swift rush had drawn him, her white arms encircling him, down with her into the gaping aperture.

Adam saw a medley of green and red lights blaze in a whirling circle, and as it sank down into the well, a pair of blazing green eyes became fixed, sank lower and lower with frightful rapidity, and disappeared, throwing upward the green light which grew more and more vivid every moment. As the light sank into the noisome depths, there came a shriek which chilled Adam's blood—a prolonged agony of pain and terror which seemed to have no end.

Adam Salton felt that he would never be able to free his mind from the memory of those dreadful moments. The gloom which surrounded that horrible charnel pit, which seemed to go down to the very bowels of the earth, conveyed from far down the sights and sounds of the nethermost hell. The ghastly fate of the African as he sank down to his terrible doom, his black face growing grey with terror, his white eyeballs, now like veined bloodstone, rolling in the helpless extremity of fear. The mysterious green light was in itself a milieu of horror. And through it all the awful cry came up from that fathomless pit, whose entrance was flooded with spots of fresh blood. Even the death of the fearless little snake-killer—so fierce, so frightful, as if stained with a ferocity which told of no living force above earth, but only of the devils of the pit—was only an incident. Adam was in a state of intellectual tumult, which had no parallel in his experience. He tried to rush away from the horrible place; even the baleful green light, thrown up through the gloomy well-shaft, was dying away as its source sank deeper into the primeval ooze. The darkness was closing in on him in overwhelming density—darkness in such a place and with such a memory of it!

He made a wild rush forward—slipt on the steps in some sticky, acrid-smelling mass that felt and smelt like blood, and, falling forward, felt his way into the inner room, where the well-shaft was not.

Then he rubbed his eyes in sheer amazement. Up the stone steps from the narrow door by which he had entered, glided the white-clad figure of Lady Arabella, the only colour to be seen on her being blood-marks on her face and hands and throat. Otherwise, she was calm and unruffled, as when earlier she stood aside for him to pass in through the narrow iron door.

CHAPTER XIX

AN ENEMY IN THE DARK

ADAM SALTON WENT for a walk before returning to Lesser Hill; he felt that it might be well, not only to steady his nerves, shaken by the horrible scene, but to get his thoughts into some sort of order, so as to be ready to enter on the matter with Sir Nathaniel. He was a little embarrassed as to telling his uncle, for affairs had so vastly progressed beyond his original view that he felt a little doubtful as to what would be the old gentleman's attitude when he should hear of the strange events for the first time. Mr. Salton would certainly not be satisfied at being treated as an outsider with regard to such things, most of which had points of contact with the inmates of his own house. It was with an immense sense of relief that Adam heard that his uncle had telegraphed to the housekeeper that he was detained by business at Walsall, where he would remain for the night; and that he would be back in the morning in time for lunch.

When Adam got home after his walk, he found Sir Nathaniel just going to bed. He did not say anything to him then of what had happened, but contented himself with arranging that they would walk together in the early morning, as he had much to say that would require serious attention.

Strangely enough he slept well, and awoke at dawn with his mind clear and his nerves in their usual unshaken condition. The maid brought up, with his early morning cup of tea, a note which had been found in the letter-box. It was from Lady Arabella, and was evidently intended to put him on his guard as to what he should say about the previous evening.

He read it over carefully several times, before he was satisfied that he had taken in its full import.

"DEAR MR. SALTON,

"I cannot go to bed until I have written to you, so you must forgive me if I disturb you, and at an unseemly time. Indeed, you must also forgive me if, in trying to do what is right, I err in saying too much or too little. The fact is that I am quite upset and unnerved by all that has happened in this terrible night. I find it difficult even to write; my hands shake so that they are not under control, and I am trembling all over with memory of the horrors we saw enacted before our eyes. I am grieved beyond measure that I should be, however remotely, a cause of this horror coming on you. Forgive me if you can, and do not think too hardly of me. This I ask with confidence, for since we shared together the danger—the very pangs—of death, I feel that we should be to one another something more than mere friends, that I may lean on you and trust you, assured that your sympathy and pity are for me. You really must let me thank you for the friendliness, the help, the confidence, the real aid at a time of deadly danger and deadly fear which you showed me. That awful man—I shall see him for ever in my dreams. His black, malignant face will shut out all memory of sunshine and happiness. I shall eternally see his evil eyes as he threw himself into that well-hole in a vain effort to escape from the consequences of his own misdoing. The more I think of it, the more apparent it seems to me that he had premeditated the whole thing—of course, except his own horrible death.

"Perhaps you have noticed a fur collar I occasionally wear. It is one of my most valued treasures—an ermine collar studded with emeralds. I had often seen the nigger's eyes gleam covetously when he looked at it. Unhappily, I wore it yesterday. That may have been the cause that lured the poor man to his doom. On the very brink of the abyss he tore the collar from my neck—that was the last I saw of him. When he sank into the hole, I was rushing to the iron door, which I pulled behind me. When I heard that soul-sickening yell, which marked his disappearance in the chasm, I was more glad than I can say that my eyes were spared the pain and horror which my ears had to endure.

"When I tore myself out of the negro's grasp as he sank into the well-hole; I realised what freedom meant. Freedom! Freedom! Not only from that noisome prison-house, which has now such a memory, but from the more noisome embrace of that hideous monster. Whilst I live, I shall always thank you for my freedom. A woman must sometimes express her gratitude; otherwise it becomes too great to bear. I am not a sentimental girl, who merely likes to thank a man; I am a woman who knows all, of bad as well as good, that life can give. I have known what it is to love and to lose. But you must not let me bring any unhappiness into your life. I must live on—as I have lived—alone, and, in addition, bear with other woes the memory of this latest insult and horror. In the meantime, I must get away as quickly as possible from Diana's Grove. In the morning I shall go up to town, where I shall remain for a week—I cannot stay longer, as business affairs demand my presence here. I think, however, that a week in the rush of busy London, surrounded with multitudes of commonplace people, will help to soften— I cannot expect total obliteration—the terrible images of the bygone night. When I can sleep easily—which will be, I hope, after a day or two—I shall be fit to return home and take up again the burden which will, I suppose, always be with me.

"I shall be most happy to see you on my return—or earlier, if my good fortune sends you on any errand to London. I shall stay at the Mayfair Hotel. In that busy spot we may forget some of the dangers and horrors we have shared together. Adieu, and thank you, again and again, for all your kindness and consideration to me.

"ARABELLA MARSH."

Adam was surprised by this effusive epistle, but he determined to say nothing of it to Sir Nathaniel until he should have thought it well over. When Adam met Sir Nathaniel at breakfast, he was glad that he had taken time to turn things over in his mind. The result had been that not only was he familiar with the facts in all their bearings, but he had already so far differentiated them that he was able to arrange them in his own mind according to their values. Breakfast had been a silent function, so it did not interfere in any way with the process of thought.

So soon as the door was closed, Sir Nathaniel began:

"I see, Adam, that something has occurred, and that you have much to tell me."

"That is so, sir. I suppose I had better begin by telling you all I know—all that has happened since I left you yesterday?"

Accordingly Adam gave him details of all that had happened during the previous evening. He confined himself rigidly to the narration of circumstances, taking care not to colour events by any comment of his own, or any opinion of the meaning of things which he did not fully understand. At first, Sir Nathaniel seemed disposed to ask questions, but shortly gave this up when he recognised that the narration was concise and self-explanatory. Thenceforth, he contented himself with quick looks and glances, easily interpreted, or by some acquiescent motions of his hands, when such could be convenient, to emphasise his idea of the correctness of any inference. Until Adam ceased speaking, having evidently come to an end of what he had to say with regard to this section of his story, the elder man made no comment whatever. Even when Adam took from his pocket Lady Arabella's letter, with the manifest intention of reading it, he did not make any comment. Finally, when Adam folded up the letter and put it, in its envelope, back in his pocket, as an intimation that he had now quite finished, the old diplomatist carefully made a few notes in his pocket-book.

"Your narrative, my dear Adam, is altogether admirable. I think I may now take it that we are both well versed in the actual facts, and that our conference had better take the shape of a mutual exchange of ideas. Let us both ask questions as they may arise; and I do not doubt that we shall arrive at some enlightening conclusions."

"Will you kindly begin, sir? I do not doubt that, with your longer experience, you will be able to dissipate some of the fog which envelops certain of the things which we have to consider."

"I hope so, my dear boy. For a beginning, then, let me say that Lady Arabella's letter makes clear some things which she intended— and also some things which she did not intend. But, before I begin to draw deductions, let me ask you a few questions. Adam, are you heart-whole, quite heart-whole, in the matter of Lady Arabella?"

His companion answered at once, each looking the other straight in the eyes during question and answer.

"Lady Arabella, sir, is a charming woman, and I should have deemed it a privilege to meet her—to talk to her—even—since I am in the confessional—to flirt a little with her. But if you mean to ask if my affections are in any way engaged, I can emphatically answer 'No!'—as indeed you will understand when presently I give you the reason. Apart from that, there are the unpleasant details we discussed the other day."

"Could you—would you mind giving me the reason now? It will help us to understand what is before us, in the way of difficulty."

"Certainly, sir. My reason, on which I can fully depend, is that I love another woman!"

"That clinches it. May I offer my good wishes, and, I hope, my congratulations?"

"I am proud of your good wishes, sir, and I thank you for them. But it is too soon for congratulations—the lady does not even know my hopes yet. Indeed, I hardly knew them myself, as definite, till this moment."

"I take it then, Adam, that at the right time I may be allowed to know who the lady is?"

Adam laughed a low, sweet laugh, such as ripples from a happy heart.

"There need not be an hour's, a minute's delay. I shall be glad to share my secret with you, sir. The lady, sir, whom I am so happy as to love, and in whom my dreams of life-long happiness are centred, is Mimi Watford!"

"Then, my dear Adam, I need not wait to offer congratulations. She is indeed a very charming young lady. I do not think I ever saw a girl who united in such perfection the qualities of strength of character and sweetness of disposition. With all my heart, I congratulate you. Then I may take it that my question as to your heart-wholeness is answered in the affirmative?"

"Yes; and now, sir, may I ask in turn why the question?"

"Certainly! I asked because it seems to me that we are coming to a point where my questions might be painful to you."

"It is not merely that I love Mimi, but I have reason to look on Lady Arabella as her enemy," Adam continued.

"Her enemy?"

"Yes. A rank and unscrupulous enemy who is bent on her destruction."

Sir Nathaniel went to the door, looked outside it and returned, locking it carefully behind him.

CHAPTER XX

METABOLISM

"AM I LOOKING grave?" asked Sir Nathaniel inconsequently when he re-entered the room.

"You certainly are, sir."

"We little thought when first we met that we should be drawn into such a vortex. Already we are mixed up in robbery, and probably murder, but—a thousand times worse than all the crimes in the calendar—in an affair of ghastly mystery which has no bottom and no end—with forces of the most unnerving kind, which had their origin in an age when the world was different from the world which we know. We are going back to the origin of superstition—to an age when dragons tore each other in their slime. We must fear nothing—no conclusion, however improbable, almost impossible it may be. Life and death is hanging on our judgment, not only for ourselves, but for others whom we love. Remember, I count on you as I hope you count on me."

"I do, with all confidence."

"Then," said Sir Nathaniel, "let us think justly and boldly and fear nothing, however terrifying it may seem. I suppose I am to take as exact in every detail your account of all the strange things which happened whilst you were in Diana's Grove?"

"So far as I know, yes. Of course I may be mistaken in recollection of some detail or another, but I am certain that in the main what I have said is correct."

"You feel sure that you saw Lady Arabella seize the negro round the neck, and drag him down with her into the hole?"

"Absolutely certain, sir, otherwise I should have gone to her assistance."

"We have, then, an account of what happened from an eye-witness whom we trust—that is yourself. We have also another account, written by Lady Arabella under her own hand. These two accounts do not agree. Therefore we must take it that one of the two is lying."

"Apparently, sir."

"And that Lady Arabella is the liar!"

"Apparently—as I am not."

"We must, therefore, try to find a reason for her lying. She has nothing to fear from Oolanga, who is dead. Therefore the only reason which could actuate her would be to convince someone else that she was blameless. This 'someone' could not be you, for you had the evidence of your own eyes. There was no one else present; therefore it must have been an absent person."

"That seems beyond dispute, sir."

"There is only one other person whose good opinion she could wish to keep—Edgar Caswall. He is the only one who fills the bill. Her lies point to other things besides the death of the African. She evidently wanted it to be accepted that his falling into the well was his own act. I cannot suppose that she expected to convince you, the eye-witness; but if she wished later on to spread the story, it was wise of her to try to get your acceptance of it."

"That is so!"

"Then there were other matters of untruth. That, for instance, of the ermine collar embroidered with emeralds. If an understandable reason be required for this, it would be to draw attention away from the green lights which were seen in the room, and especially in the well-hole. Any unprejudiced person would accept the green lights to be the eyes of a great snake, such as tradition pointed to living in the well-hole. In fine, therefore, Lady Arabella wanted the general belief to be that there was no snake of the kind in Diana's Grove. For my own part, I don't believe in a partial liar—this art does not deal in veneer; a liar is a liar right through. Self-interest may prompt falsity of the tongue; but if one prove to be a liar, nothing that he says can ever be believed. This leads us to the conclusion that because she said or inferred that there was no snake, we should look for one—and expect to find it, too.

"Now let me digress. I live, and have for many years lived, in Derbyshire, a county more celebrated for its caves than any other county in England. I have been through them all, and am familiar with every turn of them; as also with other great caves in Kentucky, in France, in Germany, and a host of other places—in many of these are tremendously deep caves of narrow aperture, which are valued by intrepid explorers, who descend narrow gullets of abysmal depth—and sometimes never return. In many of the caverns in the Peak I am convinced that some of the smaller passages were used in primeval times as the lairs of some of the great serpents of legend and tradition. It may have been that such caverns were formed in the usual geologic way—bubbles or flaws in the earth's crust—which were later used by the monsters of the period of the young world. It may have been, of course, that some of them were worn originally by water; but in time they all found a use when suitable for living monsters.

"This brings us to another point, more difficult to accept and understand than any other requiring belief in a base not usually accepted, or indeed entered on—whether such abnormal growths could have ever changed in their nature. Some day the study of metabolism may progress so far as to enable us to accept structural changes proceeding from an intellectual or moral base. We may lean towards a belief that great animal strength may be a sound base for changes of all sorts. If this be so, what could be a more fitting subject than primeval monsters whose strength was such as to allow a survival of thousands of years? We do not know yet if brain can increase and develop independently of other parts of the living structure.

"After all, the mediaeval belief in the Philosopher's Stone which could transmute metals, has its counterpart in the accepted theory of metabolism which changes living tissue. In an age of investigation like our own, when we are returning to science as the base of wonders—almost of miracles—we should be slow to refuse to accept facts, however impossible they may seem to be.

"Let us suppose a monster of the early days of the world—a dragon of the prime—of vast age running into thousands of years, to whom had been conveyed in some way—it matters not—a brain just sufficient for the beginning of growth. Suppose the monster to be of incalculable size and of a strength quite abnormal—a veritable incarnation of animal strength. Suppose this animal is allowed to remain in one place, thus being removed from accidents of interrupted development; might not, would not this creature, in process of time—ages, if necessary—have that rudimentary intelligence developed? There is no impossibility in this; it is only the natural process of evolution. In the beginning, the instincts of animals are confined to alimentation, self-protection, and the multiplication of their species. As time goes on and the needs of life become more complex, power follows need. We have been long accustomed to consider growth as applied almost exclusively to size in its various aspects. But Nature, who has no doctrinaire ideas, may equally apply it to concentration. A developing thing may expand in any given way or form. Now, it is a scientific law that increase implies gain and loss of various kinds; what a thing gains in one direction it may lose in another. May it not be that Mother Nature may deliberately encourage decrease as well as increase—that it may be an axiom that what is gained in concentration is lost in size? Take, for instance, monsters that tradition has accepted and localised, such as the Worm of Lambton or that of Spindleston Heugh. If such a creature were, by its own process of metabolism, to change much of its bulk for intellectual growth, we should at once arrive at a new class of creature—more dangerous, perhaps, than the world has ever had any experience of—a force which can think, which has no soul and no morals, and therefore no acceptance of responsibility. A snake would be a good illustration of this, for it is cold-blooded, and therefore removed from the temptations which often weaken or restrict warm-blooded creatures. If, for instance, the Worm of Lambton—if such ever existed—were guided to its own ends by an organised intelligence capable of expansion, what form of creature could we imagine which would equal it in potentialities of evil? Why, such a being would devastate a whole country. Now, all these things require much thought, and we want to apply the knowledge usefully, and we should therefore be exact. Would it not be well to resume the subject later in the day?"

"I quite agree, sir. I am in a whirl already; and want to attend carefully to what you say; so that I may try to digest it."

Both men seemed fresher and better for the "easy," and when they met in the afternoon each of them had something to contribute to the general stock of information. Adam, who was by nature of a more militant disposition than his elderly friend, was glad to see that the conference at once assumed a practical trend. Sir Nathaniel recognised this, and, like an old diplomatist, turned it to present use.

"Tell me now, Adam, what is the outcome, in your own mind, of our conversation?"

"That the whole difficulty already assumes practical shape; but with added dangers, that at first I did not imagine."

"What is the practical shape, and what are the added dangers? I am not disputing, but only trying to clear my own ideas by the consideration of yours—"

So Adam went on:

"In the past, in the early days of the world, there were monsters who were so vast that they could exist for thousands of years. Some of them must have overlapped the Christian era. They may have progressed intellectually in process of time. If they had in any way so progressed, or even got the most rudimentary form of brain, they would be the most dangerous things that ever were in the world. Tradition says that one of these monsters lived in the Marsh of the East, and came up to a cave in Diana's Grove, which was also called the Lair of the White Worm. Such creatures may have grown down as well as up. They *may* have grown into, or something like, human beings. Lady Arabella March is of snake nature. She has committed crimes to our knowledge. She retains something of the vast strength of her primal being—can see in the dark—has the eyes of a snake. She used the nigger, and then dragged him through the snake's hole down to the swamp; she is intent on evil, and hates some one we love. Result . . . "

"Yes, the result?"

"First, that Mimi Watford should be taken away at once—then—"

"Yes?"

"The monster must be destroyed."

"Bravo! That is a true and fearless conclusion. At whatever cost, it must be carried out."

"At once?"

"Soon, at all events. That creature's very existence is a danger. Her presence in this neighbourhood makes the danger immediate."

As he spoke, Sir Nathaniel's mouth hardened and his eyebrows came down till they met. There was no doubting his concurrence in the resolution, or his readiness to help in carrying it out. But he was an elderly man with much experience and knowledge of law and diplomacy. It seemed to him to be a stern duty to prevent anything irrevocable taking place till it had been thought out and all was ready. There were all sorts of legal cruxes to be thought out, not only regarding the taking of life, even of a monstrosity in human form, but also of property. Lady Arabella, be she woman or snake or devil, owned the ground she moved in, according to British law, and the law is jealous and swift to avenge wrongs done within its ken. All such difficulties should be—must be—avoided for Mr. Salton's sake, for Adam's own sake, and, most of all, for Mimi Watford's sake.

Before he spoke again, Sir Nathaniel had made up his mind that he must try to postpone decisive action until the circumstances on which they depended—which, after all, were only problematical—should have been tested satisfactorily, one way or another. When he did speak, Adam at first thought that his friend was wavering in his intention, or "funking" the responsibility. However, his respect for Sir Nathaniel was so great that he would not act, or even come to a conclusion on a vital point, without his sanction.

He came close and whispered in his ear:

"We will prepare our plans to combat and destroy this horrible menace, after we have cleared up some of the more baffling points. Meanwhile, we must wait for the night—I hear my uncle's footsteps echoing down the hall."

Sir Nathaniel nodded his approval.

CHAPTER XXI

GREEN LIGHT

WHEN OLD MR. Salton had retired for the night, Adam and Sir Nathaniel returned to the study. Things went with great regularity at Lesser Hill, so they knew that there would be no interruption to their talk.
When their cigars were lighted, Sir Nathaniel began.

"I hope, Adam, that you do not think me either slack or changeable
of purpose. I mean to go through this business to the bitter end—
whatever it may be. Be satisfied that my first care is, and shall be, the
protection of Mimi Watford. To that I am pledged; my dear boy, we who
are interested are all in the same danger. That semi-human monster out
of the pit hates and means to destroy us all—you and me certainly, and
probably your uncle. I wanted especially to talk with you to-night, for
I cannot help thinking that the time is fast coming—if it has not come
already—when we must take your uncle into our confidence. It was one
thing when fancied evils threatened, but now he is probably marked for
death, and it is only right that he should know all."

"I am with you, sir. Things have changed since we agreed to keep
him out of the trouble. Now we dare not; consideration for his feelings
might cost his life. It is a duty—and no light or pleasant one, either.
I have not a shadow of doubt that he will want to be one with us in
this. But remember, we are his guests; his name, his honour, have to be
thought of as well as his safety."

"All shall be as you wish, Adam. And now as to what we are to do?
We cannot murder Lady Arabella off-hand. Therefore we shall have to

put things in order for the killing, and in such a way that we cannot be taxed with a crime."

"It seems to me, sir, that we are in an exceedingly tight place. Our first difficulty is to know where to begin. I never thought this fighting an antediluvian monster would be such a complicated job. This one is a woman, with all a woman's wit, combined with the heartlessness of a *cocotte*. She has the strength and impregnability of a diplodocus. We may be sure that in the fight that is before us there will be no semblance of fair-play. Also that our unscrupulous opponent will not betray herself!"

"That is so—but being feminine, she will probably over-reach herself. Now, Adam, it strikes me that, as we have to protect ourselves and others against feminine nature, our strong game will be to play our masculine against her feminine. Perhaps we had better sleep on it. She is a thing of the night; and the night may give us some ideas."

So they both turned in.

Adam knocked at Sir Nathaniel's door in the grey of the morning, and, on being bidden, came into the room. He had several letters in his hand. Sir Nathaniel sat up in bed.

"Well!"

"I should like to read you a few letters, but, of course, I shall not send them unless you approve. In fact"—with a smile and a blush— "there are several things which I want to do; but I hold my hand and my tongue till I have your approval."

"Go on!" said the other kindly. "Tell me all, and count at any rate on my sympathy, and on my approval and help if I can see my way."

Accordingly Adam proceeded:

"When I told you the conclusions at which I had arrived, I put in the foreground that Mimi Watford should, for the sake of her own safety, be removed—and that the monster which had wrought all the harm should be destroyed."

"Yes, that is so."

"To carry this into practice, sir, one preliminary is required—unless harm of another kind is to be faced. Mimi should have some protector whom all the world would recognise. The only form recognised by convention is marriage!"

Sir Nathaniel smiled in a fatherly way.

"To marry, a husband is required. And that husband should be you."

"Yes, yes."

"And the marriage should be immediate and secret—or, at least, not spoken of outside ourselves. Would the young lady be agreeable to that proceeding?"

"I do not know, sir!"

"Then how are we to proceed?"

"I suppose that we—or one of us—must ask her."

"Is this a sudden idea, Adam, a sudden resolution?"

"A sudden resolution, sir, but not a sudden idea. If she agrees, all is well and good. The sequence is obvious."

"And it is to be kept a secret amongst ourselves?"

"I want no secret, sir, except for Mimi's good. For myself, I should like to shout it from the house-tops! But we must be discreet; untimely knowledge to our enemy might work incalculable harm."

"And how would you suggest, Adam, that we could combine the momentous question with secrecy?"

Adam grew red and moved uneasily.

"Someone must ask her—as soon as possible!"

"And that someone?"

"I thought that you, sir, would be so good!"

"God bless my soul! This is a new kind of duty to take on—at my time of life. Adam, I hope you know that you can count on me to help in any way I can!"

"I have already counted on you, sir, when I ventured to make such a suggestion. I can only ask," he added, "that you will be more than ever kind to me—to us—and look on the painful duty as a voluntary act of grace, prompted by kindness and affection."

"Painful duty!"

"Yes," said Adam boldly. "Painful to you, though to me it would be all joyful."

"It is a strange job for an early morning! Well, we all live and learn. I suppose the sooner I go the better. You had better write a line for me to take with me. For, you see, this is to be a somewhat unusual transaction, and it may be embarrassing to the lady, even to myself. So we ought to have some sort of warrant, something to show that we have been mindful of her feelings. It will not do to take acquiescence for granted—although we act for her good."

"Sir Nathaniel, you are a true friend; I am sure that both Mimi and I shall be grateful to you for all our lives—however long they may be!"

So the two talked it over and agreed as to points to be borne in mind by the ambassador. It was striking ten when Sir Nathaniel left the house, Adam seeing him quietly off.

As the young man followed him with wistful eyes—almost jealous of the privilege which his kind deed was about to bring him—he felt that his own heart was in his friend's breast.

The memory of that morning was like a dream to all those concerned in it. Sir Nathaniel had a confused recollection of detail and sequence, though the main facts stood out in his memory boldly and clearly. Adam Salton's recollection was of an illimitable wait, filled with anxiety, hope, and chagrin, all dominated by a sense of the slow passage of time and accompanied by vague fears. Mimi could not for a long time think at all, or recollect anything, except that Adam loved her and was saving her from a terrible danger. When she had time to think, later on, she wondered when she had any ignorance of the fact that Adam loved her, and that she loved him with all her heart. Everything, every recollection however small, every feeling, seemed to fit into those elemental facts as though they had all been moulded together. The main and crowning recollection was her saying goodbye to Sir Nathaniel, and entrusting to him loving messages, straight from her heart, to Adam Salton, and of his bearing when—with an impulse which she could not check—she put her lips to his and kissed him. Later, when she was alone and had time to think, it was a passing grief to her that she would have to be silent, for a time, to Lilla on the happy events of that strange mission.

She had, of course, agreed to keep all secret until Adam should give her leave to speak.

The advice and assistance of Sir Nathaniel was a great help to Adam in carrying out his idea of marrying Mimi Watford without publicity. He went with him to London, and, with his influence, the young man obtained the license of the Archbishop of Canterbury for a private marriage. Sir Nathaniel then persuaded old Mr. Salton to allow his nephew to spend a few weeks with him at Doom Tower, and it was here that Mimi became Adam's wife. But that was only the first step in their plans; before going further, however, Adam took his bride off to the Isle of Man. He wished to place a stretch of sea between Mimi and the White Worm, while things matured. On their return, Sir Nathaniel met them and drove them at once to Doom, taking care to avoid any one that he knew on the journey.

Sir Nathaniel had taken care to have the doors and windows shut and locked—all but the door used for their entry. The shutters were up and the blinds down. Moreover, heavy curtains were drawn across the windows. When Adam commented on this, Sir Nathaniel said in a whisper:

"Wait till we are alone, and I'll tell you why this is done; in the meantime not a word or a sign. You will approve when we have had a talk together."

They said no more on the subject till after dinner, when they were ensconced in Sir Nathaniel's study, which was on the top storey. Doom Tower was a lofty structure, situated on an eminence high up in the Peak. The top commanded a wide prospect, ranging from the hills above the Ribble to the near side of the Brow, which marked the northern bound of ancient Mercia. It was of the early Norman period, less than a century younger than Castra Regis. The windows of the study were barred and locked, and heavy dark curtains closed them in. When this was done not a gleam of light from the tower could be seen from outside.

When they were alone, Sir Nathaniel explained that he had taken his old friend, Mr. Salton, into full confidence, and that in future all would work together.

"It is important for you to be extremely careful. In spite of the fact that our marriage was kept secret, as also your temporary absence, both are known."

"How? To whom?"

"How, I know not; but I am beginning to have an idea."

"To her?" asked Adam, in momentary consternation.

Sir Nathaniel shivered perceptibly.

"The White Worm—yes!"

Adam noticed that from now on, his friend never spoke of Lady Arabella otherwise, except when he wished to divert the suspicion of others.

Sir Nathaniel switched off the electric light, and when the room was pitch dark, he came to Adam, took him by the hand, and led him to a seat set in the southern window. Then he softly drew back a piece of the curtain and motioned his companion to look out.

Adam did so, and immediately shrank back as though his eyes had opened on pressing danger. His companion set his mind at rest by saying in a low voice:

"It is all right; you may speak, but speak low. There is no danger here—at present!"

Adam leaned forward, taking care, however, not to press his face against the glass. What he saw would not under ordinary circumstances have caused concern to anybody. With his special knowledge, it was appalling—though the night was now so dark that in reality there was little to be seen.

On the western side of the tower stood a grove of old trees, of forest dimensions. They were not grouped closely, but stood a little apart from each other, producing the effect of a row widely planted. Over the tops of them was seen a green light, something like the danger signal at a railway-crossing. It seemed at first quite still; but presently, when Adam's eye became accustomed to it, he could see that it moved as if trembling. This at once recalled to Adam's mind the light quivering above the well-hole in the darkness of that inner room at Diana's Grove, Oolanga's awful shriek, and the hideous black face, now grown grey with terror, disappearing into the impenetrable gloom of the mysterious orifice. Instinctively he laid his hand on his revolver, and stood up ready to protect his wife. Then, seeing that nothing happened, and that the light and all outside the tower remained the same, he softly pulled the curtain over the window.

Sir Nathaniel switched on the light again, and in its comforting glow they began to talk freely.

CHAPTER XXII

AT CLOSE QUARTERS

"SHE HAS DIABOLICAL cunning," said Sir Nathaniel. "Ever since you left, she has ranged along the Brow and wherever you were accustomed to frequent. I have not heard whence the knowledge of your movements came to her, nor have I been able to learn any data whereon to found an opinion. She seems to have heard both of your marriage and your absence; but I gather, by inference, that she does not actually know where you and Mimi are, or of your return. So soon as the dusk fails, she goes out on her rounds, and before dawn covers the whole ground round the Brow, and away up into the heart of the Peak. The White Worm, in her own proper shape, certainly has great facilities for the business on which she is now engaged. She can look into windows of any ordinary kind. Happily, this house is beyond her reach, if she wishes—as she manifestly does—to remain unrecognised. But, even at this height, it is wise to show no lights, lest she might learn something of our presence or absence."

"Would it not be well, sir, if one of us could see this monster in her real shape at close quarters? I am willing to run the risk—for I take it there would be no slight risk in the doing. I don't suppose anyone of our time has seen her close and lived to tell the tale."

Sir Nathaniel held up an expostulatory hand.

"Good God, lad, what are you suggesting? Think of your wife, and all that is at stake."

"It is of Mimi that I think—for her sake that I am willing to risk whatever is to be risked."

Adam's young bride was proud of her man, but she blanched at the thought of the ghastly White Worm. Adam saw this and at once reassured her.

"So long as her ladyship does not know whereabout I am, I shall have as much safety as remains to us; bear in mind, my darling, that we cannot be too careful."

Sir Nathaniel realised that Adam was right; the White Worm had no supernatural powers and could not harm them until she discovered their hiding place. It was agreed, therefore, that the two men should go together.

When the two men slipped out by the back door of the house, they walked cautiously along the avenue which trended towards the west. Everything was pitch dark—so dark that at times they had to feel their way by the palings and tree-trunks. They could still see, seemingly far in front of them and high up, the baleful light which at the height and distance seemed like a faint line. As they were now on the level of the ground, the light seemed infinitely higher than it had from the top of the tower. At the sight Adam's heart fell; the danger of the desperate enterprise which he had undertaken burst upon him. But this feeling was shortly followed by another which restored him to himself—a fierce loathing, and a desire to kill, such as he had never experienced before.

They went on for some distance on a level road, fairly wide, from which the green light was visible. Here Sir Nathaniel spoke softly, placing his lips to Adam's ear for safety.

"We know nothing whatever of this creature's power of hearing or smelling, though I presume that both are of no great strength. As to seeing, we may presume the opposite, but in any case we must try to keep in the shade behind the tree-trunks. The slightest error would be fatal to us."

Adam only nodded, in case there should be any chance of the monster seeing the movement.

After a time that seemed interminable, they emerged from the circling wood. It was like coming out into sunlight by comparison with the misty blackness which had been around them. There was light enough to see by, though not sufficient to distinguish things at a distance. Adam's eyes sought the green light in the sky. It was still in about the same place, but its surroundings were more visible. It was now at the summit of what seemed to be a long white pole, near the top of which were two pendant white masses, like rudimentary arms or fins. The green light, strangely enough, did not seem lessened by the surrounding starlight, but had a clearer effect and a deeper green. Whilst they were carefully regarding this—Adam with the aid of an opera-glass—their nostrils were assailed by a horrid stench, something like that which rose from the well-hole in Diana's Grove.

By degrees, as their eyes got the right focus, they saw an immense towering mass that seemed snowy white. It was tall and thin. The lower part was hidden by the trees which lay between, but they could follow the tall white shaft and the duplicate green lights which topped it. As they looked there was a movement—the shaft seemed to bend, and the line of green light descended amongst the trees. They could see the green light twinkle as it passed between the obstructing branches.

Seeing where the head of the monster was, the two men ventured a little further forward, and saw that the hidden mass at the base of the shaft was composed of vast coils of the great serpent's body, forming a base from which the upright mass rose. As they looked, this lower mass moved, the glistening folds catching the moonlight, and they could see that the monster's progress was along the ground. It was coming towards them at a swift pace, so they turned and ran, taking care to make as little noise as possible, either by their footfalls or by disturbing the undergrowth close to them. They did not stop or pause till they saw before them the high dark tower of Doom.

CHAPTER XXIII

IN THE ENEMY'S HOUSE

SIR NATHANIEL WAS in the library next morning, after breakfast, when Adam came to him carrying a letter.

"Her ladyship doesn't lose any time. She has begun work already!"

Sir Nathaniel, who was writing at a table near the window, looked up. "What is it?" said he.

Adam held out the letter he was carrying. It was in a blazoned envelope.

"Ha!" said Sir Nathaniel, "from the White Worm! I expected something of the kind."

"But," said Adam, "how could she have known we were here? She didn't know last night."

"I don't think we need trouble about that, Adam. There is so much we do not understand. This is only another mystery. Suffice it that she does know—perhaps it is all the better and safer for us."

"How is that?" asked Adam with a puzzled look.

"General process of reasoning, my boy; and the experience of some years in the diplomatic world. This creature is a monster without heart or consideration for anything or anyone. She is not nearly so dangerous in the open as when she has the dark to protect her. Besides, we know, by our own experience of her movements, that for some reason she shuns publicity. In spite of her vast bulk and abnormal strength, she is afraid to attack openly. After all, she is only a snake and with a snake's nature, which is to keep low and squirm, and proceed by stealth and cunning. She will never attack when she can run away, although she knows well that running away would probably be fatal to her. What is the letter about?"

Sir Nathaniel's voice was calm and self-possessed. When he was engaged in any struggle of wits he was all diplomatist.

"She asks Mimi and me to tea this afternoon at Diana's Grove, and hopes that you also will favour her."

Sir Nathaniel smiled.

"Please ask Mrs. Salton to accept for us all."

"She means some deadly mischief. Surely—surely it would be wiser not."

"It is an old trick that we learn early in diplomacy, Adam—to fight on ground of your own choice. It is true that she suggested the place on this occasion; but by accepting it we make it ours. Moreover, she will not be able to understand our reason for doing so, and her own bad conscience—if she has any, bad or good—and her own fears and doubts will play our game for us. No, my dear boy, let us accept, by all means."

Adam said nothing, but silently held out his hand, which his companion shook: no words were necessary.

When it was getting near tea-time, Mimi asked Sir Nathaniel how they were going.

"We must make a point of going in state. We want all possible publicity." Mimi looked at him inquiringly. "Certainly, my dear, in the present circumstances publicity is a part of safety. Do not be surprised if, whilst we are at Diana's Grove, occasional messages come for you— for all or any of us."

"I see!" said Mrs. Salton. "You are taking no chances."

"None, my dear. All I have learned at foreign courts, and amongst civilised and uncivilised people, is going to be utilised within the next couple of hours."

Sir Nathaniel's voice was full of seriousness, and it brought to Mimi in a convincing way the awful gravity of the occasion.

In due course, they set out in a carriage drawn by a fine pair of horses, who soon devoured the few miles of their journey. Before they came to the gate, Sir Nathaniel turned to Mimi.

"I have arranged with Adam certain signals which may be necessary if certain eventualities occur. These need be nothing to do with you directly. But bear in mind that if I ask you or Adam to do anything, do not lose a second in the doing of it. We must try to pass off such moments with an appearance of unconcern. In all probability, nothing requiring such care will occur. The White Worm will not try force, though she has so much of it to spare. Whatever she may attempt to-day, of harm to any of us, will be in the way of secret plot. Some other time she may try force, but—if I am able to judge such a thing—not to-day. The messengers who may ask for any of us will not be witnesses only, they may help to stave off danger." Seeing query in her face, he went on: "Of what kind the danger may be, I know not, and cannot guess. It will doubtless be some ordinary circumstance; but none the less dangerous on that account. Here we are at the gate. Now, be careful in all matters, however small. To keep your head is half the battle."

There were a number of men in livery in the hall when they arrived. The doors of the drawing-room were thrown open, and Lady Arabella came forth and offered them cordial welcome. This having been got over, Lady Arabella led them into another room where tea was served.

Adam was acutely watchful and suspicious of everything, and saw on the far side of this room a panelled iron door of the same colour and configuration as the outer door of the room where was the well-hole wherein Oolanga had disappeared. Something in the sight alarmed him, and he quietly stood near the door. He made no movement, even of his eyes, but he could see that Sir Nathaniel was watching him intently, and, he fancied, with approval.

They all sat near the table spread for tea, Adam still near the door. Lady Arabella fanned herself, complaining of heat, and told one of the footmen to throw all the outer doors open.

Tea was in progress when Mimi suddenly started up with a look of fright on her face; at the same moment, the men became cognisant of a thick smoke which began to spread through the room—a smoke which made those who experienced it gasp and choke. The footmen began to edge uneasily towards the inner door. Denser and denser grew the smoke, and more acrid its smell. Mimi, towards whom the draught from the open door wafted the smoke, rose up choking, and ran to the inner door, which she threw open to its fullest extent, disclosing on the outside a curtain of thin silk, fixed to the doorposts. The draught from the open door swayed the thin silk towards her, and in her fright, she tore down the curtain, which enveloped her from head to foot. Then she ran through the still open door, heedless of the fact that she could not see where she was going. Adam, followed by Sir Nathaniel, rushed forward and joined her—Adam catching his wife by the arm and holding her tight. It was well that he did so, for just before her lay the black orifice of the well-hole, which, of course, she could not see with the silk curtain round her head. The floor was extremely slippery; something like thick oil had been spilled where she had to pass; and close to the edge of the hole her feet shot from under her, and she stumbled forward towards the well-hole.

When Adam saw Mimi slip, he flung himself backward, still holding her. His weight told, and he dragged her up from the hole and they fell together on the floor outside the zone of slipperiness. In a moment he had raised her up, and together they rushed out through the open door into the sunlight, Sir Nathaniel close behind them. They were all pale except the old diplomatist, who looked both calm and cool. It sustained and cheered Adam and his wife to see him thus master of himself. Both managed to follow his example, to the wonderment of the footmen, who saw the three who had just escaped a terrible danger walking together gaily, as, under the guiding pressure of Sir Nathaniel's hand, they turned to re-enter the house.

Lady Arabella, whose face had blanched to a deadly white, now resumed her ministrations at the tea-board as though nothing unusual had happened. The slop-basin was full of half-burned brown paper, over which tea had been poured.

Sir Nathaniel had been narrowly observing his hostess, and took the first opportunity afforded him of whispering to Adam:

"The real attack is to come—she is too quiet. When I give my hand to your wife to lead her out, come with us—and caution her to hurry. Don't lose a second, even if you have to make a scene. Hs-s-s-h!"

Then they resumed their places close to the table, and the servants, in obedience to Lady Arabella's order, brought in fresh tea.

Thence on, that tea-party seemed to Adam, whose faculties were at their utmost intensity, like a terrible dream. As for poor Mimi, she was so overwrought both with present and future fear, and with horror at the danger she had escaped, that her faculties were numb. However, she was braced up for a trial, and she felt assured that whatever might come she would be able to go through with it. Sir Nathaniel seemed just as usual—suave, dignified, and thoughtful—perfect master of himself.

To her husband, it was evident that Mimi was ill at ease. The way she kept turning her head to look around her, the quick coming and going of the colour of her face, her hurried breathing, alternating with periods of suspicious calm, were evidences of mental perturbation. To her, the attitude of Lady Arabella seemed compounded of social sweetness and personal consideration. It would be hard to imagine more thoughtful and tender kindness towards an honoured guest.

When tea was over and the servants had come to clear away the cups, Lady Arabella, putting her arm round Mimi's waist, strolled with her into an adjoining room, where she collected a number of photographs which were scattered about, and, sitting down beside her guest, began to show them to her. While she was doing this, the servants closed all the doors of the suite of rooms, as well as that which opened from the room outside—that of the well-hole into the avenue. Suddenly, without any seeming cause, the light in the room began to grow dim. Sir Nathaniel, who was sitting close to Mimi, rose to his feet, and, crying, "Quick!" caught hold of her hand and began to drag her from the room. Adam caught her other hand, and between them they drew her through the outer door which the servants were beginning to close. It was difficult at first to find the way, the darkness was so great; but to their relief when Adam whistled shrilly, the carriage and horses, which had been waiting in the angle of the avenue, dashed up. Her husband and Sir Nathaniel lifted—almost threw— Mimi into the carriage. The postillion plied whip and spur, and the vehicle, rocking with its speed, swept through the gate and tore up the road. Behind them was a hubbub—servants rushing about, orders being shouted out, doors shutting, and somewhere, seemingly far back in the house, a strange noise. Every nerve of the horses was strained as they dashed recklessly along the road. The two men held Mimi between them, the arms of both of them round her as though protectingly. As they went, there was a sudden rise in the ground; but the horses, breathing heavily, dashed up it at racing speed, not slackening their pace when the hill fell away again, leaving them to hurry along the downgrade.

It would be foolish to say that neither Adam nor Mimi had any fear in returning to Doom Tower. Mimi felt it more keenly than her husband, whose nerves were harder, and who was more inured to danger. Still she bore up bravely, and as usual the effort was helpful to her. When once she was in the study in the top of the turret, she almost forgot the terrors which lay outside in the dark. She did not attempt to peep out of the window; but Adam did—and saw nothing.

The moonlight showed all the surrounding country, but nowhere was to be observed that tremulous line of green light.

The peaceful night had a good effect on them all; danger, being unseen, seemed far off. At times it was hard to realise that it had ever been. With courage restored, Adam rose early and walked along the Brow, seeing no change in the signs of life in Castra Regis. What he did see, to his wonder and concern, on his returning homeward, was Lady Arabella, in her tight-fitting white dress and ermine collar, but without her emeralds; she was emerging from the gate of Diana's Grove and walking towards the Castle. Pondering on this and trying to find some meaning in it, occupied his thoughts till he joined Mimi and Sir Nathaniel at breakfast. They began the meal in silence. What had been had been, and was known to them all. Moreover, it was not a pleasant topic.

A fillip was given to the conversation when Adam told of his seeing Lady Arabella, on her way to Castra Regis. They each had something to say of her, and of what her wishes or intentions were towards Edgar Caswall. Mimi spoke bitterly of her in every aspect. She had not forgotten—and never would—never could—the occasion when, to harm Lilla, the woman had consorted even with the nigger. As a social matter, she was disgusted with her for following up the rich landowner—"throwing herself at his head so shamelessly," was how she expressed it. She was interested to know that the great kite still flew from Caswall's tower. But beyond such matters she did not try to go. The only comment she made was of strongly expressed surprise at her ladyship's "cheek" in ignoring her own criminal acts, and her impudence in taking it for granted that others had overlooked them also.

CHAPTER XXIV

A STARTLING PROPOSITION

THE MORE MIMI thought over the late events, the more puzzled she was. What did it all mean—what could it mean, except that there was an error of fact somewhere. Could it be possible that some of them—all of them had been mistaken, that there had been no White Worm at all? On either side of her was a belief impossible of reception. Not to believe in what seemed apparent was to destroy the very foundations of belief . . . yet in old days there had been monsters on the earth, and certainly some people had believed in just such mysterious changes of identity. It was all very strange. Just fancy how any stranger—say a doctor—would regard her, if she were to tell him that she had been to a tea-party with an antediluvian monster, and that they had been waited on by up-to-date men-servants.

Adam had returned, exhilarated by his walk, and more settled in his mind than he had been for some time. Like Mimi, he had gone through the phase of doubt and inability to believe in the reality of things, though it had not affected him to the same extent. The idea, however, that his wife was suffering ill-effects from her terrible ordeal, braced him up. He remained with her for a time, then he sought Sir Nathaniel in order to talk over the matter with him. He knew that the calm common sense and self-reliance of the old man, as well as his experience, would be helpful to them all.

Sir Nathaniel had come to the conclusion that, for some reason which he did not understand, Lady Arabella had changed her plans, and, for the present at all events, was pacific. He was inclined to attribute her changed demeanour to the fact that her influence over Edgar Caswall was so far increased, as to justify a more fixed belief in his submission to her charms.

As a matter of fact, she had seen Caswall that morning when she visited Castra Regis, and they had had a long talk together, during which the possibility of their union had been discussed. Caswall, without being enthusiastic on the subject, had been courteous and attentive; as she had walked back to Diana's Grove, she almost congratulated herself on her new settlement in life. That the idea was becoming fixed in her mind, was shown by a letter which she wrote later in the day to Adam Salton, and sent to him by hand. It ran as follows:

"DEAR MR. SALTON,

"I wonder if you would kindly advise, and, if possible, help me in a matter of business. I have been for some time trying to make up my mind to sell Diana's Grove, I have put off and put off the doing of it till now. The place is my own property, and no one has to be consulted with regard to what I may wish to do about it. It was bought by my late husband, Captain Adolphus Ranger March, who had another residence, The Crest, Appleby. He acquired all rights of all kinds, including mining and sporting. When he died, he left his whole property to me. I shall feel leaving this place, which has become endeared to me by many sacred memories and affections—the recollection of many happy days of my young married life, and the more than happy memories of the man I loved and who loved me so much. I should be willing to sell the place for any fair price—so long, of course, as the purchaser was one I liked and of whom I approved. May I say that you yourself would be the ideal person. But I dare not hope for so much. It strikes me, however, that among your Australian friends may be someone who wishes to make a settlement in the Old Country, and would care to fix the spot in one of the most historic regions in England, full of romance and legend, and with a never-ending vista of historical interest—an estate which, though small, is in perfect condition and with illimitable possibilities of development, and many doubtful—or unsettled—rights which have existed before the time of the Romans or even Celts, who were the original possessors. In addition, the house has been kept up to the *dernier cri*. Immediate possession can be arranged. My lawyers can provide you, or whoever you may suggest, with all business and historical details. A word from you of acceptance or refusal is all that is necessary, and we can leave details to be thrashed out by our agents. Forgive me, won't you, for troubling you in the matter, and believe me, yours very sincerely.

"ARABELLA MARCH."

Adam read this over several times, and then, his mind being made up, he went to Mimi and asked if she had any objection. She answered—after a shudder—that she was, in this, as in all things, willing to do whatever he might wish.

"Dearest, I am willing that you should judge what is best for us. Be quite free to act as you see your duty, and as your inclination calls. We are in the hands of God, and He has hitherto guided us, and will do so to His own end."

From his wife's room Adam Salton went straight to the study in the tower, where he knew Sir Nathaniel would be at that hour. The old man was alone, so, when he had entered in obedience to the "Come in," which answered his query, he closed the door and sat down beside him.

"Do you think, sir, that it would be well for me to buy Diana's Grove?"

"God bless my soul!" said the old man, startled, "why on earth would you want to do that?"

"Well, I have vowed to destroy that White Worm, and my being able to do whatever I may choose with the Lair would facilitate matters and avoid complications."

Sir Nathaniel hesitated longer than usual before speaking. He was thinking deeply.

"Yes, Adam, there is much common sense in your suggestion, though it startled me at first. I think that, for all reasons, you would do well to buy the property and to have the conveyance settled at once. If you want more money than is immediately convenient, let me know, so that I may be your banker."

"Thank you, sir, most heartily; but I have more money at immediate call than I shall want. I am glad you approve."

"The property is historic, and as time goes on it will increase in value. Moreover, I may tell you something, which indeed is only a surmise, but which, if I am right, will add great value to the place." Adam listened. "Has it ever struck you why the old name, 'The Lair of the White Worm,' was given? We know that there was a snake which in early days was called a worm; but why white?"

"I really don't know, sir; I never thought of it. I simply took it for granted."

"So did I at first—long ago. But later I puzzled my brain for a reason."

"And what was the reason, sir?"

"Simply and solely because the snake or worm *was* white. We are near the county of Stafford, where the great industry of china-burning was originated and grew. Stafford owes much of its wealth to the large deposits of the rare china clay found in it from time to time. These deposits become in time pretty well exhausted; but for centuries Stafford adventurers looked for the special clay, as Ohio and Pennsylvania farmers and explorers looked for oil. Anyone owning real estate on which china clay can be discovered strikes a sort of gold mine."

"Yes, and then——" The young man looked puzzled.

"The original 'Worm' so-called, from which the name of the place came, had to find a direct way down to the marshes and the mud-holes. Now, the clay is easily penetrable, and the original hole probably pierced a bed of china clay. When once the way was made it would become a sort of highway for the Worm. But as much movement was necessary to ascend such a great height, some of the clay would become attached to its rough skin by attrition. The downway must have been easy work, but the ascent was different, and when the monster came to view in the upper world, it would be fresh from contact with the white clay. Hence the name, which has no cryptic significance, but only fact. Now, if that surmise be true——and I do not see why not——there must be a deposit of valuable clay——possibly of immense depth."

Adam's comment pleased the old gentleman.

"I have it in my bones, sir, that you have struck——or rather reasoned out——a great truth."

Sir Nathaniel went on cheerfully. "When the world of commerce wakes up to the value of your find, it will be as well that your title to ownership has been perfectly secured. If anyone ever deserved such a gain, it is you."

With his friend's aid, Adam secured the property without loss of time. Then he went to see his uncle, and told him about it. Mr. Salton was delighted to find his young relative already constructively the owner of so fine an estate——one which gave him an important status in the county. He made many anxious enquiries about Mimi, and the doings of the White Worm, but Adam reassured him.

The next morning, when Adam went to his host in the smoking-room, Sir Nathaniel asked him how he purposed to proceed with regard to keeping his vow.

"It is a difficult matter which you have undertaken. To destroy such a monster is something like one of the labours of Hercules, in that not only its size and weight and power of using them in little-known ways are against you, but the occult side is alone an unsurpassable difficulty. The Worm is already master of all the elements except fire—and I do not see how fire can be used for the attack. It has only to sink into the earth in its usual way, and you could not overtake it if you had the resources of the biggest coal-mine in existence. But I daresay you have mapped out some plan in your mind," he added courteously.

"I have, sir. But, of course, it may not stand the test of practice."

"May I know the idea?"

"Well, sir, this was my argument: At the time of the Chartist trouble, an idea spread amongst financial circles that an attack was going to be made on the Bank of England. Accordingly, the directors of that institution consulted many persons who were supposed to know what steps should be taken, and it was finally decided that the best protection against fire—which is what was feared—was not water but sand. To carry the scheme into practice great store of fine sea-sand—the kind that blows about and is used to fill hour-glasses—was provided throughout the building, especially at the points liable to attack, from which it could be brought into use.

"I propose to provide at Diana's Grove, as soon as it comes into my possession, an enormous amount of such sand, and shall take an early occasion of pouring it into the well-hole, which it will in time choke. Thus Lady Arabella, in her guise of the White Worm, will find herself cut off from her refuge. The hole is a narrow one, and is some hundreds of feet deep. The weight of the sand this can contain would not in itself be sufficient to obstruct; but the friction of such a body working up against it would be tremendous."

"One moment. What use would the sand be for destruction?"

"None, directly; but it would hold the struggling body in place till the rest of my scheme came into practice."

"And what is the rest?"

"As the sand is being poured into the well-hole, quantities of dynamite can also be thrown in!"

"Good. But how would the dynamite explode—for, of course, that is what you intend. Would not some sort of wire or fuse be required for each parcel of dynamite?"

Adam smiled.

"Not in these days, sir. That was proved in New York. A thousand pounds of dynamite, in sealed canisters, was placed about some workings. At the last a charge of gunpowder was fired, and the concussion exploded the dynamite. It was most successful. Those who were non-experts in high explosives expected that every pane of glass in New York would be shattered. But, in reality, the explosive did no harm outside the area intended, although sixteen acres of rock had been mined and only the supporting walls and pillars had been left intact. The whole of the rocks were shattered."

Sir Nathaniel nodded approval.

"That seems a good plan—a very excellent one. But if it has to tear down so many feet of precipice, it may wreck the whole neighbour-hood."

"And free it for ever from a monster," added Adam, as he left the room to find his wife.

CHAPTER XXV

THE LAST BATTLE

LADY ARABELLA HAD instructed her solicitors to hurry on with the conveyance of Diana's Grove, so no time was lost in letting Adam Salton have formal possession of the estate. After his interview with Sir Nathaniel, he had taken steps to begin putting his plan into action. In order to accumulate the necessary amount of fine sea-sand, he ordered the steward to prepare for an elaborate system of top-dressing all the grounds. A great heap of the sand, brought from bays on the Welsh coast, began to grow at the back of the Grove. No one seemed to suspect that it was there for any purpose other than what had been given out.

Lady Arabella, who alone could have guessed, was now so absorbed in her matrimonial pursuit of Edgar Caswall, that she had neither time nor inclination for thought extraneous to this. She had not yet moved from the house, though she had formally handed over the estate.

Adam put up a rough corrugated-iron shed behind the Grove, in which he stored his explosives. All being ready for his great attempt whenever the time should come, he was now content to wait, and, in order to pass the time, interested himself in other things—even in Caswall's great kite, which still flew from the high tower of Castra Regis.

The mound of fine sand grew to proportions so vast as to puzzle the bailiffs and farmers round the Brow. The hour of the intended cataclysm was approaching apace. Adam wished—but in vain—for an opportunity, which would appear to be natural, of visiting Caswall in the turret of Castra Regis. At last, one morning, he met Lady Arabella moving towards the Castle, so he took his courage *à deux mains* and asked to be allowed to accompany her. She was glad, for her own purposes, to comply with his wishes. So together they entered, and found their way to the turret-room. Caswall was much surprised to see Adam come to his house, but lent himself to the task of seeming to be pleased. He played the host so well as to deceive even Adam. They all went out on the turret roof, where he explained to his guests the mechanism for raising and lowering the kite, taking also the opportunity of testing the movements of the multitudes of birds, how they answered almost instantaneously to the lowering or raising of the kite.

As Lady Arabella walked home with Adam from Castra Regis, she asked him if she might make a request. Permission having been accorded, she explained that before she finally left Diana's Grove, where she had lived so long, she had a desire to know the depth of the well-hole. Adam was really happy to meet her wishes, not from any sentiment, but because he wished to give some valid and ostensible reason for examining the passage of the Worm, which would obviate any suspicion resulting from his being on the premises. He brought from London a Kelvin sounding apparatus, with a sufficient length of piano-wire for testing any probable depth. The wire passed easily over the running wheel, and when this was once fixed over the hole, he was satisfied to wait till the most advantageous time for his final experiment.

In the meantime, affairs had been going quietly at Mercy Farm. Lilla, of course, felt lonely in the absence of her cousin, but the even tenor of life went on for her as for others. After the first shock of parting was over, things went back to their accustomed routine. In one respect, however, there was a marked difference. So long as home conditions had remained unchanged, Lilla was content to put ambition far from her, and to settle down to the life which had been hers as long as she could remember. But Mimi's marriage set her thinking; naturally, she came to the conclusion that she too might have a mate. There was not for her much choice—there was little movement in the matrimonial direction at the farmhouse. She did not approve of the personality of Edgar Caswall, and his struggle with Mimi had frightened her; but he was unmistakably an excellent *parti*, much better than she could have any right to expect. This weighs much with a woman, and more particularly one of her class. So, on the whole, she was content to let things take their course, and to abide by the issue.

As time went on, she had reason to believe that things did not point to happiness. She could not shut her eyes to certain disturbing facts, amongst which were the existence of Lady Arabella and her growing intimacy with Edgar Caswall; as well as his own cold and haughty nature, so little in accord with the ardour which is the foundation of a young maid's dreams of happiness. How things would, of necessity, alter if she were to marry, she was afraid to think. All told, the prospect was not happy for her, and she had a secret longing that something might occur to upset the order of things as at present arranged.

When Lilla received a note from Edgar Caswall asking if he might come to tea on the following afternoon, her heart sank within her. If it was only for her father's sake, she must not refuse him or show any disinclination which he might construe into incivility. She missed Mimi more than she could say or even dared to think. Hitherto, she had always looked to her cousin for sympathy, for understanding, for loyal support. Now she and all these things, and a thousand others— gentle, assuring, supporting—were gone. And instead there was a horrible aching void.

For the whole afternoon and evening, and for the following forenoon, poor Lilla's loneliness grew to be a positive agony. For the first time she began to realise the sense of her loss, as though all the previous suffering had been merely a preparation. Everything she looked at, everything she remembered or thought of, became laden with poignant memory. Then on the top of all was a new sense of dread. The reaction from the sense of security, which had surrounded her all her life, to a never-quieted apprehension, was at times almost more than she could bear. It so filled her with fear that she had a haunting feeling that she would as soon die as live. However, whatever might be her own feelings, duty had to be done, and as she had been brought up to consider duty first, she braced herself to go through, to the very best of her ability, what was before her.

Still, the severe and prolonged struggle for self-control told upon Lilla. She looked, as she felt, ill and weak. She was really in a nerveless and prostrate condition, with black circles round her eyes, pale even to her lips, and with an instinctive trembling which she was quite unable to repress. It was for her a sad mischance that Mimi was away, for her love would have seen through all obscuring causes, and have brought to light the girl's unhappy condition of health. Lilla was utterly unable to do anything to escape from the ordeal before her; but her cousin, with the experience of her former struggles with Mr. Caswall and of the condition in which these left her, would have taken steps—even peremptory ones, if necessary—to prevent a repetition.

Edgar arrived punctually to the time appointed by herself. When Lilla, through the great window, saw him approaching the house, her condition of nervous upset was pitiable. She braced herself up, however, and managed to get through the interview in its preliminary stages without any perceptible change in her normal appearance and bearing. It had been to her an added terror that the black shadow of Oolanga, whom she dreaded, would follow hard on his master. A load was lifted from her mind when he did not make his usual stealthy approach. She had also feared, though in lesser degree, lest Lady Arabella should be present to make trouble for her as before.

With a woman's natural forethought in a difficult position, she had provided the furnishing of the tea-table as a subtle indication of the social difference between her and her guest. She had chosen the implements of service, as well as all the provender set forth, of the humblest kind. Instead of arranging the silver teapot and china cups, she had set out an earthen teapot, such as was in common use in the farm kitchen. The same idea was carried out in the cups and saucers of thick homely delft, and in the cream-jug of similar kind. The bread was of simple whole-meal, home-baked. The butter was good, since she had made it herself, while the preserves and honey came from her own garden. Her face beamed with satisfaction when the guest eyed the appointments with a supercilious glance. It was a shock to the poor girl herself, for she enjoyed offering to a guest the little hospitalities possible to her; but that had to be sacrificed with other pleasures.

Caswall's face was more set and iron-clad than ever—his piercing eyes seemed from the very beginning to look her through and through. Her heart quailed when she thought of what would follow—of what would be the end, when this was only the beginning. As some protection, though it could be only of a sentimental kind, she brought from her own room the photographs of Mimi, of her grandfather, and of Adam Salton, whom by now she had grown to look on with reliance, as a brother whom she could trust. She kept the pictures near her heart, to which her hand naturally strayed when her feelings of constraint, distrust, or fear became so poignant as to interfere with the calm which she felt was necessary to help her through her ordeal.

At first Edgar Caswall was courteous and polite, even thoughtful; but after a little while, when he found her resistance to his domination grow, he abandoned all forms of self-control and appeared in the same dominance as he had previously shown. She was prepared, however, for this, both by her former experience and the natural fighting instinct within her. By this means, as the minutes went on, both developed the power and preserved the equality in which they had begun.

Without warning, the psychic battle between the two individualities began afresh. This time both the positive and negative causes were all in favour of the man. The woman was alone and in bad spirits, unsupported; nothing at all was in her favour except the memory of the two victorious contests; whereas the man, though unaided, as before, by either Lady Arabella or Oolanga, was in full strength, well rested, and in flourishing circumstances. It was not, therefore, to be wondered at that his native dominance of character had full opportunity of asserting itself. He began his preliminary stare with a conscious sense of power, and, as it appeared to have immediate effect on the girl, he felt an ever-growing conviction of ultimate victory.

After a little Lilla's resolution began to flag. She felt that the contest was unequal—that she was unable to put forth her best efforts. As she was an unselfish person, she could not fight so well in her own battle as in that of someone whom she loved and to whom she was devoted. Edgar saw the relaxing of the muscles of face and brow, and the almost collapse of the heavy eyelids which seemed tumbling downward in sleep. Lilla made gallant efforts to brace her dwindling powers, but for a time unsuccessfully. At length there came an interruption, which seemed like a powerful stimulant. Through the wide window she saw Lady Arabella enter the plain gateway of the farm, and advance towards the hall door. She was clad as usual in tight-fitting white, which accentuated her thin, sinuous figure.

The sight did for Lilla what no voluntary effort could have done. Her eyes flashed, and in an instant she felt as though a new life had suddenly developed within her. Lady Arabella's entry, in her usual unconcerned, haughty, supercilious way, heightened the effect, so that when the two stood close to each other battle was joined. Mr. Caswall, too, took new courage from her coming, and all his masterfulness and power came back to him. His looks, intensified, had more obvious effect than had been noticeable that day. Lilla seemed at last overcome by his dominance. Her face became red and pale—violently red and ghastly pale—by rapid turns. Her strength seemed gone. Her knees collapsed, and she was actually sinking on the floor, when to her surprise and joy Mimi came into the room, running hurriedly and breathing heavily.

Lilla rushed to her, and the two clasped hands. With that, a new sense of power, greater than Lilla had ever seen in her, seemed to quicken her cousin. Her hand swept the air in front of Edgar Caswall, seeming to drive him backward more and more by each movement, till at last he seemed to be actually hurled through the door which Mimi's entrance had left open, and fell at full length on the gravel path without.

Then came the final and complete collapse of Lilla, who, without a sound, sank down on the floor.

CHAPTER XXVI

FACE TO FACE

MIMI WAS GREATLY distressed when she saw her cousin lying prone. She had a few times in her life seen Lilla on the verge of fainting, but never senseless; and now she was frightened. She threw herself on her knees beside Lilla, and tried, by rubbing her hands and other measures commonly known, to restore her. But all her efforts were unavailing. Lilla still lay white and senseless. In fact, each moment she looked worse; her breast, that had been heaving with the stress, became still, and the pallor of her face grew like marble.

At these succeeding changes Mimi's fright grew, till it altogether mastered her. She succeeded in controlling herself only to the extent that she did not scream.

Lady Arabella had followed Caswall, when he had recovered sufficiently to get up and walk—though stumblingly—in the direction of Castra Regis. When Mimi was quite alone with Lilla and the need for effort had ceased, she felt weak and trembled. In her own mind, she attributed it to a sudden change in the weather—it was momentarily becoming apparent that a storm was coming on.

She raised Lilla's head and laid it on her warm young breast, but all in vain. The cold of the white features thrilled through her, and she utterly collapsed when it was borne in on her that Lilla had passed away.

The dusk gradually deepened and the shades of evening closed in, but Mimi did not seem to notice or to care. She sat on the floor with her arms round the body of the girl whom she loved. Darker and blacker grew the sky as the coming storm and the closing night joined forces. Still she sat on—alone—tearless—unable to think. Mimi did not know how long she sat there. Though it seemed to her that ages had passed, it could not have been more than half-an-hour. She suddenly came to herself, and was surprised to find that her grandfather had not returned. For a while she lay quiet, thinking of the immediate past. Lilla's hand was still in hers, and to her surprise it was still warm. Somehow this helped her consciousness, and without any special act of will she stood up. She lit a lamp and looked at her cousin. There was no doubt that Lilla was dead; but when the lamp-light fell on her eyes, they seemed to look at Mimi with intent—with meaning. In this state of dark isolation a new resolution came to her, and grew and grew until it became a fixed definite purpose. She would face Caswall and call him to account for his murder of Lilla—that was what she called it to herself. She would also take steps—she knew not what or how—to avenge the part taken by Lady Arabella.

In this frame of mind she lit all the lamps in the room, got water and linen from her room, and set about the decent ordering of Lilla's body. This took some time; but when it was finished, she put on her hat and cloak, put out the lights, and set out quietly for Castra Regis.

As Mimi drew near the Castle, she saw no lights except those in and around the tower room. The lights showed her that Mr. Caswall was there, so she entered by the hall door, which as usual was open, and felt her way in the darkness up the staircase to the lobby of the room. The door was ajar, and the light from within showed brilliantly through the opening. She saw Edgar Caswall walking restlessly to and fro in the room, with his hands clasped behind his back. She opened the door without knocking, and walked right into the room. As she entered, he ceased walking, and stared at her in surprise. She made no remark, no comment, but continued the fixed look which he had seen on her entrance.

For a time silence reigned, and the two stood looking fixedly at each other. Mimi was the first to speak.

"You murderer! Lilla is dead!"

"Dead! Good God! When did she die?"

"She died this afternoon, just after you left her."

"Are you sure?"

"Yes—and so are you—or you ought to be. You killed her!"

"I killed her! Be careful what you say!"

"As God sees us, it is true; and you know it. You came to Mercy Farm on purpose to break her—if you could. And the accomplice of your guilt, Lady Arabella March, came for the same purpose."

"Be careful, woman," he said hotly. "Do not use such names in that way, or you shall suffer for it."

"I am suffering for it—have suffered for it—shall suffer for it. Not for speaking the truth as I have done, but because you two, with devilish malignity, did my darling to death. It is you and your accomplice who have to dread punishment, not I."

"Take care!" he said again.

"Oh, I am not afraid of you or your accomplice," she answered spiritedly. "I am content to stand by every word I have said, every act I have done. Moreover, I believe in God's justice. I fear not the grinding of His mills; if necessary I shall set the wheels in motion myself. But you don't care for God, or believe in Him. Your god is your great kite, which cows the birds of a whole district. But be sure that His hand, when it rises, always falls at the appointed time. It may be that your name is being called even at this very moment at the Great Assize. Repent while there is still time. Happy you, if you may be allowed to enter those mighty halls in the company of the pure-souled angel whose voice has only to whisper one word of justice, and you disappear for ever into everlasting torment."

The sudden death of Lilla caused consternation among Mimi's friends and well-wishers. Such a tragedy was totally unexpected, as Adam and Sir Nathaniel had been expecting the White Worm's vengeance to fall upon themselves.

Adam, leaving his wife free to follow her own desires with regard to Lilla and her grandfather, busied himself with filling the well-hole with the fine sand prepared for the purpose, taking care to have lowered at stated intervals quantities of the store of dynamite, so as to be ready for the final explosion. He had under his immediate supervision a corps of workmen, and was assisted by Sir Nathaniel, who had come over for the purpose, and all were now staying at Lesser Hill.

Mr. Salton, too, showed much interest in the job, and was constantly coming in and out, nothing escaping his observation.

Since her marriage to Adam and their coming to stay at Doom Tower, Mimi had been fettered by fear of the horrible monster at Diana's Grove. But now she dreaded it no longer. She accepted the fact of its assuming at will the form of Lady Arabella. She had still to tax and upbraid her for her part in the unhappiness which had been wrought on Lilla, and for her share in causing her death.

One evening, when Mimi entered her own room, she went to the window and threw an eager look round the whole circle of sight. A single glance satisfied her that the White Worm in *propriâ personâ* was not visible. So she sat down in the window-seat and enjoyed the pleasure of a full view, from which she had been so long cut off. The maid who waited on her had told her that Mr. Salton had not yet returned home, so she felt free to enjoy the luxury of peace and quiet.

As she looked out of the window, she saw something thin and white move along the avenue. She thought she recognised the figure of Lady Arabella, and instinctively drew back behind the curtain. When she had ascertained, by peeping out several times, that the lady had not seen her, she watched more carefully, all her instinctive hatred flooding back at the sight of her. Lady Arabella was moving swiftly and stealthily, looking back and around her at intervals, as if she feared to be followed. This gave Mimi an idea that she was up to no good, so she determined to seize the occasion for watching her in more detail.

Hastily putting on a dark cloak and hat, she ran downstairs and out into the avenue. Lady Arabella had moved, but the sheen of her white dress was still to be seen among the young oaks around the gateway. Keeping in shadow, Mimi followed, taking care not to come so close as to awake the other's suspicion, and watched her quarry pass along the road in the direction of Castra Regis.

She followed on steadily through the gloom of the trees, depending on the glint of the white dress to keep her right. The wood began to thicken, and presently, when the road widened and the trees grew farther back, she lost sight of any indication of her whereabouts. Under the present conditions it was impossible for her to do any more, so, after waiting for a while, still hidden in the shadow to see if she could catch another glimpse of the white frock, she determined to go on slowly towards Castra Regis, and trust to the chapter of accidents to pick up the trail again. She went on slowly, taking advantage of every obstacle and shadow to keep herself concealed.

At last she entered on the grounds of the Castle, at a spot from which the windows of the turret were dimly visible, without having seen again any sign of Lady Arabella.

Meanwhile, during most of the time that Mimi Salton had been moving warily along in the gloom, she was in reality being followed by Lady Arabella, who had caught sight of her leaving the house and had never again lost touch with her. It was a case of the hunter being hunted. For a time Mimi's many turnings, with the natural obstacles that were perpetually intervening, caused Lady Arabella some trouble;

but when she was close to Castra Regis, there was no more possibility of concealment, and the strange double following went swiftly on.

When she saw Mimi close to the hall door of Castra Regis and ascending the steps, she followed. When Mimi entered the dark hall and felt her way up the staircase, still, as she believed, following Lady Arabella, the latter kept on her way. When they reached the lobby of the turret-rooms, Mimi believed that the object of her search was ahead of her.

Edgar Caswall sat in the gloom of the great room, occasionally stirred to curiosity when the drifting clouds allowed a little light to fall from the storm-swept sky. But nothing really interested him now. Since he had heard of Lilla's death, the gloom of his remorse, emphasised by Mimi's upbraiding, had made more hopeless his cruel, selfish, saturnine nature. He heard no sound, for his normal faculties seemed benumbed.

Mimi, when she came to the door, which stood ajar, gave a light tap. So light was it that it did not reach Caswall's ears. Then, taking her courage in both hands, she boldly pushed the door and entered. As she did so, her heart sank, for now she was face to face with a difficulty which had not, in her state of mental perturbation, occurred to her.

CHAPTER XXVII

ON THE TURRET ROOF

THE STORM WHICH was coming was already making itself manifest, not only in the wide scope of nature, but in the hearts and natures of human beings. Electrical disturbance in the sky and the air is reproduced in animals of all kinds, and particularly in the highest type of them all—the most receptive—the most electrical. So it was with Edgar Caswall, despite his selfish nature and coldness of blood. So it was with Mimi Salton, despite her unselfish, unchanging devotion for those she loved. So it was even with Lady Arabella, who, under the instincts of a primeval serpent, carried the ever-varying wishes and customs of womanhood, which is always old—and always new.

Edgar, after he had turned his eyes on Mimi, resumed his apathetic position and sullen silence. Mimi quietly took a seat a little way apart, whence she could look on the progress of the coming storm and study its appearance throughout the whole visible circle of the neighbourhood. She was in brighter and better spirits than she had been for many days past. Lady Arabella tried to efface herself behind the now open door.

Without, the clouds grew thicker and blacker as the storm-centre came closer. As yet the forces, from whose linking the lightning springs, were held apart, and the silence of nature proclaimed the calm before the storm. Caswall felt the effect of the gathering electric force. A sort of wild exultation grew upon him, such as he had sometimes felt just before the breaking of a tropical storm. As he became conscious of this, he raised his head and caught sight of Mimi. He was in the grip of an emotion greater than himself; in the mood in which he was he felt the need upon him of doing some desperate deed. He was now absolutely reckless, and as Mimi was associated with him in the memory which drove him on, he wished that she too should be engaged in this enterprise. He had no knowledge of the proximity of Lady Arabella, and thought that he was far removed from all he knew and whose interests he shared—alone with the wild elements, which were being lashed to fury, and with the woman who had struggled with him and vanquished him, and on whom he would shower the full measure of his hate.

The fact was that Edgar Caswall was, if not mad, close to the border-line. Madness in its first stage—monomania—is a lack of proportion. So long as this is general, it is not always noticeable, for the uninspired onlooker is without the necessary means of comparison. But in monomania the errant faculty protrudes itself in a way that may not be denied. It puts aside, obscures, or takes the place of something else—just as the head of a pin placed before the centre of the iris will block out the whole scope of vision. The most usual form of monomania has commonly the same beginning as that from which Edgar Caswall suffered—an over-large idea of self-importance. Alienists, who study the matter exactly, probably know more of human vanity and its effects than do ordinary men. Caswall's mental disturbance was not hard to identify. Every asylum is full of such cases—men and women, who, naturally selfish and egotistical, so appraise to themselves their own importance that every other circumstance in life becomes subservient to it. The disease supplies in itself the material for self-magnification. When the decadence attacks a nature naturally proud and selfish and vain, and lacking both the aptitude and habit of self-restraint, the development of the disease is more swift, and ranges to farther limits. It is such persons who become inbued with the idea that they have the attributes of the Almighty—even that they themselves are the Almighty.

Mimi had a suspicion—or rather, perhaps, an intuition—of the true state of things when she heard him speak, and at the same time noticed the abnormal flush on his face, and his rolling eyes. There was a certain want of fixedness of purpose which she had certainly not noticed before—a quick, spasmodic utterance which belongs rather to the insane than to those of intellectual equilibrium. She was a little frightened, not only by his thoughts, but by his staccato way of expressing them.

Caswall moved to the door leading to the turret stair by which the roof was reached, and spoke in a peremptory way, whose tone alone made her feel defiant.

"Come! I want you."

She instinctively drew back—she was not accustomed to such words, more especially to such a tone. Her answer was indicative of a new contest.

"Why should I go? What for?"

He did not at once reply—another indication of his overwhelming egotism. She repeated her questions; habit reasserted itself, and he spoke without thinking the words which were in his heart.

"I want you, if you will be so good, to come with me to the turret roof. I am much interested in certain experiments with the kite, which would be, if not a pleasure, at least a novel experience to you. You would see something not easily seen otherwise."

"I will come," she answered simply; Edgar moved in the direction of the stair, she following close behind him.

She did not like to be left alone at such a height, in such a place, in the darkness, with a storm about to break. Of himself she had no fear; all that had been seemed to have passed away with her two victories over him in the struggle of wills. Moreover, the more recent apprehension—that of his madness—had also ceased. In the conversation of the last few minutes he seemed so rational, so clear, so unaggressive, that she no longer saw reason for doubt. So satisfied was she that even when he put out a hand to guide her to the steep, narrow stairway, she took it without thought in the most conventional way.

Lady Arabella, crouching in the lobby behind the door, heard every word that had been said, and formed her own opinion of it. It seemed evident to her that there had been some rapprochement between the two who had so lately been hostile to each other, and that made her furiously angry. Mimi was interfering with her plans! She had made certain of her capture of Edgar Caswall, and she could not tolerate even the lightest and most contemptuous fancy on his part which might divert him from the main issue. When she became aware that he wished Mimi to come with him to the roof and that she had acquiesced, her rage got beyond bounds. She became oblivious to any danger there might be in a visit to such an exposed place at such a time, and to all lesser considerations, and made up her mind to forestall them. She stealthily and noiselessly crept through the wicket, and, ascending the stair, stepped out on the roof. It was bitterly cold, for the fierce gusts of the storm which swept round the turret drove in through every unimpeded way, whistling at the sharp corners and singing round the trembling flagstaff. The kite-string and the wire which controlled the runners made a concourse of weird sounds which somehow, perhaps from the violence which surrounded them, acting on their length, resolved themselves into some kind of harmony—a fitting accompaniment to the tragedy which seemed about to begin.

Mimi's heart beat heavily. Just before leaving the turret-chamber she had a shock which she could not shake off. The lights of the room had momentarily revealed to her, as they passed out, Edgar's face, concentrated as it was whenever he intended to use his mesmeric power. Now the black eyebrows made a thick line across his face, under which his eyes shone and glittered ominously. Mimi recognised the danger, and assumed the defiant attitude that had twice already served her so well. She had a fear that the circumstances and the place were against her, and she wanted to be forearmed.

The sky was now somewhat lighter than it had been. Either there was lightning afar off, whose reflections were carried by the rolling clouds, or else the gathered force, though not yet breaking into lightning, had an incipient power of light. It seemed to affect both the man and the woman. Edgar seemed altogether under its influence. His spirits were boisterous, his mind exalted. He was now at his worst; madder than he had been earlier in the night.

Mimi, trying to keep as far from him as possible, moved across the stone floor of the turret roof, and found a niche which concealed her. It was not far from Lady Arabella's place of hiding.

Edgar, left thus alone on the centre of the turret roof, found himself altogether his own master in a way which tended to increase his madness. He knew that Mimi was close at hand, though he had lost sight of her. He spoke loudly, and the sound of his own voice, though it was carried from him on the sweeping wind as fast as the words were spoken, seemed to exalt him still more. Even the raging of the elements round him appeared to add to his exaltation. To him it seemed that these manifestations were obedient to his own will. He had reached the sublime of his madness; he was now in his own mind actually the Almighty, and whatever might happen would be the direct carrying out of his own commands. As he could not see Mimi, nor fix whereabout she was, he shouted loudly:

"Come to me! You shall see now what you are despising, what you are warring against. All that you see is mine—the darkness as well as the light. I tell you that I am greater than any other who is, or was, or shall be. When the Master of Evil took Christ up on a high place and showed Him all the kingdoms of the earth, he was doing what he thought no other could do. He was wrong—he forgot Me. I shall send you light, up to the very ramparts of heaven. A light so great that it shall dissipate those black clouds that are rushing up and piling around us. Look! Look! At the very touch of my hand that light springs into being and mounts up—and up—and up!"

He made his way whilst he was speaking to the corner of the turret whence flew the giant kite, and from which the runners ascended. Mimi looked on, appalled and afraid to speak lest she should precipitate some calamity. Within the niche Lady Arabella cowered in a paroxysm of fear.

Edgar took up a small wooden box, through a hole in which the wire of the runner ran. This evidently set some machinery in motion, for a sound as of whirring came. From one side of the box floated what looked like a piece of stiff ribbon, which snapped and crackled as the wind took it. For a few seconds Mimi saw it as it rushed along the sagging line to the kite. When close to it, there was a loud crack, and a sudden light appeared to issue from every chink in the box. Then a quick flame flashed along the snapping ribbon, which glowed with an intense light—a light so great that the whole of the countryside around stood out against the background of black driving clouds. For a few seconds the light remained, then suddenly disappeared in the blackness around. It was simply a magnesium light, which had been fired by the mechanism within the box and carried up to the kite. Edgar was in a state of tumultuous excitement, shouting and yelling at the top of his voice and dancing about like a lunatic.

This was more than Lady Arabella's curious dual nature could stand—the ghoulish element in her rose triumphant, and she abandoned all idea of marriage with Edgar Caswall, gloating fiendishly over the thought of revenge.

She must lure him to the White Worm's hole—but how? She glanced around and quickly made up her mind. The man's whole thoughts were absorbed by his wonderful kite, which he was showing off, in order to fascinate her imaginary rival, Mimi.

On the instant she glided through the darkness to the wheel whereon the string of the kite was wound. With deft fingers she unshipped this, took it with her, reeling out the wire as she went, thus keeping, in a way, in touch with the kite. Then she glided swiftly to the wicket, through which she passed, locking the gate behind her as she went.

Down the turret stair she ran quickly, letting the wire run from the wheel which she carried carefully, and, passing out of the hall door, hurried down the avenue with all her speed. She soon reached her own gate, ran down the avenue, and with her key opened the iron door leading to the well-hole.

She felt well satisfied with herself. All her plans were maturing, or had already matured. The Master of Castra Regis was within her grasp. The woman whose interference she had feared, Lilla Watford, was dead. Truly, all was well, and she felt that she might pause a while and rest. She tore off her clothes, with feverish fingers, and in full enjoyment of her natural freedom, stretched her slim figure in animal delight. Then she lay down on the sofa—to await her victim! Edgar Caswall's life blood would more than satisfy her for some time to come.

CHAPTER XXVIII

THE BREAKING OF THE STORM

WHEN LADY ARABELLA had crept away in her usual noiseless fashion, the two others remained for a while in their places on the turret roof: Caswall because he had nothing to say, Mimi because she had much to say and wished to put her thoughts in order. For quite a while—which seemed interminable—silence reigned between them. At last Mimi made a beginning—she had made up her mind how to act.

"Mr. Caswall," she said loudly, so as to make sure of being heard through the blustering of the wind and the perpetual cracking of the electricity.

Caswall said something in reply, but his words were carried away on the storm. However, one of her objects was effected: she knew now exactly whereabout on the roof he was. So she moved close to the spot before she spoke again, raising her voice almost to a shout.

"The wicket is shut. Please to open it. I can't get out."

As she spoke, she was quietly fingering a revolver which Adam had given to her in case of emergency and which now lay in her breast. She felt that she was caged like a rat in a trap, but did not mean to be taken at a disadvantage, whatever happened. Caswall also felt trapped, and all the brute in him rose to the emergency. In a voice which was raucous and brutal—much like that which is heard when a wife is being beaten by her husband in a slum—he hissed out, his syllables cutting through the roaring of the storm:

"You came of your own accord—without permission, or even asking it. Now you can stay or go as you choose. But you must manage it for yourself; I'll have nothing to do with it."

Her answer was spoken with dangerous suavity.

"I am going. Blame yourself if you do not like the time and manner of it. I daresay Adam—my husband—will have a word to say to you about it!"

"Let him say, and be damned to him, and to you too! I'll show you a light. You shan't be able to say that you could not see what you were doing."

As he spoke, he was lighting another piece of the magnesium ribbon, which made a blinding glare in which everything was plainly discernible, down to the smallest detail. This exactly suited Mimi. She took accurate note of the wicket and its fastening before the glare had died away. She took her revolver out and fired into the lock, which was shivered on the instant, the pieces flying round in all directions, but happily without causing hurt to anyone. Then she pushed the wicket open and ran down the narrow stair, and so to the hall door. Opening this also, she ran down the avenue, never lessening her speed till she stood outside the door of Lesser Hill. The door was opened at once on her ringing.

"Is Mr. Adam Salton in?" she asked.

"He has just come in, a few minutes ago. He has gone up to the study," replied a servant.

She ran upstairs at once and joined him. He seemed relieved when he saw her, but scrutinised her face keenly. He saw that she had been in some concern, so led her over to the sofa in the window and sat down beside her.

"Now, dear, tell me all about it!" he said.

She rushed breathlessly through all the details of her adventure on the turret roof. Adam listened attentively, helping her all he could, and not embarrassing her by any questioning. His thoughtful silence was a great help to her, for it allowed her to collect and organise her thoughts.

"I must go and see Caswall to-morrow, to hear what he has to say on the subject."

"But, dear, for my sake, don't have any quarrel with Mr. Caswall. I have had too much trial and pain lately to wish it increased by any anxiety regarding you."

"You shall not, dear——if I can help it——please God," he said solemnly, and he kissed her.

Then, in order to keep her interested so that she might forget the fears and anxieties that had disturbed her, he began to talk over the details of her adventure, making shrewd comments which attracted and held her attention. Presently, *inter alia,* he said:

"That's a dangerous game Caswall is up to. It seems to me that that young man——though he doesn't appear to know it——is riding for a fall!"

"How, dear? I don't understand."

"Kite flying on a night like this from a place like the tower of Castra Regis is, to say the least of it, dangerous. It is not merely courting death or other accident from lightning, but it is bringing the lightning into where he lives. Every cloud that is blowing up here——and they all make for the highest point——is bound to develop into a flash of lightning. That kite is up in the air and is bound to attract the lightning. Its cord makes a road for it on which to travel to earth. When it does come, it will strike the top of the tower with a weight a hundred times greater than a whole park of artillery, and will knock Castra Regis into pieces. Where it will go after that, no one can tell. If there should be any metal by which it can travel, such will not only point the road, but be the road itself."

"Would it be dangerous to be out in the open air when such a thing is taking place?" she asked.

"No, little woman. It would be the safest possible place—so long as one was not in the line of the electric current."

"Then, do let us go outside. I don't want to run into any foolish danger—or, far more, to ask you to do so. But surely if the open is safest, that is the place for us."

Without another word, she put on again the cloak she had thrown off, and a small, tight-fitting cap. Adam too put on his cap, and, after seeing that his revolver was all right, gave her his hand, and they left the house together.

"I think the best thing we can do will be to go round all the places which are mixed up in this affair."

"All right, dear, I am ready. But, if you don't mind, we might go first to Mercy. I am anxious about grandfather, and we might see that—as yet, at all events—nothing has happened there."

So they went on the high-hung road along the top of the Brow. The wind here was of great force, and made a strange booming noise as it swept high overhead; though not the sound of cracking and tearing as it passed through the woods of high slender trees which grew on either side of the road. Mimi could hardly keep her feet. She was not afraid; but the force to which she was opposed gave her a good excuse to hold on to her husband extra tight.

At Mercy there was no one up—at least, all the lights were out. But to Mimi, accustomed to the nightly routine of the house, there were manifest signs that all was well, except in the little room on the first floor, where the blinds were down. Mimi could not bear to look at that, to think of it. Adam understood her pain, for he had been keenly interested in poor Lilla. He bent over and kissed her, and then took her hand and held it hard. Thus they passed on together, returning to the high road towards Castra Regis.

At the gate of Castra Regis they were extra careful. When drawing near, Adam stumbled upon the wire that Lady Arabella had left trailing on the ground.

Adam drew his breath at this, and spoke in a low, earnest whisper: "I don't want to frighten you, Mimi dear, but wherever that wire is there is danger."

"Danger! How?"

"That is the track where the lightning will go; at any moment, even now whilst we are speaking and searching, a fearful force may be loosed upon us. Run on, dear; you know the way to where the avenue joins the highroad. If you see any sign of the wire, keep away from it, for God's sake. I shall join you at the gateway."

"Are you going to follow that wire alone?"

"Yes, dear. One is sufficient for that work. I shall not lose a moment till I am with you."

"Adam, when I came with you into the open, my main wish was that we should be together if anything serious happened. You wouldn't deny me that right, would you, dear?"

"No, dear, not that or any right. Thank God that my wife has such a wish. Come; we will go together. We are in the hands of God. If He wishes, we shall be together at the end, whenever or wherever that may be."

They picked up the trail of the wire on the steps and followed it down the avenue, taking care not to touch it with their feet. It was easy enough to follow, for the wire, if not bright, was self-coloured, and showed clearly. They followed it out of the gateway and into the avenue of Diana's Grove.

Here a new gravity clouded Adam's face, though Mimi saw no cause for fresh concern. This was easily enough explained. Adam knew of the explosive works in progress regarding the well-hole, but the matter had been kept from his wife. As they stood near the house, Adam asked Mimi to return to the road, ostensibly to watch the course of the wire, telling her that there might be a branch wire leading somewhere else. She was to search the undergrowth, and if she found it, was to warn him by the Australian native "Coo-ee!"

Whilst they were standing together, there came a blinding flash of lightning, which lit up for several seconds the whole area of earth and sky. It was only the first note of the celestial prelude, for it was followed in quick succession by numerous flashes, whilst the crash and roll of thunder seemed continuous.

Adam, appalled, drew his wife to him and held her close. As far as he could estimate by the interval between lightning and thunder-clap, the heart of the storm was still some distance off, so he felt no present concern for their safety. Still, it was apparent that the course of the storm was moving swiftly in their direction. The lightning flashes came faster and faster and closer together; the thunder-roll was almost continuous, not stopping for a moment—a new crash beginning before the old one had ceased. Adam kept looking up in the direction where the kite strained and struggled at its detaining cord, but, of course, the dull evening light prevented any distinct scrutiny.

At length there came a flash so appallingly bright that in its glare Nature seemed to be standing still. So long did it last, that there was time to distinguish its configuration. It seemed like a mighty tree inverted, pendent from the sky. The whole country around within the angle of vision was lit up till it seemed to glow. Then a broad ribbon of fire seemed to drop on to the tower of Castra Regis just as the thunder crashed. By the glare, Adam could see the tower shake and tremble, and finally fall to pieces like a house of cards. The passing of the lightning left the sky again dark, but a blue flame fell downward from the tower, and, with inconceivable rapidity, running along the ground in the direction of Diana's Grove, reached the dark silent house, which in the instant burst into flame at a hundred different points.

At the same moment there rose from the house a rending, crashing sound of woodwork, broken or thrown about, mixed with a quick scream so appalling that Adam, stout of heart as he undoubtedly was, felt his blood turn into ice. Instinctively, despite the danger and their consciousness of it, husband and wife took hands and listened, trembling. Something was going on close to them, mysterious, terrible, deadly! The shrieks continued, though less sharp in sound, as though muffled. In the midst of them was a terrific explosion, seemingly from deep in the earth.

The flames from Castra Regis and from Diana's Grove made all around almost as light as day, and now that the lightning had ceased to flash, their eyes, unblinded, were able to judge both perspective and detail. The heat of the burning house caused the iron doors to warp and collapse. Seemingly of their own accord, they fell open, and exposed the interior. The Saltons could now look through to the room beyond, where the well-hole yawned, a deep narrow circular chasm. From this the agonised shrieks were rising, growing ever more terrible with each second that passed.

But it was not only the heart-rending sound that almost paralysed poor Mimi with terror. What she saw was sufficient to fill her with evil dreams for the remainder of her life. The whole place looked as if a sea of blood had been beating against it. Each of the explosions from below had thrown out from the well-hole, as if it had been the mouth of a cannon, a mass of fine sand mixed with blood, and a horrible repulsive slime in which were great red masses of rent and torn flesh and fat. As the explosions kept on, more and more of this repulsive mass was shot up, the great bulk of it falling back again. Many of the awful fragments were of something which had lately been alive. They quivered and trembled and writhed as though they were still in torment, a supposition to which the unending scream gave a horrible credence. At moments some mountainous mass of flesh surged up through the narrow orifice, as though forced by a measureless power through an opening infinitely smaller than itself. Some of these fragments were partially covered with white skin as of a human being, and others—the largest and most numerous—with scaled skin as of a gigantic lizard or serpent. Once, in a sort of lull or pause, the seething contents of the hole rose, after the manner of a bubbling spring, and Adam saw part of the thin form of Lady Arabella, forced up to the top amid a mass of blood and slime, and what looked as if it had been the entrails of a monster torn into shreds. Several times some masses of enormous bulk were forced up through the well-hole with inconceivable violence, and, suddenly expanding as they came into larger space, disclosed sections of the White Worm which Adam and Sir Nathaniel had seen looking over the trees with its enormous eyes of emerald-green flickering like great lamps in a gale.

At last the explosive power, which was not yet exhausted, evidently reached the main store of dynamite which had been lowered into the worm hole. The result was appalling. The ground for far around quivered and opened in long deep chasms, whose edges shook and fell in, throwing up clouds of sand which fell back and hissed amongst the rising water. The heavily built house shook to its foundations. Great stones were thrown up as from a volcano, some of them, great masses of hard stone, squared and grooved with implements wrought by human hands, breaking up and splitting in mid air as though riven by some infernal power. Trees near the house—and therefore presumably in some way above the hole, which sent up clouds of dust and steam and fine sand mingled, and which carried an appalling stench which sickened the spectators—were torn up by the roots and hurled into the air. By now, flames were bursting violently from all over the ruins, so dangerously that Adam caught up his wife in his arms, and ran with her from the proximity of the flames.

Then almost as quickly as it had begun, the whole cataclysm ceased, though a deep-down rumbling continued intermittently for some time. Then silence brooded over all—silence so complete that it seemed in itself a sentient thing—silence which seemed like incarnate darkness, and conveyed the same idea to all who came within its radius. To the young people who had suffered the long horror of that awful night, it brought relief—relief from the presence or the fear of all that was horrible—relief which seemed perfected when the red rays of sunrise shot up over the far eastern sea, bringing a promise of a new order of things with the coming day.

His bed saw little of Adam Salton for the remainder of that night. He and Mimi walked hand in hand in the brightening dawn round by the Brow to Castra Regis and on to Lesser Hill. They did so deliberately, in an attempt to think as little as possible of the terrible experiences of the night. The morning was bright and cheerful, as a morning sometimes is after a devastating storm. The clouds, of which there were plenty in evidence, brought no lingering idea of gloom. All nature was bright and joyous, being in striking contrast to the scenes of wreck and devastation, the effects of obliterating fire and lasting ruin.

The only evidence of the once stately pile of Castra Regis and its inhabitants was a shapeless huddle of shattered architecture, dimly seen as the keen breeze swept aside the cloud of acrid smoke which marked the site of the once lordly castle. As for Diana's Grove, they looked in vain for a sign which had a suggestion of permanence. The oak trees of the Grove were still to be seen—some of them—emerging from a haze of smoke, the great trunks solid and erect as ever, but the larger branches broken and twisted and rent, with bark stripped and chipped, and the smaller branches broken and dishevelled looking from the constant stress and threshing of the storm.

Of the house as such, there was, even at the short distance from which they looked, no trace. Adam resolutely turned his back on the devastation and hurried on. Mimi was not only upset and shocked in many ways, but she was physically "dog tired," and falling asleep on her feet. Adam took her to her room and made her undress and get into bed, taking care that the room was well lighted both by sunshine and lamps. The only obstruction was from a silk curtain, drawn across the window to keep out the glare. He sat beside her, holding her hand, well knowing that the comfort of his presence was the best restorative for her. He stayed with her till sleep had overmastered her wearied body. Then he went softly away. He found his uncle and Sir Nathaniel in the study, having an early cup of tea, amplified to the dimensions of a possible breakfast. Adam explained that he had not told his wife that he was going over the horrible places again, lest it should frighten her, for the rest and sleep in ignorance would help her and make a gap of peacefulness between the horrors.

Sir Nathaniel agreed.

"We know, my boy," he said, "that the unfortunate Lady Arabella is dead, and that the foul carcase of the Worm has been torn to pieces— pray God that its evil soul will never more escape from the nethermost hell."

They visited Diana's Grove first, not only because it was nearer, but also because it was the place where most description was required, and Adam felt that he could tell his story best on the spot. The absolute destruction of the place and everything in it seen in the broad daylight was almost inconceivable. To Sir Nathaniel, it was as a story of horror full and complete. But to Adam it was, as it were, only on the fringes. He knew what was still to be seen when his friends had got over the knowledge of externals. As yet, they had only seen the outside of the house—or rather, where the outside of the house once had been. The great horror lay within. However, age—and the experience of age—counts.

A strange, almost elemental, change in the aspect had taken place in the time which had elapsed since the dawn. It would almost seem as if Nature herself had tried to obliterate the evil signs of what had occurred. True, the utter ruin of the house was made even more manifest in the searching daylight; but the more appalling destruction which lay beneath was not visible. The rent, torn, and dislocated stonework looked worse than before; the upheaved foundations, the piled-up fragments of masonry, the fissures in the torn earth—all were at the worst. The Worm's hole was still evident, a round fissure seemingly leading down into the very bowels of the earth. But all the horrid mass of blood and slime, of torn, evil-smelling flesh and the sickening remnants of violent death, were gone. Either some of the later explosions had thrown up from the deep quantities of water which, though foul and corrupt itself, had still some cleansing power left, or else the writhing mass which stirred from far below had helped to drag down and obliterate the items of horror. A grey dust, partly of fine sand, partly of the waste of the falling ruin, covered everything, and, though ghastly itself, helped to mask something still worse.

After a few minutes of watching, it became apparent to the three men that the turmoil far below had not yet ceased. At short irregular intervals the hell-broth in the hole seemed as if boiling up. It rose and fell again and turned over, showing in fresh form much of the nauseous detail which had been visible earlier. The worst parts were the great masses of the flesh of the monstrous Worm, in all its red and sickening aspect. Such fragments had been bad enough before, but now they were infinitely worse. Corruption comes with startling rapidity to beings whose destruction has been due wholly or in part to lightning—the whole mass seemed to have become all at once corrupt! The whole surface of the fragments, once alive, was covered with insects, worms, and vermin of all kinds. The sight was horrible enough, but, with the awful smell added, was simply unbearable. The Worm's hole appeared to breathe forth death in its most repulsive forms. The friends, with one impulse, moved to the top of the Brow, where a fresh breeze from the sea was blowing up.

At the top of the Brow, beneath them as they looked down, they saw a shining mass of white, which looked strangely out of place amongst such wreckage as they had been viewing. It appeared so strange that Adam suggested trying to find a way down, so that they might see it more closely.

"We need not go down; I know what it is," Sir Nathaniel said. "The explosions of last night have blown off the outside of the cliffs—that which we see is the vast bed of china clay through which the Worm originally found its way down to its lair. I can catch the glint of the water of the deep quags far down below. Well, her ladyship didn't deserve such a funeral—or such a monument."

The horrors of the last few hours had played such havoc with Mimi's nerves, that a change of scene was imperative—if a permanent breakdown was to be avoided.

"I think," said old Mr. Salton, "it is quite time you young people departed for that honeymoon of yours!" There was a twinkle in his eye as he spoke.

Mimi's soft shy glance at her stalwart husband, was sufficient answer.